INTERNATIONAL RAVE REVIEWS FOR ONE OF THE BIGGEST SF EVENTS OF THE DECADE— PETER HAMILTON'S *THE REALITY DYSFUNCTION*

"HAMILTON PUTS [SF] BACK INTO INTERSTELLAR OVER-DRIVE. An intergalactic adventure story laced with ironies, insights, and held together by a transcending central plot."

—*The Times* (London)

"PAINTED ON THE VAST CANVAS OF CLASSIC SPACE OPERA. . . . The story builds to an explosive climax."

—*SFX*

"ELOQUENT AND INGENIOUS. . . . A host of believable charac-ters deploy against rich descriptions of worlds and living starships. Horror and heroism and even the humor are convincing. . . . Special effects run riot. . . . It all hangs together compulsively."

—*Daily Telegraph* (London)

more . . .

"THIS BOOK IS SUPER-INTELLIGENT SPACE OPERA, WROUGHT BY AN AUTHOR WHO KNOWS HIS STUFF . . . AND IT'S A RATTLING PAGE-TURNER TOO. *THE REALITY DYSFUNCTION* is an astonishing read crammed with golden-age wonders, but all depicted with an intellectual toughness that marks this as a landmark work for the 1990s."

—Stephen Baxter, author of *The Time Ships*

"BRASH, BROAD SPACE OPERA WITH MILITARY HARDWARE GALORE, FAST MOVEMENT, AND DAZZLING INVENTION. MASSIVE!"

—Gregory Benford, author of *Timescape*

PETER F. HAMILTON

THE
REALITY
DYSFUNCTION

PART 2: EXPANSION

WARNER BOOKS

A Time Warner Company

WARNER BOOKS EDITION

Aspect is a registered trademark of Warner Books, Inc.

Cover design by Don Puckey and Carol Russo
Cover illustration by Jim Burns

This Warner Books Edition is published by arrangement with Macmillan U.K.

Warner Books, Inc.
1271 Avenue of the Americas
New York, NY 10020

Visit our Web site at
http://warnerbooks.com

⦁ A Time Warner Company

Printed in the United States of America

First Paperback Printing: August, 1997

10 9 8 7 6 5 4 3 2

1

Graeme Nicholson sat on his customary stool beside the bar in the Crashed Dumper, the one furthest away from the blaring audio block, and listened to Diego Sanigra, a crewman from the *Bryant*, complain about the way the ship had been treated by Colin Rexrew. The *Bryant* was a colonist-carrier starship that had arrived at Lalonde two days ago, and so far not one of its five and a half thousand colonists had been taken out of zero-tau. It was a ruinous state of affairs, Diego Sanigra claimed, the governor had no right to refuse the colonists disembarkation. And the energy expenditure for every extra hour they spent in orbit was costing a fortune. The line company would blame the crew, as they always did. His salary would suffer, his bonus would be non-existent, his promotion prospects would be reduced if not ruined.

Graeme Nicholson nodded sympathetically as his neural nanonics carefully stored the aggrieved ramblings in a memory cell. There wasn't much which could be used, but it was good background material. How the big conflict reached down into individual lives. The kind of thing he covered so well.

Graeme had been a reporter for fifty-two of his seventy-eight years. He reckoned no journalist didactic course could teach him anything new, not now. With his experience he should have been formatting didactic courses, except there wasn't a news company editor in existence who would want junior reporters corrupted to such an extent. In every sense he was a hack reporter, with an unerring knack of turning daily misfortune into spicy epic tragedy. He went for the human underbelly every time, highlighting the suffering and misery of little people who were trampled on, the ones who couldn't fight back against the massive uncaring forces of governments, bureaucracies, and companies. It was not from any particular moral indignation, he certainly didn't see himself as championing the underdog. He simply felt emotions laid raw made for a better story, with higher audience ratings. To some degree he had even begun to look like the victims he empathized with so well; it was partly reflexive, they were less suspicious of someone whose clothes never quite fitted, who had thick ruddy skin and watery eyes.

His brand of sensationalism went down well with the tabloid broadcasts, but by concentrating on the seedy aspects he knew best, building a reputation as a specialist of dross, he found himself being squeezed out of the more prestigious assignments; he hadn't covered a half-decent story for a decade. Over the last few years his neural nanonics had been used less for sensevise recording and more for running stimulant programs. Time Universe had given him a roving assignment eight years ago, pushing him off onto all the shabby little fringe jobs that no one else with a gram of seniority would cover. Anything to keep him out of a studio, or an editorial office where his contemporaries had graduated to.

Well, no more. The joke was on the office has-beens now. Graeme Nicholson was the only man on the ground, the one with the clout, the one with the kudos. Lalonde was going to earn him the awards he'd been denied all these years; then maybe after that one of those nice cosy office seats back home on Decatur.

He had been on Lalonde for three months to do a documentary-style report on the new world frontier, and gather general sensevise impressions and locations for the company library's memory cores. Then this wonderful calamity had fallen on Lalonde. Calamitous for the planet and its people, for Rexrew and the LDC career administration staff; but for Graeme Nicholson it was manna from heaven. *It* being war, or an Ivet rebellion, or a xenoc invasion, depending on who you were talking to. He had included accounts of all three theories on the fleks *Eurydice* had taken to Avon last week. But it was strange that after two and a half weeks the Governor had still made no official announcement as to exactly what was happening up in the Quallheim and Zamjan Counties.

"That executive assistant of Rexrew's, Terrance Smith, he's talking about sending us to another phase one colony world," Diego Sanigra grumbled. He took another gulp of bitter from his tankard. "As if that's going to be any help. What would you say if you were a colonist who paid passage for Lalonde and came out of zero-tau to find yourself on Liao-tung Wan? That's Chinese-ethnic, you know, they wouldn't like the EuroChristian-types we've got stored on board."

"Is that where Terrance Smith suggested you take them?" Graeme Nicholson asked.

He gave a noncommittal grunt. "Just giving you an example."

"What about fuel reserves? Have you got enough He_3 and deuterium to get to another colony world and then return to Earth?"

Diego Sanigra started to answer. Graeme Nicholson wasn't listening too hard, he let his eyes wander round the hot crowded room. One of the spaceport shifts had just come off duty. At the moment there were few McBoeing flights. Only the three cargo ships orbiting Lalonde were being unloaded; the six colonist-carriers were waiting for Rexrew to decide what to do with their passenger complements. Most of the spaceport crews simply turned up at the start of each shift so they could keep claiming their pay.

I wonder what they feel about the end of overtime, Graeme asked himself. Might be another story there.

The Crashed Dumper certainly wasn't suffering from the troubles afflicting the rest of the city; this outlying district didn't protest or riot over Rexrew and the Ivets, it housed too many LDC worker families. There were a lot of people in tonight, drowning their sorrows. The waitresses were harried from one end of the long room to the other. The overhead fans were spinning fast, but made little impression on the heat.

Graeme heard the audio block falter, the singer's voice slowing, deepening to a weird bass rumble. It picked up again, turning the voice to a girlish soprano. The crowd clustered round started laughing, and one of them brought his fist down on it. After a moment the loud output returned to normal.

Graeme saw a tall man and a beautiful teenage girl walk past. Something about the man's face was familiar. The girl he recognized as one of the Crashed Dumper's waitresses, although tonight she was dressed in jeans and a plain cotton blouse. But the man—he was middle-aged with a neat beard and small pony-tail, wearing a smart leather jacket and ash-grey shorts, and he was very tall, almost like an Edenist.

The glass of lager dropped from Graeme's numb fingers. It hit the mayope planks and smashed, soaking his shoes and socks. "Holy shit," he croaked. The fright constricting his throat prevented the exclamation being more than a whisper.

"You all right?" Diego Sanigra asked, annoyed at being interrupted in mid-complaint.

He forced himself to look away from the couple. "Yes," he stammered. "Yes, I'm fine." Thank Christ nobody was paying any attention, if he had looked round . . . He reddened and bent down to pick up the shards of glass. When he straightened up the couple were already at the bar. Somehow they had cut straight through the crush.

Graeme ran a priority search program through his neural nanonics. Not that he could possibly be mistaken. The public figures file produced a visual image from a memory cell, recorded forty years ago. It matched perfectly.

Laton!

Lieutenant Jenny Harris twitched the reins, and the duncoloured horse gave the big qualtook tree a wide berth. Her only previous experience with the animals was her didactic course and a week in the saddle five years ago during an ESA transportation training exercise back on Kulu. Now here she was, leading an expedition through one of the toughest stretches of jungle in the Juliffe tributary network and trying to avoid the attention of a possible military invasion force at the same time. It wasn't the best reintroduction to the equestrian art. She thought the horse could sense her discomfort, he was proving awkward. A mere three hours' riding and every muscle in her lower torso was crying for relief; her arms and shoulders were stiff; her backside had gone from soreness to numbness and finally settled for a progressive hot ache.

I wonder what all this bodily offensive is doing to my implants?

Her neural nanonics were running an extended sensory analysis program, enhancing peripheral vision and threshold audio inputs, and scrutinizing them for any signs of hidden hostiles. Electronic paranoia, basically.

There had been nothing remotely threatening, except for one sayce, since they left the *Isakore*, and the sayce hadn't fancied its chances against three horses.

She could hear Dean Folan and Will Danza plodding along behind her, and wondered how they were getting on with their horses. Having the two ESA G66 Division (Tactical Combat) troops backing her up was a dose of comfort stronger than any stimulant program could provide. She had been trained in general covert fieldwork, but they had virtually been bred for it, geneering and nanonic supplements combining to make them formidable fighting machines.

Dean Folan was in his mid-thirties, a quiet ebony-skinned man with the kind of subtle good looks most of the geneered enjoyed. He was only medium height, but his limbs were long and powerful, making his torso look almost stunted by comparison. It was the boosted muscles which did that, Jenny knew; his silicon-fibre-reinforced bones had been lengthened to give him more leverage, and more room for implants.

Will Danza fitted people's conception of a modern-day soldier; twenty-five, tall, broad, with long, sleek muscles. He was an old Prussian warrior genotype, blond, courteous, and unsmiling. There was an almost psychic essence of danger emanating from him; you didn't tangle with him in any tavern brawl no matter how drunk you were. Jenny suspected he didn't have a sense of humour; but then he'd seen action in covert missions three times in the last three years. She'd accessed his file when the jungle mission was being assembled; they had been tough assignments, one had earned him eight months in hospital being rebuilt from cloned organs, and an Emerald Star presented by the Duke of Salion, Alastair II's first cousin, and chairman of the Kulu Privy Council's security commission. He had never talked about it on the journey upriver.

The nature of the jungle started to change around them. Tightly packed bushy trees gave way to tall, slender trunks with a plume of feather-fronds thirty metres overhead. A solid blanket of creepers tangled the ground, rising up to hug the lower third of the tree trunks like solid conical encrustations. It increased their visibility dramatically, but the horses had to pick their hoofs up sharply. High above their heads vennals leapt between the trees in incredible bounds, streaking up the slim trunks to hide in the foliage at the top. Jenny couldn't see how they clung to the smooth bark.

After another forty minutes they came to a small stream. She dismounted in slow tender stages, and let her horse drink. Away in the distance she could see a herd of danderil bounding away from the trickle of softly steaming water. White clouds were rolling in from the east. It would rain in an hour, she knew.

Dean Folan dismounted behind her, leaving Will Danza sitting on his horse, keeping watch from his elevated vantage point. All three of them were dressed identically, wearing a superstrength olive-green one-piece anti-projectile suit, covered with an outer insulation layer to diffuse beam weapons. The lightweight armour fitted perfectly, with an inner sponge layer to protect the skin. Thermal-shunt fibres woven into the fabric kept body temperature to a pre-set norm, which was a real blessing on Lalonde. If they were struck by a projectile slug the micro-valency generators around her waist would activate, solidifying the fabric instantly, distributing the impact, preventing the wearer's body from being pulped by automatic fire. (Jenny's only regret was that it didn't protect her from saddle sores.) The body armour was complemented by a shell-helmet which fitted with the same tight precision as the suit. It gave them all an insect appearance, with its wide goggle lenses and a small central V-shaped air-filter vent. The collar had a ring of optical sensors which could be accessed through neural nanonics, giving them a rear-view capability. They could even survive underwater for half an hour with its oxygen-recycling capacity.

The stream was muddy, its stones slimed with algae, none of which seemed to bother the horses. Jenny watched them lapping it up, and requested a drink from her shell-helmet. She sucked ice-cold orange juice from the nipple as she reviewed their location with help from the inertial guidance block.

When Dean and Will swapped position she datavised the armour suit's communications block to open a scrambled channel to Murphy Hewlett. The ESA team had split up from the Confederation Navy Marines after leaving the *Isakore*. Acting separately they thought they stood a better chance of intercepting one of the sequestrated colonists.

"We're eight kilometres from Oconto," she said. "No hostiles or locals encountered so far."

"Same with us," the marine lieutenant answered. "We're six kilometres south of you, and there's nobody in this jungle but us chickens. If Oconto's supervisor did lead fifty people in pursuit of the Ivets, he didn't come this way. There's a small savannah which starts about fifteen kilometres away, there are about a hundred homesteads out there. We'll try them."

Static warbled down the channel. Jenny automatically checked her electronic warfare suite, which reported zero activity. Must be atmospherics.

"OK. We're going to keep closing on the village and hope we find someone before we reach it," she datavised.

"Roger. I suggest we make half-hourly check-ins from now on. There isn't . . ." His signal dissolved into rowdy static.

"Hell! Dean, Will, we're being jammed."

Dean consulted his own electronic warfare block. "No activity detected," he said.

Jenny steadied her horse and put her foot in the stirrup, swinging a leg over the saddle. Will was mounting hastily beside her. All three of them scanned the surrounding jungle. Dean's horse snickered nervously. Jenny tugged at the reins to keep hers from twisting about.

"They're out there," Will said in a level tone.

"Where?" Jenny asked.

"I don't know, but they're watching us. I can feel it. They don't like us."

Jenny bit down on the obvious retort. Soldier superstitions were hardly appropriate right now, yet Will had more direct combat experience than her. A quick hardware status check showed that only the communications block was affected so far. Her electronic warfare block remained stubbornly silent.

"All right," she said. "The one thing we don't want to do is run into a whole bunch of them. The Edenists said they were most powerful in groups. Let's move out, and see if we can get outside this jamming zone. We ought to be able to move faster than them."

"Which way?" Dean asked.

"I still want to try and reach the village. But I don't think a direct route is advisable now. We'll head south-west, and curve back towards Oconto. Any questions? No. Lead off then, Dean."

They splashed over the stream, the horses seemingly eager to be on the move again. Will Danza had pulled his thermal induction pulse carbine from its saddle holster; now it was cradled in the crook of his right arm, pointing upwards. The datavised information from its targeting processor formed a quiet buzz at the back of his mind. He didn't even notice it at a conscious level, it was as much a part of the moment as the easy rhythm of the horse or the bright sunlight, making him whole.

He made up the rear of the little procession, constantly reviewing the sensors on the back of his shell-helmet. If anyone had asked him how he knew hostiles were nearby he would just have to shrug and say he couldn't explain. But instinct was pulling at him with the same irresistible impulse that pollen exerted on bees. They were here, and they were close. Whoever, or whatever, they were.

He strained round in the saddle, upping his retinal implants' resolution to their extreme. All he could see was the long thin black trunks and their verdant cone island bases, outlines wavering in the heat and unstable magnification factor.

A movement.

The TIP carbine was discharging before he even thought about it, blue target graphics sliding across his vision field like neon cell doors as he dropped the barrel in a single smooth arc. A red circle intersected the central grid square and his neural nanonics triggered a five-hundred-shot fan pattern.

The section of jungle in the central blue square sparkled with orange motes as the induction pulses stabbed against the wood and foliage. It lasted for two seconds.

"Down!" Will datavised. "Hostiles four o'clock."

He was already slithering off the horse, feet landing solidly on the broad triangular creeper leaves. Dean and Jenny obeyed automatically, rolling from their saddles to land crouched, thermal induction pulse carbines held ready. The three of them turned smoothly, each covering a different section of jungle.

"What was it?" Jenny asked.

"Two of them, I think." Will quickly replayed the memory. It was like a dense black shadow dashing out from behind one of the trees, then it split into two. That was when he fired, and the image jolted. But the black shapes refused to clarify, no matter how many discrimination programs he ran. Definitely too big for sayce, though. And they were moving towards him, using the shaggy treebases for cover.

He felt a glow of admiration, they were good.

"What now?" he datavised. Nobody responded. "What now?" he asked loudly.

"Reconnaissance and evaluation," said Jenny, who had just realized even short-range datavises were being disrupted. "We're still not out of that jamming effect."

There was a silent orange flash above her. The top third of the tree ten metres to her left began to topple over, hinging on a section of trunk that was mostly charred splinters. Just as it reached the horizontal, the rich green plumes at the top caught on fire. They spluttered briefly, belching out a ring of blue-grey smoke, then the fire really caught. Two vennals leapt out, squeaking in pain, their hides badly scorched. Before the whole length of wood crashed down, the plumes were burning with a ferocity which matched the sun.

The horses reared up, whinnying alarm. They were pulled down by boosted muscles.

Jenny realized the animals were rapidly becoming a liability as she clung on to hers. Her neural nanonics reported the suit sensors had detected a maser beam striking the tree, which was what snapped it. But there was no detectable follow-up energy strike to account for the ignition.

Dean's sensors had also detected the maser beam. He fired a fifty-shot barrage back along the line.

The fallen tree's tip fizzled out. All that was left was a tapering core of wood and a heap of ash. Blackened ground creepers smouldered in a wide circle around it.

"What the hell did that?" Dean asked.

"No data," Jenny answered. "But it isn't going to be healthy."

Globules of vivid white fire raced up the trunks of several nearby trees like some bizarre astral liquid. Bark shrivelled and peeled off in long strips behind them, the naked wood below roaring like a blast furnace as it caught alight. The flames redoubled in vehemence. Jenny, Will, and Dean were surrounded by twelve huge torches of brilliant fire.

Jenny's retinal implants struggled to cope with the vast photon flood. Her horse reared up again, fighting her, neck sweeping from side to side in an effort to make her let go, forelegs cycling dangerously close to her head. She could see the terror in its eyes. Foam sprayed out of its mouth to splatter her suit.

"Save the equipment," she shouted. "We can't hang on to the horses in this."

Will heard the order as his horse began bucking, its hind legs kicking imaginary foes. He drove his fist into its head, catching it between the eyes, and it froze for a second in stunned surprise, then slowly buckled, collapsing onto the ground. One of the blazing trees gave a single creak of warning and keeled over. It slammed down on the horse's back, breaking ribs and legs, searing its way into the flesh. Oily smoke billowed up. Will darted forward, and tugged at the saddle straps. His suit datavised an amber alert to his neural nanonics as the heat impact of the flames gusted against the outer layer.

Balls of orange flame were hurtling through the air above him, spitting greasy black liquids: vennals, fleeing and dying as their roosts were incinerated. Small withered bodies hit the ground all around, some of them moving feebly.

Dean and Jenny were still struggling with their horses, filling the air with confused curses. Will's suit sounded a preliminary caution that thermal input was reaching the limit of the handling capacity. He felt the saddle strap give, and jumped backwards, hugging the equipment packs. The suit's outer dissipator layer glowed cherry red as it radiated away the excess heat, and wisps of smoke rose from around his feet.

More trees were falling as the flame consumed the wood at a fantastic rate. For one nasty moment they were completely penned in by a rippling fence made up from solid sheets of that strange lethal white flame.

Jenny salvaged her equipment packs from her horse and let go of the bridle. It raced away blindly, only to veer to one side as another burning tree fell in its path. One of the fiery vennals landed on its back, and it charged straight into the flames, screaming piteously. She watched it tumble over. It twitched a couple of times, trying to regain its feet, then flopped down limply.

By now a ring of ground a hundred metres in diameter was burning, leaving just a small patch at the centre untouched. The three of them grouped together at the middle as the last two trees went down. Now there was only the ground creepers burning, sending up forked yellow flames and heavy blue smoke.

Jenny pulled her packs towards her and ran a systems status check. Not good. The guidance block was putting out erratic data, and the suit's laser rangefinder return was dubious. The hostiles' electronic warfare field was growing stronger. And according to her external temperature sensors, if they hadn't been wearing suits with a thermal-dispersal layer they would have been roasted alive by now.

She gripped the TIP carbine tighter. "As soon as the flames die down I want a sweep-scorch pattern laid down out to four hundred metres. Fight fire with fire. They've shown us what they can do, now it's our turn."

"All right," Will muttered happily.

Rummaging round in her packs for one of the spherical heavy duty power cells she was carrying, she plugged its coiled cable into the butt of her carbine. The other two were doing the same thing.

"Ready?" she asked. The flames were only a couple of

metres high now, the air above them swarmed with ash flakes, blotting out the sun. "Go."

They stood, shoulders together, forming a triangle. The TIP carbines blazed, sending out two hundred and fifty invisible deadly shots every second. Targeting processors coordinated the sweep parameters, overlapping their fields of fire. Neural nanonics ordered their muscles to move in precise increments, controlling the direction of the energy blitz.

A ripple of destruction roared out across the already cremated land, then started to chew its way into the vegetation beyond. Dazzling orange stars scintillated on tree trunks and creepers, desiccating then igniting the wood and tangled cords of vine. The initial ripple became a fully-fledged hurricane firestorm, exacerbated by the relentless push of the carbines.

"Burn, you mothers," Will yelled jubilantly. "Burn!"

The entire jungle was on fire around them, an avalanche of flames racing outward. One again the vennals were dying in their hundreds, plunging out of their igneous trees right into the conflagration.

Dean's neural nanonics reported that his carbine was stuttering whenever he wiped the barrel across a certain coordinate. He brought it back and held it. The shot rate declined to five a second.

"Shit. Jenny, they're locking their electronic warfare into my carbine targeting processor."

"Let me have the section," she said.

He datavised the coordinates over—no problem with communication any more. When she aimed her own TIP carbine along the line its output dropped off almost immediately, but her suit blocks were coming back on-line. "Jeeze, that electronic warfare of theirs is the weirdest."

"Want me to try?" Will asked.

"No. Finish the sweep-scorch first, we'll deal with them in a minute." She turned back to her section. Watching the invincible rampart of flame cascade over the jungle had sent her heart racing wildly. The awe that she could command such fearsome power was soaring through her veins, taking her to a dangerous high. She had to load a suppression order into her neural nanonics, which restricted the release of natural adrenalin sharply. The sweep pattern was completed, and her flesh cooled. But she still felt supreme.

A holocaust of flame raged a hundred and twenty metres away.

"OK, they've given their position away," she said. "Dean, Will: gaussguns, please. Fragmentation and electron-explosive rounds, forty–sixty ratio."

Will grinned inside his shell-helmet as he bent down to retrieve the heavy-duty weapon. The gaussgun barrel was dark grey in colour, a metre and a half long. It weighed thirty kilograms. He picked it up as if it was made from polystyrene, checked the feed tube was connected to the bulky magazine box at his feet, datavised in the ratio, and aimed it out through the shimmering flames. Dean deployed its twin beside him.

Jenny had been probing through the flames, using her TIP carbine to determine the extent and location of the dead zone simply by recording where it cut out. She datavised the coordinates over to Dean and Will: an oval area fifty metres long, roughly three hundred metres away.

"One hundred and fifty per cent coverage," she said. "Fire." Even she had to marvel at how the two men handled the weapons. The gaussguns hurled ten rounds a second, leaving the muzzle at five times the speed of sound. Yet they hardly moved as the recoil hammered at them, swaying gently from side to side. She doubted her boosted muscles could cope.

Away beyond the first rank of flames, a wide island of intact jungle erupted in violent pyrotechnics. Explosions five metres above the ground slammed out hundreds of thousands of slender crystallized carbon shrapnel blades. They scythed through the air at supersonic velocity, sharp as scalpels, stronger than diamond. Those trees which had survived the firestorm disintegrated, shredded instantly by the rabid aerial swarm. Confetti fragments blew apart like a dandelion cloud in a tornado.

The rest of the shrapnel impacted on the ground, slicing through the tangled mat of creepers, blades stabbing themselves thirty to forty centimetres down into the loose moist loam. They never had a chance to settle. EE projectiles rained down, detonating in hard vicious gouts of ionic flame. Plumes of black loam jetted up high into the ash-dimmed sky. The whole area was ruptured by steep-walled two-metre craters, undulating like a sea swell.

Looking down on the desolation, it was hard to believe even an insect could have survived, let alone any large animal.

The three ESA agents stared through the ebbing flames at the dark cyclone of loam particles and wood splinters obscuring the sun.

Jenny's neural nanonics ran a series of diagnostic programs through her suit equipment blocks. "That electronic warfare field has shut down," she said. There was a faint quaver to her voice as she contemplated the destructive forces she had unleashed. "Looks like we got them."

"And everybody knows it," Dean said flatly. "They must be able to see this fire halfway back to Durringham. The hostiles are going to come swarming to investigate."

"You're right," she said.

"They're still there," Will pronounced.

"What?!" Dean said. "You've cracked. Nothing could survive that kind of barrage, not even an army assault mechanoid. We blasted those bastards to hell."

"I'm telling you; they're still out there," Will insisted. He sounded nervous. Not like him at all.

His edginess crept in through the comfortable insulation of Jenny's suit. Listening to him she was half convinced herself. "If someone survived, that's good," she said. "I still want that captive for Hiltch. Let's move out. We'd have to investigate anyway. And we can't stay here waiting for them to regroup."

They quickly distributed the remaining ammunition and

power cells from their packs, along with basic survival gear. Each of them kept their TIP carbine; Will and Dean shouldered the gaussguns without a word of protest.

Jenny led off at a fast trot across the smouldering remnants of jungle, towards the area they had bombarded with the gaussguns. She felt terribly exposed. The fire had died down, it had nothing left to burn. Away in the distance they could see a few sporadic flames licking at bushes and knots of creeper. They were in the middle of a clearing nearly a kilometre across, the only segment of colour. Everything was black, the remnants of creepers underfoot, tapering ten-metre spikes of trees devoured by natural flames (as opposed to the white stuff the hostiles threw at them), cooked vennals that lay scattered everywhere, other smaller animals, a savagely contorted corpse of one of the horses, even the air was leaden with a seam of fine dusky motes.

She datavised her communication block to open a scrambled channel to Murphy Hewlett. To her surprise, he responded straight away.

"God, Jenny, what's happened? We couldn't raise you, then we saw that bloody great fire-fight. Are you all OK?"

"We're in one piece, but we lost the horses. I think we did some damage to the hostiles."

"Some damage?"

"Yeah. Murphy, watch out for a kind of white fire. So far they've only used it to set the vegetation alight, but our sensors can't pick up how they direct the bloody stuff. It just comes at you out of nowhere. But they hit you with an electronic warfare field first. My advice is that if your electronics start to go, then lay down a scorch pattern immediately. Flush them away."

"Christ. What the hell are we up against? First that paddle-boat illusion, now undetectable weapons."

"I don't know. Not yet, but I'm going to find out." She was surprised at her own determination.

"Do you need assistance? It's a long walk back to the boat."

"Negative. I don't think we should join up. Two groups still have a better chance to achieve our objective than one, nothing has changed that."

"OK, but we're here if it gets too tough."

"Thanks. Listen, Murphy, I'm not aiming to stay in this jungle after dark. Hell, we can't even see them coming at us in the daytime."

"Now that sounds like the first piece of sensible advice you've given today."

She referred to her neural nanonics. "There are another seven hours of daylight left. I suggest we try and rendezvous back at the *Isakore* in six hours from now. If we haven't captured a hostile, or found out what the hell is going down around here, we can review the situation then."

"I concur."

"Jenny," Dean called with soft urgency.

"Call you back," she told Murphy.

They had reached the edge of the barrage zone. Not even the tree stumps had survived here. Craters overlapped, producing a crumpled landscape of unstable cones and holes; crooked brown roots poked up into the sky from most of the denuded soil slopes. Long strands of steam, like airborne worms, wound slowly around the crumbling protrusions, sliding into the holes to pool at the bottom.

Over on the far side she watched three men emerging from the craters, scrambling sluggishly for solid ground. They helped each other along, wriggling on their bellies when the slippery loam proved impossible to stand on.

Jenny watched their progress in the same kind of bewildered daze which had engulfed her as the fantastical paddle-steamer sailed down the river.

The men reached level ground sixty metres away from the ESA team, and stood up. Two were recognizable colonist types: dungarees, thick cotton work shirts, and woolly beards. The third was dressed in some kind of antique khaki uniform: baggy trousers, calves bound up by strips of yellowish cloth; a brown leather belt round his waist sporting a polished pistol holster; a hemispherical metal hat with a five-centimetre rim.

They couldn't possibly have survived, Jenny found herself thinking, yet here they were. For one wild second she wondered if the electronic warfare field had won, and was feeding the hallucination directly into her neural nanonics.

The two groups stared at each other for over half a minute.

Jenny's electronic warfare block reported a build-up of static in the short-range datavise band. It broke the spell. "OK, let's go get them," she said.

They started to circle round the edge of the barrage zone. The three men watched them silently.

"Do you want all three?" Will asked.

"No, just one. The soldier must be equipped with the most powerful systems if he can create that kind of chameleon effect. I'd like him if we can manage it."

"I thought chameleon suits were supposed to blend in," Dean muttered.

"I'm not even sure we're seeing men," Will added. "Maybe the xenocs are disguising themselves. Remember the paddle-steamer."

Jenny ordered her suit's laser rangefinder to scan the soldier; its return should reveal the true outline to an accuracy of less than half a millimetre. The blue beam stabbed out from the side of her shell-helmet. But instead of sweeping the soldier, it broke apart a couple of metres in front of him, forming a turquoise haze. After a second the rangefinder module shut down. Her neural nanonics reported the whole unit was inoperative.

"Did you see that?" she asked. They had covered about a third of the distance round the barrage zone.

"I saw it," Will said brusquely. "It's a xenoc. Why else would it want to hide its shape?"

The distortion in the datavise band began to increase. Jenny saw the soldier start to unbuckle his holster.

"Stop!" she commanded, her voice booming out of the communication block's external speaker. "The three of you are under arrest. Put your hands on your head, and don't move."

All three men turned fractionally, focusing on her. Her neural nanonics began to report malfunctions in half of her suit's electronics.

"Screw it! We must break them up, even three of them are too powerful. Will, one round EE, five metres in front of them."

"That's too close," Dean said tensely as Will brought the gaussgun to bear. "You'll kill them."

"They survived the first barrage," Jenny said tonelessly.

Will fired. A fountain of loam spurted up into the air, accompanied by a bright blue-white sphere of flame. The blast-wave flattened some of the nearby piles of soil.

Jenny's neural nanonics reported the electronics coming back on-line. The loam subsided, revealing the three men standing firm. A faint whistle was insinuating itself into the datavise band; her neural nanonics couldn't filter it out.

"One metre," she snapped. "Fire."

The explosion sent them spinning, tottering about for balance. One fell to his knees. For the first time there was a reaction; one of the two farmer-types started snarling and shouting. His face above the beard was black, whether from loam or a flashburn she couldn't tell.

"Keep firing, keep them apart," Jenny called to Will. "Come on, run."

Explosions bloomed around the three men. Will was using the gaussgun the way riot police employed a water cannon, harrying the men as they tried to come together. Blasts that would rip a human to pieces barely affected them, at the most they tumbled backwards to sprawl on the ground. He was tempted to land a round straight on one, just to see what it would do. They scared him.

Jenny's feet pounded over the scorched creepers. The packs and the TIP carbine weighed nothing as her boosted muscles powered up and took the full load. Will was doing a good job, one of the men had been separated from the other two. He was the farmer-type who had shouted earlier.

She brought her TIP carbine round and aimed it at his left ankle, neural nanonics allowing her to compensate for the vigorous motion of her body. If they could disable him, they could chase off or kill the other two. A severed cauterized foot wasn't lethal.

Her neural nanonics triggered a single shot. She actually saw the induction pulse. A complete impossibility, her mind insisted. But a slender violet line materialized in the air ahead of her. It struck the farmer's ankle and splashed apart, sending luminous tendrils clawing up his leg. He yelled wildly, and tumbled headlong.

"Dean, subdue him," she ordered. "I want him in one piece. Will and I will fend off the other two." Her carbine's targeting circle slithered round on the soldier as she stopped running. He was taking aim with his revolver. They both fired.

Jenny saw luminous purple tapeworms writhing across the neatly pressed khaki uniform. The soldier began to jerk about as if he was being electrocuted. Then the bullet struck her with the force of a gaussgun's kinetic round. Her suit hardened instantly, and she found herself somersaulting chaotically, grey sky and black land streaking past in a confused blur. There was an instant's silence. She landed hard, and her suit unfroze. She was rolling, arms and legs jolting the ground sharply.

The gaussgun was roaring three metres away. Will was standing his ground, feet apart to brace himself, swivelling from the hip to send EE rounds chasing after each of the men.

Jenny scrambled to her feet. The soldier and one of the farmers were fifty metres away. They were facing Will, but retreating in juddering steps from the onslaught of projectiles. Somehow she had hung on to the TIP carbine, and now she lined it up. Radiant purple lines shivered across the soldier once more. He threw up his hands, as if he was physically warding off the intense energy pulses. Then both he and the farmer looked at each other. Something must have been said, because they both turned and ran towards the rim of the jungle eighty metres behind them.

Dean Folan dropped his gaussgun and backpack, which allowed him to cover the last thirty metres in two and a half seconds. In that time he fired his TIP carbine twice. The beams tore into glaring purple streamers which knocked the farmer down into the soft loam. With his opponent out for the count, Dean took the last five metres in a flying tackle, landing straight on top of him. The weight of his own body and the suit and his equipment should have been enough to finish it. But the man started to rise straight away. Dean gave a surprised yelp as he was lifted right off the ground, and went for a stranglehold, only to find a hand clamping round each wrist pulling his arms apart. He fell onto his back as the farmer regained his feet. A booted foot kicked him in the side of his ribs. His suit hardened, and he was thrown onto his belly by the force of the blow. The farmer must be a construct made entirely out of boosted muscle! His neural nanonics combat routine programs went into primary mode. He swung the TIP carbine round, and another vicious kick actually cracked the casing. But he lashed out with his free arm, knocking the farmer's other leg out from under him. The farmer went down heavily on his backside.

Somewhere in the distance the gaussgun was thumping out a stream of EE projectiles.

Both of them struggled into a semi-crouch, then launched themselves. Once again, Dean found himself losing. The farmer's impact sent him reeling backwards, fighting to keep his feet. Arms with the strength of a hydraulic ram grappled at him. His neural nanonics reviewed tactical options, and decided his physical strength was dangerously inferior. He let himself sway backwards, taking the farmer with him. Then his leg came straight up, slamming into the man's stomach. A classic judo throw. The farmer arched through the air, snarling in rage. Dean drew his twenty-centimetre fission blade and twisted round just in time to meet the man as he charged. The blade sliced down, aiming for the meat of the right forearm. It struck, cutting through the cloth sleeve. But the yellow glow faded, and it skated across the skin, scoring a shallow gash.

Dean stared at the narrow wound, partly numbed, partly shocked. Will was right, it must be a xenoc. As he watched, the skin on the forearm rippled, closing the gash. The farmer laughed evilly, teeth showing white in his grubby face. He started to walk towards Dean, arms coming up menacingly. Dean stepped inside the embrace, and ordered his suit to solidify below his shoulders. The farmer's arms closed round him in a bear hug. Composite fibres, stiffened by the suit's integral valency generators, creaked ominously as the farmer's arms squeezed. A couple of equipment blocks snapped. Instinct made Dean switch off the fission blade's power, leaving a dull black blade with wickedly sharp edges. The hostiles seemed capable of controlling and subverting any kind of electrical circuit— maybe if the knife wasn't powered up . . . He pressed the tip up into the base of the farmer's jaw.

"You can heal wounds on your arm. But can you heal your brain as it's sliced in half?" The blade was shoved up a fraction until a bead of blood welled out around the tip. "Wanna try?"

The farmer hissed in animosity. He eased off his grip around Dean's chest.

"Now keep very still," Dean said as he unlocked his suit. "Because I'm very nervous, and an accident can happen easily and quickly."

"You'll suffer," the farmer said malevolently. "You'll suffer longer than you have to. I promise."

Dean took a pace to one side, the blade remaining poised on the man's neck. "You speak English, do you? Where do you come from?"

"Here, I come from here, warrior man. Just like you."

"I don't come from here."

"We all do. And you're going to stay here. For ever, warrior man. You're never going to die, not now. Eternity in purgatory is that which awaits you. Do you like the sound of that? That's what's going to happen to you."

Dean saw Will walk behind the farmer, and touch the muzzle of the gaussgun to the back of his skull.

"I've got him," said Will. "Hey, xenoc man, one bad move, one bad word, and you are countryside." He laughed. "You got that?"

The farmer's dirty lips curled up in a sneer.

"He's got it," Dean said.

Jenny came over and studied the strange tableau. The farmer looked perfectly ordinary apart from his arrogance. She thought of his two comrades that had run into the jungle, the hundreds—thousands—more just like him out there. Maybe he had a right to be arrogant.

"What's your name?" she asked.

The farmer's eyes darted towards her. "Kingsford Garrigan. What's yours?"

"Cuff him," Jenny told Dean. "We'll take him back to the *Isakore*. You're going for a long trip, Kingsford Garrigan. All the way to Kulu." She thought she saw a flash of surprise in his eyes. "And you'd better hope your friends don't try and interfere with us. I don't know what you are, but if you attempt to screw up our electronics again, or if we have to cut and run, the first thing we drop is you. And drop you we will, from a very great height."

The farmer spat casually on her foot. Will jabbed him with the gaussgun.

Jenny opened a communication channel to the geosynchronous platform, and connected into the Kulu Embassy dumper.

"We've got you one of the hostiles," she datavised to Ralph Hiltch. "And when I say hostile, I'm not kidding."

"Fantastic. Well done, Jenny. Now get back here soonest. I've got our transport to Ombey arranged. The ESA office there has the facilities for a total personality debrief."

"I wouldn't bank on it working," she said. "He's immune to a TIP shot."

"Repeat, please."

"I said the TIP carbine doesn't hurt him, the energy pulse just breaks apart. Only physical weapons seem to have any effect. At the moment we've got him subdued with a gaussgun. He's also stronger than the G66 boys, a lot stronger."

There was a long silence. "Is he human?" Ralph Hiltch asked.

"He looks human. But I don't see how he can be. If you want my opinion, I'd guess at some kind of super bitek android. It's got to be a xenoc bitek, and a pretty advanced bitek at that."

"Christ Almighty. Datavise a full-spectrum image over, please. I'll run it through some analysis programs."

"Sure thing."

Dean had the man's hands behind his back to slide a zipcuff over his wrists. It was a figure-of-eight band of polyminium with a latch buckle at the centre. Jenny watched Dean tighten the pewter-coloured loops; no electronic lock, thank heavens, just simple mechanics.

She ordered her neural nanonics to encode the retinal pixels, and datavised the complete image over to the embassy. Infrared followed, then a spectrographic print.

Dean ejected the power magazine from his broken TIP carbine and handed it to Jenny along with the spares, then recovered his gaussgun. With Will covering their prisoner, they started walking back towards the *Isakore* at a brisk pace. Jenny aimed them off at a slight tangent, taking them quickly back into the jungle. She still felt too exposed in the firestorm clearing.

"Jenny," Ralph called after a minute. "What did the hostile say his name was?"

"Kingsford Garrigan," she replied.

"He's lying. And you're wrong about him being a xenoc android, too. I've run a search program through our records. He's a colonist from Aberdale called Gerald Skibbow."

"It is a wet, humid night here in Durringham, as they always are on this poor benighted planet. The heat clogs my throat and my skin sweats as though I have caught a fever. But still I feel cold inside, a coldness that grips the very cells of my heart." Was that a bit too purple? Oh well, the studio can always edit it out.

Graeme Nicholson was squatting on aching ankles in the deepest shadows cast by one of the spaceport's big hangars. It was drizzling hard, and his cheap synthetic suit was clinging to his flabby body. Despite the warmth of the water he really was shivering, the fat rolls of his beer belly were shaking the same way they did when he laughed.

Fifty metres away a defeated yellow light shone from an office in the spaceport's single-storey administration block. It was the only occupied office, the rest had shut long ago. With his retinal implants straining, Graeme could just make out Laton, Marie Skibbow, and two other men through the grimed glass. One of them was Emlyn Hermon, the *Yaku*'s second-in-command, who had met Marie and Laton in the Crashed Dumper. He didn't know the fourth, but he must work for the spaceport administration in some capacity.

He just wished he could listen to whatever deal they were making. But his boosted hearing was only effective inside a fifteen-metre radius. And no prize in the universe would make him creep any closer to Laton. Fifty metres was quite close enough, thank you.

"I have followed the arch-diabolist here from the city. And nothing I have seen has given me the slightest hope for the future. His interest in the spaceport can only indicate he is ready to move on. His work on Lalonde is complete. Violence and anarchy reign beyond the city. What monstrous curse he has let loose is beyond my imagination; but each new day brings darker stories down the river, sucking away the citizens' hope. Fear is his real weapon, and he possesses it in abundance."

Marie held out a small object Graeme took to be a Jovian Bank credit disk. The spaceport administration official proffered its counterpart.

"The alliance has been formed. His plan advances an-

other notch. And I cannot believe it will bring anything
other than disaster upon us. Four decades has not reduced
the fear. What has he achieved in those four decades? I ask
myself this question time and again. The only answer must
be: evil. He has perfected evil."

The office light went out. Graeme emerged from his
sheltered recess, and walked along the side of the hangar
until he could see the administration block's main entrance. The drizzle was worsening, becoming rain. His suit
felt cool, and unbearably clammy, restricting his movements. A prodigious amount of water was running off the
ezystak-panel roof overhead, splattering onto the chip-
pings round his soaking feet. Despite the physical discomfort and nagging consternation at Laton's presence, he felt
an excitement that had been absent for years. This was real
journalism: the million to one break, the hazardous follow-
up, getting the story at any cost. Those shits back in the
editing offices could never handle this, safe paunchy career creatures; and they would know it too. His real victory.

Laton and his cohorts had all emerged into the bleak
night wearing cagoules against the weather. They had their
backs to him, heading for the flight line where the indistinct outlines of the parked McBoeings formed windows
into an even graver darkness. Laton (betrayed by his
height) had his arm around Marie.

"The beauty and the beast, look. What can she see in
him? For Marie is just a simple colony girl, proud and decent, loving her new planet, working long hours like all of
this city's residents. She shares the planetary ethic of her
neighbours, striving hard to achieve a better world for her
children. Yet somehow she has stumbled. A warning that
none of us is immune to the attraction of the dark side of
human nature. I look at her, and I think: there but for the
grace of God go I."

Halfway along the McBoeings was a smaller spaceplane. It was obviously Laton's goal. Bright light shone out
of its open airlock, casting a grey smear across the ground.

A couple of maintenance crew personnel were tending the mobile support units under its nose.

Graeme sneaked up to the big undercarriage bogies of a McBoeing forty metres away, and crouched down below the broad tyres. The spaceplane was one of the small swing-wing VTOL marques starships carried in their hangars. He switched his retinal implants to full magnification and scanned the fuselage. Sure enough, the name *Yaku* was printed on the low angular tail.

Some kind of argument was going on at the foot of the steps leading up to the airlock. The administration official was talking heatedly to another man wearing a cagoule with the LDC emblem on the arm. Both of them were waving their arms around. Laton, Marie, and Emlyn Hermon stood to one side, watching patiently.

"The last obstacle has been reached. It is ironic to consider that all that stands between Laton and the Confederation is one immigration official. One man between us and the prospect of galactic tragedy."

The argument ended. A Jovian Bank disk was offered.

"Can we blame him? Should we blame him? It is a foul night. He has a family which looks to him for support. And how harmless it is, a few hundred fuseodollars to avert his eyes for one swift minute. Money which can buy food for his children in these troubled times. Money which can make life that fraction easier. How many of us would do the same? How many? Would you?" Nice touch that, involve people.

Laton and Marie went up the battered aluminium stairs, followed by a furtive Emlyn Hermon. The administration official was talking to the two ground crew.

Just as he reached the airlock hatch, Laton turned, the hood of his cagoule falling back to reveal his face in full. Handsome, well proportioned, a hint of aristocracy: Edenist sophistication, but without the cultural heritage, that essential counterbalance which made the affinity gene carriers human. It looked as though he was staring straight

at Graeme Nicholson. He laughed with a debonair raffish-
ness. Mocking.

Everyone in the Confederation who accessed the sensevise in the weeks which followed experienced the old journalist's heart thud inside his ribs. All of a sudden breath
was very hard to come by, stalling in his throat.

That pause, the derision. It wasn't an accident, chance.
Laton knew he was there, and didn't care. Graeme was too
far beneath him to care.

"He is going now. Free to roam the stars. Should I have
tried to stop him? Put myself up against a man who can
make entire worlds tremble at the mention of his name? If
you think I should, then I am sorry. For I am so frightened
of him. And I do not believe I would have made any difference, not against his strength. He would still be on his
way."

The airlock hatch shut. The two ground crew scuttled
about, hunched against the rain, unplugging the thick dark-
yellow ribbed hoses from their underbelly hatches. Compressors wound up, kicking out micro-squalls of the heavy
rain. Their reedy sibilance built steadily until the spaceplane
rocked on its undercarriage. It lifted into the murky sky.

"My duty now is to warn you all. I will do what I can,
what I must, to ensure this sensevise reaches you. So that
you know. He is coming. It is you who must fight him. I
wish you luck. Those of us left here have our own battle
against the calamity he has unleashed out in the hinterlands. It is not one for which we are well prepared, this is
not a planet of epic heroes, just ordinary people like yourselves. As always, the burden falls upon those least able to
shoulder it; for a terrible night has fallen on Lalonde, and
I do not think we will see the dawn again."

The spaceplane swooped up in a sharp climb, its wings
beginning to fold back. It arrowed into the low, bulging
cloud base, and disappeared from view.

A dozen paltry fires spluttered and hissed on the broad road
outside the Governor's dumper, the flames devouring fence

posts and broken carts that had been snatched for fuel. Little knots of protesters clustered round them under the watchful eyes of the sheriffs and deputies circling the carbotanium cone. An uneasy truce had broken out after the anger and violence of the day. The earlier barrages of stones and bottles had been answered each time by cortical-jamming impulses from the sheriffs. Thankfully the protesters had refrained from using any real weapons today. Now the chanting had stopped. The naked menace in a thousand throats screaming in unison wasn't something Colin Rexrew was accustomed to dealing with. He could never make out what they had been chanting for these last few days; he thought they weren't entirely sure themselves apart from wanting the turmoil to end. Well, so did he. Very badly.

Each time Colin Rexrew looked out of his window he could see some new plume of smoke rising from the vista of dark rooftops. Tonight the horizon was dotted with three or four fierce orange flares as buildings burned. If it wasn't for the rain and humidity Durringham would have been reduced to a single giant firestorm days ago.

And the deteriorating civic situation in the city wasn't even his real problem.

When Candace Elford came into the office Colin Rexrew was behind his desk as always, gazing vacantly at the window strip and the luckless city outside. Terrance Smith gave her a fast, expressive grimace, and they both sat down.

"I'm afraid I have now effectively lost control over a third of the city," she started.

It was the nightly situation briefing. Or the nightly crisis meeting, depending on how cynical Colin felt. The intensifying pressures seemed to make it hard to concentrate at the very times he needed his full mental resources. He would have given a lot to be able to run a stimulant program through his neural nanonics, or even escape into a MF album for a few hours like he used to in his adolescence. It would have made the strain a little easier to bear.

Not even his neural nanonics with their top of the range

managerial programs were much help. There were too
many unaccountable—downright weird—factors cropping
up to apply standard responses. Had there ever been a stage
one colony governor who had lost all control of his planet?
The memory cells held no record of any.

What a way to get into the history books.

"Is it the invaders?" he asked.

"No, as far as we can make out they are still some distance away. What we're dealing with here is mainly op-
portunist looting, and some organized grabs for power.
Nothing political, but there are some strong criminal gangs
who have been quick to take advantage of the unrest. I'd
point out that most of the districts my sheriffs have been
excluded from are on the south-eastern side of town. Those
are the newest and poorest; in other words the most disaf-
fected to begin with. The heart of the city, and more importantly the merchant and industrial sectors, remain
stable. If anything, the older residents resent the lawless-
ness. I'm looking to recruit more deputies from them."

"How long before you can start to regain control of the
south-east districts?" Terrance Smith asked.

"At the moment I'm just looking to contain the trouble,"
Candace Elford said.

"You mean you can't?"

"I didn't say that, but it isn't going to be easy. The gangs
have captured two dumpers, and their fusion generators.
We can't afford to damage them, and they know that. I lost
a lot of good people in Ozark and on the *Swithland* fiasco.
Plus we have to deal with the transient colonists. They
seem to be the biggest problem right now; they're holed up
in the docks and I can't shift them. There are barricades
across every access route and there's a lot of wanton destruction and looting going on. So half the port is currently
unusable, which has antagonized the boat captains; and I
have to deploy a lot of people to keep an eye on them."

"Starve them out," Colin said.

She nodded reluctantly. "That's one option. About the

least expensive at the moment. But it will take time, there was a lot of food stored in those warehouses."

"The merchants won't like that," Terrance Smith said.

"Screw the merchants," Colin said. "I'm sorry about the transients' gear being looted, but that doesn't excuse this kind of behaviour. We can help them eventually, but not if they're going to hamper every effort with petty-minded belligerence."

"Some families lost everything—"

"Tough shit! *We* are in danger of losing an entire planet of twenty million people. My priority is to the majority."

"Yes, sir."

There were times when Colin just felt like telling his aide: here's my seat, you take over, you with your situation summaries and cautiously formulated response suggestions. Instead, the Governor walked over to the drinks cabinet and searched through the bottles for a decent chilled white wine, and to hell with the chief sheriff's disapproval.

"Can we defend Durringham from the invaders?" he asked quietly as he flipped the neck seal and poured out a glass.

"If we had enough time to prepare, and you declared martial law, and if we had enough weapons."

"Yes or no?"

Candace Elford watched the glass in the Governor's hand. It was shaking quite badly, the wine nearly spilling. "I don't think so," she said. "Whatever it is that's out there, it's strong, well armed, and well organized. The Confederation Navy office thinks they are using some kind of sequestration technology to turn colonists into a slave army. Faced with that, I don't think we really stand much of a chance."

"Sequestration nanonics," Colin mumbled as he sank back into his chair. "Dear God, who are these invaders? Xenocs? Some exiled group from another planet?"

"I'm not one hundred per cent certain," she said. "But my satellite image analysis people found these this morning. I think it may throw a little light on the situation." She datavised an order into the office's computer. The wall-screens lit up, showing a blank section of jungle fifty kilometres west of Ozark.

The satellite had passed over in the middle of the afternoon, giving a clear bright image. Trees were compacted so tightly the jungle looked like an unbroken emerald plain. Five perfectly straight black lines began to probe across the green expanse, as if the talons of a huge invisible claw were being scored down the screen. The satellite cameras zoomed in on the head of one line, and Colin Rexrew saw trees being bulldozed into the ground. A big ten-wheeled vehicle rolled into view, grey metal glinting dully, a black bubble-cab protruding from a flat upper surface. It had a blunt wedge-shaped front that smashed through trunks without the slightest resistance. Viscous sprays of red-brown mud were being flung up by its rear wheels, caking the metal bodywork. There were another three identical vehicles following it along the track of shattered vegetation it was ripping through the jungle.

"We positively identified them as Dhyaan DLA404 landcruisers; they are made on Varzquez. Or I should say, were made. The Dhyaan company stopped producing that particular model over twenty years ago."

Colin Rexrew datavised a search order into the office computer. "The LDC never brought any to Lalonde."

"That's right. The invaders brought them. What you're seeing is the first definite proof that it is an external force behind all this. And they're heading straight towards Durringham."

"Dear God." He put his empty wineglass down on the desk, and stared at the screens. The enemy had a physical form. After weeks of helpless wrestling with an elusive, possibly imaginary, foe, it was finally real; but a reason for the invasion, logical or otherwise, was impossible to devise.

Colin Rexrew gathered up what was left of his old determination and resolve. Something tangible gave his psyche a fragment of very welcome confidence. He accessed the one neural nanonics program he had thought he would never have to use, strategic military procedure, and put it into primary mode. "We have to stop deluding ourselves we can handle this on our own. I need combat troops backed up with real fire-power. I'm going to blow these invaders right off my planet. We only need to locate the headquarters. Kill the brain and the body is irrelevant. We can see about removing the sequestration nanonics from people later."

"The LDC board will need convincing," Terrance Smith said. "It won't be easy."

"They will be told afterwards," Colin said. "You've seen those landcruisers. They'll be here in a week. We must move fast. After all, it's the board's interest I'm ultimately protecting; without Lalonde there will be no LDC."

"Where can you get troops from without going through the board?" Terrance asked.

"The same place they would ultimately get them from. We buy them on a short-term contract."

"Mercenaries?" the aide asked in surprised alarm.

"Yes. Candace, where's the nearest port we can get enough in reasonable numbers? I want armed ships, too; they can provide the fire-power back-up from low orbit. It's expensive, but cheaper than buying in strategic-defence platforms. They can also prevent any more of the invader's ships from landing."

The chief sheriff gave him a long, testing stare. "Tranquillity," she said eventually. "It's a base for blackhawks and the so-called independent traders. Where you find the ships, you find the people. Ione Saldana might be young, but she's not stupid, she won't throw out the undesirables. The plutocrats who live in the habitat have too many uses for them."

"Good," Colin said decisively. "Terrance, cancel all work on Kenyon as of now. We'll use the money earmarked for mining its main chamber. It always was bloody premature."

"Yes, sir."

"After that, you can take one of the colonist-carrier ships to Tranquillity and supervise the recruitment."

"Me?"

"You." Colin watched the protest form and die unvoiced on the younger man's lips. "I want at least four thousand general troops to re-establish order in Durringham and the immediate counties. And I also want teams of combat scouts for the Quallheim Counties. They are going to have to be the best, because they are going to be assigned the search and destroy mission in the deep jungle. Once they locate the invader's home base they can zero it for the starships' weapons. We can pound it from orbit."

"What sort of armaments are we looking for on these starships?" Terrance asked guardedly.

"Masers, X-ray lasers, particle beams, thermal inducers, kinetic harpoons, and atmospheric penetration nukes—straight fusion, I don't want any radioactives clogging the environment." He caught the aide's eye. "And no antimatter, not under any circumstances."

Terrance gave a cautious grin. "Thank you."

"What ships have we got available in orbit right now?"

"That was something I was going to mention," Terrance said. "The *Yaku* left its parking orbit this evening. It jumped outsystem."

"So?"

"Firstly, it was a cargo ship, and only fifty per cent of its cargo had been unloaded. And cargo is the one thing we are still bringing down to the spaceport. It had no reason to leave. Secondly, it had no permission to leave. There was no prior contact with our Civil Flight Control Office. The only reason I found out it had left was because Kelven Solanki got in touch with me to query it. When I checked with flight control to ask why they hadn't informed us about it, they didn't even know *Yaku* had lifted from parking orbit. It turns out someone had erased the traffic-monitor satellite data from the spaceport computer."

"Why?" Candace asked. "It's not as if we have anything that could prevent them from leaving."

"No," Colin said slowly. "But we could have asked another ship to track it. Without the monitor satellite data we don't know its jump coordinate, we don't know where it went."

"Solanki will have a copy," Terrance said. "Ralph Hiltch too, I suspect. If he was pressed."

"That's all we need, another bloody puzzle," Colin said. "See what you can find out," he told Candace.

"Yes, sir."

"Back to the original question. What other ships are available?"

Terrance consulted his neural nanonics. "There are eight left in orbit; three cargo ships, the rest colonist-carriers. And we're due for another two colonist-carriers this week, as well as a Tyrathca merchant ship sometime before the end of the month to check on their farmers."

"Don't remind me," Colin said sorely.

"I think the *Gemal* would be the best bet. That only has forty Ivets left in zero-tau. They can be transferred to the *Tachad* or the *Martijn*, both of them have spare zero-tau pods. It wouldn't take more than a few hours."

"Get onto it tonight," Colin said. "And, Candace, that means the spaceport has to be defended at all costs. We have to be able get those troops down in the McBoeings. There's nowhere else for them to land. The scouts can use VTOLs to take them direct to the Quallheim Counties, but the rest will have to use the McBoeings."

"Yes, sir, I am aware of that."

"Good, start organizing for it, then. Terrance, I want you back here in ten days. Give me one month, and I'll have these bastards begging me for surrender terms."

The gaussgun's fragmentation round hit the man full in his chest, and penetrated to a depth of ten centimetres, already starting to crater the flesh, impact shock pulverizing the entire mass of organs held within his rib cage to mucilaginous jelly. Then it exploded, silicone shrapnel reducing the entire body to a spherical cascade of scarlet cells.

Will Danza grunted in acute satisfaction. "Try rebuilding yourself out of that, my xenoc friend," he told the slippery red leaves.

The hostiles were impervious to almost any major injury. The little ESA team had found that out long ago. Gaping lacerations, severed limbs—they barely slowed the hostiles down as they emerged from the thick bushes to harass the party. Wounds closed up, bones knitted in seconds. Lieutenant Jenny Harris might insist on calling the prisoner a sequestrated colonist, but Will knew what it really was. Xenoc monster. And its friends wanted it back.

Twice in the last three kilometres Jenny Harris had been forced to order a sweep-scorch pattern. The things had been throwing that eerie white fire of theirs. Once a ball had struck Dean Folan's arm, burning through the suit's energy diffusion layer as if it wasn't there. The medical nanonic package they'd put on his arm looked like a tube of translucent green exoskeleton.

"Hey!" Dean yelled. "Get back here!"

Jenny Harris looked round. Gerald Skibbow was running into the jungle, both arms pumping wildly. "Shitfire," she muttered. He had been zipcuffed a moment ago. Dean was lining up his gaussgun.

"Mine," she called. Her blue TIP carbine targeting graphic centred on a tree five metres ahead of the running man; the shots punched straight through the slim trunk, puffs of steam and flame squirted out. Gerald Skibbow swerved frantically as the tree toppled across his path. Another volley of shots and the jungle around him caught light. One final shot on his knee knocked his legs from under him.

The three of them trotted over where he lay sprawled in the crushed muddy vines.

"What happened?" Jenny asked. She had assigned Dean to guard the prisoner. Unless a gaussgun was in his back the whole time, Gerald Skibbow felt free to cause as much trouble as possible.

Dean held up the zipcuff. It was unbroken. "I saw a hostile," he said. "I only turned away for a second."

"OK," Jenny sighed. "I wasn't blaming you." She bent over Gerald Skibbow, whose grimed face was grinning up at them, and jerked his right arm up. There was a narrow red line braceleting the wrist, an old scar. "Very clever," she told him wearily. "Next time, I'll order Dean to slice your legs off below the knee. We'll see how long it takes you to grow a new pair."

Gerald Skibbow laughed. "You don't have that much time available, Madame bitch."

She straightened up. Her spine creaked and groaned as if she was a hundred and fifty. She felt older. The fire was crackling loudly in the surrounding bushes, flames inhibited by the green twigs.

It was another four kilometres back to the *Isakore*, and the jungle was becoming progressively thicker. Vines here wrapped the trees like major arteries, creating a solid hurdle of verdant mesh between the trunks. Visibility was down to less than twenty-five metres, and that was with enhanced senses.

We're not going to make it, she realized.

They'd been expending gaussgun ammunition at a heavy rate ever since they set off. They had to, nothing else worked against the hostiles. Even the two TIP carbines were down to forty per cent of their power reserve. "Get him up," she ordered curtly.

Will clamped an arm round Gerald Skibbow's shoulder and hauled him to his feet.

White fire burst out of the ground around Jenny's feet, damp loam tearing open to spit out dazzling globules which spiralled up her legs like a liquid repelled by gravity. She screamed at the pain as her skin blistered and burned inside the anti-projectile suit. Her neural nanonics isolated the nerve strands, eliminating the raw impulses with analgesic blocks.

Will and Dean started firing their gaussguns at random into the blank impassive jungle in the vain hope of hitting a hostile. EE projectiles mashed the nearby trees. Shreds of sappy vegetation whirred through the air, forming a loose curtain behind which vivid explosions boomed.

The viscid beads of white fire evaporated as they reached Jenny's hips. She clenched her teeth against the solid ache from her legs. Frightened by the damage her neural nanonics were shielding her from. Frightened she couldn't walk. The medical program was choking up her mind with red symbols, all of them clustered around schematics of her legs like bees round honey. She felt faint.

"We can help you," silver voices whispered in chorus.

"What?" she asked, disorientated. She sat on the lumpy ground to take the strain off her legs. Her trembling muscles had been about to dump her there anyway.

"You all right, Jenny?" Dean asked. He was standing with the gaussgun pointing threateningly into the broken trees.

"Did you say something?"

"Yes, are you OK?"

"I . . ." I'm hearing things. "We've got to get out of here."

"First thing you have to do is get a medical nanonic package on those legs. I think there's enough," he said, uncertainty clouding his voice.

Jenny knew there wasn't, not to get her patched up for a hike of four kilometres under combat conditions. The neural nanonics prognosis wasn't good; the program was activating her endocrine implant, sending a potent stew of chemicals into her bloodstream. "No," she said forcefully. "We're not going to get back to the boat like this."

"We ain't going to leave you," Will said hotly.

She grinned unseen inside her shell-helmet. "Believe me, I wasn't going to ask you to. Even if the medical nanonics can get me walking, we don't have enough ordnance left to blast our way back to the *Isakore* from here."

"What then?" Will demanded.

Jenny requested a channel to Murphy Hewlett. Static crashed into her neural nanonics, that eerie whistling.

"Shitfire. I can't get the marines." She hated the idea of abandoning them.

"I think I can see why," Dean said. He pointed at the treetops. "Smoke, and plenty of it. South of here. Some distance by the look of it. They must have laid down a sweep-scorch pattern. They got troubles, too."

Jenny couldn't see any smoke. Even the leaves at the top of the trees had turned a barren grey. Her vision was tunnelling. A physiological-status request showed her endocrines were barely coping with the flayed legs. "Sling me your medical nanonics," she said.

"Right." Will fired six EE rounds into the jungle then hurriedly detached his backpack and tossed it over. He was back watching the abused trees before it reached her.

She ordered her communications block to open a channel to Ralph Hiltch, then turned the backpack seal's catch and fumbled around inside. Instead of the subliminal digital bleep that signalled the block was interfacing with the geosynchronous platform, all she heard was a monotonous buzz.

"Will, Dean, open a channel to the geosync platform, maybe a combined broadcast will get through." She picked up her TIP carbine, and pointed it at Gerald Skibbow, who was squatting sullenly beside a swath of vines four metres away. "And you, if I think you are part of the jamming effort, I will start a little experiment to see exactly how much thermal energy you can fight off. You got me, Mr. Skibbow? Is this message getting through the electronic warfare barrier?"

The communication block reported the channel to the embassy was open.

"What's happening?" Ralph Hiltch asked.

"Trouble—" Jenny broke off to hiss loudly. The medical nanonic package was contracting round her left leg, it felt as though a thousand acid-tipped needles were jabbing into the roasted gouges as the furry inner surface knitted with her flesh. She had to order the neural nanonics to block all the nerve impulses. Her legs went completely numb, lacking even the heavy vacuum feeling of chemical anaesthetics. "Boss, I hope that fall-back scheme of yours works. Because we need it pretty badly. Now, boss."

"OK, Jenny. I'm putting it in motion. ETA fifteen minutes, can you hang on that long?"

"No problem," Will said. He sounded indecently cheerful.

"Are you secure where you are?" Ralph asked.

"Our security situation wouldn't change if we moved," Jenny told him, marvelling at her own understatement.

"OK, I've got your coordinates. Use your TIP carbines to scorch a clearing at least fifty metres across. I'll need it for a landing-zone."

"Yes, sir."

"I'm on my way."

Jenny swapped her TIP carbine for Dean's gaussgun. By sitting with her back to a tree she could keep it pointed at Gerald Skibbow. The two G66 troops began slashing at the jungle with their TIP carbines.

The captain of the *Ekwan* was a middle-aged woman in a blue ship-suit, with the kind of robust, lanky figure that suggested she was from a space-adapted geneered family. The AV projector showed her floating ten centimetres above the acceleration couch in her compact cabin. "How did you know we were leaving orbit?" she asked. Her voice was slightly distorted by a curious whistle that was coming through the relay from the LDC's geosynchronous communication platform.

Graeme Nicholson smiled thinly at her puzzled tone. He diverted his eyes from the projection for a second. On the other side of Durringham spaceport's flight control centre Langly Bradburn rolled his eyes and turned back to his monitor console.

"I have a contact in the Kulu Embassy," Graeme said, returning to the projection.

"This isn't a commercial flight," the captain said, a fair amount of resentment bubbling into her voice.

"I know." Graeme had heard of the Kulu Ambassador throwing his authority around and virtually commandeering the Kulu-registered colonist-carrier. A situation which became even more interesting when he discovered from Langly that it was Cathal Fitzgerald who was in orbit making sure the captain did as she was told. Cathal Fitzgerald was one of Ralph Hiltch's people. And now, as Graeme looked through the flight control centre's window, he could see a queue of people standing on the nearby hangar apron, shoulders angled against the rain as they embarked on a passenger McBoeing BDA-9008. The entire embassy staff and dependants. "But it is only one memory flek," he said winningly. "And the Time Universe office will pay a substantial bonus when you hand it in to them, I can assure you of that."

"I haven't been told where we're going yet."

"We have offices in every Confederation system. And it would be a personal favour," Graeme emphasized.

There was a pause as the captain worked out that she would receive the entire carriage fee herself. "Very well, Mr. Nicholson. Give it to the McBoeing pilot, I'll meet him when he docks."

"Thank you, Captain, pleasure doing business with you."

"I thought you sent a flek out with the *Gemal* this morning?" Langly observed as Graeme switched off the metre-high projection pillar.

"I did, old boy. Just covering my back."

"Are people really going to be interested in a riot on Lalonde? Nobody even knows this planet even exists."

"They will. Oh, indeed they will."

Rain slammed against the little spaceplane's fuselage as it dived out through the bottom of the clouds. It made a fast rattling sound against the tough silicolithium-composite skin. Individual drops burst into streaks of steam, vaporized by the friction heat of the craft's Mach five velocity.

Looking over the pilot's shoulder Ralph Hiltch saw the

jungle blurring past below. It was grey-green, sprinkled by flexuous strands of mist. Up ahead was a broad band of brighter grey where the clouds ended, and getting broader.

"Ninety seconds," Kieron Syson, the pilot, shouted over the noise.

A loud metallic whirring filled the small cabin as the wings began to swing forward. The spaceplane pitched up at a sharp angle, and the noise of the rain impacts increased until talking was impossible. Deceleration hit three gees, forcing Ralph back into one of the cabin's six plastic seats.

Sunlight burst into the cabin with a fast rainbow flash. The sound of the rain vanished. They levelled out as their speed dropped to subsonic.

"We'll need a complete structure fatigue check after this," Kieron Syson complained. "Nobody flies supersonic through rain, half the leading edges have abraded down to their safety margins."

"Don't worry about it," Ralph told him. "It'll be paid for." He turned to check with Cathal Fitzgerald. Both of them were wearing the same model of olive green one-piece anti-projectile suits as Jenny and the two G66 troops. It had been a long time since Ralph had dressed for combat, a cool tension was compressing his body inside and out.

"Looks like your people have been having themselves a wild time," Kieron said.

Away in the southern distance a vast column of dense soot-laden smoke was rising high into the pale blue sky, a ring of flames dancing round its base. Ten kilometres to the east a kilometre-wide ebony crater had been burned out of the trees.

The spaceplane banked sharply, variable-camber wings twisting elastically to circle it round a third, smaller, blackened clearing. This one was only a hundred metres across. Small licks of flame fluttered from the fallen trees around the perimeter, and thin blue smoke formed a mushroom dome of haze. There was a small green island of withered vegetation in the exact centre.

"That's them," Kieron said as the spaceplane's guidance systems locked on to the signal from Jenny Harris's communication block.

Four people were standing on the crush of vine leaves and grass. As Ralph watched, one of them fired a gaussgun into the jungle.

"Down and grab them," he told Kieron. "And make it fast."

Kieron whistled through closed teeth. "Why me, Lord?" he muttered stoically.

Ralph heard the fan nozzles rotate to the vertical, and the undercarriage clunked as it unfolded. They were swinging round the black scorch zone in decreasing circles. He ordered his communication block to open a local channel to Jenny Harris.

"We're coming down in fifty seconds," he told her. "Get ready to run."

The cabin airlock's outer hatch hinged open, showing him the fuselage shield sliding back. A blast of hot, moist air hurtled in, along with the howl of the compressors.

"Faster, boss," Jenny shouted, her voice raw. "We've only got thirty gaussgun rounds left. Once we stop this suppression fire they'll hit the spaceplane with everything they've got."

A fine black powder was churning through the cabin like a sable sandstorm. Environment-contamination warnings sounded above the racket from the compressors, amber lights winked frantically on the forward bulkhead.

"Land us now," Ralph ordered Kieron. "Cathal, give them some covering fire, scorch that jungle."

The compressor noise changed, becoming strident. Cathal Fitzgerald moved into the airlock, bracing himself against the outer hatch rim. He began to swing his TIP carbine in long arcs. A sheet of flame lashed the darkening sky around the edge of the clearing.

"Ten seconds," Kieron said. "I'll get as close to them as I can."

Ash rose up in a cyclonic blizzard as the compressor

nozzle efflux splashed against the ground. Visibility was reduced drastically. An orange glow from the flames fluoresced dimly on one side of the spaceplane.

Jenny Harris watched the craft touch and bounce, then settle. She could just make out the name *Ekwan* on the narrow, angled tail. Ralph Hiltch and Cathal Fitzgerald were two indistinct figures hanging on to the side of the open airlock. One of them was waving madly; she guessed it was Ralph.

Will Danza fired the last of his gaussgun rounds, and dropped the big weapon. "Empty," he muttered in disgust. His TIP carbine came up, and he started adding to the flames.

"Come on, move!" Ralph's datavise was tangled with discordant static.

"Get Skibbow in," Jenny ordered Dean and Will. "I'll cover our backs." She brought her TIP carbine to bear on the soot-occluded jungle, putting her back to the spaceplane.

Will and Dean grabbed Gerald Skibbow and started to drag him towards the sleek little craft.

Jenny limped after them, trailing by several metres. The last heavy duty power cell banged against her side, its energy level down to seven per cent. She reduced the carbine's rate of fire, and fired off fifteen shots blindly. Grunting and shuffling sounds were coming down her headset, relayed by the suit's audio pick-ups. She flicked to her rear optical sensors for a moment and saw Gerald Skibbow putting up a struggle as four people tried to haul him through the spaceplane's airlock hatch. Ralph Hiltch slammed his carbine butt into Gerald's face. Blood poured out of the colonist's broken nose, dazing him long enough for Will to shove his legs through.

Jenny switched her attention back to her forward view. Five figures were solidifying out of the swirl of ash. They were stooped humanoids; like big apes, she thought. Blue targeting graphics closed like a noose around one. She fired, sending it flailing backwards.

A ball of white fire raced out of the gloom, too fast to duck. It splashed over her TIP carbine, intensifying. The weapon casing distorted, buckling as though it was made of soft wax. She couldn't free her fingers from the grip; it had melted round them. Her throat voiced a desolate cry as the terrible fire bit hard into her knuckles. The flaming remnants of the carbine fell to the ground. She held up her hand; there were no fingers or thumb, only the smoking stump of her palm. Her cry turned to a wail, and she tripped over a root protruding from the loam. The woody strand coiled fluidly round her ankle like a malicious serpent. Four dark figures loomed closer, a fifth lumbering up behind.

She twisted round on the ground. The spaceplane was twelve metres away. Gerald Skibbow was lying on the floor of the airlock with two suited figures on top of him pinning him down. He looked straight at Jenny, a gleeful sneer on his blooded lips. The root tightened its vicelike grip, cutting into her ankle. He was doing it, she knew that then.

"Lift," she datavised. "Ralph, for God's sake lift. Get him to Ombey."

"Jenny!"

"Make it mean something."

One of the dark figures landed on her. It was a man, strangely corpulent, bulky without being fat; thick matted hair covered his entire body. Then she couldn't see anything; his belly was pressed against her shell-helmet.

That quiet chorus spoke to her again. "There is no need for fear," it said. "Let us help you."

Another of the man-things gripped her knees, his buttocks squashing her damaged legs into the ground. The front of her anti-projectile suit was ripped open. It was difficult to breathe now.

"Jenny! Oh Christ, I can't shoot, they're on top of her."

"Lift!" she begged. "Just lift."

All the neural nanonics analgesic blocks seemed to have collapsed. The pain from her legs and hand was debilitating, crushing her thoughts. More ripping sounds penetrated her dimming universe. She felt hot, damp air gust across her bared crotch.

"We can stop it," the chorus told her. "We can save you. Let us in." There was a pressure against her thoughts, like a warm dry wind blowing through her skull.

"Go to hell," she moaned. She sent one final diamond-hard thought needling into her faltering neural nanonics, a kamikaze code. The order was transferred into the high-density power cell, shorting it out. She wondered if there would be enough energy left for an explosion big enough to engulf all the man-things.

There was.

The *Ekwan* fell around Lalonde's equator, six hundred kilometres above the brown and ochre streaks of the deserts which littered the continent of Sarell. With its five windmill-sail thermo-dump panels extended from its central section, the colonist-carrier was rotating slowly about its drive axis, completing one revolution every twenty minutes. A passenger McBoeing BDA-9008 was docked to an airlock tube on its forward hull.

It was a tranquil scene, starship and spaceplane sliding silently over Sarell's rocky shores and out across the deepening blues of the ocean. Thousands of kilometres ahead, the terminator cast a black veil over half of Amarisk. Every few minutes a puff of smoky yellow vapour would flash out of a vernier nozzle between the starship's thermo-dump panels, gone in an eyeblink.

Such nonchalant technological prowess created an effect which totally belied the spectacle inside the airlock tube, where children cried and threw up and red-faced parents cursed as they fended off the obnoxious sticky globules. Nobody had been given time to prepare for the departure; all they had brought with them was clothes and valuable items stuffed hastily into shoulder-bags. Children hadn't even been given anti-nausea drugs. The embassy staffers shouted back and forth in angry tones, disguising both relief at leaving Lalonde and disgust at the flying vomit. But the *Ekwan*'s crew were used to the behaviour of planet dwellers; they floated around with hand-held suction sanitizers, and cajoled the reluctant children towards one of the five big zero-tau compartments.

Captain Farrah Montgomery watched the picture projected from an AV pillar on the bridge command console, indifferent to the suffering. She'd seen it all before, a thousand times over. "Are you going to tell me where we are heading?" she asked the man strapped into her executive officer's acceleration couch. "I can start plotting our course vector. Might save some time."

"Ombey," said Sir Asquith Parish, Kulu's Ambassador to Lalonde.

"You're the boss," she said acidly.

"I don't like this any more than you."

"We've got three thousand colonists left in zero-tau. What are you going to tell them when we get to the Principality?"

"I've no idea. Though once they hear what's actually happening down on the surface I doubt they'll complain."

Captain Montgomery thought about the flek in her breast pocket with a glimmer of guilt. The reports they'd been receiving from Durringham over the past week were pretty garbled, too. Maybe they were better off leaving. At least she could transfer the responsibility to the ambassador when the line company started asking questions.

"How soon before we can leave orbit?" Sir Asquith asked.

"As soon as Kieron gets back. You know, you had no right to send him on a flight like that."

"We can wait for two more orbits."

"I'm not leaving without my pilot."

"If they're not airborne by then, you don't have a pilot any more."

She turned her head to look at him. "Just what is going on down there?"

"I wish I knew, Captain. But I can tell you I'm bloody glad we're leaving."

The McBoeing undocked as the *Ekwan* moved into the penumbra. Its pilot fired the orbital manoeuvring rockets, and it dropped away into an elliptical orbit which would intercept Lalonde's upper atmosphere. *Ekwan* started her preflight checks, testing the ion thrusters, priming the fusion tubes. The crew scurried through the life-support capsules, securing loose fittings and general rubbish.

"Got him," the navigation officer called out.

Captain Montgomery datavised the flight computer, requesting the external sensor images.

A long contrail of blue-white plasma stretched out across Amarisk's darkened eastern side, its star-head racing over the seaboard mountains. Already fifty kilometres high and rising. Bright enough to send a backwash of lame phosphorescent light skating over the snow-capped peaks.

Ekwan's flight computer acknowledged a communication channel opening.

Ralph Hiltch watched the hyped-up Kieron Syson start to relax once he could datavise the starship again. It should have been something for Ralph to be thankful about, too, communications had been impossible in the aftermath of the landing. Instead he treated it like a non-event, he expected nothing less than the communications block to work. They were owed functional circuitry.

Environment-contamination warning lights were still winking amber, though the pilot had shut off the cabin's audio alarm. The air was dry and calciferous, scratching the back of Ralph's throat. Gravity was falling off as they soared ever higher above the ocean, curving up to rendezvous with the big colonist-carrier. The prolonged bass roar of the reaction rockets was reducing.

The air they breathed was bad enough, but the human atmosphere in the spaceplane's confined cabin was murderous. Gerald Skibbow sat at the rear of the cabin, shrunk down into his plastic seat, a zipcuff restraining each wrist against the armrests, his hands white knuckled as he gripped the cushioning. He had been subdued since the air-lock hatch closed. But then Will and Dean were looking hard for an excuse to rip his head off. Jenny's death had been fast (thank God) but very, very messy.

Ralph knew he should be reviewing the memory of the ape-analogue creatures, gaining strategically critical information on the threat they faced, but he just couldn't bring himself to do it. Let the ESA office on Ombey study the memory sequence, they wouldn't be so emotionally involved. Jenny had been a damn good officer, and a friend.

The spaceplane's reaction drive cut off. Free fall left Ralph's stomach rising up through his chest. He accessed a nausea-suppression program and quickly activated it.

Huddled in his chair, Gerald Skibbow began to tremble as the forked strands of his filthy, blood-soaked beard waved about in front of his still-bleeding nose.

Ekwan's hangar was a cylindrical chamber ribbed by metal struts; the walls were composed of shadows and crinkled silver blankets. The spaceplane, wings fully retracted, eased its squashed-bullet nose through the open doors into the waiting clamp ring. Actuators slid catches into a circle of load sockets behind the radar dome, and the craft was drawn inside.

Three of *Ekwan*'s security personnel, experts at handling troublesome Ivets in free fall, swam into the cabin, coughing at the ash dust which filled the air.

Will took the zipcuffs off Gerald Skibbow. "Run, why don't you," he said silkily.

Gerald Skibbow gave him a contemptuous glance, which turned to outright alarm as he rose into the air. Hands clawed frantically for a grip on the cabin ceiling. He wound up clutching a grab loop for dear life.

The grinning security personnel closed in.

"Just tow him the whole way," Ralph told them. "And you, Skibbow, don't cause any trouble. We'll be right behind, and we're armed."

"You can't use TIP carbines in the ship," one of the security men protested.

"Oh, really? Try me."

Gerald Skibbow reluctantly let go of the grab loop, and let the men tug him along by his arms. The eight-strong group drifted out into the tubular corridor connecting the hangar to one of the life-support capsules.

Sir Asquith Parish was waiting outside the zero-tau compartment, a stikpad holding his feet in place. He gave Gerald Skibbow a distasteful look. "You lost Jenny Harris for him?"

"Yes, sir," Will said through clamped teeth.

Sir Asquith recoiled.

"Whatever sequestrated him has several ancillary energy-manipulation functions," Ralph explained. "He is lethal; one on one, he's better than any of us."

The ambassador gave Gerald Skibbow a fast reappraisal. Light strips circling the corridor outside the zero-tau compartment hatch flickered and dimmed.

"Stop it," Dean growled. He jabbed his TIP carbine into the small of Skibbow's back.

The light strips came up to full strength again.

Gerald Skibbow laughed jauntily at the shaken ambassador as the security men shoved him through the hatch. Ralph Hiltch cocked an ironic eyebrow, then followed them in.

The zero-tau compartment was a big sphere, sliced into sections by mesh decking that was only three metres apart. It didn't look finished; it was poorly lit, with bare metal girders and kilometres of power cable stuck to every surface. The sarcophagus pods formed long silent ranks, their upper surface a blank void. Most of them were activated, holding the colonists who had gambled their future on conquering Lalonde.

Gerald Skibbow was manoeuvred to an open pod just inside the hatchway. He glanced around the compartment, his head turning in fractured movements to take in the compartment. The security men holding him felt his muscles tensing.

"Don't even think of it," one said.

He was propelled firmly towards the waiting pod.

"No," he said.

"Get in," Ralph told him impatiently.

"No. Not that. Please. I'll be good, I'll behave."

"Get in."

"No."

One of the security men anchored himself to the decking grid with a toe clip, and tugged him down.

"No!" He gripped both sides of the open pod, his features stone-carved with determination. "I won't!" he shouted.

"In!"

"No."

All three security men were pushing and shoving at him. Gerald Skibbow strove against them. Will tucked a leg round a nearby girder, and smacked the butt of his TIP carbine against Gerald Skibbow's left hand. There was a crunch as the bones broke.

He howled, but managed to keep hold. His fingers turned purple, the skin undulating. "No!"

The carbine came down again. Ralph put his hands flat against the decking above, and stood on Gerald Skibbow's back, knees straining, trying to thrust him down into the pod.

Gerald Skibbow's broken hand slipped a couple of centimetres, leaving a red smear. "Stop this, stop this." Rivulets of white light began to shiver across his torso.

Ralph felt as though his own spine was going to snap, the force his boosted muscles were exerting against his skeleton was tremendous. The soles of his feet were tingling sharply, the worms of white light coiling round his ankles. "Dean, switch the pod on the second he's in."

"Sir."

The hand slipped again. Gerald Skibbow started a high-pitched animal wailing. Will hammered away at his left elbow. Firefly sparks streaked back up the carbine every time it hit, as though he was striking flint.

"Get in, you bastard," one of the security men shouted,

nearly purple from the effort, face shrivelled like a rubber
mask.

Gerald Skibbow gave way, the arm Will had hammered
on finally losing hold. He crashed down into the bottom of
the pod with an oof of air punched out through his open
mouth. Ralph cried out at the shock of the jolt that was
transmitted back up his cramped legs. The curving lid of
the pod began to slide into place, and he bent his knees
frantically, lifting his legs out of the way.

"No!" Gerald Skibbow shouted. He had begun to glow
like a hologram profile, rainbow colours shining bright in
the compartment's gloom. His voice was cut off by the lid
sliding into place, and it locked with a satisfying mechanical *click*. There was a muffled thud of a fist striking the
composite.

"Where's the bloody zero-tau?" Will said. "Where is it?"

The lid of the pod hadn't changed, there was no sign of
the slippery black field effect. Gerald Skibbow was pounding away on the inside with the fervour of a man buried
alive.

"It's on," Dean shouted hoarsely from the operator's
control panel. "Christ, it's on, it's drawing power."

Ralph stared at the sarcophagus in desperation. Work, he
pleaded silently, come on fuck you, work! Jenny died for
this.

"Switch on, you shit!" Will screamed at it.

Gerald Skibbow stopped punching the side of the pod. A
black emptiness irised over the lid.

Will let out a sob of exhausted breath.

Ralph realized he was clinging weakly to one of the
girders, the real fear had been that Gerald Skibbow would
break out. "Tell the captain we're ready," he said in a
drained voice. "I want to get him to Ombey as quickly as
we can."

2

The event horizon around *Villeneuve's Revenge* dissolved the instant the starship expanded out to its full forty-eight-metre size. Solar wind and emaciated light from New California's distant sun fell on the dark silicon hull which its disappearance exposed. Short-range combat sensors slid out of their jump recesses with smooth animosity, metallic black tumours inset with circular gold-mirror lenses. They scoured a volume of space five hundred kilometres across, hungry for a specific shape.

Data streams from the sensors sparkled through Erick Thakrar's mind, a rigid symbolic language written in monochromic light. Cursors chased through the vast constantly reconfiguring displays, closing in on an explicit set of values like circling photonic-sculpture vultures. Radiation, mass, and laser returns slotted neatly into their parameter definition.

The *Krystal Moon* materialized out of the fluttering binary fractals, hanging in space two hundred and sixty kilometres away. An inter-planetary cargo ship, eighty metres long; a cylindrical life-support capsule at one end, silver-foil-cloaked tanks and dull-red fusion-drive tube clustered at the other. Thermo-dump panels formed a ruff collar on the outside of the environmental-engineering deck just below the life-support capsule; communication dishes jutted out of a grid tower on the front of it. The ship's midsection was a hexagonal gantry supporting five rings of standard cargo-pods, some of them plugged into the environmental deck via thick cables and hoses.

A slender twenty-five-metre flame of hazy blue plasma

burnt steadily from the fusion tube, accelerating the *Krystal Moon* at an unvarying sixtieth of a gee. It had departed Tehama asteroid five days ago with its cargo of industrial machinery and micro-fusion generators, bound for the Ukiah asteroid settlement in the outer asteroid belt Dana, which orbited beyond the gas giant Sacramento. Of the star's three asteroid belts, Dana was the least populated; traffic this far out was thin. *Krystal Moon*'s sole link to civilization (and navy protection) was its microwave communication beam, focused on Ukiah, three hundred and twenty million kilometres ahead.

Erick's neural nanonics reported that pattern lock was complete. He commanded the X-ray lasers to fire.

Two hundred and fifty kilometres away, the *Krystal Moon*'s microwave dishes burst apart into a swirl of aluminium snowflakes. A long brown scar appeared on the forward hull of the life-support capsule.

God, I hope no one was in the cabin below.

Erick tried to push that thought right back to the bottom of his mind. Straying out of character, even for a second, could quite easily cost him his life. They'd drilled that into him enough times back at the academy. There was even a behavioural consistency program loaded into his neural nanonics to catch any wildly inaccurate reactions. But flinches and sudden gasps could be equally damning.

The *Villeneuve's Revenge* triggered its fusion drive, and accelerated in towards the stricken cargo ship at five and a half gees. Erick sent another two shots from the X-ray cannon squirting into the *Krystal Moon*'s fusion tube. Its drive flame died. Coolant fluid vented out of a tear in the casing, hidden somewhere in the deep shadows on the side away from the sun, the fountain fluorescing grey-blue as it jetted out from behind the ship.

"Nice going, Erick," André Duchamp commented. He had the secondary fire-control program loaded in his own neural nanonics. If the newest crew-member hadn't fired he could have taken over within milliseconds. Despite Erick's performance in the Catalina Bar, André had a single nagging doubt. After all, O'Flaherty was one of their own—after a fashion—and eliminating him didn't require many qualms no matter who you were; but firing on an unarmed civil ship . . . *You have earned your place on board,* André said silently. He cancelled his fire-control program.

Villeneuve's Revenge was a hundred and twenty kilometres from the *Krystal Moon* when André turned the starship and started decelerating. The hangar doors began to slide open. He started to whistle against the push of the heavy gee force.

He had a right to be pleased. Even though it had only been a tiny interplanetary jump, two hundred and sixty kilometres was an excellent separation distance. Since leaving Tehama, *Villeneuve's Revenge* had been in orbit around Sacramento. They had extended every sensor, focusing along the trajectory Lance Coulson had sold them until they had found the faint splash of the *Krystal Moon*'s exhaust. With its exact position and acceleration available in real time, it was just a question of manufacturing themselves a jump co-ordinate.

Two hundred and sixty kilometres, there were voidhawks that would be pushed to match that kind of accuracy.

Thermo-dump panels stayed inside the monobonded silicon hull as the *Villeneuve's Revenge* rendezvoused with *Krystal Moon.* The jump nodes were fully charged. André was cautious, they might need to leave in a hurry. It had happened before; stealthed voidhawks lying in wait, Confederation Navy Marines hiding in the cargo-pods. Not to him, though.

"Bev, give our target an active sensor sweep, please," André ordered.

"Yes, Captain," Bev Lennon said. The combat sensors sent out fingers of questing radiation to probe the *Krystal Moon.*

The brilliant lance of fusion fire at the rear of the *Villeneuve's Revenge* sank away to a minute bubble of radiant helium clinging to the tube's nozzle. *Krystal Moon* was six kilometres away, wobbling slightly from the impulse imparted by the venting coolant fluid. Thrusters flared around the rear bays, trying to compensate and stabilize.

Ion thrusters on the *Villeneuve's Revenge* fired, nudging the bulky starship in towards its floundering prey. Brendon piloted the multifunction service vehicle up out of the hangar and set off towards the *Krystal Moon*. One of the cargo-bay doors slowly hinged upwards behind him.

"Come on, Brendon," André murmured impatiently as the small auxiliary craft rode its bright yellow chemical rocket exhaust across the gap. Ukiah traffic control would know the communication link had been severed in another twelve minutes; it would take the bureaucrats a few minutes to react, then sensors would review the *Krystal Moon*'s track. They'd see the spaceship's fusion drive was off, coupled with the lack of an emergency distress beacon. That could only mean one thing. The navy would be alerted, and if the *Villeneuve's Revenge* was really unlucky a patrolling voidhawk would investigate. André was allowing twenty minutes maximum for the raid.

"It checks out clean," Bev Lennon reported. "But the crew must have survived that first X-ray laser strike, I'm picking up electronic emissions from inside the life-support capsule. The flight computers are still active."

"And they've suppressed the distress beacon," André said. "That's smart, they must know we'd slice that can in half to silence any shout for help. Maybe they'll be in a co-operative mood." He datavised the flight computer to open an inter-ship channel.

Erick heard the hiss of static fill the dimly lit bridge as the AV pillar was activated. A series of musical bleeps came with it, then the distinct sound of a child crying. He saw Madeleine Collum's head come up from her acceleration couch, turning in the direction of the communication console. Blue and red shadows flowed over her gaunt, shaven skull.

"*Krystal Moon*, acknowledge contact," André said.

"Acknowledge?" a ragged outraged male voice shouted

out of the AV pillar. "You shithead animal, two of my crew
are dead. Fried! Tina was fifteen years old!"

Erick's neural nanonics stanched the sudden damp fire
in his eyes. A fifteen-year-old girl. Great God Almighty!
These interplanetary ships were often family operated affairs, cousins and siblings combining into crews.

"Release the latches on pods DK-30-91 and DL-30-07,"
André said as though he hadn't heard. "That's all we're
here for."

"Screw you."

"We'll cut them free anyway, *Anglo*, and if we cut then
the capsule will be included. I'll open your hull up to space
like the foil on a freeze-dried food packet."

A visual check through the combat sensors showed
Erick the MSV was two hundred metres away from the
Krystal Moon. Desmond Lafoe had already fitted laser cut-
ters to the craft's robot arms; the spindly white waldos
were running through a preprogrammed articulation test.
Villeneuve's Revenge was lumbering along after the
smaller, more agile, auxiliary craft; three kilometres away
now.

"We'll think about it," said the voice.

"Daddy!" the girl in the background wailed. "Daddy,
make them go away."

A woman shushed her, sounding fearful.

"Don't think about it," André said. "Just do it."

The channel went silent.

"Bastards," André muttered. "Erick, put another blast
through that capsule."

"If we kill them, they can't release the pods."

André scowled darkly. "Scare them, don't kill them."

Erick activated one of the starship's lasers; it was designed for close-range interception, the last layer of defence against incoming combat wasps. Powerful and
highly accurate. He reduced the power level to five per
cent, and lined it up on the front of the life-support capsule. The infrared beam sliced a forty-centimetre circle out

of the foam-covered hull. Steamy gas erupted out of the breach.

André grunted at what he considered to be Erick's display of timidity, and opened the inter-ship channel again. "Release the pods."

There was no answer. Erick couldn't hear the girl any more.

Brendon guided the MSV around the rings of barrel-like cargo-pods circling the *Krystal Moon*'s mid-section. He found the first pod containing microfusion generators, and focused the MSV's external cameras on it. The latch clamps of the cradle it was lying in were closed solidly round the load pins. Sighing regretfully at the time and effort it would cost to cut the pod free, he engaged the MSV's attitude lock, keeping station above the pod, then datavised the waldo-control computer to extend the arm. Droplets of molten metal squirted out where the cutting laser sliced through the clamps, a micrometeorite swarm glowing as if they were grazing an atmosphere.

"Something's happening," Bev Lennon reported. The electronic sensors were showing him power circuits coming alive inside the *Krystal Moon*'s life-support capsule. Atmosphere was still spewing out of the lasered hole, unchecked. "Hey—"

A circular section of the hull blew out. Erick's mind automatically directed the X-ray lasers towards the hole revealed by the crumpled sheet of metal as it twirled off towards the stars. A small craft rose out of the hole, ascending on a pillar of flame. Recognition was immediate: lifeboat.

It was a cone, four metres across at the base, five metres high; with a doughnut of equipment and tanks wrapped round the nose. Tarnished-silver protective foam reflected distorted star-specks. The lifeboat could sustain six people for a month in space, or jettison the equipment doughnut and land on a terracompatible planet. Cheaper then supplying the crew with zero-tau pods, and given that the mother ship would only be operating in an inhabited star system, just as safe.

"*Merde*, now we'll have to laser every latch clamp," André complained. He could see that Brendon had cut loose half of the first pod. By his own timetable, they had nine minutes left. It was going to be a close-run thing. "Knock that bloody lifeboat out, Erick."

"No," Erick said calmly. The lifeboat had stopped accelerating. Its spent solid rocket booster was jettisoned.

"I gave you an order."

"Piracy is one thing; I'm not being a party to slaughter. There are children on that lifeboat."

"He's right, André," Madeleine Collum said.

"*Merde*! All right, but once Brendon has those pods cut free I want the *Krystal Moon* vaporized. That bloody captain has put our necks on the block by defying us, I want him ruined."

"Yes, Captain," Erick said. How typical, he thought, we can go in with lasers blazing, but if anyone fights back, that's *unfair*. When we get back to Tranquillity, I'm going to take a great deal of unprofessional pride in having André Duchamp committed to a penal planet.

They made it with forty-five seconds to spare. Brendon cut both cargo-pods free, and manoeuvred them into the waiting cargo hold in the *Villeneuve's Revenge*. X-ray lasers started to chop at the *Krystal Moon* as the MSV docked with its own cradle to be drawn gingerly into the hangar bay. The remaining cargo-pods were split open, spilling their wrecked contents out into the void. Structural spars melted, twisting as though they were being chewed. Tanks were punctured, creating a huge vapour cloud that chased outward, its fringes swirling round the retreating lifeboat.

The starship's hangar door slid shut. Combat sensors retreated back into the funereal hull. An event horizon sprang up around the *Villeneuve's Revenge*. The starship shrank. Vanished.

Floating alone amid the fragmented debris and vacuum-

chilled nebula, the lifeboat let out a passionless electromagnetic shriek for help.

The word was out even before the *Lady Macbeth* docked at
Tranquillity's spaceport. Joshua's landed the big one. On his
first Norfolk run, for Heaven's sake. How does he do it?
Something about that guy is uncanny. Lucky little sod.

Joshua led his crew into a packed Harkey's Bar. The
band played a martial welcome with plangent trumpets;
four of the waitresses were standing on the beer-slopped
bar, short black skirts letting everyone see their knickers
(or not, in one case); crews and groups of spaceport workers whistled, cheered, and jeered. One long table was
loaded down with bottles of wine and champagne in
troughs of ice; Harkey himself stood at the end, a smile in
place. Everyone quietened down.

Joshua looked round slowly, an immensely smug grin in
place. This must be what Alastair II saw from his state
coach every day. It was fabulous. "Do you want a speech?"

"NO!"

His arm swept out expansively towards Harkey. He
bowed low, relishing the theatre. "Then open the bottles."

There was a rush for the table, conversation even loud
enough to drown out Warlow erupted as though someone
had switched on a stack of AV pillars, the band struck up,
and the waitresses struggled with the corks. Joshua pushed
a bemused and slightly awestruck Gideon Kavanagh off on
Ashly Hanson, and snatched some glasses from the drinks
table. He was kissed a great many times on his way to the
corner booth where Barrington Grier and Roland Frampton
were waiting. He loaded visual images and names of three
of the girls into his neural nanonics for future reference.

Roland Frampton was rising to his feet, a slightly apprehensive smile flicking on and off, obviously worried by exactly how big the cargo was—he had contracted to buy all
of it. But he shook Joshua warmly by the hand. "I thought
I'd better come here," he said in amusement. "It would

take you days to reach my office. You're the talk of Tranquillity."

"Really?"

Barrington Grier gave him a pat on the shoulder and they all sat down.

"That Kelly girl was asking after you," Barrington said.

"Ah." Joshua shifted round. Kelly Tirrel, his neural nanonics file supplied, Collins news corp reporter. "Oh, right. How is she?"

"Looked pretty good to me. She's on the broadcasts a lot these days. Presents the morning news for Collins three times a week."

"Good. Good. Glad to hear it." Joshua took a small bottle of Norfolk Tears from the inside pocket of the gold-yellow jacket he was wearing over his ship-suit.

Roland Frampton stared at it as he would a cobra.

"This is the Cricklade bouquet," Joshua said smoothly. He settled the three glasses on their table, and twisted the bottle's cork slowly. "I've tasted it. One of the finest on the planet. They bottle it in Stoke county." The clear liquid flowed out of the pear-shaped bottle.

They all lifted a glass, Roland Frampton studying his against the yellow wall lights.

"Cheers," Joshua said, and took a drink. A dragon breathed its diabolical fire into his belly.

Roland Frampton sipped delicately. "Oh, Christ, it's perfect." He glanced at Joshua. "How much did you bring? There have been rumours . . ."

Joshua made a show of producing his inventory. It was a piece of neatly printed paper with Grant Kavanagh's stylish signature on the bottom in black ink.

"Three thousand cases!" Roland Frampton squeaked, his eyes protruded.

Barrington Grier gave Joshua a sharp glance, and plucked the inventory from Roland's hands. "Bloody hell," he murmured.

Roland was dabbing at his forehead with a silk handkerchief. "This is wonderful. Yes, wonderful. But I wasn't expecting quite so much, Joshua. Nothing personal, it's just that first-time captains don't normally bring back so much. There are arrangements I have to make . . . the bank. It will take time."

"Of course."

"You'll wait?" Roland Frampton asked eagerly.

"You were very good to me when I started out. So I think I can wait a couple of days."

Roland's hand sliced through the air, he ended up making a fist just above the table. Determination visibly returned his old spark. "Right, I'll have a Jovian Bank draft for you in thirty hours. I won't forget this, Joshua. And one day I want to be told how you did it."

"Maybe."

Roland drained his glass in one gulp and stood up. "Thirty hours."

"Fine. If I'm not about, give it to one of the crew. I expect they'll still be here."

Joshua watched the old man weave a path through the excited crowd.

"That was decent of you," Barrington said. "You could have made instant money going to a big commercial distribution chain."

Joshua flashed him a smile, and they touched glasses. "Like I said, he gave me a break when I needed it."

"Roland Frampton doesn't need a break. He thought he was doing you a favour agreeing to buy your cargo. First-time captains on the Norfolk run are lucky if they make two hundred cases."

"Yeah, so I heard."

"Now you come back with a cargo worth five times as much as his business. You going to tell us how you did it?"

"Nope."

"Didn't think so. I don't know what you've got, young Joshua. But by God, I wish I had shares in you."

He finished his glass and treated Barrington to an iniquitous smile. He handed over the small bottle of Norfolk Tears. "Here, with compliments."

"Aren't you staying? It's your party."

He looked round. Warlow was at the centre of a cluster of girls, all of them giggling as one sat on the crook of his outstretched arm, her legs swinging well off the floor. Ashly was slumped in a booth, also surrounded by girls, one of them feeding him dainty pieces of white seafood from a plate. He couldn't even spot the others. "No," he said. "I have a date."

"She must be quite something."

"They are."

The *Isakore* was still anchored where they had left it, prow wedged up on the slippery bank, hull secure against casual observation by a huge cherry oak tree which overhung the river, lower branches trailing in the water.

Lieutenant Murphy Hewlett let out what could well have been a whimper of relief when its shape registered. His retinal implants were switched to infrared now the sun had set. The fishing boat was a salmon-pink outline distorted by the darker burgundy flecks of the cherry oak leaves, as if it was hidden behind a solidified waterfall.

He hadn't really expected it to be there. Not a quantifiable end, not to this mission. His mates treated his name as a joke back in the barracks. Murphy's law: if anything can go wrong, it will. And it had, this time as no other.

They had been under attack for five hours solid now. White fireballs that came stabbing out of the trees without warning. Figures that lurked half seen in the jungle, keeping pace, never giving them a moment's rest. Figures that weren't always human. Seven times they'd fallen back to using the TIP carbines for a sweep-scorch pattern, hacking at the jungle with blades of invisible energy, then tramping on through the smouldering vine roots and cloying ash.

All four of them were wounded to some extent. Nothing seemed to extinguish the white fire once it hit flesh. Murphy was limping badly, his right knee enclosed by a medical nanonic package, his left hand was completely useless, he wasn't even sure if the package could save his fingers.

But Murphy was most worried about Niels Regehr; the lad had taken a fireball straight in the face. He had no eyes nor nose left, only the armour suit sensors enabled him to see where he was going now, datavising their images directly into his neural nanonics. But even the neural nanonics pain blocks and a constant infusion of endocrines couldn't prevent him from suffering bouts of hallucination and disorientation. He kept shouting for *them* to go away and leave him alone, holding one-sided conversations, even quoting from prayers.

Murphy had detailed him to escort their prisoner; he could just about manage that. She said her name was Jacqueline Couteur, a middle-aged woman, small, overweight, with greying hair, dressed in jeans and a thick cotton shirt. She could punch harder than any of the supplement-boosted marines (Louis Beith had a broken arm to prove it), she had more stamina than them, and she could work that electronic warfare trick on their suit blocks if she wasn't being prodded with one of their heavy-calibre Bradfield chemical-projectile rifles.

They had captured her ten minutes after their last contact with Jenny Harris. That was when they'd let the horses go. The animals were panicking as balls of white fire arched down out of the sky, a deceitfully majestic display of borealis rockets.

Something made a slithering sound in the red and black jungle off to Murphy's right. Garrett Tucci fired his Bradfield, slamming explosive bullets into the vegetation. Murphy caught the swiftest glimpse of a luminous red figure scurrying away; it was either a man with a warm cloak spread wide, or else a giant bat standing on its hind legs.

"Bloody implants are shot," he muttered under his breath. He checked his TIP carbine's power reserve. He was down to the last heavy-duty power cell: twelve per cent. "Niels, Garrett, take the prisoner onto the boat and get the motor going. Louis, you and I are laying down a sweep-scorch. It might give us the time we need."

"Yes, sir," he answered.

Murphy felt an immense pride in the tiny squad. Nobody could have done better, they were the best, the very best. And they were his.

He drew a breath, and brought the TIP carbine up again. Niels was shoving his Bradfield's muzzle into the small of Jacqueline Couteur's back, urging her towards the boat. Murphy suddenly realized she could see as well as them in the dark. It didn't matter now. One of the day's smaller mysteries.

His TIP carbine fired, nozzle aimed by his neural nanonics. Flames rose before him, leaping from tree to tree, incinerating the twigs, biting deeply into the larger branches. Vines flared and sparkled like fused electrical cables, swinging in short arcs before falling to the ground and writhing ferociously as they spat and hissed. A solid breaker of heat rolled around him, shunted into the ground by his suit's dispersal layer. Smoke rose from his feet. The medical nanonic package around his knee datavised a heat-overload warning into his neural nanonics.

"Come on, Lieutenant!" Garrett shouted.

Through the heavy crackling of the flames Murphy could hear the familiar chugging sound of the *Isakore*'s motor. The suit's rear optical sensors showed him the boat backing out from under the cherry oak, water boiling ferociously around its stern.

"Go," Murphy told Louis Beith.

They turned and raced for the *Isakore*. Murphy could just targeting graphics circling his back.

We'll never make it, not out of this.

Flames were rising thirty metres into the night behind them. *Isakore* was completely free of the cherry oak. Niels was leaning over the gunwale, holding out a hand. The green-tinted medical nanonic package leaching to his face looked like some massive and grotesque wart.

Water splashed around his boots. Once he nearly slipped on the mud and tangled snowlily fronds. But then he was clinging to the side of the wooden boat, hauling himself up onto the deck.

"Holy shit, we made it!" He was laughing uncontrollably, tears streaming out of his eyes. "We actually bloody made it." He pulled his shell-helmet off, and lay on his back, looking at the fire. A stretch of jungle four hundred metres long was in flames, hurling orange sparks into the black sky far above.

The impenetrable water of the Zamjan shimmered with long orange reflections. Garrett was turning the boat, aiming the prow downriver.

"What about the Kulu team?" Louis asked. He'd taken his shell-helmet off, showing a face glinting with sweat. His breathing was heavy.

"I think that was a sonic boom we heard this afternoon," Murphy said, raising his voice above the flames. "Those Kulu bastards, always one move ahead of everyone else."

"They're soft, that's all," Garrett shouted from the wheel-house. "Can't take the pressure. We can. We're the fucking Confed fucking Navy fucking Marines." He whooped.

Murphy grinned back at him; fatigue pulled at every limb. He'd been using his boosted muscles almost constantly, which meant he'd have to make sure he ate plenty of high-protein rations to regain his proper blood energy levels. He loaded a memo into his neural nanonics.

His communication block let out a bleep for the first time in five hours; the datavise told him that there was a channel to the navy ELINT satellite open.

"Bloody hell," Murphy said. He datavised the block: "Sir, is that you, sir?"

"Christ, Murphy," Kelven Solanki's datavise gushed into his mind. "What's happening?"

"Spot of trouble, sir. Nothing we can't handle. We're back on the boat now, heading downriver."

Louis gave an exhausted laugh, and flopped onto his back.

"The Kulu team evacuated," Kelven Solanki reported. "Their whole embassy contingent upped and left in the *Ekwan* this evening. Ralph Hiltch called me from orbit to say there wasn't enough room on the spaceplane to pick you up."

Murphy could sense a great deal of anger lying behind the lieutenant-commander's smooth signal. "Doesn't matter, sir; we got you a prisoner."

"Fantastic. One of the sequestrated ones?"

Murphy glanced over his shoulder. Jacqueline Couteur was sitting on the deck with her back to the wheel-house. She gave him a dour stare.

"I think so, sir, she can interfere with our electronics if we give her half a chance. She's got to be watched constantly."

"OK, when can you have her back in—" Kelven Solanki's datavise vanished under a peal of static. The communications block reported the channel was lost.

Murphy picked up his TIP carbine and pointed it at Jacqueline Couteur. "Is that you?"

She shrugged. "No."

Murphy looked back at the fire on the bank. They were half a kilometre away now. People were walking along the shoreline where the *Isakore* had been anchored. The big cherry oak was still standing, intact, a black silhouette against the blanket of flame.

"Can they affect our electronics from here?"

"We don't care about your electronics," she said. "Such things have no place in our world."

"Are you talking to them?"

"No."

"Sir!" Garrett yelled.

Murphy swung round. The people on the shore were standing in a ring, holding hands. A large ball of white fire emerged from the ground in their midst and curved over their heads, soaring out across the river.

"Down!" Murphy shouted.

The fireball flashed overhead, making the air roil from its passage, bringing a false daylight to the boat. Murphy ground his teeth together, anticipating the strike, the pain as it vaporized his legs or spine. There was a clamorous

BOOM from behind the wheel-house, the boat rocked violently, and the light went out.

"Oh shit, oh shit." Garrett was crying.

"What is it?" Murphy demanded. He pulled himself onto his feet.

The boxy wooden structure behind the wheel-house was a smoking ruin. Fractured planks with charred edges pointed vacantly at the sky. The micro-fusion generator it had covered was a shambolic mass of heat-tarnished metal and dripping plastic.

"You will come to us in time," Jacqueline Couteur said calmly. She hadn't moved from her sitting position. "We have no hurry."

The *Isakore* drifted round a bend in the river, water gurgling idly around the hull, pulling the fire from view. A duet of night and silence closed over the boat, a void surer than vacuum.

Ione wore a gown of rich blue-green silk gauze. A single strip of cloth which clung to her torso then flared and flowed into a long skirt, it forked around her neck, producing two ribbonlike tassels that trailed from each shoulder. Her hair had been given a damp look, it was bound up and held in place at the back by an exquisite red flower brooch, its tissue-thin petals carved from some exotic stone. A long platinum chain formed a cobweb around her neck.

The trouble with looking so elegant, Joshua thought, was that part of him just wanted to stare at her, while the other part wanted to rip the dress to shreds so he could get at the body beneath. She really did look gorgeous.

He ran a finger round the collar on his own black dinner-jacket. It was too tight. And the butterfly tie wasn't straight.

"Leave it alone," Ione said sternly.

"But—"

"Leave it. It's fine."

He dropped his hand and glowered at the lift's door. Two Tranquillity serjeants were in with them, making it seem crowded. The door opened on the twenty-fifth floor of the StOuen starscraper, revealing a much smaller lobby than usual. Parris Vasilkovsky's apartment took up half of the floor, his offices and staff quarters took up the other half.

"Thanks for coming with me," Joshua said as they stood in front of the apartment door. He could feel the nerves building in the base of his stomach. This was the real big time he was bidding for now. And Ione on his arm ought to impress Parris Vasilkovsky. Precious little else would.

"I want to be with you," Ione murmured.

He leant forward to kiss her.

The muscle membrane opened, and Dominique was standing behind it. She had chosen a sleeveless black gown with a long skirt and a deep, highly revealing V-neck. Her thick honey-blonde hair had been given a slight wave, curling around her shoulders. Broad scarlet lips lifted in appreciation as she caught the embrace.

Joshua straightened up guiltily, though his errant eyes remained fixed on Dominique's cleavage. A host of memories started to replay through his mind without any assistance from his neural nanonics. He'd forgotten how impressive she was.

"Don't mind me," Dominique said huskily. "I adore young love."

Ione giggled. "Evening, Dominique."

The two girls kissed briefly. Then it was Joshua's turn.

"Put him down," Ione said in amusement. "You might catch something. Heaven only knows what he got up to on Norfolk."

Dominique grinned as she let go. "You think he's been bad?"

"He's Joshua; I *know* he's been bad."

"Hey!" Joshua complained. "That trip was strictly business."

Both girls laughed. Dominique led the way into the apartment. Joshua saw her skirt was made up from long panels, split right up to the top of her hips. The fabric swayed apart as she walked, giving Joshua brief glimpses of her legs, and a pair of very tight white shorts.

He held back on a groan. It was going to be hard to concentrate tonight without that kind of distraction.

The dining-room had two oval windows to show Mirchusko's dusky crescent—south of the equator two huge white cyclone swirls were crashing, in a drama which had been running for six days. Slabs of warmly lit coloured glass paved the polyp walls from floor to ceiling, each with an animal engraved on its surface by fine smoky grooves. Most of them were terrestrial—lions, gazelles, elephants, hawks—though several of the more spectacular non-sentient xenoc species were included. The grooves moved at an infinitesimal speed, causing the birds to flap their wings, the animals to run; their cycles lasted for hours. The table was made from halkett wood (native to Kulu), a rich gold in colour, with bright scarlet grain. Three antique silver candelabras were spaced along the polished wood, with slender white candles tipped by tiny flames.

There were six people at the dinner. Parris himself sat at the head of the table, looking spruce in a black dinner-jacket. The formal evening attire suited him, complementing his curly silver-grey hair to give him a distinguished appearance. At the other end of the table was Symone, his current lover, a beautiful twenty-eight-year-old whose geneered chromosomes had produced a dark walnut skin and hair a shade lighter than Dominique's, a striking and delightful contrast. She was eight months pregnant with Parris's third child.

Joshua and Dominique sat together on one side of the table. And Dominique's long legs had been riding up and down his trousers all through the meal. He had done his best to ignore it, but his twitching mouth had given him away to Ione, and, he suspected, Symone as well.

Opposite them were Ione and Clement, Parris's son. He was eighteen, lacking his big sister's miscreant force, but quietly cheerful. And handsome, Ione thought, though not in the mould of Joshua's wolfish ruggedness; his younger face was softer, framed with fair curly hair that was recognizably Parris's. He had just returned from his first year at university on Kulu.

"I haven't been to Kulu yet," Joshua said as the white-jacketed waiter cleared the dessert dishes away, assisted by a couple of housechimps.

"Wouldn't they let you in?" Dominique asked with honeyed malice.

"The Kulu merchants form a tight cartel, they're hard to crack."

"Tell me about it," Parris said gruffly. "It took me eight years before I broke in with fabrics from Oshanko, until then my ships were going there empty to pick up their nanonics. That costs."

"I'll wait until I get a charter," Joshua said. "I'm not going to try head-butting that kind of organization. But I'd like to play tourist sometime."

"You did all right penetrating Norfolk," Dominique said, eyes wide and apparently innocent over her crystal champagne glass.

"Hey, neat intro," he said enthusiastically. "We just slid into that subject, didn't we? I never noticed."

She stuck her tongue out at him.

"You got off lightly, Joshua," Parris said. "Me, I get lumbered with her subtlety all day every day."

"I would have thought she was old enough to have left home by now," he said.

"Who'd have her?"

"Good point."

Dominique lobbed a small cluster of grapes at her father. Parris caught them awkwardly, laughing. One went bouncing off across the moss carpet. "Make me an offer for her, Joshua, anything up to ten fuseodollars considered."

He saw the warning gleam in Dominique's eye. "I think I'll decline, thanks."

"Coward." Dominique pouted.

Parris dropped the grapes onto a side plate, and wiped

his hand with a napkin. "So how did you do it, Joshua? My captains don't get three thousand cases, and the Vasilkovsky line has been making the Norfolk run for fifty years."

Joshua activated a neural nanonics memory cell. "Confidentiality coverage. Agreed?" His gaze went round the table, recording everyone saying yes. They were legally bound not to repeat what they heard now. Although quite what he could do about Ione was an interesting point, since her thought processes were Tranquillity's legal system. "I traded something they needed: wood." He explained about the mayope.

"Very clever," Dominique drawled when he finished, though there was a note of respect in amongst the affected languor. "Brains as well as balls."

"I like it," Parris said. He studied his cut-crystal glass. "Why tell us?"

"Supply and demand," Joshua said. "I've found a valuable hole in the market, and I want to fill it."

"But the *Lady Macbeth* hasn't got the capacity to do it by herself," Clement said. "Right?"

Joshua had wondered how smart the lad was. Now he knew. A real chip off the Vasilkovsky block. "That's right. I need a partner, a big partner."

"Why not go to a bank?" Dominique asked. "Charter some ships for yourself."

"There's a loose end which needs tying up."

"Ah," Parris, showing some real interest at last, leant forward in his seat. "Go on."

"The power mayope has over Norfolk lies in keeping it a monopoly, that way we can keep the price high. I have a provisional arrangement with a distributor on Norfolk who's agreed to take as much as we can ship in. What we need to do next is pin down the supply to a single source, one that only we can obtain. That is going to take upfront money, the kind which can't be explained away to bank auditors."

"You can do that?"

"Parris, I have never been on a planet more corrupt than Lalonde. It's also very primitive and correspondingly poor. If you, with all your money, went there, you would be its king."

"No, thank you," Parris said sagely.

"Fine, but with money pushed into the right credit disks we can guarantee that no one else gets an export licence. OK, it won't last for ever, administration people move on, traders will offer counter-bribes when they find what we're doing; but I figure we ought to get two of Norfolk's conjunctions out of it. Two conjunctions where your ships are filled to capacity with Norfolk Tears."

"Every ship? I do have quite a few."

"No, not every ship. We have to walk a fine line between greed and squeeze. My Norfolk distributor will give us most favoured customer status, that's all. It'll be up to us to work out exactly how much we can squeeze them for before they start to protest. You know how jealously they guard their independence."

"Yes." Parris nodded thoughtfully.

"And what about Lalonde?" Ione asked quietly. Her glass was dangling casually between thumb and forefinger, she rocked it from side to side, swirling the champagne around the bottom.

"What about Lalonde?" Joshua asked.

"Its people," Symone said. "It doesn't sound as though they get a very good deal out of this. The mayope is their wood."

Joshua gave her a polite smile. Just what I need, bleed-ing hearts. "What do they get at the moment?"

Symone frowned.

"He means they get nothing," Dominique said.

"We're developing their market for them," Joshua said. "We'll be pumping hard cash into their economy. Not much by our standards, I admit, but to them it will buy a lot of things they need. And it will go to the people too, the colonists who are breaking their backs to tame that world, not just the administration staff. We pay the loggers upriver in the hinterlands, the barge captains, the timber-yard workers. Them, their families, the shops they buy stuff from. All of them will be better off. We'll be better off. Norfolk will be better off. It's the whole essence of trade. Sure, banks and governments make paper money from the deal, and we slant it in our favour, but the bottom line is that people benefit." He realized he was staring hard at Symone, daring her to disagree. He dropped his eyes, almost embarrassed.

Dominique gave him a soft, and for the first time, sincere kiss on his cheek. "You really did pick yourself the best, didn't you?" she said challengingly to Ione.

"Of course."

"Does that answer your question?" Parris asked his lover, smiling gently at her.

"I guess it does."

He started to use a small silver knife to peel the crisp rind from a date-sized purple fruit. Joshua recognized it as a saltplum from Atlantis.

"I think Lalonde would be in capable hands if we left it to Joshua," Parris said. "What sort of partnership were you looking for?"

"Sixty-forty in your favour," he said amicably.

"Which would cost me?"

"I was thinking of two to three million fuseodollars as an initial working fund to set up our export operation."

"Eighty-twenty," Dominique said.

Parris bit into the saltplum's pink flesh, watching Joshua keenly.

"Seventy-thirty," Joshua offered.

"Seventy-five-twenty-five."

"I get that percentage on all Norfolk Tears carried by the Vasilkovsky Line while our mayope monopoly is in operation."

Parris winced, and gave his daughter a small nod.

"If you provide the collateral," she said.

"You accept my share of the mayope as collateral, priced at the Norfolk sale value."

"Done."

Joshua sat back and let out a long breath. It could have been a lot worse.

"You see," Dominique said wickedly. "Brains as well as breasts."

"And legs," Joshua added.

She licked her lips provocatively, and took a long drink.

"We'll get the legal office to draw up a formal contract tomorrow," Parris said. "I can't see any problem."

"The first stage will be to set up an office on Lalonde and secure that mayope monopoly. The *Lady Mac* has still got to be unloaded, then she needs some maintenance work, and we're due a grade-E CAB inspection as well thanks to someone I met at Norfolk. Not a problem, but it takes time. I ought to be ready to leave in ten days."

"Good," said Parris. "I like that, Joshua. No beating around, you get straight to it."

"So how did you make your fortune?"

Parris grinned and popped the last of the saltplum into his mouth. "Given this will hopefully develop into quite a large operation, I'll want to send my own representative with you to Lalonde to help set up our office. And keep an eye on this upfront money of mine you'll be spending."

"Sure. Who?"

Dominique leaned over until her shoulder rubbed against Joshua's, a hand made of steel flesh closed playfully on his upper thigh. "Guess," she whispered salaciously into his ear.

Durringham had become ungovernable, a city living on spent nerves, waiting for the final crushing blow to fall.

The residents knew of the invaders marching and sailing downriver, everyone had heard the horror stories of xenoc enslavement, of torture and rape and bizarre bloodthirsty ceremonies; words distorted and swollen with every kilometre, like the river down which they travelled. They had also heard of the Kulu Embassy evacuating its personnel in one madcap night, surely the final confirmation—Sir

Asquith wouldn't do that unless there was no hope left.
Durringham, their homes and jobs and prosperity, was in
the firing line of an unknown, unstoppable threat, and they
had nowhere to run. The jungle belonged to the invaders,
the seven colonist-carrier starships orbiting impotently
overhead were full, they couldn't offer an escape route.
There was only the river and the virgin sea beyond.

The second morning after Ralph Hiltch made his dash to
the relative safety of the *Ekwan*, the twenty-eight paddle-
boats remaining in the frightened city's circular harbours
set off in convoy downriver. Price of a ticket was one thousand fuseodollars per person (including a child). No destination was named: some talked about crossing the ocean to
Sarell; Amarisk's northern extremity was mooted. It didn't
matter, leaving Durringham was the driving factor.

Given the exorbitant price the captains insisted on, and
the planet's relative poverty, it was surprising just how
many people turned up wanting passage. More than could
be accommodated. Tempers and desperation rose with the
brutal sun. Several ugly scenes flared as the gangplanks
were hurriedly drawn up.

Frustrated in their last chance to escape, the crowd
surged towards the colonists barricaded in the transients'
dormitories at the other end of the port. Stones were flung
first, then Molotovs.

Candace Elford dispatched a squad of sheriffs and newly
recruited deputies, armed with cortical jammers and laser
rifles, to quell this latest in a long line of disturbances. But
they ran into a gang ransacking a retail district. The tactical street battle which followed left eight dead, and two
dozen injured. They never got to the port.

That was when Candace finally had to call up Colin
Rexrew and admit that Durringham was out of control.
"Most urban districts are forming their own defence committees," she datavised. "They've seen how little effect the
sheriffs have against any large-scale trouble. All the riots
we've had these last few weeks have shown that often
enough, and everyone's heard about the *Swithland* posse.

They don't trust you and me to defend them, so they're going to do it for themselves. There's been a lot of food stockpiled over the last couple of weeks. They all think they're self-sufficient, and they're not letting anyone over their district's boundary. That's going to cause trouble, because I'm getting reports of people in the outlying villages to the east abandoning their land and coming in looking for a refuge. Our residents aren't letting them through. It's a siege mentality out there. People are waiting for Terrance Smith to come back with a conquering army, and hoping they can hold out in the meantime."

"How far away are the invaders?"

"I'm not sure. We're judging their progress by the way our communications with the villages fail. It's not constant, but I'd say their main force is no more than ten or fifteen kilometres from Durringham's eastern districts. The majority are on foot, which should give us two or three days' breathing space. Of course, you and I know there are nests of them inside the city as well. I've had some pretty weird stories about bogeymen and poltergeists coming in for days now."

"What do you want to do?" Colin asked.

"Revert to guarding our strategic centres; the spaceport, this sector, possibly both hospitals. I'd like to say the port as well, but I don't think I've got the manpower. There have been several desertions this week, mostly among the new deputies. Besides, nearly all of the boats have left now; there's been a steady exodus of fishing craft and even some barges since the paddle-boat convoy cast off this morning, so I can't see a lot of point."

"OK," Colin said with his head in his hands. "Do it." He glanced out of the office window at the sun-lashed rooftops. There was no sign of any of the usual fires that had marked the city's torment over the last weeks. "Can we hang on until Terrance returns?"

"I don't know. At the moment we're so busy fighting each other that I couldn't tell you what sort of resistance we can offer to the invaders."

"Yeah. That sounds like Lalonde through and through."

Candace sat behind her big desk, watching the situation
reports paint unwelcome graphics across the console displays, and issuing orders through her staff. There were
times when she wondered if anyone out there was even receiving them, let alone obeying them.

Half of her sheriffs were deployed around the spaceport,
spending the afternoon digging in, and positioning some
large maser cannons to cover the road. The rest took up position around the administration district in the city, covering the governor's dumper, the sheriff's headquarters,
various civic buildings, and the Confederation Navy office. Five combined teams of LDC engineers and sheriffs
went round all the remaining dumpers they could reach,
powering down the fusion generators. If the invaders
wanted Durringham's industrial base, such as it was,
Rexrew was determined to thwart them. The He$_3$ and deuterium fuel was collected and put into storage at the spaceport. By midafternoon the city was operating on
electron-matrix power reserves alone.

That more than anything else brought home the reality
of the situation to the majority. Fights and squabbles between gangs and districts ended, those barricades which
had been erected were strengthened, sentry details were finalized. Everyone headed home, the roads fell silent. The
rain which had held off all day began to slash down. Beneath its shroud of miserable low cloud, Durringham held
its breath.

Stewart Danielsson watched the rain pounding away on
the office windows as the conditioner hummed away efficiently, sucking the humidity from the air. He had made the
office his home over the last week; Ward Molecular had
seen a busy time of it. Everybody in town was keen to have
the ancillary circuits on their electron-matrix cells serviced, especially the smaller units which could double as
rifle power magazines at a pinch. He'd sold a lot of interface cables as well.

The business was doing fine. Darcy and Lori would be

pleased when they got back. They hadn't actually said he could sleep over when they left him in charge, but with the way things were it was only right. Twice he'd scared off would-be burglars.

His sleeping-bag with the inflatable mattress was comfy, and the office fridge was better than the one in his lodgings; he'd brought the microwave cooker over from the cabin out back of the warehouse. So now he had all the creature comforts. It was turning into a nice little sojourn. Gaven Hough stayed late most nights, keeping him company. Neither of them had seen Cole Este since the night after the first anti-Ivet riot. Stewart wasn't much bothered by that.

Gaven opened the door in the glass partition wall and stuck his head round. "Doesn't look like Mr. Crowther is coming to pick up his unit now, it's gone four."

Stewart stretched himself, and turned the processor block off. He'd been trying to keep their work records and payments up to date. It had always seemed so easy when Darcy was handling it. "OK, we'll get closed up."

"We'll be the last in the city. There's been no traffic outside for the last two hours. Everyone else has gone home, scared of these invaders."

"Aren't you?"

"No, not really. I haven't got anything an army would want."

"You can stay here tonight. I don't think it'll be safe walking home through this town now, not with the way people are on edge. There's enough food."

"Thanks. I'll go and shut the doors."

Stewart watched the younger man through the glass partition as he made his way past the workbenches to the warehouse's big doors. I ought to be worried, he thought, some of the rumours flying around town are blatantly unreal, but something is happening upriver. He gave the warehouse a more thoughtful glance. With its mayope walls it was strong enough to withstand any casual attempt at damage. But there were a lot of valuable tools and equipment inside, and everybody knew that. Maybe we should be boarding the windows up. There was no such thing as an insurance industry on Lalonde, if the warehouse went so did their jobs.

He turned back to the office windows, giving them a more objective appraisal; the frames were heavy enough to nail planks across.

Someone was walking down the muddy road outside. It was difficult to see with the way the rain was smearing the glass, but it looked like a man dressed in a suit. A very strange suit; it was grey, with a long jacket, and there was no seal up the front, only buttons. And he wore a black hat that looked like a fifty-centimetre column of brushed velvet. His right hand gripped a silver-topped cane. Rain bounced off him as though his antique clothes were coated in frictionless plastic.

"Stewart!" Gaven called from somewhere in the warehouse. "Stewart, come back here."

"No. Look at this."

"There's three of them in here. Stewart!"

The native panic in Gaven's voice made him turn reluctantly from the window. He squinted through the partition wall. It was dark in the cavernous warehouse, and Gaven had shut the wide doors. Stewart couldn't see where he'd got to. Humanoid shapes were moving around down by the stacks of crates; bigger than men. And it was just too gloomy to make out quite what—

The window behind him gave a loud grating moan. He whirled round. The frames groaned again as though they had been shoved by a hurricane blast. But the rain was falling quite normally outside. It couldn't be the wind. The man in the grey suit was standing in the middle of the road, cane pressing into the mud, both hands resting on the silver pommel. He stared directly at Stewart.

"Stewart!" Gaven yelled.

The window-panes cracked, fissures multiplying and interlacing. Animal reflex made Stewart spin round, his arms coming up to protect his head. *They're going to smash!*

A two and a half metre tall yeti was standing pressed up against the glass of the partition wall. Its ochre fur was matted and greasy, red baboon lips were peeled back to show stained fangs. He gagged at it in amazement, recoiling.

All the glass in the office shattered at once. In the instant before he slammed his eyelids shut, he was engulfed by a beautiful prismatic cloud of diamonds, sparkling and shimmering in the weak light. Then the slivers of glass penetrated his skin. Blood frothed out of a thousand shallow cuts, staining every square centimetre of his clothes a bright crimson. His skin went numb as his brain rejected outright the shocking level of pain. His sight, the misty vermilion of tightly shut eyes, turned scarlet. Pain stars flared purple. Then the universe went harrowingly black. Through the numbness he could feel hot coals burning in his eye sockets.

"Blind, I'm blind!" He couldn't even tell if his voice was working.

"It doesn't have to be like that," someone said to him. "We can help you. We can let you see again."

He tried to open his eyelids. There was a loathsome sensation of thin tissues ripping. And still there was only blackness. Pain began to ooze its way inwards, pain from every part of his body. He knew he was falling, plummeting to the ground.

Then the pain in his legs faded, replaced by a blissful liquid chill, as if he was bathing in a mountain tarn. He was given his sight back, a spectral girl sketched against the infinite darkness. It looked as though she was made up from translucent white membranes, folded with loving care around her svelte body, then flowing free somehow to become her fragile robes as well. She was a sublime child, in her early teens, poised between girlhood and womanhood, what he imagined an angel or fairy would be like. And she danced all the while, twirling effortlessly from foot to foot, more supple and graceful than any ballerina; her face blessed by a bountiful smile.

She held out her arms to him, ragged sleeves floating softly in the unfelt breeze. "See?" she said. "We can stop it hurting." Her arms rose, palms pressing together above her head, and she spun round again, lightsome laughter echoing.

"Please," he begged her. "Oh, please."

The pain returned to his legs, making him cry out. His siren vision began to retreat, skipping lightly over the emptiness.

She paused and cocked her head. "Is this what you want?" she asked, her dainty face frowning in concern.

"No! Back, come back. Please."

Her smile became rapturous, and her arms closed around him in a celebratory embrace. Stewart gave himself up to her balmy caresses, drowning in a glorious tide of white light.

Ilex coasted out of its wormhole terminus a hundred thousand kilometres above Lalonde. The warped gateway leading out of space-time contracted behind the voidhawk as it refocused its distortion field. Sensors probed round cautiously. The bitek starship was at full combat stations alert.

Waiting tensely on his acceleration couch in the crew toroid, Captain Auster skimmed through the wealth of data which both the bitek and electronic systems gathered. His primary concern was that there were no hostile ships within a quarter of a million kilometres, and no weapon sensors were locking on to the voidhawk's hull. A resonance effect in *Ilex*'s distortion field revealed various ship-sized masses orbiting above Lalonde, then there were asteroids, satellites, moons, boulder-sized debris. Nothing large was in the starship's immediate vicinity. It took a further eight seconds for *Ilex* and Ocyroe, the weapons-systems officer, working in tandem, to confirm the absence of any valid threat.

OK, let's go for a parking orbit; seven hundred kilometres out, Auster said.

Seven hundred? *Ilex* queried.

Yes. Your distortion field won't be so badly affected at that altitude. We can still run if we have to.

Very well.

Together their unified minds arrived at a suitable flight vector. *Ilex* swooped down the imaginary line towards the bright blue and white planet.

"We're going into a parking orbit," Auster said aloud for the benefit of the three Adamist naval officers on the bridge. "I want combat stations maintained at all times; and please bear in mind who could be here waiting for us." He allowed an overtone of stern anxiety to filter out to the Edenist crew to emphasize the point. "Ocyroe, what's our local space situation?"

"Nine starships in a parking orbit, seven colonist-carriers and two cargo ships. There are three interplanetary fusion drive ships en route from the asteroid Kenyon, heading for Lalonde orbit. Nothing else in the system."

"I can't get any response from Lalonde civil flight control," said Erato, the spaceplane pilot. He looked up from the communication console he was operating. "The geosynchronous communication platform is working, as far as I can tell. They just don't answer."

Auster glanced over at Lieutenant Jeroen van Ewyck, the Confederation Navy Intelligence officer they had brought with them from Avon. "What do you think?"

"This is a backward planet anyway, so their response isn't going to be instantaneous. But given the contents of those fleks I'd rather not take any chances. I'll try and contact Kelvin Solanki directly through the navy ELINT satellites. Can you see if you can get anything from your planetside agents?"

"We'll broadcast," Auster said.

"Great. Erato, see what the other starship captains can tell us. It looks like they must have been here some time if there are this many left in orbit."

Auster added his own voice to *Ilex*'s affinity call, spanning the colossal distance to the gas giant. Aethra answered straight away; but the immature habitat could only confirm the data which Lori and Darcy had included in their flek to the Edenist embassy on Avon. Since Kelven Solanki had transmitted the files to Murora there had only been the usual weekly status updates from Lalonde. The last one, four days ago, had contained a host of information on the colony's deteriorating civil situation.

Can you tell us what's happening? Gaura asked through the affinity link between Aethra and *Ilex*. He was the chief of the station supervising the habitat's growth out at the lonely edge of the star system.

Nobody is answering our calls, Auster said. **When we know something, *Ilex* will inform you immediately.**

If Laton is on Lalonde he may make an attempt to capture and subvert Aethra. He has had over twenty years to perfect his technique. We have no weaponry to resist him. Can you evacuate us?

That will depend on the circumstances. Our orders from the First Admiral's office are to confirm his existence and destroy him if at all possible. If he has become powerful enough to defend himself against the weapons we are carrying, then we must jump back to Fleet Headquarters and alert them. That takes priority over everything. Auster extended a burst of sympathy.

We understand. Good luck with your mission.

Thank you.

Can you sense Darcy and Lori? Auster asked *Ilex*.

No. They do not answer. But there is a melodic in the affinity band which I've never encountered before.

The voidhawk's perceptive faculty expanded into Auster's mind. He perceived a distant soprano voice, or a soft whistle; the effect was too imprecise to tell. It was an adagio, a slow harmonic which slipped in and out of mental awareness like a radio signal on a stormy night.

Where is it coming from? Auster asked.

Ahead of us, *Ilex* said. **Somewhere on the planet, but it's skipping about. I can't pin it down.**

Keep tuned in to it, and if you track down its origin let me know right away.

Of course.

Jeroen van Ewyck datavised his console processor to point one of *Ilex*'s secondary dishes at a navy ELINT satellite orbiting Lalonde, then opened a channel down to the office in Durringham. There was nothing like the usual bit rate available, the microwave beam emitted by the navy office was well below standard strength. A flustered rating answered, and switched the call straight through to Kelven Solanki.

"We're here in response to the flek you sent on the *Eurydice*," Jeroen van Ewyck said. "Can you advise us of the situation on the planet, please?"

"Too late," Kelven datavised. "You're too bloody late."

Auster ordered the bitek processor in his command console to patch him into the channel. "Lieutenant-Commander Solanki, this is Captain Auster. We were dispatched as soon as we were refitted for this mission. I can assure you the Admiralty took the report from you and our Intelligence operatives very seriously indeed."

"Seriously? You call sending one ship a serious response?"

"Yes. We are primarily a reconnaissance and evaluation mission. In that respect, we are considered expendable. The Admiralty needs to know if Laton's presence has been confirmed, and what kind of force level is required to deal with the invasion."

There was a moment's pause.

"Sorry if I shouted off," Kelven said. "Things are getting bad down here. The invaders have reached Durringham."

"Are these invaders acting under Laton's orders?"

"I've no idea yet." He started to summarize the events of the last couple of weeks.

Auster listened with growing dismay, a communal emotion distributed equally around the other Edenists on board. The Adamists too, if their facial expressions were an accurate reflection of their thoughts.

"So you still don't know if Laton is behind this invasion?" Auster asked when he finished.

"No. I'd say not; Lori and Darcy had virtually written him off by the time they got to Ozark. If it is him backing the invaders, then he's pulling a very elaborate double bluff. Why did he warn Darcy and Lori about this energy virus effect?"

"Have you managed to verify that yet?" Jeroen van Ewyck asked.

"No. Although the supporting circumstantial evidence we have so far is very strong. The invaders certainly have a powerful electronic warfare technology at their fingertips, and it's in widespread use. I suppose Kulu will be the place to ask; the ESA team managed to get their prisoner outsystem."

Typical of the ESA, Erato said sourly.

Auster nodded silently.

"How bad are conditions in the city?" Jeroen van Ewyck asked.

"We've heard some fighting around the outlying districts this evening. The sheriffs are protecting the spaceport and the government district. But I don't think they'll hold out for more than a couple of days. You must get back to Avon and inform the First Admiral and the Confederation Assembly what's happening here. At this point we still can't discount xenocs being involved. And tell the First Admiral that Terrance Smith's mercenary army must be prevented from landing here, as well. This is far beyond the ability of a few thousand hired soldiers to sort out."

"That goes without saying. We'll evacuate you and your staff immediately," Auster said.

Forty-five of them? Ocyroe asked. **That's pushing our life-support capacity close to the envelope.**

We can always make a swallow direct to Jospool, That's only seven light-years away. The crew toroid can support us for that long.

"There's some of the ratings and NCOs I'd like to get

off," Kelven Solanki datavised. "This wasn't supposed to be a front-line posting. They're only kids, really."

"No, all of you are coming," Auster said flatly.

"I'd like to capture one of these sequestrated invaders if possible," Jeroen van Ewyck put in quickly.

What about the marines, Erato? Auster asked. **Do you think it's worth a try?**

I'll fly recovery if we can spot them, the pilot said. His thoughts conveyed a rising excitement.

Auster acknowledged his leaked feelings with an ironic thought. Pilots were uniformly a macho breed, unable to resist any challenge, even Edenist ones.

The Juliffe basin is proving difficult to resolve, *Ilex* said with a note of annoyance. **My optical sensors are unable to receive a clearly defined image of the river and its tributaries for about a thousand kilometres inland.**

It's night over the basin, and we're still seventy thousand kilometres away, Auster pointed out.

Even so, the optical resolution should be better than this.

"Commander Solanki, we're going to attempt to recover the marines as well," Auster said.

"I haven't been able to contact them for over a day. God, I don't even know if they're still alive, let alone where they are."

"None the less, they are our naval personnel. If there's any chance, we owe them the effort."

The statement drew him a startled glance from Jeroen van Ewyck and the other two Adamists on the bridge. They quickly tried to hide their gaffe. Auster ignored it.

"Christ but— All right," Kelven Solanki datavised. "I'll fly the recovery myself, though. No point in risking your spaceplane. It was me who ordered them in there to start with. My responsibility."

"As you wish. If our sensors can locate their fishing boat, do you have an aircraft available?"

"I can get one. But the invaders knocked out the last

plane to fly into their territory. One thing I do know is that they've got some lethal fire-power going for them."

"So has *Ilex*," Auster said bluntly.

Joshua Calvert fell back onto the translucent sheet and let out a heartfelt breath. The bed's jelly-substance mattress was rocking him gently as the waves slowed. Sweat trickled across his chest and limbs. He gazed up at the electrophorescent cell clusters on Ione's ceiling. Their ornate leaf pattern was becoming highly familiar.

"That's definitely one of the better ways of waking up," he said.

"One?" Ione unwrapped her legs from his waist and sat back on his legs. She stretched provocatively, hands going behind her neck.

Joshua groaned, staring at her voraciously.

"Tell me another," she said.

He sat up, bringing his face twenty centimetres from hers. "Watching you," he said in a throaty voice.

"Does that turn you on?"

"Yes."

"Solo, or with another girl?" She felt his muscles tighten in reflex. Well, that's my answer, she thought. But then she'd always known how much he enjoyed threesomes. It wasn't Joshua's cock which was hard to satisfy, just his ego.

He grinned; the Joshua rogueish-charm grin. "I bet this conversation is going to turn to Dominique."

Ione gave his nose a butterfly kiss. They just couldn't fool each other; it was a togetherness similar to the one she enjoyed with the habitat personality. Comforting and eerie at the same time. "You mentioned her name first."

"Are you upset about her coming to Lalonde with me?"

"No. It makes sound business sense."

"You do disapprove." He stroked the side of her breasts tenderly. "There's no need to be jealous. I have been to bed with Dominique, you know."

"I know. I watched you on that big bed of hers, remember?"

He cupped her breasts and kissed each nipple in turn. "Let's bring her to this bed."

She looked down on the top of his head. "Not possible, sorry. The Saldanas eradicated the gay gene from their DNA three hundred years ago. Couldn't risk the scandal, they are supposed to uphold the ten commandments throughout the kingdom, after all."

Joshua didn't believe a word of it. "They missed erasing the adultery gene, then."

She smiled. "What's your hurry to hit the mattress with her? The two of you are going to spend a week locked up in that zero-gee sex cage of yours."

"You are jealous."

"No. I never claimed to have an exclusive right to you. After all, I didn't complain about Norfolk."

He pulled his head back from her breasts. "Ione!" he complained.

"You reeked of guilt. Was she very beautiful?"

"She was . . . sweet."

"Sweet? Why, Joshua Calvert, I do believe you're getting romantic in your old age."

Joshua sighed and dropped back on the mattress again. He wished she'd make up her mind whether she was jealous or not. "Do I ask about your lovers?"

Ione couldn't help the slight flush that crept up her cheeks. Hans had been fun while it lasted, but she'd never felt as free with him as she did with Joshua. "No," she admitted.

"Ah hah, I'm not the only one who's guilty, by the looks of it."

She traced a forefinger down his sternum and abdomen until she was stroking his thighs. "Quits?"

"Yes." His hands found her hips. "I brought you another present."

"Joshua! What?"

"A gigantea seed. That's an aboriginal Lalonde tree. I

saw a couple on the edge of Durringham, they were eighty metres tall, but Marie said they were just babies, the really big ones are further inland from the coast."

"*Marie* said that, did she?"

"Yes." He refused to be put off. "It should grow all right in Tranquillity's parkland. But you'll have to plant it where the soil is deep and there's plenty of moisture."

"I'll remember."

"It'll grow up to the light-tube eventually."

She pulled a disbelieving face.

I will have to run environmental compatibility tests first, Tranquillity said. Our biosphere is delicately balanced.

So cynical. "Thank you, Joshua," she said out loud.

Joshua realized he had regained his erection. "Why don't you just ease forward a bit?"

"I could give you a treat instead," Ione said seductively. "A real male fantasy come true."

"Yes?"

"Yes. There's a girlfriend of mine I'd like you to meet. We go swimming together every morning. You'd like that, watching us get all wet and slippery. She's younger than me. And she never, ever wears a swimming costume."

"Jesus." Joshua's face went from greed to caution. "This isn't on the level," he decided.

"Yes, it is. She's also very keen to meet you. She likes it a lot when people wash her. I do it all the time, sliding my hands all over her. Don't you want to join me?"

He looked up at Ione's mock-innocent expression, and wondered what the hell he was letting himself in for. Gay gene, like bollocks. "Lead on."

They had walked fifty metres down the narrow sandy path towards the cove, Ione's escort of three serjeants an unobtrusive ten paces behind, when Joshua stopped and looked round. "This is the southern endcap."

"That's right," she said slyly.

He caught up with her as she reached the top of the

bluff. The long, gently curving cove below looked tremendously enticing, with a border of shaggy palm trees and a tiny island offshore. Away in the distance he could see the elaborate buildings of the Laymil project campus.

"It's all right," she said. "I won't have you arrested for coming here."

He shrugged and followed her down the bluff. Ione was running on ahead as he reached the sand. Her towelling robe was flung away. "Come on, Joshua!" Spray frothed up as her feet reached the water.

A naked girl, a tropical beach. Irresistible. He dropped his own robe and jogged down the slope. Something was moving behind him, something making dull thudding sounds as it moved, something heavy. He turned. "Jesus!"

A Kiint was running straight at him. It was smaller than any he'd seen before, about three metres long, only just taller than him. Eight fat legs were flipping about in a rhythm which was impossible to follow.

His feet refused to budge. "Ione!"

She was laughing hysterically. "Morning, Haile," she called at the top of her voice.

The Kiint lumbered to a halt in front of him. He was looking into a pair of soft violet eyes half as wide as his own face. A stream of warm damp breath poured from the breathing vents.

"Er . . ."

One of the tractamorphic arms curved up, the tip formshifting into the shape of a human hand—slightly too large.

"Well, say hello, then," Ione said; she had walked up to stand behind him.

"I'll get you for this, Saldana."

She giggled. "Joshua, this is my girlfriend, Haile. Haile, this is Joshua."

Why has he so much stiffness? Haile asked.

Ione cracked up, nearly doubling over as she laughed. Joshua gave her a furious glare.

Not want to shake hands? Not want to initiate human

greetings ritual? Not want to be friends? The Kiint sounded mournfully disappointed.

"Joshua, shake hands. Haile's upset you don't want to be friends with her."

"How do you know?" he asked out of the corner of his mouth.

"Affinity. The Kiint can use it."

He put his hand up. Haile's arm reached out, and he felt a dry, slightly scaly, bud of flesh flow softly around his fingers. It tickled. His neural nanonics were executing a priority search through the xenoc files he had stored in a memory cell. The Kiint could hear.

"May your thoughts always fly high, Haile," he said, and gave a slight formal bow.

I have much likening for him!

Ione gave him a calculating stare. I might have known that charm of his would work on xenocs too, she thought.

Joshua felt the Kiint's flesh deliver a warm squeeze to his hand, then the pseudo-hand peeled back. The itchy sensation it left in his palm seemed to spread up along his spine and into his skull.

"Your new girlfriend," he said heavily.

Ione smiled. "Haile was born a few weeks ago. And boy, does she grow fast."

Haile started to push Ione towards the water, flat triangular head butting the girl spiritedly, beak flapping. One of her tractamorphic arms beckoned avidly at Joshua.

He grinned. "I'm coming." His scalp felt as if he'd been in the sun too long, an all-over tingle.

"The water eases her skin while she's growing," Ione said as she skipped ahead of the eager Kiint. "She needs to bathe two or three times a day. All the Kiint houses have interior pools. But she loves the beach."

"Well, I'll be happy to help scrub her while I'm here."

Much gratitude.

"My pleasure," Joshua said. He stopped. Haile was standing at the edge of the water, big eyes regarding him attentively. "That was you."

Yes.

"What was?" Ione asked, she looked from one to the other.

"I can hear her."

"But you don't have an affinity gene," she said, surprised, and maybe a little indignant.

Joshua has thoughts of strength. Much difficulty to effect interlocution, but possible. Not so with most humans. Feel hopelessness. Failure sorrow.

He swaggered. "Strong thoughts, see?"

"Haile hasn't quite mastered our language, that's all," Ione smiled with menace. "She's confused strength with simplicity. You have very elementary thoughts."

Joshua rubbed his hands together determinedly, and walked towards her. Ione backed away, then turned and ran giggling into the water. He caught her after six metres, and the two of them fell into the small clear ripples whooping and laughing. Haile plunged in after them.

Much joyness. Much joyness.

Joshua was interested by how well the young Kiint could swim. He would have considered her body too heavy to float, but she could move at a fair speed; her tractamorphic arms spread out into flippers, and angled back along her flanks. Ione wouldn't let her go out to the little island, saying it was still too far, which ruling Haile accepted with rebellious sulks.

I have seen some of the all-around's park space, she told Joshua proudly as he rubbed the dorsal ridge above her rump. **Ione has shown me. So much to absorb. Adventureness fun. Envy Joshua.**

Joshua didn't quite understand how to collect his thoughts into a voice Haile could understand, instead he simply spoke. "You envy me? Why?"

Venture as you please. Fly to stars so distant. Welcome sights so strange. I want this, muchness!

"I don't think you'd fit in the *Lady Mac*. Besides, human ships that can carry Kiint have to be licensed by your government. I haven't got that licence."

Sadness. Anger. Frustration. I may not venture beyond adult defined constraints. Much growth before I can.

"Bumming round the universe isn't all it's cracked up to be. Most of the Confederation planets are pretty tame, and travelling on a starship is boring; dangerous too."

Danger? Excitement query?

Joshua moved down towards Haile's flexible neck. Ione was grinning at him over the xenoc's white back.

"No, not excitement. There's a danger of mechanical failure. That can be fatal."

You have excitement. Achievement. Ione narrated many voyages you have undertaken. Triumph in Ruin Ring. Much gratification. Such boldness exhibited.

Ione turned her giggle into a cough. **You're a flirt, girl.**

Incorrect access mode to human males, query? Praise of character, followed by dumb admiration for feats; your instruction.

Yes, I did say that, didn't I. Perhaps not quite so literally, though.

"That was a while ago now," Joshua said. "Of course, life was pretty tricky in those days. One wrong move and it could have been catastrophic. The Ruin Ring is an ugly place. You've gotta have determination to be a scavenger. It's a lonely existence. Not everyone can take it."

You achieved legend status. Most famous scavenger of all.

Don't push it, Ione warned.

"You mean the Laymil electronics stack? Yeah, it was a big find, I earned a lot of money from that one."

Much cultural relevance.

"Oh, yeah, that too."

Ione stopped rubbing Haile's neck and frowned. "Joshua, haven't you accessed the records we've been decoding?"

"Er, what records?"

"Your electronics stack stored Laymil sensevise recordings. We've uncovered huge amounts of data on their culture."

"Great. That's good news."

She eyed him suspiciously. "They were extremely advanced biologically. Well ahead of us on the evolutionary scale; they were almost completely in harmony with their habitat environment, so now we have to question just how artificial their habitats were. Their entire biology, the way they approached living organisms, is very different to our own perception. They revered any living entity. And their psychology is almost incomprehensible to us; they could be both highly individual, and at the same time submerge themselves into a kind of mental homogeneity. Two almost completely different states of consciousness. We think they may have been genuine telepaths. The research project geneticists are having furious arguments over the relevant gene sequence. It is similar to the Edenist affinity gene, but the Laymil psychology complements it in a way which is impossible to human Edenist culture. Edenists retain a core of identity even after they transfer their memories into the habitat personality at death, whereas the Laymil willingness to share their most private selves has to be the product of considerable mental maturity. You can't engineer behavioural instinct into DNA."

"Have you found out what destroyed their habitats yet?" Joshua asked. Haile shuddered below his hand, a very human reflex. He felt a burst of cold alarm invading his thoughts. "Hey, sorry."

Fright. Scared feel. So many deaths. They had strength. Still were defeated. Query cause?

"I wish I knew," Ione said. "They seemed to celebrate life, much more than we do."

The *Isakore* was bobbing about inertly on the Zamjan as though it was a log of elegantly carved driftwood, ripples slopping against the hull with quiet insistence. They had rigged up a couple of oarlike outriggers to steer with during the first day—the rudder alone was no good. And they'd managed to stick more or less to the centre of the river. It was eight hundred metres wide here, which gave them some leeway when the current began to shift them towards one of the banks.

According to Murphy Hewlett's inertial-guidance block they had floated about thirty kilometres downriver since the micro-fusion generator had been taken out. The current had pushed them with dogged tenacity the whole time, taking them away from the landing site and the burnt antagonistic jungle. Only another eight hundred plus kilometres to go.

Jacqueline Couteur had been no trouble, spending her time sitting up in the prow under the canvas awning. If it hadn't been for the ordeal they'd been through, the price they'd paid in their own pain and grief, to capture her, Murphy would have tied the useless micro-fusion generator round her neck and tossed her overboard. He thought she knew that. But she was their mission. And they were still alive, and still intact. Until that changed, Lieutenant Murphy Hewlett was going to obey orders and take her back to Durringham. There was nothing else left, no alternative purpose to life.

Nobody had tried to interfere with them, although their communication channels were definitely being jammed (none of the other equipment blocks were affected). Even the villages they had sailed past had shown no interest. A couple of rowing dinghies had ventured close the first morning, but they'd been warned off with shots from one of the Bradfields. After that the *Isakore* had been left alone.

It was almost a peaceful voyage. They'd eaten well, cleaned and reloaded the weapons, done what they could about their wounds. Niels Regehr swam in and out of lucidity, but the medical nanonic package clamped over his face was keeping him reasonably stable.

Murphy could just about allow himself to believe they would return to Durringham. The placid river encouraged that kind of foolish thinking.

As night fell at the end of the second day he sat at the stern, holding on to the tiller they had fixed up, and doing his best to keep the boat in the centre of the river. At least with this job he didn't have to use his leg with its achingly stiff knee, though his left hand was incapable of gripping the tiller pole. The clammy air from the water made his fatigues uncomfortably sticky.

He saw Louis Beith making his way aft, carrying a flask. A medical nanonic package made a broad bracelet around his arm where Jacqueline Couteur had broken the bone and it glimmered dimly in the infrared spectrum.

"Brought you some juice," Louis said. "Straight out the cryo."

"Thanks." Murphy took the mug he held out. With his retinal implants switched to infrared, the liquid he poured from the flask was a blue so deep it was nearly black.

"Niels is talking to his demons again," Louis said quietly.

"Not much we can do about it, short of loading a somnolence program into his neural nanonics."

"Yeah, but Lieutenant; what he says, it's like it's for real, you know? I thought people hallucinating don't make any sense. He's even got me looking over my shoulder."

Murphy took a swallow of the juice. It was freezing, numbing the back of his throat. Just perfect. "It bothers you that bad? I could put him under, I suppose."

"No, not bad. It's just kinda spooky, what with everything we saw, and all."

"I think that electronic warfare gimmick the hostiles have affects our neural nanonics more than we like to admit."

"Yeah?" Louis brightened. "Maybe you're right." He stood with his hands on his hips, staring ahead to the west. "Man, that is some meteorite shower. I ain't never seen one that good before."

Murphy looked up into the cloudless night sky. High above the *Isakore*'s prow the stars were tumbling down from their fixed constellations. There was a long broad slash of them scintillating and flashing. He actually smiled, they looked so picturesque. And the hazy slash was still growing as more of them hit the atmosphere, racing eastwards. It must be a prodigious swarm gliding in from interplanetary space, the remains of some burnt-out comet that had disintegrated centuries ago. The meteorites furthest away were developing huge contrails as they sizzled their way downwards. They were certainly penetrating the atmosphere a long way, tens of kilometres at least. Murphy's smile bled away. "Oh my God," he said in a tiny dry voice.

"What?" Louis asked happily. "Isn't that something smooth? Wow! I could look at that all night long."

"They're not meteorites."

"What?"

"They're not meteorites. Shit!"

Louis looked at him in alarm.

"They're bloody kinetic harpoons!" Murphy started to run forwards as fast as his knee would allow. "Secure yourself!" he shouted. "Grab something and hold on. They're coming down right on top of us."

The sky was turning to day overhead, blackness flushed away by a spreading stain of azure blue. The contrails to the west were becoming too bright to look at. They seemed to be lengthening at a terrific rate, cracks of sunlight splitting open across the wall of night.

Kinetic harpoons were the Confederation Navy's standard tactical (non-radioactive) planetary surface assault weapon. A solid splinter of toughened, heat-resistant composite, half a metre long, needle sharp, guided by a cruciform tail, steered by a processor with preprogrammed flight vector. They carried no explosives, no energy charge; they destroyed their target through speed alone.

Ilex accelerated in towards Lalonde at eight gees, following a precise hyperbolic trajectory. The apex was reached twelve hundred kilometres above Amarisk, two hundred kilometres east of Durringham. Five thousand harpoons were expelled from the voidhawk's weapons cradles, hurtling towards the night-masked continent below. *Ilex* inverted the direction of its distortion field's acceleration wave, fighting Lalonde's gravity. Stretched out on their couches, the crew raged impotently against the appalling gee force, nanonic supplement membranes turning rigid to hold soft weak human bodies together as the voidhawk dived away from the planet.

The harpoon swarm sheered down through the atmosphere, hypervelocity friction ablating away the composite's outer layer of molecules to leave a dazzling ionic tail over a hundred kilometres long. From below it resembled a rain of fierce liquid light.

Their silence was terrifying. A display of such potency should sound like the roar of an angry god. Murphy clung to one of the rails along the side of the wheel-house, squinting through squeezed-up eyelids as the solid sheet of vivid destruction plummeted towards him. He heard Jacqueline Couteur moaning in fear, and felt a cheap, malicious satisfaction. It was the first time she had shown the slightest emotion. Impact could only be seconds away now.

The harpoons were directly overhead, an atmospheric river of solar brilliance mirroring the Zamjan's course. They split down the centre, two solid planes of light diverging with immaculate symmetry, sliding down to touch the jungle away in the west then racing past the *Isakore* at a speed too fast even for enhanced human senses to follow. None of them, not one, landed in the water.

Multiple explosions obliterated the jungle. Along both sides of the Zamjan gouts of searing purple flame streaked upwards as the harpoons struck the earth, releasing their colossal kinetic energy in a single devastating burst of heat. The swath of devastation extended for a length of seven kilometres along the banks, reaching a kilometre and a half inland. A thick filthy cloud of loam and stone and wood splinters belched up high into the air, blotting out the heat flashes. The blast-wave rolled out in both directions, flattening still more of the jungle.

Then the sound broke over the boat. The roar of the explosions overlapped, merging into a single sonic battering-ram which made every plank on the *Isakore* twang as if it was an overtuned guitar string. After that came the eternal thunderclap of the air being ripped apart by the harpoons' plunge; sound waves finally catching up with the weapons.

Murphy jammed his hands across his stinging eardrums. His whole skeleton was shaking, joints resonating painfully.

Debris started to patter down, puckering the already distressed surface of the river. A sprinkling of fires burnt along the banks where shattered trees lay strewn among deep craters. Pulverized loam and wood hung in the air, an obscure black fog above the mortally wounded land.

Murphy slowly lowered his hands, staring at the awful vision of destruction. "It was our side," he said in dazed wonder. "We did it."

Garrett Tucci was at his side, jabbering away wildly. Murphy couldn't hear a thing. His ears were still ringing vociferously. "Shout! Datavise! My ears have packed up."

Garrett blinked, he held up his communications block. "It's working," he yelled.

Murphy datavised his own block, which reported the channel to the ELINT satellite was open.

A beam of bright white light slid over the *Isakore*, originating from somewhere above. Murphy watched as the beam swung out over the water, then tracked back towards the boat. He looked up, beyond surprise. It was coming from a small aircraft hovering two hundred metres overhead, outlined by the silver stars. Green, red, and white strobes flashed on the tips of its wings and canards. His neural nanonics identified the jet-black planform, a BK133.

Murphy's communication block bleeped to acknowledge a local channel opening. "Murphy? Are you there, Murphy?"

"Sir? Is that you?" he asked incredulously.

"Expecting someone else?" Kelven Solanki datavised.

The beam found the *Isakore* again, and remained trained on the deck.

"Have you still got your prisoner?"

"Yes, sir." Murphy glanced at Jacqueline Couteur, who was staring up at the aircraft, shielding her eyes against the spotlight.

"Good man. We'll take her back with us."

"Sir, Niels Regehr is injured pretty badly. I don't think he can climb a rope ladder."

"No problem."

The BK133 was descending carefully, wings rocking in the thermal microbursts generated by the harpoons' impact. Murphy could feel the compressor jets gusting against his face, a hot dry wind, pleasant after the river's humidity. He saw a wide hatch was open on the side of the fuselage. A man in naval fatigues was slowly winching down towards the *Isakore*.

Floodlights on the roof of the navy office showed the grounds around the building were thick with people. All of them seemed to be looking up into the night sky.

Murphy watched them through the BK133's open midfuselage hatch as Kelven Solanki piloted it down onto the roof pad. A wedge-shaped spaceplane was sitting on one side of the roof, wings retracted; it only just fitted, tail and nose were overhanging the edges. It was one of the most welcome sights he had seen in a long long while.

"Who are all those people?" he asked.

"Anyone who saw *Ilex*'s spaceplane taking the staff away earlier," Vince Burtis said. He was the nineteen-year-old navy rating who had winched the marine squad to safety. To him the invasion was exactly what he had signed on for, adventure on alien worlds; he was enjoying himself. Murphy hadn't the heart to disillusion him. The kid would realize soon enough.

"I guess they want to leave too," Vince Burtis said soberly.

The BK133 settled on the roof. Kelven datavised the

flight computer to power down the internal systems. "Everyone out," he said.

"Hurry, please." Erato's appeal was relayed through his communication block. "I'm in touch with the sheriffs outside. They say the crowd is already at the door."

"They shouldn't be able to get in," Kelven datavised.

"I think some of the sheriffs may be with them," Erato said hesitantly. "They're only human."

Kelven released his straps and hurried back into the cabin. Vince Burtis was guiding Niels Regehr's tentative footsteps, helping him down through the hatch. Garrett Tucci and Louis Beith were already out, marching Jacqueline Couteur towards the spaceplane at gunpoint.

Murphy Hewlett gave his superior a tired smile. "Thank you, sir."

"Nothing to do with me. If the *Ilex* hadn't shown up you'd still be paddling home."

"Is everyone else from the office out?"

"Yes, the spaceplane made a couple of flights earlier this evening, we're the last," Kelven said.

They both hopped down onto the roof. The noise of the spaceplane's compressors rose, obscuring the sound of the crowd below. Kelven did his best to ignore the sensation of guilt. He had made a lot of friends among Lalonde's civil administration staff. Candace Elford had turned over the BK133 as soon as he asked, no questions. Surely some people could have been taken up to the orbiting colonist-carriers.

Who though? And who would choose?

The best—the only—way to help Lalonde now was through the Confederation Navy.

The stairwell door on the other side of the BK133 burst open. People began to spill out onto the roof, shouting frantically.

"Oh, Christ," Kelven said under his breath. He could see three or four sheriffs among them, armed with cortical jammers, one had a laser hunting rifle. The rest were civilians. He looked round. Vince Burtis and Niels Regehr were halfway up the stairs to the airlock. One of the *Ilex*'s crew was leaning out, offering a hand to Niels. Vince was staring over his shoulder in shock.

"Get in," Kelven datavised, waving his arms.

Two sheriffs were rounding the nose of the BK133, more people were crouched low scuttling under the fuselage. Still more were running out of the open door. There must have been thirty on the roof.

"Wait for us."

"You can carry one more."

"I have money, I can pay."

Murphy aimed his Bradfield into the air and fired off two shots. The heavy-calibre weapon was startlingly loud. Several people threw themselves down, the rest froze.

"Don't even think about it," Murphy said. The Bradfield lined up on one of the ashen-faced sheriffs. A cortical jammer fell from the man's hands.

The noise of the spaceplane's compressors was becoming strident.

"There's no room on board. Go home before anyone gets hurt."

Kelven and Murphy started backing towards the spaceplane. A young brown-skinned woman who had crawled under the BK133 straightened up, and walked towards them defiantly. She was holding a small child in front of her, it couldn't have been more than two years old. Plump face and wide liquid eyes.

Murphy just couldn't bring himself to point the Bradfield at her. He reached the foot of the spaceplane's aluminium stairs.

"Take him with you," the woman called. She held the child out. "For Jesus's sake, take my son, if you have a gram of pity in you. I'm begging you!"

Murphy's foot found the first step. Kelven had a hand on his arm, guiding him back.

"Take him!" she shrieked over the swelling compressor efflux. "Take him, or shoot him."

He shuddered at her fervour. She meant it, she really meant it.

"It would be a kindness. You know what will happen to him on this cursed planet." The child was crying, squirming about in her grip.

The other people on the roof were all motionless, watching him with hard, accusing eyes. He turned to Kelven Solanki, whose face was a mask of torment.

"Get him," Kelven blurted.

Murphy dropped the Bradfield, letting it skitter away across the silicon roof. He datavised a codelock into its controlling processor so no one could turn it on the spaceplane, then grabbed the child with his right hand.

"Shafi," the woman shouted as he raced up the stairs. "His name's Shafi Banaji. Remember."

He barely had a foot in the airlock when the spaceplane lifted, its deck tilting up immediately. Hands steadied him, and the outer hatch slid shut.

Shafi's baggy cotton trousers were soiled and stinking; he let out a long fearful wail.

3

Including Tranquillity, there were only five independent (non-Edenist) bitek habitats to be found within the boundaries of the Confederation. After Tranquillity, probably the most well known, or notorious depending on your cultural outlook and degree of liberalism, was Valisk.

Although they were both, technically, dictatorships, they occupied opposite ends of the political spectrum, with the dominant ideologies of the remaining three habitats falling between them, a well-deserved mediocrity. Tranquillity was regarded as elitist, or even regal given its founder: industrious, rich, and slightly raffish, with a benevolent, chic ruler, it emphasized the grander qualities of life, somewhere you aspired to go if you made it. Valisk was older, its glory days over, or at the very least in abeyance: it played host to a more decadent population; money here (and there was still plenty) came from exploiting the darker side of human nature. And its strange governorship repelled rather than attracted.

It hadn't always been so.

Valisk was founded by an Edenist Serpent called Rubra. Unlike Laton, who terrorized the Confederation two and a half centuries later, his rebellion was of an altogether more constructive nature. He was born in Machaon, a habitat orbiting Kohistan, the largest gas giant in the Srinagar star system. After forty-four years, he abandoned his culture and his home, sold his not inconsiderable share in his family's engineering enterprise, and emigrated to a newly opened Adamist asteroid settlement in Kohistan's trailing Trojan cluster.

It was a period of substantial economic growth for the star system. Srinagar had been colonized by ethnic-Hindus in 2178 during the Great Dispersal, a hundred and sixteen years earlier. Basic industrialization had been completed, the world was tamed, and people were looking for new ways of channelling their energies. All across the Confederation emerging colony planets were exploiting space resources and increasing their wealth dramatically. Srinagar was eager to be numbered among them.

Rubra started with six leased interplanetary cargo ships. Like all Serpents he was a high achiever in his chosen field (nearly always to Edenist embarrassment, for so many of them chose crime). He made a small fortune supplying the Trojan cluster's small but wealthy population of engineers and miners with consumer goods and luxuries. He bought more ships, made a larger fortune, and named his expanding company Magellanic Itg—joking to his peers that one day he would trade with that distant star cluster. By 2306, after twelve years of steady growth, Magellanic Itg owned manufacturing stations and asteroid-mining operations, and had moved into the interstellar transport market.

At this point Rubra germinated Valisk in orbit around Opuntia, the fourth of the system's five gas giants. It was a huge gamble. He spent his company's entire financial reserves cloning the seed, mortgaging half of the starships to boot. And bitek remained technology *non grata* for the major religions, including the Hindu faith. But Srinagar was sufficiently Bolshevik about its new economic independence from its sponsoring Govcentral Indian states, and energetic enough in its approach to innovation, to cast a blind eye to proscriptions announced by fundamentalist Brahmians on a distant imperialist planet over two centuries earlier. Planet and asteroid governments saw no reason to impose embargoes against what was rapidly evolving into one of the system's premier economic assets. Valisk became, literally, a corporate state, acting as the home port for Magellanic Itg's starship fleet (already one of the largest in the sector) and dormitory town for its industrial stations.

Although Valisk was a financially advantageous location from which Rubra could run his flourishing corporate empire, he needed to attract a base population to the habitat to make it a viable pocket civilization. Industrial stations were therefore granted extremely liberal weapons and research licences and Valisk started to attract companies specializing in military hardware. Export constraints were almost non-existent.

Rubra also opened the habitat to immigration for "people who seek cultural and religious freedom", possibly in reaction to his own formal Edenist upbringing. This invitation attracted several nonconformist religious cults, spiritual groups, and primitive lifestyle tribes, who believed that a bitek environment would fulfil the role of some benevolent Gaia and provide them free food and shelter. Over nine thousand of these people arrived over the course of the habitat's first twenty-five years, many of them drug- or stimulant-program addicts. At this time, Rubra, infuriated with their unrepentant parasitical nature, banned any more from entering.

By 2330 the population had risen to three hundred and fifty thousand. Industrial output was high, and many interstellar companies were opening regional offices inside.

Then the first blackhawks to be seen in the Confederation began to appear, all of them registered with Magellanic Itg, and captained by Rubra's plentiful offspring. Rubra had pulled off a spectacular coup against both his competitors and his former culture. Voidhawk bitek was the most sophisticated ever sequenced; copying it was a triumph of genetic retro-engineering.

With blackhawks now acting as the mainstay of his starship fleet, Rubra was unchallengeable. A large-scale cloning programme saw their numbers rising dramatically; neural symbionts were used to give captaincies to Adamists who had no qualms about using bitek, and there were many. By 2365 Magellanic Itg ceased to use anything other than blackhawks in its transport fleet.

Rubra died in 2390, one of the wealthiest men in the Confederation. He left behind an industrial conglomerate used as an example by economists ever since as the classic corporate growth model. It should have carried on. It had the potential to rival the Kulu Corporation owned by the Saldana family. Ultimately it might even have equalled the Edenist He_3 cloud-mining operation. No physical or financial restrictions existed to limit its inherent promise; banks were more than willing to advance loans, the markets existed, supplied by its own ships.

But in the end—after the end—Rubra's Serpent nature proved less than benign after all. His psychology was too different, too obsessional. Brought up knowing his personality pattern would continue to exist for centuries if not millennia, he refused to accept death as an Adamist. He transferred his personality pattern into Valisk's neural strata.

From this point onward company and habitat started to degenerate. Part of the reason was the germination of the other independent habitats, all of whom offered themselves as bases for blackhawk mating flights. The Valisk/Magellanic Itg monopoly was broken. But the company's industrial decline, and the habitat's parallel deterioration, was due principally to the inheritance problem Rubra created.

When he died he was known to have fathered over a hundred and fifty children, a hundred and twenty-two of whom were carefully conceived *in vitro* and gestated in exowombs; all had modifications made to their affinity gene, as well as general physiological improvements. Thirty of the exowomb children were appointed to Valisk's executive committee, which ran both the habitat and Magellanic Itg, while the remainder, along with the rapidly proliferating third generation, became blackhawk pilots. The naturally conceived children were virtually disinherited from the company, and many of them returned to the Edenist fold.

Even this nepotistic arrangement shouldn't have been too much trouble. There would inevitably be power struggles within such a large committee, but strong characters would rise to the top, simple human dynamics demanded it. None ever did.

The alteration Rubra had made to their affinity gene was a simple one; they were bonded to the habitat and a single family of blackhawks alone. He robbed them of the Edenist general affinity. The arrangement gave him access to their minds virtually from the moment of conception, first through the habitat personality, then after he died, as the habitat personality.

He shaped them as they lay huddled in the metal and composite exowombs, and later in their innocent childhood; a dark conscience nestled maggot-fashion at the centre of their consciousness, examining their most secret thoughts for deviations from the path he had chosen. It was a dreadfully perverted version of the love bond which existed between voidhawks and their captains. His descendants became little more than anaemic caricatures of himself at his prime. He tried to instil the qualities which had driven him, and wound up with wretched neurotic inadequates. The more he attempted to tighten his discipline, the worse their dependence upon him became. A slow change manifested in the habitat personality's psychology. In his growing frustration with his living descendants he became resentful; of their lives, of their bodily experiences, of the emotions they could feel, the humanness of glands and hormones running riot. Rubra was jealous of the living.

Edenist visits to the habitat, already few and far between, stopped altogether after 2480. They said the habitat personality had become insane.

Dariat was an eighth-generation descendant, born a hundred and seventy-five years after Rubra's body died. Physically he was virtually indistinguishable from his peer group; he shared the light coffee-coloured skin and raven hair that signalled the star system's ethnic origin. A majority of Valisk's population originated insystem, though few of them were practising Hindus. Only his indigo eyes marked him out as anything other than a straight Srinagar genotype.

He never knew of his calamitous inheritance until his teens, although even from his infancy he knew in his heart he was different; he was better, superior to all the other children in his day club. And when they laughed at him, or teased him, or sent him to Coventry, he laid into them with a fury that none of them could match. He didn't know where it came from himself, only that it lay within, like some slumbering lake-bottom monster. At first he felt shame at the beatings he inflicted, blood for a five-year-old is a shocking sight; but even as he ran home crying a different aspect of the alien ego would appear and soothe him, calming his pounding heart. There was nothing wrong, he was assured, no crime committed, only rightness. They shouldn't have said what they did, catcalled and sneered. You were right to assert yourself, you are strong, be proud of that.

After a while the feelings of guilt ebbed away. When he needed to hit someone he did it without remorse or regret. His leadership of the day club was undisputed, out of fear rather than respect.

He lived with his mother in a starscraper apartment; his father had left her the year he was born. He knew his father was important, that he helped to manage Magellanic Itg; but whenever he paid mother and son one of his dutiful visits he was subject to moody silences or bursts of frantic activity. Dariat didn't like him, the grown-up was weird. I can do without him, the boy thought, he's weak. The conviction was as strong as one of his didactic imprints. His father stopped visiting after he was twelve years old.

Dariat concentrated on science and finance subjects when he began receiving didactic courses at ten years old, although right at the back of his mind was the faintest notion that the arts might just have been equally appealing. But they were despicable moments of weakness, soon swallowed by the pride he felt whenever he passed another course assessment. He was headed for great things.

At fourteen the crux came. At fourteen he fell in love.

Valisk's interior did not follow the usual bitek habitat convenience of a tropical or sub-tropical environment. Rubra had decided on a scrub desert extending out from the base of the northern endcap, then blending slowly into hilly savannah plain of terrestrial and xenoc grasses before the standard circumfluous salt-water reservoir at the base of the southern endcap.

Dariat was fond of hiking round the broad grasslands with their subtle blend of species and colours. The children's day club which he used to dominate had long since broken up. Adolescents were supposed to join sports groups, or general interest clubs. He had trouble integrating, too many peers remembered his temper and violence long after he had stopped resorting to such crude methods. They shunned him, and he told himself he didn't care. Somebody told him. In dreams he would find himself walking through the habitat talking to a white-haired old man. The old man was a big comfort, the things he said, the encouragement he gave. And the habitat was slightly different, richer, with trees and flowers and happy crowds, families picnicking.

"It's going to be like this once you're in charge," the old man told him numerous times. "You're the best there's been for decades. Almost as good as me. You'll bring it all back to me, the power and the wealth."

"This is the future?" Dariat asked. They were standing on a tall altar of polyp-rock, looking down on a circular starscraper entrance. People were rushing about with a vigour and purpose not usually found in Valisk. Every one of them was wearing a Magellanic Itg uniform. When he lifted his gaze it was as though the northern endcap was transparent; blackhawks flocked around their docking rings, loaded with expensive goods and rare artefacts from a hundred planets. Further out, so far away it was only a hazy ginger blob, Magellanic Itg's failed Von Neumann machine spun slowly against the gas giant's yellow-brown ring array.

"It could be the future," the old man sighed regretfully. "If you will only listen how."

"I will," Dariat said. "I'll listen."

The old man's schemes seemed to coincide with the pressure of conviction and certainty which was building in his own mind. Some days he seemed so full of ideas and goals he thought his skull must surely burst apart, whilst on other occasions the dream man's long rambling speeches seemed to have developed a tangible echo, lasting all day long.

That was why he enjoyed the long bouts of solitude provided by the unadventurous interior. Walking and exploring obscure areas was the only time the raging thoughts in his brain slowed and calmed.

Five days after his fourteenth birthday he saw Anastasia Rigel. She was washing in a river that ran along the floor of a deep valley. Dariat heard her singing before he saw her. The voice led him round some genuine rock boulders onto a shelf of naked polyp which the water had scoured of soil. He squatted down in the lee of the boulders, and watched her kneeling at the side of the river.

The girl was tall and much much blacker than anyone he'd seen in Valisk before. She appeared to be in her late teens (seventeen, he learned later), with legs that seemed to be all bands of muscle, and long jet-black hair that was arranged in ringlets and woven with red and yellow beads. Her face was narrow and delicate with a petite nose. There were dozens of slim silver and bronze bracelets on each arm.

She was only wearing a blue skirt of some thin cotton. A brown top of some kind lay on the polyp beside her. Dariat caught some fleeting glimpses of high pointed breasts as she rubbed water across her chest and arms. It was even better than accessing bluesense AV fleks and tossing off. For once he felt beautifully calm.

I'm going to have her, he thought, I really am. The certainty burned him.

She stood up, and pulled her brown top on. It was a sleeveless waistcoat made from thin supple leather, laced up the front. "You can come out now," she said in a clear voice.

Just for a moment he felt wholly inferior. Then he trotted towards her with a casualness that denied she had just caught him spying. "I was trying not to alarm you," he said.

She was twenty centimetres taller than him; she looked down and grinned openly. "You couldn't."

"Did you hear me? I thought I was being quiet."

"I could feel you."

"Feel me?"

"Yes. You have a very anguished spirit. It cries out."

"And you can hear that?"

"Lin Yi was a distant ancestress."

"Oh."

"You have not heard of her?"

"No, sorry."

"She was a famous spiritualist. She predicted the Big One2 quake in California back on Earth in 2058 and led her followers to safety in Oregon. A perilous pilgrimage for those times."

"I'd like to hear that story."

"I will tell it if you like. But I don't think you will listen. Your spirit is closed against the realm of Chi-ri."

"You judge people very fast. We don't stand much of a chance, do we?"

"Do you know what the realm of Chi-ri is?"

"No."

"Shall I tell you?"

"If you like."

"Come then."

She led him up the river, bracelets tinkling musically at

every motion. They followed the tight curve of the valley; after three hundred metres the floor broadened out, and a Starbridge village was camped along the side of the river.

Starbridge was the remnants of the cults and tribes and spiritualists who had moved into Valisk during its formative years. They had slowly amalgamated down the decades, bonding together against the scorn and hostility of the other inhabitants. Now they were one big community, united spiritually with an *outré* fusion of beliefs that was often incomprehensible to any outsider. They embraced the primitive existence, living as tribes of migrants, walking round and round the interior of the habitat, tending their cattle, practising their handicraft, cultivating their opium poppies, and waiting for their nirvana.

Dariat looked out on the collection of ramshackle tepees, stringy animals with noses foraging the grass, children in rags running barefoot. He experienced a contempt so strong it verged on physical sickness. He was curious at that, he had no reason to hate the Starbridge freakos, he'd never had anything to do with them before. Even as he thought that, the loathing increased. Of course he did, slimy parasites, vermin on two legs.

Anastasia Rigel stroked his forehead in concern. "You suffer yet you are strong," she said. "You spend so much time in the realm of Anstid."

She brought him into her tepee, a cone of heavy handwoven cloth. Wicker baskets ringed the walls. The light was dim, and the air dusty. The valley's pinkish grass was matted, dry and dying underfoot. He saw her sleeping roll bundled up against one basket, a bright orange blanket with pillows that had some kind of green and white tree motif embroidered across them, haloed by a ring of stars. He wondered if that was what he'd do it on, where he'd finally become a real man.

They sat crosslegged on a threadbare rug and drank tea, which was like coloured water, and didn't taste of much. Jasmine, she told him.

"What do you think of us?" she asked.

"Us?"

"The Starbridge tribes."

"Never really thought about you much," Dariat said. He was getting itchy sitting on the rug, and it was pretty obvious there weren't going to be any biscuits with the tea.

"You should. Starbridge is both our name and our dream, that which we seek to build. A bridge between stars, between all peoples. We are the final religion. They will all come to us eventually; the Christians and Muslims and Hindus and Buddhists, even the Satanists and followers of Wicca; every sect, every cult. Each and every one of them."

"That's a pretty bold claim."

"Not really. Just inevitable. There were so many of us, you see, when Rubra the Lost invited us here. So many beliefs, all different, yet really all the same. Then he turned on us, and confined us, and isolated us. He thought he would punish us, force us to conform to his materialistic atheism. But faith and dignity is always stronger than mortal oppression. We turned inwards for comfort, and found we had so much that we shared. We became one."

"Starbridge being the one?"

"Yes. We burned the old scriptures and prayer books on a bonfire so high the flames reached right across the habitat. With them went all the ancient prejudices and the myths. It left us pure, in silence and darkness. Then we rebirthed ourselves, and renamed what we knew was real. There is so much that old Earth's religions have in common; so many identical beliefs and tenets and wisdoms. But their followers are forced apart by names, by priests who have grown decadent and greedy for physical reward. Whole peoples, whole planets who denounce one another so that a few evil men can wear robes of golden cloth."

"That seems fairly logical," Dariat said enthusiastically. "Good idea." He smiled. From where he was sitting he could see the whole side of her left breast through the waistcoat's lace-up front.

"I don't think you have come to faith that quickly," she said with a trace of suspicion.

"I haven't. Because you haven't told me anything about it. But if you were telling the truth about hearing my spirit, then you've got my full attention. None of the other religions can offer tangible proof of God's existence."

She shifted round on the rug, bracelets clinking softly. "Neither do we offer proof. What we say is that life in this universe is only one segment of the great journey a spirit undertakes through time. We believe the journey will finish when a spirit reaches heaven, however you choose to define that existence. But don't ask how close this universe is to heaven. That depends on the individual."

"What happens when your spirit reaches heaven?"

"Transcendence."

"What sort?"

"That is for God to proclaim."

"God. Not a goddess, then?" he asked teasingly.

She grinned at him. "The word defines a concept, not an entity, not a white man with a white beard, nor even an earth mother. Physical bodies require gender. I don't think the instigator and sovereign of the multiverse is going to have physical and biological aspects, do you?"

"No." He finished the tea, relieved the cup was empty. "So what are these realms?"

"While the spirit is riding a body it also moves through the spiritual realms of the Lords and Ladies who govern nature. There are six realms, and five Lords and Ladies."

"I thought you said there was only one heaven?"

"I did. The realms are not heaven, they are aspects of ourselves. The Lords and Ladies are not God, but they are of a higher order than ourselves. They affect events through the wisdoms and deceits they reveal to us. But they have no influence on the physical reality of the cosmos. They are not the instigators of miracles."

"Like angels and demons?" he asked brightly.

"If you like. If that makes it easier to accept."

"So they're in charge of us?"

"You are in charge of yourself. You and you alone chose where your spirit roams."

"Then why the Lords and Ladies?"

"They grant gifts of knowledge and insight, they tempt. They test us."

"Silly thing to do. Why don't they leave us alone?"

"Without experience there can be no growth. Existence is evolution, both on a spiritual and a personal level."

"I see. So which is this Chi-ri I'm closed against?"

Anastasia Rigel climbed to her feet and went over to one of the wicker baskets. She pulled out a small goatskin bag. If she was aware of his hungry look following her every move she never showed it. "These represent the Lords and Ladies," she said as she sat back down. The bag's contents were tipped out. Six coloured pebble-sized crystals bounced on the rug. They had all been carved, he saw; cubes with their faces marked by small runes. She picked up the red one. "This is for Thoale, Lord of destiny." The blue crystal was held up, and she told him it was for Chi-ri, Lady of hope. Green was for Anstid, Lord of hatred. Yellow for Tarrug, Lord of mischief. Venus, Lady of love, was as clear as glass.

"You said there were six realms," he said.

"The sixth is the emptiness." She proffered a jet-black cube, devoid of runes. "It has no Lord or Lady, it is where lost spirits flee." She crossed her arms in front of herself, fingers touching her shoulders, bracelets falling to the crook of her elbows. She reminded Dariat of a statue of Shiva he'd seen in one of Valisk's four temples; Shiva as Nataraja, king of dancers. "A terrible place," Anastasia Rigel murmured coolly.

"You don't think I have any hope?" he asked, suddenly annoyed at this primitive paganish nonsense again.

"You resist it."

"No, I don't. I've got lots of hope. I'm going to run this habitat one day," he added. She ought to be impressed by that.

Her head was shaken gently, hair partly obscuring her

face. "That is Anstid deceiving you, Dariat. You spend so much time in his realm, he has an unholy grip upon your spirit."

"How do you know?" he said scornfully.

"These are called Thoale stones. He is the Lord I am beholden to. He shows me what is to unfold." A slight, droll smile flickered over her lips. "Sometimes Tarrug intervenes. He shows me things I should not see, or events I cannot understand."

"How do the stones work?"

"Each face is carved with the rune of a realm. I read the combinations, how they fall, or in the case of the emptiness where it falls in relation to the others. Would you like to know what your future contains?"

"Yeah. Go on."

"Pick up each crystal, hold it in your hands for a moment, try to impress it with your essence, then put it in the bag."

He picked up the clear one, naturally. Love Lady. "How do I impress it?"

She just shrugged.

He squeezed the crystals one at a time, feeling increasingly stupid, and dropped them in the goatskin bag. Anastasia Rigel shook the bag, then tipped the crystals out.

"What does it say?" Dariat asked, a shade too eagerly for someone who was supposed to be sceptical.

She stared at them a while, eyes flicking anxiously between the runes. "Greatness," she said eventually. "You will come to greatness."

"Hey, yeah!"

Her hand came up, silencing him. "It will not last. You shine so bright, Dariat, but for such a short time, and it is a dark flame which ignites you."

"Then what?" he asked, disgruntled.

"Pain, death."

"Death?"

"Not yours. Many people, but not yours."

Anastasia Rigel didn't offer to sleep with him that time.

Nor any of his visits during the month which followed. They walked round the savannah together, talking inanities, almost as brother and sister. She would tell him about the Starbridge philosophy, the idiosyncrasies of the realms. He listened, but became lost and impatient with a worldview which seemed to have little internal logic. In return he told her of his father, the resentment and the confusion of loss; mainly in the hope she'd feel sorry for him. He took her down into a starscraper; she said she'd never been in one before. She didn't like it, the confining walls of the apartments, although she was fascinated by the slowly spinning starfield outside.

The sexual tension died down from its initial high-voltage peak, though it was never laid to rest. It became a sort of game, jibes and smirks, played for points that neither knew how to win. Dariat enjoyed her company a lot. Someone who treated him fairly, who took time to hear what he said. Because she wanted to. He could never quite understand what she got out of the arrangement. She read his future several times, though none of the readings ever proved quite as dire as the first.

Dariat spent more and more time with her, almost divorcing himself from the culture lived out in the starscrapers and industrial stations (except for keeping up on his didactic courses). The portentous aspirations in his mind lost their grip when he was in her presence.

He learnt how to milk a goat, not that he particularly wanted to. They were smelly, bad-tempered creatures. She cooked him fish which she caught in the streams, and showed him which plants had edible roots. He found out about the tribe's way of life, how they sold a lot of their handicrafts to starship crews, chiefly the rugs and pottery, how they shunned technology. "Except for nanonic medical packages," she said wryly. "Amazing how many women become technocrats around childbirth time." He went to some of their ceremonies, which seemed little more than open air parties where everyone drank a strong distilled spirit, and sang gospel hymns late into the night.

One evening, when she was wearing just a simple white cotton poncho, she invited him into her tepee. He felt all the sexual heat return as the outline of her body was revealed through the fabric by the light of the tepee's meagre oil lamp. There was some kind of clay pot in the centre with a snakelike hose coming from the side. It was smoking docilely, filling the air with a funny sweet and sour scent.

Anastasia took a puff on the pipe, and shivered as if she'd swallowed a triple whisky. "Try some," she said, her voice rich with challenge.

"What is it?"

"A wide gate into Tarrug's realm. You'll like it. Anstid won't. He'll lose all control over you."

He looked at the crimped end of the tube, still wet from her mouth. He wanted to try it. He was frightened. Her eyes were very wide.

She tipped her head back, expelling two long plumes of smoke from her nostrils. "Don't you want to explore the realm of mischief with me?"

Dariat put the tube in his mouth and sucked. The next minute he was coughing violently.

"Not so hard," she said. Her voice sounded all furred. "Take it down slow. Feel it float through your bones."

He did as he was told.

"They're hollow, you know, your bones." Her smile was wide, shining like the light-tube against her black face.

The world spun round. He could feel the habitat moving, stars whipping round faster and faster, smearing across space. Smeared like cream. He giggled. Anastasia Rigel gave him a long, knowing grin, and took another drag on the tube.

Space was pink. Stars were black. Water smelt of cheese. "I love you," he told her. "I love you, I love you." The tepee walls were palpitating in and out. He was in the belly of some huge beast, just like Jonah.

Bloody hell.

"What did you say?"

Shit, I can't filter . . . What's green? What are you—

"My hands are green," he explained patiently.

"Are they?" Anastasia Rigel asked. "That's interesting."

What has she given you?

"Tarrug?" Dariat asked. Anastasia had said that was who they were going to visit. "Hello, Tarrug. I can hear him. He's talking to me."

Anastasia Rigel was at right angles to him. She pulled the poncho off over her head, sitting crosslegged and naked on the rug. Now she was totally upside-down. Her nipples were black eyes following him.

"That's not Tarrug you hear," she said. "That's Anstid."

"Anstid. Hi!"

What is it? What is in that bloody pipe? Wait, I'm reviewing the local memory . . . Oh, fuck, it's salfrond. I can't hold onto your thoughts when you're tripping on that, you little prick.

"I don't want you to."

Yes, you do. Oh, believe me you do, boy. I've got the keys to every dark door in this kingdom, and you're the golden protégé. Now stop smoking that mind-rotting crap.

Dariat very deliberately stuck the tube in his mouth, and inhaled until his lungs were about to burst. His cheeks puffed out. Anastasia Rigel leant forwards and took the tube from between his lips. "Enough."

The tepee was spinning in the opposite direction to the habitat, and outside it was raining shoes. Black leather shoes with scarlet buckles.

Shit! I'm going to kill that little black junkie bitch for this. It's high bloody time I shoved the Starbridge tribes out of the airlock. Dariat, stand up, boy. Walk outside, get some fresh air. There's some medical nanonic packages in the village, the headman's got some. They can straighten out your blood chemistry.

Dariat's giggles returned. "Piss off."

GET UP!

"No."

Weakling! Always bloody weaklings. You're no better than your bastard father.

Dariat squeezed his eyes shut. The colours were behind his eyelids too. "I am not like him."

Yes, you are. Weak, feeble, pathetic. All of you are. I should have cloned myself when I had the chance. Parthenogenetics would have solved all this bullshit. Two fucking centuries of weaklings I've had to endure. Two centuries, fuck it.

"Go away!" Even stoned, he could tell this wasn't part of the trip. This was more. This was much much worse.

"Is he hurting you, baby?" Anastasia Rigel asked.

"Yes."

I'll fucking cripple you if you don't get up. Smash your legs, shred your hands to ribbons. Do you like the sound of that, boy? A life spent grubbing round like a snail. Can't walk, can't feed yourself, can't wipe your arse.

"Stop it," Dariat screamed.

Get up!

"Don't listen to him, baby. Close your mind."

Tell that bitch from me, she's dead.

"Please, both of you, stop it. Leave me alone."

Get up.

Dariat tried to rise. He got up to his knees, then fell into Anastasia's lap.

"You're mine now," she said gladly.

No, you're not. You're mine. Always mine. You can never leave. I won't allow you to.

Her hands ran over his clothes, opening seals. Kisses with the sharp cold impact of hailstones fell on his face. "This is what you wanted, what you always wanted," she breathed in his ear. "Me."

The nauseating colour stripes blitzing his sight swirled into blackness. Her hot skin sliding up and down against him. Weight pressing against every part of him. He was doing it! He was fucking! Tears poured out of his eyes.

"That's right, baby. Up inside me. Purge him. Purge him

with me. Fly, fly into Venus and Chi-ri. Leave him behind. Free yourself."

Always mine.

Dariat woke feeling awful. He was lying on the stiff tousled grass of the tepee without a stitch of clothing. The entrance flap was open, a slice of bright morning light sliding through. A heavy dew mottled his legs. Something had died and decomposed in his mouth, his tongue by the feel of it. Anastasia Rigel was lying beside him. Naked and beautiful. Arms tucked up against her chest.

Last night. I fucked her. I did it!

He tried to smother an ecstatic laugh.

Feeling better?

Dariat screamed. It was inside his head. Anstid. The realm demigod.

He jerked around, hugging himself, biting his lower lip so hard he drew blood.

Don't be an idiot. I'm not a bloody spirit bogeyman. There's no such thing. Religion is a psychological crutch for mental inadequates. Spiritualism is for mental paraplegics. Think what that makes your girlie friend.

"What are you?"

Anastasia Rigel woke up, blinking against the light. She ran her hand through her wild hair and sat up, looking at him with a curious expression.

I'm your ancestor.

"A lost spirit from the emptiness?" he asked, wide eyed with fright.

Give me one more word of mythology and I really will have your legs broken. Now think logically. I'm your ancestor. Who can I be?

Information from his didactic history courses tumbled into his thoughts. "Rubra?" The idea didn't make him feel any better at all.

Well done. Now stop panicking, and stop shivering. I don't normally talk direct to someone your age, I like to let you have sixteen years to yourself. But I'm not

going to allow you to become a dopehead. Do not ever smoke that stuff again. Understand?

"Yes, sir."

Stop vocalizing. Concentrate your thoughts.

"What are you saying, baby?" Anastasia Rigel asked. "Are you still tripping?"

"No. It's Rubra, he's . . . We're talking."

She pulled the white poncho round herself, giving him an alarmed look.

I've got plans for you, boy, Rubra said. Big plans. You're destined for Magellanic itg's executive committee.

I am?

Yes. If you play your cards right. If you do as you're told.

I will.

Good. Now I've been lenient letting you sow your oats with dinky little Anastasia. I can understand that, she's got a nice body, good tits, pretty face. I had a sex drive myself, once. But you've had your fun now; so put your clothes on and say goodbye. We'll find someone a bit more suitable.

I can't leave her. Not after . . . last night.

Take a real good look at yourself, boy. Rutting with a bubblehead primitive on a filthy mat in a tepee. Some friend, she filled your brain with two kinds of shit. That's not how Valisk's future ruler is going to behave. Is it?

No, sir.

Good boy.

He started to pick up his clothes.

"Where are you going?" she asked.

"Home."

"He told you to."

"I . . . What is there here?"

She gave him a forlorn look over the white poncho which was still clasped to her body. "Me. Your friend. Your lover."

He shook his head.

"I'm human. That's more than he is."

Come on. Leave.

Dariat pulled on his shoes. He paused by the entrance flap.

"It's Anstid," she said in a mournful tone. "That's who you really talk to."

Pseudobabble. Ignore her.

Dariat walked slowly out of the village. Some of the elders gave him strange looks as he passed their steaming cooking pits. They couldn't understand. Why would anyone leave Anastasia's bed?

That's their trouble, boy. They're too backward. The real world is beyond them. I really must get round to cleaning them out one day.

Now Dariat knew what he was, what he was destined for, the didactic courses took on a whole new level of importance. He listened to Rubra's advice on the specializations he needed, the grades he had to achieve. He became obedient, and a shade resentful at his own compliance. But what else was there? Starbridge?

In return for acquiescence Rubra taught him how to use the affinity bond with the habitat. How to access the sensitive cells to see what was going on, how he could call on vast amounts of processing power, the tremendous amount of stored data that was available.

One of the first things Rubra did was to guide him through a list of possible replacement girls, eager to bury the lingering traces of yearning for Anastasia Rigel. Dariat felt like a voyeuristic ghost, watching the prospective candidates through the sensitive cells; seeing them at home, talking to their friends. Some of them he watched having sex with their boyfriends, two with other girls, which was exciting. Rubra didn't seem to object to these prolonged observations. At least it meant he didn't have to pay for bluesense fleks any more.

One girl he chanced on was nice, Chilone, nine months

older than him. As black as Anastasia (which was what first caught his attention), but with dark auburn hair. Shy and pretty, who talked a lot about sex and boys with her girl friends.

Still he hesitated from meeting her, even though he knew her daily routine, knew her interests, what to say, which day clubs she belonged to. He could contrive a dozen encounters.

Get on with it, Rubra told him after a week of cautious scrutiny. **Screw her brains out. You don't think Anastasia's still pining over you, do you?**

What?

Try using the sensitive cells around the tepee.

That was something he'd never done, not using the habitat's perception faculty to spy on her. But the tone Rubra used had a hint of cruel amusement in it.

Anastasia had a lover, Mersin Columba, another Starbridge. A man in his forties; overweight, balding, with white pallid skin. They looked horrible locked together. Anastasia flinched silently as she lay underneath his pumping body.

The old white-hot infantile fury rose into Dariat's mind. He wanted to save her from the repellent humiliation; his beautiful girl who had loved him.

Take my advice. Go find young Chilone.

Like juvenile Edenists, it hadn't taken Dariat long to discover how to fox the habitat's sensitive cells. Unless Rubra's principal personality pattern was concentrating on him in particular, the autonomous monitoring of the subroutines could be circumvented.

Dariat used the sensitive cells to follow Mersin Columba out of the tepee. The podgy oaf had a smug smile on his face as he made his way down to the stream. Anastasia Rigel was curled up on her rug, staring at nothing.

Mersin Columba made his way down the valley before stripping off his shirt and trousers. He splashed into a wide pool, and began to wash off the smell and stains of sex.

The first blow from Dariat's wooden cudgel caught him

on the side of his head, tearing his ear. He grunted and
dropped to his knees. The second blow smashed across the
crown of his skull.

Stop it!

Dariat aimed another blow; laughing at the surprise on
the man's face. Nobody does that to my girl. Nobody does
that to me! A cascade of blows rained down on Mersin
Columba's unprotected head. Rubra's furious demands
were reduced to a wasp's buzz at the back of Dariat's raging mind. He was vengeance. He was omnipotent, more
than any realm Lord. He struck and struck, and it felt good.

The water pushed at Mersin Columba's inert body. Long
ribbons of blood wept from the battered head, turned to tattered curlicues by the current. Dariat stood over him. The
bloody length of wood dropped from his fingers.

I didn't realize what I'd created with you, Rubra said.
The silent voice lacked its usual conviction.

Dariat shivered suddenly. His heart was pumping hard.
**Anastasia is mine. Well, she certainly doesn't belong to
poor old Mersin Columba any more, and that's a fact.**

The body had drifted five metres downstream. Dariat
thought it looked repugnant, sickly white, bloated.

Now what? he asked sullenly.

**I'd better get some housechimps to tidy up. And
you'd better make tracks.**

Is that it?

**I'm not going to punish you for killing a Starbridge.
But we're going to have to work on that temper of
yours. It can be useful, but only if it's applied properly.**

For the company.

**Yes. And don't you forget it. Don't worry, you'll im-
prove with age.**

Dariat turned and walked away from the river. He hiked
up out of the valley and spent the afternoon wandering
aimlessly around the savannah.

His thoughts were glacial. He had killed a man, but there
was no remorse, no sense of guilt. No sense of satisfaction,

either. He felt nothing, as if the whole incident was an act he'd seen on an AV recording.

When the light-tube began to dim into brassy twilight he turned and made his way towards the Starbridge village.

Where do you think you're going? Rubra asked.

She's mine. I love her. I'm going to have her. Tonight, always.

No. Only I am for always.

You can't stop me. I don't care about the company. Keep it. I never wanted it. I want Anastasia.

Don't be a fool.

Dariat detected something then, a strand of emotion wound up with the mental voice: anxiety. Rubra was worried.

What's happened?

Nothing's happened. Go home. It's been a hellish day.

No. He tried to use the sensitive cells to show him the village. Nothing, Rubra was blocking his affinity.

Go home.

Dariat started running.

Don't, boy!

It was over a kilometre back to the valley. The pink and yellow grass came up to his waist in places, blades whipping his legs. He reached the brow of the slope and looked down in dismay. The village was packing up, moving on. Half of the tepees were already down, folded into bundles and put on the carts. Animals were being rounded up. All the fire pits were out. It was a crazy time to be moving. Night was almost here. His sense of calamity redoubled.

Dariat sprinted down the steep slope, falling twice, grazing his knees and shins. He didn't care. Faces turned to watch as he dashed towards Anastasia's tepee.

He was shouting her name as he shoved the entrance flap aside.

The rope had been tied to the apex of the tepee. She must have used a stack of her wicker baskets to stand on. They were scattered all over the floor.

Her head was tilted to one side, the rope pressing into her left cheek, just behind the ear. She swayed slightly from side to side, the tepee's poles letting out quiet creaks.

Dariat stared at her for some immeasurable time. He didn't understand why. Not any of it.

Come on, boy. Come on home.

No. You did this. You made me leave her. She was mine. This would never have happened if you'd stayed out of my life. Tears were pouring down his cheeks.

I am your life.

You're not. Not not not. He closed out the voice. Refusing to hear the pleas and threats.

One of the wicker baskets had a piece of paper lying on top. It was weighted down by Anastasia's goatskin bag. Dariat picked it up, and read the message she'd written.

Dariat, I know it was you. I know you thought you did it for me. You didn't. You did it because it's what Anstid wanted, he will never allow you an alliance with Thoale. I thought I could help you. But I see I can't; I'm not strong enough to defy a realm Lord. I'm sorry.

I can't see any purpose in staying in this universe any more. I'm going to free my spirit and continue my flight towards God. The Thoale stones are my gift to you; use them please. You have so many battles to fight. Seeing the future may help you win some.

I want you to know I loved you for all the time we were together.

Anastasia Rigel

He loosened the thong at the top of the bag and spilled the six crystals onto the dusty rug. The five which were carved with runes landed with the blank face uppermost. He slowly picked them up, and threw them again. They came up blank. The empty realm, where lost spirits go.

Dariat fled the Starbridge village. He never went back. He stopped taking didactic courses, refused to acknowledge Rubra's affinity bond, argued a lot with his mother, and moved into a starscraper apartment of his own at fifteen.

There was nothing Rubra could do. His most promising protégé for decades was lost to him. The affinity window into Dariat's mind remained closed; it was the most secure block the habitat personality pattern had ever known, remaining in place even while the boy slept. After a month of steady pressure Rubra gave up, even Dariat's subconscious was sealed against subliminal suggestions. The block was more than conscious determination, it was a profound psychological inhibition. Probably trauma based.

Rubra cursed yet another failure descendant, and switched his priority to a new fledgeling. Monitoring of Dariat was assigned to an autonomic sub-routine. Occasional checks by the personality's principal consciousness revealed a total drop-out, a part-time drunk, part-time hustler picking up beer money by knowing people and where to find them, getting involved with deals which were dubious even for Valisk. Dariat never got a regular job, living off the starscraper food pap, accessing MF albums, sometimes for days on end. He never approached a girl again.

It was a stand-off which lasted for thirty years. Rubra had even stopped his intermittent checks on the wrecked man. Then the *Yaku* arrived at Valisk.

The *Yaku*'s emergence above Opuntia six days after it left Lalonde never raised a query. None of Graeme Nicholson's fleks had yet reached their destination when the cargo starship asked for and was granted docking permission. As far as both the habitat personality and the Avon Embassy's small Intelligence team (the only Confederation observers Rubra would allow inside) were concerned it was just another cargo starship visiting a spaceport which handled nearly thirty thousand similar visits a year.

Yaku had emerged a little further away from Valisk than was normal, and its flight vector required a more than average number of corrections—the fusion drive was fluctuating in an erratic fashion. But then a lot of the Adamist starships using Valisk operated on the borderline of CAB spaceworthiness requirements.

It docked at a resupply bay on the edge of the three-kilo-metre-wide disk which was the habitat's non-rotational spaceport. The captain requested a quantity of He₃ and deuterium, as well as oxygen, water, and some food. Spaceport service companies were contracted within ten minutes of its arrival.

Three people disembarked. Their passport fleks named them as Marie Skibbow, Alicia Cochrane, and Manza Balyuzi; the last two were members of *Yaku*'s crew. All three cleared Valisk's token immigration and customs carrying small bags with a single change of clothing.

The *Yaku* undocked four hours later, its cryogenic tanks full, and flew down towards Opuntia. Whatever its jump coordinate was, the gas giant was between it and Valisk when it activated its energy patterning nodes. No record of its intended destination existed.

Dariat was sitting up at the bar in the Tabitha Oasis when the girl caught his eye. Thirty years of little exercise, too much cheap beer, and a diet of starscraper gland synthesized pastes had brought about a detrimental effect on his once slim physique. He was fat verging on obese, his skin was flaky, his hair was dulled by a week's accumulation of oil. Appearance wasn't something he paid a lot of attention to. A togalike robe covered a multitude of laxities.

That girl, though: teenaged, long limbed, large breasted, exquisite face, bronzed, strong. Wearing a tight white T-shirt and short black skirt. He wasn't alone in watching her. The Tabitha Oasis attracted a tough crew. Girl like that was a walking gang-bang invitation. It had happened before. But she hadn't got a care in the world, there was an *élan* to her which was mesmerizing. All the more surprising, then, was her table companion.

Anders Bospoort: physically her counterpart; late twenties, slab muscles, the best swarthy face money could buy. But he didn't have her youthful exuberance, his mouth and

eyes smiled (for that money they ought to) but there was
no emotion powering the expression. Anders Bospoort was
in almost equal proportions gigolo, pimp, pusher, and bluesense star.

Strange she couldn't see that. But he could pile on the
charm when necessary, and the expensive wine bottle sitting on the table between them was nearly empty.

Dariat beckoned the barkeeper over. "What's her
name?"

"Marie. Arrived on a ship this afternoon."

That explained a lot. Nobody had warned her. Now the
wolves of the Tabitha Oasis were circling the camp-fire,
enjoying her elaborate seduction. Later they would be able
to share the corruption of youth, sensevising Anders
Bospoort's boosted penis sliding up between her legs.
Have her surprise and pleading in their ears. Feel the ripe
body molested by powerful skilled hands.

Maybe Anders wasn't so stupid, Dariat thought, bringing her here was a good advert. He could ask an easy ten
per cent over the odds for her flek.

The barkeeper shook his head sadly. He was three times
Dariat's age, and he'd spent his every year in Valisk. He'd
seen it all, so he claimed, every human foible. "Pity, nice
girl like that. Someone should tell her."

"Yeah. Anywhere else, and someone might." Dariat
looked at her again. Surely a girl with her beauty couldn't
be that naïve about men?

Anders Bospoort extended a gracious arm as they rose from
the table. Marie smiled and accepted it. He thought she
looked glad at the opportunity to stay close. The gazes she
drew from the men of the Tabitha Oasis weren't exactly coy.
His size and measured presence was a reassurance. She was
safe with him.

They walked across the vestibule outside the bar, and
Anders datavised the starscraper's mechanical systems
control processor for a lift.

"Thank you for taking me there," Marie said.

He saw the excitement in her eyes at the little taste of the illicit. "I don't always go there. It can get a little rough. Half of the regulars have Confederation warrants hanging over them. If the navy ever comes visiting Valisk the population on penal planets would just about double overnight."

The lift arrived. He gestured her through the open doors. Halfway there, and it was going so smoothly. He'd been a perfect gentleman from the moment they met outside the Apartment Allocation Office (always the best place to pick up clean meat), every word clicking flawlessly into place. And she'd been drawn closer and closer, hypnotized by the old Bospoort magic.

She glanced uncertainly at the floor as the doors closed, as if she'd only just realized how far from her home and family she was. All alone with her only friend in the whole star system. No going back for her now.

He felt a tightening in his stomach as the anticipation heightened. This would all go on the flek; the prelude, the slow-burning conquest. People appreciated the build in tension. And he was an artiste supreme.

The doors opened to the eighty-third floor.

"It's a walk down two floors," Anders told her apologetically. "The lifts don't work below here. And the maintenance crews won't come down to fix them. Sorry."

The vestibule hadn't been cleaned for a long time and rubbish was accumulating in the corners. There was graffiti on the walls, a smell of urine in the air. Marie looked round nervously, and stayed close to Anders' side.

He guided her to the stairwell. The light was dim, a strip of electrophorescent cells on the wall whose output had faded to an insipid yellow. Dozens of big pale moths whirred incessantly against it. Water leaked down the walls from cracks in the polyp. A cream-coloured moss grew along the edge of every step.

"It's very kind of you to let me stay with you," Marie ventured.

"Just until you get your own apartment sorted out. There

are hundreds of unused ones. It's one of life's greater mysteries why it always takes so long for the Allocation Office to assign one."

Nobody else was using the stairs. Anders very rarely got to meet any of his neighbours. The bottom of the starscraper was perfect for him. No quick access, everyone stayed behind closed doors to conduct their chosen business in life, and no questions were ever asked. The cops Magellanic Itg contracted to maintain a kind of order in the rest of Valisk didn't come down here.

They left the stairwell on his floor, and he datavised a code at his apartment door. Nothing happened. He flashed her a strained smile, and datavised the code again. This time it opened, juddering once or twice as it slid along its rails. Marie went in first. Anders deliberately kept the inside lights low, and codelocked the door behind him—at least the processor acknowledged that. He put his arm round her shoulder and steered her into the biggest of the three bedrooms. That door was codelocked too.

Marie walked into the middle of the room, eyes straying to the double bed. There were long velvet straps fixed to each corner.

"Take your clothes off," Anders told her. An uncompromising sternness appeared in his voice. He datavised an order to the overhead light panel, but it remained at its lowest level. Shit! And she was obediently stripping off. Nothing for it, he'd have to stay with the deep shadows and hope everyone found it erotic.

"Now take mine off," he ordered. "Slowly."

He could feel her hands trembling as she pushed the shirt off his broad shoulders, which made a nice touch. Nervous ones were always more responsive.

His eyes ran over her with expert tracking as she walked ahead of him to the bed, capturing every square centimetre of flesh on display. When she was lying on the water mattress his hands traced the same route. Then his boosted cock was swelling to its full length, and he focused on her face to make sure he captured her fear. That was always a big turn on for the punters.

Marie was smiling.

The lights sprang up to full intensity.

Anders twisted round in confusion. "Hey—"

At first he thought someone had crept up and snapped handcuffs round his wrists, but when he looked he saw it was Marie's elegant feminine hands gripping him.

"Let go." The pain as she squeezed harder was frightening. "Bitch! Let go. Christ—"

She laughed.

He looked back down at her, and gasped. She was sprouting hair right across her chest and stomach, thick black bristles that scratched and pricked his skin where he lay on top of her. Individual strands began to harden. It was like lying on a hedgehog hide. The long tips were puncturing his own skin, needling in through the subcutaneous layers of fat.

"Fuck me, then," she said.

He tried to struggle, but all that did was push more needle spines into his abdomen. Marie let go of one wrist. He hit her then, on the side of her ribs, and her flesh gave way below his fist. When he brought his hand away it was covered in yellow and red slime. The spines piercing him turned to worms, slick and greasy, licking round inside the swath of puncture holes down his torso. Blood trickled out.

Anders let out an insane howl. She was rotting below him, skin melting away into a putrescent crimson film of mucus. It was acting like glue, sticking him to her. The stench was vile, stinging his eyes. He puked, the wine from the Tabitha Oasis splattering down on her deliquescing face.

"Kiss me."

He bucked and floundered against her, weeping helplessly, praying to a God he hadn't addressed in over a decade. The worms were wriggling between his abdominal muscles, twining round tendon fibres. Blood and pus

squelched and intermingled, forming a sticky glue which
wedded them belly to belly like Siamese twins.

"Kiss me, Anders."

Her free hand clamped onto the back of his skull. It felt
like there was nothing left on it but bone. Sludge dripped
into his coiffured hair.

"No!" he whimpered.

Her lips had dribbled away like candle wax, leaving a
wide gash in the bubbling corruption that was her face. The
teeth were a permanent grin. His head was being forced
down towards her. He saw her teeth parting, then they were
rammed against his own face.

The kiss. And hot, black, gritty liquid surged up out of
her throat. Anders couldn't scream any more. It was in his
own mouth, kneading its way down his air passage like a
fat, eager serpent.

A voice from nowhere said: "We can stop it."

The liquid detonated into his lungs. He could feel it, hot
and rancid inside his chest, swelling out to invade every
delicate cavity. His ribcage heaved at the alien pressure
from within. He had stopped struggling.

"She'll kill you unless you let us help. She's drowning
you."

He wanted to breathe. He wanted air. He would do anything to breathe. Anything.

"Then let us in."

He did.

Using the sensitive cells in the polyp above Anders
Bospoort's bed, Dariat watched as the injuries and manifes-
tations reversed themselves. Marie's glutinous skin hardened, bristles retracting. The wounds down Anders
Bospoort's abdomen closed up. They became what they
were before: satyr and seraph.

Anders began to stroke himself, hands tracing lines of
muscle across his chest. He looked down on his body with
a childlike expression of awe which swiftly became a
broad grin. "I'm magnificent," he whispered. "Utterly

magnificent." The accent was different to Anders' usual. Dariat couldn't quite place it.

"Yes, you look pretty good," she replied indifferently. She sat up. The sheets were stained a faint pink below her back.

"Let me have you."

Her mouth wrinkled up with indecision.

"Please. You know I need to. Hell, it's been seven hundred years. Show a little compassion here."

"All right then." She lay back down. Anders started to lick her body, reminding Dariat of a feeding dog. They fucked for twenty minutes, Anders rutting with a fervour he'd never shown in any of his fleks. Electric lights and household equipment went berserk as they thrashed about. Dariat quickly checked the neighbouring apartments; a stimulant-program writer was yelling in frustration as his processors crashed at tremendous speed; a clone merchant's vats seethed and boiled as regulators fried the fragile cell clusters which they were wired up to. Doors all around the vestibule opened and shut like guillotines. He had to launch a flurry of subversive affinity orders into the floor's neural cells to prevent the local personality subroutines from alerting Rubra's principal consciousness.

When he arrived, puffing heavily, outside the apartment, Marie and Anders Bospoort were getting dressed. He used a black-market customized processor block to break the door's codelock, and walked straight in.

Marie and Anders looked up in alarm. They ran out of the bedroom. The processor block died in Dariat's hand and the apartment was plunged into pitch darkness.

"The dark doesn't bother me," he said loudly. The sensitive cells showed him the two of them were walking towards him menacingly.

"Nothing will bother you from now on," Marie replied.

The belt of his toga robe began to tighten round his belly. "Wrong. Firstly you won't be able to tyrannize me like you did poor old Anders, I'm not that weak. Secondly, if I die Rubra will see exactly what's been going on, and what you are. He might be crazy, but he'll fight like a lion to defend his precious habitat and corporation. Once he knows you exist you've lost ninety per cent of your advantage. You'll never take over Valisk without my help."

The lights came back on. His belt loosened. Marie and Anders regarded him with expressionless faces.

"It's only thanks to me he doesn't know already. You obviously don't understand much about bitek. I can help there as well."

"Perhaps we don't care if he knows," Anders said.

"OK, fine. You want me to lift the limiter orders I put on this floor's sensitive cells?"

"What do you want?" Marie asked.

"Revenge. I've waited thirty years for you. It's been so long, so very tiring; I nearly broke on more than one occasion. But I knew you would come in the end."

"You expected me?" she asked derisively.

"What you are, yes."

"And what am I?"

"The dead."

4

Gemal emerged from its jump six hundred and fifty thousand kilometres above Mirchusko, where the gas giant's gravity anchored it in a slightly elliptical orbit; Tranquillity, in its lower circular orbit, was trailing by two hundred thousand kilometres. Oliver Llewelyn, the colonist-carrier's captain, identified his starship to the habitat personality, and requested approach and docking permission.

"Do you require assistance?" Tranquillity asked.

"No, we're fully functional."

"I don't get many colonist-carrier vessels visiting. I thought you might have been making an emergency maintenance call."

"No. This flight is business."

"Does your entire passenger complement wish to apply for residency?"

"Quite the opposite. The zero-tau pods are all empty. We've come to hire some military specialists who live here."

"I see. Docking and approach request granted. Please datavise your projected vector to spaceport flight control."

Terrance Smith datavised a sensor access request into the starship's flight computer, and watched the massive bitek habitat growing larger as they accelerated towards rendezvous in a complex manoeuvre at two-thirds of a gee. He opened a channel to the habitat's communication net, and asked for a list of starships currently docked. Names and classifications flowed through his mind. A collation program sorted through them, indicating possibles and probables.

"I didn't realize this was such a large port," he said to Oliver Llewelyn.

"It has to be," the captain replied. "There are at least five major family-owned civil carrier fleets based here purely because of the tax situation, and most of the other line companies have offices in the habitat. Then you've got to consider the residents. They import one hell of a lot; everything you need to live the good life, from food to clothes to pretentious art. You don't think they'll eat the synthesized pulp the starscrapers grow, do you?"

"No, I suppose not."

"A lot of ships pick up contracts for them, bringing stuff in from all over the Confederation. And of course Tranquillity is the Confederation's principal base for blackhawk mating flights now Valisk is falling from favour with the captains. The eggs gestate down in the big inner ring. It all adds together. The Lords of Ruin have built it into one of the most important commercial centres in this sector."

Terrance looked across the bridge. Seven acceleration couches were arranged in a petal pattern on its composite decking, and only one of them was empty. The compartment had an industrial look, with cables and ducts fixed to the walls rather than being tucked neatly out of sight behind composite panels. But then that was a uniform characteristic throughout the *Gemal* and her sister ships which shuttled between Earth and stage one colony worlds. They were bulk carriers whose cargo happened to be people, and the line companies didn't waste money on cosmetic finishes.

Captain Llewelyn was lying inertly on his acceleration couch, surrounded by a horseshoe of bulky consoles; a well-built sixty-eight-year-old oriental with skin as smooth as any adolescent. His eyes were shut as he handled the datavise from the flight computer.

"Have you been here before?" Terrance asked.

"I stopped over two days, that was thirty-five years ago when I was a junior officer in a different company. Don't suppose it's changed much. Plutocrats put a lot of stock in stability."

"I'd like you to talk to the other captains for me, the independent trader starships we want to hire. I haven't exactly done this kind of work before."

Oliver Llewelyn snorted softly. "You let people know what kind of flight you're putting together, then start flashing that overloaded Jovian Bank credit disk around, and you'll be beating them off with a stick."

"What about the mercenaries and general troops?"

"The captains will put you in touch. Hell, the combat boosted will pay the captains for an introduction. You want my advice, delegate. Find yourself ten or twenty officer types with some solid experience, and let them recruit troops for you. Don't try and do it all yourself. We haven't got time, for a start. Rexrew gave us a pretty tight schedule."

"Thanks."

"You're paying, remember?"

"Yeah." It had taken twenty thousand fuseodollars just to get Oliver Llewelyn to agree to take the *Gemal* to Tranquillity. "Not part of my LDC contract," the captain had said stubbornly. Money was easier than datavising legal requirements at him. Terrance suspected it was going to cost a lot more to take the *Gemal* back to Lalonde. "You sound like you know what you're talking about," he said, mildly intrigued.

"I've flown a lot of different missions in my time," the old captain said indifferently.

"So where do I meet these starship captains?"

Oliver Llewelyn accessed a thirty-five-year-old file in his neural nanonics. "We'll start at Harkey's Bar."

Fifteen hours later Terrance Smith had to admit that Oliver Llewelyn had been perfectly correct. He didn't need to make any effort, the people he wanted came to him. Like iron to a magnet, he thought, or flies to shit. He was sitting in a wall booth, feeling like an old-style tsar holding court, receiving petitions from eager subjects. Harkey's Bar was full with starship crews hunched around tables, or concentrating in small knots at the bar. There was also a scattering of the combat boosted in the room. He had never seen them before, not in the flesh—if that's what it could be called. Several of them resembled cosmoniks, with a tough silicon outer skin, and dual—even triple—lower arms, sockets customized for weapons. But the majority had a sleeker appearance than the cosmoniks, whose technology they pilfered; they'd been sculpted for agility rather than blunt EVA endurance, although Terrance could see one combat boosted who was almost globular, his (her?) head a neckless dome, with a wrap-around retinal strip, grainy auburn below its clear lens. The lid rippled constantly, a blink moving round and round. There were four stumpy legs, and four arms, arranged symmetrically. The arms were the most human part of the modified body, since only two of them ended in burnished metal sockets. He tried not to stare at the assembled grotesqueries, not to show his inner nerves.

The bar's atmosphere was subdued, heavy with anticipation. It was long past the time the band were usually jamming on stage, but tonight they were drinking back in the kitchen, resigned to a blown gig.

"Captain André Duchamp," Oliver Llewelyn said. "Owner of the *Villeneuve's Revenge.*"

Terrance shook hands with the smiling round-faced captain. There was some contradiction in his mind that such a jovial-seeming man should want to join a military mission. "I need starships capable of landing a scout team on a terracompatible planet, then backing them up with tactical ground strikes," he said.

André put his wineglass down squarely on the table. "The *Villeneuve's Revenge* has four X-ray lasers and two electron-beam weapons. Planetary bombardment from low orbit will not be a problem."

"There could also be some anti-ship manoeuvres required from you. Some interdiction duties."

"Again, monsieur, this is not a problem from my personal position; we do have combat-wasp launch-cradles. However, you would have to provide the wasps themselves. And I would require some reassurance that we will not be involved in any controversial action in a system where Confederation Navy ships are present. As a commercial vessel I have no licence to carry such items."

"You would be operating under government licence, which allows you to carry any weapons system quite legitimately. This entire mission is completely legal."

"So?" André Duchamp gave him a quizzical glance. "This is excellent news. A legal combat mission is one I will welcome. As I say, I have no objection to conducting anti-ship engagements. May I ask which government you represent?"

"Lalonde."

André Duchamp had a long blink while his neural nanonics almanac file reviewed the star system. "A stage one colony world. Interesting."

"I am negotiating with several astroengineering companies with stations here at Tranquillity for combat wasps," Terrance Smith said. "There will also be several nuclear-armed atmospheric-entry warheads to be taken on the mission. Would you be prepared to carry and deploy them?"

"*Oui.*"

"In that case, I believe we can do business, Captain Duchamp."

"You have yet to mention money."

"I am authorized to issue a five hundred thousand fuseodollar fee for every ship which registers for Lalonde naval duty, payable on arrival at our destination. Pay for an individual starship is three hundred thousand fuseodollars per month, with a minimum of two months' duty guaranteed. There will be bonuses for enemy starships and spaceplanes destroyed, and a completion bonus of three hundred thousand fuseodollars. We will not, however, be providing insurance cover."

André Duchamp took a leisurely sip of wine. "I have one further question."

"Yes?"

"Does this *enemy* use antimatter?"

"No."

"Very well. I would haggle the somewhat depressing price . . ." He cast a glance around the crowded room, crews not quite watching to see what the outcome would be. "But I feel I am not in a strong bargaining position. Today it is a buyer's market."

From his table on the other side of the bar Joshua watched André Duchamp rise from Terrance Smith's booth. The two of them shook hands again, then André went back to the table where his crew were waiting. They all went into a tight huddle. Wolfgang Kuebler, captain of the *Maranta*, was shown to Smith's booth by Oliver Llewelyn.

"That looks like five ships signed up," Joshua said to his crew.

"Big operation," Dahybi Yadev said. He drained his beer glass and sat it down on the table. "Starships, combat-boosted mercs, enhanced troops; that's a long, expensive shopping list. Big money involved."

"Lalonde can't be paying, then," Melvyn Ducharme said. "It doesn't have any money."

"Yes, it does," Ashly Hanson said quietly. "A colony world is a massive investment, and a very solid one if you get in early enough. A healthy percentage of my zero-tau maintenance trust-fund portfolio is made up from development company shares, purely for the long-term stability they offer. I've never, ever heard of a colony failing once the go-ahead has been given. The money may not be floating around the actual colonists themselves, but the amount of financial resources required simply to initiate such a venture runs close to a trillion fuseodollars. And Lalonde has been running for over a quarter of a century, they'd even started an asteroid industrial settlement project. Remember? The development company has the money; more than enough to hire fifteen independent traders and a few thousand mercenary troops. I doubt it would even cause a ripple in their accountancy program."

"What for, though?" Sarha Mitcham asked. "What couldn't the sheriffs handle by themselves?"

"The Ivet riots," Joshua said. Even he couldn't manage any conviction. He shrugged under the sceptical looks the others gave him. "Well, there was nothing else while we were there. Marie Skibbow was worried about the scale of the civil disturbance. Nobody quite knew what was happening upriver. And the number of troops this Smith character is trying to recruit implies some kind of ground action is required."

"Hard to believe," Dahybi Yadev muttered. "But the actual mission objective won't be known until after they've jumped away from Tranquillity. Simple security."

"All right," Joshua said. "We all know the score. With Parris Vasilkovsky backing us on the mayope venture we have a chance to make macro money. And at the same time, with the money we made from the Norfolk run we certainly don't need to hire on with any mercenary fleet." He looked at each of them in turn. "Given the circumstances, we can hardly take *Lady Mac* to Lalonde ahead of the fleet. I've heard that Terrance Smith has ordered a batch of combat wasps from the McBoeing and Signal-Yakovlev industrial stations. He's clearly expecting some kind of conflict after they arrive. So the question is, do we go with him to find out what's happening, and maybe protect our interest, or do we wait here for news? We'll take a vote, and it must be unanimous."

Time Universe's Tranquillity office was on the forty-third floor of the StCroix starscraper. It was the usual crush of offices, studios, editing rooms, entertainment suites, and electronic workshops; a micro-community where individual importance was graded by allocated desk space, facility size, and time allowance. Naturally, given the make-up of the habitat's population, it had a large finance and commerce bureau, but it also provided good Confederationwide news coverage.

Oliver Llewelyn walked into the wood-panelled lobby at ten thirty local time the day after the *Gemal* had docked. The receptionist palmed him off on a junior political correspondent called Matthias Rems. In the composite-walled office Matthias used to assemble his reports he produced the flek Graeme Nicholson had given him and named a carriage fee of five thousand fuseodollars. Matthias wasn't stupid, the fact that the *Gemal*'s captain had come direct from Lalonde was enough to warrant serious attention. By now the entire habitat knew about the mercenary fleet being assembled by Terrance Smith, though its purpose remained unknown. Rumour abounded. Lalonde was immediate news; plenty of Tranquillity residents would have LDC shares sleeping in their portfolios. First-hand sensevises of the planet and whatever was happening there would have strong ratings clout. Ordinarily Matthias Rems might have hesitated about the shameless rip-off fee (he guessed correctly that Llewelyn had already been paid), especially after he accessed the company personnel file on Graeme Nicholson; but given the circumstances he knuckled under and paid.

After the captain left, Matthias slotted the flek into his desktop player block. The sensevise recording was code-locked, so Graeme Nicholson had obviously considered it important. He pulled Nicholson's personal code from his file, then sat back and closed his eyes. The Crashed Dumper invaded his sensorium; its heat and noise and smell, the taste of a caustic local beer tarring his throat, unaccustomed weight of a swelling belly. Graeme Nicholson held the fragments of a broken glass in his hand, his arms and legs trembling slightly; both eyes focused unwaveringly on a tall man and lovely teenage girl over by the crude bar.

Twelve minutes later a thoroughly shaken Matthias Rems burst in on Claudia Dohan, boss of Time Universe's Tranquillity operation.

The ripple effect of Graeme Nicholson's flek was similar to the sensation Ione's appearance had caused the previous year, in every respect save one. Ione had been a feel-good item: Laton was the antithesis. He was terror and danger, history's nightmare exhumed.

"We have to show a sense of responsibility," a twitchy Claudia Dohan said after she surfaced from the sensevise. "Both the Confederation Navy and the Lord of Ruin must be told."

The AV cylinder on her desktop processor block chimed. "Thank you for your consideration," Tranquillity said. "I have informed Ione Saldana about Laton's reappearance. I suggest you contact Commander Olsen Neale yourself to convey the contents of the flek."

"Right away," Claudia Dohan said diligently.

Matthias Rems was glancing nervously round the office, disturbed by the reminder of the habitat personality's perpetual vigilance.

Claudia Dohan broke the news on the lunchtime programme. Eighteen billion fuseodollars was wiped off share values on Tranquillity's trading floor within quarter of an hour of the sensevise being broadcast. Values crept back up during the rest of the afternoon as brokers assessed possible war scenarios. By the end of the day seven billion fuseodollars had been restored to prices—mainly on astro-engineering companies which would benefit from armaments sales.

The Time Universe office had done its work well, considering the short period it had in which to prepare. Its current affairs channel's usual afternoon schedule was replaced by library memories of Laton's earlier activities and earnest studio panel speculation. While Tranquillity's residents were being informed, Claudia Dohan started hiring starships to distribute copies of Graeme Nicholson's flek across the Confederation. This time she had a small lever against the captains, unlike Ione's very public appearance; she had a monopoly on Laton's advent and they were bidding against each other to deliver fleks. By the evening she had dispatched eighteen starships to various planets (Kulu, Avon, Oshanko, and Earth being the principals). Those Time Universe offices would in turn send out a second wave of fleks. Two weeks ought to see the entire Confederation brought up to speed. And warned, Claudia Dohan thought, Time Universe alone alerting the human and xenoc races to the resurgent danger. A greater boost to company fortunes simply wasn't possible.

She took the whole office out to a five-star meal that night. This coup, following so soon after Ione, should bring them all some heady bonuses, as well as boosting them way ahead of their contemporaries on the promotion scale. She was already thinking of a seat on the board for herself.

But it was a hectic afternoon. Matthias Rems (making his debut as a front-line presenter) introduced forty-year-old recordings of the broken Edenist habitat Jantrit, its shell cracked like a giant egg where the antimatter had detonated. Its atmosphere jetted out of a dozen breaches in the five-hundred-metre-thick polyp, huge grey-white plumes which acted like rockets, destabilizing the cylinder's ponderous rotation. The wobble built over the period of a few hours, until it developed into an uncontrollable tumble. On the outside, induction cables lashed round in anarchic hundred-kilometre arcs, preventing even the most agile voidhawks from rendezvousing. Inside, water and soil were tossed about, acting like a permanent floating earthquake. Starscrapers, weakened by the blast, broke off like rotten icicles, whirling away at terrific velocities. And all the while their air grew thinner.

Some people were saved as the voidhawks and Adamist starships hurtled after the spinning starscrapers. Eight thousand out of a population of one and a quarter million. Even then utter disaster might have been averted. The dying Edenists should have transferred their memories into the habitat personality. But Laton had infected Jantrit's neuron structure with his proteanic virus and its rationality was crumbling as trillions upon trillions of cells fell to the corruption every second. The other two habitats orbiting the gas giant were too far away to provide much assistance; personality transference was a complex function, distance and panic confused the issue. Twenty-seven thousand Edenists managed to bridge the gulf; three thousand patterns were later found to be incomplete, reduced to traumatized childlike entities. Voidhawks secured another two hundred and eighty personalities, but the bitek starships didn't have the capacity to store any more, and they were desperately busy anyway, chasing the starscrapers.

For Edenists it was the greatest tragedy since the founding of their culture. Even Adamists were stunned by the scale of the disaster. A living sentient creature thirty-five kilometres in length mind-raped and killed, nearly one and a quarter million people killed, over half a million stored personality patterns wiped.

And it had all been a diversion. A tactic to enable Laton and his cohorts to flee without fear of capture after their coup failed. He used the community's deaths as a cover; there was no other reason for it, no grand strategic design.

Every voidhawk, every Confederation Navy ship, every asteroid settlement, every planetary government searched for Laton and the three blackhawks he had escaped with.

He was cornered two months later in the Ragundan system: three blackhawks, armed with antimatter and refusing to surrender. Three voidhawks and five Confederation Navy frigates were lost in the ensuing battle. An asteroid settlement was badly damaged with the loss of a further eight thousand lives when the blackhawks tried to use it as a hostage, threatening to bomb it with antimatter unless the navy withdrew. The naval flotilla's commanding admiral called their bluff.

As with all space engagements there was nothing left of the vanquished but weak nebulas of radioactive molecules. There was no body to identify. But it couldn't have been anyone else.

Now it seemed there must have been four blackhawks. Nobody could mistake that tall, imperious man standing on the steps of the *Yaku*'s spaceplane, laughing at a cowering Graeme Nicholson.

The guests Matthias Rems invited into the studio, a collection of retired navy officers, political professors, and weapons engineers, observed that Laton's actual goal had never been declared. Speculation had been rife for years after the event. It obviously involved some kind of physical (biological) and mental domination, subverting the Edenists through the (fortunately) imperfect proteanic virus he had developed. Changing them and the habitats. But to what grandiose ideal had been thought for ever unknown. The studio debate concentrated on whether Laton was behind the current conflict on Lalonde, and if it was the first stage in his bid to impose his will on the Confederation again. Graeme Nicholson had certainly believed so.

Laton was different to the kind of planetary disputes like Omuta and Garissa; the perennial squabbling between asteroid settlements and their funding companies over autonomy. Laton wasn't a violence-tinged argument over resources or independence, he was after people, individuals. He wanted to get into your genes, your mind, and alter you, mould you to his own deviant construct. Laton was deadly personal.

One of the keenest observers of the Time Universe programmes was Terrance Smith. The Laton revelation had come as a profound shock. He, and the *Gemal*'s crew, became the objects of intense media interest. Hounded every time he left the colonist-carrier, he eventually had to appeal to Tranquillity for privacy. The habitat personality agreed (a resident's freedom from intrusion was part of the original constitution Michael Saldana had written), and the reporters were called off. They promptly switched their attention to anyone who had signed on as a member of the mercenary fleet, all of whom protested (truthfully) that they knew nothing of Laton.

"What do we do?" Terrance Smith asked in a bleak voice. He was alone with Oliver Llewelyn on the *Gemal*'s bridge. Console holoscreens were showing the Time Universe evening news programme, cutting between a studio presenter and segments of Graeme Nicholson's recording. The captain was someone whose opinion Terrance valued, in fact he'd grown heavily dependent on him during the last couple of days. There weren't many other people he confided in.

"You don't have many options," Oliver Llewelyn pointed out. "You've already paid the registration fee to twelve ships, and you've got a third of the troops you wanted. Either you go ahead as originally planned, or you cut and run. Doing nothing isn't a valid alternative, not now."

"Cut and run?"

"Sure. You've got enough money in the LDC's credit account to lose yourself. Life could get very comfortable for you and your family." Oliver Llewelyn watched Terrance Smith closely, trying to anticipate his reaction. The notion obviously appealed, but he didn't think the bureaucrat would have enough backbone.

"I . . . No, we can't. There are too many people depending on me. We have to do something to help Durringham. You weren't down there, you don't know what it was like that last week. These mercenaries are the only hope they've got."

"As you wish." Pity, Oliver Llewelyn thought, a great pity. I'm getting too old for this kind of jaunt.

"Do you think fifteen ships is enough to go up against Laton?" Terrance Smith asked anxiously. "I have the authority to hire another ten."

"We're not going up against Laton," Oliver Llewelyn said patiently.

"But—"

The captain gestured at one of the console holoscreens. "You accessed Graeme Nicholson's sensevise. Laton has left Lalonde. All your mercenaries are faced with is a big mopping-up operation. Leave Laton to the Confederation; the navy and the voidhawks will be going after him with every weapon they've got."

The notion of taking on Laton was something the starship captains had been discussing among themselves. Only three were sufficiently alarmed to return Terrance Smith's registration fee. He had no trouble in attracting replacements, and bringing the number of the fleet up to nineteen—six blackhawks, nine combat-capable independent traders, three cargo carriers, and the *Gemal* itself. Virtually none of the general troops or the combat-boosted mercenaries resigned. Fighting Laton's legions, being on the *right* side, gave the whole enterprise a kudos like few others; old hands and fresh youngsters queued up to sign on.

Three and a half days after he arrived, Terrance Smith had all he came for. The one request from Commander Olsen Neale to hold off and wait for a Confederation naval investigatory flight was smilingly refused. Durringham needs us now, Terrance told him.

Ione and Joshua walked down one of Tranquillity's winding valleys in the late afternoon, dew-heavy grass staining their sandals. She was wearing a long white cotton skirt and a matching camisole, a loose-fitting outfit which allowed the air to circulate over her warm skin. Joshua just wore some long dark mauve shorts. His skin was tanning nicely, she thought, he was almost back to his old colour. They had spent most of his stopover outside; swimming with Haile, riding, walking, having long sexual adventures. Joshua seemed to get very turned on having sex beside and in the bountiful streams meandering through the habitat.

Ione stopped at a long pool which formed the intersection of two streams. It was lined by mature rikbal trees, whose droopy branches stroked the water with their long, thin leaves. They were all in flower, bright pink blooms the size of a child's fist.

Gold and scarlet fish slithered through the water. It was tranquillity, Ione thought, small t, created by big T; name chasing form, name creating form. The lake—the whole park—was a pause from the habitat's bustle; the habitat was a pause from the Confederation's bustle. If you wanted it to be.

Joshua pushed her gently against a rikbal trunk, kissing her cheek, her neck. He opened the front of her camisole.

Hair fell down across her eyes, she was wearing it longer these days. "Don't go," she said quietly.

His arms dropped inertly to his sides, head slumping forwards until his brow touched hers. "Good timing."

"Please."

"You said you weren't going to dump this possessive scene on me."

"This isn't being possessive."

"What then? It sounds like it."

Her head came up sharply, pink spots burning on both cheeks. "If you must know, I'm worried about you."

"Don't be."

"Joshua, you're flying into a war zone."

"Not really. We're flying escort duty for a troop convoy, that's all. The soldiers and combat boosted are in at the hard edge."

"Smith wants the starships to provide ground strikes; he's bought combat wasps for interdiction missions. That's the hard edge, Joshua, that's the dead edge. Bloody hell, you're going up against Laton in an antique wreck that barely rates its CAB spaceworthiness licence. And there's no reason. None. You don't need mayope, you don't need Vasilkovsky." She held his arm, imploring. "You're rich. You're happy. Don't try and tell me you're not. I've watched you for three years. You've never had so much fun as when you gallivanted around the galaxy in the *Lady Macbeth*. Now look at what you're doing. Paper deals, Joshua. Making paper money you can never spend. Sitting behind a desk, that's your destination. That's where you're flying to, Joshua, and it isn't you."

"Antique, huh?"

"I didn't mean—"

"How old is Tranquillity, Ione? At least I own the *Lady Mac*, it doesn't own me."

"I'm just trying to shock some sense into you. Joshua, it's Laton you're facing. Don't you watch the AV recordings? Didn't you access Graeme Nicholson's sensevise?"

"Yes. I did. Laton isn't on Lalonde. He left on the *Yaku*. Did you miss that bit, Ione? If I wanted to go on suicide flights I'd chase after the *Yaku*. That's where the danger is. That's where the navy heroes are going. Not me, I'm protecting my own interests."

"But you don't need it!" she said. God, but he could be bonehead stubborn at times.

"You mean you don't."

"What?"

"Not convenient, is it? Me having that much money. That much money would mean I make the decisions, I make the choices. It gives me control over my life. Where does that fit into your cosy scenario of us, Ione? I won't be so easy to manipulate then, will I?"

"Manipulate! One glimpse of a female nipple and your fly seal bursts apart from the pressure. That's how complicated your personality is. You don't need manipulating, Joshua, you need hormone suppressors. All I'm doing is trying to think ahead for you, because God knows you can't do it for yourself."

"Jesus, Ione! Sometimes I can't believe you're bonded to a cubic kilometre of neuron cells, you don't display the IQ of an ant most days. This is my *chance*, I can make it. I can be your equal."

"I don't want an equal." Ione jammed her mouth shut. She'd nearly done it, nearly said: "I just want you." But torture wouldn't bring that from her lips, not now.

"Yeah, so I noticed," he said. "I started with a broken-down ship. I made that work, I earned a living flying it. And now I'm moving on, moving up. That's life, Ione. Growing, evolving. You should try it sometime." He turned and stomped off through the trees, sweeping the hanging branches aside impatiently. If she wanted to say sorry, she could damn well come after him and do it.

Ione watched him go, and fumbled with the front of her

camisole. What an arsehole. He might be psychic, but only at the expense of common sense.

I'm so sorry, Tranquillity said gently.

She sniffed hard. **What about?**

Joshua.

There's no reason. If he wants to go, let him. See if I care.

You do care. He is right for you.

He doesn't think so.

Yes, he does. But he is prideful. As are you.

Thanks for nothing.

Don't cry.

Ione glanced down, seeing her hands as blobs. Her eyes were horribly warm. She wiped at them vigorously. God, how could I have been so stupid? He was just supposed to be a fun stud. Nothing more.

I love you, Tranquillity said, so full of cautious warmth that Ione had to smile. Then she winced as her stomach churned, and promptly threw up. The bile was acid and disgusting. She cupped her hands to capture some of the cool pool water so she could rinse her mouth out.

You are pregnant, Tranquillity observed.

Yes. The last time Joshua came back, before he made the Norfolk run.

Tell him.

No! That would only make it worse.

You are both fools, Tranquillity said with unaccustomed ardour.

Stars slid across the window behind Commander Olsen Neale. Choisya was the only one of Mirchusko's moons visible, a distant grey-brown crescent sliver peeping up over the bottom of the oval every three minutes. Erick Thakrar didn't like the sight of the starfield, it was too close, too easy to reach. He wondered, briefly, if he was developing a space-phobia. It wasn't unheard of, and there were a lot of associations involved. That horrified, distraught voice coming from the *Krystal Moon*; a fifteen-year-old girl. What had

Tina looked like? It was a question he'd been asking himself a lot recently. Did she have a boyfriend? What mood fantasy bands did she cherish? Had she enjoyed her life on the old interplanetary vessel? Or did she find it intolerable?

What the fuck was she doing in the forward compartment below the communication dishes?

"The micro-fusion generators were handed directly over to the *Nolana* as soon as we docked," Erick said. "They never even passed through Tranquillity's cargo-storage facility. Which means there was no data work, no port manager's inspection. And of course we were all on board the *Villeneuve's Revenge* until the transfer was finished. I couldn't get a message out to you."

"We'll track the *Nolana*, of course," Olsen Neale said. "See where the generators go. It should expose the distribution net. You've done well," he added encouragingly. The young captain looked haggard, nothing like the bright eager agent who had wangled himself a berth on the *Villeneuve's Revenge* those long months ago.

It hits us all in the end, son, Olsen Neale thought soulfully to himself. We deliberately bring ourselves down to their level so we can blend in, and sometimes it costs just too much. Because nothing can go lower than human beings.

Erick remained unmoved by the compliment. "You can have Duchamp and the rest of the crew arrested immediately," he said. "My neural nanonics recording of our attack on the *Krystal Moon* will be more than enough to convict them. I want you to tell the prosecutor to ask for maximum penalties. We can have them all committed to a penal planet. The whole lot of them, and that's better than they deserve."

And it transfers your guilt, as well, Neale thought silently. "I don't think we can do that right now, Erick," he said.

"What? Three people have died just so that you have enough evidence against Duchamp. Two of them I killed myself."

"I'm truly sorry, Erick, but circumstances have changed somewhat radically since your mission began. Have you accessed Time Universe's Lalonde sensevise?"

Erick gave him a demoralized stare, guessing what was coming. "Yes."

"Terrance Smith has signed on the *Villeneuve's Revenge* for his mercenary fleet. We've got to have somebody there, Erick. It's a legal mission for a planetary government, there's nothing I can do to prevent them from leaving. Christ, this is Laton we're talking about. I was about ten years old when he destroyed Jantrit. One and a quarter million people just so he could make a clean getaway, and the habitat itself; the Edenists had never lost a habitat before, their life expectancy is measured in millennia. And now he's had nearly forty years to perfect his megalomaniac schemes. Shit, we don't even know what they are; but what I've heard about Lalonde is enough to frighten me. I'm scared, Erick, I've got a family. I don't want him to get his hands on them. We have to know where he went on the *Yaku*. Nothing is more important than that. Piracy and flogging off black-market goods are totally irrelevant by comparison. The navy has to find him and exterminate him. Properly this time. Until he's dead, we have no other goal. I've already sent a flek to Avon, a courier left on a blackhawk an hour after the Time Universe people told me about their recording."

Erick's brow crinkled in surprise.

Olsen Neale gave a modest smile. "Yes, a blackhawk. They're fast, they're good. And Laton will ultimately have them too if we don't stop him. Their captains are just as unnerved by him as we are."

"All right." Erick gave up. "I'll go."

"Anything. Any piece of data. What he's done out in the Lalonde hinterlands. Where the *Yaku* went. Just anything."

"I'll get whatever I can."

"You could try asking this journalist, Graeme Nicholson." He shrugged at Erick's expression. "The man's smart, resourceful. If anyone on that planet had the presence of mind to track the *Yaku*'s jump coordinate, it'll be him."

Erick rose to his feet. "OK."

"Erick . . . take care."

The heavy curtains in Kelly Tirrel's bedroom were drawn across the two oval windows. Ornate wall-mounted glass globes emitted a faint turquoise light. It made the white bed-sheets shimmer as if they were the surface of a moonlit lake; human skin was dark and tantalizing.

Kelly let Joshua run his hands over her, parting her legs so he could probe the damp cleft hidden below her tangle of pubic hair.

"Nice," she purred, squirming over the rumpled sheets.

His teeth shone as he parted his lips. "Good."

"If you take me with you, there will be five days of this. Nonstop; and in free fall, too."

"A powerful argument."

"Money as well. Collins will pay triple rate for my passage."

"I'm already rich."

"So get richer."

"Jesus, you're a pushy bitch."

"Is that a complaint? Did you want to be with someone else tonight?"

"Er, no."

"Good." Her hand slid round his balls. "This is the one for me, Joshua. This is my make or break chance. I blew the Ione story because of someone not a million kilometres from here." Her fingers tightened slightly. "Opportunities like this don't come to a place like Tranquillity three times in a life. If I pull it off I'll be made; top of the seniority table, good assignments, a decent bureau posting, a real salary. You owe me this, Joshua. You owe me very big."

"Suppose the mercenaries don't want you with them?"

"You leave them to me. The way I'll pitch it at them, they'll eat up the offer. Heroes up against frightening odds helping to flatten Laton, rogues with a heart of gold, sensevised into every home in the Confederation. Come on!"

"Jesus." There was still an uncomfortable pressure round his balls, long red nails touching his scrotum, a little too sharply to be described as tickling. She wouldn't. Would she? Her smart, expensive grey-blue Crusto suit was folded neatly over a chair by the dresser. It had been taken off with military regimentation as she *prepared* for sex.

She probably would. Jesus.

"Of course I'll take you."

Thumb and forefinger nipped one ball impishly.

"Yow!" His eyes watered. "You don't think you're getting carried away with this idea, do you? I mean, there are career moves and career moves. Landing on a hostile planet behind enemy lines is pushing company loyalty to extremes."

"Crap." Kelly rolled onto one elbow and glared at him. "Did you see who Time Universe had introducing their studio segments? Matthias bastard Rems, that's who. Just because he was in the right place at the right time. That lucky little shit. He's younger than me, barely out of his nursery pen. And they gave him three days prime scheduling time. And market research says he's popular because he's *boyish*. Some women like that, it turns out. Eighty-year-old virgins, I should think. The reason Time Universe won't let him record sensevises is because then we'd all know for sure he hasn't got any balls."

"Not a problem in your case, is it?"

It came out before he could think. Kelly spent a hot violent twenty minutes making him wish it hadn't.

The nineteen starships under Terrance Smith's command assembled a thousand kilometres beyond Tranquillity's spaceport: the *Gemal* with five thousand general troops, three cargo clippers carrying their equipment and supplies, and fifteen combat-capable ships, six of which were blackhawks.

Tranquillity watched their drives come on, and the flotilla moved in towards Mirchusko at one gee. The Adamist starships employed a single-file formation (with *Gemal* leading) which the blackhawks encircled insolently. Strategic-defence sensor-platforms detected a vast amount of encrypted data traffic being exchanged between the ships as communication channels were tested and combat tactics exchanged.

They curved around the gas giant, heading towards its penumbra. Their drive exhausts shortened and vanished while they were still a hundred and eighty-four thousand kilometres above the unruly cloudscape, coasting towards the jump co-ordinate. Tranquillity saw the faint blue flickers of ion jets perfecting their orbital tracks; then the thermo-dump panels and sensor clusters began to withdraw. The blackhawks rushed away from the main convoy, freed of the constraints imposed by their Adamist partners, expanding in a perfectly spaced rosette. Then the bitek starships performed their swallow manoeuvre, jumping on ahead to scout for any possible trouble. Space reverberated with the gravity-wave backwash of their wormhole interstices snapping shut behind them, impinging on the habitat's sensitive mass-detection organs.

Gemal jumped. Tranquillity noted its spacial location and velocity vector. The trajectory was aligned exactly on Lalonde. One by one the remaining starships fell into the same jump coordinate and triggered their energy patterning nodes, squeezing themselves out of space-time.

5

Since the advent of its independence in 2238, Avon's government had contracted civil astroengineering teams to
knock fifteen large (twenty- to twenty-five-kilometre diameter) stony iron asteroids into high orbit above the planet
using precisely placed and timed nuclear explosions. Fourteen of them followed the standard formula of industrialization adopted throughout the Confederation. After their orbits
were stabilized with a perigee no less than a hundred thousand kilometres, their ores had been mined out and the refined metal sent down to the planet below in the form of
giant lifting bodies which coasted through the atmosphere to
a splash-glide landing in the ocean. The resulting caverns
were expanded, regularized into cylindrical shapes, the surface sculpted into a landscape, sealed, then turned into habitable biospheres. At the same time the original ore
refineries would gradually be replaced by more sophisticated industrial stations, allowing the asteroid's economy to
shift its emphasis from the bulk production of metals and
minerals to finished micro-gee engineered products. The refineries moved on to a fresh asteroid in order to satisfy the
demand of the planetary furnaces and steel mills, keeping
the worst aspects of raw-material exploitation offplanet
where the ecological pollution on the aboriginal biota was
zero.

Anyone arriving at a terracompatible planet in the Confederation could tell almost at a glance how long it had
been industrialized by the number of settled asteroids in
orbit around it.

Avon had been opened for colonization to ethnic Canadians in 2151 during the Great Dispersal, and conformed to the usual evolutionary route out of an agrarian economy into industrialization in slightly less than a century. A satisfactory achievement, but nothing remarkable. It remained a pedestrian world until 2271 when it played host to the head of state conference called to discuss the worrying upsurge in the use of antimatter as a weapon of mass destruction. From that conference was born the Confederation, and Avon seized its chance to leapfrog an entire developmental stage by offering itself as a permanent host for the Assembly. Without any increase in exports, foreign currency poured in as governments set up diplomatic missions; and the lawyers, interstellar companies, finance institutions, influence peddlers, media conglomerates, and lobbyists followed, each with their own prestige offices and staff and dependents.

There was also the Confederation Navy, which was to police the fragile new-found unity between the inhabited stars. Avon contributed to that as well, by donating to the Assembly an orbiting asteroid named Trafalgar which was in the last phase of mining.

Trafalgar was unique within the Confederation in that it had no industrial stations after the miners moved out. It was first, foremost, and only, a naval base, developing from a basic supply and maintenance depot for the entire Confederation Navy (such as it was in the early days) up to the primary military headquarters for the eight hundred and sixty-two inhabited star systems which made up the Confederation in 2611. When First Admiral Samual Aleksandrovich took up his appointment in 2605 it was the home port for the 1st Fleet and headquarters and training centre for the Marine Corps. It housed the career Officer Academy, the Engineering School, the Navy Technical Evaluation Office, the First Admiral's Strategy Office, the Navy Budget Office, the principal research laboratories for supralight communications, and (more quietly) the headquarters of the Fleet Intelligence Arm. A black and grey peanut shape, twenty-one kilometres long, seven wide, rotating about its long axis; it contained three cylindrical biosphere caverns which housed a mixed civilian and military population of approximately three hundred thousand. There were non-rotational spaceports at each end: spheres two kilometres in diameter, the usual gridwork of girders and tanks and pipes, threaded with pressurized tubes carrying commuter cars, and docking-bays ringed by control cabins. Their surface area was just able to cope with the vast quantity of spaceship movements. The spindles were both fixed to Trafalgar's axis at the centre of deep artificial craters two kilometres wide which the voidhawks used as docking-ledges.

As well as its responsibility for defence and anti-pirate duties across the Confederation it coordinated Avon's defence in conjunction with the local navy. The strategic-defence platforms protecting the planet were some of the most powerful ever built. Given the huge numbers of government diplomatic ships, as well as the above average number of commercial flights using the low-orbit docking stations, security was a paramount requirement. There hadn't been an act of piracy in the system for over two and a half centuries, but the possibility of a suicide attack against Trafalgar was uppermost in the minds of navy tacticians. Strategic sensor coverage was absolute out to a distance of two million kilometres from the planetary surface. Reaction time by the patrolling voidhawks was near instantaneous. Starships emerging outside designated areas took a formidable risk in doing so.

Ilex was calling for help even before the wormhole terminus closed behind it. Auster had ordered the voidhawk to fly straight to Avon, over four hundred light-years from Lalonde. Even for a voidhawk, the distance was excessive. *Ilex* needed to recharge its energy patterning cells after ten swallows, which involved a prolonged interval of ordinary flight to allow its distortion field to concentrate the meagre wisps of radiation which flittered through the interstellar medium.

The voyage had taken three and a half days. There were sixty people on board, and the bitek life-support organs were rapidly approaching their critical limit. The air smelt bad, membrane filters couldn't cope with the body gases, CO_2 was building up, oxygen reserves were almost exhausted.

Trafalgar was five thousand kilometres away when the wormhole terminus sealed. Legally, it should have been a hundred thousand. But a long sublight flight to a docking-ledge would have pushed *Ilex*'s life-support situation from critical to catastrophic.

The asteroid immediately went to defence condition C2, allowing the duty officer to engage all targets at will. Nuclear-pumped gamma-ray lasers locked onto the voidhawk's hull within three-quarters of a second of the wormhole opening.

Every Edenist officer in Trafalgar's strategic-defence command-centre heard *Ilex*'s call. They managed to load a five-second delay order into the defence platforms. Auster gave a fast resume of the voidhawk's situation. The delay was extended for another fifteen seconds while the duty officer made her evaluation. A squadron of patrol voidhawks closed on *Ilex* at ten gees.

"Stand down," the duty officer told the centre, and datavised a lockdown order into the fire-command computer. She looked across at the nearest Edenist. "And tell that idiot captain from me I'll fry his arse off next time he pulls a stunt like this."

Ilex swooped in towards Trafalgar at five gees as traffic control cleared a priority approach path ahead of it. Six patrol voidhawks spiralled round it like over-protective avian parents, all seven bitek starships exchanging fast affinity messages of anxiety, interest, and mild rebuke. The northern axial crater was a scene of frantic activity while *Ilex* chased the asteroid's rotation, looping around the globular non-rotating spaceport to fly in parallel to the spindle. It settled on a titanium pedestal with eight balloon-tyre maintenance vehicles and crew buses racing towards it, bouncing about in the low gravity.

Lalonde's navy office personnel disembarked first, hurrying along the airlock tube to the waiting bus, all of them taking deep gulps of clean, cool air. A medic team carried Niels Regehr off in a stretcher, while two paediatric nurses soothed and patted a blubbering Shafi Banaji. Environment-maintenance vehicles plugged hoses and cables into the crew toroid's umbilical sockets, sending gales of fresh air gusting through the cabins and central corridor. Resenda, *Ilex*'s life-support officer, simply vented the fouled atmosphere they'd been breathing throughout the voyage, and grey plumes jetted up out of the toroid, seeded with minute water crystals that sparkled in the powerful lights mounted on the spindle to illuminate the crater.

Once the first bus trundled away, a second nosed up to the airlock. A ten-strong marine squad in combat fatigues and armed with chemical projectile guns marched on board. Rhodri Peyton, the squad's captain, saluted an exhausted, unwashed, and unshaven Lieutenant Murphy Hewlett.

"This is her?" he asked sceptically.

Jacqueline Couteur stood in the middle of the corridor outside the airlock, with Jeroen van Ewyck and Garrett Tucci training their Bradfields on her. She was even dirtier than Murphy, the check pattern of her cotton shirt almost lost below the engrained grime picked up in the jungle.

"I'm tempted to let her show you what she can do," Murphy said.

Kelven Solanki stepped forwards. "All right, Murphy." He turned to the marine captain. "Your men are to have at least two weapons covering her at all times. She's capable of emitting an electronic warfare effect, as well as letting loose some kind of lightning bolt. Don't try to engage her in physical combat, she's quite capable of ripping you apart."

One of the marines snickered at that. Kelven didn't have the energy left to argue.

"I'll go with her," Jeroen van Ewyck said. "My people need to be briefed anyway, and I'll let the science officers know what's required."

"What is required?" Jacqueline Couteur asked.

Rhodri Peyton turned, and gave a start. In place of the dumpy middle-aged woman there was a tall, beautiful, twenty-year-old girl wearing a white cocktail gown. She gave him a silent entreating look, the maiden about to be offered to the dragon. "Help me. Please. You're not like them. You're not an emotionless machine. They want to hurt me in their laboratories. Don't let them."

Garrett Tucci jabbed the Bradfield into her back. "Pack it in, bitch," he said roughly.

She twisted, like an AV projection with a broken focus, and the old Jacqueline Couteur was standing there, a mocking expression on her face. Her jeans and shirt were now clean and pressed.

"My God," Rhodri Peyton gasped.

"Now do you see?" Kelven asked.

The now nervous marine squad escorted their prisoner along the connecting tube to the bus. Jacqueline Couteur sat beside one of the windows, five guns lined up on her. She watched the bare walls of sterile rock impassively as the bus rolled back across the crater and into a downward sloping tunnel that led deep into the asteroid.

First Admiral Samual Aleksandrovich hadn't set foot on his native Russian-ethnic birth planet Kolomna for the last fifty-three of his seventy-three years; he hadn't been back for a holiday, nor even his parents' funeral. Regular visits might have been deemed inappropriate given that Confederation Navy career officers were supposed to renounce any national ties when they walked through the academy entrance; for a First Admiral to display any undue interest would have been a completely unacceptable breach of diplomatic etiquette. People would have understood his attending the funerals, though. So everyone assumed he was applying the same kind of steely discipline to his private affairs that ruled his professional life.

They were all wrong. Samual Aleksandrovich had never been back because there was nothing on the wretched planet with its all-over temperate climate which interested him, not family nor culture nor nostalgic scenery. The reason he left in the first place was because he couldn't stand the idea of spending a century helping his four brothers and three sisters run the family fruit-farming business. The same geneering which had produced his energetic one metre eighty frame, vivid copper hair, and enhanced metabolism, bestowed a life expectancy of at least a hundred and twenty years.

By the time he was nineteen years old he had come to realize that such a life would be a prison sentence given the vocations available on a planet just emerging from its agrarian phase. A potentially blessed life should not be faced with such finite horizons, for if it was it would turn from being a joy into a terrible burden. Variety was sanity. So on the day after his twentieth birthday he had kissed his parents and siblings goodbye, walked the seventeen kilometres into town through a heavy snowfall, and signed on at the Confederation Navy recruitment office.

Metaphorically, and otherwise, he had never looked back. He had never been anything other than an exemplary officer; he'd seen combat seven times, flown anti-pirate interdictions, commanded a flotilla raiding an illegal antimatter-production station, and gained a substantial number of distinguished service awards. But appointment to the post of First Admiral required a great deal more than an exemplary record. Much as he hated it, Samual Aleksandrovich had to play the political game; appearing before Assembly select committees, giving unofficial briefings to senior diplomats, wielding Fleet Intelligence information with as much skill as he did the rapier (he was year champion at the academy). His ability to pressure member states was admired by the Assembly President's staffers, as much for its neatness as the millions of fuseodollars saved by circumventing fleet deployment to trouble spots; and their word counted for a great deal more than the Admiralty, who advanced the names of candidates to the Assembly's Navy Committee.

In the six years he had held the office he had done a good job keeping the peace between sometimes volatile planetary governments and the even more mercurial asteroid settlements. Leaders and politicians respected his toughness and fairness.

A great deal of his renowned even-handed approach was formed when at the age of thirty-two he was serving as a lieutenant on a frigate that had been sent to Jantrit to assist the Edenists in some kind of armed rebellion (however unbelievable it sounded at the time). The frigate crew had watched helplessly while the antimatter was detonated, then spent three days in exhausting and often fruitless manoeuvres to rescue survivors of the tragedy. Samual Aleksandrovich had led one of the recovery teams after they rendezvoused with a broken starscraper. With heroic work that won him a commendation he and his crew-mates saved eighteen Edenists trapped in the tubular honeycomb of polyp. But one of the rooms they forced their way into was filled with corpses. It was a children's day club that had suffered explosive decompression. As he floated in desolated horror across the grisly chamber, he realized the Edenists were just as human as himself, and just as fallible. After that the persistent snide comments from fellow officers about the tall aloof bitek users annoyed him intensely. From then on he devoted himself body and soul to the ideal of enforcing the peace.

So when the *Eurydice* had docked at Trafalgar carrying a flek from Lieutenant-Commander Kelven Solanki about the small possibility (and he had been most unwilling to commit himself) that Laton was still alive and stirring from his self-imposed exile, First Admiral Samual Aleksandrovich had taken a highly personal interest in the Lalonde situation.

Where Laton was concerned, Samual Aleksandrovich

exhibited neither his usual fairness nor a desire for justice to be done. He just wanted Laton dead. And this time there would be no error.

Even after his staff had edited down Murphy Hewlett's neural nanonics recording of the marine squad's fateful jungle mission, to provide just the salient points, there was three hours of sensorium memory to access. When he surfaced from Lalonde's savage heat and wearying humidity, Samual Aleksandrovich remained lost in thought for quarter of an hour, then took a commuter car down to the Fleet Intelligence laboratories.

Jacqueline Couteur had been isolated in a secure examination room. It was a cell cut into living rock with a transparent wall of metallized silicon whose structure was reinforced with molecular-binding-force generators. On one side it was furnished with a bed, wash-basin, shower, toilet, and a table, while the other side resembled a medical surgery with an adjustable couch and a quantity of analysis equipment.

She sat at the table, dressed in a green clinical robe. Five marines were in the cell with her, four of them carrying chemical-projectile guns, the fifth a TIP carbine.

Samual Aleksandrovich stood in front of the transparent wall looking at the drab woman. The monitoring room he was in resembled a warship's bridge, a white composite cube with a curved rank of consoles, all facing the transparent wall. The impersonality disturbed him slightly, an outsized vivarium.

Jacqueline Couteur returned his stare levelly. She should never have been able to do that, not a simple farmer's wife from a backwoods colony world. There were diplomats with eighty years of experienced duplicity behind them who broke into a sweat when Samual Aleksandrovich turned his gaze on them.

He likened the experience to looking into the eyes of an Edenist habitat mayor at some formal event, when the consensus intellect of every adult in the habitat looked back at him. Judging.

Whatever you are, he thought, you are not Jacqueline Couteur. This is the moment I've dreaded since I took my oath of office. A new threat, one beyond anything we know. And the burden of how to deal with it will inevitably fall heaviest on my navy.

"Do you understand the method of sequestration yet?" he asked Dr Gilmore, who was heading the research team.

The doctor made a penitent gesture. "Not as yet. She's certainly under the control of some outside agency, but so far we haven't been able to locate the point where it interfaces with her nervous system. I'm a neural nanonics expert, and we've got several physicists on the team. But I'm not entirely sure we even have a specialization to cover this phenomenon."

"Tell me what you can."

"We ran a full body and neural scan on her, looking for implants. You saw what she and the other sequestrated colonists could do back on Lalonde?"

"Yes."

"That ability to produce the white fireballs and electronic warfare impulses must logically have some kind of focusing mechanism. We found nothing. If it's there it's smaller than our nanonics, a lot smaller. Atomic sized, at least, maybe even sub-atomic."

"Could it be biological? A virus?"

"You're thinking of Laton's proteanic virus? No, nothing like that." He turned and beckoned to Euru.

The tall black-skinned Edenist left the monitor console he was working at and came over. "Laton's virus attacked cells," he explained. "Specifically neural cells, altering their composition and DNA. This woman's brain structure remains perfectly normal, as far as we can tell."

"If she can knock out a marine's combat electronics at over a hundred metres, how do you know your analysis equipment is giving you genuine readings?" Samual Aleksandrovich asked.

The two scientists exchanged a glance.

"Interference is a possibility we've considered," Euru

admitted. "The next stage of our investigation will be to acquire tissue samples and subject them to analysis outside the range of her influence—if she lets us take them. It would require a great deal of effort if she refused to cooperate."

"Has she been cooperative so far?"

"For most of the time, yes. We've witnessed two instances of visual pattern distortion," Dr Gilmore said. "When her jeans and shirt were removed she assumed the image of an apelike creature. It was shocking, but only because it was so unusual and unexpected. Then later on she tried to entice the marines to let her out by appearing as an adolescent girl with highly developed secondary sexual characteristics. We have AV recordings of both occasions; she can somehow change her body's photonic-emission spectrum. It's definitely not an induced hallucination, more like a chameleon suit's camouflage."

"What we don't understand is where she gets the energy to produce these effects," Euru said. "The cell's environment is strictly controlled and monitored, so she can't be tapping Trafalgar's electrical power circuits. And when we ran tests on her urine and faeces we found nothing out of the ordinary. Certainly there's no unusual chemical activity going on inside her."

"Lori and Darcy claimed Laton warned them of an energy virus," Samual Aleksandrovich said. "Is such a thing possible?"

"It may well be," Euru said. His eyes darkened with emotion. "If that *creature* was telling the truth he would probably have been attaching the nearest linguistic equivalents to a totally new phenomenon. An organized energy pattern which can sustain itself outside a physical matrix is a popular thesis with physicists. Electronics companies have been interested in the idea for a long time. It would bring about a radical transformation in our ability to store and manipulate data. But there has never been any practical demonstration of such an incorporeal matrix."

Samual Aleksandrovich switched his glance back to the

woman behind the transparent wall. "Perhaps you are looking at the first."

"It would be an extraordinary advance from our present knowledge base," Dr Gilmore said.

"Have you asked the Kiint if it is possible?"

"No," Dr Gilmore admitted.

"Then do so. They may tell us, they may not. Who understands how their minds work? But if anyone knows, they will."

"Yes, sir."

"What about her?" Samual Aleksandrovich asked. "Has she said anything?"

"She is not very communicative," Euru said.

The First Admiral grunted, and activated the intercom beside the cell's door. "Do you know who I am?" he asked.

The marines inside the cell stiffened. Jacqueline Couteur's expression never changed; she looked him up and down slowly.

"I know," she said.

"Who exactly am I talking to?"

"Me."

"Are you part of Laton's schemes?"

Was there the faintest twitch of a smile on her lips? "No."

"What do you hope to achieve on Lalonde?"

"Achieve?"

"Yes, achieve. You have subjugated the human population, killed many people. This is not a situation I can allow to continue. Defending the Confederation from such a threat is my responsibility, even on a little planet as politically insignificant as Lalonde. I would like to know your motives so that a solution to this crisis may be found which does not involve conflict. You must have known that ultimately your action would bring about an armed response."

"There is no 'achievement' sought."

"Then why do what you have done?"

"I do as nature binds me. As do you."

"I do what my duty binds me to do. When you were on

the *Isakore* you told the marines that they would come to you in time. If that isn't an objective I don't know what is."

"If you believe I will aid you to comprehend what has happened, you are mistaken."

"Then why did you allow yourself to be captured? I've seen the power you possess; Murphy Hewlett is good, but not that good. He couldn't get you here unless you wanted to come."

"How amusing. I see governments and conspiracy theories are still inseparable. Perhaps I'm the lovechild of Elvis and Marilyn Monroe come to sue the North American Govcentral state in the Assembly court for my rightful inheritance."

Samual Aleksandrovich gave her a nonplussed look. "What?"

"It doesn't matter. Why did the navy want me here, Admiral?"

"To study you."

"Precisely. And that is why I am here. To study you. Which of us will learn the most, I wonder?"

Kelven Solanki had never envisaged meeting the First Admiral quite so early in his career. Most commanders were introduced, certainly those serving in the 1st Fleet. But not lieutenant-commanders assigned to minor field-diplomat duties. Yet here he was being shown into the First Admiral's office by Captain Maynard Khanna. Circumstances muted the sense of excitement. He wasn't sure how the First Admiral viewed his handling of events on Lalonde, and the staff captain had given him no clues.

Samual Aleksandrovich's office was a circular chamber thirty metres across, with a slightly domed ceiling. Its curving wall had one window which looked out into Trafalgar's central biosphere cavern, and ten long holoscreens, eight slowly flicking through images from external sensors and the remaining two showing tactical displays. The ceiling was ribbed with bronze spars, with a fat AV cylinder protruding from the apex resembling a crystalline stalactite. There were two clusters of furniture; a huge teak desk with satellite chairs; and a sunken reception area lined by padded leather couches.

Maynard Khanna showed him over to the desk where the First Admiral was waiting. Auster, Dr Gilmore, Admiral Lalwani, the Fleet Intelligence chief, and Admiral Motela Kolhammer, the 1st Fleet Commander, were all sitting before the desk in the curved blue-steel chairs that had extruded out of the floor like pliable mercury.

Kelven stood to attention and gave a perfect salute, very conscious of the five sets of eyes studying him. Samual Aleksandrovich smiled thinly at the junior officer's obvious discomfort. "At ease, Commander." He gestured at one of the two new chairs formatting themselves out of the floor material. Kelven removed his cap, tucked it under his arm, and sat next to Maynard Khanna.

"You handled Lalonde quite well," the First Admiral said. "Not perfectly, but then you weren't exactly prepared for anything like this. Under the circumstances I'm satisfied with your performance."

"Thank you, sir."

"Bloody ESA people didn't help," Motela Kolhammer muttered.

Samual Aleksandrovich waved him quiet. "That is something we can take up with their ambassador later. Though I'm sure we all know what the outcome will be. Regrettable or not, you acted properly the whole time, Solanki. Capturing one of the sequestrated was exactly what we required."

"Captain Auster made it possible, sir," Kelven said. "I wouldn't have got the marines out otherwise."

The voidhawk captain nodded thankfully in acknowledgement.

"None the less, we should have given your situation a higher priority to begin with, and provided you with adequate resources," Samual Aleksandrovich said. "My mistake, especially given who was involved."

"Has Jacqueline Couteur confirmed Laton's existence?"

Kelven asked. Part of him was hoping that the answer was going to be a resounding no.

"She didn't have to." Samual Aleksandrovich sighed ponderously. "A blackhawk"—he paused, raising his bushy ginger eyebrows in emphasis—"has just arrived from Tranquillity with a flek from Commander Olsen Neale. Under the circumstances I can quite forgive him for using the ship as a courier. If you would like to access the sensevise."

Kelven sank deeper into the scoop of his chair as Graeme Nicholson's recording played through his brain. "He was there all along," he said brokenly. "In Durringham itself, and I never knew. I thought the *Yaku*'s captain left orbit because of the deteriorating civil situation."

"You are not in any way to blame," Admiral Lalwani said.

Kelven glanced over at the grey-haired Edenist woman. There was an inordinate amount of sympathy and sadness in the tone.

"We should never have stopped checking, all those years ago," she continued. "The presence of Darcy and Lori on Lalonde was a rather miserable token to appease our paranoia. Even we were guilty of wishing Laton dead. The hope overwhelmed reason and rational thought. All of us knew how resourceful he was, and we knew he had acquired data on Lalonde. The planet should have been thoroughly searched. Our mistake. Now he has returned. I don't like to think of the price we will all have to pay before he is stopped this time."

"Sir, Darcy and Lori seemed very uncertain that he was behind this invasion," Kelven said. "Laton actually warned them of this illusion-creating ability the sequestrated have."

"And Jacqueline Couteur agrees he isn't a part of this," Dr Gilmore said. "That's one of the few things she will admit to."

"I hardly think we can take her word for it," Admiral Kolhammer said.

"Precise details are for later," Samual Aleksandrovich said. "What we have with Lalonde is shaping up into a major, and immediate, crisis. I'm tempted to ask the Assembly President to declare a state of emergency; that would put national navies at my disposal."

"In theory," Admiral Kolhammer said drily.

"Yes, and yet anything less may not suffice. This undetectable sequestration ability has me deeply worried. It has been used so freely on Lalonde, hundreds of thousands of people, if not millions. How many people does the agency behind it intend to subjugate? How many planets? It is a threat which the Assembly cannot be allowed to ignore in favour of its usual horse trading." He considered the option of total mobilization before reluctantly dismissing it. There wasn't enough evidence to convince the president, not yet. It would come eventually, he was in no doubt of that. "For the moment we will do what we can to contain the spread of this plague, whilst trying to find Laton. The flek from Olsen Neale also went on to report that Terrance Smith has met with some success in recruiting mercenaries and combat-capable starships for Governor Rexrew. That blackhawk made excellent time from Tranquillity; a little over two days, the captain told me. So we may just be able to put a brake on Lalonde before it gets totally out of hand. Terrance Smith's ships are scheduled to depart from Tranquillity today. Lalwani, you estimate it will take them a week to reach Lalonde?"

"Yes," she said. "It took the *Gemal* six days to get from Lalonde to Tranquillity. With the starships in Smith's fleet having to match formation after each jump, a single extra day is a conservative estimate. Even a navy flotilla would be hard pushed to match that. And those are not front-line ships."

"Apart from the *Lady Macbeth*," Maynard Khanna said in a quiet voice. "I accessed the list of ships Smith recruited; the *Lady Macbeth* is a ship I am familiar with." He glanced at the First Admiral.

"I know that name . . ." Kelven Solanki ran a search program through his neural nanonics. "The *Lady Macbeth* was orbiting Lalonde when the trouble first broke out upriver."

"That wasn't mentioned in any of your reports," Lalwani said. Her slim forehead showed a frown.

"It was a commercial flight. Slightly odd, the captain wanted to export aboriginal wood, but as far as we could tell perfectly legitimate."

"This name does seem to be popping up with suspicious regularity," Maynard Khanna said.

"We should be able to look into it easily enough," Samual Aleksandrovich said. "Commander Solanki, the principal reason I asked you here was to inform you that you are to act as an adviser to the squadron which will blockade Lalonde."

"Sir?"

"We're launching a dual programme to terminate this threat. The first aspect is a Confederationwide alert for Laton. We have to know where the *Yaku* went, where it is now."

"He won't stay on board," Lalwani said. "Not after he reaches a port. But we'll find him. I'm organizing the search now. All the voidhawks in the Avon system will be conscripted and dispatched to alert national governments. I've already sent one to Jupiter; once the habitat consensus is informed, every voidhawk in the Sol system will be used to relay the news. I estimate it will take four to five days to blanket the Confederation."

"Time Universe will probably beat you to it," Admiral Kolhammer said gruffly.

Lalwani smiled. The two of them were sparring partners from way back. "In this case I wouldn't mind in the least."

"Be a lot of panic. Stock markets will take a tumble."

"If it makes people take the threat seriously, so much the better," Samual Aleksandrovich said. "Motela, you are to assemble a 1st Fleet squadron, a large one, to be held on fifteen-minute-departure alert. When we find Laton, eliminating him is going to be your problem."

"What problem?"

"I admire the sentiment," Samual Aleksandrovich said with a touch of censure. "But kindly remember he escaped from us last time, when we were equally hungry for blood. That mistake cannot be repeated. This time I shall require proof, even though it will no doubt be expensive. I imagine Lalwani and Auster will agree."

"We do," Lalwani said. "All Edenists do. If there is any risk in confirming the target is Laton, then we will bear it."

"In the meantime, I want Lalonde to be completely isolated," Samual Aleksandrovich said. "The mercenary force is not to be allowed to land, nor do I want any surface bombardments from orbit. Those colonists have suffered enough already. The solution to this sequestration lies in discovering the method by which it is implemented, and devising a counter. Brute force is merely dumping plutonium in a volcano. And I suspect the mercenaries would simply be sequestrated themselves should they land. Dr Gilmore, this is your field."

"Not really," the doctor said expressively. "But we shall put our female subject through an extensive series of experiments to see if we can determine the method of the sequestration and how to cancel it. However, judging by what we know so far, which is virtually nothing, I have to say an answer is going to take a considerable time to formulate. Though you are quite right to instigate a quarantine. The less contact Lalonde has with the rest of the Confederation the better, especially if it turns out Laton isn't behind the invasion."

"The doctor has a point," Lalwani said. "What if the Lalonde invasion is the start of a xenoc incursion, and Laton himself has been sequestrated?"

"I'm keeping it in mind," Samual Aleksandrovich said. "We need to know more, either from the Couteur woman or Lalonde itself. Our principal trouble remains what it has always been: reaction time. It takes us far too long to amass any large force. Always our conflicts are larger than they would have been if we had received a warning of problems and threats earlier in their development. But just this once, we may actually be in luck. Unless there was some supreme diplomatic foul-up, Meredith Saldana's squadron was due to leave Omuta three days ago. They were in the system mainly for pomp and show, but they carried a full weapons load. A squadron of front-line ships already assembled and perfectly suited to these duties; we couldn't have planned it better. It'll take them five days to get back to Rosenheim. Captain Auster, if *Ilex* can get there before they dock at 7th Fleet headquarters and all the crews go on leave, then Meredith might just be able to get to Lalonde before Terrance Smith. And if not before, then certainly in time to prevent the bulk of the mercenary troops from landing."

"*Ilex* will certainly try, First Admiral," Auster said. "I have already asked for auxiliary fusion generators to be installed in the weapons bays. The energy patterning cells can be recharged directly from them, reducing the flight time between swallows considerably. We should be ready to depart in five hours, and I believe we can make the two-day deadline."

"My thanks to *Ilex*," Samual Aleksandrovich said formally.

Auster inclined his head.

"Lieutenant-Commander Solanki, you'll travel with Captain Auster, and carry my orders for Rear-Admiral Saldana. And I think we can manage a promotion to full commander before you go. You've shown considerable initiative over the last few weeks, as well as personal courage."

"Yes, sir, thank you, sir," Kelven said. The promotion barely registered, some irreverent section of his mind was counting up the number of light-years he had flown in a week. It must be some kind of record. But he was going back to Lalonde, and bringing his old friends help. That felt good. I've stopped running.

"Add an extra order that the *Lady Macbeth* and her crew is to be arrested," Samual Aleksandrovich told Maynard

Khanna. "They can try explaining themselves to Meredith's Intelligence officers."

The *Santa Clara* materialized a hundred and twenty thousand kilometres above Lalonde, almost directly in line between the planet and Rennison. Dawn was racing over Amarisk, half of the Juliffe's tributary network flashing like silver veins in the low sunlight. The early hour might have accounted for the lack of response from civil traffic control. But Captain Zaretsky had been to Lalonde before, he knew the way the planet worked. Radio silence didn't particularly bother him.

Thermo-dump panels slid out of the hull, and the flight computer plotted a vector which would deliver the starship to a five hundred kilometre equatorial orbit. Zaretsky triggered the fusion drive and the ship moved in at a tenth of a gee. *Santa Clara* was a large cargo clipper, paying a twice-annual visit to the Tyrathca settlements, bringing new colonists and shipping out their rygar crop. There were over fifty Tyrathca breeders on board, all of them shuffling round the cramped life-support capsules; the dominant xenocs refused to use zero-tau pods (though their vassal castes were riding the voyage in temporal suspension). Captain Zaretsky didn't particularly like being chartered by Tyrathca merchants, but they always paid on time, which endeared them to the ship's owners.

Once the *Santa Clara* was underway, he opened channels to the nine starships in parking orbit. They told him about the riots, and rumours of invaders, and the fighting in Durringham which had lasted four days. There had been no information coming up from the city for two days now, they said, and they couldn't decide what to do.

Zaretsky didn't share their problem. *Santa Clara* had a medium-sized VTOL spaceplane in its hangar, his contract didn't call for any contact with the human settlements. Whatever rebellion the Ivets were staging, it didn't affect him.

When he opened a channel to the Tyrathca farmers on

the planet they reported a few skirmishes with humans who were "acting oddly;" but they had prepared their rygar crop, and were waiting for the equipment and new farmers the *Santa Clara* was bringing. He acknowledged the call, and continued the slow powered fall into orbit, the *Santa Clara*'s fusion exhaust drawing a slender thread of incandescence across the stars.

Jay Hilton sat on the rock outcrop fifty metres from the savannah homestead cabin, her legs crossed, head tipped back to watch the starship decelerating into orbit, and mournful curiosity pooling in her eyes. The weeks of living with Father Horst had brought about a considerable change in her appearance. For a start her lush silver-white hair had been cropped into a frizz barely a centimetre long, making it easier to keep clean. She had cried bucketfuls the day Father Horst took the scissors to it. Her mother had always looked after it so well, washing it with special shampoo brought from Earth, brushing it to a shine each night. Her hair was her last link with the way things used to be, her last hope that they might be that way again. When Father Horst had finished his snipping she knew in her heart that her most precious dream, that one day she'd wake up to find everything had returned to normal, was just a stupid child's imagination. She had to be tough now, had to be adult. But it was so hard.

I just want Mummy back, that's all.

The other children looked up to her. She was the oldest and strongest of the group. Father Horst relied on her a great deal to keep the younger ones in order. A lot of them still cried at night. She heard them in the darkness, crying for their lost parents or siblings, crying because they wanted to go back to their arcology where none of this horrid confusion and upset happened.

Dawn's rosy crown gave way to a tide of blue which swept across the sky, erasing the stars. Rennison faded to a pale crescent, and the starship's exhaust became more difficult to see. Jay unfolded her legs and clambered down off the rocks.

The homestead on the edge of the savannah was a simple wooden structure, its solar-cell roof sheets glinting in the strong morning light. Two of the dogs, a Labrador and an Alsatian, were out and about. She patted them as she went up the creaking wooden stairs to the porch. The cows in the paddock were making plaintive calls, their udders heavy with milk.

Jay went in through the front door. The big lounge whiffed strongly—of food, and cooking, and too many people. She sniffed the air suspiciously. Someone had wet their bedding again, probably more than one.

The floor was a solid patchwork of sleeping-bags and blankets, their occupants only just beginning to stir. Grass stuffing from the makeshift mattresses of canvas sacks had leaked out again.

"Come on! Come on!" Jay clapped her hands together as she pulled the reed blinds open. Streamers of gold-tinged sunlight poured in, revealing children blinking sleep from their eyes, wincing at the brightness. Twenty-seven of them were crammed together on the mayope floorboards, ranging from a toddler about two years old up to Danny, who was nearly the same age as Jay. All of them with short haircuts and rough-tailored adult clothes which never quite fitted. "Up you get! Danny, it's your gang's turn to do the milking. Andria, you're in charge of cooking this morning: I want tea, oatmeal, and boiled eggs for breakfast." A groan went up, which Jay ignored; she was just as fed up with the changeless diet as they were. "Shona, take three girls with you and collect the eggs, please."

Shona gave a timid smile as well as she could, grateful for being included in the work assignments and not being treated any differently to the others. Jay had drilled herself not to flinch from looking at the poor girl. The six-year-old's face was covered in a bandage mask of glossy translucent epithelium membrane, with holes cut out for her eyes and mouth and nose. Her burn marks were still a livid pink below the overlapping membrane strips, and her hair was only just beginning to grow back. Father Horst said she ought to heal without any permanent scarring, but he was forever grieving over the lack of medical nanonic packages.

Coughs and grumbles and high-pitched chattering filled the room as the children struggled out of bed and into their clothes. Jay saw little Robert sitting brokenly on the side of his sleeping-bag, head in his hands, not bothering to get dressed. "Eustice, you're to get this room tidied up, and I want all the blankets aired properly today."

"Yes, Jay," she answered sullenly.

The outside door was flung open as five or six children rushed out laughing, and ran for the lean-to, which they used as a toilet.

Jay picked her way over the rectangles of bedding to Robert. He was only seven, a black-skinned boy with fluffy blond hair. Sure enough, the navy blue pants he wore were damp.

"Pop down to the stream," she said kindly. "There will be plenty of time to wash before breakfast."

His head was lowered even further. "I didn't mean to," he whispered, on the verge of tears.

"I know. Remember to wash out your sleeping-bag as well." She caught the sound of someone giggling. "Bo, you help him take the bag down to the stream."

"Oh, Jay!"

"It's all right," Robert said. "I can manage."

"No, you won't, not if you want to be back in time for breakfast." The big table was already being pulled out from the kitchen corner by three of the boys, scraping loudly across the floor. They were shouting for people to get out of the way.

"Don't see why I should have to help him," Bo said intransigently. She was an eight-year-old, meaty for her age, with chubby red cheeks. Her size was often deployed to help boss the smaller children around.

"Chocolate," Jay said in warning.

Bo blushed, then stalked over to Robert. "Come on then, you."

Jay knocked once on Father Horst's door and walked in. The room had been the homestead's main bedroom when they moved in; it still had a double bed in it, but most of the floor space was taken up with packets, jars, and pots of food they'd taken from the other deserted homestead cabins. Clothes and cloth and powered tools, anything small or light enough to be carried, filled the second bedroom in piles that were taller than Jay.

Horst was getting up as the girl came in. He'd already got his trousers on, thick denim jeans with leather patches, a working man's garment, requisitioned from one of the other savannah homesteads. She picked up the faded red sweatshirt from the foot of the bed and handed it to him. He had lost a lot of weight—a lot of fat—over the last weeks; slack bands of flesh hung loosely from his torso. But even the folds were shrinking, and the muscles they covered were harder than they had ever been, though at night they felt like bands of ignescent metal. Horst spent most of every day working, hard manual work; keeping the cabin in shape, repairing and strengthening the paddock fence, building a chicken run, digging the latrines; then in the evening there would be prayers and reading lessons. At night he dropped into bed as if a giant had felled him with its fist. He had never known a human body could perform such feats of stamina, least of all one as old and decrepit as his.

Yet he never wavered, never complained. There was a fire in his eyes that had been ignited by his predicament. He was embarked on a crusade to survive, to deliver his charges to safety. The bishop would be hard pressed to recognize that dreamy well-meaning Horst Elwes who had left Earth last year. Even thinking about his earlier self with its disgusting self-pity and weaknesses repelled him.

He had been tested as few had ever been before, his faith thrown onto towering flames that had threatened to reduce him to shreds of black ash so powerful was the doubt and insecurity fuelling them: but he had emerged triumphant. Born of fire, and reforged, his conviction in self, and Christ the Saviour, was unbreakable.

And he had the children to thank. The children who were now his life and his task. The hand of God had brought them together. He would not fail them, not while there was a breath left in his body.

He smiled at Jay who was as grave faced as she always was at the break of day. The sounds of the usual morning bedlam were coming through the door as bedding was put away and the furniture brought out.

"How goes it today, Jay?"

"Same as always." She sat on the end of the bed as he pulled on his heavy hand-tooled boots. "I saw a starship arrive. It's coming down into low orbit."

He glanced up from his laces. "Just one?"

"Uh huh," she nodded vigorously.

"Ah well, it's not to be today, then."

"When?" she demanded. Her small beautiful face was screwed up in passionate rage.

"Oh, Jay." He pulled her against him, and rocked her gently as she sniffled. "Jay, don't give up hope. Not you." It was the one thing he promised them, repeating it every night at prayers so they would believe. On a world far away lived a wise and powerful man called Admiral Aleksandrovich, and when he heard what terrible things had happened on Lalonde he would send a fleet of Confederation Navy starships to help its people and drive away the demons who possessed them. The soldiers and the navy crews would come down in huge spaceplanes and rescue them, and then their parents, and finally put the world to rights again. Every night Horst said it, with the door locked against the wind and rain, and the windows shuttered against the dark empty savannah. Every night he believed and they believed. Because God would not have spared them if it was not for a purpose. "They will come," he promised. He kissed her forehead. "Your mother will be so proud of you when she returns to us."

"Really?"

"Yes, really."

She pondered this. "Robert wet his bed again," she said.

"Robert is a fine boy." Horst stomped on the second boot. They were two sizes too large, which meant he had to wear three pairs of socks, which made his feet sweat, and smell.

"We should get him something," she said.

"Should we now? And what's that?"

"A rubber mat. There might be one in another cabin. I could look," she said, eyes all wide with innocence.

Horst laughed. "No, Jay, I haven't forgotten. I'll take you out hunting this morning, and this time it will be Danny who stays behind."

Jay let out a squeal of excitement and kicked her legs in the air. "Yes! Thank you, Father."

He finished tying his laces and stood up. "Don't mention the starship, Jay. When the navy comes it will be in a mighty flotilla, with their exhaust plumes so strong and bright they will turn night into day. Nobody will mistake it. But in the meantime we must not pour cold water on the others' hopes."

"I understand, Father. I'm not as dumb as them."

He ruffled her hair, which she pretended not to like, wriggling away. "Come along now," he said. "Breakfast first. Then we'll get our expedition sorted out."

"I suppose Russ will come with us?" she asked in a martyred voice.

"Yes, he will. And stop thinking uncharitable thoughts."

The children already had most of the bedding off the floor. Two boys were sweeping up the dried grass from the sack mattresses (Must find a better replacement, Horst thought). Eustice's voice could be heard through the open door, yelling instructions to the children airing the linen outside.

Horst helped to pull the big table into the middle of the room. Andria's team were scurrying round the kitchen corner, tending the equipment and the meal. The big urn was

urning. He caught himself before brooding turned to
...ancholia; he wouldn't need to go back, the navy would
...me. And don't ever think anything different.

...ay bounded up to walk beside him, adjusting her stride
...match his. She gave him a sideways smile, then returned
...r gaze to the front, perfectly content.

...Horst felt his own tensions seeping away. Having her so
...ose was like the time right after that dreadful night. She
...d screamed and fought him as he pulled her away from
...uth and Jackson Gael. He had forced her through the vil-
...age towards the jungle, only once looking back. He saw it
...ll then, in the light of the fire which pillaged their sturdy
...ranquil village, snuffing out their ambitions of a fair fu-
...ure as swiftly as rain dissolved the mud castles the chil-
...ren built on the riverbank. Satan's army was upon them.
...lore figures were marching out of the dark shadows into
...e orange light of the flames, creatures that even Dante in
...s most lucid fever-dreams had never conceived, and the
...reams of the ensnared villagers rose in a crescendo.

...Horst had never let Jay look back, not even after they
...ched the trees. He knew then that waiting for the hunt-
...party to return was utter folly. Laser rifles could not
...m the demon legions Lucifer in his wrath had loosed
...n the land.

...hey had carried on far into the jungle, until a numbed,
...ified Jay had finally collapsed. Dawn found them hud-
...together in the roots of a qualtook tree, soaked and
...ering from a downpour in the night. When they eased
...way cautiously back towards Aberdale and hid them-
...s in the vines ringing the clearing they saw a village
...a dream.

...eral buildings were razed to the ground. People
...d by without paying them a glance. People Horst
...his flock, who should have been overwrought by the
...e. That was when he knew Satan had won, his
...had possessed the villagers. What he had seen at
...ceremony had been repeated here, again and again.
...re's Mummy?" Jay asked miserably.

just starting to boil, and the three IR plates were heating up
the boiling pans ready for the eggs.

Once again Horst gave a fast prayer of thanks that the
solar-powered equipment functioned so well. It was easy
enough for the children to use without hurting themselves,
and most of them had helped their mothers with the cooking before. All they needed was some direction, as they did
in every task he set them. He didn't like to think how he
would have coped if the homestead hadn't been empty.

It took another fifteen minutes before Andria's cooking
party were ready to serve breakfast. Several of the eggs
Shona brought back were broken, so Horst himself scrambled them up in a pan on a spare IR plate. It was easier to
feed Jill, the toddler, that way.

The tea was finally ready, and the eggs boiled. Everyone
lined up with their mug and cutlery and eggcup, and filed
past the kitchen bar which doubled as a serving counter.
For a few wonderful minutes the room was actually quiet
as the children drank, and cracked their eggs open, and
pulled faces as they munched the dry oatmeal biscuits,
dunking them in the tea to try and soften them up first.
Horst looked round his extended family and tried not to
feel frightened at the responsibility. He adored them in a
way he had never done with his parishioners.

After breakfast it was wash time, with the extra two
tanks he had installed in the rafter space struggling to provide enough hot water. Horst inspected them all to make
sure they were clean and that they had jell-rinsed their
teeth. That way he could have a few words with each of
them, make them feel special, and wanted, and loved. It
also gave him the chance to watch for any sign of illness.
So far there had been remarkably little, a few colds, and
one nasty outbreak of diarrhoea a fortnight ago, which he
suspected was from a batch of jam that had come from another homestead.

The morning would follow its standard pattern while he
and Jay were away. Clothes to be washed in the stream and
hung out to dry. Hay to be taken into the cows, corn to be

measured out into the chicken-run dispensers (they never did that very well), lunch to be prepared. When he went away it was always the packets of protein-balanced meals from Earth—all they had to do was put them in the microwave for ninety seconds, and nothing could go wrong. Sometimes he allowed a group to pick elwisie fruit from the trees on the edge of the jungle. But not today; he gave Danny a stern lecture that no one was to wander more than fifty metres from the cabin, and someone must be on watch the whole time in case a kroclion turned up. The plains carnivores hadn't often plagued the homesteads, but his didactic memory showed what a menace the lumbering animals could be. The boy nodded earnestly, eager to prove his worth.

Horst was still suffering from stings of doubt when he led the group's one horse from its stable. He trusted Jay to be left in charge, she acted far older than her years. But he had to hunt for meat, there were hardly any fish in the nearby stream. If they stuck to the cache of food in his bedroom it would be gone within ten days; it existed to supplement what he killed and stored in the freezer, and acted as an emergency reserve just in case he ever did get ill. And Jay deserved a break from the homestead, she hadn't been away since they arrived.

He took two other children with him as well as Jay. Mills, an energetic eight-year-old from Schuster village, and Russ, a seven-year-old who simply refused to ever leave Horst's side. The one and only time he had gone hunting without him the boy had run off into the savannah and it had taken the whole afternoon to find him.

Jay was grinning and waving and playing up to her jealous friends when they set off. The savannah grass quickly rose up around their legs; Horst had made Jay wear a pair of trousers instead of her usual shorts. A thick layer of mist started to lift from the waving stalks and blades now the sun was rising higher into the sky. Haze broke the visibility down to less than a kilometre.

"This humidity is worse than the Juliffe back in Dur-

ringham," Jay exclaimed, waving her hand f front of her face.

"Cheer up," Horst said. "It might rain later."

"No, it won't."

He glanced round to where she was walking i he was making through the stiff grass. Bright eye mischievously at him from below the brim of hei sun-hat.

"How do you know?" he asked. "It always Lalonde."

"No, it doesn't. Not any more, not during the da

"What do you mean?"

"Haven't you noticed? It only ever rains at night

Horst gave her a perplexed stare. He was about her not to be silly. But then he couldn't remember th time he'd rushed indoors to shelter from one of Lalo... ferocious downpours—a week, ten days? He had an u comfortable feeling it might even have been longer. "No hadn't noticed," he said temperately.

"That's all right, you've had a lot on your mind

"I certainly have." But the chirpy mood w now.

I should have noticed, he told himself. But th gards the weather as something suspicious? He was important though, he just couldn't think Surely they couldn't change the weather.

Horst made it a rule that he was never a than four hours. That put seven other hor within reach (eight counting the ruins o building) as well as allowing enough time deril or some vennals. Once he had shot a wild, and they'd eaten ham and bacon f week. It was the most delicious meat he restrial beasts were pure ambrosia com and bland aboriginal animals.

There was hardly anything of any ins now, he had stripped them pretty other couple of visits there wou'

"I have no idea," he said truthfully. There were fewer people than there should have been, maybe seventy or eighty out of the population of five hundred. They acted as though devoid of purpose, walking slowly, looking round in befogged surprise, saying nothing.

The children were the exception. They ran around between the somnolent, shuffling adults, crying and shouting. But they were ignored, or sometimes cuffed for their trouble. Horst could hear their distraught voices from his sanctuary, deepening his own torment. He watched as a girl, Shona, trailed after her mother pleading for her to say something. She tugged insistently at the trousers, trying to get her to stop. For a moment it looked like she had succeeded. Her mother turned round. "Mummy," Shona squealed. But the woman raised a hand, and a blast of white fire streamed from her fingers to smite the girl full in the face.

Horst cringed, crossing himself instinctively as she dropped like a stone, not even uttering a cry. Then anger poured through him at his own cravenness. He stood up and strode purposefully out of the trees.

"Father," Jay squeaked behind him. "Father, don't."

He paid her no heed. In a world gone mad, one more insanity would make no difference. He had sworn himself to follow Christ, a long time ago, but it meant more to him now than it ever had. And a child lay suffering before him. Father Horst Elwes was through with evasions and hiding.

Several of the adults stopped to watch as he marched into the village, Jay scuttling along behind him. Horst pitied them for the husks they were. The human state of grace had been drained from their bodies. He could tell, accepting the gift of knowledge as his right. Six or seven villagers formed a loose group standing between him and Shona, their faces known but not their souls.

One of the women, Brigitte Hearn, never a regular churchgoer, laughed at him, her arm rising. A ball of white fire emerged from her open fingers and raced towards him. Jay screamed, but Horst stood perfectly still, face resolute.

The fireball started to break apart a couple of metres away from him, dimming and expanding. It burst with a wet crackle as it touched him, tiny strands of static burrowing through his filthy sweatshirt. They stung like hornets across his belly, but he refused to reveal his pain to the semicircle of watchers.

"Do you know what this is?" Horst thundered. He lifted the stained and muddied silver crucifix that hung round his neck, brandishing it at Brigitte Hearn as though it was a weapon. "I am the Lord's servant, as you are the Devil's. And I have His work to do. Now stand aside."

A spasm of fright crossed Brigitte Hearn's face as the silver cross was shaken in front of her. "I'm not," she said faintly. "I'm not the Devil's servant. None of us are."

"Then stand aside. That girl is badly hurt."

Brigitte Hearn glanced behind her, and took a couple of steps to one side. The other people in the group hurriedly parted, their faces apprehensive, one or two walked away. Horst gestured briefly at Jay to follow him, and went over to the fallen girl. He grimaced at the singed and blackened skin of her face. Her pulse was beating wildly. She had probably gone into shock, he decided. He scooped her up in his arms, and started for the church.

"I had to come back," Brigitte Hearn said as Horst walked away. Her body was all hunched up, eyes brimming with tears. "You don't know what it's like. I had to."

"It?" Horst asked impatiently. "What is it?"

"Death."

Horst shuddered, almost breaking his stride. Jay looked round fearfully at the woman.

"Four hundred years," Brigitte Hearn called out falteringly. "I died four hundred years ago. Four hundred years of nothing."

Horst barged into the small infirmary at the back of the church, and laid Shona down on the wooden table which doubled as an examination bed. He snatched the medical processor block from its shelf and applied a sensor pad to the nape of her neck. The metabolic display appeared as he described her injuries to the processor. Horst read the results and gave the girl a sedative, then started spraying a combination analgesic and cleansing fluid over the burns.

"Jay," he said quietly. "I want you to go into my room and fetch my rucksack from the cupboard. Put in all the packets of preprocessed food you can find, then the tent I used when we first arrived, and anything else you think will be useful to camp out in the jungle—the little fission blade, my portable heater, that kind of stuff. But leave some space for my medical supplies. Oh, and I'll need my spare boots too."

"Are we leaving?"

"Yes."

"Are we going to Durringham?"

"I don't know. Not straight away."

"Can I go and fetch Drusilla?"

"I don't think it's a good idea. She'll be better off here than tramping through the jungle with us."

"All right. I understand."

He heard her moving about in his room as he worked on Shona. The younger girl's nose was burnt almost down to the bone, and the metabolic display said only one retina was functional. Not for the first time he despaired the lack of nanonic medical packages; a decent supply would hardly have bankrupted the Church.

He had flushed the dead skin from Shona's burns as best he could, coating them in a thin layer of corticosteroid foam to ease the inflammation, and was binding her head with a quantity of his dwindling stock of epithelium membrane when Jay came back in carrying his rucksack, It was packed professionally, and she had even rolled up his sleeping-bag.

"I got some stuff for myself," she said, and held up a bulging shoulder-bag.

"Good girl. You didn't make the bag too heavy, did you? You might have to carry it a long way."

"No, Father."

Someone knocked timidly on the door post. Jay shrank into the corner of the infirmary.

"Father Horst?" Brigitte Hearn poked her head in. "Father, they don't want you here. They say they'll kill you, that you can't defend yourself against all of them."

"I know. We're leaving."

"Oh."

"Will they let us leave?"

She swallowed and looked over her shoulder. "Yes. I think so. They don't want a fight. Not with you, not with a priest."

Horst opened drawers in the wooden cabinet at the back of the infirmary, and started shoving his medical equipment into the rucksack. "What are you?" he asked.

"I don't know," she said woefully.

"You said you had died?"

"Yes."

"What is your name?"

"Ingrid Veenkamp, I lived on Bielefeld when it was a stage one colony world, not much different to this planet." She twitched a smile at Jay. "I had two girls. Pretty, like you."

"And where is Brigitte Hearn now?"

"Here, in me. I feel her. She is like a dream."

"Possession," Horst said.

"No."

"Yes! I saw the red demon sprite. I witnessed the rite, the *obscenity* Quinn Dexter committed to summon you here."

"I'm no demon," the woman insisted. "I lived. I am human."

"No more. Leave this body you have stolen. Brigitte Hearn has a right to her own life."

"I can't! I'm not going back there. Not to that."

Horst took a grip on his trembling hands. Thomas had known this moment, he thought, when the disciple doubted his Lord's return, when in prideful arrogance he refused to believe until he had seen the print of nails in His hand.

"Believe," he whispered. "Jesus is the Christ, the Son of God; and that believing ye might have life through His name."

The Brigitte/Ingrid woman bowed her head.

Horst asked the question that should never be asked: "Where? Where, damn you!"

"Nowhere. There is nothing for us. Do you hear? Nothing!"

"You lie."

"There is nothing, just emptiness. I'm sorry." She took an unsteady breath, seemingly gathering up a remnant of dignity. "You must leave now. They are coming back."

Horst shut the flap on his rucksack and sealed it. "Where are the rest of the villagers?"

"Gone. They hunt fresh bodies for other souls trapped in the beyond, it has become their quest. I haven't the stomach for it, nor have the others who remained in Aberdale. But you take care, Father. Your spirit is hale, but you could never withstand one of us for long."

"They want more people to possess?"

"Yes."

"But why?"

"Together we are strong. Together we can change what is. We can destroy death, Father. We shall bring eternity into existence here on this planet, perhaps even across the entire Confederation. I shall stay as I am for all time now; ageless, changeless. I am alive again, I won't give that up."

"This is lunacy," he said.

"No. This is wonder, it is our miracle."

Horst pulled his rucksack onto his back, and picked Shona up. Several adults had started to gather around the church. He walked down the steps pointedly disregarding them, Jay pressing into his side. They stared at him, but no one made a move. He turned and headed for the jungle, mildly surprised to see Ingrid Veenkamp walking with him.

"I told you," she said. "They lack nerve. You will be safer if I am with you. They know I can strike back."

"Would you?"

"Perhaps. For the girl's sake. But I don't think we will find out."

"Please, lady," Jay said, "do you know where my mummy is?"

"With the others, the pernicious ones. But don't look for her, she is no longer your mother. Do you understand?"

"Yes," she mumbled.

"We'll get her back for you, Jay," Horst said. "One day, somehow. I promise."

"Such faith," Ingrid Veenkamp said.

He thought she was mocking, but there was no trace of a smile on her face. "What about the other children?" he asked. "Why haven't you possessed them?"

"Because they are children. No soul would want a vessel so small and frail, not when there are plentiful adults to be had. Millions on this planet alone."

They had reached the fields, and the soft loam was clinging to Horst's feet in huge claggy lumps. With the weight of the rucksack and Shona conspiring to push him into the ground he wasn't even sure he could make it to the first rank of trees. Sweat was dripping from his forehead at the effort. "Send the children after me," he wheezed. "They are hungry and they are frightened. I will take care of them."

"You make a poor Pied Piper, Father. I'm not even sure you'll last until nightfall."

"Mock and scorn as you like, but send them. They'll find me. For God knows I'll not be able to travel far or fast."

She dipped her head briefly. "I'll tell them."

Horst staggered into the jungle with Jay beside him, her big shoulder-bag knocking against her legs. He managed another fifty metres through the inimical vines and undergrowth, then sank panting painfully to his knees, face perilously red and hot.

"Are you all right?" Jay asked anxiously.

"Yes. We'll just have to take it in short stages, that's all. I think we're safe for now."

She opened the shoulder-bag's seal. "I brought your cooler flask, I thought you might need it. I filled it with the high-vitamin orange juice you had in your room."

"Jay, you are a twenty-four-carat angel." He took the flask from her and drank some of the juice; she had set the thermostat so low it poured like slushy snow. They heard someone pushing their way through the undergrowth behind them, and turned. It was Russ and Andria, the first of the children.

Trudging across the savannah wasn't quite the holiday Jay had told herself it would be. But it was lovely being away from the homestead, even if it was only going to be for a few hours. She longed to ride the horse, too; though there was no way she was going to plead with Father Horst in front of the boys.

They arrived at the Ruttan family's old homestead after forty minutes' walking. Untended, it had suffered from Lalonde's rain and winds. The door which had been left open had swung to and fro until the hinges broke, and now it lay across the small porch. Animals (probably sayce) had used it for shelter at some time, adding to the disarray inside.

Jay waited with the two boys while Father Horst went in, carrying his laser hunting rifle, and checked over the three rooms. The abandoned cabin was eerie after the noise and bustle of their own homestead. She heard a distant rumble, and looked up, thinking it was approaching thunder. But the sky remained a perfect basin of blue. The noise grew louder, swelling out of the west.

Father Horst emerged from the homestead carrying a wooden chair. "It sounds like a spaceplane," he said.

The grimed window-panes were rattling in their frames. Jay searched the sky frantically as the sound began to fade into the east. But there was nothing to be seen, the spaceplane was too high. She gave the distant mountains to the south a forlorn glance. It must have been going to the Tyrathca farmers, she thought.

"Have a hunt round," Horst said. "See if you can find anything useful; you might try the barn as well. I'm going to the roof to cut the solar-cell sheets down." He put the chair down under the eaves, and stood on it, squirming his way up onto the roof.

There was nothing much in the cabin; fans of grey fungus had established a foothold in the cracks between the planks, and greenish ripples of mould patterned the damp mattresses. She pulled a couple of clay mugs out from under one of the beds, and Russ found some shirts in a box below the kitchen workbench.

"They'll be all right once we wash them," Jay declared, holding up the smelly, soiled garments.

They had more luck in the barn: two sacks of protein-concentrate cakes used to feed young animals that had just come out of hibernation, and Mills discovered a small fission-blade saw behind a pile of old cargo-pods. "Good work!" Horst told them as he clambered down. "And look what I got, all three sheets. We'll be able to heat the water tanks up in half the time now."

Jay rolled up the solar-cell sheets while he lifted the sacks into the plough horse's big saddle-bags.

Horst handed round his chill flask full of icy elwisie juice, then they set off again. Jay was glad of her hat. The sunlight was scorchingly hot on her arms and back, air rippled and shimmered all around. I never thought I'd miss the rains.

There was a river to cross before they reached the Soebergs' homestead. It was less than a metre deep, but about fifteen metres wide. A fast, steady flow from the mountains, winding in broad curves along the savannah's gentle contours. The bottom was smooth rock and rounded pebbles. Snowlily plants were growing right across it, their long fronds waving in the current. Flower buds as big as her head bobbed on the surface, the first splits starting to appear in their sides.

Jay and Horst took their boots off, and waded across clinging to the side of the horse. The water was invigorating, numbing her toes. She could easily believe it must have come directly from the snow peaks themselves, she wouldn't have been surprised to see nuggets of ice bobbing about. After she sat on the bottom of the bank and dried her feet she thought she could walk for another hundred kilometres. Her skin was still tingling delightfully when they started up the bank.

They had been walking for another ten minutes when Horst held up his hand. "Mills, Russ, come down off the horse," he said with quiet insistence.

The tone he used set up an uncomfortable prickling along Jay's spine. "What is it?" she asked.

"The Soebergs' homestead. I think."

She peered over the tops of the wavering grass stems. There was something up ahead, a white silhouette against the indistinct horizon, but the sun-roiled air made it hard to tell exactly what.

Horst fished his optical intensifier from a pocket. It was a curving band of black composite that fitted over his eyes. He studied the scene ahead for a while, his right forefinger adjusting the magnification control.

"They are coming back," he said in a soft murmur.

"Can I see?" she asked.

He handed her the band. It was large and quite heavy; the edges annealed to her skin with a pinching sensation.

She thought she was looking at some kind of AV recording, a drama play perhaps. Sitting in the middle of the savannah was a lovely old three-storey manor house, surrounded by a wide swath of tidy lawns. It was made of white stone, with a grey slate roof and large bay windows. Several people were standing under the portico.

"How do they do that?" Jay asked, more curious than alarmed.

"When you sell your soul to Satan, the material rewards are generous indeed. It is what he asks in return you should fear."

"But Ingrid Veenkamp said—"

"I know what she said." He removed the band from her face, and she blinked up at him. "She is a lost soul, she knows not what she does. Lord forgive her."

"Do they want our homestead too?" Jay asked.

"I shouldn't think so. Not if they can build that in a week." He sighed, and took one final look at the miniature mansion. "Come along, we'll see if we can find a nice fat danderil. If we get back early I'll have time to mince the meat, and you can have burgers tonight. What do you say?"

"Yeah!" the two boys chanted in chorus, grinning.

They turned round, and started to trek back across the heat-soaked savannah to the homestead.

Kelven Solanki floated through the open hatch into the *Arikara*'s bridge. The blue-grey compartment was the largest he'd ever seen in a warship before. As well as the normal flight crew it had to accommodate the admiral's twenty-strong squadron-coordination staff. Most of their couches were empty now. The flagship was orbiting Takfu, the largest gas giant in the Rosenheim star system, taking on fuel.

Commander Mircea Kroeber was stretched out along his couch, supervising the fuelling operation with three other crew-members. Kelven had seen the cryogenic tanker as *Ilex* docked with the huge flagship. A series of spherical tanks stacked on top of a reaction drive section, and sprouting thermo-dump panels like the wings of a mutant butterfly.

The squadron of twenty-five ships was in formation around the *Arikara*, holding station five hundred kilometres away from Uhewa, the Edenist habitat which was re-supplying them with both fuel and consumables. It was just one of the priority operations *Ilex*'s arrival in the star system had kicked off ten hours ago. Rosenheim's planetary government had immediately placed a restriction on all starship passengers and crew wanting to visit the surface. They now had to go through a rigorous screening process to make sure Laton wasn't amongst them, creating a vast backlog in the low orbit port stations. The system's asteroid settlements had swiftly followed suit. Reserve naval officers were being called up, and the 7th Fleet elements present in the system had been put on alert status along with the national navy.

Kelven was beginning to feel like a plague carrier, infecting the Confederation with panic.

Rear-Admiral Meredith Saldana was hanging in front of a console in the C&C section of the bridge, his soles touching the decking's stikpads. He was wearing an ordinary naval ship-suit, but it seemed so much smarter on him, braid stripes shining brightly on his arm. A couple of his staff officers were in attendance behind him. One of the console's AV projection pillars was emitting a low-frequency laser sparkle. When Kelven looked straight at it he saw Jantrit breaking apart.

Meredith Saldana datavised a shutdown order at the console as Kelven let the stikpad claim his shoes. The Rear-Admiral was six centimetres taller than him, and possessed a more distinguished appearance than the First Admiral. Could the Saldanas sequence dignity into their genes?

"Commander Kelven Solanki reporting as ordered, sir."

Meredith Saldana gave him a frank stare. "You are my Lalonde advisory officer?"

"Yes, sir."

"Just been promoted, Commander?"

"Yes, sir."

"It always shows."

"Sir, I have your orders flek from the First Admiral." Kelven held it out.

Meredith Saldana took the black coin-sized disk with some reluctance. "I don't know which is worse. Three months of these ridiculous ceremonial fly-bys and flag-waving exercises in the Omutan system, or a combat mission which is going to get us shot at by unknown hostiles."

"Lalonde needs our help, sir."

"Was it bad, Kelven?"

"Yes, sir."

"I suppose I'd better access this flek, hadn't I? All we've received so far are the emergency deployment orders from Fleet headquarters and the news about Laton showing up again."

"There is a full situation briefing included, sir."

"Excellent. If we run to schedule we should be departing for Lalonde in eight hours. I've requested another three voidhawks assigned to the squadron for liaison and interdiction duties. Is there anything else you think I need immediately? This mission's code rating gives me the authority to requisition almost any piece of hardware the navy has in the system."

"No, sir. But you will have a fourth extra voidhawk, *Ilex* has been assigned to the squadron as well."

"You can never have too many voidhawks," Meredith said lightly. There was no response from the young commander. "Carry on, Kelven. Find yourself a berth, and get settled in. Report for duty here to me an hour before departure time, you can give me a first-hand account of what we can expect. I always feel a lot happier being brought up to date by someone with hands-on experience. Meanwhile I suggest you get some sleep, you look like you need it."

"Yes, sir, thank you, sir."

Kelven twisted his feet free of the stikpad, and pushed off towards the hatch.

Meredith Saldana watched him manoeuvre through the open oval without touching the rim. Commander Solanki seemed to be a very tense man. But then I'd probably be the same in his place, the admiral thought. He held up the flek with a sense of foreboding, then slotted it into his couch player to find out exactly what he was up against.

Horst was always glad to get back to the homestead and greet his scampish charges; after all, when all was said and done, they were only children. And profoundly shocked children at that. They should never be left on their own, and if he had his way they never would. Practicality dictated otherwise, of course, and there had never yet been any major disaster while he was roaming the savannah for meat and foraging the other homesteads. To some extent he had grown blasé about his trips. But this time, after encountering the possessed out at the Soeberg homestead, he had forced the return pace, stopping only to kill a danderil, his mind host to a whole coven of thoughts along the theme of what if.

When he topped a small rise six hundred metres away and saw the familiar wood cabin with the children sporting around outside he felt an eddy of relief. Thank you, Lord, he said silently.

He slowed down for the last length, giving Jay a respite. Sweat made her blue blouse cling to her skinny frame. The heat was becoming a serious problem. It seemed to have banished the hardy chikrows back into the jungle. Even the danderil he'd shot had been sheltering in the shade of one of the savannah's scarce trees.

Horst blinked up at the unforgiving sky. Surely they don't mean to burn this world to cinders? They have form now, stolen bodies; and all the physical needs, urges, and failings which go with them.

He squinted at the northern horizon. There seemed to be an effete pink haze above the jungle, dusting the sharp seam between sky and land, like the flush of dawn refracted over a deep ocean. The harder he tried to focus upon it, the more insubstantial it became.

He couldn't believe it was a natural meteorological *rara avis*. More an omen. His humour, already tainted by the Soeberg homestead, sank further.

Too much is happening at once. Whatever polluted destiny they are manufacturing, it is reaching its zenith.

They were a hundred metres from the cabin when the children spotted them. A scrum of small bodies came running over the grass, Danny in the lead. Both of the homestead's dogs chased around them, barking loudly.

"Freya's here," the boy yelled out at the top of his voice. "Freya's here, Father. Isn't it wonderful?"

Then they were all clinging to him, shouting jubilantly and smiling up with enthusiasm as he laughed and patted them and hugged them. For a moment he revelled in the contact, the hero returning. A knight protector and Santa Claus rolled into one. They expected so much of him.

"What did you find in the cabins, Father?"

"You were quick today."

"Please, Father, tell Barnaby to give my reading tutor block back."

"Was there any more chocolate?"

"Did you find any shoes for me?"

"You promised to look for some story fleks."

With his escort swirling round and chattering happily, Horst led the horse over to the cabin. Russ and Mills had slithered off its back to talk with their friends.

"When did Freya arrive?" Horst asked Danny. He remembered the dark-haired girl from Aberdale, Freya Chester, about eight or nine, whose parents had brought a large variety of fruit trees with them. Kerry Chester's grove had always been one of the better maintained plots around the village.

"About ten minutes ago," the boy said. "It's great, isn't it?"

"Yes. It certainly is." Remarkable, in fact. He was surprised she had survived this long. Most of the children had turned up during the first fortnight while they were still camping in a glade a kilometre away from Aberdale. Five of them walking from Schuster. They had said a woman was with them for most of the journey—Horst suspected it was Ingrid Veenkamp. Several others, the youngest ones, he had found himself as they wandered aimlessly through the jungle. He and Jay made a regular circuit of the area round the village in the hope of finding still more. And for every one they did save he suffered the images of ten more lost in the ferocious undergrowth, stalked by sayce and slowly starving to death.

At the end of a fortnight it was obvious that the messy, hot, damp glade was totally impractical as a permanent site. By that time he had over twenty children to look after. It was Jay who suggested they try a homestead cabin, and four days later they were safely installed. Only five more children had turned up since then, all of them in a dreadful state as they tramped down the overgrown track between Aberdale and the savannah. Dispossessed urchins, totally unable to fend for themselves, sleeping in the jungle and stealing food from the village when they could, which wasn't anything like often enough. The last had been Eustice, two weeks ago when Horst skirted the jungle on a hunting trip; a skeleton with skin, her clothes reduced to tattered grey rags. She couldn't walk, if the Alsatian hadn't scented her and raised the alarm she would have been dead inside of a day. As it was, he had nearly lost her.

"Where is Freya?" Horst asked Danny.

"Inside, Father, having a rest. I said she could use your bed."

"Good lad. You did the right thing."

Horst let Jay and some of the girls lead the horse over to the water trough, and detailed a group of boys to remove the danderil carcass he'd secured to its back. Inside the cabin it was degrees cooler than the air outside, the thick double layer of mayope planks which made up the walls and ceiling proving an efficient insulator. He said a cheery hello to a bunch of children sitting around the table who were using a reading tutor block, and went into his own room.

The curtains were drawn, casting a rich yellow light throughout the room. There was a small figure lying on the bed wearing a long navy-blue dress, legs tucked up. She didn't appear starved, or even hungry. Her dress was as clean as though it had just been washed.

"Hello, Freya," Horst said softly. Then he looked at her

fully, and even more of the savannah's warmth was drained from his skin.

Freya raised her head lazily, brushing her shoulder-length hair from her face. "Father Horst, thank you so much for taking me in. It's so kind of you."

Horst's muscles froze the welcoming smile on his face. She was one of them! A possessed. Below the healthy deeply tanned skin lay a wizened sickly child, the dark dress hid a stained adult's T-shirt. The two images overlapped each other, jumping in and out of focus. They were enormously difficult to distinguish, obscured by a covering veil which she drew over his mind as well as his eyes. Reality was repugnant, he didn't want to see, didn't want truth. A headache ignited three centimetres behind his temple.

"All are welcome here, Freya," he said with immense effort. "You must have had a terrible time these last weeks."

"I did, it was horrible. Mummy and Daddy wouldn't speak to me. I hid in the jungle for ages and ages. There were berries and things to eat. But they were always cold. And I sometimes heard a sayce. It was really scary."

"Well, there are no sayce around here, and we have plenty of hot food." He walked along the side of the bed towards the dresser below the window, every footfall magnified to a strident thump in the still room. The noise of the children outside had perished. There was just the two of them now.

"Father?" she called.

"What do you want here?" he whispered tightly, his back towards her. He was afraid to pull the curtains open, afraid there might be nothing outside.

"It is a kindness." Her voice was deepening, becoming a morbid atonality. "There is no place for you on this world any more. Not as you are. You must change, become as us. The children will come to you one at a time when you call. They trust you'

"A trust that will never be betrayed." He turned round,

Bible in hand. The leather-bound book his mother had given him when he became a novice; it even had a little inscription she had written in the cover, the black ink fading to a watery blue down the decades.

Freya gave him a slightly surprised look, then sneered. "Oh, poor Father! Do you need your crutch so badly? Or do you hide from true life behind your belief?"

"Holy Father, Lord of Heaven and the mortal world, in humility and obedience, I do ask Your aid in this act of sanctification, through Jesus Christ who walked among us to know our failings, grant me Your blessing in my task," Horst incanted. It was so long ago since he had read the litany in the Unified prayer-book; and never before had he spoken the words, not in an age of science and universal knowledge, living in an arcology of crumbling concrete and gleaming composite. Even the Church questioned their need: they were a relic of the days when faith and paganism were still as one. But now they shone like the sun in his mind.

Freya's contempt descended into shock. "What?" She flung her legs off the bed.

"My Lord God, look upon Your servant Freya Chester, fallen to this unclean spirit, and permit her cleansing; in the name of the Father, the Son, and the Holy Ghost." Horst made the sign of the cross above the furious little girl.

"Stop it, you old fool. You think I fear that, your blind faith?" Her control over her form was slipping. The healthy clean image flickered on and off like a faulty light, exposing the frail malnourished child underneath.

"I beseech You to grant me Your strength, O Lord; so that her soul may be saved from damnation."

The Bible burst into flames. Horst groaned as the heat gnawed at his hand. He dropped it to the floor where it sputtered close to the leg of the bed. His hand was agony, as though it was dipped in boiling oil.

Freya's face was screwed up in determination, great rubberlike folds of skin distorting her pretty features almost beyond recognition. "Fuck you, priest." The obscenity seemed ludicrous coming from a child. "I'll burn your mind out of your skull. I'll cook your brain in its own blood." Her possessed shape shimmered again. The lame Freya below was choking.

Horst clutched at his crucifix with his good hand. "In the name of our Lord Jesus Christ, I order you, servant of Lucifer, to be gone from this girl. Return to the formless nothing where you belong."

Freya let out a piercing shriek. "How did you know!"

"Begone from this world. There is no place in the sight of God for those who would dwell in Evil."

"How, priest?" Her head turned from side to side, neck muscles straining as though she was fighting some invisible force. "Tell me . . ."

Heat was building along Horst's spine. He was sweating profusely, frightened she really would burn him. It was like the worst case of sunburn he had ever known, as though his skin was splitting open. His clothes would catch fire soon, he was sure.

He thrust the crucifix towards the girl. "Freya Chester, come forth, come into the light and the glory of our Lord."

And Freya Chester was solidly before him, thin sunken face racked by pain, spittle on her chin. Her mouth was working, struggling around complex words. Terror pounced from her black eyes.

"Come, Freya!" Horst shouted jubilantly. "Come forth, there is nothing to fear. The Lord awaits."

"Father." Her voice was tragically frail. She coughed, spewing out a meagre spray of saliva and stomach juices. "Father, help."

"In God we trust, to deliver us from evil. We seek Your justice, knowing we are not worthy. We drink of Your blood, and eat of Your flesh so we may share in Your glory. Yet we are but the dust from which You made us. Guide us from our errors, Lord, for in ignorance and sin we know not what we do. And we ask for Your holy protection."

For one last supremely lucid moment the demon possessor returned. Freya glared at him with a ferocity which withered his resolution by its sheer malice.

"I won't forget you," she ground out between her curled lips. "Never in all eternity will I forget you, priest."

Unseen hands scrabbled at his throat, tiny fingers, like an infant's. Blood emerged from the grazes sharp nails left around his Adam's apple. He held the crucifix on high, defiant that Christ's symbol would triumph.

Freya let out a last bellow of rage. Then the demon spirit was gone in a blast of noxious arctic air which blew Horst backwards. Neatly stacked piles of food packets went tumbling over, the bedlinen took flight, loose articles stampeded off the dresser and table. There was a bang like a castle door slamming in the face of an invading army.

Freya, the real Freya, all crusty sores, ragged clothes, and bony famined figure, was stretched out on the bed, emitting quiet gurgles from her chapped mouth. She started to cry.

Horst clambered to his feet, hanging on to the edge of the bed for support. He drew a gasping breath, his body aching inside and out, as though he had swum an ocean.

Jay and a troop of frantic children rushed in, shouting in a confused babble.

"It's all right," he told them, dabbing at the scratch marks on his throat. "Everything's all right now."

When Jay awoke the next morning she was surprised to see she had overslept. She hardly ever did that, the few minutes alone to herself at the start of each morning were among the most precious of the day. But it had to be dawn. A pale tinge of hoary light was creeping into the cabin's main room around the reed blinds. The other children were all still sound asleep. She quickly pulled on her shorts, boots, and an adult-sized shirt she had altered to something approximating her own size, and slipped quietly out of the door. Thirty sec-

onds later she ran back in shouting for Father Horst at the
top of her voice.

Far above the lonely savannah cabin, the long vivid contrails of thirteen starship fusion drives formed a cosmic
mandala across the black pre-dawn sky.

6

Lewis Sinclair had been born in 2059. He lived in Messopia, one of the first purpose-built industrial/accommodation/leisure complexes to be constructed on Spain's Mediterranean coast; a cheerless mathematical warren of concrete, glass, and plastic which covered five square kilometres and sheltered ninety thousand people against the ferocious armada storms which were beginning to plague Earth. It was a heavily subsidized experiment by the European Federal Parliament, by that time desperate to tackle the cancerous underclass problem thrown up by the continent's eighty-five million unemployed. Messopia was a qualified success; its medium-scale engineering industries provided only a minimal return for investors, but it provided a foretaste of the huge arcologies which in the centuries to come would house, protect, and employ Earth's dangerously expanded population.

His path through life was never going to be anything other than troublesome; born to low-income parents, who were only in the new microcosm city because of the parliamentary law requiring a socially balanced population. There was no real niche for him in an enterprise geared so resolutely towards the middle-class job/family/home ethic. He played truant from school, turned to crime, drugs, violence. A textbook delinquent, one of thousands who ran through Messopia's architecturally bankrupt corridors and malls.

It could have been different, if the education system had caught him early enough, if he had had the strength to hold out against peer pressure, if Messopia's technocrat designers had been less contemptuous of the social sciences. The opportunities existed. Lewis Sinclair lived in an age of quite profound technological and economic progress, and never really knew it, let alone shared in it. The first batches of asteroid-mined metal were starting to supplement depleted planetary reserves; biotechnology was finally living up to its initial promise; crude examples of the affinity bond were being demonstrated; more and more non-polluting fusion plants were coming on-stream as the supplies of He_3 mined from Jupiter's atmosphere increased. But none of it reached down to his level of society. He died in 2076, seventeen years old; one year after the bitek habitat Eden was germinated in orbit around Jupiter, and one year before the New Kong asteroid settlement began its FTL stardrive research project. His death was as wasteful as his life, a fight with power-blade knives in a piss-puddled subterranean warehouse, him and his opponent both high on synthetic crack. The fight was over a thirteen-year-old girl they both wanted to pimp.

He lost, the power blade chopping through his ribs to slice his stomach into two unequal portions.

And Lewis Sinclair made the same discovery as every human eventually made. Death was not the end of being. In the centuries that followed, spent as a virtually powerless astral entity suspended in dimensional emptiness, perceiving and envying mortals in their rich physical existence, he simply wished it were so.

But now Lewis Sinclair had returned. He wore a body again, weeping for joy at such simple magnificence as raindrops falling on his upturned face. He wasn't going to go back into the deprivation which lay after physical life, not ever. And he had the power to see that it was so; him and all the others, acting in combination, they were supreme badasses.

There was more to him than before, more than the strength which flesh and blood provided. Part of his soul was still back there in the terrible empty gulf; he hadn't emerged fully into life, not yet. He was trapped like a butterfly unable to complete the transformation from dirt-bound pupa to wing-free ephemeral. Often he felt as though the body he had possessed was simply a biological sensor mechanism, a mole's head peeking out from the earth, feeding sensations back to his feeling-starved soul via an incorporeal umbilical cord. Strange energistic vortices swirled around the dimensional twist where the two continua intermingled, kinking reality. The bizarre effect was usable, bending to his will. He could alter physical structures, sculpt energy, even prise open further links back into the extrinsic universe. His mastery of this power was increasing gradually, but its wild fluxes and resonances caused havoc in cybernetic machinery and electronic processor blocks around him.

So he watched through the spaceplane's narrow curving windscreen as the *Yaku* (now operating under a forged registration) dwindled against the sharp-etched stars, and felt his new muscles relaxing below the seat webbing. The spaceplane systems were an order of magnitude simpler than the *Yaku*'s, and critical malfunctions were highly unlikely now. Starflight was a disturbing business, so very technical. His dependency on the machines which his very presence disrupted was unnerving. With some luck he would never have to venture across the interstellar gulf again. He and his five colleagues riding down to the surface would be sufficient to conquer this unsuspecting world, turning it into a haven for other souls. Together they would make it their own.

"Retro burn in five seconds," Walter Harman said.

"OK," Lewis said. He concentrated hard, feeling round a chorus of distant voices with the peculiar cell cluster in this body's brain. **We're coming down now,** he told Pernik Island.

I look forward to your arrival, the island personality replied.

The affinity voice sounded clear and loud in his mind. Bitek functioned almost flawlessly despite the energistic turmoil boiling around his cells. It was one reason for selecting this particular planet.

The manoeuvring rockets at the rear of the little spaceplane fired briefly, pushing him down into the angle of the seat. The conditioning grille above his head was emitting an annoyingly loud whine as the fan motor spun out of control. His fingers tightened their grip on the armrests.

Walter Harman claimed to have been a spaceplane pilot back in the 2280s, serving in the Kulu Navy. As only three of them had even been in space before, his right to pilot the spaceplane went unchallenged. The body he used belonged to one of *Yaku*'s crew, possessed within minutes of Lewis boarding the starship. It was equipped with neural nanonics, which unlike bitek proved almost useless in the constant exposure to the hostile energistic environment a possession generated, so Walter Harman had activated the spaceplane's manual-control system, an ergonomic joystick which deployed from the console in front of the pilot's seat. A projection pillar showed trajectory graphics and systems information, updating constantly as he muttered instructions to the flight computer.

The spaceplane rolled, and Lewis saw the mass of the planet slide round the windscreen. They were over the terminator now, heading into the penumbra.

Night was always their best time, putting mortal humans at a disadvantage, adding to their own potency. Something about the darkness embraced their nature.

The spaceplane shook gently as the upper atmosphere began to strike the heatshield belly. Walter Harman pitched them up at a slight angle, and swung the wings out a few degrees, beginning the long aerobrake glide downwards.

They were still in the darkness when they dropped below subsonic. Lewis could see a hemispherical bauble of light glinting on the horizon ahead.

"Your approach is on the beam," the island personality informed them over the microwave channel. "Please land on pad eighteen." A purple and yellow flight vector diagram appeared on the console's holoscreen.

"Acknowledged, Pernik," Walter Harman said.

A three-dimensional simulacrum of the island materialized inside Lewis's skull, an image far sharper than the porno holographs he used to peddle back in Messopia. He automatically knew which pad eighteen was. A burst of doubt and anxiety blossomed in his mind, which he did his best to prevent from leaking back down the affinity bond to the island personality. This Edenist consensual set-up was so smooth. He worried that they might be taking on more than they could reasonably expect to accomplish.

The island personality had accepted his explanation that he was representing his merchant family enterprise from Jospool. Not every Edenist used the voidhawks to carry freight, there simply weren't enough to go round.

Lewis studied the mental simulacrum. Pad eighteen was close to the rim and the floating quays, there would be machinery there. It would be easy.

Pernik's coating of moss made the two-kilometre disk a black hole in the faintly phosphorescent ocean. Pale yellow radiance shone from a few windows in the accommodation towers, and floodlights illuminated all the quays. It was 4 a.m. local time, most of the inhabitants were asleep.

Walter Harman set the spaceplane down on pad eighteen with only a minor wobble.

Welcome to Pernik, the personality said formally.

Thank you, Lewis replied.

Eysk is approaching. His family runs one of our premier fishing enterprises. He should be able to fill your requirements.

Excellent, Lewis said. **My thanks again for receiving me so promptly. I have spent weeks on that Adamist starship; it was becoming somewhat claustrophobic. I understand.**

Lewis wasn't sure, but he thought there was a mild dose of puzzlement in the personality's tone. Too late now, though, they were down. Excitement was spilling into his blood. His part of the scheme was by far the most important.

The airlock opened with a couple of jerky motions as the actuators suffered power surges. Lewis went down the aluminium stairs.

Eysk was walking across the polyp apron towards pad eighteen. A ridge of electrophorescent cells circling the pad were casting an austere light over the spaceplane. Lewis could see very little of the island beyond; there was one accommodation tower forming a slender black rectangle against the night sky, and the sound of waves sloshing against the rim came from the other side of the spaceplane.

"Keep him busy," Lewis ordered Walter Harman as the pilot followed him down the stairs.

"No problem, I've got a thousand dumb questions lined up. Atlantis hadn't been discovered when I was alive."

Lewis reached the landing pad and tensed—this was it, make or break time. He had altered his facial features considerably during the starflight; that old journalist back on Lalonde had given him a nasty moment. He waited for the approaching Edenist to shout an alarm to the island.

Eysk gave a slight bow in greeting, and directed an identity trait at Lewis. He waited politely for Lewis to return the punctilio.

Lewis didn't have one. He hadn't known. His only source of data on Edenist customs was far beyond his grasp.

Deep down at the centre of his brain there was a presence, the soul which used to own the body he now possessed. A prisoner held fast by the manacle bonds of Lewis's thoughts.

All of the possessors had a similar prisoner, visualized as a tiny homunculus contained within a sphere of cephalic glass. They pleaded and they begged to be let out, to come back; annoying background voices, a gnat's buzz across consciousness. The possessed could use them, torment them with glimpses of reality in return for information, learning how to blend in with the modern, starkly alien society into which they had come forth.

But the centre of Lewis's mind contained only a heavy

darkness. He hadn't told the others that, they were all so boastful of how they controlled their captives, so he just brazened it out. The soul he had usurped as he came to this body neither entreated nor threatened. Lewis knew it was there, he could sense the surface thoughts, cold and hard, formidable with resolution. Waiting. The entity frightened him, he had come to possess the body the same way he had walked Messopia's corridors, The King of Strut—thinking he could handle it. Now the first fractures of insecurity in his hyped-up confidence were multiplying. The usurped soul's personality was far stronger than him; he could never have withstood such dread isolation, not simply beyond sensation, but knowing sensation was possible. What kind of person could?

Are you all right? Eysk asked kindly.

I'm sorry. I think it may have been something I ate. And the ride down was a god-fucking bitch.

Eysk's eyebrow rose. **Indeed?**

Yeah, feel like I'm gonna puke. Be all right in a minute.

I do hope so.

"This is Walter Harman," Lewis said out loud, knowing he was making a colossal balls-up of things. "A pilot, so he claims. After that flight, think I'm going to ask the captain for a dekko at his licence." He laughed at his witticism.

Walter Harman smiled broadly, and put out his hand. "Pleasure to meet you. This is one hell of a planet. I've never been here before."

Eysk seemed taken aback. "Your enthusiasm is most gratifying. I hope you enjoy your stay."

"Thanks. Say, I tasted some gollatail a year back, have you got any round here?"

I'm just going for a walk, get some air, Lewis said. Down in his memories were a thousand hangovers; he gathered together the phantom sensation of nausea and cranial malaise, then broadcast them into the affinity band. **It ought to clear my head.**

Eysk flinched at the emetic deluge. **Quite.**

"I'd like to try some again, maybe take back a stock of my own," Walter Harman prompted. "Old Lewis here can tell you what our ship's rations are like."

"Yes," Eysk said. "I believe we have some." His gaze never left Lewis's back.

"Great, that's just great."

Lewis stepped over the half-metre ridge of electrophorescent cells around the pad, and headed towards the island's rim. There was one of the floating quays ahead, a twenty-metre crane to one side for lifting smaller boats out of the water.

Sorry about this, Lewis told the island personality. **A flight has never had this effect before.**

Do you require a medical nanonic package?

Let's leave it a minute and see. Sea wind always was the best cure for headaches.

As you wish.

Lewis could hear Walter Harman chattering away inanely behind him. He reached the metal railing that guarded the rim, and stood beside the crane. It was a spindly column and boom arrangement made from monobonded carbon struts, lightweight and strong. But heavy enough for his purpose. He closed his eyes, focusing his attention on the structure, feeling its texture, the rough grain of carbon crystals held together with hard plies of binding molecules. Atoms glowed scarlet and yellow, their electrons flashing in tight fast orbits.

Miscreant energistic pulses raced up and down the struts, sparking between molecules. He felt the others in the spaceplane cabin lending their strength, concentrating on a point just below the boom pivot. The carbon's crystalline lattice began to break down. Spears of St Elmo's fire flickered around the pivot.

A tortured creaking sound washed across the rim of the island. Eysk looked round in confusion, peering against pad eighteen's glare.

Lewis, move now please, the island personality said.

Unidentified static discharge on the crane. It is weak-ening the structure.

Where? He played it dumb, looking round, looking up.

Lewis, move.

The compulsion almost forced his legs into action. He fought it with bursts of mystification, then panic. Remembering the power blade as it descended, the sight of blood and chips of bone spewing out of the wound. It hadn't happened to him, it was some horror holo he was watching on the screen. Distant. Remote.

Lewis!

Carbon shattered with a sudden thunderclap. The boom jerked, then began to fall, curving down in that unreal slow motion he'd seen once before. And nothing had to be faked any more. Fear staked him to the ground. A yell started to emerge from his lips—

—Mistake. Your greatest and your last, Lewis. When this body dies my soul will be free. And then I can return to possess the living. And when that happens I will have the same power as you. After that we shall meet as equals, I promise you—

—as the edge of the boom smashed into his torso. There was no pain, shock saw to that. Lewis was aware of the boom finishing its work, crushing him against the polyp. Body ruined.

His head hit the ground with a brutish smack, and he gazed up mutely at the stars. They started to fade.

Transfer, Pernik ordered. The mental command was thick with sympathy and sorrow.

His eyes closed.

Pernik awaited. Lewis saw it through a long dark tunnel, a vast bitek construct glowing with the gentle emerald aura of life. Colourful phantom shapes slithered below its translucent surface, tens of thousands of personalities, at once separate and in concord: the multiplicity. He felt himself drifting towards it along the affinity bond, his energistic nexus abandoning the mangled body to infiltrate the naked colossus. Behind him the dark soul rose as smoothly as a shark seeking wounded prey to re-inherit the dying body. Lewis's tightly whorled thoughts quaked in fright as he reached the island's vast neural strata. He penetrated the surface, and diffused himself throughout the network, instantly surrounded by a babble of sights and sounds. The multiplicity murmuring amongst itself, autonomic subroutines emitting pulses of strictly functional information.

His dismay and disorientation was immediately apparent. Ethereal tentacles of comfort reached out to reassure him.

Don't worry, Lewis. You are safe now . . .
—
What are you?

The multiplicity recoiled from him, a tide of thoughts in swift retreat, leaving him high and dry. Splendidly alone. Emergency autonomic routines to isolate him came online, erecting axon blockades around the swarm of neural cells in which he resided.

Lewis laughed at them. Already his thoughts were spread through more cells than the body which he'd abandoned had contained. The energistic flux resulting from such possession was tremendous. He thought of fire, and began to extend himself, burning through the multiplicity's simplistic protection, seeping through the neural strata like a wave of searing lava, obliterating anything in his path. Cell after cell fell to his domination. The multiplicity shrieked, trying to resist him. Nothing could. He was bigger than them, bigger than worlds. Omnipotent. The cries began to die away as he engulfed them, receding as though they were falling down some shaft that pierced clean to the planet's core. Squeezing. Compressing their fluttering panicked thoughts together. The polyp itself was next, contaminated by swaths of energy seething out of the transdimensional twist. Organs followed, even the thermal potential cables dangling far below the surface. He possessed every living cell of Pernik. At the heart of his triumphant mind the multiplicity lay silent, stifled.

He waited for a second, savouring the nirvana-high of absolute mastery. Then the terror began.

Eysk had started to run towards the rim as the crane creaked and groaned. Pernik showed him the boom starting to topple down. He knew he was too late, that there was nothing he could do to save the strangely idiosyncratic Edenist from Jospool. The boom picked up speed, slamming into the apparently dumbfounded Lewis. Eysk closed his eyes, mortified by the splash of gore.

Calm yourself, the personality said. **His head survived the impact. I have his thoughts.**

Thank goodness. Whatever caused the crane to fail like that? I've never seen such lightning on Atlantis before.

It . . . I . . .

Pernik?

The mental wail which came down the affinity link seemed capable of bursting Eysk's skull apart. He dropped to his knees, clamping his hands to his head, vision washed out by a blinding red light. Steel claws were burrowing up out of the affinity link, ripping through the delicate membranes inside his brain, shiny silver smeared with blood and viscid cranial fluid.

"Poor Eysk," a far-off chorus spoke directly into his mind—so very different to affinity, so very insidious. "Let us help you." The promise of pain's alleviation hummed in the air all around.

Even numbed and bruised he recognized the gentle offer for the Trojan it was. He blinked tears from his eyes, closing his mind to affinity. And he was abruptly alone, denied even an echo of the emotional fellowship he had shared for his entire life. The grotesque mirage of the claw vanished. Eysk let out a hot breath of relief. The polyp below his trembling hands was glowing a sickly pink—that was real.

"What—"

Hairy cloven feet shuffled into view. He gasped and looked up. The hominid creature with a black-leather wolf's head howled victoriously and reached down for him.

Laton opened his eyes. His crushed, faltering body was suffused with pain. It wasn't relevant, so he ignored it. There wasn't going to be much time before oxygen starvation started to debilitate his reasoning. Physical shock was already making concentration difficult. He quickly loaded a sequence of localized limiter routines into the neuron cells buried beneath the polyp on which he was pinned by the twisted crane boom. Developed for his Jantrit campaign, their sophistication was orders of magnitude above the usual diversionary orders juvenile Edenists employed to avoid parental supervision. Firstly he regularized the image which the surrounding sensitive cells were supplying to the neural strata, freezing the picture of his body.

At that point his heart gave its last beat. He could sense the desperate attempts by the multiplicity to ward off Lewis's subsumption of the island. Laton was banking everything on the primitive street boy using brute force to take over. Sure enough Lewis's eerily potent, but crude, thought currents flowed through the neural strata below, flushing every other routine before him; though even his augmented power failed to root out Laton's subversive routines. They were symbiotic rather than parasitic, working within the controlling personality not against it. It would take a highly experienced Edenist bitek neuropathologist to even realize they were there, let alone expunge them.

Laton's lips gave a final quirk of contempt. He cleared a storage section in the neuron cells, and transferred his personality into it. His final act before consciousness and memory sank below the polyp was to trigger the proteanic virus infecting every cell in his body.

Mosul dreamed. He was lying in bed in his accommodation tower flat, with Clio beside him. Mosul woke. He looked down fondly at the sleeping girl; she was in her early twenties with long dark hair and a pretty flattish face. The sheet had slipped from her shoulders, revealing a pert rounded breast. He bent over to kiss the nipple. She stirred, smiling dreamily as his tongue traced a delicate circle. A warm overspill of gently erotic images came foaming out of her drowsy mind.

Mosul grinned in anticipation, and woke. He frowned down in puzzlement at the sleeping girl beside him. The bedroom was illuminated by a sourceless rosy glow. It shaded Clio's silky skin a dark burgundy colour. He shook the sleep from his head. They had been making love for hours last night, he was entitled to some lassitude after that.

She responded eagerly to his kisses, throwing aside the sheet so he could feast on the sight of her. Her skin hardened and wrinkled below his touch. When he looked up in alarm she had become a cackling white-haired crone.

The pink light shifted into bright scarlet, as though the room was bleeding. He could see the polyp walls palpitating. In the distance a giant heartbeat thudded.

Mosul woke. The room was illuminated by a sourceless rosy glow. He was sweating, it was intolerably hot.

Pernik, I'm having a nightmare . . . I think. Am I awake now?

Yes, Mosul.

Thank goodness. Why is it so hot?

Yes, you are having a nightmare. My nightmare.

Pernik!

Mosul woke, jerking up from the bed. The bedroom walls were glowing red; no longer safe hard polyp but a wet meat traced with a filigree of purple-black veins. They oscillated like jelly. The heartbeat sounded again, louder than before. A damp acrid smell tainted the air.

Pernik! Help me.

No, Mosul.

What are you doing?

Clio rolled over and laughed at him. Her eyes were featureless balls of jaundiced yellow. "We're coming for you,

Mosul, you and all your kind. Smug arrogant bastards that you are."

She elbowed him in the groin. Mosul shouted at the vicious pain, and tumbled off the raised sponge cushion which formed his bed. Sour yellow vomit trickled out of his mouth as he writhed about on the slippery floor.

Mosul woke. It was real this time, he was sure of that. Everything was dangerously clear to his eyes. He was lying on the floor, all tangled up in the sheets. The bedroom glowed red, its walls raw stinking meat.

Clio was locked in her own looped nightmare, hands raking the top of the bed, staring sightlessly at the ceiling. Unformed screams stalled in her throat, as though she was choking. Mosul tried to get up, but his feet slithered all over the slimed quaking floor. He directed an order at the door muscle membrane. Too late he saw its shape had changed from a vertical oval to a horizontal slash. A giant mouth. It parted, giving him a brief glimpse of stained teeth the size of his feet, then thick yellow vomit discharged into the bedroom. The torrent of obscenely fetid liquid hit him straight on, lifting him up and throwing him against the back wall. He didn't dare cry out, it would be in his mouth. His arms thrashed about, but it was like paddling in glue. There seemed no end to the cascade, it had risen above his knees. Clio was floundering against the wall a couple of metres away, her body spinning in the hard current. He couldn't reach her. The vomit's heat was powerful enough to enervate his muscles, and the stomach acid it contained was corroding his skin. It had risen up to his chest. He struggled to stay upright. Clio had disappeared below the surface, not even waking from her nightmare. And still more poured in.

As far as Lewis Sinclair was aware, Laton's corpse lay perfectly still under the crumpled crane boom. Not that he bothered to check. Pernik Island was big, much larger than his imagination had ever conceived it, and for someone with his background difficult to comprehend. Every second yelled for his attention as he sent out phobic fantasies through his affinity bonds with the slumbering populace, invading their dreams, breaking their minds wide open with insane fear so more souls could come through and begin their reign of possession. He ignored the bitek's tedious minutiae—autonomic organ functions, the monitoring routines which the old multiplicity employed, enacting muscle membrane functions. All he cared about was eliminating the remaining Edenists; that task received his total devotion.

The island's cells glimmered a faint pink as a result of the energistic arrogation, even the shaggy coat of moss shone as though imbued with firefly luminescence. Pernik twinkled like a fabulous inflamed ruby in the funereal gloom of Atlantis's moonless night, sending radiant fingers probing down through the water to beckon curious fish. An observer flying overhead would have noticed flashes of blue light pulsing at random from the accommodation tower windows, as though stray lightning bolts were being flung around the interior.

Long chill screams reverberated around the borders of the park, emerging from various archways at the base of the towers. By the time they reached the rim they had blended into an almost musical madrigal, changes in pitch matching the poignant lilt of the waves washing against the polyp.

Housechimps scampered about, yammering frantically at each other. Their control routines had been wiped clean by Lewis's relentless purge of the multiplicity and all its subsidiaries, and long-suppressed simian tribal traits were surfacing. Fast, violent fights broke out among them as they instinctively fled into the thicker spinneys growing in the park.

The remaining sub-sentient servitor creatures, all eighteen separate species necessary to complement the island's static organs, either froze motionless or performed their last assigned task over and over again.

Unnoticed amid the bedlam and horror, Laton's corpse was quietly dissolving into protoplasmic soup.

Edenist biotechnicians examining the wreckage of Jantrit had called the process Laton used to doctor the habitat's neural strata a proteanic virus. In fact, it was far more complex than that. Affinity-programmable organic molecules was a term one researcher used.

Deeply disturbed by the technology and its implications, the Jovian consensus released little further information. Research continued, a classified high-priority project, which concentrated on developing methods to warn existing habitats of the sub-nanonic weapon being deployed against them, and a means of making future habitats (and people) immune. Progress over the intervening forty years was slow but satisfactory.

Of course, unknown to the Edenists, at the same time Laton was equally busy on Lalonde refining his process, and meeting with considerable success.

In its passive state, the updated proteanic virus masqueraded as inert organelles within his body cells—no matter what their nature, from liver to blood corpuscles, muscles to hair. When his last affinity command activated them, each organelle released a batch of plasmids (small, artificially synthesized DNA loops) and a considerable quantity of transcription factors, proteins capable of switching genes on or off. Once the plasmids had been inserted into the cell's DNA, mitosis began, forcing the cells to reproduce by division. Transcription factors switched off the human DNA completely, as well as an entire series of the new plasmids, leaving them to be carried passively while just one type of plasmid was activated to designate the function of the new cell. It was a drastic mutation. Hundreds of thousands of Laton's cells were already dying, millions more were killed by the induced mitosis; but over half fissioned successfully, turning into specialist diploid gametes.

They spilled out of the arms, legs, and collar of his one-piece ship-suit in a magenta sludge, draining away from stubborn clusters of dead cells that retained their original pattern—kernels of lumpy organs, slender ribs, a rubbery dendritic knot of veins. As they spread across the polyp they started to permeate the surface, slipping through microscopic gaps in the grainy texture, seeping down towards the neural stratum four metres below. Pernik's nutrient capillaries and axon conduits speeded their passage.

Four hours later, when dawn was breaking over the condemned island, the majority of the gametes had reached the neural stratum. Stage two of the proteanic virus was different. A gamete would penetrate a neural cell's membrane and release the mission-specific plasmid Laton had selected (he had four hundred to choose from). The plasmid was accompanied by a transcription factor which would activate it.

Mitosis produced a neuron cell almost identical to the original it replaced. Once begun, the reproduction cycle was unstoppable; new cells started to supplant old at an ever-increasing rate. A chain reaction of subtle modification began to ripple out from the rim of the island. It went on for a considerable time.

Admiral Kolhammer was almost correct about Time Universe beating the Edenists to inform the Confederation about Laton. Several dozen star systems heard the news from the company first. Governments were put in an embarrassing position of knowing less than Time Universe until the voidhawks carrying diplomatic fleks from Admiral Aleksandrovich and the Confederation Assembly President arrived, clarifying the situation.

Naturally enough, public perception was focused almost exclusively on Laton: the threat from the past risen like the devil's own phoenix. They wanted to know what was being done to track him down and exterminate him. They were quite vociferous about it.

Presidents, kings, and dictators alike had to release statements assuring their anxious citizens that every resource was being deployed to locate him.

Considerably less attention was drawn to the apparent persona sequestration of Lalonde's population. Graeme

Nicholson hadn't placed much emphasis on the effect, keeping it at the rumour level. It wasn't until much later that news company science editors began to puzzle about the cost-effectiveness of sequestrating an entire backward colony world, and question exactly what had happened in the Quallheim Counties. Laton's presence blinded them much as it did everyone else. He was on Lalonde, therefore Lalonde's uprising problem was instigated by him. QED.

Privately, governments were extremely worried by the possibility of an undetectable energy virus that could strike at people without warning. Dr Gilmore's brief preliminary report on Jacqueline Couteur was not released for general public access.

Naval reserve officers were called in, warships were placed on combat alert and brought up to full flight-readiness status. Laton gave governments the excuse to instigate rigorous screening procedures for visiting starships. Customs and Immigration officers were told to be especially vigilant for any electronic warfare nanonics.

There was also an unprecedented degree of cooperation between star systems' national groupings to ensure that the warning reached everybody and was taken seriously. Within a day of a flek courier voidhawk arriving, even the smallest, most distant asteroid settlement was informed and urged to take precautions.

Within five days of Admiral Lalwani dispatching the voidhawks, the entire Confederation had been told, with just a few notable exceptions. Most prominent of these were starships in transit.

Oenone raced in towards Atlantis at three gees. There were only sixty cases of Norfolk Tears left clamped into its lower hull cargo bay. Since leaving Norfolk, Syrinx had flown to Auckland, a four-hundred-light-year trip. Norfolk Tears increased in price in direct proportion to the distance from Norfolk, and Auckland was one of the richer planets in its sector of the Confederation. She had sold sixty per cent of her cargo to a planetary retailer, and another thirty per cent to a family merchant enterprise in one of the system's Edenist habitats. It was the first shipment the Auckland system had seen for fifteen months, and the price it raised had been appropriately phenomenal. They had already paid off the Jovian Bank loan and made a respectable profit. Now she was back to honour her deal with Eysk's family.

She looked through *Oenone*'s sensor blisters at the planet as they descended into equatorial orbit. Cool blues and sharp whites jumbled together in random splash patterns. Memories played below her surface thoughts, kindled by the sight of the infinite ocean. Mosul's smiling face.

We're not going to stay very long, are we? *Oenone* asked plaintively.

Why? she teased. Don't you like talking to the islands? They make a change from habitats.

You know why.

You stayed in Norfolk orbit for over a week.

I had lots of voidhawks to talk to. There are only fifteen here.

Don't worry. We won't stay long. Just enough time to unload the Norfolk Tears, and for me to see Mosul.

I like him.

Thank you for the vote of confidence. While we're here, would you ask the islands to see if anyone has a cargo they need shipping outsystem.

I'll start now.

Can you give me a link through to Mosul first, please.

It is midnight on Pernik. The personality says Mosul is unobtainable at the moment.

Oh dear. I wonder what her name is?

Syrinx.

Yes?

Pernik is wrong.

What do you mean? Mosul is available?

No, I mean the personality is different, altered. There is no joy in its thoughts.

Syrinx opened her eyes and stared round the contoured

walls of her cabin. Familiar trinkets she had picked up on
her voyages were lined up in glass-fronted alcoves. Her
eyes found the fifteen-centimetre chunk of whalebone
carved into a squatting Eskimo which Mosul had given her.
But *Oenone*'s unease was too unsettling for the crude
statue to register the way it usually did, bringing forth a
warm recollection intrinsic to both of them.

**Perhaps there has been an accident on one of the
fishing boats,** she suggested.

Then the grief should be shared, as is proper.

Yes.

Pernik hides behind a facade of correctness.

Is Eysk available?

One moment.

Syrinx felt the voidhawk's mind reach out, then Eysk
was merging his thoughts with her. Still the same old kind-
hearted family elder, with that deeper layer of toughness
that made him such a shrewd businessman.

Syrinx, he exclaimed happily, **we were wondering
where you had got to.**

Did you think I'd skipped out on you?

Me? He projected mock horror. **Not at all. The arrest
warrant we had drawn up was a mere precaution.**

She laughed. **I've brought your cases of Norfolk
Tears.**

How many?

Sixty.

**Ah well, my family will be through that lot before the
week's out. Are you coming down tonight?**

Yes, if it's not too late.

**Not at all. I'll have some servitors lined up to unload
your flyer by the time you get down.**

Fine. Is everything all right on the island?

There was a moment's hesitation, a thought-flash of bemused incomprehension. **Yes. Thank you for asking.**

Is Mosul there?

Sex, that's all you young people think of.

We learn by example. Is he there?

Yes. But I don't think Clio will welcome an interruption right now.

Is she very pretty?

Yes. He generated an image of a girl's grinning face, half hidden by long dark hair. **She's bright, too. They are on the point of formalizing the arrangement.**

I'm happy for him, for both of them.

Thank you. Don't tell Mosul I said so, but she'll make a splendid addition to the family.

That's nice. I'll see you in a couple of hours.

I'll look forward to it. Just remember, Mosul learnt everything he knows from me.

As if I could forget. She broke the contact.

Well? Oenone asked.

I don't know. Nothing I could put my finger on, but he was definitely stilted.

Shall I ask the other islands?

Goodness, no. I'll find out what's troubling them once I'm down. Mosul will tell me, he owes me that much.

Hooked into the flyer's sensors, Syrinx couldn't be sure, but Pernik appeared aged somehow. Admittedly it was darkest night, but the towers had a shabby look, almost mouldered. They put her in mind of Earth's Empire State Building, now carefully preserved in its own dome at the centre of the New York arcology. Structurally sound, but unable to throw off the greying weight of centuries.

Thirty-two years old, and you see everything in such jaded terms, she told herself wearily. Pity that Mosul had formed a permanent attachment, though. He would have made a good father.

She clucked her tongue in self-admonition. But then her mother had conceived two children by the time she was thirty.

There's always Ruben, Oenone suggested.

It wouldn't be fair to him, not even to ask. He'd feel obligated to say yes.

I would like you to have a child. You are feeling incomplete. It upsets you. I don't like that.

I am not feeling incomplete!

You haven't even prepared any zygotes for my children yet. You should think about these things.

Oh goodness. You're starting to sound like Mother.

I don't know how to lie.

Rubbish!

Not to you. And it was you who was thinking of Mosul in that light.

Yes. Syrinx stopped trying to argue, it was stupidly blinkered. What would I do without you?

Oenone wrapped her thoughts with a loving embrace, and for a moment Syrinx imagined the flyer's ion field had leaked inside the cabin, filling it with golden haze.

They landed on one of the pads in the commercial section. The electrophorescent-cell ridge around the metal grid shone with a strong pink radiance. Few of the accommodation tower windows were lit.

It looks like they're in mourning, Syrinx said to Oxley in singular engagement mode as she walked down the aluminium stair. They had flown down alone so that the little flyer could carry more cargo, but it was still going to take three trips to bring all sixty cases down.

Yes. He glanced about, frowning. **There aren't many fishing boats in dock, either.**

Eysk and Mosul walked out of the shadows beyond the ridge.

Syrinx forgot everything else as Mosul sent out a burst of rapturous greeting, mingled with mischievously erotic subliminals.

She put her arms around him and enjoyed a long kiss.

I'd like to meet her, she told him. **Lucky thing that she is.**

You shall.

They stood about on the pad, chatting idly, as the island's lizard-skinned housechimps unloaded the first batch of cases under Oxley's careful direction and stacked them on a processor-controlled flat-top trolley. When all eighteen cases were on, the drone trundled off towards one of the low warehouse domes ringing the park.

Do you want me to bring the rest down tonight? Oxley asked.

Please, Eysk said. **I have already organized sales with other families.**

The pilot nodded, winked at Syrinx, who was still standing with Mosul's arm around her shoulder, and went back into the flyer. Sitting in the command seat he linked his mind with the controlling processor array.

Something was affecting the coherent magnetic-field generation. It took a long time to form, and he had to bring compensator programs on-line. By the time he finally lifted from the pad the fusion generator was operating alarmingly close to maximum capacity.

He almost turned back there and then. But once he rose above a hundred metres the field stabilized rapidly. He had to cut the power levels back. Diagnostic programs reported the systems were all functioning flawlessly.

With a quick curse directed at all Kulu-produced machinery, he ordered the flight computer to design an orbital-injection trajectory that would bring him to a rendezvous with *Oenone*.

See you in three hours, Syrinx called as the sparkling artificial comet performed a tight curve around the accommodation towers before soaring up into the night sky.

Three hours! Oxley let his groan filter back down the affinity link.

You're professionals. You can handle it.

He put the flyer into a steep climb. One thing about an oceanic world, there was no worry about supersonic-boom footprints stomping all over civic areas. He was doing Mach two by the time he was fifteen kilometres away.

Pernik vanished from his affinity perception. Ordinarily a contact would simply fade with distance until it was no more. But this was different, like steel shutters slamming into place. Oxley was over a hundred and fifty years old, in his time he'd visited almost ninety per cent of the Confederation, and he had never known an Edenist habitat to react in such a manner. It was alien to the whole creed of consensual unity.

He switched in the aft sensors. A luminous red pearl haunted the horizon, sending shimmer-spears of light dancing across the black water.

"What is . . ." The words dried up at the back of his throat.

Pernik? he demanded. **Pernik, what is going on? What is that light?**

The silence was total. There wasn't the slightest trace of the personality's thoughts left anywhere in the affinity band.

Syrinx?

Nothing.

***Oenone*, something's happening on Pernik, can you reach Syrinx?**

She is there, the worried voidhawk answered. **But I cannot converse with her. Something is interfering.**

Oh, heavens. He banked the flyer round, heading back for the island.

Affinity broadened out from the single tenuous thread to the orbiting voidhawk, offering him the support of innumerable minds combining into a homogenized entity, buoying him up on a tide of intellect. He wasn't alone, and he wasn't anxious any more. Doubts and personal fears bled away, exchanged for confidence and determination, a much-needed reinforcement of his embattled psyche. For a moment, flying over the gargantuan ocean in a tiny machine, he had been horribly lonely; now his kind had joined him, from the eager honoured enthusiasms of sixteen-year-olds up to the glacial thoughts of the islands themselves. He felt like a child again, comforted by the loving arms of an adult, wiser and stronger. It was a reconfirmation of Edenism which left him profoundly grateful for the mere privilege of belonging.

This is Thalia Island, Oxley, we are aware of Pernik's

withdrawal from affinity and we are summoning a planetary consensus to deal with the problem.

That red lighting effect has me worried, he replied. The flyer had dropped below subsonic again. Pernik gleamed a sickly vermilion eight kilometres away.

Around the planet, consensus finalized, bringing together every sentient entity in an affinity union orchestrated by the islands. Information, such as it had, was reviewed, opinions formed, discussed, discarded, or elaborated. Two seconds after considering the problem the consensus said: We believe it to be Laton. A ship of the same class as the *Yaku* arrived last night and sent a spaceplane down to the island. From that time onward Pernik's communication has declined by sixty per cent.

Laton? The appalled question came from *Oenone* and its crew.

Yes. The Atlantean consensus summarized the information that had been delivered by a voidhawk two days earlier. As we have no orbital stations our checks on arriving ships were naturally less than ideal, depending solely on civil traffic control satellite-platform sensors. The ship has of course departed, but the spaceplane remained. Pernik and its population must have been sequestrated by the energy virus.

Oh no, Oxley cried brokenly. Not him. Not again.

Ahead of him, Pernik issued a brilliant golden light, as though sunrise had come to the ocean. The flyer gave a violent lurch to starboard, and began to lose height.

Syrinx watched the little flyer disappear into the east. The night air was cooler than she remembered from her last visit, bringing up goosebumps below her ship-tunic. Mosul, who was dressed in a baggy sleeveless sweatshirt and shorts, seemed completely unaffected. She eyed him with a degree of annoyance. Macho outdoors type.

This Clio was a lucky woman.

Come along, Eysk said. The family is dying to meet

you again. You can tell the youngsters what Norfolk was like.

I'd love to.

Mosul's arm tightened that bit extra round her shoulder as they headed for the nearest tower. Almost proprietary, she thought.

Mosul, she asked on singular engagement, **what's wrong down here? You all seem so tense.** It was a struggle to convey the emotional weight she wanted.

Nothing is wrong. He smiled as they passed under the archway at the foot of the tower.

She stared at him, dumbfounded. He had answered on the general affinity band, an extraordinary breach of protocol.

Mosul caught her expression, and sent a wordless query.

This is . . . she began. Then her thoughts flared in alarm. *Oenone*, she couldn't perceive *Oenone*! "Mosul! It's gone. No, wait. I can feel it, just. Mosul, something is trying to block affinity."

"Are they?" His smile hardened into something which made her jerk away in consternation. "Don't worry, little Syrinx. Delicate, beautiful little Syrinx, so far from home. All alone. But we treasure you for the gift you bring. We are going to welcome you into a brotherhood infinitely superior to Edenism."

She spun round, ready to run. But there were five men standing behind her. One of them—she gasped—his head had grown until it was twice the size it should be. His features were a gross caricature, cheeks deep and lined, eyes wide and avian; his nose was huge, coming to a knife edge that hung below his black lips, both ears were pointed, rising above the top of his skull.

"What are you?" she hissed.

"Don't mind old Kincaid," Mosul said. "Our resident troll."

It was getting lighter, the kind of liquid redness creeping across the island's polyp which she associated with Duchess-night on Norfolk. Her legs began to shake. It was shameful, but she was so alone. Never before had she been denied the community of thoughts that was the wonder of Edenism. *Oenone!* The desperate shout crashed around the confines of her own skull. *Oenone,* **my love. Help me!**

There was an answer. Not coherent, nothing she could perceive, decipher. But somewhere on the other side of the blood-veiled sky the voidhawk cried in equal anguish.

"Come, Syrinx," Mosul said. He held out his hand. "Come with us."

It wasn't Mosul. She knew that now.

"Never."

"So brave," he said pityingly. "So foolish."

She was physically strong, her genes gave her that much. But there were seven of them. They half carried, half pushed her onwards.

The walls became strange. No longer polyp but stone. Big cubes hewn from some woodland granite quarry; and old, the age she thought she had seen on the approach flight. Water leaked from the lime-encrusted mortar, sliming the stone.

They descended a spiral stair which grew narrower until only one of them could march beside her. Syrinx's shiptunic sleeve was soon streaked with water and coffee-coloured fungus. She knew it wasn't real, that it couldn't be happening. There was no "down" in an Atlantean island. Only the sea. But her feet slipped on the worn steps, and her calves ached.

There was no red glow in the bowels of the island. Flaming torches in black iron brands lighted their way. Their acrid smoke made her eyes water.

The stairway came out onto a short corridor. A sturdy oak door was flung open, and Syrinx shoved through. Inside was a medieval torture chamber.

A wooden rack took up the centre of the room; iron chains wound round wheels at each end, manacles open and waiting. A brazier in one corner was sending out waves of heat from its radiant coals. Long slender metal instruments were plunged into it, metal sharing the furnace glow.

The torturer himself was a huge fat man in a leather jerkin. Rolls of hairy flesh spilled over his waistband. He stood beside the brazier, cursing the slender young woman who was bent over a pair of bellows.

"This is Clio," Mosul's stolen body said. "You did say you wanted to meet her."

The woman turned, and laughed at Syrinx.

"What is the point?" Syrinx asked weakly. Her voice was very close to cracking.

"This is in your honour," the torturer said. His voice was a deep bass, but soft, almost purring. "You, we shall have to be very careful with. For you come bearing a great gift. I don't want to damage it."

"What gift?"

"The living starship. These other mechanical devices for sailing the night gulf are difficult for us to employ. But your craft has elegance and grace. Once we have you, we have it. We can bring our crusade to new worlds with ease after that."

FLEE! Flee, *Oenone*. Flee this dreadful world, my love. And never come back.

"Oh, Syrinx." Mosul's handsome face wore the old sympathetic expression she remembered from such a time long ago now. "We have taken affinity from you. We have sent Oxley away. We have taken everybody from you. You are alone but for us. And believe me, we know what being alone does to an Edenist."

"Fool," she sneered. "That wasn't affinity, it is love which binds us."

"And we shall love the *Oenone* too," a musical chorus spoke to her.

She refused to show any hint of surprise. "*Oenone* will never love you."

"In time all things become possible," the witching chorus sang. "For are we not come?"

"Never," she said.

The corpulent paws of Kincaid the troll tightened around her arms.

Syrinx closed her eyes as she was forced towards the rack. This is not happening therefore I can feel no pain. This is not happening therefore I can feel no pain. Believe it!

Hands tore at the collar of her ship-tunic, ripping the fabric. Hot rancid air prickled her skin.

This is NOT happening therefore I can feel no pain. Not not not—

Ruben sat at his console station in *Oenone*'s bridge along with the rest of the crew. There were only two empty seats. Empty and accusing.

I should have gone down with her, Ruben thought. Maybe if I could have provided everything she needed from life she wouldn't have gone running to Mosul in the first place.

We all share guilt, Ruben, the Atlantean consensus said. **And ours is by far the larger failing for letting Laton come to this world. Your only crime is to love her.**

And fail her.

No. We are all responsible for ourselves. She knows that as well as you do. All individuals can ever do is share happiness wherever they can find it.

We're all ships that pass in the night?

Ultimately, yes.

Consensus was so large, so replete with wisdom, he found it easy to believe. An essential component of the quiddity.

She is in trouble down there, he said. **Frightened, alone. Edenists shouldn't be alone.**

I am with her, *Oenone* said. **She can feel me even though we cannot converse.**

We are doing what we can, the consensus said. **But this is not a world equipped for warfare.**

The part of Ruben which had joined with the consensus was suddenly aware of Pernik igniting to solar splendour—and he was sitting strapped into a metal flea that spun and tossed erratically as it fell from the sky.

SYRINX! *Oenone* cried. **Syrinx. Syrinx. Syrinx. Syrinx. Syrinx.**

The voidhawk's affinity voice was a thunderclap roar howling through the minds of its crew. Ruben thought he would surely be deafened. Serina sat with her mouth gaping wide, hands clamped over her ears, tears streaming down her face.

Oenone, **restrain yourself,** the consensus demanded.

But the voidhawk was beyond reason. It could feel its captain's pain, her hopelessness as the white-hot metal seared into her flesh with brutal intricate skill while in her heart she thought of nothing but their love. Lost in helpless rage its distortion effect twisted and churned like a frenzied captured beast pummelling at its cage bars.

Gravity rammed Ruben down into his seat, then swung severely. His arms outside the webbing were sucked up towards the ceiling, their weight quadrupling. *Oenone* was tumbling madly, its energy patterning cells sending out vast random surges of power.

Tula was yelling at the voidhawk to stop. Loose pieces of junk were hurtling round the bridge—cups and plastic meal trays, a jacket, cutlery, several circuit wafers. Gravity was fluctuating worse than a roller-coaster ride. One moment they appeared to be hanging upside-down, the next they were at right angles, and always weighing too much. A spinning circuit wafer sliced past Edwin, nicking his cheek. Blood squirted out.

Ruben could just make out the calls of the other voidhawks in orbit above Atlantis, trying to calm their rampant cousin. They all started to alter course for a rendezvous. Together their distortion fields could probably nullify *Oenone*'s supercharged flailings.

Then the most violent convulsion of all kicked the crew toroid. Ruben actually heard the walls give a warning creak. One of the consoles buckled, big skinlike creases appearing in its composite sides as it concertinaed down towards the decking. Coolant fluid and sparks burst out of the cracks. He must have blacked out for a second.

Gravity was at a forty-degree angle to the horizontal when he came to, and holding steady.

I'm coming. I'm coming. I'm coming, *Oenone* was braying.

Horrified, Ruben linked into the voidhawk's sensor blisters. They were heading down towards Atlantis at two and a half gees. Reaction to the berserker power thundering through the energy patterning cells made the muscles in his arms and legs bunch like hot ropes.

Fast-moving specks were rising above the hazy blue-white horizon, skimming over the atomic fog of the thermosphere like flat stones flung across a placid sea. The other voidhawks: their calls redoubled in urgency. But *Oenone* was immune to them, to the Atlantean consensus' imperious orders. Rushing to help its beloved.

They're too far away, Ruben realized in dismay, they won't reach us in time.

The consensus relaxed its contact with Oxley, allowing him complete independence to pilot the floundering flyer, letting his instinct and skill attempt to right the craft unencumbered. He shot order after order into the bitek processors, receiving a stream of systems information in return. The coherent magnetic generators were failing, databuses were glitched, the fusion generator was powering down, electron-matrix crystal power reserves were dropping. Whatever electronic warfare techniques Pernik had, they were the best he had ever encountered, and they were trying to kill him.

He concentrated on the few control channels which remained operational, reducing the spin and flattening out the dive. The faltering magnetic fields squeezed and pushed at glowing ion streams, countering the corkscrew trajectory. Black ocean and lustrous island chased each other round the sensor images at a decreasing rate.

There was no panic. He treated it as though it was just

another simulation run. An exercise in logic and competence set by the CAB to try and trip him.

At the back of his mind he was aware of further pandemonium breaking out amid the consensus. A ghost image lying across the flyer's sensor input visualization showed him *Oenone* plummeting towards the planet.

With only a kilometre of altitude left the flyer lost its spin. The nose was dangerously low. He poured the final power reserves into raising it, using the craft's ellipsoid surface as a blunt wing, gaining a degree of lift in an attempt to glide-curve away from the island. Distance was his only chance of salvation now. Streaks of reflected starlight blurred on the sable water below, growing closer. There was no sign of the electronic warfare assault abating.

Pernik's resplendent silhouette winked out. Silence detonated into the affinity consensus, absorbing the entire planet's mental voice.

Into the emptiness came a single devastating identity trait.

Your attention, please, Laton said. **We don't have much time.** *Oenone*, **resume your orbit now.**

The flyer's crashed systems abruptly sprang back into zealous life. And a shock-numbed Oxley was pressed deep into his seat as it vaulted back into the sky.

Lewis Sinclair watched keenly as the torturer manipulated Syrinx's mangled leg with a pair of ruddy glowing tongs and a mallet. She wasn't screaming so loudly now. The fight was going out of her. But not the spirit, he suspected. She was one tough lady. He had seen the type before back in Messopia; cops mainly, the special forces mob, hard-eyed and dedicated. A pusher Lewis worked for had captured one once, and it didn't matter what was done to the man, they couldn't get him to tell them anything.

Lewis didn't think the possessed were going to gain control of the voidhawk through Syrinx. But he didn't say anything, let them sweat it. It wasn't so much his problem, possessing the island gave him a measure of security a mere human body could never offer. The range of physical sensations and experiences available to him was truly astonishing.

The sensitive cells woven through the polyp were fantastically receptive; people with their mundane eyes and ears and nose were almost insensate by comparison. His consciousness roved at random through the huge structure, tasting and sampling. He was getting the hang of splitting himself into multiples, supervising a dozen actions at once.

Syrinx groaned again as the souls from beyond sang into her mind with their strange icy promises. And Lewis saw a girl standing at the back of the dungeon. The quake her presence sent through his psyche perceptibly rocked the entire island, as though it had ridden over a tidal wave. It was her! The girl from Messopia, Thérèse, the one he'd fought and died over.

Thérèse was tall for thirteen, skinny, with breasts that had been pushed into maturity by a course of tailored growth hormones. Long raven hair, brown eyes, and a pretty, juvenile face with just the right amount of cuteness; everybody's girl next door. She was wearing black leather shorts to show off her tight little arse, and her breasts were almost falling out of a scarlet halter top. Her pose was indolent, chewing at her gum, one hand on her hip.

Where the hell did she come from? Lewis asked.

What? the possessed Eysk asked.

Her. Thérèse. There, behind you.

Eysk turned round, then frowned angrily at the ceiling. **Very funny. Now fuck off.**

But—

Thérèse gave a bored sigh and sauntered out of the dungeon.

Can't you see her?

None of them answered him. He knew she was real, he could hear her *clicking* walk, feel the weight of her black stilettos on his polyp, olfactory cells picked up the sugary whiff of gum on her exhaled breath. She walked away from the dungeon, down a long corridor. For some reason it was difficult to keep his perception focused on her. She was only walking, but she seemed to be moving so fast. He barely noticed as the polyp of the corridor gave way to concrete. The light became a harsh electric yellow coming from bulbs on the ceiling, each one cupped by a protective wire cage. She hurried on ahead of him, feet sending out that regular *click click click* as her stilettos rapped the ground. His filthy jeans restricted his movements, clinging to his legs as he trailed after her. The air was cooler here, he could see his breath emerging as white streamers.

Thérèse slipped through a big set of grey-painted metal doors ahead. Lewis followed her into the empty subterranean warehouse in Messopia five hundred and fifty years ago. He gagged. It was a square chamber, sixty metres to a side, twenty metres high, rough poured concrete ribbed with steel beams coated in red-oxide paint. Striplights cast a feeble moon-white glow from on high. As before, leaking sewage pipes dripped rank liquids onto the floor.

She stood in the middle of the floor, looking at him expectantly.

He glanced down, seeing his body for the first time. "Oh no," he said in a desperate voice. "This isn't happening."

Loud, positive footsteps sounded from the far end of the warehouse. Lewis didn't wait to see who was emerging from the gloom, he spun round. There was no door any more, just a concrete wall. "Jesus Almighty. Fuck!"

"Hello, Lewis."

His body was compelled to turn, leg muscles working like dead meat fired by a cattle prod. He bit hard on his trembling lip.

Thérèse had gone. The person walking towards him was the body he had possessed on Lalonde.

"You're dead," Lewis whispered through a fear-knotted throat.

Laton merely smiled his superior smile. "Of all the people resident in this universe today, Lewis, you should know there is no such thing as death."

"I'm in charge here," Lewis yelled. "I am Pernik." He tried to fling the white fire, to conjure up energistic devastation, to flay the zombie to its stinking corrupt bones and beyond.

Laton halted five metres away. "You were Pernik. I told you once that we would meet again as equals. I lied. You cannot even begin to conceive the processes involved in your manifestation within this universe. You are a Neanderthal out of time, Lewis. You believed brute force was the key to conquest. Yet you failed to even think about the source of your energistic power. I know, I've been analysing your tiresomely sluggish thoughts ever since you possessed my body."

"What have you done to me?"

"Done? Why, Lewis, I have made you a part of me. Possession of the possessor. It is possible given the right circumstances. In this case I simply corrupted Pernik's neural stratum with my biological weapon. The neuron cells and nerve paths only conduct my thought impulses now. You can kill the cells, but you can't subvert them. It's a question of coding, you see. I know the codes, you don't. And please don't ask me for them, Lewis, it's nothing as simple as a number. You now operate only as a subsidiary part of me, you only think because I allow you to. That is how I summoned you here."

"I think because I am! I have been me for centuries, you bastard."

"And were you to go back there to the beyond, you would be you again. Free and independent. Do you want to go, Lewis? That is your escape from my bondage. In this universe you require a physical, living biological matrix in which to function. You may depart now if you wish."

A weight pulled at Lewis's belt. When he looked down he saw it was the power-blade knife hanging in its sheath. "No." He shook his head feebly, quailing at the prospect. "No, I won't. That's what you want. Without me Pernik would be free again. I'm going to stop that, I'm going to beat you."

"Don't flatter yourself, Lewis. I will never allow you to resume your barbaric act of sodomy. You think of yourself as strong, as purposeful. You are entirely incorrect. You and the other returners have a nebulous plan to re-establish yourselves permanently in this physical universe. You do so because of your own quite pathetic psychological weaknesses."

Lewis snarled at his tall tormentor. "So fucking smart, aren't you. Let's see what you're like after a hundred fucking years of nothing; no food, no breathing, no touch, just fucking nothing. You'll be begging to join us, shithead."

"Really?" Laton's smile no longer contained even a vestige of humour. "Think what you are, Lewis. Think what all the returners are. Then ask yourself, where is the rest of the human race? The hundreds of billions who have died since the day our ancestors first struck two flints together, from the time we watched the glaciers retreating as we battled with mammoths."

"They're with me, billions of them. They're waiting for their chance. And when they get into this universe they're gonna come gunning for you, shithead."

"But they're not with you in the beyond, Lewis, there are nothing like enough souls to account for everyone. You cannot lie to me, you are part of me. I know. They're not there. Ask yourself who and why, Lewis."

"Fuck you." Lewis drew the knife from its scabbard. He thumbed the switch in a smooth motion and the silver blade emitted a dangerous buzz.

"Lewis, kindly behave yourself; this is my perceptual reality, after all."

Lewis watched the solid blade curve round towards his fingers. He dropped the knife with a yell. It vanished before it reached the floor, making as little fuss as a snowflake landing on water. "What do you want with me?" He raised his clenched fists, knowing that it was all futile. He wanted to pound his knuckles into the concrete.

Laton took another few paces towards him. And Lewis

came to realize just how imposing the big Edenist was. It was all he could do not to back away.

"I want to make amends," Laton said. "At least part way. I doubt I will ever be fully forgiven in this universe, not for my crime. And it was a crime, I admit that now. You see, from you I have learnt how wrong I was before. Immortality is a notion we all grasp at because we can sense that there is continuity beyond death. It is an imperfect realization due to the weakness of the fusion between this continuum and the state of emptiness which follows. So much of our misunderstanding of life is rooted in this, so many wasted opportunities, so much religious claptrap born. I was wholly wrong to try and achieve a physical life extension, when corporeal life is but the start of existence. I was no better than a monkey trying to grasp a hologram banana."

"You're mad!" Lewis shouted recklessly. "You're fucking mad!"

Laton became pitying. "Not mad, but very human. Even in this hiatus state I have emotions. And I have weaknesses. One of them is the desire for revenge. But then you know all about that, don't you, Lewis? Revenge is a prime motivator; glands or no glands, chemical fury or otherwise. You burnt for it in the empty beyond, revenge on the living for the crime of living.

"Well, now I shall have my revenge for the agonies and degradations you so joyfully submitted my kind to. My kind being the Edenists. For I am one. At the end. Flawed, but proud of them, their silly pride and honour. They are a basically peaceful people, those of Pernik more than most, and you delighted in shattering their sanity. You also destroyed my children, and you revelled in it, Lewis."

"I still do! I hope it fucking hurt you watching! I hope the memory makes you scream at nights. I want you in pain, you shit, I want you weeping. If I'm part of your memories then you won't ever be able to forget, I won't let you."

"Oh, Lewis, haven't you learnt anything yet?" Laton

drew his own knife from a scabbard he brought into existence. Its wickedly thrumming power-blade was half a metre long. "I'm going to free Syrinx and warn the Atlantean consensus as to the exact nature of the threat they face. However, the remaining possessed do present a slight problem. So I need you to overcome them, Lewis. I shall consume you, completely."

"Never! I won't help."

Laton took a pace forwards. "It isn't a question of choice. Not on your part."

Lewis tried to run. Even though he knew it was impossible. The concrete closed in, shrinking the warehouse to the size of a tennis court, a room, a cube five metres across.

"I require control of the energistic spillover, Lewis. The power which comes from colliding continua. For that I must have the you which is you. I must complete my possession."

"No!" Lewis raised his arms as the blade came whistling down. Once again there was the dreadful grinding sound as bone was pierced and fragmented. A flash of intolerable pain followed by the devastating numbness. His blood spilled onto the floor in great spurts from his elbow stump.

"Goodbye, Lewis. It may be some time before we encounter one another again. But none the less I wish you luck in your search for me."

Lewis had collapsed twitching into a corner, soles of his boots slipping on his own blood. "Bastard," he spat through white lips. "Just do it. Get it over with and laugh, you shithead prick sucker."

"Sorry, Lewis. But like I told you, I shall consume you in your entirety. It's almost a vampiric process, really— though I expect that particular irony is sadly lost on you. And in order for the transfer to work you must remain conscious for the entire feast." Laton gave him a lopsided, half-apologetic smile.

The true meaning of what the Edenist was saying finally

sank in. Lewis started to scream. He was still screaming when Laton picked up his severed arm and bit into it.

Pernik's illumination returned to normality with eye-jarring suddenness. The accommodation towers blazed with diamond-blue light from every window, winding pathways through the park were set out by orange fairy lanterns, circular landing pads glowed hotly around the entire rim, the floating quays were like fluorescent roots radiating out into the opaque glassy water.

Oxley thought it looked quite magnificent. So cruelly treacherous, that a creation of such beauty could play host to the most heinous evil.

Land immediately please, Oxley, Laton said. **I don't have much time. They are resisting me.**

Land? Oxley felt his throat snarl up as outrage vied with a shaky form of laugh. **Show me where you are, and I'll come to you, Laton. I'll be doing around Mach twenty when we embrace. Show yourself!**

Don't be a fool. I am Pernik now.

Where's Syrinx?

She lives. *Oenone* will confirm that. But you must pick her up now, she requires urgent medical attention.

***Oenone*?** He sent the querying thought lancing upwards, while at the back of his mind he was aware of Laton delivering a vast quantity of information to the Atlantean consensus.

The voidhawk registered as a subdued jumble of thoughts. It had stopped its crazed descent; now it was rising laboriously up out of the mesosphere, its distortion effect generating barely a tenth of a gee.

***Oenone*, is she alive?**

Yes.

The emotional discharge in the voidhawk's thought brought tears to his eyes.

Oxley, Ruben called, **if there's any chance . . . please.**

OK. He studied the island. Pinpricks of light were blooming and dying right across it, stars with a lifetime measurable in fractions of a second. It looked quite magical, though he didn't like to dwell too hard upon what their cause would be.

Consensus, should I go in?

Yes. No other spaceplanes can reach Pernik in time. Trust Laton.

That was it, the universe had finally gone totally insane. **Oh, shit. OK, I'm taking the flyer down.**

Fires had taken hold in the central park when Oxley piloted the flyer down onto one of the pads. He could see a spaceplane further along the row, wings retracted, lying on its side with its undercarriage struts sticking up in the air and its fuselage cracked open around the midsection. Bodies were sprawled on the polyp around the base of the nearest accommodation tower; most of them looked as though they had been caught in a firestorm, skin blackened, faces unrecognizable, clothes still smoking.

An explosion sounded in the distance, and a ball of orange flame rolled out of a window on the other side of the park.

They are learning, Laton said impassively. **Grouped together they can ward off my energistic assaults. It won't do them any good in the long run, of course.**

Oxley's nerves were raw edged. He still thought this was some giant trap. The steel-clad jaws would snap shut any second; conversation might just be the trigger. **Where's Syrinx?**

Coming. Open the flyer airlock.

He felt the consensus balance his insecurities with an injection of urbane courage. Somehow he was giving the order to cut the ion field and open the airlock.

Faint shouts and the drawn out screeching of metal under tremendous stress penetrated the cabin. Oxley sniffed the air. Mingled with the brine was a frowsty putrescence which furred the roof of his mouth. With his hand clamped firmly over his nose he made his way aft.

Someone was walking towards the flyer. A giant, three

metres tall, hairless, naked skin a frail cream colour, virtually devoid of facial features. It was holding a figure in its outstretched arms.

"Syrinx," he gasped. He could feel *Oenone* pushing behind his eyes, desperate to see.

Three-quarters of her body was engulfed by green medical nanonic packages. But even that thick covering couldn't disguise the terrible damage inflicted on her limbs and torso.

The nanonic packages do not function well in this environment, Laton said as the giant mounted the flyer's airstairs. **Once you are airborne their efficiency will recover.**

Who did this?

I do not know their names. But I assure you the bodies they possessed have been rendered nonfunctional.

Oxley backed into the cabin, too shaken to offer further comment. Laton must have loaded an order into the flight-control processors, because the front passenger seat hinged open to form a flat couch. It was the one designed for transporting casualty cases. Basic medical monitor and support equipment slid out from recesses in the cabin wall above it.

The giant laid Syrinx down gently, then stood, its head touching the cabin ceiling. Oxley wanted to rush over to her, but all he could do was stare dumbly at the hulking titan. Its blank face crawled as though the skin was boiling. Laton looked down at him.

"Go to the Sol system," the simulacrum said. "There are superior medical facilities available there in any case. But the Jovian consensus must be informed of the true nature of the threat these returning souls pose to the Confederation; indeed to this whole section of the galaxy. That is your priority now."

Oxley managed to jerk a nod. "What about you?"

"I will hold the possessed off until you leave Pernik. Then I will begin the great journey." The big lips pressed together in compassion. "If it is of any comfort, you may tell our kind I am now truly sorry for Jantrit. I was utterly and completely wrong."

"Yes."

"I do not ask forgiveness, for it would not be in Edenism's power to grant. But tell them also that I came good in the end." The face managed a small, clumsy smile. "That ought to set the cat among the pigeons."

The giant turned and clumped out of the cabin. When it reached the top of the airlock stairs it lost all cohesion. A huge gout of milky white liquid sloshed down onto the metal grid of the landing pad, splattering the flyer's landing gear struts.

The flyer was five hundred kilometres from Pernik and travelling at Mach fifteen up through the ionosphere when the end came.

Laton waited until the diminutive craft was beyond any conceivable blast range, then used his all-pervasive control to release every erg of chemical energy stored in the island's cells simultaneously. It produced an explosion to rival an antimatter planetbuster strike. Several of the tsunami which raced out from the epicentre were powerful enough to traverse the world.

7

It was a quiet evening in Harkey's Bar. Terrance Smith's bold little fleet had departed the previous day, taking with it a good many regulars. The band audibly lacked enthusiasm, and only five couples were dancing on the floor. Gideon Kavanagh sat at one table; the medical nanonic package preparing his stump for a clone graft was deftly covered by a loose-fitting purple jacket. His companion was a slim twenty-five-year-old girl in a red cocktail dress who giggled a lot. A group of bored waitresses stood at one end of the bar, talking among themselves.

Meyer didn't mind the apathetic atmosphere for once. There were some nights when he really didn't feel like maintaining the expected image of combination raconteur, bon viveur, ace pilot, and sex demon—the qualities that independent starship captains were supposed to possess in abundance. He was too old to be keeping up that kind of nonsense.

Leave it to the young ones like Joshua, he thought. Although with Joshua it was hardly an act.

Nor was it always an artificial pose for you, *Udat* said.

Meyer watched one of the young waitresses swish past the end of the booth, an oriental with blonde hair whose long black skirt was split up to her hips. He didn't even feel remotely randy, just appreciative of the view. **Those days seem to be long gone,** he told the blackhawk with an irony that wasn't entirely insincere.

Cherri Barnes was sitting in the booth with him; the two of them sharing a chilled bottle of imported white Valencay wine. Now there was a woman he felt perfectly comfortable with. Smart, attractive, someone who didn't feel compelled to talk into any silences, a good crew member too; and they'd been to bed on several occasions over the years. No incompatibility there.

Her company lightens you, *Udat* proclaimed. That makes me happy.

Oh, well, as long as you're happy . . .

We need a flight. You are growing restless. I am eager to leave.

We could have gone to Lalonde.

I think not. Such missions do not sit well with you any more.

You're right. Though Christ knows I would have liked a crack at that bastard Laton. But I suppose that's something else best left to Joshua and his ilk. Though what he wanted to go for after the money he pulled in on the Norfolk run beats me.

Perhaps he feels he has something to prove.

No. Not Joshua. There's something odd going on there. And knowing Joshua, money is at the root of it. But no doubt we'll hear about it in due course. In the meantime the Lalonde mission has left a pleasing shortage of starships docked here. Finding a charter should be relatively easy.

There were those Time Universe charters available. Claudia Dohan specifically wanted blackhawks to deliver the fleks of Graeme Nicholson's sensevise. Time was of the essence, she said.

Those charters were all rush and effort.

It would have been a challenge.

If I'd wanted my mother as a permanent companion rather than a blackhawk I would never have left home.

I am sorry. I have upset you.

No. It's this Laton business. It has me worried. Fancy him turning up again after all this time.

The navy will find him.

Yeah. Sure.

"What are you two talking about?" Cherri asked.

"Huh? Oh, sorry," he grinned sheepishly. "It's Laton, if you must know. Just thinking of him running round free again . . ."

"You and fifty billion others." She picked up one of the menu sheets. "Come on, let's order. I'm starving."

They chose a chicken dish with side salad, along with a second bottle of wine.

"The trouble is, where can you travel to that's guaranteed safe?" Meyer said after the waitress departed. "Until the Confederation Navy finds him, the interstellar cargo market is going to be very jumpy. Our insurance rates are going to go through the roof."

"So shift to data-courier work. That way we don't have to physically dock with any stations. Alternatively, we just fetch and carry cargo between Edenist habitats."

He shifted his wineglass about on the table, uncomfortable with the idea. "That's too much like giving in, letting him win."

"Well, make up your mind."

He managed a desultory smile. "I dunno."

"Captain Meyer?"

He glanced up. A smallish black woman was standing at the end of the booth's table, dressed in a conservative grey suit; her skin was black enough to make Cherri seem white. He guessed she was in her early sixties. "That's me."

"You are the owner of the *Udat*?"

"Yes." If it had been anywhere else but Tranquillity, Meyer would have pegged her as a tax inspector.

"I am Dr Alkad Mzu," she said. "I wonder if I could sit with you for a moment? I would like to discuss some business."

"Be my guest."

He signalled to a waitress for another wineglass, and poured out the last of the bottle when it arrived.

"I require some transportation outsystem," Alkad said.

"Just for yourself? No cargo?"

"That is correct. Is it a problem?"

"Not for me. But the *Udat* doesn't come cheap. In fact, I don't think we've ever carried just one passenger before."

We haven't, *Udat* said.

Meyer quashed a childish grin. "Where do you want to travel? I can probably give you a quote straight away."

"New California." She sipped her wine, peering at him over the rim of the glass.

Out of the corner of his eye, Meyer could see Cherri frowning. There were regular commercial flights to the New Californian system from Tranquillity three or four times a week, and more non-scheduled charter flights on top of that. The Laton scare hadn't stopped any departures yet. He was suddenly very curious about Alkad Mzu.

OK, let's see how badly she wants to get there. "That would be at least three hundred thousand fuseodollars," he told her.

"I expected it to be about that," she replied. "Once we arrive, I may wish to pick up some cargo to carry on to a further destination. Could you supply me with the *Udat*'s performance and handling parameters, please?"

"Yes, of course." He was only slightly mollified. Taking a cargo on somewhere was a viable excuse for an exclusive charter. But why not travel to New California on a regular civil flight, then hire a starship after she arrived? The only reason he could think of was that she specifically wanted a blackhawk. That wasn't good, not good at all. "But *Udat* is only available for civil flights," he stressed the word lightly.

"Naturally," Alkad Mzu said.

"That's all right then." He opened a channel to her neural nanonics and datavised the blackhawk's handling capacity over.

"What sort of cargo would we pick up?" Cherri asked. "I'm the *Udat*'s cargo officer, I may be able to advise on suitability."

"Medical equipment," Alkad said. "I have some type-definition files." She datavised them to Meyer.

The list expanded in his mind, resembling a three-dimensional simulacrum of magnified chip circuitry, with every junction labelled. There seemed to be an awful lot of it. "Fine," he said, slightly at a loss. "We'll review it later." Have to run it through an analysis program, he thought.

"Thank you," Alkad said. "The journey from New California will be approximately two hundred light-years, if you'd care to work out a quote based on the cargo's mass and environmental requirements. I will be asking other captains for quotes."

"We'll be tough to beat," he said smoothly.

"Is there any reason why we can't know where we're going?" Cherri asked.

"My colleagues and I are still in the preliminary planning stage of the mission. I'd prefer not to say anything more at this time. But I shall certainly inform you of our destination before we leave Tranquillity." Alkad stood up. "Thank you for your time, Captain. I hope we see each other again. Please datavise your full quote to me at any time."

"She hardly touched her wine," Cherri said as the doctor departed.

"Yes," Meyer said distantly. Five other people were leaving the bar. None of them space industry types. Merchants? But they didn't look rich enough.

"Are we putting in a formal bid?"

"Good question."

I would like to visit New California, *Udat* said hopefully.

We've been before. You just want to fly.

I do. It is boring sitting on this ledge. *Udat* relayed an image of whirling stars as seen from Tranquillity's docking-ledge, speeded up, always tracing the same circles. The edge of the habitat's spaceport disk started to grey, then crumbled and broke apart with age.

Meyer grinned. What an imagination you have. I'll get us a charter soon. That's a promise.

Good!

"I think we need to know a little bit more about this Mzu woman," he said out loud. "No way is she on the level."

"Oh, really?" Cherri cooed; she cocked her head on one side. "You noticed that, did you?"

Ione let go of the image. Her apartment rematerialized around her. Augustine was walking determinedly across the dining-room table towards the remains of the salad she had pushed away, moving at a good fifty centimetres a minute. At the back of her mind she was aware of Alkad Mzu standing in the vestibule of the thirty-first floor of the StMartha starscraper waiting for a lift. There were seven Intelligence agency opera-tives hanging around in the park-level foyer above her, alerted by their colleagues in Harkey's Bar. Two of them—a female operative from New Britain, and the second-in-command of the Kulu team—resolutely refused to make eye contact. Strange really. For the last three weeks they had spent most of their off-duty hours in bed together screwing each other into delirious exhaustion.

In my history courses I recall an incident in the twen-tieth century when the American CIA tried to get rid of a Caribbean island's Communist president by giving him an exploding cigar, Ione said.

Yes? Tranquillity asked loyally.

Six hundred years of progress—human style.

Would you like me to inform Meyer that Alkad Mzu will not be granted an exit visa?

Informing him I'll blow him and the *Udat* out of exis-tence if he leaves with her would be more to the point. But no, we won't do anything yet. How many captains has she contacted now?

Sixty-three in the last twenty months.

And every contact follows the same pattern, she mused. A request for a charter fee quote to carry her to a star system, then picking up a cargo to take onwards. But never the same star system; and it was Joshua who was asked to quote for Garissa. Ione tried not to consider the implications of that. It *had* to be coincidence.

I am sure it is, Tranquillity said.

I was leaking. Sorry.

There was never any follow-up to her meeting with Joshua.

No. But what is she doing? I wonder.

I have two possible explanations. First, she is aware of the agency observers—and it would be hard to believe she is not—and she is simply having fun at their expense.

Fun? You call that fun? Threatening to recover the Alchemist?

Her home planet has been annihilated. If the humour is somewhat rough, that is to be expected.

Of course. Go on.

Secondly, she is attempting to produce a range of escape options which exceed the observers' ability to keep track of. Sixty-three is an excessive number of captains to contact even for a warped game.

But she must know it isn't possible to confuse you.

Yes.

Strange woman.

A very intelligent woman.

Ione reached over to her discarded plate, and began shredding one of the lettuce leaves. Augustine crooned adoringly as he finally reached the pile of shreds, and started to munch at them.

Is it possible for her to circumvent your observation? Apparently Edenists can induce localized blindspots in their habitats' perception.

I would say it is extremely unlikely. No Edenist has ever succeeded in evading me, and there were many attempts in your grandfather's day.

Really? She perked up.

Yes, by their Intelligence agency operatives. All failed. And I acquired some valuable information on the nature of localized circumvention patterns they employed. Fortunately I do not use quite the same thought

routines as Edenist habitats, so I am relatively insusceptible. And Alkad Mzu does not have affinity.

Are we sure? She was missing for some time between Garissa's destruction and turning up here, four years. She could have had neuron symbionts implanted.

She did not. A complete medical body scan is required for health-insurance coverage for all Laymil project staff when they start work. She has neural nanonics, but no affinity symbionts. Nor any other implants, for that matter.

Oh. I'm still unhappy over these continual encounters with starship captains. Perhaps if I had a private word with her . . . explain how upsetting it is.

That might work.

Did Father ever meet her?

No.

I'll think about what to say then, I don't want to come over all heavy handed. Perhaps I could invite her for a meal, keep it informal.

Certainly. She always maintains her social propriety.

Good. In the meantime, I'd like you to double the number of serjeants we keep in her immediate vicinity. With Laton running loose in the Confederation, we really don't want to add to Admiral Aleksandrovich's troubles right now.

Meyer and Cherri Barnes took a lift up from Harkey's Bar to the StMartha's foyer. He walked with her down a flight of stairs to the starscraper's tube station, and datavised for a carriage.

"Are we going back to the hotel or *Udat*?" Cherri asked.

"My hotel flat has a double bed."

She grinned, and tucked his arm round hers. "Mine too."

The carriage arrived, and he datavised the control processor to take them to the hotel. There was a slight surge of acceleration as it got under way. Meyer sank deeper into his cushioning; Cherri still hadn't let go of him.

His neural nanonics informed him a file stored in one of the memory cells was altering. Viral safeguard programs automatically isolated the cell. According to the menu, the file was the cargo list Alkad Mzu had datavised to him.

The viral safeguard programs reported the change had finished; tracer programs probed the file's new format. It wasn't hostile. The file had contained a time-delay code which simply re-arranged the order of the existing information into something entirely different. A hidden message.

Meyer accessed the contents.

"Holy shit," he muttered fifteen seconds later.

Now that would be a real challenge, *Udat* said excitedly.

Ombey was the newest of Kulu's eight principality star systems. A Royal Kulu Navy scoutship discovered the one terracompatible planet in 2457, orbiting a hundred and forty-two million kilometres from its G2 star. After an ecological certification team cleared its biosphere as non-harmful, it was declared a Kulu protectorate and opened for immigration by King Lukas in 2470. Unlike other frontier worlds, such as Lalonde, which formed development companies and struggled to raise investment, Ombey was funded entirely by the Kulu Royal Treasury and the Crown-owned Kulu Corporation. Even at the beginning it couldn't be described as a stage one colony. It couldn't even be said to have gone through a purely agrarian phase. A stony iron asteroid, Guyana, was manoeuvred into orbit before the first settler arrived, and navy engineers immediately set about converting it into a base. Kulu's larger astroengineering companies brought industry stations to the system to gain a slice of the military contracts involved, and to take advantage of the huge start-up tax incentives on offer. The Kulu Corporation began a settlement on an asteroid orbiting the gas giant Nonoiut, which assembled a cloudscoop to mine

He₃. As always within the Kingdom, the Edenists were excluded from germinating a habitat and building an adjunct cloudscoop, a prohibition rationalized by the Saldanas on religious grounds.

By the time the first wave of farmers arrived, the already substantial government presence produced a large ready-made consumer base for their crops. Healthcare, communications, law enforcement, and didactic education courses, although not quite up to the level of the Kingdom's more developed planets, were provided from day one. Forty hectares of land were given to each family, along with a generous low-interest loan for housing and agricultural machinery, with the promise of more land for their children. Basic planetary industrialization was given a high priority, and entire factories were imported to provide essentials for the engineering and construction business. Again, government infrastructure contracts provided a massive initial subsidy. The company and civil workers arriving during the second ten-year period was equal to the number of farmers.

In 2500 its population rose above the ten million mark, and it officially lost its protectorate status to become a principality, governed by one of the King's siblings.

Ombey was a meticulously planned endeavour, only possible to a culture as wealthy as the Kulu Kingdom. The Saldanas considered the investment costs more than worthwhile. Although the Principality didn't start to show a return for over ninety years, it allowed them to expand their family dynasty as well as their influence, both physical (economic and military) and political, inside the Confederation. It made their position even more secure, although by that time a republican revolution was virtually impossible. And it was all done without conflict or opposition with neighbouring star systems.

By 2611 there were twelve settled asteroids in orbit and two more on their way. Planetary population was a fraction under two hundred million, and the twelve settled asteroids in the system's dense inner belt were home to another two million people. Subsidies and loans from Kulu had long since ended, self-sufficiency both industrially and economically had been reached in 2545, exports were accelerating. Ombey was a thriving decent place to live, bristling with justified optimism.

Captain Farrah Montgomery had expected the flight from Lalonde to take four days. By the time the *Ekwan* finally jumped into the Ombey system, emerging two hundred thousand kilometres above the planet's surface, they had been in transit for eight. The big colonist-carrier had endured a multitude of irritating systems failures right from the very first minute of getting underway. Mechanical components had broken down, electrical circuits suffered a rash of surges and drop-outs. Her crew had been harried into short-tempered despair as they attempted patchwork repairs. Most worrying, the main fusion tubes produced erratic thrust levels, adding to the difficulty of reaching plotted jump coordinates, and increasing the flight duration drastically.

Fuel levels, while not yet critical, were uncomfortably low.

Sensors slid out of their jump recesses, and Captain Montgomery performed a preliminary visual orientation sweep. Ombey's solitary moon, Jethro, was rising above the horizon, a large grey-yellow globe peppered with small deep craters, and streaked with long white rays. They were above the planet's night side; the Blackdust desert continent straddling the equator was a huge ebony patch amid oceans that reflected jaundiced moonlight. On the eastern side of the planet the coastline of the Espartan continent was picked out by the purple-white lights of towns and cities; there were fewer urban sprawls in the interior, declining to zero at the central mountain range.

After Captain Montgomery had cleared their arrival with civil flight control, Ralph Hiltch contacted the navy base on Guyana, and requested docking permission along with a code four status alert. *Ekwan* closed on the asteroid at one and a quarter gravities, holding reasonably steady.

The base admiral, Pascoe Farquar, after receiving Ralph's request, backed by Sir Asquith, authorized the alert. Non-essential personnel were cleared from the habitation cavern the navy used. Commercial traffic was turned away. Xenobiology, nanonic, and weapons specialists began to assemble an isolation confinement area for Gerald Skibbow.

The *Ekwan* docked at Guyana's non-rotating spaceport amid a tight security cordon. Royal Marines and port personnel worked a straight five-hour shift to bring the *Ekwan*'s three thousand grumbling, bewildered colonists out of zero-tau and assign them quarters in the navy barracks. Ralph Hiltch and Sir Asquith spent most of that time in conference with Pascoe Farquar and his staff. After he accessed sensorium recordings Dean Folan made during the jungle mission, as well as the garbled reports of Darcy and Lori claiming Laton was on Lalonde, the admiral decided to raise the alert status to code three.

Ralph Hiltch watched the last of the fifty armour-suited marines floating into the *Ekwan*'s large zero-tau compartment. They were all muscle boosted and qualified in free fall combat routines; eight of them carried medium-calibre automatic recoilless projectile carbines. The sergeants followed Cathal Fitzgerald's directions and started positioning them in three concentric circles surrounding Gerald Skibbow's zero-tau pod, with five on the decks either side in case he broke through the metal grids. Extra lights had been attached to the nearby support girders, beams focused on the one pod in the compartment which was still encased by an absorptive blackness, casting a weird jumble of multiple shadows outside the encircling ring of marines.

Ralph's neural nanonics were relaying the scene to the admiral and the waiting specialists. It made him slightly self-conscious as he anchored himself to a girder to address the marine squad.

"This might look excessive for one man," he said to the marines, "but don't drop your guard for an instant. We're not entirely sure he is human, certainly he has some lethal energy-projecting abilities that come outside anything we've encountered before. If it's any comfort, free fall does seem to unnerve him slightly. Your job is just to escort him down to the isolation area that's been prepared. Once he's there, the technical people will take over. They think the cell they've prepared will be able to confine him. But getting him there could get very messy."

He backed away from the pod, noting the half-apprehensive faces of the first rank of marines.

God, they look young. I hope to hell they took my warning seriously.

He checked his own skull-helmet, and took a deep breath. "OK, Cathal, switch it off."

The blackness vanished from the pod revealing the smooth cylindrical composite sarcophagus. Ralph strained to hear the manic battering which Skibbow had been giving the pod before the zero-tau silenced him. The compartment was quiet apart from the occasional scuffling of the marines as they craned for a glimpse.

"Open the lid."

It began to slide back. Ralph braced himself for Skibbow to burst out of the opening like a runaway combat wasp with a forty-gee drive. He heard a wretched whimpering sound. Cathal gave him a puzzled glance.

God, did we get the right pod?

"All right, stay back," Ralph said. "You two," he indicated the marines with the carbines, "cover me." He pulled himself cautiously across the grid towards the pod, still expecting Skibbow to spring up. The whimpering grew louder, interspersed with low groans.

Very, very carefully, Ralph eased himself up the side of the pod, and peeked in. Ready to duck down fast.

Gerald Skibbow was floating listlessly inside the curving cream-white composite coffin. His whole body was trembling. He clutched his shattered hand to his chest. Both eyes were red rimmed, blood was still oozing from his mashed nose. The smell of jungle mud and urine clogged in Ralph's nose.

Gerald continued his weak gurglings, bubbles of saliva forming at the corner of his mouth. When Ralph manoeuvred himself right over the pod there was no reaction from the unfocused eyes.

"Shit."

"What's happened?" Admiral Farquar datavised.

"I don't know, sir. It's Skibbow all right. But it looks like he's gone into some kind of shock." He waved a hand in front of the colonist's filthy, bloody face. "He's virtually catatonic."

"Is he still dangerous, do you think?"

"I don't see how he could be, unless he recovers."

"All right, Hiltch. Have the marines take him down to the isolation area as quickly as possible. I'll have an emergency medical team there by the time you arrive."

"Yes, sir." Ralph pushed himself away, allowing three marines to pull the still unresisting Skibbow from the zero-tau pod. His neural nanonics informed him the asteroid was being stood down to code six status.

I don't understand, he thought bleakly, we brought a walking nuke on board, and wind up with a pants-wetting vegetable. Something wiped that sequestration from him. What?

The marine squad departed the compartment noisily, joking and catcalling. Relieved they hadn't been needed after all. With one hand holding idly on a girder, Ralph hung between the two decking grids long after the last of them left, staring at the zero-tau pod.

Three hours after Guyana's alert status was reduced to code six, life inside had almost returned to normal. Civilians with jobs in the military-run cavern were allowed to resume their duties. Restrictions on communication and travel were lifted from the other two caverns. Spaceships were permitted to dock and depart, although the spaceport where the *Ekwan* was berthed was still off-limits to anything but navy ships.

Three and a half hours after the marines delivered a virtually comatose Gerald Skibbow to the isolation cell, Captain Farrah Montgomery walked into the small office Time Universe maintained on Guyana and handed over Graeme Nicholson's flek.

It was an hour after the maids had served Cricklade's breakfast, and Duke was already rising across a sky that was ribbed with slender bands of flimsy cloud. Duchess-night had seen the first sprinkling of rain since the midsummer conjunction. The fields and forests glimmered and shone under their glace coating of water. Aboriginal flowers, reduced to wizened brown coronets after discharging their seeds, turned to a pulpy mess and started to rot away. Best of all, the dust had gone from the air. Cricklade's estate labourers had started their morning in a cheerful mood at the omen. Rain this early meant the second crop of cereals should produce a good heavy harvest.

Louise Kavanagh didn't care about the rain, nor the prospect of an impending agricultural bounty. Not even Genevieve's playful enthusiasm could summon her for their usual stroll in the paddock. Instead, she sat on the toilet in her private bathroom with her panties round her ankles and her head in her hands. Her long hair hung lankly, tasselled ends brushing her shiny blue shoes. It was stupid to have hair so long, she thought, stupid, snobbish, impractical, a waste of time, and insulting.

Why should I have to be preened and groomed like I'm a pedigree show horse? It's a wicked, filthy tradition treating women like that. Just so that I look the classic-beauty part for some ghastly clot-head young "gentleman". What do looks matter, and especially looks that come from a pseudo-mythical past on another planet? I already have my man.

She clenched her stomach muscles again, squeezing her guts hard as she held her breath. Her nails dug into her palms painfully with the effort. Her head started to shake, skin reddening.

It didn't make the slightest difference. She let the air out of her straining lungs in a fraught sob.

Angry now, she squeezed again. Let out her breath.

Squeezed.

Nothing.

She wanted to cry. Her shoulders were shivering, she even had the hot blotches round her eyes, but there were no tears left. She was all cried out.

Her period was at least five days overdue. And she was so regular.

She was pregnant with Joshua's baby. It was wonderful. It was horrible. It was . . . a wretched great mess.

"Please, Jesus," she whispered. "What we did wasn't really a sin. It wasn't. I love him so. I really do. Don't let this happen to me. Please."

There was nothing in the world she wanted more than to have Joshua's baby. But not *now*. Joshua himself still seemed like a gorgeous fantasy she had made up to amuse herself during the long hot months of Norfolk's quiescent summer. Too perfect to be real, the kind of man who melted her inside even as he set her on fire with passion. A passion she didn't quite know she had before. Previous daydreams of romance had all sort of blurred into vague unknowns after her tall, handsome champion kissed her. But lying in bed at night the memory of Joshua's cunning hands exploring her naked body brought some most unladylike flushes below the sheets. There hadn't been a day gone by when she didn't visit their little glade in Wardley Wood, and the smell of dry hay always kindled a secret glow of arousal as she thought of their last time together in the stable.

"Please, my Lord Jesus."

Last year one of the girls at the convent school, a year older than Louise, had moved away from the district rather abruptly. She was from one of Stoke County's more important families, her father was a landowner who had sat on the local council for over a decade. Gone to stay with a wealthy sheep-farming relative on the isle of Cumbria, the Mother Superior had told the other pupils, where she will learn the practical aspects of house management which will adequately prepare her for the role of marriage. But everyone knew the real reason. One of the Romany lads, in Stoke for the rose crop, had tumbled her in his caravan. The girl's family had been more or less shunned by decent folk after that, and her father had to resign his council seat, saying it was due to ill health.

Not that anyone would dare do that to any branch of the Kavanagh family. But the whispers would start if she took a sudden holiday; the tarnish of shame would never be lifted from Cricklade. And Mummy would cry because her daughter had let her down frightfully badly. And Daddy would . . . Louise didn't like to think what her father would do.

No! she told herself firmly. Stop thinking like that. Nothing terrible is going to happen.

"You know I'm coming back," Joshua had told her as they lay entwined by the side of the sun-blessed stream. And he said he loved her.

He would return. He *promised*.

Everything would be all right after that. Joshua was the one person in the galaxy who could face up to her father unafraid. Yes, everything would be fine just as soon as he arrived.

Louise brushed her—fearsomely annoying—hair from her face, and slowly stood up. When she looked in the mirror she was an utter ruin. She started to tidy herself up, pulling up her panties, splashing cold water on her face. Her light flower-pattern dress with its long skirt was badly creased. Why couldn't she wear trousers, or even shorts? She could just imagine Nanny's reaction to that innocent suggestion. Legs on public display? Good grief! But it would be so much more practical in this weather. Lots of the women working in the groves did; girls her age, too. She started to plait her hair. That would be something else which changed after she was married.

Married. She grinned falteringly at her reflection. Joshua was going to be in for a monumental shock when he returned and she told him the stupendous news. But, ultimately, he would be happy and rejoice with her. How could he not? And they would be married at the end of summer (which was as quick as decency versus a swelling belly could allow), when the Earth flowers were at their peak and the granaries were full from the second harvest. Her bulge probably wouldn't show, not with an adequately designed dress. Genevieve would adore being chief bridesmaid. There would be huge marquees on the lawns for the reception. Family members she hadn't seen for years. It would be the biggest celebration in Stoke County for decades, everyone would be happy and they would dance under the neon-red night sky.

People might guess because of the speed. But Joshua was going to be her father's business partner in this exciting mayope venture. He was rich, of good blood (presumably—how else would he inherit a starship?), a fine manager able to take on Cricklade. An eminently suitable (if unusual) match for the Cricklade heir. Their marriage wouldn't be that extraordinary. Her reputation would remain intact. And the Kavanaghs' respectability would remain unblemished.

After the wedding they could travel Norfolk's islands for their honeymoon. Or maybe even to another planet in his starship. What was important was that she wouldn't have the baby here, with everyone noting the date of birth.

Real life could match up to her most fantastical daydreams. With a fabulous husband, and a beautiful baby.

If Joshua . . .

Always, *if Joshua* . . .

Why did it have to be like that?

The lone Romany caravan stood beside a tall Norfolk-aboriginal pine in a meadow which until recently had been a site for more than thirty similar caravans. Rings of flat reddish stones confined piles of ash, cold now. Grass along the bank of the little stream was trampled down where horses and goats had drunk and people had scooped water into pails. Several piles of raw earth marked the latrines, their conical sides scored with fresh runnels, evidence of last Duchess-night's rain.

The caravan, a hybrid of traditional design riding modern lightweight wheels, had seen more prosperous times. Its jaunty and elaborate paintwork was fading, but the wood was sound. Three goats were tethered to its rear axle. Two horses waited outside, one a mud-spotted piebald shire-horse with a wild shaggy mane which was used to pull the caravan, the other a black riding stallion, its coat sleek and glossy, the expensive leather saddle on its back polished to a gleam.

Grant Kavanagh stood inside the caravan, stooping so he didn't knock his head on the curving ceiling. It was dark and faintly dusty, smelling of dried herbs. He enjoyed that, it brought back sharp memories of his teenage years. Even now, the sight of the Romany caravans winding their way through Cricklade's wolds as midsummer approached always made him feel incredibly randy.

The girl pulled back the heavy curtains hanging on a cord across the middle of the caravan. Her name was Carmitha, twenty years old, with a big broad-shouldered body, which, Grant knew with depressing instinct, would be horribly overweight in another six or seven years. Rich black hair hanging below her shoulders harmonized with dark, smooth skin. She had changed into a flimsy white skirt and loose-fitting top.

"That looks fantastic," he said.

"Why, thank you, kind sir." She curtsied, and giggled effusively.

Grant drew her closer and started to kiss her. His hands fumbled with the buttons down the front of her blouse.

She pushed him away gently, and removed his hands, kissing the knuckles lightly. "Let me do that for you," she said coquettishly. Her fingers moved down to the top button in a slow, taunting caress. He looked in delight as her body was exposed. He pulled her down onto the bed, immensely gratified by her ardour.

The caravan squeaked as it started rocking. A hurricane

lantern hanging from a brass chain on the ceiling clanged loudly as it swayed gently to and fro. He barely heard it above Carmitha's exuberant whoops of joy.

After a time which was nowhere near long enough, he came in drastic shudders, his spine singing raptures. Carmitha quickly squealed, claiming multiple orgasms were nearly making her swoon.

He collapsed onto the bed, prickly blankets scratching his back. Dust mingled with sweat and trickled among the curly hair on his chest.

By God but summer conjunction makes life worth living, he thought. A time when he could prove himself again and again. The Tear crop had been one of the best ever; the estate had made its usual financial killing. He had tumbled nearly a dozen young girls from the grove teams. The meteorological reports were predicting a humid month ahead, which meant a good second harvest. Young Joshua's audacious mayope proposal could only add to the family's wealth and influence.

The only blot on the horizon was the reports coming out of Boston on the disturbances. It looked like the Democratic Land Union was stirring up trouble again.

The Union was a motley collection of reformists and political agitators, a semi-subversive group who wanted to see land distributed "fairly" among the People, the foreign earnings from the sale of Norfolk Tears invested with social relevance, and full democracy and civil rights awarded to the population. And free beer on Friday nights, too, no doubt, Grant thought caustically. The whole blessing of a Confederation of eight hundred plus planets was that it gave people a massive variety of social systems to choose from. What the Democratic Land Union activists failed to appreciate was that they were free to leave for their damned Communistic workers' paradise as soon as the workshy little buggers earned enough cash to pay their passage. But oh no, they wanted to liberate Norfolk, no matter how much damage and heartache they caused in the process of peddling their politics of envy.

A chapter of the Democratic Land Union had tried to spread its sedition in Stoke County about ten years ago. Grant had helped the county's chief constable round them up. The leaders had been deported to a Confederation penal planet. Some of the nastier elements—the ones found with home-made weapons—had been handed over to a squad of special operations constables from the capital, Norwich. The rest, the pitiful street trash who handed out leaflets and drank themselves into a coma on the Union-supplied beer, had been given fifteen years' hard labour in the polar work gangs.

There hadn't been sight or sign of them on Kesteven ever since. Some people, he thought sagely, just never learn. If it works, don't try and fix it. And Norfolk worked.

He kissed the crown of Carmitha's head. "When do you leave?"

"Tomorrow. Most of my family has already left. There is fruit-picking work in Hurst County. It pays well."

"And after that?"

"We'll winter over in Holbeach. There are many deep caves in the cliffs above the town. And some of us get jobs in the harbour market gutting fish."

"Sounds like a good life. Don't you ever want to settle down?"

She shrugged, thick hair sloshing about. "Be like you, tied to your cold stone palace? No thanks. There might not be much to see in this world, but I want to see it all."

"Better make the most of the time we've got, then."

She crawled on top of him, calloused hands closing round his limp penis.

There was a pathetic scratching knock on the caravan's rear door. "Sir? Are you there, sir?" William Elphinstone asked. The voice was as quavery as the knock.

Grant chopped back on an exasperated groan. *No, I'm not in here, that's why my bloody horse is outside.* "What do you want?"

"Sorry to bother you, sir, but there's an urgent phone call

for you at the house. Mr. Butterworth said it was important, it's from Boston."

Grant frowned. Butterworth wasn't going to send anyone after him unless it was genuinely important. The estate
manager knew full well what he was up to at a slack time
like this. He was also wily enough not to come looking
himself.

I wonder what young Elphinstone has done to annoy
him, Grant thought irreverently.

"Wait there," he shouted. "I'll be with you in a minute."
He deliberately took his time dressing. No damn way was
he going to come dashing out of the caravan tucking his
shirt into his trousers and give the lad something to tell all
the other junior estate managers.

He straightened his tweed riding jacket, smoothed down
his muttonchops with his hands, and settled his cap. "How
do I look?"

"Masterful," Carmitha said from the bed.

There was no detectable irony. Grant fished around in
his pocket and found two silver guineas. He dropped the
gratuity into a big china bowl sitting on a shelf beside the
door as he went out.

Louise watched her father and William Elphinstone ride up
to the front door. Grooms appeared, and took charge of the
horses. From the way the animals were sweating it had been
a hard ride. Her father hurried into the house.

Poor old Daddy, always busy.

She strolled over to where William was talking to the
grooms, both boys younger than her. He saw her coming
and dismissed them. Louise stroked the black stallion's
flank as the big animal was led past her.

"Whatever is all the fuss about?" she asked.

"Some call from Boston. Mr. Butterworth thought it important enough to send me out looking for your father."

"Oh." Louise started to move away. Rather annoyingly,
William walked in step with her. She wasn't in the mood
for company.

"I've been asked to the Newcombes' bash on Saturday evening," he said. "I thought it might be rather fun. They're not quite our people, but they set a decent table. There will be dancing afterwards."

"That's nice." Louise always hated it when William tried to put on graces. "Our people" indeed! She went to school with Mary Newcombe.

"I hoped you would come with me."

She looked at him in surprise. Eagerness and anxiety squabbled over his face. "Oh, William, that's jolly nice of you to ask. Thank you. But I really can't. Sorry."

"Really can't?"

"Well, no. The Galfords are coming to dinner on Saturday. I simply must be there."

"I thought that perhaps now he's left, you might find more time for my company."

"Now who's left?" she asked sharply.

"Your friend, the gallant starship captain."

"William, you really are talking the most appalling tosh. Now I've said I can't attend the Newcombes' party with you. Kindly leave the subject."

He stopped and took hold of her arm. She was too surprised to say anything. People simply did not take such liberties.

"You always found plenty of time for him," he said in a flat tone.

"William, desist this instant."

"Every day, it was. The two of you galloping off to Wardley Wood."

Louise felt the blood rising to her cheeks. What did he know? "Remove your hand from me. Now!"

"You didn't mind his hands."

"William!"

He gave her a humourless smile and let go. "I'm not jealous. Don't get me wrong."

"There is nothing to be jealous of. Joshua Calvert was a guest and friend of my father's. That is the end of the matter."

"Some fiancés would think otherwise."

"Who?" she squawked.

"Fiancés, my dearest Louise. You must be aware there is some considerable speculation upon whom you are to marry. All I'm saying is that there are some Kesteven families of good breeding, and eligible sons, who would take exception to your . . . shall we call it, indiscretion."

She slapped him. The sound rang across the lawn as her palm struck his cheek. "How dare you!"

He dabbed at his cheek with the fingers of his right hand, a look of distaste on his face. The imprint of her palm was clearly etched in pink. "What an impetuous creature you are, Louise. I had no idea."

"Get out of my sight."

"Of course, if that's what you wish. But you might like to consider that should word get out, your currently enviable position may well become less than secure. I don't want to see that happen, Louise, I really don't. You see, I am genuinely very fond of you. Fond enough to make allowances."

She seemed utterly incapable of movement, condemned to stand there in front of him, gaping in astonishment. "You . . ." It came out in a crushed gasp. For a distressing instant she thought she was going to faint.

William knelt in front of her.

No, she thought, oh no no no, this can't be happening. Joshua bloody Calvert, where are you?

"Marry me, Louise. I can obtain your father's approval, have no fear of that. Marry me, and we can have a wonderful future together here at Cricklade." He held his hand out, face soft with expectancy.

She drew herself up into the most regal pose she could manage. And very clearly, very calmly said: "I would sooner shovel bullock manure for a living." One of Joshua's better expressions, though admittedly not verbatim.

William paled.

She turned on a heel and walked away. Her back held straight.

"This is not the last time we shall pursue this topic," he called after her. "Believe me, dearest Louise, I will not be defeated in my suit for you."

Grant Kavanagh sat himself down behind the desk in his study and picked up the phone. His secretary had put a call through to Trevor Clarke, Kesteven's lord lieutenant. Grant didn't like the implications of that one jot.

"I need you to bring Stoke's militia to Boston," Trevor Clarke said as soon as they had exchanged greetings. "A full turnout, please, Grant."

"That might be difficult," Grant said. "This is still a busy time here. The rosegroves need pruning, and there's the second grain crop to drill. We can hardly take able men from the land."

"Can't be helped. I'm calling in all the county militias."

"All of them?"

" 'Fraid so, old chap. We've blacked it from the news, you understand, but the situation in Boston, frankly, doesn't look good."

"What situation? You're not seriously telling me that bloody Union rabble worries you?"

"Grant . . ." Trevor Clarke's voice dropped an octave. "Listen, this is totally confidential, but there are already five districts in Boston that have been completely taken over by this mob, rendered ungovernable. We have a state of open insurrection here. If we send the police in to re-establish order they don't come out again. The city is under martial law, insofar as we can enforce it. I'm worried, Grant."

"Dear Christ! The Democratic Land Union has done this?"

"We're not sure. Whoever these insurrectionists are, they seem to be armed with energy weapons. That means offplanet complicity. But it's hard to believe the Union could ever organize something like that. You know what they're like, hotheads smashing up tractors and ploughs. Energy weapons break every letter in our constitution; they are everything this society was set up to avoid."

"An outside force?" Grant Kavanagh could hardly believe what he was hearing.

"It may be. I have asked the Chancellor's office in Norwich to request the Confederation Navy squadron extends its duty tour. Fortunately the personnel are all still here having their shore leave. The squadron commander is recalling them back up to orbit now."

"What good is that?"

"The navy starships can make damn sure nothing else is delivered to the insurrectionists from outsystem. And as a last resort they can provide our ground forces with strike power."

Grant sat perfectly still. Ground forces. Strike power. It was unreal. Through the windows he could see Cricklade's peaceful wolds, rich and verdant. And here he was calmly talking about virtual civil war. "But God's teeth, man, this is a city we're talking about. You can't use starship weapons against Boston. There are a hundred and twenty thousand people living there."

"I know," Trevor Clarke said mordantly. "One of the militia's major assignments will be to help evacuate the civilians. You will be minimizing casualties, Grant."

"Have you told the Chancellor what you're planning? Because if you haven't, I damn well will."

There was a silence which lasted for several seconds. "Grant," Trevor Clarke said gently, "it was the Chancellor's office that recommended this action to me. It must be done while the insurrectionists are concentrated in one place, before they have a chance to spread their damnable revolution. So many people are joining them. I . . . I never thought there was so much dissatisfaction on the planet. It has to be stopped, and stopped in a way that forbids repetition."

"Oh, my God," Grant Kavanagh said brokenly. "All right, Trevor, I understand. I'll call in the militia captains this afternoon. The regiment will be ready for you by to-morrow."

"Good man, Grant. I knew I could rely on you. There will be a train to collect you from Colsterworth Station. We'll billet you in an industrial warehouse outside town. And don't worry, man, the starships are only a last resort. I expect we'll only need one small demonstration and they'll cave in."

"Yes. I'm sure you're right." Grant returned the pearl-handled phone to its cradle, a morbid premonition telling him it could never be that simple.

The train had six passenger carriages, room enough for all of the Stoke county militia's seven hundred men. It took them twenty-five minutes to embark. The station was a scene of pure chaos; half of the town's streets were clogged with carts, carriages, buses, and farm-ranger vehicles. Families took a long time saying goodbye. Men were shifty and irritable in their grey uniforms. Complaints about ill-fitting boots rippled up and down the platform.

Louise and Marjorie were pressed against the wall of the station with a pile of kitbags on one side, and olive-green metal ammunition boxes on the other. Some of the boxes had date stamps over ten years old. Three hard-faced men were guarding the ammunition, stumpy black guns cradled in their arms. Louise was beginning to regret coming, Genevieve hadn't been allowed.

Mr Butterworth, in his sergeant-major's uniform, marched up and down the platform, ordering people about. The train was gradually filled; work teams began to load the kitbags and ammunition into the first carriage's mail compartment.

William Elphinstone came down the platform, looking very smart in his lieutenant's uniform. He stopped in front of them. "Mrs Kavanagh," he said crisply. "Louise. It looks like we're off in five minutes."

"Well, you mind you take great care, William," Marjorie said.

"Thank you. I will."

Louise let her gaze wander away with deliberate slowness. William looked slightly put out, but decided this wasn't the time to make an issue of it. He nodded to Marjorie and marched off.

She turned to her daughter. "Louise, that was extremely rude."

"Yes, Mother," Louise said unrepentantly. How typical of William to volunteer even though it wasn't his militia, she thought. He only did it to be covered in glory, so he would seem even more acceptable to Daddy. And he would never be in the front line sharing the risk with the poor common troops, not him. Joshua would.

Marjorie gave her daughter a close look at the unexpected tone, seeing the sulky stubborn expression on her usually placid face. So Louise doesn't like William Elphinstone. Can't say I blame her. But to be so public was totally out of character. Louise's decorum was always meticulously formal and correct, gratingly so. Suddenly, despite all the worry of Boston, she felt delighted. Her daughter wasn't the meek-minded little mouse any more. She wanted to cheer out loud. And I wonder what started this episode of independent thinking, though I've a pretty shrewd idea. Joshua Calvert, if you laid one finger on her . . .

Grant Kavanagh strode vigorously along the side of the train, making sure his troops were settled and everything was in place. His wife and daughter were waiting dutifully at the end of the platform. Both of them quite divine, Marjorie especially.

Why do I bother with those little Romany tarts?

Louise's face was all melancholic. Frightened, but trying not to show it. Trying to be brave like a good Kavanagh. What a wonderful daughter. Growing up a treat. Even though she had been a bit moody these last few days. Probably missing Joshua, he thought jovially. But that was just another reminder that he really would have to start thinking seriously about a decent bloodmatch for her. Not yet though, not this year. Cricklade Manor would still echo with her laughter over Christmas, warming his heart.

He hugged her, and her arms wrapped round his waist. "Don't go, Daddy," she whispered.

"I have to. It won't be for long."

She sniffed hard, and nodded. "I understand."

He kissed Marjorie, ignoring the whistles and cheers which rang out from the carriages at the rear of the train.

"Now don't you try and prove anything," she said in that weary half-censorious way which meant she was scared to the core. So he said, "Of course I won't, I'll just sit in the command tent and let the youngsters get on with it."

Marjorie put her arm around Louise as they waved the train out of the station. The platform was a solid mass of women with handkerchiefs flapping from frantic wrists. She wanted to laugh at how silly they must all look to the men on the train. But she didn't because she was a Kavanagh, and must set an example. Besides, she might have started crying at the futility and stupidity of it all.

In the clear sky above, silver lights flashed and twisted as the navy squadron changed formation and orbital inclination so that Boston was always in range to one of their number.

Dariat was nerving himself up to commit suicide. It wasn't easy. Suicide was the culmination of failure, of despair. Since the return of the dead from the realm of emptiness, his life had become inspiring.

He watched the couple make their cautious way down the starscraper's fetid stairwell. Kiera Salter had done well seducing the boy, but then what fifteen-year-old male could possibly resist Marie Skibbow's body? Kiera didn't even have to enhance the physique she had possessed. She just put on a mauve tank top and a short sky-blue skirt and let nature wreak havoc on the boy's hormone balance—as she had done with Anders Bospoort.

The monitoring sub-routine assigned to observe Horgan flowed through the neural cells behind the stairwell's polyp walls, spreading out through the surrounding sectors to interface with the starscraper's existing routines. An invisible, all-encompassing guardian angel. It was checking for threats, the possibility of danger. Horgan was another of Rubra's myriad descendants. Cosseted, privileged, and cherished; his mind silently, stealthily guided into the correct academic spheres of interest, and bequeathed a breathtaking arrogance for one so young. He had all the hallmarks of conceit endemic to Rubra's tragic protégés. Horgan was proud and lonely and foul tempered. A lanky youth with dark Asian skin, and giveaway indigo eyes, if his chromosomes had granted him the muscle weight to back up his narcissistic personality he would have been involved in as many fights as the young Dariat.

Naturally he admitted no surprise when Kiera/Marie confided her attraction to him. A girl like that was his due.

Kiera and Horgan stepped out of the stairwell onto the eighty-fifth-floor vestibule.

Dariat felt the monitoring routine flood into the apartment's stratum of neural cells and interrogate the autonomic routines within, reviewing local memories. This was the crux. It had taken him two days to modify the apartment's routines. None of his usual evasions had ever had to withstand examination by such a large personality sub-routine before, it was virtually sentient in its own right.

There was no alarm, no bugle for help to Rubra's principal consciousness. The monitor routine saw only an empty apartment waiting for Horgan.

"They are coming," Dariat told the others in Anders Bospoort's bedroom. All three possessed were with him. Ross Nash who rode in Bospoort's own body, a Canadian from the early twentieth century. Enid Ponter, from the Australian-ethnic planet Geraldton, dead for two centuries, who occupied Alicia Cochrane's mortal form. And Klaus Schiller, possessing Manza Balyuzi's body, a German who muttered incessantly about his Führer, and seemingly angered at having to take on an Asian appearance. The body was now markedly different to the image contained in his passport flek the day he disembarked from the *Yaku*. His skin was blanching; jet-black hair streaked with expanding tufts of fine blond strands; the gentle facial features shifting to rugged bluntness, eyes azure blue. He had even grown a couple of centimetres taller.

"And Rubra?" Enid Ponter asked. "Does he know?"

"My disruption routines have worked. The monitor can't see us."

Ross Nash looked slowly round the bedroom, almost as though he was sniffing a trace of some exotic scent in the air. "I sense it. Behind the walls, there is a coldness of heart."

"Anstid," Dariat said. "That's what you sense. Rubra is just an aspect of him, a servant."

Ross Nash made no attempt to hide his disgust.

None of them really trusted him, Dariat knew. They were strong enemies who had agreed a precarious truce because of the damage they could each inflict on the other. Such a stand-off could never last long. Human doubts and insecurities gnawed at such restraints, chafing at reasonableness. And the stakes on both sides were high, accelerating the devout need to see treachery in every hesitant breath and wary footstep.

But he would prove his worthiness as few had done before. Entrusting them with not merely his life, but his death as well. It was all so absurdly logical.

He needed their awesome powers of manifestation, and at the same time retain his affinity. Their power came from death, therefore he must die and possess a body with the affinity gene. So simple when you say it quick. And completely mad. But then what he had seen these last few days defied sanity.

Horgan and Kiera entered the apartment. They were kissing even as the door closed.

Dariat concentrated hard, his affinity strumming the new neural routines alive with a delicate harmony of deceit. The image of the twined figures was incorporated into one of them. An illusive fallacy; generated by a misappropriated section of the habitat's neural cells massing ten times that of the human brain. Small in relation to the total mass of the neural strata, but enough to make the illusion perfect, giving the phantom Horgan and Kiera weight and texture and colour and smell. Even body heat. The sensitive cells registered that as they started to tug each other's clothes off with the typical impatience of teenagers in lust.

Most difficult of all for Dariat to mimic was the constant flow of emotion and feeling Horgan emitted unconsciously into the affinity band. But he managed it, by dint of careful memory and composition. The monitor routine looked on with tranquil disinterest.

There was a split in Dariat's mind, like alternative quantum-cosmology histories, two realities diverging. In one, Horgan and Kiera raced for the bedroom, laughing, clothes flying. In the other . . .

Horgan's eyes blinked open in surprise. The kiss had delivered every promise her body made. He was primed for the greatest erotic encounter of his life. But now she was sneering contemptuously. And four other people were coming into the lounge from one of the bedrooms. Two of the men were huge, in opposite directions.

Horgan barely paid them any attention. He had heard of deals like this, whispered terrors amongst the kids in the day clubs. Snuffsense. The bitch had set him up as the meat they would rape to death. He turned, his leg muscles already taut.

Something—strange, like a hard ball of liquid—hit him on the back of the head. He was falling, and in the distance a choir of infernal angels was singing.

Dariat stood aside as Ross Nash hauled the semiconscious Horgan into the bedroom. He tried not to stare at the boy's feet, they were floating ten centimetres in the air.

"Are you ready?" Kiera asked, her tone dripping with disdain.

He walked past her into the bedroom. "Do we get to screw afterwards?"

Dariat had favoured an old-fashioned capsule you swallowed rather than a transfusion pad or medical package. It was black—naturally—two centimetres long. He had acquired it from his regular narkhal supplier. A neurotoxin, guaranteed painless, she promised. As if he could complain if it wasn't.

He grinned at that. And swallowed, almost while his conscious mind was diverted. If it did hurt she was due for some very pointed lessons on consumer rights from an unexpected direction.

"Get on with it," he told the figures grouped round the bed. Tall and reedy, they were now, mud-brown effigies a sculptor had captured through a blurred lens. They bent over the spread-eagled boy and sent cold fire writhing up and down his spine.

The poison was fast acting. Guaranteed. Dariat was losing all feeling in his limbs. Sight greyed out. His hearing faded, which was a relief. It meant he didn't have to listen to all that screaming. "Anastasia," he muttered. How easy it would be to join her now. She only had a thirty-year head start, and what was that compared to infinity? He could find her.

Death.

And beyond.

A violent jerk of both body and mind. The universe blew away in all directions at once, horrifying in its immensity. Silence shrouded him; a silence he considered only possible in the extremity of intergalactic space. Silence without heat or cold, without touch or taste. Silence singing with thoughts.

He didn't look around. There was nothing to look with, nowhere to look, not in this, the sixth realm. But he knew, was aware of, what shared this state with him, the spirits Anastasia had told him about as they sat in her tepee so long ago.

Nebulous minds wept tears of emotion, their sorrow and lamentation splashing against him. And whole spectra of hatreds; jealousy and envy, but mostly self-loathing. They were spirits, all of them, lost beyond redemption.

Outside of this was colour, all around, but never present. Untouchable and taunting. A universe he was pleased to call real. The realm of the living. A wondrous, beautiful place, a corporeality crying out for belonging.

He wanted to beat against it, to demand entry. He had no hands, and there was no wall. He wanted to call to the living to rescue him. He had no voice.

"Help me!" his mind shrieked.

The lost spirits laughed cruelly. Their numbers pressed against him, vast beyond legion. He had no single defined location, he found, no kernel with a protective shell. He was everywhere at once, conjunctive with them. Helpless against their invasion. Lust and avarice sent them prising and clawing at his memories, suckling the sweet draught of sensations he contained. A poor substitute for intrinsicality, but still fresh, still juicy with detail. The only sustenance this arcane continuum boasted.

"Anastasia, help me."

They adored his most shameful secrets, for they carried the strongest passion—stolen glances at women through the habitat sensitive cells, masturbating, the hopeless yearning for Anastasia, impossible promises made in the depth of night, hangovers, gluttony, glee as the club smashed against Mersin Columba's head, Anastasia's vital body hot against him, limbs locking together. They drank it all, deriding him even as they idolized him for the glimpse of life he brought.

Time. Dariat could sense it going by outside. Seconds, mere seconds had elapsed. Here, though, it had little relevance. Time was the length of every memory, governed by perception. Here it was defied as his rape went on and on. A rape which wasn't going to end. Not ever. There were too many of them for it to end.

He would have to abide by it, he realized in dread. And join in. Already he craved the knowledge of warmth, of touch, of smell. Memories of such treasures were all around. He had only to reach out—

The bedroom was damp and cold, its furniture cheap. But he couldn't afford anything more. Not now. The dismissal papers were still in his jacket pocket. The last pay packet was in there with it, but slim now. It had been fatter this afternoon. Before he went to the bar, doing what any man would.

Debbi was rising from the bed, blinking drowsily up at him. Voice like a fucking cat, complaining complaining complaining. Where had he been with his no-good friends? Did he know what time it was? How much had he drunk? Like she always did.

So he told the bitch to shut up, because for once he was utterly pissed off with all the grief she gave him. And when she didn't quieten down he hit her. Even that didn't do it. She was shrieking real loud now, waking up the whole goddamn neighbourhood. So he hit her again, harder this time.

—to devour the pitiful echoes of sensation.

"Holy Anstid, help me your eternal servant. For pity's sake. Help!"

Laughter, only laughter. So he raged back and lost himself from the mockery in—

The sun glinting off the Inca temple that rose unchallenged into the sky. It was greater than any cathedral he had ever seen. But its builders were now a nation quelled before Spain's might. And the wealth inside the broken city was beyond that of kings. A life of glory awaited its conquerors.

His armour acted like a furnace in the heat. And the gash on his leg was host to strange brown pustular styes, spores of accursed jungle. Already he was frightened he wouldn't live to see Spain's shores again.

—which wasn't an answer. Calamity and pain were thin substitutes for the explosion of experience which lay in the vaguely perceived extrinsic universe.

Ten seconds. That was all the time that had passed there since he died. And how long had some of the spirits been here? How could they stand it—

Centuries which ache like a lover's heart laid still. To leech and leech what is new to find only that which is stale. Yet even such an insipid taste surpasses the hell which lies further from the taunting glimmer of the lost home of our flesh. Madness and dragons lie in wait for those that venture away from what we discern. Safer to stay. Safer to suffer the known rather than the unknown.

—Dariat could distinguish bursts of Horgan's pain, flashing into the nothingness of the sixth realm like flames licking through black timber. They came from where the spirits were clustered thickest, as though they were dogs fighting for scraps of the rarest steak.

Colours were stronger there, oozing through cracks that curved across dimensions. And the lost spirits howled in a unison of hatred, tempting and taunting Horgan to accede, to surrender. Maidens promised oceans of pleasure while malefactors threatened eternities of torment.

The cracks from which the rich slivers of pain emerged were growing wider as Kiera, Ross, Enid, and Klaus exerted their power.

"Mine," Dariat proclaimed in defiance. "He is mine. Prepared for me. He belongs to me."

"No, mine."

"Mine."

"Mine."

"Mine," rose the cry.

"Kiera, Ross, help me. Let me come back." He knew he could not stay here. Cool quiet darkness called, away from the universe of birth. Where Anastasia had gone, where they would meet again. To linger here with only the memories of yesterday's dreams as a reason was insanity. Anastasia was brave enough to venture forth. He could follow in her wake, unworthy though he was.

"Stop it, I beg," Horgan called. "Rescue me."

The uniformity in which Dariat was suspended began to warp. A tight narrow funnel resembling a cyclone vortex that led down into the fathomless unknowable heart of a gas giant. Spirits were compelled towards it, into it. Dariat was one of them, pressed ever tighter against—

A poorly cobbled street with cottages on either side. It was raining hard. His bare feet were numb with cold. Wood smoke hung in the air, wisps from the chimneys swirled low by the wind. Water was soaking his ragged coat and making his cough worse. His thin chest vibrated as the air bucked in his throat. Ma had taken to giving him sad smiles whenever he told her how bad it felt inside.

Beside him his little sister was sniffling. Her face was barely visible below her woollen bonnet and above her coat collar. He held her hand in his as she tottered along unquestioningly. She looked so frail, worse than him. And winter was only just beginning. There never seemed to be enough broth; and the portions they had were made mostly from vegetables. It didn't fill the belly. Yet there was meat in the butchers.

Townsfolk walked along with them as the church bell pealed incessantly, summoning them. His sister's wooden clogs made dull rapping sounds against the cobbles. They were full with water, swelling her small white feet, and making the sores worse.

Da earned a good wage labouring in the squire's fields. But there was never extra money to spend on food.

The worn penny piece with Queen Victoria's face was clutched in his free hand. Destined for the smiling, warmly dressed pastor.

It just didn't seem right.

"Please," Horgan called, weaker now, thoughts bruised by the pain.

Dariat slid in towards the boy. "I'll help, I'll help," he lied. Light trickled through from the far end of the tunnel,

flickering and shifting, glowing like sunlight shining
through stained glass into a dusty church. But the other
spirits were promising the boy salvation as well—

*Cold claimed the whole world. There was no such thing as
warmth, not even inside his stiff, stinking furs. In the distance the ice wall glared a dazzling silver-white as the sun
beat upon it. The others of the tribe were spread out across
the grassy plain, sloshing their way through ice-mushed
puddles. And glimpsed up ahead through the tall, swaying
spires of grass was the mammoth.*

"Come then, Dariat," Ross Nash called.

Dariat saw his thoughts take form, become harder, as
groping fingers of energy reached for him. He was
strengthened from the touch, given weight, given volume;
hurtling past the other spirits, victory rapturous in his
mind. They howled and cursed as he was sucked down and
down. Faster—in.

Even midnight-blackness was a sight to rejoice.

Eyelids blinked away tears of joy. Pain was glorious because it was real. He moaned at the wounds scored across
his thin body, and felt a strange sensation of dry fluid bathe
his skin. It flowed where his mind directed. So he put forth
his will and watched the lacerations close. Yes!

Oh, my darling Anastasia, you were right all along. And
always I doubted, at the core, in my secret spirit. What
have I done?

Kiera smiled scornfully down at him. "Now you will
forget your feeble quest for revenge against Rubra, and
work with us to capture Magellanic Itg's blackhawks with
your affinity so we may spread ourselves across the stars.
Because to lose now will mean returning to the incarcera-
tion of the beyond. You were there for fifteen seconds,
Dariat. Next time it will be for ever."

Ione didn't sleep. Her body was drowsy, and her eyelids
were heavy enough to remain closed. But her mind floated

at random through the habitat's perception images. She re-acquainted herself with favourite slices of landscape, checking on the residents as they slumbered or partied or worked their way through the small hours. Young children were already stirring, yawning staff arrived at the restaurants which served breakfast. Starships came and (a lower number than normal) went from the spaceport outside. A couple of oddball scavenger craft were rising slowly out of the Ruin Ring along Hohmann transfer orbits which would bring them to an eventual rendezvous with the habitat. Mirchusko was ninety per cent full, its ochre-on-saffron storm-bands bold against the starfield. Five of its seven major moons were visible, various lacklustre crescents strung out across the ring plane.

Far inside the gossamer ribbon of the Ruin Ring two dozen blackhawks were rushing towards the gas giant's equator on a mating flight. Three eggs had already been ejected into Mirchusko's thick inner rings. She listened to their awed, inquisitive exchanges with the blackhawks who had helped stabilize them; whilst racing on ahead their dying parent radiated sublime gratification.

Life goes on, Ione thought, even in dire times like these.

A sub-routine pervading the lakeside house warned her Dominique was approaching the bedroom. She dismissed the habitat perception and opened her eyes. Clement was lying on the furred air mattress beside her, mouth open, eyes tight shut, snoring softly.

Ione recalled the night fondly. He was a good lover, enthusiastic, knowledgeable, slightly selfish—but that was most likely due to his age. And for all the enjoyment, he wasn't Joshua.

The muscle membrane door opened to allow Dominique in. She was dressed in a short royal-purple robe, carrying a tray. "So how was my little brother?" She leered down at the two naked bodies.

Ione laughed. "Growing up big and strong."

"Really? You should abolish incest, I could find out for myself then."

"Ask the bishop. I only do civil and financial laws. Morals are all down to him."

"Breakfast?" Dominique asked, perching on the end of the bed. "I've got juice, toast, coffee, and quantat slices."

"Sounds fine." Ione nudged Clement awake, and ordered the window to clear. The glass lost its deep hazel tint to reveal the placid lake at the foot of the cliff. Tranquillity's axial light-tube was just starting to fluoresce its way up through the orange spectrum.

"Any word in about Laton?" Dominique asked. She sat cross-legged facing Ione and Clement, pouring juice and handing round toast.

"Nothing to add to what the navy voidhawk brought yesterday," Ione said. It was one of the reasons she had turned to Clement, for the comfort of physical contact, the need to be wanted. She had accessed the Confederation Navy's classified report on the energy virus with growing concern.

As soon as Tranquillity reported the contents of Graeme Nicholson's flek she had placed an order for another ten strategic-defence platforms from the industrial stations orbiting outside the spaceport, supplementing the thirty-five which already protected the habitat. The companies were glad of the work, starship component manufacturing was slowing along with the declining number of flights. It didn't take a military genius to work out that Laton was going to try and spread his revolution; and Tranquillity was almost on a direct line between Lalonde and Earth, the core of the Confederation. The first pair of new platforms were nearly ready to deploy, with the rest being completed over another six days. And she was already wondering if she should order more.

Within an hour of the navy voidhawk delivering the warning flek from Trafalgar, she had hired twelve blackhawks to act as close-range patrol vessels, and equipped them with nuclear-armed combat wasps from Tranquillity's reserve stocks. She was thankful there were enough of the bitek craft available to charter. But then since her grandfather opened the habitat as a base for mating flights the blackhawks and their captains had been pretty loyal to Tranquillity and the Lord of Ruin.

What with the extra defences and the patrols, the habitat was developing a siege mentality in the wake of Terrance Smith's departure.

But were her precautions enough?

"How is the alert hitting the Vasilkovsky Line?" Ione asked.

Dominique took a drink of juice. "Hard. We've got twenty-five ships idle in Tranquillity's dock right now. No merchant is going to risk sending cargo until they know for sure Laton isn't at the destination. Three of our captains arrived yesterday, all from different star systems. They all said the same thing. Planetary governments are virtually quarantining incoming starships, asteroid governments too. Give it another week, and interstellar trade will have shut down altogether."

"They'll find the *Yaku* by then," Clement said, tearing a corner off his toast. "Hell, they've probably found it already. The navy voidhawk said it was a Confederationwide alert. No ship is ever more than ten days from a star system. I bet a navy squadron is blowing it to smithereens right now."

"That's what gets me the most," Ione said. "No knowing, having to wait for days for any news."

Dominique leant forwards and squeezed her knee. "Don't worry. The 7th Fleet squadron will stop him from becoming involved. They'll all be back here in a week with their tails between their legs complaining they didn't get a chance to play soldier."

Ione looked up into deep, surprisingly understanding eyes. "Yeah."

"He'll be all right. He's the only man I know who could lie his way out of a supernova explosion. Some leftover megalomaniac isn't going to be a problem."

"Thanks."

"Who?" Clement asked around a full mouth, looking from one girl to another.

Ione bit into a slice of her orange-coloured quantat. It had the texture of a melon, but tasted like spicy grapefruit. Dominique was grinning roguishly at her over a coffee-cup.

"Girls' talk," Dominique said. "You wouldn't understand."

Clement threw a quantat rind at her. "It's Joshua. You've both got the hots for him."

"He's a friend," Ione said. "And he's in way over his silly little head, and we're worried about him."

"Don't be," Clement said briskly. "Joshua showed me round the *Lady Macbeth*. She's got more combat potential than a front-line frigate, and Smith armed her with combat wasps before they left. Anyone damn stupid enough to go up against that starship is dead meat."

Ione gave him a kiss. "Thank you, too."

"Any time."

They ate the rest of their breakfast in companionable peace. Ione was debating what to do for the rest of the day when Tranquillity called. That was the thing with being the absolute ruler of a bitek habitat, she reflected, you don't really have to do anything, thoughts were acted on instantly. But there was the human side to consider. The Chamber of Trade was nervous, the Financial and Commerce Council more so, ordinary people didn't know what was going on. Everybody wanted reassurance, and they expected her to provide it. She had done two interviews with news companies yesterday, and there were three delegations who wanted personal audiences.

Parker Higgens is requesting an immediate interview, Tranquillity told her as she was finishing her coffee. **I recommend you grant it.**

Oh, you do, do you? Well, I think there are more important things for me to attend to right now.

I believe this to be more important than the Laton crisis.

What? It was the ambiguity which made her sit up straighter on the furry bed. Tranquillity was emitting a strong impression of discomfort, as if it was unsure of a subject. Unusual enough to intrigue her.

There has been some remarkable progress with the Laymil sensorium recordings in the last seventy hours. I did not wish to trouble you with the project while you were involved with upgrading my defence and soothing the residents. That may have been my mistake. Last night some of the researchers made an extremely important find.

Which is? she asked avidly.

They believe they have located the Laymil home planet.

The path leading from the tube station to the octagonal Electronics Division building was littered with ripe bronze berries fallen from the tall chuantawa trees. They crunched softly as Ione's shoes helped flatten them further into the stone slabs.

Project staff emerging from the stations gave her the faintly guilty glance of all workers arriving early and finding the boss already in.

Oski Katsura greeted her at the entrance, dressed in her usual white lab smock, one of the few people in the habitat who never seemed perturbed by Ione's escort of serjeants. "We haven't made an announcement yet," she said as they went inside. "Some of the implications are only just sinking in."

The hall where the Laymil stack was kept had changed considerably since Ione's first visit. Most of the experimental electronic equipment had been cleared out. Processor blocks and AV projectors were lined up along the benches, forming individual research stations, each with a rack of fleks. Workshop cubicles behind the glass wall had been converted into offices. The impression was one of academic endeavour rather than out and out scientific pioneering.

"We use this mainly as a sorting centre now," Oski Katsura said. "As soon as they have been decrypted, the sensorium memories are individually reviewed by a panel of experts drawn from every discipline we have here at the project. They provide a rough initial classification, cataloguing incidents and events depicted, and decide if there is anything which will interest their profession. After that the relevant memory is datavised to an investigatory and assessment committee which each division has formed. As you can imagine, most of it has been sent to the Cultural and Psychology divisions. But even seeing their electronics used in the intended context of mundane day-to-day operation has been immensely useful to us here. And the same goes for most of the physical disciplines—engineering, fusion, structures. There's something in most memories for all of us. I'm afraid a final and exhaustive analysis is going to take a couple of decades at least. All we are doing for now is providing a preliminary interpretation."

Ione nodded silent approval. Tranquillity's background memories were revealing how hard the review teams were working.

There were only five other people in the hall, as well as Lieria. They had all been working through the night, and now they were clustered round a tray from the canteen, drinking tea and eating croissants. Parker Higgens rose as soon as she came in. His grey suit jacket was hanging off the back of one of the chairs, revealing a crumpled blue shirt. All-night sessions were obviously something the old director was finding increasingly difficult to manage. But he proffered a tired smile as he introduced her to the other four. Malandra Sarker and Qingyn Lin were Laymil spaceship experts, she a biotechnology systems specialist, while his field was the mechanical and electrical units the xenocs employed in their craft. Ione shook hands while Tranquillity silently supplied profile summaries of the two. Malandra Sarker struck her as being young for the job at twenty-eight, but she had her doctorate from the capital university on Quang Tri, and references which were impeccable.

Ione knew Kempster Getchell, the Astronomy Division's chief; they had met during the first round of briefings, and on several formal social occasions since then. He was in his late sixties, and from a family which lacked any substantial geneering. But despite entropy's offensive, leaving him with greying, thinning hair, and a stoop to his shoulders, he projected a lively puckish attitude, the complete opposite to Parker Higgens. Astronomy was one of the smallest divisions in the Laymil project, concerned mainly with identifying stars which had Laymil-compatible spectra, and searching through radio astronomy records to see if any abnormality had ever been found to indicate a civilization. Despite frequent requests, no Lord of Ruin had ever agreed to fund the division's own radio-telescope array. They had to make do with library records from universities across the Confederation.

Kempster Getchell's assistant was Renato Vella, a swarthy thirty-five-year-old from Valencia, on a four-year sabbatical from one of its universities. He acted both excited and awed when Ione greeted him. She wasn't quite sure if it was her presence or their discovery which instigated his jitters.

"The Laymil home planet?" Ione asked Parker Higgens, permitting a note of scepticism to sound.

"Yes, ma'am," the director said. The joy that should have been present at making the announcement was missing, he seemed more apprehensive than triumphant.

"Where is it?" she asked.

Parker Higgens traded a pleading glance with Kempster Getchell, then sighed. "It used to be here, in this solar system."

Ione counted to three. "Used to be?"

"Yes."

Tranquillity? What is going on?

Although it is an extraordinary claim, the evidence does appear to be slanted in their favour. Allow them to complete their explanation.

All right. "Go on."

"It was a recording that was translated two days ago,"

Malandra Sarker said. "We found we had got the memory of a Laymil spaceship crew-member. Naturally we were delighted, it would give us a definite blueprint for one of their ships, inside and out, as well as the operating procedures. Up until now all we've had is fragments of what we thought were spaceship parts. Well we found out what a Laymil ship looks like all right." She datavised one of the nearby processor blocks; its AV pillar shone an image into Ione's eyes.

The Laymil ship had three distinct sections. At the front were four white-silver metal ovoids; the large central unit was thirty metres long, with the three twenty-metre units clustered around it—obviously life-support cabins. The midsection was drum shaped, its sides made up from interlaced stone-red pipes packed so tightly there was no chink between them, an almost intestinal configuration. Five black heat-radiation tubes protruded at right angles from its base, spaced equally around the rim. At the rear was a narrow sixty-metre-long tapering fusion tube, with slim silver rings running along its length at five-metre intervals. Right at the tip, around the plasma exhaust nozzle, was a silver foil parasol.

"Is it organic?" Ione asked.

"We think about eighty per cent," Qingyn Lin said. "It matches what we know of their use of biotechnology."

Ione turned away from the projection.

"It is a passenger ship," Malandra Sarker said. "From what we can make out, the Laymil didn't have commercial cargo ships, although there are some tankers and specialist industrial craft."

"This would seem to be correct," Lieria said, speaking through the small white vocalizer block held in one of her tractamorphic arms. "The Laymil at this cultural stage did not have economic commerce. Technical templates and DNA were exchanged between clan units, but no physical or biotechnology artefacts were traded for financial reward."

"The thing is," Malandra Sarker said, sinking down into

a chair, "it was leaving a parking orbit around their home planet to fly to Mirchusko's spaceholms."

"We always wondered why the ship fuel tanks we found were so large," Qingyn Lin said. "There was far too much deuterium and He$_3$ stored for simple inter-habitat voyages, even if they made fifteen trips in a row without refuelling. Now we know. They were interplanetary spaceships."

Ione gave Kempster Getchell a questioning look. "A planet? Here?"

A wayward smile formed on his lips, he appeared indecently happy about the revelation. "It does look that way. We checked the star and planet positions gathered from the spacecraft's sensor array most thoroughly. The system we saw is definitely this one. The Laymil home planet used to orbit approximately one hundred and thirty-five million kilometres from the star. That does put it rather neatly between the orbits of Jyresol and Boherol." He pouted sadly. "And here I've spent thirty years of my life looking at stars with spectra similar to this one. All the time it was right under my nose. God, what a waste. Still, I'm back on the cutting edge of astrophysics now, and no mistake. Trying to work out how you make a planet disappear . . . ho, boy."

"All right," Ione said with forced calm. "So where is it now? Was it destroyed? There isn't an asteroid belt between Jyresol and Boherol. There isn't even a dust belt as far as I know."

"There is no record of any extensive survey being made of this system's interplanetary medium," Kempster said. "I checked our library. But even assuming the planet had literally been reduced to dust, the solar wind would have blown the majority of particles beyond the Oort cloud within a few centuries."

"Would a survey now help?" she asked.

"It might be able to confirm the dust hypothesis, if the density is still higher than is usual. But it would depend on when the planet was destroyed."

"It was here two thousand six hundred years ago," Renato Vella said. "We know that from analysing the position of the other planets at the time the memory was recorded. But if we are to look for proof of the dust I believe we would be better off taking surface samples from Boherol and the gas giant moons."

"Good idea, well done, lad," Kempster said, patting his younger assistant on the shoulder. "If this wave of dust was expelled outwards then it should have left traces on all the airless bodies in the system. Similar to the way sediment layers in planetary core samples show various geological epochs. If we could find it, we would get a good indication of when it actually happened as well."

"I don't think it was reduced to dust," Renato Vella said.

"Why not?" Ione asked.

"It was a valid idea," he said readily. "There aren't many other ways you can make something that mass disappear without trace. But it's a very theoretical solution. In practical terms the energy necessary to dismantle an entire planet to such an extent is orders of magnitude above anything the Confederation could muster. You have to remember that even our outlawed antimatter planetbuster bombs don't harm or ablate the mass of a terracompatible-sized planet, they just wreck and pollute the biosphere. In any case an explosion—multiple explosions even—wouldn't do the trick, they would just reduce it to asteroidal fragments. To turn it into dust or preferably vapour you would need some form of atomic disrupter weapon, probably powered by the star—I can't think what else would produce enough energy. That or a method of initiating a fission chain reaction in stable atoms."

"Perfect mass-energy conversion," Kempster muttered, his eyebrows beetled in concentration. "Now there's an idea."

"And why wasn't the same method used against the Laymil habitats?" Renato Vella said, warming to his theme. "If you have a weapon which can destroy a planet so thoroughly as to eradicate all traces of it, why leave the remnants of the habitats for us to find?"

"Yes, yes, why indeed?" Kempster said. "Good point, lad, well done. Good thinking."

His assistant beamed.

"We still think the habitats destroyed themselves," Parker Higgens said. "It fits what we know, even now." He looked at Ione, visibly distressed. "I think the memory may show the start of the planet's destruction. There is clearly some kind of conflict being enacted on the surface as the ship leaves orbit."

"Surely that was an inter-clan dispute, wasn't it?" Qingyn Lin asked dubiously. "That's what it sounded like to me."

"You are all mistaken in thinking of this problem purely in terms of the physical," Lieria said. "Consider what we now know. The planet is confirmed to have been in existence at the same time the habitats were broken. The Laymil entity whose memory we have accessed is concerned about the transformation in the life-harmony gestalt which is being propagated across an entire continent. A drastic metaphysical change which threatens nothing less than the entire Laymil racial orientation. Director Parker Higgens is correct, these events cannot be discounted as coincidence."

Ione glanced round the group. None of them looked as though they wished to contradict the Kiint. "I think I'd better review this memory myself." She sat in the chair next to Malandra Sarker. **Show me.**

As before, the Laymil body hardened around her own, an exoskeleton which did not—could never—fit. The recording quality was much higher than before. Oski Katsura and her team had been working long hours on the processors and programs required to interpret the stored information. There were hardly any of the black specks which indicated fragmentary data drop-outs. Ione relaxed deeper into the chair as the sensorium buoyed her along.

The Laymil was a shipmaster, clan-bred for a life traversing the barren distance between the spaceholm constellation and Unimeron, the prime lifehost. It hung at the hub of the ship's central life-support ovoid as the drive was readied for flight. There was nothing like the human arrangement of decks and machinery, present even in void-hawks. The protective metal shell contained a biological nest-womb, a woody growth honeycombed with chambers and voyage-duration pouches for travellers, creating an ex-otic organic grotto. Chambers were clustered together without logic, like elongated bubbles in a dense foam; the walls had the texture of tough rubber, pocked with hun-dreds of small holes to restrain hoofs, and emitting a fresh green radiance. Organs to maintain the atmosphere and re-cycle food were encased in the thicker partitions.

The all-pervasive greenness was subtly odd to Ione's human brain. Tubular buttress struts curved through the chamber around the Laymil body, flaring out where they merged with a wall. Its three hoofs were pushed into holes, buttocks resting on a grooved mushroom-stool; its hands were closed on knobby protrusions. A teat stalactite hung centimetres from the feeding mouth. The position was rock solid and immensely comfortable, the nest-womb had grown into a flawlessly compatible layout with the ship-master's body. All three heads slid around in slow weaving motions, observing small opaque composite instrument panels that swelled out of the wall. Ione found it hard to tell where the plastic began and the cells ended; the cellu-lar/mechanical fusion was seamless, as though the womb-nest was actually growing machinery. Panel-mounted lenses projected strange graphics into the Laymil's eyes, in a fashion similar to human AV projectors.

As the heads moved they provided snatched glimpses into other chambers through narrow passageways. She saw one of the Laymil passengers cocooned in its voyage-du-ration pouch. It was swaddled in translucent glittery mem-branes that held it fast against the wall, and a waxy hose supplying a nutrient fluid had been inserted into its mouth, with a similar hose inserted into its anus, maintaining the digestive cycle. A mild form of hibernation.

The Laymil shipmaster's thoughts were oddly twinned,

as though the recording was of two separate thought patterns. On a subsidiary level it was aware of the ship's biological and mechanical systems. It controlled them with a processor's precision, preparing the fusion tube for ignition, maintaining attitude through small reaction thrusters, computing a course vector, surveying the four nest-wombs. There was a similarity here to the automatic functions a human's neural nanonics would perform; but as far as she could ascertain the shipmaster possessed no implants. This was the way its brain was structured to work. The ship's biotechnology was sub-sentient, so, in effect, the shipmaster was the flight computer.

On an ascendant level its mind was observing the planet below through the ship's sensor faculty. Unimeron was remarkably similar to a terracompatible world, with broad blue oceans and vast white cloud swirls, the poles home to smallish ice-caps. The visual difference was provided by the continents; they were a near-uniform green, even the mountain ranges had been consumed by the vegetation layer. No piece of land was wasted.

Vast blue-green cobweb structures hung in orbit, slightly below the ship's thousand-kilometre altitude. These were the skyhavens, most two hundred kilometres in diameter, some greater, rotating once every five or more hours, not for artificial gravity but simply to maintain shape. They were alive, conscious with vibrant mentalities, greater than that of a spaceholm even. A combination of spaceport and magnetosphere energy node, with manufacturing modules clumped around the hub like small bulbous tangerine barnacles. But the physical facets were just supplementary to their intellectual function. They formed an important aspect of the planet's life-harmony, smoothing and weaving the separate continental essence thoughts into a single unified planetwide gestalt. Mental communication satellites, though they contributed to the gestalt as well, sang to distant stars. That voice was beyond Ione completely, both its message and its purpose, registering as just a vague cadence on the threshold of perception. She felt a little darker for its absence, the Laymil shipmaster considered it magnificent.

The skyhavens were packed close together, with small variants in altitude, allowing them to slide along their various orbital inclinations without ever colliding. No segment of the planet's sky was ever left open. It was an amazing display of navigational exactitude. From a distance it looked as though someone had cast a net around Unimeron. She tried to gauge the effort involved in their growth, a planet-girdling structure, and failed. Even for a species with such obvious biotechnology and engineering supremacy the skyhavens were an awesome achievement.

"Departure initiation forthcoming," the shipmaster called.

"Venture boldness reward," the skyhaven essence replied. "Anticipate hope."

Unimeron's terminator was visible now, blackness biting into the planet. Nightside continents were studded with bright green lightpoints, smaller than human cities, and very regular. One southern continent, curving awkwardly around the planet's mass away from the ship's sensors, had delicate streamers of phosphorescent red mist meandering along its coastal zones with exploratory tendrils creeping further inland. The edges were visibly palpitating like the fringes of a terrestrial jellyfish as they curled and flowed around surface features, yet all the while retaining a remarkable degree of integrity. There was none of the braiding or churning of ordinary clouds. Ione considered the effect quite delightful, the mist looked alive, as though the air currents were infected with biofluorescent spoors.

But the Laymil shipmaster was physically repelled by the sight. "Galheith clan essence asperity woe." His heads bobbed around in agitation, letting out low hoots of distress. "Woe. Folly acknowledgement request."

"No relention," the skyhaven essence answered sadly.

As their orbits took them over the continent, the skyhavens would hum in dismay. The life-harmony of Unimeron was being disrupted, with the skyhavens refusing to disseminate the Galheith clan essence into the gestalt. It was too radical, too antagonistic. Too different. Alien and antithetical to the harmony ethos that had gone before.

A tiny flare of sharp blue-white light sprang out of the red mist, dying down quickly.

"**Reality dysfunction,**" the shipmaster called in alarm.

"**Confirm.**"

"**Horror woe. Galheith research death essence tragedy.**"

"**Concord.**"

"**Impetuosity woe release. Reality dysfunction exponential. Prime lifehost engulfed fear.**"

"**Reality dysfunction counter. Spaceholm constellation prime essence continuation hope.**"

"**Confirm. Hope carriage.**" The shipmaster quickly reviewed the other Laymil hibernating in the nest-wombs; both mental traits converging for the evaluation. "**Essencemasters condition satisfactory. Hope reality dysfunction defeat. Hope Galheith atonement.**"

"**Hope joined. Rejoice unity commitment.**"

Where the flare of light had sprung, the jungle was now alight. Ione realized the glimmer of orange must be a firestorm easily over ten kilometres wide.

The spaceship was crossing the terminator. Skyhavens ahead glowed a fragile platinum as the Van Allen radiation belt particles gusted across their web strands.

"**Departure initiation,**" the shipmaster announced. Ionized fuel was fired into the fusion drive's magnetic pinch. A jet of plasma slowly built up. Information streamed into the Laymil's brain, equations were performed, instructions were pushed into the nest-womb's neurons and the coincident hardware's circuits. There was never any doubt, any self-questioning. The terms did not apply.

Unimeron began to shrink behind the ship. The shipmaster focused his attention on the spaceholm constellation, and the frail song of welcome it emitted, so much quieter than the prime lifehost's joyous spirit.

And the memory expired.

Ione blinked free of the stubbornly persistent, green-polluted images. Emotions and sensations were harder to discard.

"What is a reality dysfunction?" she asked. "The shipmaster seemed frightened half to death by it."

"We don't know," Parker Higgens said. "There has never been any reference to it in any of the other memories."

"Ione Saldana, I believe the term reality dysfunction refers to a massive malevolent violation within the Laymil life-harmony essence," Lieria said. "The nature of the Galheith clan was being radically altered by it. However, the impression conveyed by the memory is that it is more than a mental reorientation, it also incorporated a distortion within the local physical matrix. Example: the energy flare."

"It was a weapon?" She shot a tense glance at the two astronomers.

Kempster scratched at his shadow of stubble. "That flare definitely started a fire, so I would have to say yes. But one forest fire is a little different from something which can cause a planet to vanish."

"If it went on to spread through the entire planet's life essence, as seems more than likely," Malandra Sarker said, "then it would have Unimeron's entire technical resources at its disposal. Placed on a war footing, a race like that would have a frightening armaments-production wherewithal."

"I disagree," Renato Vella said. "Granted they could build fleets of ships, and hundreds of thousands of nukes, probably antimatter too. But they are not that much further advanced than us. I still maintain the energy required to destroy a planet is beyond this level of technology."

I was just thinking of the Alchemist, Ione said to Tranquillity. She was almost afraid to mention it in case Lieria could intercept the thought. What was it Captain Khanna said? One idea in a lifetime is all it takes. The Laymil might not have had the initial physical resources, but what about the mental potential of a planetary mind devoted to weapons design?

The possibility is an alarming one, Tranquillity agreed. **But why would they turn it on themselves?**

Good question. "Even if they built a weapon, why would they turn it on themselves?"

The group regarded her with puzzled faces—a child innocently flooring adult logic with a simple question. Then Renato Vella smiled suddenly. "We've been assuming it was destroyed, how about if they just moved it instead?"

Kempster Getchell chuckled. "Oh my boy, what a wonderful notion."

"I bet it would require less energy than obliteration."

"Good point, yes."

"And we've seen they can build massive space structures."

"We are evading the point," Parker Higgens said sternly. "We believe this reality dysfunction, whatever it is, is behind both the removal of the Laymil planet and the suicide of the spaceholms. Our priority now has to be to establish what it was, and if it still exists."

"If the planet was moved, then the reality dysfunction is still around," Renato Vella said, refusing to be deflected. "It is wherever the planet is."

"Yes, but what is it?" Oski Katsura asked with some asperity. "It seems to be many things, some kind of mental plague and a weapon system at the same time."

"Oh shit," Ione said out loud as she and Tranquillity made the connection simultaneously. "Laton's energy virus."

Tranquillity allowed the group to access the report from Dr Gilmore through the hall's communication net processors, giving the images direct to Lieria via affinity.

"My God," Parker Higgens said. "The similarities are startling."

"Similarities, hell," Kempster half-shouted. "That fucker's come back!"

The director flinched at the astronomer's coarse anger. "We can't be sure."

"I'm sorry, Parker, but I cannot in all sincerity consider this to be a coincidence," Ione told him.

"I concur," Lieria said.

"The Confederation, specifically the First Admiral, must be informed immediately," Ione said. "That goes without question. The navy must understand that they are not facing Laton himself but something far more serious. Parker, you will act as my representative in this matter; you have both the authority and knowledge necessary to convey the severity of this reality dysfunction to the First Admiral."

He looked shocked at first, then bowed. "Yes, ma'am."

"Oski, prepare copies of every Laymil memory we have. The rest of you put down what observations you can for the navy staff, whatever you think may help. Tranquillity is recalling one of the patrol blackhawks now, it will be ready to leave for Avon in an hour. I will ask the Confederation Navy office to provide an officer to escort you, Parker, so you had better get ready. Time is important here."

"Yes, ma'am."

Ione Saldana, I also request a blackhawk to convey one of my colleagues home to Jobis, Lieria said. **I judge these events to be of sufficient portent to warrant informing my race.**

Yes, of course. She was aware of Tranquillity summoning a second armed blackhawk back to the docking-ledges even as she acknowledged the Kiint's request. All the remaining resident blackhawks would have to be conscripted for patrol duties now, she thought tersely, probably the independent traders too. Then a stray thought struck. **Lieria, did the Kiint ever hear the skyhavens' starsong?**

Yes.

The finality of the tone stopped Ione from enquiring further. But only for now, she promised herself. I've had enough of this mystic superiority crap they keep peddling.

"Kempster, that red mist over Unimeron's southern continent, was that a part of the reality dysfunction, do you think? There's no mention of it being present on Lalonde."

"Its nature would suggest so," Kempster said. "I can't see that it's a natural phenomenon, not even on that planet. Possibly a secondary effect, a by-product of the interaction with Unimeron's life essence, but definitely connected. Wouldn't you agree, lad?"

Renato Vella had been lost in deep contemplation ever since he accessed Dr Gilmore's report. Now he nodded briefly. "Yes, it is likely."

"Something on your mind?" the old astronomer asked, his cheerfulness reasserting itself.

"I was just thinking. They could build living space structures that completely encircled their world, yet this reality dysfunction still defeated them. Their spaceholms were so frightened of it they committed suicide rather than submit. What do you think is going to happen to us when we confront it?"

8

"Jesus, what's all that red gunk in the air? I don't remember that from the last time we were here. It's almost as if it's glowing. The bloody stuff's covering the whole of the Juliffe tributary network, look." Joshua abandoned the *Lady Mac*'s sensor input and turned to Melvyn Ducharme on the acceleration couch next to his.

"Don't look at me, I'm just a simple fusion engineer. I don't know anything about meteorology. Try the mercs, they're all planet-bred."

"Humm," Joshua mused. Relations between the *Lady Mac*'s crew and the mercenary scout team they were carrying hadn't been exactly optimal during the voyage. Both sides kept pretty much to themselves, with Kelly Tirrel acting as diplomatic go-between—when she was out of the free-fall sex cage. That girl had certainly lived up to her side of the bargain, he thought contentedly.

"Anybody care to hazard a guess?" he called.

The rest of the crew on the bridge accessed the images, but no one volunteered an opinion.

Amarisk was slowly turning round into their line of sight as they closed on the planet. Nearly half of the continent was already in daylight. From where they were, still a hundred thousand kilometres out, the Juliffe and most of its tributaries were smothered in a nebulous red haze. At first inspection it had looked as though some unique refraction effect was making the water gleam a bright burgundy. But once the *Lady Mac*'s long-range optical sensors were focused on Lalonde, that notion had quickly been dispelled. The effect was caused by thousands of long narrow

cloud bands in the air above the surface of the water, clinging to the tributary network's multiple fork pattern with
startling accuracy. Although, Joshua realized, the bands
were much broader than the actual rivers themselves;
where the first band started, just inland from the mouth of
the Juliffe, it was almost seventy kilometres across.

"I've never seen anything like it on any planet," Ashly
said flatly. "Weird stuff; and it is glowing, Joshua. You can
see it stretching beyond the terminator, all the way to the
coast."

"Blood," Melvyn intoned solemnly. "The river's awash
with blood, and it's starting to evaporate."

"Shut it," Sarha snapped. The idea was too close to the
thoughts bubbling round in her own mind. "That's not
funny."

"Do you think it's hostile?" Dahybi asked. "Something
of Laton's?"

"I suppose it must be connected with him," Joshua admitted uneasily. "But even if it is hostile, it can't harm us
at this distance. It's strictly lower atmosphere stuff. Which
means it may be a hazard for the merc scouts, though.
Sarha, tell them to access the image, please." They were
less likely to insult a woman.

A grumbling Sarha requested a channel to the lounge in
capsule C where the seven mercenary scouts and Kelly Tirrel were lying on acceleration couches as the *Lady Mac* accelerated in towards Lalonde. There was a gruff
acknowledgment from her AV pillar, and Joshua grinned in
private.

The flight computer alerted him that a coded signal was
being transmitted from the *Gemal*. "We've detected an unknown atmospheric phenomenon above Amarisk," Terrance Smith said pedantically.

"Yeah, those red clouds sticking to the tributaries,"
Joshua answered. "We see it too. What do you want us to
do about it?"

"Nothing yet. As far as we can make out it is simply polluted cloud, presumably coming from the river itself. If a

sensor sweep shows it to be radioactive then we will re-
assess the landing situation. But until then, proceed as ordered."

"Aye, aye, Commodore," Joshua grunted when the channel was closed.

"Polluted cloud," Melvyn said in contempt.

"Biological warfare," Ashly suggested in a grieved tone.
"Not nice. Typical of Laton, mark you. But definitely not
nice."

"I wonder if it's his famed proteanic virus?" Dahybi
said.

"Doubt it, that was microscopic. And it didn't glow in
the dark, either. I'd say it has to be radioactive dust."

"Then why isn't the wind moving it?" Sarha asked.
"And how did it form in the first place?"

"We'll find out in due course," Warlow said with his
usual pessimism. "Why hurry the process?"

"True enough," Joshua agreed.

The Lady Mac was heading in towards the planet at a
steady one gee. As soon as each ship in the little fleet had
emerged from its final jump into the Lalonde system, it had
accelerated away from the coordinate, the whole fleet
spreading out radially at five gees to avoid presenting an
easy target grouping. Now they were holding a roughly
circular formation twenty thousand kilometres wide, with
Gemal and the cargo ships at the centre.

The six blackhawks were already decelerating into low
orbit above Lalonde to perform a preliminary threat assessment. Bloody show-offs, Joshua thought. Lady Mac
could easily match their six gee manoeuvres if she wasn't
encumbered with escort duties.

Even with naval tactics programs running in primary
mode, Terrance Smith was ever cautious. The lack of any
response from Durringham was extremely bad news, although admittedly half anticipated. What had triggered the
fleet commander's paranoia was the total absence of any
orbital activity. The colonist-carrier starships had gone,
along with the cargo ships. The inter-orbit craft from

Kenyon were circling inertly in a five-hundred-kilometre equatorial parking orbit, all systems powered down—even their navigation beacons, which was contrary to every CAB regulation in the flek. Of the sheriff's office's ageing observation satellite there was no trace. Only the geosynchronous communication platform and civil spaceflight traffic monitoring satellites remained active, their onboard processors sending out monotonously regular signals. He lacked the transponder interrogation code to see if the navy ELINT satellites were functional.

After a quick appraisal, Smith had ordered a descent into a thousand-kilometre orbit. His fleet moved in, the combat-capable starships dumping small satellites in their wake to form an extensive high-orbit gravitonic-distortion-detector network. If any starship emerged within five hundred thousand kilometres of the planet, the satellites would spot it.

The blackhawks released a quintet of military-grade communication satellites as they raced towards the planet. Ion engines pushed the comsats into geostationary orbit, positioning them to give complete coverage of the planet, with overlapping reception footprints covering Amarisk in its entirety.

Twenty thousand kilometres out from Lalonde, the blackhawks split into two groups and swept into a seven-hundred-kilometre orbit at differing inclinations. Each of them released a batch of fifteen observation satellites, football-sized globes that decelerated further, lowering themselves into a two-hundred-kilometre orbit; their parallel tracks provided a detailed coverage sweep over a thousand kilometres wide. The blackhawks themselves, with their powerful sensor blisters augmented by electronic scanner pods, were integrated into the effort to reconnoitre Durringham and the Juliffe tributary basin. The intention was to compile a comprehensive survey with a resolution below ten centimetres for the mercenary scouts to use.

"It's virtually impossible," Idzerda, the captain of the blackhawk *Cyanea*, told Terrance Smith after the first pass.

"That red cloud is completely opaque, except for the edges where it thins out, and even there the images we're receiving of the land below are heavily distorted. I'm not even sure cloud is the word for it. It doesn't move like cloud should. It's almost as if a film of electrophorescent cells has been solidified into the air. Spectrographic analysis is useless with that light it emits. One thing we have noticed; we ran a comparison with the old cartography memory from the sheriff's observation satellite which you supplied. The cloud is brightest over towns and villages. Durringham shines like there's a star buried under there. There is no way of telling what is going on below it. The only villages we can even see are the ones furthest up the tributaries where the glow peters out. And they are wrong."

"Wrong?" Terrance Smith asked.

"Yes. They're the most recently settled, the most primitive ones, right?"

"Yes."

"We've seen stone houses, gardens, domelike structures, metalled roads, heck, even windmills. None of it was there on the old images you gave us, and they were only recorded a month ago."

"That can't possibly be correct," Terrance said.

"I know that. So either the whole lot are holograms, or it's an illusion loaded directly into the observation satellite processors by this electronic warfare gimmick you warned us about. Although we can't see how it disrupts the blackhawks' optical sensors as well. The people who put up that cloud have got some startlingly potent projection techniques. But why bother? That's what we don't understand. What's the point of these illusions?"

"What about power emission centres?" Terrance Smith asked. "It must take a lot of energy to generate a covering layer like that red cloud."

"We haven't found any. Even with their electronic jamming we should be able to spot the flux patterns from a medium-sized fusion generator. But we haven't."

"Can you locate the jamming source?"

"No, sorry, it's very diffuse. But it's definitely ground based. It only affects us and the satellites when we're over Amarisk."

"Is the red cloud radioactive?"

"No. We're fairly sure of that. No alpha, beta, or gamma emission."

"What about biological contamination?"

"No data. We haven't attempted to sample it."

"Make that your priority," Terrance said. "I have to know if it's safe to send the combat scout teams down."

On its following pass, the *Cyanea* released two atmospheric probes. The vehicles were modified versions of the marque used by planet-survey missions, three-metre delta-wing robots with the central cylindrical fuselage crammed full of biological sampling and analysis equipment.

Both of them pitched up to present their heatshield bellies to the atmosphere, curving down towards the surface as they aerobraked. Once they had fallen below subsonic velocity, airscoop intake ramps hinged back near the nose, and their compressor engines whirred into silent life. A preprogrammed flight plan sent them swooping over the first fringes of the red cloud, fifteen kilometres to the south-east of Durringham. Encrypted data pulsed up to the newly established bracelet of communication satellites.

The air was remarkably clear, with humidity thirty per cent down on Lalonde's average. Terrance Smith accessed the raw image from a camera in the nose of one probe. It looked as though it was flying over the surface of a red dwarf star. A red dwarf with an azure atmosphere. The cloud, or haze—whatever—was completely uniform, as though, finally, an electromagnetic wavefront had come to rest and achieved mass, then someone had polished it into a ruby surface. There was nothing to focus on, no perspective, no constituent particles or spores; its intensity was mechanically constant. An optically impenetrable layer floating two kilometres above the ground. Thickness unknown. Temperature unknown. Radiating entirely in the bottom end of the red spectrum.

"No real clouds anywhere above it," Joshua murmured. Like most of the fleet's crews he had accessed the datavise from the atmospheric probes. Something had bothered him about that lack; ironically, more than the buoyant red blanket itself. "Amarisk always had clouds."

Sarha quickly ran a review of the images the fleet had recorded on their approach, watching the cloud formations. "Oh my Lord, they split," she said disbelievingly. "About a hundred kilometres offshore the clouds split like they've hit something." She ran the time-lapse record for them, letting the tumbling clouds sweep through their neural nanonics' visualization. Great billowing bands of cumulus and stratocumulus charged across the ocean towards Amarisk's western shoreline, only to branch and diverge, raging away to the north and south of the Juliffe's mouth.

"Jesus. What would it take to do that? Not even Kulu tries to manipulate its climate." Joshua switched back to a real-time view from *Lady Mac*'s sensor clusters. A cyclone was being visibly sawed into two unequal sections as it pirouetted against the invisible boundary. He ordered the flight computer to open a channel to the *Gemal*.

"Yes, we've seen it," Terrance Smith said. "It has to be tied in with the red cloud cover. Obviously the invaders have a highly sophisticated method of energy manipulation."

"No shit? The point is, what are you going to do about it?"

"Destroy the focal mechanism."

"Jesus, you can't mean that. This fleet can't possibly go into orbit now. With that kind of power available they'll be able to smash us as soon as we're within range. Hell, they can probably pull us down from orbit. You'll have to abort the mission."

"It's ground based, Calvert, we're sure of that. It can't be anywhere else. The blackhawks can sense the mass of anything larger than a tennis ball in orbit, you can't disguise mass from their distortion fields. All we have to do is send in the combat scout teams to locate the invader's bases. That's what we planned on doing all along. You knew that when you signed on. Once we find the enemy, the starships can bombard them from orbit. That's what you're here for, Calvert. Nobody promised you an easy ride. Now hold formation."

"Oh, Jesus." He looked round the bridge to make sure everyone shared his dismay. They did. "What do you want to do? At five gees I can get us to a suitable jump coordinate in twelve minutes—mark."

Melvyn looked thoroughly disgusted. "That bloody Smith. His naval programs must have been written by the most gung-ho admiral in the galaxy. I say jump."

"Smith has a point," Warlow rumbled.

Joshua glanced over at the big cosmonik in surprise. Of everyone, Warlow had been the least eager to come.

"There is nothing hostile in orbit," the bass voice proclaimed.

"It can chop up a bloody cyclone," Ashly shouted.

"The red cloud is atmospheric. Whatever generates it affects lower atmospheric weather. It is planet based, centred on Amarisk. The blackhawks have not been destroyed. Can we really desert the fleet at this juncture? Suppose Smith and the others do liberate Lalonde? What then?"

Jesus, he's right, Joshua thought. You knew you were committed after you took the contract. But . . . Instinct. That bloody obstinate, indefinable mental itch he suffered from—and trusted. Instinct told him to run. Run now, and run fast.

"All right," he said. "We stay with them, for now. But at the first—and I really mean *first*, Warlow—sign of the shit hitting the fan, then we are out of orbit at ten gees. Commitment or no commitment."

"Thank God somebody's got some sense," Melvyn murmured.

"Sarha, I want a constant monitor of all the observation satellite data from now on. Any other shit-loopy atmospheric happenings pop up and I want to be informed immediately."

"Yes, Captain."

"Also, Melvyn, set up a real-time review program of the grav-detector satellite's data. I don't intend us to be dependent on the *Gemal* informing us whether we've got company."

"Gotcha, Joshua," Melvyn sang.

"Dahybi, nodes to be charged to maximum capacity until further notice. I want to be able to jump within thirty seconds."

"They aren't designed for long-term readiness—"

"They'll last for five days in that state. It'll be settled one way or another by then. And I have the money for maintenance."

Dahybi shrugged his shoulders against the couch webbing. "Yes, sir."

Joshua tried to relax his body, but eventually gave up and ordered his neural nanonics to send overrides into his muscles. As they began to slacken he accessed the fleet's command communication channels again, and started to format a program which would warn him if one of the ships dropped out of the network unexpectedly. It wasn't much, but it might be worth a couple of seconds.

The atmospheric probes began to lose height, sliding down towards the surface of the red cloud. "Systems are functioning perfectly," the flight's controlling officer reported. "There's no sign of the electronic warfare effect." She flew them to within five metres of the top, then levelled them out. There was no reaction from the serene red plain. "Air analysis is negative. Whatever holds the boundary together seems to be impermeable. None of it is drifting upwards."

"Send the probes in," Terrance ordered.

The first probe eased its way towards the surface, observed by cameras on the second. As it touched the top of the layer a fan of red haze jetted up behind it, arcing with slow smoothness, like powder-fine dust in low gravity.

"It is a solid!" Terrance exclaimed. "I knew it."

"Nothing registering, sir, no particles. Only water vapour, humidity rising sharply."

The probe sank deeper, vanishing from its twin's view. Its data transmission began to fissure.

"High static charge building up over the fuselage," the control officer reported. "I'm losing it."

The probe's datavise dissolved into garbage, then cut off. Terrance Smith ordered the second one down. They didn't learn anything new. Contact was lost twenty-five seconds after it ploughed into the cloud.

"Static-charged vapour," Terrance said in confusion. "Is that all?"

Oliver Llewelyn cancelled the datavise from *Gemal*'s flight computer. The bridge was dimly lit, every officer lying on an acceleration couch, eyes closed as they helped coordinate the fleet's approach. "It reminds me of a gas giant's rings," the captain said. "Minute charged particles held together with a magnetic flux."

"The blackhawks say there is no magnetic flux, only the standard planetary magnetic field," Terrance corrected automatically. "Was there any sign of biological activity?" he asked the flight control officer on the *Cyanea*.

"No, sir," she said. "No chemicals present either. Just water."

"Then why is it glowing?"

"I don't know, sir. There must be a light-source of some kind deeper inside, where the probes can't reach."

"What are you going to do?" Oliver Llewelyn asked.

"It's a screen, a canopy; they're covering up whatever they're doing below. It's not a weapon."

"It might only be a screen. But it's beyond our ability to create. You can't commit your forces against a total unknown, and certainly not one of that magnitude. Standard military doctrine."

"There are over twenty million people down there, including my friends. I can't leave without at least making one attempt to find out what's going on. Standard military doctrine is to scout first. That's what we'll do." He drew a breath, entering the newly formatted data from the probes into his neural nanonics and letting the tactics program draw up a minimum-risk strategy for physical evaluation of the planetary situation. "The combat scout teams go in as originally planned, although they land well clear of the red cloud. But I'm altering the search emphasis. Three teams into the Quallheim Counties to find the invader's landing site and base; that section of the mission hasn't changed. Then nine teams are to be distributed along the rest of the Juliffe tributaries to appraise the overall status of the population and engage targets of opportunity. And I want the last two teams to investigate Durringham's spaceport; they now have two objectives. One, find out if the McBoeing spaceplanes are still available to effect a landing for the general troops we're carrying in the *Gemal*. Secondly, I want them to access the records in the flight control centre and find out where the starships went. And why."

"Suppose they didn't go anywhere?" Oliver Llewelyn said. "Suppose Captain Calvert is right, and your invaders can just reach up and obliterate ships in orbit?"

"Then where is the wreckage? The blackhawks have cat-alogued every chunk of matter above the planet, there's nothing incongruous this side of Rennison's orbit."

Oliver Llewelyn showed him a morbid grin. "Lying in the jungle below that red cloud."

Terrance was becoming annoyed with the captain's con-stant cavils. "They were unarmed civil ships, we're not. And that makes a big difference." He put his head back down on the couch's cushioning, closed his eyes, and began to datavise the revised landing orders through the secure combat communication channels.

The fleet decelerated into a one-thousand-kilometre orbit, individual ships taking up different inclinations so that Amarisk was always covered by three of them. Repeated sweeps by the swarm of observation satellites had revealed no new information on ground conditions below the red cloud. The six blackhawks rose up from their initial seven-hundred-kilometre orbit to join the rest of the starships, their crews quietly pleased at the extra distance between them and the uncanny aerial portent.

After one final orbit, alert for any attack from the invaders, the mercenary scout teams clambered into the waiting spaceplanes, and Terrance Smith gave the final go ahead to land. As each starship crossed into the umbra its spaceplane undocked and performed a retro-burn which pushed it onto an atmosphere interception trajectory. They reached the mesosphere nine thousand kilometres west of Amarisk and aerobraked over the nightside ocean, sending a multitude of hypersonic booms crashing down over the waves.

Brendon couldn't keep his attention away from the red cloud. He was piloting the spaceplane from the *Villeneuve's Revenge*, taking the six-strong mercenary scout team down to their designated drop zone a hundred kilometres east of Durringham. The cloud had been visible to the forward sensors when they were still six hundred kilometres offshore. From there it hadn't been so bad, a colossal meteorological marvel. Now though, up close, the sheer size was intimidating him badly. The thought that some entity had constructed it, deliberately built a lightway of water vapour in the sky, was acutely disconcerting. It hung twenty kilometres off the starboard wing, inert and immutable. Far ahead he could just see the first fork as it split to follow one of the tributaries. That more than anything betrayed its artificiality, the fact that it had intent.

As the spaceplane eased down level with it he could see the land underneath. Unbroken jungle, but dark, tinted a deep maroon.

"It's blocking a lot of light under there," said Chas Paske, the mercenary team's leader.

"Oui," Brendon agreed, without looking round. "The computer estimates it's about eight metres thick at the edge, getting thicker deeper in, though," he reported.

"Probably three or four hundred metres at the centre, over the river itself."

"What about the electronic warfare field?"

"It's there all right, I'm having some trouble with the flight control processors, and the communication channel is suffering from interference, the bit rate is way down."

"As long as we can transmit the coordinates for the starships to bombard," Chas Paske said. "That's all we need."

"*Oui*. Landing in three minutes."

The spaceplane was approaching the natural clearing they had chosen. Brendon checked with the blackhawks, which were still supervising the observation. He was assured there was no human activity within at least two kilometres of the clearing.

Qualtook and baby giganteas ringed their allocated landing site. Inside them, burnt and broken stumps were still visible through the mantle of vines, evidence of the fire which had raged decades ago. The spaceplane nosed its way cautiously over the edge of the trees, as if afraid of what it might find. Birds took to the air in dismay at the huge predator shape and the clarion squealing it emitted. A radar pulse slashed across the ground, slicing straight through the vine leaves to uncover the extent of the stumps. Landing struts unfolded from the fuselage, and after a minute of jostling to avoid the more hazardous protrusions it settled gently on the ground, compressor nozzles blasting dusty fountains of dead leaves and twigs into the air.

Even as silence stole back into the clearing the outer airlock hatch was opening. Chas Paske led his team out. Five disc-shaped aerovettes swooped into the sky, rim-mounted sensors probing the encircling jungle for motion or infrared signatures.

The mercenaries began to unload their equipment from the open belly holds. They were all boosted, their appearance way outside the human norm. Chas Paske was bigger than any cosmonik, his synthetic skin the colour of weather-worn stone. He didn't bother with clothes other than weapon belts and equipment straps.

"Hurry it up," Brendon said. "The jamming is getting worse, I can hardly get a signal through to the satellites."

Pods and cases began to accumulate on the battered carpet of vines. Chas was hauling down a portable zero-tau pod containing an affinity-bonded eagle when an aerovette datavised him that there was a movement among the trees. He picked up a gaussrifle. The aerovette was hovering a metre over the trees, providing him an image of heads bobbing about through the undergrowth. Nine of them, making no attempt to hide.

"Hey," a woman's voice shouted.

The mercenaries were fanning out, positioning the aerovettes to provide maximum coverage.

"The blackhawks said there was no one here," Chas Paske said. "For Christ's sake."

"It's the optical distortion," Brendon replied. "It's worse than we thought."

The woman emerged into the clearing. She shouted again and waved. More people came out of the trees behind her, women and a couple of boys in their early teens. All of them in dirty clothes.

"Thank God you're here," she said as she hurried over to Chas. "We waited and waited. It's terrible back there."

"Hold it," Chas said.

She didn't hear him, or ignored him. Looking down to pick her way over thick tangles of vines. "Take us away. Up to the starships, anywhere. But get us off this planet."

"Who the hell are you? Where do you come from?" At the back of his mind Chas thought how odd it was that his appearance didn't affect her. People normally showed at least some doubt when they saw his size and shape. This woman didn't.

His neural nanonics cautioned him that the gaussrifle's targeting processor was malfunctioning. "Stop," he bellowed when she was six metres away. "We can't take any chances; you may have been sequestrated. Now, where are you from?"

She jerked to a halt at the volume he poured into his voice. "We're from the village," she said, slightly breathless. "There's a whole group of them devils back there."

"Where?"

The woman took another pace forward and pointed over her shoulder. "There." Another step. "Please, you must help us." Her haggard face was imploring.

All five aerovettes fell out of the sky. The ground below Chas Paske's feet began to split open with a wet tearing sound, revealing a long fissure from which bright white light shone upwards. Neural nanonics overrode all natural human feelings of panic, enforcing a smooth threat response from his body. He jumped aside, landing beside the smiling woman. She hit him.

Terrance Smith had lost contact with three of the eleven spaceplanes which had landed, and the remaining three in the air were approaching the Quallheim Counties. The observation satellites were unable to provide much information on the fate of those that had been silenced, the images they produced of the drop zones were decaying by the minute. None of them had crashed, though, the blackout had come after they landed. Encouraged by his tactics program, which estimated forty per cent losses at the first landing attempt, Terrance assumed the worst, and contacted the last three spaceplanes.

"Change your principal drop zone to one of the backups," he ordered. "I want you to land at least a hundred and fifty kilometres from the red cloud."

"It's moving!" Oliver Llewelyn shouted as Terrance was receiving acknowledgements from the pilots.

"What is?"

"The red cloud."

Terrance opened a channel to the processor array which was correlating the observation satellite images. Whorls and curlicues were rippling along the edges of the red bands, flat streamers, kilometres long, were shooting out horizontally, like solar prominences. The eerie symmetry of the velvet-textured clouds was rupturing, their albedo fluctuating as vast serpentine shadows skated erratically from side to side.

"It knows we're here," Oliver Llewelyn said. "We've agitated it."

For one brutally nasty second Terrance Smith had the idea that the massive formation of forking cloud bands was alive, a gas-giant entity that had migrated across interplanetary space from Murora. Damn it, the thing did resemble the kind of convoluted storm braids which curled and clashed in week-long hostilities among the hydrogen and frozen ammonia crystals of gas-giant atmospheres. "Don't be absurd," he said. "Something is deliberately causing those disturbances. This may be our best chance yet to discover how they shape that thing. Get onto the blackhawk captains, I want every sensor we have available focused on it. There has to be some kind of energy modulation going on down there. Something has to register on some spectrum we're covering."

"Want to bet?" Oliver Llewelyn muttered under his breath. He was beginning to wish he had never agreed to fly the *Gemal* for Smith, and to hell with the legalities of refusing. Some things were more important than money, starting with his life. He grudgingly began datavising instructions round the blackhawks.

The communication links with another two spaceplanes dropped out. But three had landed their mercenary teams without incident and were already back in the air.

It is possible, Terrance told himself fiercely as the pearl-white specks soared to safety above the tangled tributary basin. We can find out what's happening down there.

He observed the red cloud sending huge pseudostorm streamers boiling ferociously out across the jungle. A navigational graphics overlay revealed the position of the spaceplanes still on the ground. The largest swellings were heading for the landing zones with unerring accuracy.

"Come on," he urged them through clenched teeth. "Get up. Get out of there."

"Sensors report no energy perturbation of any kind," Oliver Llewelyn said.

"Impossible. It's being directed. What about the sensors the invaders used to track our spaceplanes, have we detected those?"

"No."

Five more spaceplanes were back in the air, streaking away from the grasping claws of red cloud. Two of them were ones they had lost contact with earlier. Terrance heard a cheer go round the *Gemal*'s bridge, and added his own whoop of exhilaration.

Now the mission was starting to come together. With the combat scout teams on the ground they would have targets soon. They could start hitting back.

The last three spaceplanes landed in the Quallheim Counties. One of them was from the *Lady Macbeth*.

The *Villeneuve's Revenge* had the standard pyramid structure of four life-support capsules at its core. They were spherical, divided into three decks, with enough volume to make life for the crew of six very agreeable. Fifteen passengers could be accommodated with only a modest reduction in comfort. None of the six mercenaries they had brought to Lalonde had complained. The fittings, like the rest of the ship's systems, could be classed as passable with plenty of room for improvement, upgrading, or preferably complete replacement.

Erick Thakrar and Bev Lennon sailed headfirst through the ceiling hatch of the lounge deck above the spaceplane hangar. The compartment's surfaces were coated in a thin grey-green foam with stikpads at regular intervals, though most of them had lost their cohesiveness. Furniture was all lightweight composite that had been folded back neatly into alcoves, producing a floor made up of labelled squares, hexagons, and circles like some mismatched mosaic. Walls were principally storage lockers, broken by hatchways into personal cabins, the red panels of emergency equipment cubicles, and inbuilt AV player blocks with their projector pillars. There was a watery vegetable smell in the air. Only two of the lightstrips were on. Several purple foil food wrappers were drifting through the air like lost aquatic creatures, with a couple more clamped against the roof grilles by the gentle air flow. A black flek was spinning idly. It all added up to lend the lounge a discarded appearance.

Erick slapped casually at the plastic-coated ladder stretching between floor and ceiling, angling for the floor hatch. His neural nanonics reported André Duchamp opening a direct communication channel.

"He's docking now," the captain datavised. "Or attempting to."

"How is the communication link? Can you get anything from inside?"

"Nothing. It's still a three per cent bit rate, just enough to correlate docking procedures. The processors must have been bollocksed up quite badly."

Erick glanced over his shoulder at Bev, who shrugged. The two of them were armed; Bev with a neural jammer, Erick a laser pistol he hoped to God he wouldn't have to use.

The spaceplane had emerged from the upper atmosphere and re-established contact with a weak signal from a malfunctioning reserve transmitter. Brendon claimed the craft had been subject to a ferocious electronic warfare attack which had decimated the on-board processors. They only had his word for it, the link had barely enough power to broadcast his message, a full-scale datavise to assess the internal electronic damage was impossible.

In view of the known sequestration ability of the invaders, André Duchamp wasn't taking any chances.

"That *anglo* Smith should have anticipated this," André grumbled. "We should have had an examination procedure set up."

"Yes," Erick agreed. He and Bev traded a grin.

"Typical of this bloody bodge-up mission," André chuntered on. "If he wants proper advice he should have experienced people like me on his general staff, not that arsehole Llewelyn. I could have told him you need to be careful when it comes to sequestration. Fifty years of experience, that's what I've got, that counts for a hell of a lot more than any neural nanonics tactics program. I've had every smartarse weapon in the Confederation thrown at me, and I'm still alive. And he goes and chooses a Celt who makes a living from flying the brain dead. *Merde!*"

Bev's legs cleared the rim of the hatch into the lounge, and he datavised a codelock at it. The carbotanium hatch slid shut, its seal engaging with a solid clunk.

"Come on, then," Erick said. He slipped through the floor hatch into the lower deck. His neural nanonics provided him with an image from the starship's external sensor clusters. The spaceplane was floundering, just metres away from the hull. Without a full navigational datalink, Brendon was having a great deal of trouble inserting the spaceplane's nose into the hangar's docking collar. Novice pilots could do better, Erick thought, wincing as reaction-control thrusters fired hard, seconds before the radar dome tip scraped the hull. "Ye gods. We might not have anything left to inspect at this rate."

The lower deck was severely cramped, comprising an engineering shop for medium-sized electromechanical components, a smaller workshop for electronic repairs, two airlocks, one for the spaceplane hangar, one for EVA work, storage bins, and space armour lockers. Its walls were naked titanium, netted with conduits and pipes.

"Collar engaged," André said. "Madeleine is bringing him in now."

The whine of actuators carried faintly through the starship's stress structure into the lower deck. Erick accessed a camera in the hangar, and saw the spaceplane being pulled into the cylindrical chamber. A moth crawling back inside a silver chrysalis. The retracted wings had a clearance measured in centimetres.

He datavised orders into the hangar systems processors. When the spaceplane came to rest, power lines, coolant hoses, and optical cables plugged into umbilical sockets around its fuselage.

"There's very little data coming out," Erick said, scanning the docking operations console holoscreen to see the preliminary results of the diagnostic checks. "I can't get any internal sensors to respond."

"Is that the processors or the sensors themselves which are malfunctioning?" André asked.

"Difficult to tell," Bev said, hanging from a grab hoop behind Erick to look over his shoulder. "Only ten per cent of the internal databuses are operational, we can't access the cabin management processors to see where the fault lies. God knows how Brendon ever piloted that thing up here. He's missing half of his control systems."

"Brendon is the best," Madeleine Collun said.

The console's AV pillar bleeped, showing a single communication circuit was open from the spaceplane. Audio only.

"Anyone out there?" Brendon asked. "Or have you all buggered off to lunch?"

"We're here, Brendon," Erick said. "What's your situation?"

"The atmosphere is really bad, total life-support failure as far as I can make out . . . I'm gulping oxygen from an emergency helmet . . . Get that airlock connected now . . . This is killing my lungs . . . I can smell some kind of plastic burning . . . Acid gas . . ."

"I can't cycle the cabin atmosphere for him," Erick datavised to André. "Our pumps are working and the hose seals are confirmed, but the spaceplane pressure valves won't open, there's no environmental circuit."

"Get him into the airlock, then," André said. "But don't let him into the life-support cabin, not yet."

"Aye, aye."

"Come on!" Brendon shouted.

"On our way, Brendon."

Bev ordered the airlock tube to extend. The spaceplane's fuselage shield panel slid back to reveal the circular airlock hatch below.

"Lucky that worked," Erick muttered.

Bev was staring into the AV pillar's projection, watching the airlock tube seal itself to the hatch rim. "It's a simple power circuit. Nothing delicate about that."

"But there's still a supervising processor— Hell." Environment sensors inside the airlock tube were picking up traces of toxic gases as the spaceplane's hatch swung open. The console holoscreen switched to a camera inside the metal tube. A curtain of thin blue smoke was wafting out of the hatch. A flickering green light shone inside the cabin. Brendon appeared, pulling himself along a line of closely spaced grab hoops. His yellow ship's one-piece was smeared with dirt and soot. The copper-mirror visor of the shell-helmet he was wearing covered his face, it was connected to a portable life-support case.

"Why didn't he put his spacesuit on?" Erick asked.

Brendon waved at the camera. "God, thanks, I couldn't have lasted much longer. Hey, you haven't opened the hatch."

"Brendon, we have to take precautions," Bev said. "We know the invaders can sequestrate people."

"Oh, sure, yes. One moment." He started coughing.

Erick checked the environmental readings again. Fumes were still pouring out of the spaceplane cabin; the airlock tube filters could barely cope.

Brendon opened his visor. His face was deathly white, sweating heavily. He coughed again, flinching at the pain.

"Christ," Erick muttered. "Brendon, datavise a physiological reading please."

"Oh God it hurts." Brendon coughed again, a hoarse croaking sound.

"We've got to get him out," Bev said.

"I don't get any response from his neural nanonics," Erick said. "I'm trying to datavise them through the airlock tube's processor but there isn't even a carrier code acknowledgement."

"Erick, he's in trouble!"

"We don't know that!"

"Look at him."

"Look at Lalonde. They can build rivers of light in the sky. Faking up one injured crewman isn't going to tax them."

"For God's sake." Bev stared at the holoscreen. Brendon was juddering, one hand holding a grab loop as he vomited. Sallow globules of fluid burped out of his mouth, splashing and sticking to the dull-silver wall of the tube opposite.

"We don't even know if he's alone," Erick said. "The hatch into the spaceplane isn't shut. It won't respond to my orders. I can't even shut it, let alone codelock it."

"Captain," Bev datavised. "We can't just leave him in there."

"Erick is quite right," André replied regretfully. "This whole incident is highly suspicious. It is convenient for somebody who wants to get inside the ship. Too convenient."

"He's dying!"

"You may not enter the airlock while the hatch into the spaceplane remains open."

Bev looked round the utilitarian lower deck in desperation. "All right. How about this? Erick goes up into the lounge and codelocks that hatch behind him, leaving me in here. That way I can take a medical nanonic in to Brendon, and I can check out the spaceplane cabin to make sure there aren't any xenoc invaders on board."

"Erick?" André asked.

"I've no objection."

"Very well. Do it."

Erick swam up into the empty lounge, and poised himself on the ladder. Bev's face was framed by the floor hatch, grinning up at him. "Good luck," Erick said. He datavised a codelock at the hatch's seal processor, then turned the manual fail-safe handle ninety degrees.

Bev twisted round as soon as the carbotanium square closed. He pulled a medical nanonic package from a first aid case on the wall. "Hold on, Brendon. I'm coming in." Red environmental warning lights were flashing on the panel beside the circular airlock tube hatch. Bev datavised his override authority into the management processor, and the hatch began to swing back.

Erick opened a channel into the lounge's communication net processor, and accessed the lower deck cameras. He watched Bev screw up his face as the fumes blew out of the open hatchway. Emerald green light flared out of the spaceplane's cabin, sending a thick, blindingly intense beam searing along the airlock tube to wash the lower deck. Caught full square, Bev yelled, his hands coming up instinctively to cover his eyes. A ragged stream of raw white energy shot along the centre of the green light, smashing into him.

The camera failed.

"Bev!" Erick shouted. He sent a stream of instructions into the processor. A visualization of the lower deck's systems materialized, a ghostly reticulation of coloured lines and blinking symbols.

"Erick, what's happening?" André demanded.

"They're in! They're in the fucking ship. Codelock all the hatches now. Now, God damn it!"

The schematic's coloured lines were vanishing one by one. Erick stared wildly at the floor, as if he could see what was happening through the metal decking. Then the lounge lights went out.

"Five minutes until we land at our new drop zone, and the tension in the cabin is really starting to bite," Kelly Tirrel subvocalized into a neural nanonics memory cell. "We know something has happened to at least five other spaceplanes. What everyone is now asking themselves is, will the extra distance protect us? Do the invaders only operate below their protective covering of red cloud?"

She accessed the spaceplane's sensors to observe the magnificent, monstrous spectacle again. Thousand-kilometre-long bands of glowing red nothingness suspended in the air. Astounding. This far inland they were slim and complex, interwoven like the web of a drunken spider above the convoluted tributaries. When she had seen them from orbit, calm and regular, they had intimidated her; up close and churning like this they were just plain frightening.

Coiling belts were edge-on with the starboard wing, growing larger as they spun through the sky towards the spaceplane. It was an excellent image, a little bit too realistic for peace of mind. But then the spaceplane's sensor array was all military-grade. Long streamlined recesses on both sides of the fuselage belly were now holding tapering cylindrical weapons pods—maser cannons providing a three-hundred-and-sixty-degree cover, an electronic warfare suite, and a stealth envelope. They weren't quite an assault fighter, but neither were they a sitting duck like some of the spaceplanes.

Typical that Joshua would have a multi-role spaceplane. No! Thank God Joshua had a multi-role spaceplane.

Forty minutes into the descent, and already she missed him. You're so weak, she swore at herself.

Kelly was starting to have serious second thoughts about the whole assignment. Like all war correspondents, she supposed. Being on the ground was very different to sitting in the office anticipating being on the ground. Especially with the appearance of that red cloud.

The seven mercenaries had discussed that appearance ad nauseam the whole way in from the emergence point. Reza Malin, the team's leader, had seemed almost excited by the prospect of venturing below it. Such adverse circumstances were a challenge, he said. Something new.

She had taken time to get to know all of them reasonably well. So she knew what Reza said wasn't simple bravado.

He had been a Confederation Navy Marine at one time. An officer, she guessed; he wasn't very forthcoming about that period of his life, nor subsequent contracts as a marshal on various stage one colony planets. But he must have been good at the second oldest profession, money in large quantities had paid for a considerable number of physical enhancements and alterations. Now he was one of the elite. Like a cosmonik, blurring the line between machine and human. The kind of hyper-boosted composite the mundane troops stored in zero-tau on the *Gemal* aspired to become.

Reza Malin retained a basic humanoid shape, although he was now two metres tall, and proportionally broad. His skin was artificial, a tough neutral grey-blue impact-resistant composite with a built-in chameleon layer. He didn't bother with clothes any more, and there were no genitalia (rather, no external genitalia, Kelly recorded faithfully). Cybernetic six-finger claws replaced his natural hands. Both forearms were wide, with integral small-calibre gaussrifles, his skeleton rigged to absorb recoil. Like Warlow, his face was incapable of expression. Black glass bubble-shields covered both eyes; the nose was now a flat circular intake which could filter chemical and biological agents. The back and sides of his bald skull were studded with a row of five sensor implants, smooth centimetre-wide ulcerlike bulges.

Despite the lack of expression, she learned a lot from his voice, which was still natural. Reza wasn't easily flustered. That and a civilized competence, the way the other six followed his orders without question, gave her more confidence than she would otherwise have had in the scouting mission. In the final analysis, she realized, she trusted him with her life.

The spaceplane banked sharply. Kelly was aware of Ashly Hanson focusing the optical sensors on a small river three kilometres below. The silvery water had a curious speckling of white dots.

"What does he think he's doing?" Pat Halahan asked. The team's second in command was sitting in the seat next to her. A ranger-scout, as he described himself, slimmer and smaller than Reza, but with the same blue-grey skin, and powerful adipose legs. Each forearm had twin wrists, one for ordinary hands, one a power data socket for plug-ins—weapons or sensors. His senses were all enhanced, with a raised rim of flesh running from the corner of his eyes right around the back of his skull.

"Hey, what's happening, Ashly?" he called out. Electronic warfare was a thought all the mercenaries were sharing.

"I'm going to land us here," Ashly said.

"Any particular reason?" Reza Malin asked with quiet authoritativeness. "The surveyed back-up landing site is another seventy kilometres south-east."

"Listen, anyone who can create that damn cloud can intercept our communications without even trying. They'll have every site Terrance Smith ever reviewed marked in a big red circle that says 'hit this'."

There was a moment's silence.

"Smart man," Pat Halahan muttered to Kelly. "I wish we'd had him on the Camelot operation. Lost a lot of good people because the general hired too many virgins."

"Go ahead," Reza said.

"Thank you," Ashly sang back. The spaceplane dived steeply, spiralling at an angle which sent Kelly's stomach pressing up against her collar bones. "Are you quite sure you want to land?" the pilot asked. "You ask me, we're in way over our heads. Terrance Smith couldn't organize a gang-bang in a brothel."

"If Smith is going to beat the invaders, the starships have to know where to hit them," Reza said. "For that you need us. We always go in at the shit end. It's what we're good at."

"Whatever you say."

"Don't worry about us. Ultra-tech never works well in jungle terrain, nature is just too damn messy. And I don't think I've seen many jungles worse than this one. They can probably swat us with some energy blast, even lob a baby-nuke on us if they're feeling particularly bitchy. But they've got to find us first. And rooting us out of that forest wilderness is going to be tricky, I'll make bloody sure of that. You just make sure you and young Joshua stay intact to pick us up afterwards."

"If I'm alive, I'll pick you up."

"Good, I'll hold you to that."

The spaceplane's yaw angle reversed as it performed an abrupt roll. Kelly clung to the armrests with white knuckles as the webbing shifted its hold around her body. This wasn't a clean aerodynamic dive, it was a death plummet.

"How you doing, Kell?" Sewell shouted, sounding hugely amused. Sewell was one of the team's three combat-adept types, and looked it. Standing two metres thirty, his leathery skin matt-black, and woven through with a web of energy absorption/dispersal fibres. His head was virtually globular, a glossy shell that protected his sensors, sitting on a short neck. Trunklike upper arms supported dual elbows; he had attached heavy-calibre gaussrifles to the top joints.

Chuckles went round the cabin. Kelly realized her eyes were tight shut, and forced herself to open them. The spaceplane was shaking.

"You should eat, take your mind off it," Sewell crowed. "I've got some big gooey slices of strawberry creamcake in my pack. Want some?"

"When you were boosted, the doctors wired your neural nanonics to your liver," she said. "It was one fuck of a lot smarter than your brain, bollockhead."

Sewell laughed.

A judder ran through the cabin as the wings began to sweep out.

"Irradiate the drop zone, Ashly, please," Reza said.

"Affirmative."

"There might be civilians down there," protested Sal Yong, another of the combat-adepts.

"Doubt it," Ashly said. "The nearest village is fifty kilometres away."

"We're not on a Red Cross mission, Sal," Reza said.

"Yes, sir."

The spaceplane twisted again.

Great swaths of maser radiation poured out of the unblemished sky around the small shallow river. Hundreds of birds dropped to the ground or splashed into the water, charred feathers smoking; vennals tumbled from the trees, limbs still twitching; sayce howled briefly as their hides wizened and cracked, then died as their brains broke apart from the intense heat; danderil nibbling at the vegetation collapsed, their long elegant legs buckling as their viscera boiled. The verdant emerald leaves of the trees and vines turned a darker, bruised shade of green. Flowers shrivelled up. Berries and fruit burst open in puffs of steam.

The spaceplane came down fast and level. It actually landed in the river, undercarriage struts crushing the stony bed, nose jutting over the grassy bank. Steam and spray erupted from the water as it was struck by the compressor jets, sending a large circular wave sloshing outwards over the bank.

Sewell and Jalal were first out, the two big combat-adept mercenaries didn't wait for the aluminium airlock stairs to extend. They jumped down into the lathery water, covering the quiet wilting trees with their gaussrifles, and sprinted ashore. The half-metre depth didn't even slow them down.

Reza released a couple of aerovettes, ordering them to scan the immediate jungle. The stealthed, disc-shaped aerial combat robots were a metre and a half wide, their central section a curving mesh-grid to protect the wide-cord contra-rotating fans in the middle. Five infrared lasers were mounted around their rim, along with a broad passive-sensor array. They hummed softly and slipped through the air, climbing up to traverse the top of the nearby trees.

Pat Halahan and Theo Connal were second to emerge, following the first two mercenaries ashore. Theo Connal had a short body, one and a half metres tall, boosted for jungle roving. His skin was the same tough chameleon envelope as Reza and Pat, but his legs and arms were disproportionately long. Both feet were equipped with fingers instead of toes. He walked with an apeish stoop. Even his bald head portrayed simian characteristics, with a tiny button nose, squashed circle mouth, and slanted eyes, heavily lidded.

He activated the chameleon circuit when he landed in the water, and scrambled up the shallow incline of the bank. Only a faint mauve optical shimmer betrayed his silhouette. As soon as he reached a tree he seemed to embrace it, then levitated, spiralling round the trunk. At which point the spaceplane sensors lost him, even the infrared.

"My God," Kelly said. She had wondered why Reza had included someone as basically harmless-looking as Theo on the team. A small buzz of excitement began in her belly. This kind of flawless professionalism was darkly enticing; it was easy to see how combat missions became so narcotic.

Another pair of aerovettes skimmed off over the trees.

Sal Yong and Ariadne, the second ranger, came down the airlock steps. Ariadne was the only other female on the team, although her gender was obscured like all the others. There was very little difference between her and Pat, maybe lacking just a few centimetres in height, and her sensor band was broader.

"Now or never, Kelly," Reza said.

"Oh, now," she said, and stood up. "Definitely." The visor of her shell-helmet slid down. Collins had given her carte blanche on selecting her equipment back in Tranquillity, so she had asked for Reza's advice and bought what he suggested. After all, it was in his own interest not to have a liability tramping through the jungle with the scout team. "Keep it simple, and make it the best," he'd said. "You're not combat trained, so all you have to do is keep up with us and stay undetected."

"I can load combat programs into my neural nanonics," she'd offered generously.

Reza simply laughed.

She had wound up with a one-piece suit of rubbery

body-armour, produced in the New Californian system, that would protect her from a modest level of attack from both projectile and energy beam weapons. Reza had taken her to an armourer who serviced mercenary equipment, and had a chameleon layer added.

More aerovettes whirred overhead as she hurried down the airlock steps into the river. Steam hung in the air. She was glad of the shell-helmet's air filters, cremated birds bobbed around her ankles.

Pat Halahan and Jalal were unloading the gear from the forward cargo hold.

"Help them," Reza ordered Kelly. He was wading through the shallows, carrying some composite containers. A nylon harness held a black metallic sphere about twenty centimetres in diameter to his right side, just above his equipment belt. Kelly wondered what it was, her neural nanonics couldn't identify it, there were no visible features to assist the search and comparison program. None of the other mercenaries had one. She knew this wasn't the time to ask.

The spaceplane's steps were already folding back into the fuselage. She set to, stacking the metal cases and composite containers on the muddy grass of the bank.

Reza and Pat carried a trunk-sized zero-tau pod ashore. The black negating surface evaporated to reveal a white plastic cylinder. It split open, and a mahogany-coloured geneered hound lumbered out. Kelly thought its fangs could probably cut through her armour suit.

Reza knelt down beside the big beast and ruffled its head fondly with his hand. "Hello, Fenton. How are you, boy?"

Fenton yawned, pink tongue hanging limply between his front fangs.

"Go have a look round for me. Go on."

Reza patted his hindquarters as he rose. Fenton swung his neolithic head round to give his master a slightly maligning look, but trotted off obediently into the undergrowth.

Kelly had been standing perfectly still. "He's well trained," she said vaguely.

"He's well bonded," Reza replied. "I have affinity neuron symbionts fitted."

"Ah."

Pat and Jalal were wading ashore with a second zero-tau pod.

"*Adieux*," Ashly datavised.

The spaceplane lifted with a brassy shriek. Vigorous geysers of water sprouted under the compressor nozzles, splashing up against the carbotanium fuselage. Then it was above the trees, undercarriage folding up, and the geysers withering away to white-foam ripples.

Kelly tracked her shell-helmet sensors round the forbidding wall of water-basted jungle. Oh, crap, I'm committed now.

She watched the spaceplane pitch up nearly to the vertical and accelerate away into the eastern sky at high speed. Her neural nanonics said they had landed less than three minutes ago.

The explosion was large enough for the *Gemal*'s ordinary sensor clusters to pick it up as the starship fell into the planet's umbra, leaving Amarisk behind. For the vastly more sensitive observation satellites in low orbit it registered as a savage multi-spectrum glare, overloading some scanners.

Terrance Smith's neural nanonics informed him it was the spaceplane from the blackhawk *Cyanea*, which had been landing a scout team in the Quallheim Counties. It had been on the ground when the blast happened. "What the hell did that?" he demanded.

"No idea," Oliver Llewelyn replied.

"Shit. It was over seventy kilometres from the nearest piece of red cloud. Did the scout team get clear?"

"No response from any of their personal communicator blocks," one of the bridge's communication officers reported.

"Bugger." His neural nanonics' strategic display showed

him the remaining four spaceplanes climbing into orbit. Seven more had already docked with their parent starships. Two were manoeuvring for a rendezvous.

"Do you want to divert a spaceplane for a rescue?" Oliver asked.

"Not without confirmation that someone is alive down there. It was a hell of an explosion. The electron matrices must have shorted out."

"Neat trick if you can do it," Oliver said. "They have a lot of safeguards built in."

"Do you suppose that electronic warfare—"

"Sir, message from the *Villeneuve's Revenge*," the communications officer said. "Captain Duchamp says the invaders have boarded his ship."

"*What?*"

"That was one of the spaceplanes we lost contact with," Oliver said.

"You mean they're up in orbit?" Terrance asked.

"Looks like it."

"Christ." He datavised the processor managing the command communication channels, ready to issue a general alert. But his neural nanonics informed him a couple of starships were leaving their assigned orbital slots. When he requested the strategic display it showed him *Datura* and *Gramine* under acceleration, rising out of the thousand-kilometre orbit. His fist hit the acceleration couch cushioning. "What is happening?"

"The spaceplanes from both the *Datura* and *Gramine* experienced communication difficulties," Oliver said in a strained voice. He glanced over at Terrance Smith. The ordinarily prim bureaucrat looked haunted.

"Cut them out of our communication net," Terrance ordered. "Now. I don't want them to access our observation satellite data."

"They're running," Oliver said. "They must be heading for a jump coordinate."

"Not my problem."

"The hell it isn't. If they are xenocs, you'll be letting them loose in the Confederation."

"If they have the technology to put together that cloud, they already have bloody starships. My concern and mission is Lalonde. I'm not sending the blackhawks to intercept them, we don't have the numbers to send ships off on wild-goose chases."

"Their drives aren't right," Oliver said. "They aren't burning the fuel cleanly. Look at the spectroscopic analysis."

"Not now, fuck it!" Terrance shouted. He glared at Oliver. "Contribute something positive or shut up." His neural nanonics linked him in to the communication processor, opening direct channels to the remaining starships. "This is an emergency warning," he datavised. Even as the painful phrase emerged, he wondered how many listeners were still under his command.

The *Lady Macbeth*'s bridge was completely silent as Terrance Smith's voice came out of the AV pillars.

"Oh, Jesus," Joshua moaned. "This is all we need."

"It looks like *Datura* and *Gramine* are preparing to jump," Sarha said. "Sensor clusters and thermo-dump panels are retracting." She frowned. "Most of them, anyway. Their thrust is very erratic. They should be above the five-thousand-kilometre gravity-field boundary in another four minutes."

"This invasion force is too big, isn't it," Joshua said. "We're not going to save Lalonde, not with what we've got."

"Looks that way," Dahybi said in a subdued tone.

"Right then." Joshua's mind was immediately full of trajectory graphics. A whole range of possible jump coordinates to nearby inhabited star systems popped up.

You'll be abandoning Kelly, a voice in his head said.

It's her choice.

But she didn't know what was happening.

He instructed the flight computer to retract the thermo-dump panels. Fully extended, the panels couldn't withstand high-gee acceleration. And if he was going to run, he wanted to do it fast.

"As soon as Ashly returns we're leaving," he announced.

"What about the merc team?" Warlow asked. "They are dependent on us knocking out the invader's bases."

"They knew the risks."

"Kelly is with them."

Joshua's mouth tightened into a hard line. The crew were looking at him with a mixture of sympathy and concern.

"I'm thinking of you, too," he said. "The invaders are coming up here after us. I can't order you to stay in these circumstances. Jesus, we gave it our best shot. There isn't going to be any mayope again. That's all we ever really came for."

"We can make one attempt to pick them up," Sarha said. "One more orbit. A hundred minutes isn't going to make much difference."

"And who's going to tell Ashly he has to go down there again? The invaders will know he's coming down for a pick-up."

"I'll pilot the spaceplane down," Melvyn said. "If Ashly doesn't want to."

"She's my friend," Joshua said. "And it's my spaceplane."

"If there's any trouble in orbit, then we'll need you, Joshua," Dahybi said. The slightly built node specialist was uncharacteristically firm. "You're the best captain I've ever known."

"This is both melodramatic and unnecessary," Warlow said. "You all know that Ashly will pilot it."

"Yes," Joshua said.

"Joshua!" Melvyn shouted.

But Joshua's neural nanonics were already feeding him an alarm. The gravitonic distortion warning satellites were recording nine large gaps in space being forcibly opened.

Thirty-five thousand kilometres above Lalonde, the voidhawks from Meredith Saldana's 7th Fleet squadron had arrived.

An electronic warfare technique that can knock out power circuits as well as processors? What the hell have we come up against?

A single gleam of bright pale green light shone up into the lounge through the inspection window in the middle of the floor hatch. There was movement below.

"Erick, what's happening?" André Duchamp datavised.

The channel to the lounge's net processor was thick with interference. Erick's neural nanonics had to run a discriminator program to make any sense of the captain's signal.

"We're getting power drop-outs all over the ship!" Madeleine called.

Erick pushed off from the ladder, and grasped the floor hatch's handle to steady himself. Very gingerly he edged his face over the fifteen centimetre diameter window and directly into the beam of light. A second later he was airborne, arms and legs cycling madly as a twisted shout burst from his lips. He hit the ceiling. Bounced. Grabbed at the ladder as his body spasmed in reaction.

Erick had looked into hell. It was occupied by goblinesque figures with hideous bone faces, long, reedy limbs, large arthritis-knobbed hands. They dressed in leather harnesses sewn together with gold rings. A dozen at least, boiling out of the airlock tube. Grinning with tiny pointed teeth.

Three of them had clung to Bev, yellow talon fingers slashing rents in his ship-suit. His head had been flung back, mouth open in black horror as the abdominal gashes spewed entrail strands of translucent turquoise jelly. And suicide-terror shone in his eyes.

"Did you see that?" Erick wailed.

"See what? *Merde*! The net is screwed, our databuses are glitched. I'm losing all control."

"Dear God, they're xenocs. They're fucking xenocs!"

"Erick, *enfant*, dear child, calm down."

"They're killing him! They love it!"

"Calm! You are an officer on my ship. Now calm. Report!"

"There's twelve—fifteen of them. Humanoid. They've got Bev. Oh, God, they're chopping him to pieces." Erick shifted a stored sedative program into primary mode, and immediately felt his breathing regularize. It seemed heartless, callous even, wrapping Bev's suffering away behind an artificial cliff of binary digits. But he needed to be calm. Bev would understand.

"Are they heavily armed?" André asked.

"No. No visible weapons. But they must have something in the spaceplane, that light I saw—"

All six electronically operated bolts on the floor hatch thudded back together. The metallic bang rang clear across the lounge.

"God . . . André, they just cracked the hatch's codelock." He stared at it, expecting the manual bolts to slide open.

"But none of the systems processors are working in that capsule!"

"I know that! But they cracked it!"

"Can you get out of the lounge?"

Erick turned to the ceiling hatch and datavised the code at it. The bolts remained stubbornly in place. "The hatch won't respond."

"Yet they can open it," André said.

"We can cut through it," Desmond Lafoe suggested.

"Our hatches and the capsule decking have a monobonded carbon layer sandwiched in," Erick replied. "You'd never get a fission blade through that stuff."

"I can use a laser."

"That will allow them into the other capsules, and the bridge," André said. "I cannot permit that."

"Erick's trapped in there."

"They will not take my ship."

"André—" Madeleine said.

"*Non*. Madeleine, Desmond, both of you into the

lifeboats. I will stay. Erick, I am so sorry. But you understand. This is my ship."

Erick thumped the ladder, grazing his knuckles. This life-support capsule's lifeboats were accessed from the lower deck. "Sure." You murdering pirate bastard. What the fuck do you know about honour?

Someone started hammering on the floor hatch.

They'll be through soon, Erick thought, monobonded carbon or not. Count on it.

"Call Smith for help," Desmond said. "Hell, he's got five thousand troops on the *Gemal*, armed and itching to kill."

"It will take time."

"You got an alternative?"

Erick looked round the lounge, inventorying everything in sight—cabins, lockers filled with food and clothes, emergency equipment cubicles. All he had was a laser pistol.

Think!

Open the floor hatch and pick them off one at a time as they come through?

He aimed the laser at a cabin door, and pressed the trigger stud. A weak pink beam stabbed out, then flickered and died. Several small blisters popped and crackled where it had struck the composite.

"Bloody typical," he said out loud.

Look round again. Come on, there must be something. Those dreary months spent on CNIS initiative courses. Adapt, improvise. Do something.

Erick dived across the intervening space to a wall of lockers, catching a grab loop expertly. There wasn't much in the emergency cubicle: medical nanonics, pressure patches, tools, oxygen bottles and masks, torch, processor blocks with ship's systems repair instructions, fire extinguishers, hand-held thermal sensor. No spacesuit.

"Nobody said it was going to be easy."

"Erick?" André asked. "What is happening?"

"Got an idea."

"Erick, I have spoken with Smith. Several other ships have been hijacked. He is taking some of his troops out of zero-tau, but it will be at least another thirty minutes before anyone can rendezvous with us."

The lounge was getting lighter. When Erick looked over his shoulder he saw a ring of small hemispherical blue flames chewing at a patch of the hard grey-green foam on the floor decking. Little twisters of smoke writhed out from the edge. When a circle of titanium roughly a metre in diameter had been exposed it began to glow a dull orange. "No good, Captain. They're coming through the decking, some sort of thermal field. We haven't got five minutes."

"Bastards."

Erick opened the tool-box, and took out a fission-blade knife. Please, he prayed. The blade shone a cool lemon when he thumbed the actuator. "Sweet Jesus, thank you."

He flew cleanly through the air. A stikpad anchored him near the middle of the ceiling. He pushed the fission blade into the reinforced composite conditioning duct, and started to saw a circle about thirty centimetres wide.

"Madeleine? Desmond?" he datavised. "Are you in spacesuits yet?"

"Yes," Desmond replied.

"You want to do me a *real* big favour?"

"Erick, they cannot stay on board," André warned.

"What do you want, Erick?" Desmond asked.

"Hauling out of here. Soon."

"I forbid it," André said.

"Stuff you," Desmond retorted. "I'm coming down, Erick. You may count on me, you know you can."

"Desmond, if they break into the lounge I will scuttle the ship," André datavised. "I must do it before they glitch the flight computer."

"I know. My risk," Desmond replied.

"Wait to see if they break out of the lounge first," Erick said. "That'll give Desmond a chance to get clear if this doesn't work."

There was no answer.

"You owe me that! I'm trying to save your ship, damn you."

"*Oui, d'accord.* If they get out of the lounge."

The yellow patch on the floor had turned white. It started to hiss, bulging up in the centre, rising into a metre-high spike of light. A ball of fire dripped off the end, gliding up to hit the ceiling where it broke into a cluster of smaller globes that darted outwards.

Erick ducked as several rushed past. He finished cutting a second circle out of the duct and moved along.

Another ball of fire dripped off the spike. Then another. The patch was spreading out over the floor decking, scorching away more of the foam.

"I'm by the hatch, Erick," Desmond datavised.

The empty lounge was awhirl with small beads of white fire. They had stung Erick several times now, vicious skewers of pain that charred out a centimetre-wide crater of skin. He glanced at the ceiling hatch's inspection window to see the sensor-studded collar of an SII spacesuit pressed against it, and waved.

Erick had cut eight holes in the duct when he heard a shrill creaking sound rise above the hiss. When he glanced down he saw the floor decking itself had started to distend. The metal was cherry red, swelling and distorting like a cancerous volcano.

He watched, mesmerized, as the top burst open.

"Erick," a voice called out of the rent. "Let us out, Erick. Don't make it hard on yourself. It's not you we want."

The triangular rips of radiant metal began to curl back like petals opening to greet the dawn. Shapes scuttled about in the gloom below.

Erick kicked away from the stikpad that was holding him to the ceiling. He landed beside the floor hatch.

"We want the ship, Erick, not you. You can go in peace. We promise."

A big bloodshot eye with a dark green iris was looking

at him through the floor hatch's inspection window. It blinked, and the lounge lights came back on.

Erick gipped the manual lock handle, twisted it ninety degrees, and pulled up.

The possessed came up through the open hatch, cautiously at first, glancing round the sweltering smoky lounge with wide eyes. Their skin was as white as bleached bone, stretched tight over long wiry muscles. Oily black hair floated limply. They started to advance towards him, grinning and chittering.

"Erick," they cooed and giggled. "Erick, our friend. So kind to let us in when we knocked."

"Yeah, that's me," Erick said. He had positioned himself beside one of the cabin doors, a silicon-fibre strap round his waist tethering him to a grab hoop. Level with his shoulder, the environment control panel's cover swung free. Erick's right hand rested on a fat red lever inside. "Your friend."

"Come with us," the one in front said as they floated sedately towards him. "Come join us."

"I don't think so." Erick yanked the atmosphere-vent lever down.

The vent system on board a starship was included as a last resort to extinguish fire. It dumped the affected life-support capsule's air straight out of the hull, cutting off oxygen to the flames and killing them dead. And because of the danger a fire represented inside the confined cabin space of a starship, the vent was designed to be quick acting, evacuating an entire deck within a minute.

"NO!" The leader of the possessed screamed in fury and panic. His hands were flung forwards towards Erick in a futile belated attempt to stop the lever clicking home. Spears of white fire arced out of his fingertips.

The panel, its lever, the circuitry behind Erick's hand, and a half metre circle of wall composite flamed into ruin. Molten metal and a fount of incendiary composite blasted outwards.

Erick cried out in agony as his entire right arm was

flayed down to the bone. His neural nanonics responded instantly, erecting an analgesic block. But the shock was too much, he lurched away from consciousness, only to have stimulant programs bully him back. Menus and medical physiological schematics appeared inside his dazed fragile mind. Options flashed in red. Demands for drugs and treatments to be administered at once. And a single constant pressure alarm.

The very air itself howled like a tormented banshee in its rush to escape from the lounge. Thin, layered sheets of smoke drifting around the ruddy cone torn in the floor condensed to form airborne whirlpools underneath the five ceiling grilles. They spun at a fantastic rate, betraying the speed of the air molecules as they were sucked into the duct.

The possessed were in turmoil, clinging desperately at grab hoops and each other, their assumed shapes withering like glitched AV projections to reveal ordinary bodies underneath. All of them were buffeted savagely by the tempest force drawing them inexorably towards the ceiling. One flew up through the hatch from the lower deck, curving helplessly through the air to slam against a ceiling grille. Suction held him there, squirming in pain.

Another lost hold of a grab hoop, to be sucked backwards up to a grille. Both of them tried to push their way off, only to find it was impossible. The strength that the external vacuum exerted was tremendous. They could feel themselves being pulled through the narrow metal bands of the grille. Sharp edges cut their clothes and began shredding the flesh underneath. Ripples of blue and red energy shimmered around their bodies for a short time, delaying the inevitable; but the exertion proved too much, and the ghostlight quickly faded. The bands of metal sawed down to their ribs. Strips of lacerated flesh were torn off. Blood burst free from a hundred broken veins and arteries, foaming away down the conduit. Organs started to swell through the gaps between the ribs.

Erick activated the Confederation Navy's emergency

vacuum-survival program stored in his neural nanonics. His heart began to slow; muscles and organs were shut down, reducing the amount of oxygen they took from his blood, extending the time which the brain could be kept alive. He hung inertly from the strap fastening him to the wall, limbs pulled towards the ceiling. The charred remnant of his right hand broke off and smacked against a grille.

Blood oozed from the blackened meat of his upper arm.

Scraps of paper, clothing, tools, miscellaneous litter, and personal items from the cabins and lower deck plunged through the lounge to crash into the grilles. There might have been enough material to block them, at least long enough for the possessed to rally and try and shut down the vent or retreat back into the spaceplane. But the extra holes Erick had cut into the duct allowed an unrestricted flow of smaller articles into space. Tattered ribbons of water from the shower and taps in the bathroom poured through the open door to streak through the nearest hole.

The uproarious torrent of air began to abate.

Through pain-hazed eyes, Erick had watched the group's leader turn from semi-naked ogre to a podgy forty-year-old man in dungarees as the micro-storm raged. He was hanging onto a grab loop two metres away, legs pointing up rigidly at the nearest grille, trousers and shirt flapping madly. His mouth worked, bellowing curses and obscenities that were snatched away. A red glow grew around his hand, bloodlight shining through the skin, illuminating the bones within. Mucus and saliva streamed from his nose, joining the flood of debris and liquids vanishing into the duct. The seepage began to turn pink, then crimson.

Now the glow from his hand was fading along with the sound and the fury of the evacuating air. He fixed Erick with a disbelieving stare as tears began to bubble and boil from the surface of his eyes. Balls of blood were spitting out of his nostrils with each beat of his heart.

The last wisp of air vanished.

Erick swung round as the force waned, rotating languidly on the end of the tether strap. The physiological medical schematic his neural nanonics were displaying appeared to be a red statue, except for the right arm which was completely black. Each turn swept the lounge into view. He saw the surviving possessed struggling through the solid cloud of junk that filled the achingly silent compartment. It was difficult to tell which of them were alive. Corpses—two badly mutilated—floated and tumbled and collided with the ones trying to reach the floor hatch. Dead or alive, everyone was weeping blood from their pores and orifices as capillaries ruptured and membranes tore from the immense pressure gradient. They were acting out a bizarre three-dimensional wrestling match in slow motion, with the hatch as their prize. It was macabre. It swam from his view.

Next time round there were fewer movements. Their faces—those he would remember without any help from his neural nanonics image-storage program. Turning.

They were slowing, running down like mechanoids suffering a power drain. The vacuum was turning foggy with fluid. He realized some of it was his own. Red. Very red.

Turning.

All purposeful movement had ceased within the lounge. There was only the gentle stirring of soggy dross.

Around and around. And the redness was fading to grey with the ponderous solemnity of a sunset.

Around.

Ilex and its eight cousins flew into a standard defence sphere formation two and a half thousand kilometres wide. Their distortion fields flared out to sample the masses and structure of local space. In their unique perceptive spectrum Lalonde hung below them like a deep shaft bored into the uniformity of space, radiating weak gravity streams to bind its three smaller moons and Kenyon, as it in turn was bound to the bright blue-white star. The interplanetary medium was rich with solar and electromagnetic energy; Van Allen belts encircling the planet shone like sunlight striking an angel's wings. Starships and spaceplanes were revealed in orbit, dense knots in the fabric of space-time, pulsing hotly with electrical and magnetic forces.

Electronic sensors detected a barrage of narrow-beam maser radiation flying between small high-orbit sensor satellites, communication-relay satellites, and the starships. Terrance Smith was being informed of their presence, but there was no hostile response. Satisfied there was no immediate threat, the voidhawks maintained their relative positions for another ninety seconds.

Near the centre of the formation a zone of space the size of a quark warped to an alarming degree as its mass leapt towards infinity, and the first frigate emerged. The remaining twenty warships jumped insystem over the next six minutes. It was a textbook-sharp manoeuvre, giving Admiral Meredith Saldana the widest possible number of tactical options. All he needed was the relevant data to evaluate.

The normal background murmur of voices on Arikara's bridge died away into a shocked hush as the first sensor scans came in. Amarisk occupied the centre of the planet's daylight hemisphere, the red cloud bands above the Juliffe resembling a jagged thunderbolt captured in mid-discharge.

"Was there ever anything like that on this God-blighted planet before?" Meredith Saldana asked in a voice that strained for reasonableness.

"No, sir," Kelven replied.

"Then it is part of the invasion, a new phase?"

"Yes, sir. It looks that way."

"Captain Hinnels, do we know what it is?" the Admiral asked.

The staff science officer looked round from a discussion with two of the sensor evaluation team. "Haven't got a clue, Admiral. It's definitely optically radiant, but we're not picking up any energy emission. Of course, we're still a long way off. It's rearranging the local weather patterns, too."

Meredith datavised for the sensor image again, and grunted when he saw the clouds being parted like candyfloss curtains. "How much power would that take?"

"It would depend on the focal accuracy—" Hinnels broke off at the Admiral's gaze. "Controlling the weather over a quarter of a continent? A hundred, two hundred gigawatts at least, sir; I can't be more specific, not until I understand how they apply it."

"And they have that much power to spare," Meredith mused out loud.

"More importantly, where's it coming from?" Kelven said. "Durringham had thirty-five fusion generators in the dumpers, and three smaller units in the navy office. Their entire power output didn't add up to more than twenty megawatts."

"Interesting point, Commander. You think there has been a massive landing operation since you left?"

"Shipping generators in would be the logical answer."

"But?"

"I don't believe it. The amount of organization necessary to set it up would be incredible, not to mention the number of starships involved. And you saw the flek of Jacqueline Couteur, she can summon up energy from nowhere."

The admiral gave him a dubious stare. "There is a difference between flinging fireballs and this." His hand waved expansively at one of the big bridge holoscreens showing the planet.

"A difference of scale, sir. There are twenty million people on Lalonde."

Meredith didn't like either alternative. Both implied forces immeasurably superior to that available to his squadron. Probably superior to the whole damn navy, he thought in apprehension. "Hinnels? Give me an evaluation. Is it safe to move the squadron closer?"

"Given the capability the invaders are demonstrating,

I'd say it's not safe even being here, Admiral. Moving into low orbit will obviously increase the risk, but by how much I wouldn't like to say."

"Thank you," Meredith said acidly. He knew he shouldn't take out his anxiety on the crew. But damn, that red cloud was unnerving. The size of it.

"Very well, we shall attempt to accomplish the First Admiral's orders and halt any use of force by Smith's starships, with the proviso that at the first sign of aggression from the invaders we withdraw at once. I'm not committing the squadron to fight that . . . whatever it is." He was aware of the relieved looks flashing round the bridge, and diplomatically ignored them. "Lieutenant Kanuik, have you completed a status review of the mercenary ships?"

"Yes, sir."

Meredith datavised the computer for a tactical situation display. The mercenary starships seemed to be in considerable disarray, with three under power, heading out of orbit. Probably running for a jump coordinate. Small VTOL spaceplanes were docked to five of the blackhawks. The Adamist craft left in orbit all had their hangar doors open. Another two spaceplanes were rising up from the planet. He cursed silently. They must have landed their scout teams already.

One of the Adamist starships was venting heavily, a grey jet of atmospheric gas shooting out of the hull. Its ion thrusters glowed bright blue to compensate the wayward thrust.

He saw a blackhawk's purple vector line begin to curl up like a corkscrew. Long-range optical sensors showed him the bitek starship tumbling and twisting hectically.

"Sir!"

He cancelled the datavise. Lieutenant Rhoecus, his staff voidhawk coordination officer, was wincing. "One of the blackhawks, it's . . ." The Edenist puffed his cheeks out and jerked up from his acceleration couch as though someone had thumped him in the belly. "Its captain is being attacked . . . tortured. There are voices. Singing. The blackhawk's frightened." He closed his eyes, teeth gritted. "They want the captain."

"Who does?"

Rhoecus shook his head. "I don't know. It's fading. I had the impression of thousands speaking to the captain. It was almost like a habitat multiplicity."

"Signal from the *Gemal*, Admiral," a communications rating said. "Terrance Smith wants to talk to you."

"Does he now? Put him on."

Meredith looked into his console's AV projection pillar, seeing an exceptionally handsome man with perfectly arranged black hair. Corporate clone, the Admiral thought. Although the usual smooth flair of competence endemic to the type was in danger of crumbling. Terrance Smith looked like a man under a great deal of pressure.

"Mr Smith, I am Admiral Saldana, commander of this squadron; and under the authority invested in me by the Confederation Assembly I am now ordering you to suspend your military operation against Lalonde. Recall all your personnel from the planetary surface and do not attempt to engage the invader's forces. I also require you to hand over all combat wasps and nuclear devices to the navy. The starships currently under your command are free to leave this system once they have complied with my instructions, except for the *Lady Macbeth*, which is now under arrest. Do you understand?"

"They're up here."

"Pardon me?"

Terrance Smith's eyes flicked to one side, glancing at someone out of pick-up range. "Admiral, the invaders are up here. They came up in the spaceplanes that took my scout teams down. They're sequestrating my crews."

Meredith took a second to compose himself. Four minutes into the mission, and already it was catastrophe. "Which crews? Which starships?" He suddenly looked across the bridge at Lieutenant Rhoecus. "Is that what was happening to the blackhawk captain? Sequestration?"

"It could be, yes," the startled Edenist replied.

"I want two voidhawks on that blackhawk, now. Restrain it, I don't want it to leave this system. They are authorized to engage it with combat wasps if it resists. Deploy the remaining voidhawks to prevent any of the Adamist starships from leaving. Commander Kroeber."

"Sir?"

"Squadron to move in now. Full interception duties, I want those starships neutralized. Alert the marine squads, have them stand by for boarding and securement."

"Aye, aye, sir."

He turned back to the AV pillar. "Mr Smith."

"Yes, Admiral?"

"Which ships have been taken over?"

"I don't know for certain. The only ones which haven't sent spaceplanes down to the surface are the *Gemal*, the *Lythral*, the *Nicol*, and the *Inula*. But the *Cyanea*'s spaceplane never made it back."

"Admiral," Kelven interjected.

"Yes, Commander?"

"We don't know the *Gemal* didn't send a spaceplane down. There is no visible evidence of sequestration, certainly not over a communication channel."

Gravity returned to the *Arikara*'s bridge as the fusion drive came on, building swiftly. The Admiral squirmed his shoulders, trying to get completely comfortable before the high gees squashed him. "Point taken, Commander Solanki, thank you. Commander Kroeber, all starships are to be intercepted, no exceptions."

"Aye, aye, sir."

Meredith checked the tactical situation display again. There was only one spaceplane which hadn't rendezvoused with its parent starship now. "And tell that spaceplane to remain where it is. It is not to dock. Solanki, start working out how we are going to restrain any starship crew-members that have been sequestrated."

"Sir, if this sequestration produces the same energy-control ability in the crews that it has in Jacqueline Couteur, I recommend the marines aren't sent into the ships at all."

"I'll bear that in mind. However, we will certainly have to make at least one attempt."

"Admiral," Lieutenant Rhoecus called through gritted teeth. "Another blackhawk captain is being sequestrated."

"Acknowledged, Lieutenant." Meredith reviewed the tactical display again, observing the blackhawk's crazed course, a moth caught in a tornado. "Send a voidhawk to intercept, full interdiction authority." That was a third of his voidhawk force committed already. He needed the rest to contain the Adamist starships. If any more blackhawks were taken over he would have to order a combat wasp launch. They would probably fight back.

With his options diminishing before his eyes, Meredith let out a pained hiss of breath as the Arikara accelerated past six gees. Sensors reported another mercenary starship's fusion drive igniting.

Ashly Hanson came through the airlock tube from the spaceplane and drifted straight into the barrel of a laser rifle. Warlow was holding it, aiming it directly at his forehead.

"Sorry," the hulking cosmonik boomed. "But we have to be sure."

Ashly realized there was a fission saw plugged into his spare left elbow socket, a glowing saffron blade nearly a metre long.

"Sure of what?"

Warlow rotated his principal left arm around the blade. He held a processor block in his hand. "Datavise something into this."

"Like what?"

"Anything, doesn't matter."

Ashly datavised a copy of the spaceplane's maintenance record.

"Thanks. It was Joshua's idea. From the reports we've had it looks like they can't use their neural nanonics."

"Who can't?"

"Spaceplane pilots who have been sequestrated."

"Oh, God. I knew it, they can intercept our communications."

"Yes." Warlow executed a perfect mid-air roll, and headed for the airlock tube. "I'm going to check the spaceplane's cabin, make sure you didn't bring any up. Nothing personal."

Ashly eyed the deck's ceiling hatch. It was locked, red LEDs blinking to show the manual bolts were engaged on the other side. "The invaders are up in orbit?"

"Yes. Busy hijacking starships."

"What's Smith doing about it?"

"Nothing. A naval squadron has arrived, it is in their hands now. They have aborted our mission. Oh, and we're under arrest, too." His diaphragm rattled a metallic approximation of a chuckle.

"The whole fleet? They can't do that. We're operating under *bona fide* contract to the Lalonde government."

"No, just the *Lady Mac*."

"Why us?" But he was talking to a pair of disappearing horned feet.

"Erick? Erick, are you receiving this?"

"His organs are critical, heading for all-out cellular collapse. For God's sake cancel that suspension program."

"Got it. Physiological data coming through."

"Program the nanonic packages for total cranial function support. We have to sustain the brain. André, where the hell's that plasma? He's lost litres of blood."

"Here, Madeleine. Erick, you wonderful crazy *Anglo*. You got them, do you hear me? You got them!"

"Mesh the infuser with his carotid."

"It was magnificent. Pull one little lever and all of them, *baboom*, dead."

"Shit. Desmond, slap a nanonic package on that stump, the epithelium membrane isn't strong enough, he's leaking plasma everywhere."

"His lungs are filling up too, they must be ruptured. Up

the oxidization factor. His brain is still showing electrical activity."

"It is? Oh, thank God."

"Erick, don't try and datavise. We've got you. We won't let you go."

"Do you want to put him in zero-tau?"

"Hell, yes. We're days from a decent hospital. Just let me try and get him stabilized first."

"Erick, my dear one, don't you worry about a thing. For this I will buy you the best, the greatest, clone body in Tranquillity. I swear. Whatever the cost."

"Shut *up*, Captain. He's in enough shock as it is. Erick, I'm going to put you back under. But don't worry, everything is going to be just fine."

The last of the six aerovettes stopped transmitting. Reza Malin upped his cranial audio receptors to full sensitivity, trying to hear the noise of the little vehicle's impact. The sounds of the jungle invaded his brain—insect chirps, animal warbles, leaves crackling—filtered and reduced by discrimination programs. He counted to ten, but there was no crash.

"We're on our own now," he said. The aerovettes had been sent off to the west at a fast walking pace as a decoy, giving the scout team time to melt away into the jungle. He had guessed the invaders could track anything electronic; as Ashly said, if they could create the cloudbands, they could do almost anything. They weren't invincible though, the fact that the team had landed was proof of that. But they were definitely going to provide a formidable challenge. Possibly the greatest Reza would ever face. He liked that idea.

His two hounds, Fenton and Ryall, were slinking through the undergrowth two hundred metres ahead of the scout team, sniffing out people. So far the jungle had been deserted. Pat Halahan's affinity-bonded harpy eagle, Octan, was skimming the treetops, retinal implants alert for the slightest motion below the fluttering leaves. The animals provided a coverage almost as good as the aerovettes.

The team was following a danderil track, heading roughly north-east towards its operational target, the Quallheim Counties. Sal Yong was leading, brushing through the dense vines with barely a sound. With his chameleon circuit activated it looked as though a heavy miniature breeze was whirling along the track. The other six followed quickly (Theo was up overhead somewhere), all of them loaded down with packs, even Kelly. He was pleased to see she was keeping up. If she didn't, it would be a maser pulse through her brain, which would upset some of the team. But he wasn't having a liability of a reporter holding them back. He wondered if she realized that, if it lent a note of urgency to her steps. Probably. She was smart enough, and her bureau chief would certainly have known the deal. So would Joshua, for all his youth, wise beyond his years.

Fenton arrived at a river, and peered out of the bushes lining the steep bank. Reza requested a chart from his inertial-guidance block, and confirmed their position.

"Pat, there's a river one eighty metres ahead, it leads into the Quallheim eventually. Send Octan along it to check for any boat traffic."

"Right." The voice seemed to emerge from a small qualtook tree.

"Are we going to use it?" Ariadne asked, a clump of knotted tinnus vines.

"Yes, providing Octan says nobody else is. It's narrow enough, good tree cover. We can cut a day off our time." He called silently to his hounds, and ordered them to cut back behind the team, covering their rear.

They reached the river three minutes later, and stood at the top of the four-metre bank.

"What is that stuff?" Jalal asked.

The water was clotted with free-floating fleshy leaves, pure white discs a couple of metres in diameter, a tiny purple star in their centre. Each had an upturned rim of a few centimetres, natural coracles. They bobbed and spun and sailed calmly along with the current, undulating with the swell. Some overlapped, some collided and rebounded, but they all kept moving along. Upstream or downstream, whichever way the team looked, the river was smothered in them.

Kelly smiled inside her shell-helmet as the daylight dream of her Lalonde didactic course came slithering into her conscious thoughts. "They're snowlilies," she said. "Quite something, aren't they? Apparently they all bloom at the same time then drift downstream to drop their kernel. It really screws up the Juliffe basin for boat traffic while they're in season." She tracked her retinal implants along the river. It was all going into a neural nanonics memory cell, scenes of Lalonde. Capturing the substance of a place was always important, it gave the report that little edge, adding to reality.

"They're a bloody nuisance," Reza said curtly. "Sewell, Jalal, activate the hovercraft; Pat, Ariadne, point guard."

The two combat-adepts unslung the big packs they were carrying, and took out the programmed silicon craft, cylinders sixty centimetres long, fifteen wide. They slithered down the bank to the water's edge.

Kelly focused on the sky downstream. At full magnification the northern horizon was stained a pale red. "It's close," she said.

"An hour away," Reza said. "Maybe two. This river winds a crooked course."

Sewell shoved a couple of snowlilies aside and dropped his cylinder into the clear patch of water. The hovercraft began to take shape, its gossamer-thin silicon membrane unfolding in a strict sequence, following the pattern built into its molecules. A flat boat-shaped hull was activated first, five metres long, fifteen centimetres thick. Water was pumped into its honeycomb structure, ballast to prevent it from blowing away. The gunwales started to rise up.

Theo Connal dropped lightly to the ground beside

Kelly. She gave a slight start as he turned off his chameleon circuit.

"Anything interesting?" Reza asked.

"The cloud is still shifting about. But it's slower now."

"Figures, the spaceplanes have gone."

"All the birds are flying away from it."

"Don't blame 'em," Pat said.

Kelly's communication block reported that a signal was being beamed down from the geostationary satellites, coded for their team. It was a very powerful broadcast, completely non-directional.

"Kelly, Reza, don't respond to this," Joshua said. "It looks like our communications are wide open to the invaders, which is why I'm transmitting on a wide footprint, a directional beam will pinpoint you for them. OK, situation update; we've got big problems up here. Several spaceplanes were taken over while they were on the ground, the invaders are now busy hijacking starships, but nobody can tell which ones. You know Ashly wasn't sequestrated, so that means you should be able to trust me. But don't take orders from anyone else, especially don't broadcast your location. Problem two, a navy squadron has just arrived and shut down the strike mission. Jesus, it's a total fucking shambles in orbit right now. Some of the hijacked ships are trying to run for a jump coordinate, I've got voidhawks blocking the *Lady Mac*'s patterning nodes, and two of my fellow combat-capable trader starships are heading up to intercept the navy squadron.

"Your best bet is to turn round from that cloud and just keep going, out into the hinterlands somewhere. There's no point in trying to locate the invader's bases any more. I'll do my best to pick you up in a day or two, if this cock-up gets sorted by then. Stay alive, that's all you have to worry about now. I'll keep you informed when I can. Out."

The two hovercraft had finished erecting themselves.

Sewell and Jalal were unpacking the energy matrices and superconductor fan motors ready to slot them into place.

"Now what?" Ariadne asked. The team had all gathered around Reza.

"Keep going," he said.

"But you heard what Joshua said," Kelly exclaimed. "There's no point. We have no orbital fire-power back-up, and no mission left. If we just manage to survive for the next few days it's going to be a bloody miracle."

"You still haven't grasped it yet, have you, Kelly?" Reza said. "This is bigger than Lalonde; this isn't about doing a dirty job for money, not any more. These invaders are going to challenge the entire Confederation. They have the power. They can change people, their minds, their bodies; mould whole planets into something new, something that we have no part in. Some time soon those ships in orbit are going to have to try and attack, to put a stop to it all. It doesn't matter whether it is Smith or the navy squadron. If the invaders aren't stopped here, they'll keep on coming after us. Sure we can run, but they'll catch us, if not out in the hinterlands than back at Tranquillity, or even Earth if you want to run that far. But not me. Everyone has to make a stand eventually, and mine is right here. I'm going to find a base and let the ships know."

Kelly held her tongue, she could well imagine how Reza would react to her wheedling.

"More like it!" Sal Yong proclaimed.

"OK," Reza said. "Finish fitting out the hovercraft, and get our gear stowed."

It took a surprisingly short five minutes to complete their preparations and clamber in. Fully assembled the hovercraft was a simple affair, with a big fan at the rear and two cycloidal impellers filling the skirt with air. It was steered mechanically, by vanes behind the fan.

Kelly sat on a bench at the rear of her craft, riding with Sal Yong, Theo Connal, and Ariadne. Now the decision

9

One thing Princess Kirsten had always insisted on after ascending to the throne of the Principality of Ombey was keeping breakfast a family affair. Crises could come and go, but giving the children quality time was sacrosanct.

Burley Palace, where she ruled from, was situated at the top of a gently sloping hill in the middle of Ombey's capital, Atherstone. Its pre-eminent location gave the royal apartments at the rear of the sprawling stone edifice a grand view over the parks, gardens, and elegant residential buildings which made up the city's eastern districts. Away in the distance was the haze-blurred line of deeper blue that was the ocean.

Atherstone was only fifteen degrees south of the equator, putting it firmly in the tropical climate belt, but the early morning breeze coming in off the ocean kept the temperature bearable until about ten o'clock. So Kirsten had the servants set the table on the broad, red-tiled balcony outside her bedroom, where she could sit amid the yellow and pink flowers of the aboriginal tolla vines that choked the back of the palace, and have a leisurely hour with her husband and three natural-born children.

Zandra, Emmeline, and Benedict were aged seven, five, and three respectively, the only naturally conceived children she and Edward had produced. Their first five offspring had been gestated in exowombs after the zygotes had been carefully geneered to the latest physiological pinnacle which the Kulu geneticists had achieved. It was the Saldana family way; incorporating the freshest advances into each new generation, or at least that part of it destined had been made, she was quite glad to be free of the pack and walking through the jungle.

Reza's lead hovercraft moved out from the bank, skimming easily over the snowlilies, and turned downstream. Fenton and Ryall sat in the prow, blunt heads thrust out into the wind as they picked up speed.

to actually hold high office. Always the elder children, following the old Earth European aristocratic tradition.

Kirsten's first five children would probably live for around two hundred years, whereas she herself and the natural-born three could only hope for about a hundred and eighty years. She had been sixty-six in 2608, when she was crowned in Atherstone Cathedral, two months after her brother Alastair II had assumed the throne on Kulu. As the ninth child, she had always been destined (barring an accident among her older brothers and sister) to rule Ombey, the newest principality.

Like all her nine exowomb siblings, and the five natural-born children of her mother and father, she was tall and physically robust; geneering gave her dark red hair and an oval face with well-rounded cheeks—and of course a thin nose with a tip that curved down.

But geneering could only provide the physical stamina necessary for the stresses resulting in a century of wielding the supreme authority vested in a reigning monarch. She had been in training for the intellectual challenge from birth; first loaded up with the theory, endless politics and economics and management didactic courses, then five years at Nova Kong University learning how to apply them. After serving a twelve-year naval commission (compulsory for all senior Saldanas) she was given divisional management positions in the Kulu Corporation, the massive kingdom-wide utilities, transport, engineering, energy, and mining conglomerate founded by Richard Saldana when he settled Kulu (and still owned solely by the king), graduating up to junior cabinet posts. It was a career designed with the sole intent of giving her unrivalled experience on the nature and use of power for when she came to the throne.

Only the siblings of the reigning monarch ruled the Kingdom's principalities on his behalf, keeping the family in direct command. The hierarchy was long established and extraordinarily successful in binding together nine star systems which were physically spread over hundreds of light-years. The only time it had ever come near to failure was when Crown Prince Michael germinated Tranquillity; and the Saldana family would never let anything like that happen again.

Kirsten came out onto the balcony the morning after the *Ekwan*'s arrival feeling distinctly edgy. Time Universe had been triumphantly broadcasting its Laton exclusive since yesterday evening. She had given the news programmes a quick scan after she woke, and the deluge hadn't yet abated. Speculation over the *Ekwan* and Guyana's code two alert was red hot. For the first time since her coronation she found herself considering censorship as an option for calming the mounting media hysteria. Certainly there would have to be some sort of official statement before the day was over.

She pushed up the voluminous sleeves of her rising robe and looked out over the superb lawns with their mixture of terrestrial and xenoc flower-beds, and the artificial lakes graced by black swans. The sky was a deep indigo, without any cloud. Another gorgeous, balmy day; if not in paradise, then as close as she would ever see. But the sunshine panorama left her unmoved. Laton was a name which carried too many adolescent fear-images with it. Her political instinct was telling her this wasn't a crisis that would blow over in the night. Not this one.

That same political instinct which had kept the Saldana family securely on their various thrones for four hundred years.

The children's nanny brought her excitable charges out of the nursery, and Kirsten managed to smile and kiss them all and make a fuss. Edward lifted little Benedict into his lap, while she seated Emmeline next to her own chair. Zandra sat at her place and reached eagerly for the jug of dorze juice.

"Grace first," Kirsten admonished.

"Oh, Mummy!"

"Grace."

Zandra sighed woundedly, clasped her hands together and moved her lips. "Now can I eat?"

"Yes, but don't bolt it." She signalled one of the four attendant footmen to bring her own tea and toast.

Edward was feeding Benedict slim slices of bread along with his boiled egg. "Is the news still all Laton?" he asked over Emmeline's head.

"Yes," Kirsten said.

He pulled a sympathetic face, and dangled another bread soldier in front of a cheerful Benedict.

They had been married forty years. A good marriage by any reasonable standards, let alone an institution as odd as a royal marriage. Edward was old money, titled as well, and an ex-navy officer who had served with some distinction. He was also geneered, which was a big plus; the court liked matches with the same range of life expectancy—it made things tidy. They hadn't quite been pushed into it by the family, but the pressure had been there for someone like him. All the senior Saldanas displayed for public consumption the Christian monogamy ideal. Divorce was, of course, out of the question. Alastair was head of Kulu's Church, Defender of the Faith throughout the Kingdom. Royalty didn't break the commandments, not publicly.

However, she and Edward enjoyed a relationship of mutual respect, and trust, and even considerable fondness. Maybe love had been there too at the start of it, forty years ago. But what they had now was enough to carry them through the next century together without bitterness and regret. Which was an achievement in itself. When she thought of her brother Claude's marriage . . .

"Mummy's thinking again," Emmeline announced loudly.

Kirsten grinned. "Thinking what to do with you."

"What?" Emmeline squealed.

"Depends what you've done wrong."

"Nothing! Ask Nanny, I've been good. All day."

"She pinched Rosy Oldamere's swimming towel yesterday," Zandra said. Emmeline burst into giggles. "You said you wouldn't tell."

"It was so funny. Miss Eastree had to lend Rosy hers, she was shivering all over."

"Her skin was turning blue," Emmeline said proudly.

"Who's Laton?" Zandra asked.

"A bad man," Edward said.

"Is he on Ombey?"

"No," Kirsten said. "Now eat your rice chips."

Her neural nanonics gave a silent chime, which warned her from the start it was going to be bad news; her equerry would never allow a datavised message through unless it was serious, not at breakfast. She accessed the Defence and Security Council datapackage.

"Trouble," she said resentfully.

Edward glanced over as she rose.

"I'll help get them ready for day club," he said.

"Thanks." He was a good man.

She walked through the private apartments and emerged into the wide marbled corridor which led to the cabinet offices, drawing startled looks and hurried bows from staff who were in early. She was still dressed in her turquoise and grey rising robe.

The official reception room was a decagonal chamber with a vaulting roof that dripped chandeliers. A horizontal sheet of sunlight was pouring in through a ring of azure windows halfway up the walls. Pillars were inlaid with gold and platinum under a lofriction gloss which kept the metal permanently agleam. Holoprints of impossibly violent stellar events alternated with oil paintings around the walls. There were no modern dreamphase or mood-effusion works; the Saldanas always favoured antiquity for the intimation of timeless dignity it gave.

Three people were waiting for her in the middle of the black tushkwood tile floor. Sylvester Geray was at their head; her equerry, a thirty-six-year-old captain wearing his Royal Kulu Navy dress uniform. Hopelessly formal, she always thought, but he hadn't put a foot wrong since he took up the post three months after her coronation.

The other two, both wearing civilian suits, were a less welcome sight. Roche Skark, the director of the ESA office on Ombey, smiled politely at his princess and inclined his head. Despite geneering, he was a rotund man, in his eighties, and twenty centimetres shorter than Kirsten. He had held his post for thirteen years, dealing with threats and perceived threats throughout the sector with pragmatism and a judicious application of abstruse pressure on the people who counted. Foreign governments might grumble endlessly about the ESA and its influence and meddling in local internal politics, but there was never any solid proof of involvement. Roche Skark didn't make the kind of elementary mistakes which could lead to the diplomatic embarrassment of his sovereign.

Jannike Dermot, on the other hand, was quite the opposite of the demure ESA director. The fifty-year-old woman wore a flamboyant yellow and purple cord stripe suit of some expensive silk-analogue fabric, with her blonde hair arranged in a thick, sweep-back style. It was the kind of consummate power dressing favoured by corporate executives, and she looked the part. However, her business was strictly the grubbier side of the human condition: she was the chief of the Internal Security Agency on Ombey, responsible for the discreet maintenance of civil order throughout the principality. Unlike its more covertly active sister agency, the ISA was mostly concerned with vetting politicians and mounting observations on subversives or anyone else foolish enough to question the Saldana family's right to rule. Ninety-five per cent of its work was performed by monitor programs; fieldwork by operatives was kept to a minimum. Also within its province was the removal of citizens deemed to be enemies of the state; which—contrary to popular myth—was actually a reasonably benign affair. Only people who advocated and practised violence were physically eliminated, most were simply and quietly deported to a Confederation penal planet from which there was never any return.

Quite where the boundaries of the respective agencies' operational fields were drawn tended to become a little blurred at times, especially in the asteroid settlements or the activities of foreign embassy personnel. Kirsten, who chaired Ombey's Defence and Security Council, often found herself arbitrating such disputes between the two. It always privately amused her that despite the nature of their work the agencies were both basically unrepentant empire-building bureaucracies.

"Sorry to disturb you, ma'am," Sylvester Geray said. "The matter was deemed urgent."

"Naturally," Kirsten said. She datavised a code at one set of high double doors, and gestured for them to follow. "Let's get on with it."

The doors opened into her private office. It was a tastefully furnished room in white and powder blue, though lacking in the ostentation of the formal State Office next door where she received diplomats and politicians. French windows looked out into a tiny walled garden where fountains played in a couple of small ornamental ponds. Glass-fronted cabinets and bookshelves stood around the walls, heavy with exquisite gifts from visitors and institutions who enjoyed her patronage. A malachite bust of Alastair II sat on a pedestal in an alcove behind her desk (Allie looking over her shoulder, as always). A classic Saldana face, broadly handsome, with a gravity the sculptor had captured perfectly. She remembered her brother practising that sombre poise in the mirror when he was a teenager.

The doors swung shut and Kirsten datavised a codelock at them. The processor in her desk confirmed the study was now physically and electronically secure.

"The datapackage said there has been a new development in the *Ekwan* case," she said as she sat in her high-backed chair behind the desk.

"Yes, ma'am," Jannike Dermot said. "Unfortunately there has."

Kirsten waved a hand for them to sit. "I didn't think it would be good news."

"I'd like to bring in Admiral Farquar," Sylvester Geray said.

"Of course." Kirsten datavised the processor for a security level one sensenviron conference and closed her eyes.

The illusion was of a curving featureless white chamber with a central oval table; Kirsten sat at the head, with Roche Skark and Pascoe Farquar on one side, and Jannike Dermot and Sylvester Geray on the other. Interesting that the computer should be programmed to seat the two agency directors opposite each other, she thought.

"I would like to formally request a system-wide code two defence alert," the Admiral said as his opening gambit.

Kirsten hadn't been expecting that. "You believe Laton will attack us?" she asked mildly. Only she could issue a code two alert, which allowed the military to supersede all civil administration, and requisition whatever personnel and materials it required. Basically it was a declaration of martial law. (A code one alert was a full declaration of war, which only Alastair could proclaim.)

"It's a little more complicated than that, ma'am," the Admiral said. "My staff have been reviewing the whole Lalonde-Laton situation. Now this reporter Graeme Nicholson has confirmed Laton was present on the planet, we have to begin to consider other factors, specifically this energy virus which the Edenists reported."

"I find it quite significant they wanted their findings to be known," Roche Skark said. "In fact they actually requested that we should be told. Which is an unusual step given the Kingdom's standard relationship with Edenism. They obviously considered the threat dangerous enough to exceed any political differences. And considering what happened to our G66 troops in Lalonde's jungle I believe they were totally justified."

"Our analysis of both Jenny Harris's jungle mission and subsequent events on Lalonde suggests that the energy virus and this prevalent sequestration are the same thing," said the Admiral. "What we are dealing with is an invisible force that can take over human thought processes and bestow an extremely advanced energy manipulation ability. Sophisticated enough to act as an electronic warfare field, and construct those white fireballs out of what appears to be thin air."

"I reviewed parts of the jungle mission," Kirsten said. "The physical strength those people had was phenomenal. Are you suggesting anyone who is infected will acquire similar capabilities?"

"Yes, ma'am."

"How is the energy virus transmitted?"

"We don't know," the Admiral admitted. "Though we do consider the fact that Laton called it a virus to be significant. The very nature of the term virus, whether employed in the biological or software sense, implies a pattern that can reproduce itself within its host, usually at an exponential rate. But again, I'm not sure. We really are working in the dark on this one, putting together appraisals from observed data. There has to be a priority to discover its exact nature."

"We can find out relatively easily," Jannike Dermot said. "The answer is in Gerald Skibbow's memory—how he was infected and sequestrated, how the energy virus behaves, what its limits are. I consider him to be the key to alleviating our lack of knowledge."

"Has he recovered yet?" Kirsten asked.

"No. The doctors say he is suffering from a case of profound trauma; it's touch and go if he ever will recover his full intellectual faculties. I want him to undergo a personality debrief."

"Is that wise, in his state?"

The ISA director showed no emotion. "Medically, no, not making him relive the events. But a debrief will provide us with the information we require."

It was a responsibility Kirsten could have done without; Skibbow was somebody's child, probably had children of his own. For a moment she thought of Benedict sitting in

Edward's lap. "Proceed," she said, trying to match the ISA director's impersonality.

"Thank you, ma'am."

"The report from Lalonde said it was Laton himself who warned the Edenists of this energy virus? He claimed he was being attacked by it."

"That's right, ma'am," Admiral Farquar said. "Which is what makes our current problem even more acute."

"You think he was telling the truth, that it is a xenoc incursion?"

"Under the circumstances, I have to give it strong consideration. Which is why I want a code two alert. It will give me the resources to defend the Ombey system should they back up the virus with a physical invasion."

Kirsten felt her palms tingle, that earlier unsettling notion that this wasn't just an ordinary crisis was abruptly resumed. "What do you mean: back up the virus?"

The Admiral flicked a glance at Roche Skark. "It is a possibility that the *Ekwan* brought it to Ombey," he said.

"Oh, dear God. Do you have any proof?"

"We are ninety per cent convinced Gerald Skibbow has been purged, although none of the science team can offer an explanation as to how that happened. However, in their haste to get him here, the Lalonde Embassy's Intelligence team may have overlooked the fact that some of their own people were carrying it. After all, Graeme Nicholson's report confirms that Laton—presumably a sequestrated Laton—was in Durringham the day they left. We have to assume the virus was also present in the city's population at that time."

"When the Admiral's staff informed me of this probability, my Guyana operatives immediately tried to round up the *Ekwan*'s crew and all the embassy staff," the ISA director said. "Three embassy people were unaccounted for: Angeline Gallagher, Jacob Tremarco, and Savion Kerwin. We subsequently found that all three took a spaceplane down to Ombey as soon as the code three restrictions were lifted. We know they landed at Pasto Spaceport seven hours ago. The spaceplane which brought them down suffered from several systems failures and processor glitches during the flight."

"*Ekwan*'s flight from Lalonde was one long list of malfunctions. But since it docked at Guyana its systems have functioned smoothly," the Admiral said.

"And the spaceplane?" Kirsten asked, guessing.

"When my people arrived at the spaceport it was in the line company's engineering hangar," Jannike Dermot said. "The maintenance crews couldn't find a thing wrong with it."

"And there was some difficulty with the zero-tau pod when Gerald Skibbow was put in it," Roche Skark added. "The implication is that this energy virus isn't quite under control, it interferes with nearby electronic equipment on a permanent basis."

"So what you're telling me is that they're down here," Kirsten said.

"Yes, ma'am," the ISA director acknowledged. "I'm afraid we have to assume they are. We're hunting them, of course. I've already alerted the police."

"What about the others who were on board the *Ekwan*?"

"As far as we can tell, they have not been infected."

"Exactly how do you tell?"

"Those that have neural nanonics can use them. We thought that if the energy virus does have an unrestrained capacity to interfere with circuitry then implants would be the first to suffer a loss of efficiency."

"Good idea," she said.

"The rest of *Ekwan*'s complement of colonists are being brought into close proximity with delicate electronics. So far none of the processor arrays have been affected, but we're repeating the procedure every few hours just to be sure."

"What about people the three from the embassy came into contact with while they were in Guyana?"

"We have reviewed the spaceport crews," the Admiral said. "And we're drawing up a schedule now to run the entire asteroid population through these assessments. Including myself, no exceptions."

"I see."

"Will you declare a code two alert, ma'am?"

"I would point out that a code two alert will allow me to quarantine the Xingun continent," Jannike Dermot said. "It is unlikely that Gallagher, Tremarco and Kerwin have left yet. I can shut down all air transport to and from the rest of Ombey. I can also order all road traffic to be suspended, though it may prove difficult to enforce in practice. We might get lucky and trap them in Pasto City itself."

Kirsten summoned up the emergency statutes file from a memory cell and began to review it. Her neural nanonics started to chart a course of action, balancing necessity against the chaos that would come with an attempt to suspend all Ombey's civil and industrial activities. "Without direct evidence of a physical threat I cannot issue a code two alert," she said. "However, I am declaring a code three alert, and a biohazard isolation order for the orbiting asteroids. I want them insulated from each other, from the planet, and from incoming starships. Our orbital facilities are essential to our defence, and I agree that they must be safeguarded against the carriers of this virus. Admiral Farquar, you are to order and enforce a complete quarantine as of now. All civil spacecraft in transit to return to their port of origin.

"Your primary military task is the defence of Ombey and the orbital asteroids with their associated strategic-defence systems. A code three alert will give you the authority to mobilize our resident naval reserve forces; although if it is to mean anything the quarantine order must apply equally to the fleet. Crews will have to be rearranged to ensure that personnel from different asteroid bases are not mixed together. The navy's secondary role will be guarding against further risk of infiltration within the star system as a whole. That means all incoming starships to be refused docking permission.

"As to Xingu, I agree that it should be segregated from

the rest of the planet. Sylvester, you are to inform the Xingun continental parliament's speaker that there is now a state of civil emergency in existence. Shut down its air transport links now. And I do mean now, all planes in the air to return to their departure airport. Admiral, if any refuse to comply you are ordered to shoot them out of the sky. Use the low-orbit strategic-defence platforms."

"Yes, ma'am."

Kirsten watched Sylvester Geray's image freeze as he started to datavise her orders into the secure government communication net. "Roche, do you believe the embassy three are going to try and spread the virus among our population?"

"Their actions so far indicate that is their main goal, yes, ma'am."

"So it's not just them we're looking for, we're going to have to round up anyone they came into contact with?"

"Yes, ma'am. Speed in this instance is going to be essential; the faster they are caught, the fewer possible contamination cases we will have to worry about. It's an exponential problem again. If they go free for too long then it may well escalate beyond our ability to contain, as it did on Lalonde."

"Jannike, do the police on Xingu have sufficient resources to track them down?"

"I believe so, ma'am," the ISA director said.

"May I suggest we use someone more familiar with people who have been sequestrated by the virus?" Roche Skark said smoothly. "I'm sure the civil authorities are capable, Jannike, but I feel hands-on experience will be of immense benefit in this instance. Someone who is perfectly aware of the urgency, and knows how to react should things turn ugly. And judging by Lalonde that may well happen."

The ISA director stared at him levelly. "One of your agents, you mean?"

"It is a logical appointment. I recommend Ralph Hiltch is sent to Xingu to oversee the search."

"Him? The man who didn't even know Laton was on Lalonde, the greatest criminal psychopath the Confederation has ever known!"

"I feel that's slightly unfair, Madam Director. The Confederation and the Edenists believed Laton was dead after the navy destroyed his blackhawks. How many corpses are you currently investigating?"

"Enough," Kirsten said. "That will do, both of you. In this situation I think every resource has to be deployed without prejudice; I'd like to believe we can deal with this incident better than a stage one colony planet. That was a good suggestion, Roche; have Ralph Hiltch sent to Pasto immediately. He is to liaise with the civil authorities there, with a brief to advise and assist with the capture of the embassy personnel and identification of anyone else who has been sequestrated."

"Thank you, ma'am. I'll inform him at once."

"I just hope he can contain them," she said, allowing her deeper worries to surface momentarily. "If not, he could be facing a one-way trip."

The cloudband which lay over the Quallheim was a muddy rouge colour when seen from the underside, streaked with long rusty gold ridges as though it was reflecting the twilight rays of a sinking sun. It grew ever broader, the frayed edges stirring and flexing in disquiet as it swam out lazily over the sweltering jungle.

Kelly, casually accustomed to the enormousness of Tranquillity, was dumbfounded by its size. To the west and east there was no visible end, the band could encircle the world for all those sitting in the hovercraft knew. Straight ahead, to the north, there might have been a hairline of blue sky above the black treetops. Amarisk was slipping gently into a deep luminous cavern.

Thunder, strident bass rumbles that echoed strangely, taking a long time to fade, had been audible for the last twenty minutes as the two hovercraft eased their way towards the Quallheim over the buoyant mass of snowlilies coating the unnamed tributary. There was no sign of any lightning.

The hovercraft slipped under the tempestuous lip of cloud, and red-tinged darkness tightened around them like a noose. With the morning sun high in the sky, the transition into shadow was abrupt, leaving none of the scout team in any doubt of the change. Kelly couldn't help a shiver inside her armour even though the suit kept her skin temperature at a comfortable constant.

Reza's communication block reported it had lost the geosynchronous communication-satellite's beacon. They were cut off from Smith, Joshua, and the navy squadron.

Trees lining the bank became dark and sullen, even the flowers which eternally sprouted from the vines lost their perky glimmer. Snowlilies were the rancid colour of drying blood. High overhead large flocks of birds were embarking on their first ever migration, flapping and gliding towards the brightness sleeting down beyond the cloud.

"The cloud stretches across the heavens like the Devil's own wedding veil. It is the coming of an immortal penumbra as Lalonde is eclipsed by a force before which nature trembles in fear. The planet is being forcibly wedded to a dark lord, and the prospect of cold alien offspring issuing forth is one which gnaws menacingly at the team's fragile spirit."

"Please!" Sal Yong protested loudly. "I want to eat sometime today." The big combat-adept mercenary was sitting on the bench ahead of Kelly, shoulders slewed so the front of his rounded, dull-gloss head was aligned on her.

"Sorry," she said. She hadn't been aware she was talking out loud. "This is crazy, you know. We should be running the opposite way."

"Life is crazy, Kell. Don't let that stop you from enjoying it." He swung his doughty shoulders back.

"The problem is, I'd like to go on enjoying it, preferably for decades."

"Then why come here?" Ariadne asked. She was sitting

next to Sal Yong, steering the hovercraft with a small joystick.

"Born stupid, I guess."

"I've been with Reza for a decade now," the female ranger scout said. "I've seen atrocities and violence even your scoop-happy company would never show for public consumption. We've always made it home. He's the best combat scout team leader you'll ever meet."

"On a normal mission, yes. But this bloody thing—" Her arm rose to take in the cloud and gloomy jungle with an extravagant sweep. "Look at it, for Christ's sake. Do you really think a couple of well-placed maser blasts from orbit are going to knock it out? We need the whole Confederation Navy armed with every gram of antimatter they've ever confiscated."

"Still got to have somewhere to shoot that antimatter down at," Sal Yong said. "The navy would have to send the marines in if we weren't already here shovelling shit. Think of the money we're saving the Confederation taxpayer."

Beside Kelly, Theo broke into a high-pitched chuckle. He even sounds like a monkey, she thought.

"Regular marines couldn't handle this," Ariadne said cheerfully, guiding the hovercraft round a rock. "You'd need the Trafalgar Greenjackets. Special-forces types, boosted like us."

"Bunch of knuckle shufflers, all theory and drills," Sal Yong said witheringly. The two of them started arguing over the merits of various regiments.

Kelly gave up. She just couldn't get through to them. Perhaps that was what made mercenaries so different, so fascinating. It wasn't just the physical supplement boosting, it was the attitude. They really didn't care about the odds, staking their life time and again. That would make a good follow-up story back at Tranquillity; interview some ex-mercs, find out why they had quit. She loaded a note in her neural nanonics. The pretence of normality. Keep the mind busy so it doesn't have time to brood.

The hovercraft arrived at the Quallheim itself after another forty minutes. It was four or five times the width of the tributary, over two hundred and fifty metres broad. Both banks were overrun with tall trees that leant over the river at sharp angles, plunging aerial roots and thick vines into the water. Snowlilies lay three deep on the surface, moving at an infinitesimal pace. Where the tributary emptied into the Quallheim they formed a mushy metre-high dune on top of the water.

Now the scout team headed upriver, keeping close to the northern bank and the paltry cover of the trees. Reza seemed more concerned about lying exposed to the cloud than proximity to possible hostiles on the land. With nothing but the lightly furrowed carpet of snowlilies opening out like an empty ten-lane motorway ahead, the hovercraft began to pick up speed.

It was dark on the river, under the centre of the cloud-band, an occultation which made all the team switch to infrared vision. The trees blocked any sight of the natural sunlight beyond it. Thunder was a constant companion, booms slithering up and down the river like the backwash of some vast creature burrowing its way through the vermilion vapour above. Big insects, similar to terrestrial dragonflies but without wings, skipped across the snowlilies, only to be hurled tumbling by the wind of the hovercraft's passage. Vennals, burning with a pink-blue radiance of charcoal embers, hung in the branches of the trees, watching the small convoy rush past with wide, soft eyes.

Towards the middle of the morning, Reza stood up and signalled the second hovercraft towards the northern bank where there was a break in the trees. Ariadne rode the craft up the lush grass to a halt next to its twin. Fenton and Ryall were already bounding off into the undergrowth.

"I didn't want to datavise," Reza said when they all gathered round. "And from now on we'll operate a policy of minimal electronic emission. Ariadne, have you detected any broadcasts from the invaders?"

"Not yet. I've had our ELINT blocks scanning since we landed. The electromagnetic spectrum is clean. If they're communicating it's either by ultra-tight beam, or fibre optics."

"They could be using affinity, or an analogue," Pat said.

"In that case, you can forget homing in on them," she said. "Nobody can intercept that kind of transmission."

"What about the blackhawks?" Jalal asked. "Could they detect it?"

"No good," Pat said. "They can't even detect the bond between me and Octan, let alone some xenoc variant."

"Never mind," Reza said. "The Quallheim Counties were the origin of the invasion. There has to be a large base station around here somewhere. We'll find it. In the meantime, there is a village called Pamiers a couple of kilometres ahead. Pat says Octan has located it."

"That's right," Pat Halrahan said. "He's circling it now, at a reasonable distance. The whole place is illuminated with white light, yet there is no break in the cloud overhead. There are houses there as well, about thirty or forty proper stone buildings alongside the wood shacks the colonists build."

"Smith said there were buildings like that in villages the observation satellites did manage to view," Reza said.

"Yeah, but I can't see where they came from," Pat said. "There are no roads at all, no way to bring the stone in."

"Air or river," Sewell suggested.

"Invade a planet then airlift in stone houses for the population?" Pat said. "Come on, this is weird, but not insane. Besides, there is no sign of any construction activity. The grass and paths haven't been churned up. And they should have been, the houses have only been here a fortnight at most."

"They could be something like our programmed silicon," Kelly said, and rapped a gloved knuckle on the hard gunwale behind her. "Assembled in minutes, and easily airlifted in."

"They look substantial," Pat said with vague unease. "I

know that's not an objective opinion, but that's the way it feels. They're solid."

"How many people?" Reza asked.

"Twenty or twenty-five walking about. There must be more inside."

"OK, this is our first real chance to obtain serious Intelligence data as to what's going on down here," Reza said. "We're going to deactivate the hovercraft and cut through the jungle around the back of Pamiers. After we've reached the river again and set up a retreat option, I'll take Sewell and Ariadne with me into the village, while the rest of you provide us with some cover. Assume anyone you meet is hostile and sequestrated. Any questions?"

"I'd like to come into Pamiers with you," Kelly said.

"Your decision," Reza said indifferently. "Any real questions?"

"What information are we looking for?" Ariadne asked.

"Intent and capability," Reza said. "Also physical disposition of their forces, if we can get it."

Hackles raised inside her armour, Kelly let the team shove a couple of hovercraft electron matrices into her pack before they all set off again. Reza didn't want them to walk in single file, for fear of ambush; instead they fanned out through the trees with chameleon circuits on, avoiding animal paths. There was a method of trekking through the raw jungle, Kelly learnt, and for her it was always walking where Jalal walked. He seemed to instinctively find the easiest way around trees and thick undergrowth, avoiding having to force his way against the clawing branches and heavy loam. So she kept her helmet sensors focused on the low-power UV pin-point light at the nape of his neck, and bullied her legs to keep up.

It took them fifty minutes to skirt the village and wind up back at the river. Sewell and Jalal set to activating the hovercraft at the top of a short slope above the water. Kelly dumped her pack into the locker at the rear of the second craft, and felt as though she could fly without the extra weight. With equipment stowed, the team fitted their weapons, checked power and projectile magazines, and set off back towards Pamiers.

Reza found the first corpse two hundred metres short of the village clearing. It was Ryall who smelt it for him, a sharp tang of dead flesh which even the jungle's muggy air couldn't disguise. He sent the hound veering off towards it. Ryall promptly smelt another corpse, causing Reza to hurriedly damped down his reception of the hound's olfactory sense.

It was a child, about five or six, he guessed. Ryall had found it sitting huddled up at the foot of a mayope tree. Age was hard to determine; there wasn't a lot left, so he had to go by size. Insects and humidity had accelerated the decomposition, though it was strange no animal had disturbed it. According to his didactic memory, sayce were supposed to be fairly brutal carnivores.

He led Sewell, Kelly, and Ariadne through the trees to the body, and dispatched Ryall to the second.

"It's a girl," Ariadne said after examining the remains. She held up a nondescript length of filthy, dripping-wet fabric. "This is a skirt."

Reza wasn't going to argue. "How did she die?" he asked.

"There are no broken bones, no sign of violence. Judging by the way she's curled up between the roots I'd say she crawled here to die. Poisoned? Starving? No way of knowing now."

"Scared of the invaders," Reza said thoughtfully. "They probably didn't bother to sequestrate the children."

"You mean the adults just ignored her?" Kelly asked in disgust.

"Ignored her, or drove her away. A child like this wouldn't walk around in the jungle by herself. The village had been established long enough for her to pick up basic jungle lore."

Ryall trotted up to the second corpse, emitting a warm feeling of satisfaction as his muzzle touched the putrefying flesh. Reza picked up the sense of accomplishment and expanded the affinity band allowing himself to see through the hound's enhanced retinas. "It's another kid," he told them. "A bit older, there's a baby in its arms." Ryall could scent more decaying meat in the humid air, three or four blends, all subtly different. Closer to the river, Fenton had picked up a further series of traces. "My God," Reza growled in a dismayed whisper. "They're everywhere, all around."

A village like Pamiers would start off with a population of about five hundred. Say two hundred families, and they've been here a couple of years. That would mean about a hundred and fifty children.

He stood, scanning the jungle. Slender yellow target graphics slid up over the black and red image in an uncomplicated, unprogrammed reflex. He wanted to shoot something dead. His neural nanonics ordered a slight endocrine effusion, stabilizing the sudden hormonal surge.

"Come on, she can't help us any more," he said, and began pushing briskly through the bushes and vines towards the village. He turned his chameleon circuit off, and after a few paces the others followed suit.

Pamiers followed the standard configuration of settlements along the Juliffe's tributaries. A semicircular clearing chopped out of the jungle along the side of the river. Crude single-storey houses clustered together in no particular order at the centre, along with larger barns, a church, a meeting hall, an Ivet compound. Wooden jetties ventured ten or fifteen metres into the water, with a few fishing skiffs tied up. Fields and plots ringed the outside, a surfeit of crops pushing out of rich black loam.

However, Pamiers' layout was all that remained recognizable as the four of them stepped out of the trees.

"Where is this light coming from?" Kelly asked, looking round in surprised confusion. As Pat had reported, the village bathed luxuriantly in a bright pool of sunlight, and yellow pollen was thick in the air. She scanned the cloud overhead, but there was no break. Thunder, muted while they were in the trees, rolled insistently around them once more.

Ariadne walked on a few paces, activating her full implant sensor suite as well as the specialist blocks clipped to her belt. She turned a complete circle, sampling the environment. "It's omnidirectional. We're not even leaving shadows. See?"

"Like an AV projection," Reza said.

"Yes and no. The spectrum matches Lalonde's sun."

"Let's go see what those new houses are made of," he said.

Pamiers' fields had been left untended. Terrestrial plants were fighting a fierce battle for light and height with the vines that had surged out of the jungle to reclaim their native territory. Fruit was hanging in mouldy white clusters.

Yet inside the ring of fields, the grass around the houses was short and tidy, studded with what looked suspiciously like terrestrial daisies. When he had studied the sheriff's satellite images on the flight from Tranquillity Reza had seen the way the village clearings were worn down and streaked with muddy runnels. Grass and weeds grew in patchy clumps. But this was an even, verdant carpet that matched Tranquillity's parkland for vitality.

Stranger still were the houses.

Apart from three burnt-out ruins, the original wooden shacks had been left standing, their planks bleached a pale grey, shuttered windows open to the weather, bark slates slipping and curling, solar-cell panels flapping loosely. They were uninhabited, that was obvious at a glance. Mosses, tufts of grass, and green moulds were tucked into corners and flourishing promisingly. But jammed at random between the creaky cabins were the new structures. None of them was the same, with architectural styles ranging across centuries—a beautiful two-storey Tudor cottage, an Alpine lodge, a Californian millionaire's cinderblock ranch, a circular black landcoral turret, a marble and silverglass pyramid, a marquee which resembled a cross between a Bedouin tent and a medieval European pavilion, complete with heraldic pennants fluttering on tall poles.

"Having some trouble with my blocks," Ariadne said. "Several malfunctions. Guido and communications are right out."

"If it begins to affect the weapons we'll pull back," Reza cautioned. "Keep running diagnostic programs."

They cleared the fields and started to walk over the grass. Ahead of them a woman in a long blue polka-dot dress was pushing a waist-high gloss-black trolley that had a white parasol above it, and huge spindly wheels with chrome wire spokes. Whatever it was, it was impossibly primitive. Reza loaded the image's pixel pattern into his neural nanonics with an order to run a comparison search program through his encyclopaedia. Three seconds later the program reported it was a European/North American style pram *circa* 1910–50.

He walked over to the woman, who was humming softly. She had a long face that was crudely painted in so much make-up it was almost a clown's mask, with dark brown hair worn in a severe bun, encased by a net. She smiled up happily at the four members of the team, as though their weapons and equipment and boosted form were of no consequence.

That simpleton smile was the last straw for Reza, whose nerves were already stretched painfully thin. Either she was retarded, or this whole village was an incredibly warped trap. He activated his short-range precision sensors, and scanned her in both electromagnetic and magnetic spectrums, then linked the return into a fire-command protocol. Any change in her composition (such as an implant switching on or a neural nanonics transmission) and his forearm rifle would slam five EE rounds into her. The rest of his sensors were put into a track-while-scan mode, allowing his neural nanonics to keep tabs on the other villagers he could see walking about among the buildings behind her. He had to use four back-up units, several principal sensors had packed up altogether. The overall resolution was way down on the clarity he was used to.

"What the fucking hell's going on here?" he demanded.

"I have my baby again," she said in a lilting tone. "Isn't he gorgeous?"

"I asked you a question. And you will now answer."

"Do as he says," Kelly said hastily. "Please."

The woman turned to her. "Don't worry, my dear. You can't hurt me. Not now, not any more. Would you like to see my baby? I thought I'd lost him. I lost so many back then. It was horrible, all those dead babies. The midwives tried to stop me seeing them; but I looked just the same. They were all perfect, so beautiful, my babies. An evil life it was." She bent forwards over the pram and lifted out a squirming bundle draped in lacy white cloth. The baby cooed as she held it out.

"Where have you come from?" Reza asked. "Are you the sequestration program?"

"I have my life back. I have my baby back. That's what I am."

Ariadne stepped forward. "I'm going to get a sample from one of those buildings."

"Right," Reza said. "Sewell, go with her."

The two of them walked round the woman and started off towards the nearest house, a whitewashed Spanish hacienda.

The baby let out a long gurgle, smiling blithely, feet kicking inside the wrap. "Isn't he just adorable," the woman said. She tickled his face with a finger.

"One more time," Reza said. "What are you?"

"I am me. What else could I be?"

"And that?" He pointed to the cloud.

"That is part of us. Our will."

"Us? Who is us?"

"Those who have returned."

"Returned from where?"

She rocked the baby against her chest, not even looking up. "From hell."

"She's either nuts, or she's lying," Reza said.

"She's been sequestrated," Kelly said. "You won't get anything out of her."

"So sure of yourselves," the woman said. She gave Kelly a sly look as she cuddled the baby. "So stupid. Your starships have been fighting among themselves. Did you know that?"

Reza's neural nanonics' optical-monitor program reported more people were appearing from the houses. "What do you know about it?"

"We know what we feel, the pain and the iron fire. Their souls weeping in the beyond."

"Can we check?" Kelly asked urgently.

"Not from here."

The woman laughed, a nervous cackle. "There aren't many left to check, my dear. You won't hear from them again. We're taking this planet away, right away. Somewhere safe, where the ships can never come to find us. It will become paradise, you know. And my baby will be with me always."

Reza regarded her with a chill of foreboding. "Yes, you are a part of this," he said quietly. The yellow target graphics locked on to her torso. "What is happening here?"

"We are come, and we are not going to leave. Soon the whole world will be hiding from the sky. From *heaven*. And we shall live on in peace for ever."

"There will be more of this red cloud?"

The woman slowly tilted her head back until she was staring straight up. Her mouth fell open as though in wonder. "I see no clouds." She started to laugh wildly.

Reza saw Ariadne had reached the hacienda. The ranger scout was bending over, scraping at the wall with some kind of tool. Sewell was standing behind her, the long gaussrifle barrels he had plugged into his lower elbow sockets swivelling from side to side in an automatic sweep pattern.

"Ariadne," Reza bellowed. "Get back here. We're leaving now."

The woman's laughter chopped off. "No, you're not." She dropped the baby.

It was Reza's infrared sensors which caught the change. A wave of heat emerged right across her body and started to flow like a film of liquid, rushing along her arms as she brought them up, becoming denser, hotter.

His left forearm's gaussgun fired five electron explosive rounds just as a white light ignited around her hands. There was three metres between them. Impact velocity alone would have been enough to tear her body apart, with the EEs detonating as well there was nothing left for the last three rounds to hit.

Kelly's armour hardened protectively as the blast wave slammed into her. Then she screamed as a jet of spumescent gore slopped across the front of the paralysed fabric.

"Sewell, zero the area!" Reza shouted.

The twin heavy-calibre gaussrifles the big combat-adept mercenary carried began to blaze, squirting out a barrage of EE projectiles. Emerald-green laser beams emerging from Reza and Ariadne snapped on and off, traversing the clearing in a strobe waltz as their lighter weapons picked off targets.

Kelly's armour unlocked. She fell to her knees, centimetres from the baby. Her hand went out instinctively, twitching the blood-soaked lace aside to see if it was still alive.

There was a vennal inside the wrap. The little xenoc creature had been distorted, its vulpine skull swollen and moulded into a more globular shape, scales melded together and stretched. They were losing their distinctive blue-green pigmentation, fading to pale pink. Its forepaws had become chubby, tiny human hands scrabbled feebly at the air. Squeals of terror emerged from its toothless mouth.

Her neural nanonics were unable to quell her stomach spasm in time. An emergency program triggered the shell-helmet's quick-release seal, and the visor sprang open. She vomited onto the neatly mown grass.

Sewell ran backwards across the grass, making almost

as much speed as he could travelling forward. An autonomic locomotion program took care of that, guiding his feet round possible obstacles, leaving his conscious thoughts free to assist with target selection.

The first fire sequence had ripped into the houses, smashing them apart in plumes of ionic flame and smoke. Even Sewell, who was aiming for maximum destruction, was surprised by the devastating effect the rifles inflicted. As soon as the first EE projectile hit the buildings their bright colours switched off, leaving behind a neutral grey. The rifles laid down a comprehensive fire pattern. Walls and roofs buckled and collapsed, sending out billowing clouds of thick dust, support timbers splintered then seemed to crumble. Within seconds the whole area had been reduced to pulverized rubble. The old shacks bent and bowed before the pressure blasts; they were far sturdier than the new houses. Several keeled over, wood twisting and shrieking. Slate-tile roofs somersaulted, intact walls slewed through the air rippling like giant mantas.

Sewell switched to the people, concentrating on coordinates where the target-allocation program had located individuals. The feed tubes from his backpack magazine hummed smoothly as they supplied the gaussrifles with fresh ammunition. There had been eighteen people visible to his sensors before Reza's shouted order. He pumped airburst shrapnel rounds after them as they dived for cover amid the shattered houses.

Infrared sensors showed him eccentric waves of heat shimmering amid the expanding dust. White fire, like an earthbound comet, streaked towards him. Boosted muscles flung him aside. The gaussrifles swung round to the origin, compensating for his dive. EE projectiles pummelled the area.

"Up, you bitch!" Reza yelled at Kelly. "Back to the hovercraft."

She rolled over, seeing a fermenting red cloudscape sky lit by green lasers and white fireballs. Fear and hatred fired her limbs and she jerked to her feet. The houses were a flattened circle belching smoke and dust. White fire raged in a spiral maelstrom above them, slinging out splinters that arced overhead. Trees fell and fire bloomed where they struck the wall of jungle. Sewell and Ariadne were charging towards her, both firing back into the rubble.

Kelly took three paces towards the trees then stopped. She pulled her nine-millimetre automatic pistol from her holster in one smooth movement. The gun's familiarization and targeting program went into primary mode, and she fired two bullets into the mutated vennal. Then she sprinted after Reza, neural nanonics releasing a torrent of adrenalin and amphetamines into her bloodstream.

Pain stabbed into the back of Ariadne's left thigh as the fireball struck her. Neural nanonics erected an analgesic block straight away. Compensator programs shifted her balance, favouring her right leg, activating those left thigh muscles which remained functional. Valves in the veins and arteries of her pelvis and knee sealed, limiting the blood loss. Her speed was barely reduced. She caught up with Kelly just as a fireball hit the reporter in the side of her ribs.

Kelly's armour gleamed an all-over ruby as it tried to disperse the energy. A circle of the suit flared as it melted. The fire lingered round the rent, chewing at the exposed skin. She stumbled and fell, rolling on the damp loam of an overgrown strawberry patch, beating wildly at the flame with her gauntlets.

"Keep going," Ariadne shouted. Her targeting program located another figure moving through the thinning dust cloud. The TIP pistol plugged into her wrist socket fired a burst of energy at it.

The entire left side of Kelly's ribs had gone numb, frightening her at a deeper level than programs or chemicals could relieve. None of the mercenaries were slowing down. *They're not going to help me!*

Kelly ordered her neural nanonics to override her trembling muscles and scrambled to her feet. Her integral medical program was signalling for attention. She ignored it and ran on. The clearing's sourceless sunlight went out, plunging her back into the stark red and black landscape of the infrared image.

It took her eight minutes to reach the hovercraft. Eight minutes of furiously punching vines out of her way and skidding on mud while the three mercenaries hurled out a barrage of fire through the jungle to cover their retreat. Eight minutes of white fireballs twisting and swerving round trunks, pursuing the team with the tenacity of smart seeker missiles. Of thunder roaring overhead and flinging down stupendous lightning bolts that rocked the ground. Sudden impossible gusts of wind rising from nowhere to slap her around like a lightweight doll. Of neural nanonic programs and endocrine implant effusions assuming more and more control of her body as its natural functions faltered under the unrelenting demands of her flight.

One hovercraft was already rushing down the slope into the snowlily-congested river when she arrived at the little glade.

"Bastards!" she yelled weakly.

Lightning struck twenty metres behind her, sending her sprawling. Reza was sitting behind the second hovercraft's control panel, hand playing over the switches. The impeller fans began to spin, forcing air into the skirt. It began to rise slowly upwards,

Sewell and Sal Yong stood on either side of it, their gaussrifles blasting away at unseen targets.

Kelly started to crawl. The first of the white fireballs shot out of the trees, curving round to drop on the hovercraft. Lightning flashed down again. A mayope tree toppled over with a sepulchral splintering. It crashed down ten metres behind her, one of the upper boughs coming down straight on top of her legs. Her armour stiffened, and her bent knees were pushed sharply into the yielding loam.

"Wait!" Kelly begged in a rasp. "For fuck's sake, you shitheads. Wait!"

The hovercraft's skirt was fully inflated, twigs and

leaves were thrown out from under the thick rubbery fabric. Sewell hopped over the gunwale.

"Jesus God, I can't move. Help me!" Her vision contracted to a tunnel with the hovercraft at the far end.

"Help me!"

Sewell was standing in the middle of the hovercraft. One of his gaussrifles turned towards her. Leaves and small branches rustled and slithered like serpents over her legs, she could feel them coiling round her calves. Then Sewell fired. The explosions sent her cartwheeling over the ground. She slammed into something hard. It grated along the side of her armour suit. Moving. Hovercraft! Her hands scrabbled with animal passion against it. And she was being lifted effortlessly into the air. Rationality ended there and she kicked and flailed against the air. "No! No! No!"

"Easy there, Kell, I've got you."

Her world spun round as the big mercenary dumped her unceremoniously on the floor of the hovercraft. She gagged, limbs juddering as the neural nanonics stopped sending out compulsive overrides. After a minute she began to sob, the quivering muscle motions starting deep in her belly and emerging through her mouth.

"You made it," Sal Yong said later. How much later Kelly didn't know, her mind was furred with tranquillizers, thoughts slow. She tried to sit up, and winced at the bands of pain tightening around her ribs. A medical diagram unfolded inside her skull. Her body's decay in unwelcome detail.

"The tree!" she barked hoarsely.

"We got it," Sewell said. "Shitfire, but that was weird."

"You were going to leave me!" Panic set her skin crawling. Blue lights flashed silently around the physiological display. More tranquillizers.

"You're going to have to learn to keep up, Kell," Reza said in his normal level tones. "We're on a combat mission. I told you when we started, I can't spare anyone for baby-sitting duties."

"Yes." She flopped back down. "So you did. I'm sorry."

I simply didn't realize you were serious, that you would leave a fellow human being behind, to face . . . that.

"Hey, you did all right," Sal Yong said. "Lotsa people would have screwed up, they had all that shit thrown at them."

"Oh, thanks."

There were mechanical clunks from somewhere behind her as Sewell detached his gaussrifles. "Let's see about getting that armour off you, Kell. You look like you could do with some field aid." She felt him touch the suit's seal catch, and then humid sticky air was sliding over her skin. Her helmet came off, and she blinked dizzily.

Sewell was sitting on a bench above her, holding a couple of medical nanonic packages. Kelly avoided looking at her ribs; the physiological display was bad enough.

"Looks like I'm not the only one," she said, smiling bravely. His artificial skin was pitted with small deep blackened craters where the white fire had struck, including a long score on the side of his glossy head. Blood and fluid dribbled out of the cracks each time he moved. "Or are you going to say they're just flesh wounds?"

"Nothing critical."

"Oh, crap, I'm drowning in macho culture."

"You can put your gun down now, Kell."

The nine-millimetre pistol was still in her hand, fingers solidified round its grip. She gave it a bewildered stare. "Right. Good idea."

He tilted her gently on her right side, then peeled the covering off the nanonic package. It moulded itself to her left side, curving round to cover her from her navel to her spine. The colours of her physiological display changed, reds diluting to amber, as it began knitting itself to her wound.

"Where are we going?" she asked. The hovercraft was moving faster than it had before. Humidity was making her sweat all over, the smell of vegetation was rank, itching her throat. Lying half-naked racing through a xenoc jungle being chased by monsters and cut off from any hope of rescue. She knew she ought to be reduced virtually to hysterics, yet really it was almost funny. You wanted a tough assignment, my girl.

"Aberdale," Reza said. "According to the LDC's chief sheriff, that's where the first reported trouble started."

"Of course," Kelly answered. There was a strange kind of strength on the far side of utter despair, she found, or maybe it was just the tranquillizers.

"Kell?"

She closed her leaden eyelids. "Yes."

"Why did you shoot the baby?"

"You don't want to know."

The navy squadron closed on Lalonde at seven gees, crews prone on their acceleration couches with faces screwed up against the lead-weighted air which lay on top of them. When they were seventeen thousand kilometres out, the fusion flames died away and the starships rotated a hundred and eighty degrees in a virtuoso display of synchronization, ion thrusters crowning them in a triumphant blue haze. The *Arikara* and the *Shukyo* released twenty combat communication-relay satellites, streaking away at ten gees to englobe the planet. Then the warships began to decelerate.

As the merciless gee force returned to *Arikara*'s bridge Meredith Saldana accessed the tactical display. The voidhawks had performed small swallow manoeuvres, taking them to within two and a half thousand kilometres of the planet and curving into orbit ahead of the Adamist warships to which such short-range precision jumps were impossible. But the mercenary fleet was leading the bitek starships a merry dance. Three blackhawks were racing away from Lalonde, striving for the magic two thousand kilometre altitude where they would be outside the influence of the planet's gravitational field, allowing them to swallow away. Voidhawks were in pursuit. Four of the nine combat-capable independent traders were also under acceleration. Two of them, *Datura* and *Cereus*, were heading on a vector straight towards the squadron at two and a half gees. They wouldn't respond to any warning calls from the *Arikara*, nor Terrance Smith.

"*Haria, Gakkai*, go to defensive engagement status, please," Meredith datavised. The situation display showed him the two frigates end their deceleration burn, flip over, and accelerate ahead of the rest of the squadron.

"What is the state of the remaining mercenary ships?" the Admiral enquired.

"Smith claims the starships remaining in orbit are obeying his orders, and therefore haven't been hijacked," said Lieutenant Franz Grese, the squadron Intelligence officer.

"What do you think?"

"I think Commander Solanki was right, and we'd better be very careful, Admiral."

"Agreed. Commander Kroeber, we'll send a marine squad into the *Gemal* first. If we can verify that Smith himself hasn't been hijacked or sequestrated it may just make our job that bit easier."

"Aye, aye, sir."

The tactical situation warned him the *Datura* and *Cereus* were launching combat wasps. Meredith observed in astonishment as each of them released a salvo of thirty-five; according to the accompanying identification codes the starships were small vehicles, forty to forty-five metres in diameter. They couldn't have held back any reserves—what absurd tactics. The drone armaments began to accelerate from their launch craft at twenty gees.

"No antimatter, Admiral," datavised Second Lieutenant Clark Lowie, the *Arikara*'s weapons officer. "Fusion drives only."

That's something, Meredith thought. "What's their storage capacity?"

"Best estimate would be forty combat wasps maximum, Admiral."

"So they haven't left any for their own defence?"

"Looks that way, sir."

Haria and *Gakkai* launched a counter salvo; eighty combat wasps leaping ahead to intercept the incoming hostiles at twenty-seven gees. Purple, red, and green vector lines sprang up in Meredith's mind, as if someone was performing laser acupuncture right across his skull. The combat wasps started to squirt megawatt electronic warfare pulses at each other. Active and kinetic submunitions began to scatter. Two disc-shaped swarms formed, five hundred kilometres across, alive with deceitful impulses and infrared signatures. Electron beams flashed out, perfectly straight lightning bolts glaring against the starfield. The first explosions flared. Kiloton nuclear devices were detonated on each side. Smaller explosions followed as combat wasps blew apart under the prodigious energy impact.

A second, smaller, salvo was launched by the frigates, compensating for the loss.

"Admiral, the *Myoho* reports the blackhawk it's chasing is about to swallow outsystem," Lieutenant Rhoecus called. "Request permission to follow."

"Granted. Follow and interdict; it is not to come into contact with inhabited Confederation territory."

"Aye, aye, sir."

A vast circle of space burst into pyrotechnic oblivion as the two antagonistic combat wasp swarms collided, as though a giant wormhole had been torn open into the heart of a nearby star. The annular plasma storm eddied violently, radiating down through the visible spectrum in seconds until only nebulous violet mists were left.

Arikara's sensor clusters struggled to burn through the conflagration and present an accurate representation of events through the tactical situation display. Some submunitions from both sides had survived. Now they were accelerating towards their intended targets. All four combatant ships began high-gee evasive manoeuvres.

Myoho and its blackhawk disappeared from the display. *Granth* and *Ilex* both fired a volley of combat wasps at their respective prey.

Haria's masers began to fire as the remaining submunitions closed on it. Small vivid explosions peppered nearby space. Rail guns thumped out a stream of steel spheres which formed a last-ditch kinetic umbrella. Eight surviving submunitions drones detected it, three of them were gamma-pulse lasers. A second before they struck the umbrella they fired.

Large oval sections of the frigate's hull turned cherry red under the radiation assault. Molecular-binding generators maxed out as they fought to keep the monobonded silicon's structure intact. The energy-dispersal web below the silicon struggled to absorb and redistribute the intense influx. All the sensor clusters either melted or had their electronics burnt out by the gamma-ray deluge. Replacement clusters rose immediately; but the starship was blind for a period of three seconds.

In that time the remaining five submunitions hit the kinetic umbrella. They disintegrated instantly, but hypervelocity fragments kept coming. With the sensors unable to see them and direct the frigate's close-range weapons they struck the hull and vaporized. The binding generators, already heavily stressed, couldn't handle the additional loading. There were half a dozen localized punctures. Fists of plasma punched inwards. Internal systems melted and fused as they were exposed. Fuel tanks ripped open sending hundred-metre fountains of vaporizing deuterium shooting out.

"*Bellah*, assist, please," Commander Kroeber ordered. "Rescue and recovery." The stricken frigate's emergency beacon was howling across the distress bands. The life-support capsules should have easily withstood the strike. Even as he requested more information from the computer the sensor image showed him ion thrusters firing to slow the frigate's wayward tumble.

With all of their combat-wasp stocks exhausted in the first salvo, *Datura* and *Cereus* were left with only short-range masers to defend themselves against the assault from the frigates' drones. The electronic warfare barrage was unrelenting as the drones closed at twenty gees, defeating the starships' sensors. The two mercenary starships exploded within seconds of each other.

A cheer went round the *Arikara*'s bridge. Meredith felt like joining in.

"Admiral, another blackhawk is leaving orbit," Lieutenant Rhoecus said.

Meredith cursed, he really couldn't spare another voidhawk. A quick check on the tactical display revealed little information, the blackhawk was on the other side of Lalonde from the squadron. "Which is the nearest voidhawk?"

"The *Acacia*, Admiral."

"Can they hit it with combat wasps?"

"They have a launch window, but estimate only a thirty per cent chance of success."

"Tell them to launch, but remain in orbit."

"Aye, aye, sir."

"*Bellah* reports survivors from the *Haria* have been detected, Admiral," Commander Kroeber said. "They're matching velocities."

"Good. Hinnels, has there been any reaction from the Juliffe cloud bands?"

"Nothing specific, sir. But they've been growing wider at a constant rate, the area they're covering has increased by one and a half per cent since we arrived. It adds up to a respectable volume."

Another combat-wasp battle raged high above Lalonde's terminator as the drones from the *Granth* encountered defences fired by their prey. Then the blackhawk vanished down a wormhole interstice. Three seconds later *Granth* followed.

"Damn," Meredith muttered.

But the *Ilex* was having better luck. Its combat-wasp salvo had forced the blackhawk it was chasing to flee back down towards the planet.

The Admiral requested a channel to the *Gemal*. "We shall be boarding you first, Smith. Any resistance and the marines will shoot to kill, understood?"

"Yes, Admiral," Terrance Smith replied.

"Have you received any updates from the teams you landed?"

"Not yet. I expect most of them were sequestrated," he added gloomily.

"Tough. I want you to broadcast a message that their mission is over. We will pick up any survivors if at all possible. But none of them is to attempt to penetrate under the cloud, no hunting of enemy bases. This is now a Confederation Navy problem. I don't want the invaders antagonized unduly." Not while my squadron is so close to that bloody cloud, he finished silently. It was the sheer quantity of power involved again. Frightening. And the berserk way the hijacked ships were behaving didn't help.

"I'm not sure I can guarantee that, Admiral," Smith said.

"Why not?"

"I issued the team leaders with kiloton nukes. It would give them a fall-back in case the starships were unable to provide strike power. I was worried the captains might balk at bombarding a planetary surface."

If it hadn't been for the fierce gee force Meredith would have put his head in his hands. "Smith, if you get out of this with your life, it won't be on my account."

"Well, fuck you!" Terrance Smith yelled. "You Saldana bastard, why do you think I had to hire these people in the first place? It's because Lalonde is too poor to rate decent navy protection. Where were you when the invaders landed? You would never have come to help us put down that first insurrection, because it didn't affect your precious financial interests. Money, that's what you shits respect. What the hell would you know about ordinary people suffering? You were born with a silver spoon in your mouth that's so big it's sticking out through your arse. The only reason you're here now is because you're frightened the invasion might spread to worlds you own, that it might hit your credit balance. I'm doing what I can for *my* people."

"And that includes nuking them, does it?" Meredith asked. He'd been subject to anti-Saldana bigotry for so long now the insults never even registered. "They're sequestrated, you cretin, they don't even know they're your people any more. This invasion isn't going to be beaten by brute force. Now, you will broadcast that message, make the mercenary teams turn back."

The tactical display sounded an alarm. A broad fan of curving purple vector lines were rising high over Wyman, Lalonde's small arctic continent. Someone behind the planet had launched a salvo of fifty-five combat wasps.

"My God," Meredith muttered. "Lowie, what are they aimed at?"

"Unclear, Admiral. There is no single target, it's a rogue salvo. But from the vectors I'd say they were seeking to engage anything in the thousand-kilometre orbit . . . Bloody hell."

A second salvo, of equal size, was curving round the south pole.

"Jesus, that's a neat pincer movement," Joshua said. At some ridiculous private level he was delighted he didn't need any intervention from his neural nanonics to remain calm. He felt his mind function with that same cool reserve which had manifested itself back in the Ruin Ring when Neeves and Sipika appeared.

This is me, what I am: a starship captain.

The *Lady Mac*'s three fusion drives came on almost without conscious thought. "Stand by for combat gees," he warned.

"How many?" Sarha asked nervously.

"How high is up?"

Other starships were getting under way, retracting their thermo-dump panels. Three of them launched combat wasps in a defensive cluster formation.

"Remain in orbit," Smith ordered over the command net. "The navy squadron will provide us with protective cover from the salvo."

"Like bollocks they will," Joshua said. The squadron was still four minutes from orbital injection. A sensor scan revealed blackhawks and voidhawks alike racing up for a higher altitude; the slower Adamist starships were following, with three exceptions, *Gemal* one of them.

The gee force in *Lady Mac*'s bridge passed five gees. Ashly groaned in dismay. "My bones can't take this."

"You're younger than me," Warlow countered.

"I'm more human, too."

"Wimp."

"Castrated mechanoid."

Sarha suddenly noticed the trajectory Joshua had loaded into the flight computer. "Joshua! Where the hell are you taking us?"

Lady Mac was rising above the equatorial plane at seven gees, decreasing altitude at the same time.

"We're going under them."

"This trajectory is going to graze the atmosphere!"

He watched more of the mercenary starships launching combat wasps. "I know." It had been an instinctive manoeuvre, opposing every tactic program in the flight computer's memory core; they all said altitude was the key in orbital combat situations, giving you more room to manoeuvre, more flexibility. Everyone else in the little mercenary fleet was clinging to that doctrine, escaping from Lalonde with fusion drives operating way out on the limit. "Dad was always telling me about this one," he said in what he hoped was a confident manner. "He always used it in a scrape. *Lady Mac*'s still about, isn't she?"

"Your bloody father isn't!" Sarha had to datavise, she couldn't expel enough air from her lungs to talk. The acceleration had reached nine gees. She hadn't known even *Lady Mac* could produce that kind of drive level. Every internal membrane supplement had turned rock hard. An arterial implant at the base of her neck was injecting oxygen into her bloodstream, making sure her brain didn't starve. She couldn't ever remember having to use it before. Joshua Calvert, we are not a bloody combat wasp!

"Look, it's very simple," he explained, trying to sort out the logic in his own mind. As usual, rationality was trailing well behind impetuosity. "Combat wasps are designed for deep-space operations. They can't operate in the atmosphere."

"We are designed for deep-space operations!"

"Yes, but we're spherical."

Sarha couldn't snarl, she would have dislocated her jaw bone; but she managed to grate her teeth together.

Lady Macbeth flew over the Sarell continent in forty-five seconds, arching down sharply towards the brown and yellow volcanic deserts. She was three hundred kilometres in altitude when she passed over the northern coastline; the north pole was two and a half thousand kilometres ahead. Seven hundred kilometres above, and four thousand kilometres ahead, the combat wasp salvo spotted her. Six of them abruptly altered course and dived down.

"Here they come," Joshua said. He fired eight of *Lady Mac*'s combat wasps, programming them for a tight defence-shield formation. The drones leapt upwards at twenty gees, scattering submunitions almost immediately.

Aft sensors showed the starships in orbit behind and above were releasing more and more combat wasps. Even the *Gemal* was breaking out of its thousand-kilometre orbit, the old colonist-carrier could only make one and a half gees. And there was no escort, Joshua saw sadly. Far away to the east, barely above the horizon, there was a volley of explosions followed by the unmistakable larger smeared detonation of a starship. Wonder who that was? It didn't seem to matter much, only that it wasn't him.

"Melvyn, keep monitoring the grav-detector satellite data. I want to know if any ships start jumping outsystem, and if possible where to."

"I'm on it, Joshua."

"Dahybi, I can't believe the voidhawks can keep jamming our nodes with all this going on, the second they slip I want to know."

"Yes, Captain."

The sensors showed Joshua the attacking combat wasps releasing their submunitions. Particle beams lanced out from both swarms. "OK, everybody, here we go." He shot an order directly into the drive deflector coils, and *Lady Mac* lurched downwards.

Meredith Saldana caught the crazy flight vector developing and datavised a request into the tactical situation computer for confirmation. The vector was recomputed and verified. Half of the squadron's frigates would be unable to produce a nine-gee thrust. "Who's that idiot?" he asked in reflex.

"*Lady Macbeth*, sir," Lieutenant Franz Grese said. "None of the others have triple-fusion drives."

"Well, if they all suicide on us I shall be a very happy man."

It wasn't looking good. He had already changed the squadron's operational orbit from one thousand kilometres to two thousand three hundred, which would give them a superior look-down shoot-down position—but only if the mercenary ships stayed put. Injection was in ninety seconds. Combat wasps were being launched at a prodigious rate from the mercenary fleet. Intelligence and tactics programs couldn't say which were defensive and who was attacking whom. Each of his squadron's ships had launched a defence cluster salvo.

One of the voidhawks exploded with appalling savagery, and the victorious blackhawk skirted its roiling debris plume to vanish into a wormhole interstice.

"Who?" he asked Rhoecus.

"*Ericra*, but they saw the combat-wasp barrage approaching. *Ilex* has their memory patterns safe."

Even now, after all the truths he had seen in his cosmopolitan life, Meredith felt the old twang of prejudice. Upon death, souls departed this life for ever. It was the Christian way. They were not to be ensnared in a mockery of God's living creatures.

You can leave the Kingdom, he acknowledged jadedly, but it never leaves you.

Go in peace, he prayed silently for the dead Edenists. *Wherever you roam.*

On a more pertinent level he was down to six void-hawks.

"Combat wasps have locked on to the *Gemal*, sir," Clarke Lowie reported.

The gee force on the bridge was reducing rapidly as the *Arikara* slid into orbit.

Thank Christ for small mercies, Meredith thought. "Commander Kroeber, squadron to engage all combat wasps launched by the mercenary fleet. We'll sort out who's friendly and who isn't when events become a little less immediate."

"Aye, aye, sir."

Arikara trembled as a salvo was fired.

"Issue a blanket order for all mercenary starships to cease acceleration and evasive manoeuvres as soon as the combat wasps have been cleared. Failure to comply will result in naval fire."

"Aye, aye, sir."

When the *Lady Mac* reached one hundred kilometres' altitude Joshua withdrew all but five sensor clusters. Wyman's fjord-etched coastline was directly below. Three hundred kilometres overhead, the two combat-wasp swarms were firing a fusillade of kinetic missiles and coherent radiation at each other. They clashed at a closing speed of over seventy kilometres per second. A patch of sky burst into pure white atomic fury, bringing a transient dawn to the arctic continent's month-long night underneath.

Eleven submunitions broke through to descend on the *Lady Macbeth* with cybernetic mayhem in their silicon brains. Two of them were one-shot gamma pulsers. They tracked the hurtling starship as it buffeted its way through the upper atmosphere, then discharged the energy in their electron matrices with one swift burst. The resulting gamma-ray beam lasted for a quarter of a second.

A sheath of ions had already built up around the *Lady Macbeth*'s hull, a tangerine fluorescence that radiated away from the forward fuselage in hypersonic ripples. But they were swiftly lost against the incandescent streams of energized helium emerging from the fusion tubes. The stratosphere reeled from the unrestrained tumult of the starship's passage. Her exhaust stretched out over a hundred and fifty kilometres behind her, evanescing into titanic electrical storms which lashed the sharp icy steppes seventy-five kilometres below with a vigour that threatened to split the glaciers open to the bedrock. Insubstantial green and scarlet borealis spectres cavorted over the ice-encrusted continent in a display which rivalled the bands over the Juliffe in scale.

"Breakthrough!" Warlow cried.

Systems schematics filled Joshua's mind, laced with red symbols. The hull's molecular-binding generators, already labouring with the burden imposed by the ion sheath, had overloaded in half a dozen places as the gamma pulses drilled into the monobonded silicon.

He switched back to the flight management display. The thrust from one of the fusion tubes was reducing. "Any physical violation?" The thought of needles of blazing atmospheric gases searing in over the delicate modules and tanks at this velocity was terrifying. Neural nanonics effused an adrenalin antidote into his bloodstream.

"Negative, it's all energy seepage. But there's some heavy component damage. Losing power from generator two, and I've got cryogenic leakages."

"Compensate, then, just keep us functional. We'll be through the atmosphere in another twenty seconds."

Sarha was already datavising a comprehensive list of instructions into the flight computer, closing pipes and tanks, isolating damaged sub-components, pumping vaporized coolant fluid from the malfunctioning generator into emergency dump stores. Warlow began to help her, prioritizing the power circuits.

"Three nodes are out, Joshua," Dahybi reported.

"Irrelevant." He took the starship down to sixty kilometres.

The nine remaining kinetic missile drones followed.

They were, as Joshua said, intended for deep space operation: basically a sensor cluster riding on top of fuel tanks and a drive unit. There was no streamlining, no outer fuselage; in a vacuum there was no need for such refinements. All they had to do was collide with their victim, mass and velocity would obey Newton's equations and combine to complete the task. But now they were flying through the mesosphere, a medium implacably alien and hostile. Ionization started to accumulate around their blunt circular sensor heads as the gas thickened, turning to long tongues of violet and yellow flame which licked back along the body. Sensors burnt away in seconds, exposing the guidance electronics to the radiant incoming molecules. Blinded, crippled, subject to intolerable heat and friction pressures, the kinetic drones detonated in garish starburst splendour twenty kilometres above the *Lady Macbeth*.

The *Arikara*'s tactical situation display showed their vectors wink out almost simultaneously. "Very smart," Meredith said grudgingly. It took a hell of a nerve to pilot a starship like that—nerve and egomaniacal self-confidence. I doubt I would have that much gumption.

"Stand by. Evasive manoeuvring," Commander Kroeber said.

And Meredith had no more time to reflect on the singular antics of Joshua Calvert. Punishing gravity returned abruptly to the flagship's bridge. A third salvo of combat wasps leaped out of their launch-tubes.

Lady Macbeth soared out of the mesosphere, throwing off her dangerous cloak of glowing molecules. Behind her, Wyman's ice-fields glimmered under eerie showers of ethereal light. Combat-sensor clusters rose out of their hull recesses on short stalks, their golden-lensed optical scanners searching round.

"We're in the clear. Thank you, sweet Jesus." Joshua reduced the thrust from the fusion drives until it was a merely uncomfortable three gees. Their trajectory was taking them straight away from the planet at a high inclination. There were no combat wasps within four thousand kilometres. I *knew* the old girl could do it. "Told you so," he sang at the top of his voice.

"Awesome," Ashly said, and meant it.

On the couch next to Joshua, Melvyn shook his head in dazed admiration despite the gee force.

"Thanks, Joshua," Sarha said gently.

"My pleasure. Now, damage assessments please. Dahybi, can we jump?"

"I'll need time to run more diagnostics. But even if we can jump it isn't going to be far. Those three nodes were physically wrecked by the gamma pulses. Our energy patterns will have to be recalculated. Ideally, we need to replace the nodes first."

"We're only carrying two spares. I'm not made of money. Dad always jumped with nodes damaged and—"

"Don't," Sarha pleaded. "Just for once, Joshua. Let's deal with the present, OK?"

"Somebody's jumped outsystem," Melvyn said. "The grav-detector satellites registered at least two distortions while we were performing our dodo impersonation, I think there may have been a wormhole interstice opened as well. I can't tell for sure, half of the satellites have dropped out."

"There is no jamming from the voidhawks any more," Dahybi said.

"OK, great. Warlow, Sarha, how are our systems coping?"

"Number two generator's out," Warlow said. "I've shut it down. It took the main strike from the gamma rays. Lucky really, most of the energy was absorbed by its casing. We'll have to dump it when we dock, it's got a half-life longer than some geological eras now."

"And I'd like you to stop using the number one fusion-drive tube," Sarha said. "The injection ionizers are damaged. Other than that, nothing serious, we've got some leaks and some component glitches. But none of the life-support capsules were breached, and our environmental-maintenance equipment is fully functional."

"Got another jumper," Melvyn called out.

Joshua reduced thrust to one gee, cutting drive tube one altogether, then accessed the sensors. "Jesus, will you look at that?"

Lalonde had acquired its own ring, gloriously radiant stripes of fusion fire twining together to form a platinum amulet of immense complexity. Over five hundred combat wasps were in flight, and thousands of submunitions wove convoluted trajectories. Starships initiated high-gee evasive manoeuvres. Nuclear explosions blossomed.

The *Lady Macbeth*'s magnetic and electromagnetic sensors were recording impulses nearly off the scale. It was a radiative inferno.

"Two more wormhole interstices opening," Melvyn said. "Our bitek comrades are leaving in droves."

"I think we'll join them," Joshua said. Just for once in her life, Sarha might be right, he conceded. It was the now which counted. *Lady Mac* was already two thousand kilometres in altitude, and rising steeply from the pole; he shifted their inclination again, carrying them further north of the ecliptic and away from the conflict raging above the planet's equatorial zones. Another three thousand kilometres and they would be out of the influence of Lalonde's gravity field, and free to jump. He made a mental note to travel an additional five hundred klicks—no point in stressing the nodes, given their state. About a hundred seconds at their current acceleration. "Dahybi, how is the patterning coming?"

"Reprogramming. Another two minutes. You really don't want to rush me with this one, Joshua."

"Fine, the further we are from the gravity field the better."

"What about the mercs?" Ashly said. It wasn't loud, but his level voice carried the bridge easily.

Joshua banished the display showing him possible jump coordinates. He turned his head and glared at the pilot. Why was there always one awkward bastard? "We can't! Jesus, they're killing each other back there."

"I promised them, Joshua. If they were alive I said I

would go down and pick them up. And you said something
similar in your message."

"We'll come back."

"Not in this ship, not in a week. If we dock at a port, it'll
take a month to refit. That's without any hassle from the
navy. They won't be alive in two days, not down there."

"The navy said they'd pick up any survivors."

"You mean that same navy which right now is shooting
at our former colleagues?"

"Jesus!"

"There isn't going to be a combat wasp left in thirty
minutes," the pilot said reasonably. "Not at the rate they're
expending them. All we have to do is sit tight for a couple
of hours out here."

Instinct pushed Joshua, *repelled* him from Lalonde and
the red cloud bands. "No," he said. "I'm sorry, Ashly, but
no. This is too big for us." The coordinate display flipped
up in his mind.

Ashly looked desperately round the bridge for an ally.
His eyes found Sarha's guilty expression.

She let out an exasperated sigh. "Joshua?"

"Now what!"

"We should jump to Murora."

"Where?" His almanac file produced the answer,
Murora was the largest gas giant in the Lalonde system.
"Oh."

"Makes sense," she said. "There's even an Edenist station in orbit to supervise their new habitat's growth. We
can dock there and replace the failed nodes with our
spares. Then we can jump back here in a day or so and do
a fast fly-by. If we get an answer from the mercs, and the
navy doesn't shoot us on sight, Ashly can go down to pick
them up. If not, we just head straight back to Tranquillity."

"Dahybi, what do you think?" Joshua asked curtly. Most
of his anger was directed at himself; he should have
thought of Murora as an alternative destination.

"Gets my vote," the node specialist said. "I really don't

want to try an interstellar jump unless we absolutely have to."

"Anybody else object? No? OK, nice idea, Sarha." For the third time, the jump coordinate display appeared in his mind. He computed a vector to align the *Lady Mac* on the gas giant, eight hundred and fifty-seven million kilometres distant.

Ashly blew Sarha a kiss across the bridge. She grinned back.

Lady Macbeth's two remaining fusion drives powered down. Ion thrusters matched her course to the Murora jump coordinate with tiny nudges. Joshua fired a last coded message at the geostationary communications satellites, then the dish antenna and various sensor clusters started to sink down into their jump recesses.

"Dahybi?" Joshua asked.

"I've programmed in the new patterns. Look at it this way, if they don't work, we'll never know."

"Fucking wonderful." He ordered the flight computer to initiate the jump.

Two kinetic missiles hammered into the frigate *Neanthe*, almost severing it in half. When the venting deuterium and glowing debris cleared, *Arikara*'s sensors observed *Neanthe*'s four life-support capsules spinning rapidly. Still intact. Kinetic missiles found two of them while a one-shot pulser discharged eighty kilometres away, stabbing another with a beam of coherent gamma radiation.

Admiral Saldana clenched his teeth in helpless fury. The battle had rapidly escalated out of all control, or even sanity. All the mercenary ships had fired salvos of combat wasps, there was simply no way of telling which were programmed to attack ships (or which ships) and which were for defence.

The tactical situation computer estimated over six hundred had now been launched. But communications were poor even with the dedicated satellites, and sensor data was degraded by the vast amount of electronic warfare signals emitted by everybody's combat wasps. One of the bridge ratings had said they'd be better off with a periscope.

When it came, the explosion was intense enough to outshine the combined photonic output of the six hundred-plus fusion drives whirling round above Lalonde. An unblemished radiation nimbus expanded outwards at a quarter of the speed of light, engulfing starships, combat wasps, submunitions, and observation satellites with complete dispassion; hiding their own detonation behind a shell of scintillating molecules. When it was five hundred kilometres in diameter it began to thin, swirling with secondary colours like a solar soap bubble. It was three thousand kilometres ahead of the *Arikara*, yet it was potent enough to burn out every one of the sensors which the flagship had orientated on that sector of space.

"What the hell was that?" Meredith asked. The fear was there again, as always. Antimatter.

Seven gees slammed him down in his couch as the starship accelerated away from the planet and the dwindling explosion.

Clark Lowie and Rhys Hinnels reviewed the patchy tactical situation data leading up to the explosion. "It was one of their starships which imploded, sir," Clarke Lowie said after a minute's consultation. "The patterning nodes were activated."

"But it was only three thousand kilometres above Lalonde."

"Yes, sir. They must have known that. But they took out the *Shukyo* and the *Bellah*. I'd say it was deliberate."

"Suicide?"

"Looks that way, sir."

Five ships. He had lost five ships, and God knows how much damage inflicted on the rest of them. Mission elapsed time was twenty-three minutes, and most of that had been spent flying into orbit from the emergence point.

"Commander Kroeber, withdraw all squadron ships

from orbit immediately. Tell them to rendezvous at the jump coordinate for Cadiz."

"Aye, aye, sir."

A direct repudiation of the First Admiral's orders, but there was no mission left, not any more. And he could save some crews by retreating now. He had that satisfaction, for himself.

The gravity plane shifted slightly as the *Arikara* came round onto its new vector, then reduced to five gees. Another salvo of combat wasps was fired as enemy drones curved round to intercept them.

Madness. Utter madness.

The river was one of the multitude of smaller unnamed tributaries that covered the south-western region of the colossal Juliffe basin. Its roots were the streams wandering round the long knolls which made up the land away to the south of Durringham, merging and splitting a dozen times until finally becoming a single steadfast river two hundred kilometres from the Juliffe itself.

At the time the spaceplanes brought down the mercenary scout teams there was still a respectable current running through it, the deflected rains hadn't yet begun to affect the flow of water. In any case, the lakes and swamps which accounted for a third of its length formed a considerable reservoir, capable of sustaining the level for months.

The snowlilies, too, were relatively unaffected. The only difference the red cloud made was to extend the period it took for the aquatic leaves to ripen and break free of their stems. But where it ran through the thickest jungle that made up the majority of the Juliffe basin, the snowlilies seemed almost as numerous as always. Certainly they managed to cover the river's thirty-metre width, even if they weren't layered two or three deep as they had been in previous seasons.

Where the tributary ran through a quiet section of deepest jungle, one of the snowlilies five metres from the bank bulged up near the centre, then tore. A fist with grey water-resistant artificial skin punched through and began to widen the tear. Chas Paske broke the surface, and looked round.

The banks on either side of him were steep walls made from the knotted roots of cherry oak trees. Tall trunks straddled the summit, their white bark stained magenta from the light filtering through the tenebrous canopy far overhead. As far as the combat-boosted mercenary could see there was nobody around. He struck out for the shore.

His left thigh had been badly damaged by the white fire flung by the women who'd ambushed them. It was one reason for diving into the river as his team fled from the spaceplane's landing zone. Nothing else seemed to extinguish the vile stuff.

Their shrill, delighted laughter had reverberated through the trees as the mercenaries crashed through the undergrowth. If he had just been granted another minute to unload their gear, establish a perimeter defence formation, the outcome would have been so very different. They had enjoyed it, those vixen women, that was the terrifying part of it, calling happily to each other as the mercenaries ran in panic. It was a game to them, exhilarating sport.

They weren't people as he understood. Chase Paske was neither a superstitious nor religious man. But he knew that whatever evil had befallen Lalonde had nothing to do with Laton, nor was it going to be solved by Terrance Smith and his rag-tag forces.

He reached the bank and started to climb. The roots were atrociously slippery, his left leg dangled uselessly, and his arms and back were badly burnt, debilitating the boosted muscles. It was a slow process, but by jamming his elbows and right knee into crannies he could lever and pull himself upwards.

The women, it appeared, hadn't understood the feats a boosted metabolism was capable of. He could survive for an easy four hours underwater without taking a breath. A useful trait when chemical and biological agents were being used.

Chas scrambled up the last couple of metres to the top of the woody bank, and rolled into the lee of a crooked trunk. Only then did he start to review the bad news his neural nanonics medical program was supplying.

The shallow flesh burns he could ignore for now—although they would need treating eventually. Almost half of his outer thigh had been burnt away, and the dull glint of his silicolithium femur was visible through the minced and charred muscle tissue. Nothing short of a total rebuild was going to get his leg functioning again. He started picking long white wormanalogues from the lairs they were burrowing into the naked wound.

He didn't even have his pack with him when the women attacked. There was only his personal equipment belt. Which was better than nothing, he thought phlegmatically. It contained two small neural nanonic packages, which he wrapped round the top of his thigh like an old-fashioned bandage. They didn't cover half the length of the wound, but they would stop poisoned blood and aboriginal bacteria from getting into the rest of his circulatory system. The remainder of it was going to fester, he realized grimly.

Taking stock, he had a first aid kit, a laser pistol with two spare power magazines, a small fission-blade knife, a hydrocarbon analyser to tell him which vegetation contained toxins his metabolism couldn't filter, a palm-sized thermal inducer, and five EE grenades. He also had his guido block, a biological/chemical agent detector block, and an electronic warfare detector block. No communications block, though, which was a blow; he couldn't check in with Terrance Smith to request evacuation, or even find out if any other members of his team had survived.

Finally there was the kiloton fusion nuke strapped to his side in its harness. A black carbotanium sphere twenty centimetres in diameter, thoroughly innocuous looking.

Chas did nothing for five minutes while he thought about his situation; then he began to cut strips of wood from the cherry oaks to form a splint and a crutch.

* * *

Hidden behind its event horizon, the singularity came into being two hundred and twenty thousand kilometres above Murora, its intense mass density bending the course of nearby photons and elementary particles in tight curves. It took six milliseconds to expand from its initial subatomic size out to fifty-seven metres in diameter. As it reached its full physical dimensions the internal stresses creating the event horizon ceased to exist.

Lady Macbeth fell in towards the gas giant, ion thrusters squirting out long spokes of cold blue fire to halt the slight spin caused by venting coolant gases. Thermo-dump panels stretched wide to glow a smoky cardinal red as they disposed of the excess thermal energy acquired during the starship's frantic flight through Lalonde's polar atmosphere. Sensor clusters swept the local environment for hazards while star trackers fixed their exact position.

Joshua exhaled loudly, allowing his relief to show. "Well done, Dahybi. That was good work under pressure."

"I've been in worse situations."

He refused to rise to the bait. "Sarha, have you locked down those malfunctioning systems yet?"

"We're getting there," she said blandly. "Give me another five minutes."

"Sure." After the harsh acceleration of Lalonde orbit, free fall was superbly relaxing. Now, if she'd just give him a massage . . .

"That was one hell of a scrap back there," Melvyn said.

"We're well out of it," Warlow rumbled.

"Feel sorry for the scout teams, trapped on a planet full of people who behave like that." Melvyn stopped and winced, then gave Joshua a cautious glance.

"She knew what she was going down to," Joshua said. "And I meant what I said about going back to check."

"Reza Malin knew what he was about," Ashly said. "She'll be safe enough with him."

"Right." The flight computer datavised an alarm into Joshua's neural nanonics. He accessed the sensor array.

Murora's storm bands were smears of green and blue,

mottled with the usual white ammonia cyclones. A thick whorl of ochre and bronze rings extended from the cloud tops out to a hundred and eighty thousand kilometres, broken by two major divisions. The gas giant boasted thirty-seven natural satellites, from a quartet of hundred-kilometre ring-shepherds up to five moons over two thousand kilometres in diameter; the largest, M-XI, named Keddie, had a thick nitrogen methane atmosphere.

Aethra had been germinated in a two hundred thousand kilometre orbit, far enough outside the fringes of the ring to mitigate any danger of collision from stray particles. The seed had been brought to the system in 2602 and attached to a suitable mineral-rich asteroid; it would take thirty years to mature into a structure capable of supporting a human population, and another twenty years to reach its full forty-five-kilometre length. After nine years of untroubled development it was already three and a half kilometres long.

In the same orbit, but trailing five hundred kilometres behind the young habitat, was the supervisory station, occupied by fifty staff (it had accommodation for a thousand). The Edenists didn't use bitek for such a small habitational environment; it was a carbotanium wheel seven hundred and fifty metres in diameter, eighty metres wide, containing three long gardens separated by blocks of richly appointed apartments. Its hub was linked to a large non-rotating cylindrical port, grossly under-used, but built in anticipation of the traffic which would start to arrive once the habitat reached its median size and He_3 cloud-scoop mining began in Murora's atmosphere. During the interim there were just two inter-orbit vessels docked, which the station staff used to commute to Aethra on their inspection tours.

Lady Macbeth had emerged forty thousand kilometres away from the solitary Edenist outpost, a jump accuracy Joshua was entirely satisfied with considering the conditions. Her sensors focused on the station in time to see it break apart. The rim had been sliced open in several places, allowing the atmosphere to jet out. Small thrusters were still firing in a useless attempt to halt the ominous wobble which had developed. Optical sensors revealed trees, bushes, and oscillating slicks of water rushing out of the long gashes.

"Like the Ruin Ring," Joshua whispered painfully.

Small circular spots on the carbotanium shell glowed crimson. The tough metal was visibly undulating as the structure's seesaw fluctuations increased. Then one of the cryogenic fuel-storage tanks in the non-rotating port exploded, which triggered another two or three tanks. It was hard to tell the exact number, the entire station was obscured by the white vapour billowing out.

As the cloud dispersed large sections of the wheel tumbled out of the darkening centre.

A hundred kilometres away, two fusion drives burnt hotly against the icy starscape, heading for the immature habitat. One of the ships was emitting a steady beat of microwaves from its transponder.

"They're here already," Melvyn said. "Bloody hell. They must have jumped before we did."

"That is the *Maranta*'s transponder code," Warlow said without any notable inflection. "Why would Wolfgang leave it transmitting?"

"Because he's not the captain any more," Ashly said. "Look at the vectors. Neither of them is maintaining a steady thrust. Their drives are unstable."

"They're going to kill the habitat, aren't they?" Sarha said. "Just like Laton did all those years ago. Those bastards! It can't hurt them, it can't hurt anybody. What kind of sequestration is this?"

"A bad one," Warlow grumbled at an almost subliminal volume. "Very bad."

"I'm picking up lifeboat beacons," Melvyn said with a rush of excitement. "Two of them. Somebody escaped."

Joshua, who had felt eager triumph at their successful jump to Murora and anger at the station's violation, was left empty, leaving his mind in an almost emotion-free state. His crew was looking at him. Waiting. Dad never mentioned this part of captaining a ship.

"Melvyn, Sarha; recalibrate the injection ionizers for the number one fusion tube. Whatever thrust we can get, please. I'm going to need it. Ashly, Warlow, get down to the airlock deck. We won't have much time to bring them on board, make sure they come through as fast as possible."

Warlow's couch webbing peeled back immediately. The cosmonik and the pilot went through the floor hatch as though they were in a race.

"Dahybi, recharge the nodes. I'll jump outsystem as soon as we have them on board." *If* we get them on board.

"Yes, Captain."

"Stand by for combat gees. Again!"

On the other side of hugely complex schematic diagrams, Sarha smiled knowingly at the hard-used martyred tone.

Lady Macbeth's fusion drives ignited, driving the ship towards the twirling wreckage of the station. Thermo-dump panels hurried back into their recesses as the gee force climbed. The starship's sensors tracked the two fusion drives forty thousand kilometres ahead. Joshua was wondering how long it would take for them to spot the rescue attempt. If they use the sensors the way they do the fusion drives they may never see us. *Maranta* was only accelerating at half a gee.

Melvyn and Sarha finished their work on fusion tube number one, and gave him control, warning it wouldn't last for long. Joshua brought *Lady Mac* up to five gees, and held her there.

"They're launching combat wasps," Dahybi said.

Joshua observed the flight computer plotting purple vector lines. "That's odd." The six combat wasps were flying around Aethra, forming a loose ring. Their drives went off when they were two hundred kilometres from the habitat, coasting past it. Submunitions burst out from two, and accelerated towards the slowly rotating cylinder.

"Kinetic missiles," Joshua said. "What the hell are they doing?"

Bright orange explosions rippled across the rust-red polyp surface.

"Injuring it," Sarha said with terse determination. "That kind of assault won't destroy it, but they'll inflict a lot of harm. Almost as if they're deliberately mutilating it."

"Injuring it?" Dahybi asked. The normally composed node specialist was openly incredulous. "What for? People injure. Animals injure. Not habitats. You can't hurt them like you can a mammal."

"That's what they're doing," Sarha insisted.

"It does look that way," Joshua said.

The *Maranta*'s drive came on again, followed a few seconds later by the second ship.

"They've seen us," Joshua said. It had taken eight minutes, which was appallingly sloppy detection work. *Lady Mac* was over halfway towards the lifeboats. Less than twenty thousand kilometres away now. The other ships were barely five hundred kilometres distant from the squealing beacons. "This is where it gets interesting." He launched eight combat wasps and upped the *Lady Mac*'s acceleration to seven gees. The drones shot ahead at twenty-five gees. An answering salvo of twelve emerged from the two starships.

"Shit," Joshua exclaimed. "They're running for Aethra."

"Clever," Melvyn said. "We can't use the nukes when they're close to it."

"No, but I can still use the gamma pulsers for offence." He fired off a string of coded instructions to the combat wasps. "And it may give us the time we need to pick up the lifeboats. None of their combat wasps are targeting them." He thought for a moment. "Sarha, broadcast a tight-beam warning to the lifeboats. Tell them to deactivate their beacons now. Anyone warped enough to maim a habitat won't think twice about snuffing refugees."

The first combat-wasp conflict took place five thousand kilometres from Aethra, a ragged rosette of plasma sprawling across six hundred kilometres. Joshua watched several attackers come through unscathed and launched another salvo of five drones, programming three to form a defence-shield formation. The bridge's gravity plane shifted sharply as he initiated an evasion manoeuvre.

The children were crying with their voices and minds. Gaura broadcast a soothing harmonic in the general affinity band, adding to the compulsion of the other adults. What I need, he thought, is someone to calm me.

The lifeboat was a sturdy cylinder ten metres long and four wide. It had no propulsion system apart from the solid-fuel booster to fire it clear of any conceivable emergency, and reaction thrusters to hold it stable while the refugees waited for rescue. Like all the systems on the station it was spacious and well equipped. There were eight seats, lockers with enough food for a fortnight, and a month-long oxygen supply. For Edenists, even disasters would be inconvenient rather than dangerous.

Such arrogance, he cursed inside the confines of his own skull, such stupid blind faith in our technological prowess.

Right now there were fourteen adults and five children crammed inside. There hadn't been time for them to reach another lifeboat. With a hubris which hindsight revealed to be quite monstrous, the disasters which the designers anticipated had all been natural. Even a meteorite strike would leave most of the wheel intact, and evacuation would be a calm rational process.

What had never been even a theoretical contingency was insane Adamist starships slicing the station apart with lasers.

It had all happened so fast. Now little Gatje and Haykal hugged Tiya, their mother, faces distraught as she kept them anchored. The air was too hot, it stank of vomit. Aethra couldn't hide its torment over the kinetic missile attack that bit deep into its shell from the young impressionable minds. Candre's death convulsions as she went through explosive decompression was still causing wintry shivers along Gaura's spine. The combined psychological stresses of the last fifteen minutes was going to leave a trauma scar that would take a long time to heal even for the well-balanced psyche of an Edenist.

And it was all his fault. As station chief he should have taken precautions. He had known about the civil strife on Lalonde. Yet he had done nothing.

It is not your fault, Aethra said softly into his mind. **Who could have anticipated this?**

I should have.

From the information you had, this was not predictable.

I had enough data from *Ilex*. It was chaos on the planet when they left.

These starships did not come from Lalonde. They are mercenaries, recruited elsewhere.

I could still have done something. Put people into apartments closer to the lifeboats. Something! How are Candre and the others?

I have them. But now is not a good time to begin raising my consciousness to multiplicity status.

No. And you? How are you?

I was angry, frightened. Now I feel sorrow. It is a sad universe where such wanton acts can take place.

I'm sorry we brought you into existence. You have done nothing to deserve this.

I am glad I live. And I may yet continue to live. None of the craters is more than twenty metres deep. I have lost a lot of nutrient fluid though, and my mineral-digestion organs have been damaged from the shock-waves.

Gaura's hand squeezed the grab hoop he was holding. Fury and helplessness were alien to him, but he felt them now with a daunting strength. The physical damage can be repaired. It will be repaired, never doubt that. Not as long as one Edenist remains alive.

Thank you, Gaura. You are a fine supervisor. I am privileged to have you and your staff attend the dawn

of my intellect. And one day Gatje and Haykal shall run around in my park. I will enjoy their laughter.

A solid beam of intolerable white light stabbed into the lifeboat through its one small, heavily shielded port. Space was being devastated by another hail of fusion explosions. The children started crying again.

Through Aethra's much-degraded perception he saw the long white fusion exhaust of the third Adamist starship decelerating towards them. With its tremendous velocity it had to be a warship, but there had been no contact apart from the curt woman telling them to switch off the beacon. Who were they? Who were the other two? Why had they attacked Aethra?

Not knowing was difficult for an Edenist.

You will soon be safe, Aethra said. It widened its broadcast to include the Edenists on both lifeboats. **All of you will be safe.**

Gaura met his wife's frightened stubborn eyes. **I love you,** he said for her alone.

The blast light was fading. He looked out of the port, his mind welcoming inquisitive contacts, showing the children their solidly real rescuer approaching.

Whoever the pilot was, he was coming very close. And moving far too fast.

Space directly outside the lifeboat was filled with the brilliant fusion exhaust. Gaura flinched, jerking back from the port. **It's going to hit!**

There were screams behind him. Then the exhaust vanished, and a huge spherical starship was a hundred metres away, small sensor clusters sticking out of its dark silicon hull like metallized insect antenna. Its equatorial ion thrusters exhaled fountains of sparkling blue ions, halting its minute drift.

Bloody hell! It was a collective sentiment from the adults.

The starship rolled towards the lifeboat as though there was a solid surface below it. And its extended airlock tube was suddenly coming round to clang against the hatch.

Gaura took a moment to recover his poise. A voidhawk would be very hard put to match that display of precision manoeuvring.

The lifeboat's bitek processors reported the short-range inter-ship channel was picking up a transmission.

"You people in the lifeboat, as soon as the hatch opens we want you through the tube and into the lounge," commanded the female voice they'd heard earlier. "Make it fast! We're running out of combat wasps and we've got to pick your friends up as well."

The hatch seal popped and it swung back. Little Gatje squealed in alarm as one of the biggest cosmoniks Gaura had ever seen floated in the airlock tube.

It's all right, he told his dismayed daughter. **He's a . . . friend. Really.**

Gatje clutched at the fabric of her mother's suit. **Promise, Daddy?**

"Shift your bastard arses through here now!" Warlow bellowed.

The children gulped into fearful silence.

Gaura couldn't help it, after all the horror they'd been through to be greeted by such utter normality, he started to laugh. **I promise.**

"Oh, Jesus, they've cracked it," Joshua told the three crew-members left on the bridge when *Lady Mac* rendezvoused with the second lifeboat. Another combat wasp was curving round over Aethra's bulk, accelerating sharply. "I knew they'd work out the numbers game eventually." He fired a salvo of three drones in defence. It was a terrible ratio. One which the *Lady Mac* could only ever lose. Three defenders was an absolute minimum to guarantee an attacker didn't get through. If he could just have flown evasive manoeuvres, or attacked, or been able to run, the numbers would have shifted back towards something near favourable.

"Jesus!" The fourth solo combat wasp appeared from behind Aethra. He had to launch another three from *Lady Mac*'s diminishing reserves.

"Fifteen left," Sarha said with morbid cheerfulness.

The starship's maser cannons fired at a kinetic missile that was sixty kilometres away. Five nuclear-tipped submunitions exploded perilously close to Aethra, reducing the latest attacking combat wasp to its subatomic constituents.

"Did you have to tell us that?" Melvyn said laboriously.

"You mean you didn't know?"

"Yes. But I could always hope I was wrong."

Joshua accessed a camera on the airlock deck. Warlow had anchored himself to a stikpad beside the airlock tube. He was grabbing people as they came out and slinging them into the chamber. Ashly and one of the Edenist men were on a stikpad below the ceiling hatch, catching then shoving the human projectiles up into the lounge above.

"How many more to come, Warlow?" Joshua datavised.

"Six. That makes forty-one in total."

"Wonderful. Stand by for combat acceleration the second the airlock seals." He sounded the audio warning so the Edenists would know. The flight computer showed his plot of an open-ended vector heading away from Murora. At eight gees they could outrun the other starships easily, and jump outsystem. That kind of prolonged acceleration would be tough on the Edenists (no sinecure for the crew, either), but it was one hell of a lot better than staying here.

"Joshua, Gaura has asked me to say some of the children are very young, they can't possibly survive high gees," Warlow datavised. "Their bones aren't strong enough."

"Jesus shit! Kids? How old? How many gees?"

"One girl was about three. There were a couple of five-year-olds as well."

"Fuck it!"

"What is it?" Sarha asked, real concern darkening her sea-green eyes for the first time since they'd entered the Lalonde system.

"We're not going to make it."

The fifth solo combat wasp appeared from behind Aethra. Seven of the *Lady Mac*'s submunition drones detonated their nuclear explosives in immediate response. Joshua launched two more.

"Even if we jump without an alignment trajectory, from here, it'll take us fifteen seconds to retract the sensors and prime the nodes," he said. "We'll be blind for ten seconds. It's not long enough."

"So run," Sarha said. "Fire every last combat wasp at them and go. *Lady Mac* can make eight gees even with tube one down. *Maranta* can't make more than four gees. We can get clear."

"That vector's already loaded. But we've got kids on board. Shit! Shit! Shit!" He saw the last Edenist being yanked out of the airlock tube by Warlow. The flight computer was shutting the hatch before his feet were fully clear.

Do something, and do it now, Joshua Calvert, he told himself. Because you're going to be dead in twenty seconds if you don't.

His mind ordered the flight computer to start the fusion tube ignition sequence.

Another whole two seconds to think in.

There was nothing in the tactics programs, even Dad had never dug himself a hole this deep in the shit.

Can't run, can't fight, can't jump out, can't hide . . .

"Oh yes I can!" he whooped.

The fusion drives came on, and the *Lady Mac* accelerated down the vector plot that sprang from Joshua's mind even as the idea unrolled. Three gees, heading straight in towards the gas giant.

"Joshua!" Dahybi complained. "We can't jump if you take us inward."

"Shut up."

Dahybi settled back and started into a recital of a scripture he remembered from his youth. "Yes, Captain."

"Warlow, activate the three zero-tau pods we've got in capsule C, and cram the children in. You've got four minutes maximum before we start accelerating properly."

"Right, Joshua."

The sensors reported that four combat wasps were pursuing them. Joshua fired an answering salvo of five. He could hear Dahybi muttering something that sounded like a prayer, it had the right dirge-like resonance.

"They're coming after us," Melvyn said a minute later.

Maranta and its cohort were accelerating away from Aethra.

"That's the *Gramine*," Sarha said after studying the image. "Look at the angle its drive is deflected through. There isn't another starship that can do that. Wissler was always boasting about their combat agility."

"Just wonderful, Sarha, thanks," Joshua proclaimed. "You got any other morale boosters for us?"

Warlow climbed the ladder into the lounge deck, boosted muscles lifting him easily against the heavy gravity. Carbon composite rungs creaked in dismay under his tripled weight. There were Edenists packed solid across the lounge floor, none of the acceleration couches had been activated—not that there were enough anyway. They didn't have neural nanonics, the cosmonik realized. And because of it their children whimpered and snivelled in wretched distress without any cushioning below them.

He walked over to the smallest girl, who was lying wide-eyed and terribly pale beside her mother. "I'm putting her into zero-tau," he announced shortly, and bent down. He had plugged a pair of cargo-handling arms into his elbow sockets before coming up the ladder, they had wide metal manipulator forks which would act as a good cradle. The girl started crying again. "There will be none of this acceleration in the pod. Explain to her. She must not squirm when I pick her up. Her spine will break."

Be brave, Tiya told her daughter. **He will take you to a safe place where you won't hurt so.**

He's horrible, Gatje replied as the metal prongs slid underneath her.

You will be all right, Gaura said, reinforcing the pacific mental subliminal Tiya was radiating.

Warlow took care to keep Gatje's spine level, supporting her head with one set of forks while the other three arms were positioned under her torso and legs. He lifted gingerly.

"Can I help?" Gaura asked, levering himself onto his elbows. His neck felt as though it was being slowly compressed in a hydraulic vice.

"No. You are too weak." Warlow clumped out of the lounge, an outlandish faerie-legend figure walking amongst the prone hurting bodies with a grace completely at variance with his cumbersome appearance.

There were seven children under ten years old. It took him nearly five minutes to shift them from the lounge to the zero-tau pods. His neural nanonics monitored their flight on a secondary level. The attacking starships were matching *Lady Mac*'s three-gee acceleration. Combat-wasp submunitions produced a continual astral fire of plasma between them.

Lady Mac swept over the fringes of the ring, two thousand kilometres above the ecliptic as Warlow lowered the last child into the zero-tau pod.

"Thank Christ for that," Joshua said when the pod was enveloped by the black field. "OK, people, stand by for high acceleration."

Lady Mac's thrust increased to seven gees, tormenting the Edenists in the lounge still further. For all the stamina of their geneered bodies they had never been supplemented to withstand the onerous burden of combat spaceflight.

Maranta and *Gramine* began to fall behind. Sensors showed three more combat wasps eating up the distance.

"Jesus, how many of the fucking things have they got left?" Joshua asked as he launched four of the *Lady Mac*'s remaining six drones in response.

"I estimate ten," Melvyn datavised. "Possibly more."

"Wonderful." Joshua angled the *Lady Mac* down sharply towards the rings.

The slow moving pack of dusty ice chunks reflected an unaccustomed radiance as the three starships streaked past.

After millennia of stasis, stirred only by the slow heartbeat of the gas giant's magnetosphere, the ring's micrometre dust was becoming aroused by the backwash of electromagnetic pulses from the fusion bombs exploding above it. Dark snowflake-crystal patterns rippled elegantly over its surface. The temperature rose by several fractions of a degree, breaking up the unique and fantastically delicate valency bonds between disparate atoms which free fall and frigidity had established. Behind the starships, the rings quivered like a choppy sea before the storm was unleashed.

Those on board the *Lady Macbeth* able to receive the sensor images watched with numbed fascination as the ring particles grew larger, changing from a grainy mist to a solid plain of drifting mud-yellow boulders. It took up half of the image; they were close enough now to make it seem like the floor of the universe.

The penultimate combat wasp darted out of the *Lady Macbeth*'s launch-tubes. Submunitions ejected almost at once, scattering like a shoal of startled fish. A hundred kilometres behind her, twenty-seven fusion bombs arrayed in an ammonite maculation detonated simultaneously, throwing up a temporary visual and electronic barrier. She turned, unseen by her pursuers, triple drive exhausts scoring vast arcs across the stars. Then the three barbs of superenergized helium were searing into the ice and rock of the ring. No physical structure was capable of withstanding that starcore temperature. The agitated surface cratered and geysered as though a depth charge had been set off far below.

Lady Macbeth dived straight into the rings, decelerating at eleven gees.

10

The watchers were there when Alkad Mzu arrived at the shoreline of Tranquillity's circumfluous salt-water sea. As always they remained several hundred metres behind, innocuous fellow hikers enjoying the balmy evening, even a couple on horses trekking along the wilder paths of the habitat. She counted eight of them as she walked along the top of the steep rocky escarpment to the path which led down to the beach. This cove was one of the remoter stretches of the northern shoreline; a broad curve of silver-white sand two kilometres long, with jutting headlands of polyp-rock cliffs. Several small islands were included within the bay's sweeping embrace, tenanted by willowy trees and a fur of colourful wild flowers. A river emptied over the escarpment two hundred metres from the path where she stood, producing a foaming waterfall which fell into a rock pool before draining away over the sands. Overhead, the giant habitat's light-tube had languished to an apricot ember strung between its endcap hubs. Vitric water caught the final rays to produce a soft-focus copper shimmer across the wavelets.

Alkad picked her way carefully along the shingle-strewn path. An accident now would be the ultimate irony, she thought. There was the familiar nagging ache in her left leg, exacerbated by the rough incline.

Her retinal implants located a pair of adolescent lovers in the dunes at the far end of the beach. Craving solitude amid the deepening shadows, their dark entwined bodies were oblivious to the world, and nearly invisible. The girl's baby-blonde hair provided a rich contrast to her ebony skin, while the boy reminded Alkad of Peter as he stroked and caressed his willing partner. An omen, though Alkad Mzu no longer really believed in deities.

She reached the warm, dry sands and adjusted the straps of her lightweight backpack. It was the one she had brought with her to the habitat twenty-six years ago; it contained the cagoule and flask and first aid kit which she carried unfailingly on every ramble through the interior. By now the routine of her hike was scribed in stone. If she hadn't worn it, the Intelligence agencies would have been suspicious.

Alkad cut across the dunes at an angle, aiming for the middle of the beach, her feet leaving light imprints in the powdery sand. Three watchers made their way down the path behind her, the rest carried on walking along the top of the escarpment. And—a recent development, this—a couple of Tranquillity serjeants stood impassively at the foot of the escarpment beside the waterfall. She only saw them against the craggy polyp because of their infrared emission. They must have been positioned there in anticipation of her route.

It wasn't entirely unexpected. Tranquillity would have informed Ione Saldana about all those agency-teasing meetings with starship captains. The girl was erring on the side of caution, which was quite acceptable. She did have the rest of the population to think about, after all.

Alkad peered ahead, out over the huge grey valley of water to the southern shore, searching. There, to the right, twenty degrees up the curve. The Laymil project campus was a unique splash of opal light on the darkened terraces of the southern endcap. Such a shame, really, she thought with a tinge of regret. The work had been an interesting challenge, interpreting and extrapolating xenoc technology from mere fragments of clues. She had made friends there, and progress. And now the whole campus was animated with the discovery of the Laymil sensorium memories that young scavenger had found. It was an exciting time to be a project researcher, full of promise and reward.

In another life she could easily have devoted herself to it.

Alkad reached the water's edge as the light-tube cooled to a smirched platinum. Ripples sighed contentedly against the sand. Tranquillity really was a premium place to live. She shrugged out of her backpack, then touched the seal on her boots and started to pull them off.

Samuel, the Edenist Intelligence operative, was six metres from the foot of the scarp path when he saw the lone figure by the water bend over to take her boots off. That wasn't part of the humdrum formula which governed Mzu's activities. He hurried after Pauline Webb, the CNIS second lieutenant, who had reached the beach ahead of him. She dithered in the grove of palm trees which huddled along the base of the escarpment, debating whether to break cover and walk openly on the sands.

"It looks like she's going for a swim," he said.

Pauline gave him a cursory nod. The CNIS and the Edenists cooperated to a reasonable degree in their observation.

"At night?" she said. "By herself?"

"The doctor is a solitary soul, but I concede this isn't the most sensible thing she's ever done." Samuel was thinking back to that morning when the news of Omuta's sanctions being lifted had appeared in the AV projection at Glover's restaurant.

"So what do we do?"

Monica Foulkes, the ESA operative, caught up with them. She increased the magnification factor of her retinal implants just as Alkad Mzu pulled her sweatshirt off over her head. "I don't know what you two are panicking over. Nobody as smart as Dr Mzu would choose drowning as a method of suicide. It's too prolonged."

"Maybe she is just going for a quick swim," Pauline suggested, without much hope. "It's a pleasant enough evening."

Samuel kept watching Mzu. Now her boots and clothes were off she was removing the contents of her backpack and dropping them on the sand. It was the casual way she did it which bothered him; as if she was without a care. "I somehow doubt it."

"We're going to look particularly stupid charging over there to rescue her if all she's doing is taking a dip to cool off," Monica groused.

The middle-aged Edenist's lips pursed in amusement. "You think we don't look stupid anyway?"

She scowled, and ignored him.

"Does anyone have any relevant contingency orders?" Pauline asked.

"If she wants to drown herself, then I say let her," Monica said. "Problem solved at long last. We can all pack up and go home then."

"I might have known you'd take that attitude."

"Well, I'm not swimming after her if she gets into trouble."

"You wouldn't have to," Samuel said, without shifting his gaze. "Tranquillity has affinity-bonded dolphins. They'll assist any swimmers that get into difficulties."

"Hoo-bloody-rah," Monica said. "Then we can have another twenty years of worrying about who the daft old biddy will talk to and what she'll say."

Alkad datavised a code to the processor in her empty backpack. The seal around the bottom opened, and the composite curled up revealing the hidden storage space. She reached in to remove the programmable silicon spacesuit which had lain there undisturbed for twenty-six years.

Ione, Tranquillity said urgently. **We have a problem developing.**

"Excuse me," Ione said to her cocktail party guests. They were members of the Tranquillity Banking Regulatory Council, invited to discuss the habitat's falling revenue which the massive decrease in starship movements was causing. Something needed to be done to halt the stock market's wilder fluctuations, so she had thought an informal party was the best way of handling it. She turned instinctively to face her apartment's window wall and the shoals of yellow and green fish nosing round the fan of light it threw across the dusky sand. **What?**

It's Alkad Mzu. Look.

The image fizzed up into her mind.

Samuel frowned as Mzu drew some kind of object from deep inside her backpack. It looked ridiculously like a football, but with wings attached. Even with his retinal implants on full magnification he couldn't quite make it out. "What is that?"

Mzu fastened the collar round her neck, and bit down on the nozzle of the respirator tube. She datavised an activation code into the suit's control processor. The black ball flattened itself against her upper chest and started to flow over her skin.

Both the other Intelligence operatives turned to look at the sharpness in Samuel's voice. The two serjeants began to walk forwards over the beach.

Ione! Tranquillity's thoughts rang with surprise, turning to alarm. **I can sense a gravitonic-distortion zone building.**

So? she asked. Every starship emerging above Mirchusko registered in the habitat's mass-sensitive organs. There was no requirement for the usual network of strategic warning grav-distortion-detector satellites which guarded ordinary asteroid settlements and planets, Tranquillity's perception of local space was unrivalled, making threat response a near-instantaneous affair. **Is the starship emerging too close? Arm the strategic-defence platforms.**

No use. It's—

At first Samuel mistook it for a shadow cast by an evening cloud. There was still enough pearly radiance coming from the light-tube to give the circumfluous sea a sparse shimmer, a cloud would produce exactly that patch of darkness. But there was only one patch of darkness; and when he glanced up the air was clear. Then the noise began, a distant thunderclap which lasted for several seconds, then chopped off abruptly. A brilliant star shone at the centre of the darkness, sending long radials of frigid white light into the habitat.

Mzu was silhouetted perfectly against the white blaze reflected off the sea, encased in the black skin of the space-suit, a consummate monochrome picture.

Shock immobilized Samuel's body for a precious second. Out of the centre of the fading star a blackhawk came skimming silently over the sea towards Mzu; a compressed ovoid one hundred and thirty metres long, with a horse-shoe life-support section moulded round the rear dorsal bulge. Its blue polyp hull was marbled with an imperial-purple web.

"Jesus wept!" Pauline said in an aghast whisper. "It jumped inside. It's come right into the fucking habitat!"

"Get her!" Monica cried. "For Christ's sake stop the bitch!" She ran forwards.

"No, stop! Come back," Samuel yelled. But Pauline was already charging out of the trees after the ESA agent, boosted muscles accelerating her to a phenomenal speed. "Oh, shit." He started to run.

Meyer saw the small spacesuited woman standing at the water's edge, and *Udat* obligingly angled round towards her. Tension had condensed his guts into a solid lump. Swallowing *inside* a habitat, it had to be the craziest stunt in the history of spaceflight. Yet they'd done it!

We are in, *Udat* observed sagely. **That's halfway.**

And don't I know it.

WHAT ARE YOU DOING? Tranquillity's outraged broadcast thundered into the blackhawk's mind.

Meyer winced. Even *Udat*'s calm thoughts fluttered.

The woman is a political dissident being persecuted by the Kulu ESA, Meyer replied with shaky bravado. **Of all people, Ione Saldana should sympathize with that. We're taking her where she will be safe.**

STOP IMMEDIATELY. I WILL NOT PERMIT THIS. UDAT, SWALLOW OUT NOW. The force of the mental compulsion which the habitat personality exerted was in-credible. Meyer felt as though someone had smashed a meat hook into his skull to pull his brain out by the roots. He groaned, clutching at the cushioning of his acceleration couch, heart pounding in his ears.

STOP!

"Keep going," he gasped. His nose started to bleed. Neural nanonics sent out a flurry of metabolic overrides.

Alkad waded through the shallows as the blackhawk descended, gliding fastidiously round one of the cove's small islands. She hadn't grasped how big the bitek creature was. To see that almighty bulk suspended so easily in the air was an uncanny marvel. Its rounded nose was streaked with long frost rays as the sea's humidity gusted over polyp which was accustomed to the radiative chill of deep space. A huge patch of water below the hull began to foam and churn as the distortion field interacted with it. She suddenly felt as though the horizontal was rolling. *Udat* turned through ninety degrees, and tilted sharply, bringing the portside wing of its life-support horseshoe down towards the water. An airlock slid open. Cherri Barnes stood inside, wearing her spacesuit. Orange silicon-fibre straps tethered her securely to the sides of the small chamber. She threw a rope-ladder down.

On the beach five figures were racing over the dunes.

Ione said: **Kill her.**

The serjeants pulled laser pistols from their holsters. Alkad Mzu already had her foot on the first rung.

Udat's maser cannon fired.

Monica Foulkes pounded hard across the sand, neural nanonics commands and boosted muscles meshing so that her body ate the distance effortlessly, a hundred and fifty metres in nine seconds. The prime order of the ESA's Tranquillity operation was to prevent Mzu from leaving, that took precedence over everything. It didn't look like Monica was going to get to the blackhawk in time, Mzu had started to claw her way up the rocking ladder. She reviewed which of her weapon implants would have the best chance; the trouble was most of them were designed for unobtrusive close-range work. And that bloody Lunar SII spacesuit didn't help. It would have to be a microdart, and hope the tip penetrated. She was aware of the serjeants off to her left pulling out their laser pistols.

A metre-wide column of air fluoresced a faint violet, drawing a line from a silver bubble on the blackhawk's lower hull to a serjeant. The bitek servitor blew apart in an explosion of steam and carbon granules. Fifteen metres behind it, where the beam struck the beach, a patch of sand became a puddle of glass, glowing a vivid rose-gold.

Over-hyped nerves sent Monica diving for cover the instant the beam appeared. She hit the loose sand, momentum ploughing a two and a half metre long furrow. There were two near-simultaneous thuds behind her as Samuel and Pauline flung themselves down. The second serjeant erupted into a black-grain mist with a loud burping sound as the maser hit it. Monica's mind gibbered as she waited, head buried in the sand. At least with that power rating it'll be quick . . .

A wind began howling over the dunes.

Samuel raised his head to see his worst expectation confirmed. A wormhole interstice was opening around the nose of the blackhawk. Alkad Mzu was halfway up the rope-ladder.

You must not take her from here, he pleaded with the starship. **You must not!**

The interstice widened, a light-devouring tunnel boring through infinity. Air streamed in.

"Hang on!" Samuel shouted to the two women agents.

COME BACK! Tranquillity commanded.

Meyer, his mind twinned with the blackhawk, quailed under the habitat's furious demand. It was too much, the storm voice had raged inside his skull for what seemed like days, bruising his neurons with its violence. Welcome surrender beckoned—to hell with Mzu, nothing was worth this. Then he felt local space twisting under the immense distortion which *Udat's* energy patterning cells exterted. A pseudoabyss leading into freedom opened before him. **Go,** he ordered. The cold physical blackness outside invaded his mind, plunging him into glorious oblivion.

A small but ferocious hurricane set Alkad spinning like a runaway propeller at the end of her precarious silicon-fibre ladder. "Wait!" she datavised in mounting terror. "You're supposed to wait till I'm in the airlock." Her digitalized vehemence made no impression on *Udat*. The air buoyed her up as though she had become weightless, swinging her round until the ladder was horizontal. Oscillating gravity was doing terrible things to her inner ears. Screaming air tried to tear her from the ladder. Neural nanonics pumped muscle-lock orders into her hands and calves to reinforce her grip. She could feel ligaments ripping. Collar sensors showed her the fuzzy rim of the wormhole interstice sliding inexorably along the hull towards her. "No. In the name of Mary, wait!" And then Dr Alkad Mzu was suddenly presented with every physicist's dream opportunity: observing the fabric of the universe from the outside.

Monica Foulkes heard Samuel's shouted warning and instinctively grabbed a tuft of reedy dune grass. The wind surged with impossible strength. Gravity shifted round until the beach was above her. Monica wailed fearfully as sand fell up into the sky. She felt herself following it, feet pulled into the air and sliding round to point at the interstice surrounding the blackhawk's nose. The grass clump made an awful slow tearing sound. Her hips and chest left the ground. Sand was blasting directly into her face. She couldn't see, couldn't breathe. The grass clump moved several centimetres. "OhdearGodpreservemeee!"

A long-fingered hand clamped around her free wrist. The grass clump left the sand with a sharp sucking noise, its weight wrenching her arm out towards the blackhawk. For an eternal second Monica hung splayed in the air as the sand scudded around her. Someone groaned with pained effort.

The wormhole interstice closed behind *Udat*.

Sand, water, mangled vegetation, and demented fish

cascaded down out of the sky. Monica landed flat on her belly, breath knocked out of her. "Oh my God," she wheezed. When she looked up, the haggard Edenist was crouched on his knees, panting heavily as he clutched his wrist. "You"—the words were difficult to form in her throat—"you held on to me."

He threw her a nod. "I think my wrist is broken."

"I would have . . ." She shuddered, then gave a foolish jittery laugh. "God, I don't even know your name."

"Samuel."

"Thank you, Samuel."

He rolled onto his back and sighed. "Pleasure."

Are you all right? Tranquillity asked the Edenist.

My wrist is very painful. She's heavy.

Your colleagues are approaching. Three of them are carrying medical nanonic packages in their aid kits. They will be with you shortly.

Even after all this time spent in Tranquillity, he couldn't get used to the personality's lack of empathy. Habitats were such an essential component of Edenism. It was disconcerting to have one treat him in this cavalier fashion. **Thank you.**

"I didn't think voidhawks and blackhawks could operate in a gravity field," Monica said.

"They can't," he told her. "This isn't gravity, it's centrifugal force. It's no different to the docking-ledges they use outside."

"Ah, of course. Have you ever heard of one coming inside a habitat before?"

"Never. A swallow like that requires phenomenal accuracy. From a strictly chauvinistic point of view I hate to say this, but I think it would be beyond most voidhawks. Even most blackhawks, come to that. Mzu made an astute choice. This was a very well thought out escape."

"Twenty-six years in the making," Pauline said. She climbed slowly to her feet, shaking her cotton top, which had been soaked by the falling water. A fat blue fish, half a metre long, was thrashing frantically on the sand by her shoes. "I mean that woman had us fooled for twenty-six goddamn years. Acting out the role of a flekhead physics professor with all the expected neuroses and eccentricities slotting perfectly into place. And we believed it. We patiently watched her for twenty-six years and she behaved exactly as predicted. If my home planet had been blown to shit, I'd behave like that. She never faltered, not once. But it was a twenty-six-year charade. Twenty-six goddamn years! What kind of a person can do that?"

Monica and Samuel exchanged an anxious look.

"Someone pretty obsessive," he said.

"Obsessive!" Pauline's face darkened. She leant over to pick the big fish up, but it squirmed out of her hands. "Keep bloody still," she shouted at it. "Well, God help Omuta now she's loose in the universe again." She finally succeeded in grabbing hold of the fish. "You do realize that thanks to our sanctions they haven't got a defensive system which can even fart loudly?"

"She won't get far," Monica said. "Not with this Laton scare closing down all the starship flights."

"You hope!" Pauline staggered off towards the waterline with her wriggling burden.

Monica clambered to her feet and brushed the sand off her clothes, shaking it out of her hair. She looked down at the lanky Edenist. "Dear me, CNIS entrance standards have really gone downhill lately."

He grinned weakly. "Yeah. But you know she's right about Mzu. The good doctor had us all fooled. Clever lady. And now there's going to be hell to pay."

She put her hand under his shoulder and helped him up. "I suppose so. One thing's for certain, there's going to be a mad scramble to catch her. Every government is going to want her tucked away on their own planet in order to safeguard democracy. And, my new friend, there are some democrats in this Confederation I don't ever want to find her."

"Us, for instance?"

Monica hesitated, then gave her head a rueful shake. "No. But don't tell my boss I said that."

Samuel watched the two agents on horseback galloping across the beach toward them. Right now he couldn't even remember which services they belonged to. Not that it mattered. In a few hours they'd all be going their separate ways again. "Damn, Tranquillity really was the only place for her, wasn't it?"

"Yes. Come on, let's see if these two have got anything for your wrist. I think that's Onku Noi on the second horse. The Imperial Oshanko mob are always loaded down with gadgets."

According to his neural nanonics' timer function it was high noon. But Chas Paske wasn't sure how to tell any more. There hadn't been any fluctuation in the red cloud's lambent emission since he started walking—hobbling, rather. The black and red jungle remained mordantly uninviting. Every laboured step was accompanied by the incessant hollow rolls and booms of thunder from high above.

He had managed to splint his leg, after a fashion: five laths of cherry oak wood that stretched from his ankle to his pelvis, lashed into place by ropy vines. The thigh wound was still a real problem. He had bound it with leaves, but every time he looked it seemed to be leaking capacious amounts of ichor down his shin. And it was impossible to keep the insects out. Unlike what appeared to be every other living creature, they hadn't abandoned the jungle. And devoid of other targets, they massed around him—mosquito-analogues, maggot-analogues, things with legs and wings and pincers that had no analogue. All of them suckling at his tender flesh. Twice now he'd changed the leaves, only to find a seething mass of tiny black elytra underneath. Flies crawled round his skin burns as though they were the only oases of nourishment in a barren world.

According to his guidance block he had come two and a half kilometres in the last three hours. It was hard going through the virgin undergrowth which lay along the side of the river. His crutch kept getting snagged by the thick cords that foamed over the loam. Slender low-hanging branches had a knack of catching the splint laths.

He picked the small wrinkled globes of abundant vine fruit as he went, chewing constantly to keep his fluid and protein levels up. But at this rate it was going to take him weeks to get anywhere.

Durringham was his ultimate goal. Whatever resources and wealth existed on this misbegotten planet, they resided in the capital. Scouting it had been his team's mission. He saw no reason to abandon that assignment. Sitting waiting to die in the jungle wasn't a serious option. Recovery and evacuation was obviously out of the question now. So, there it was, an honourable solution; one which would keep him occupied and motivated, and, should he achieve the impossible and make it, might even accomplish something worthwhile. Chas Paske was going to go down swinging.

But for all his determination he knew that he was going to have to find an easier way to travel. The medical program was releasing vast amounts of endocrines from his implants, analgesic blocks had been thrown across a good twenty per cent of his nerve fibres. Boosted metabolism or not, he couldn't keep expending energy at this rate.

He accessed his guidance block and summoned up the map. There was a village called Wryde fifteen hundred metres downstream on the other bank. According to the LDC file it had been established nine years ago.

It would have to do.

He plucked another elwisie fruit, and limped on. One advantage of the thunder was that no one would hear the racket he made ploughing through the vegetation.

The light was visible long before the first of the houses. A welcome gold-yellow nimbus shrouding the river. Snowlilies glinted and sparkled with their true opulence. Chas heard a bird again, the silly surprised warble of a chikrow. He lowered himself in tricky increments, and started to slither forward on his belly.

Wryde had become a thriving, affluent community, far beyond the norm for a stage one colony planet. The town nestled snugly in a six-square-kilometre clearing that had been turned over to dignified parkland. It was comprised of large houses built from stone or brick or landcoral, all of them the kind of elegantly sophisticated residence that a merchant or wealthy farmer would own. The main street was a handsome tree-lined boulevard, bustling with activity: people wandering in and out of the shops, sitting at the tables of pavement cafés. Horse-drawn cabs moved up and down. An impressive red-brick civic hall stood at one end, four storeys high, with an ornate central clock tower. He saw some kind of sports field just outside the main cluster of houses. People dressed all in white were playing a game he didn't know while spectators picnicked round the boundary. Close to the jungle at the back of the park, five windmills stood alongside a lake, their huge white sails turning steadily even though there was very little breeze. Grandiose houses lined the riverbank, lawns extending down to the water. They all had boat-houses or small jetties; rowing-boats and sailing dinghies were moored securely against the sluggish tide of snowlilies. Larger craft had been drawn up on wooden slipways.

It was the kind of community every sane person would want to live in; small-town cosiness, big-city stability. Even Chas, lying in muddy loam under a bush on the opposite bank, felt the subtle attraction of the place. By simply existing it offered the prospect of belonging to a perpetual golden age.

His retinal implants showed him the sunny, happy faces of the citizens as they went about their business. Scanning back and forth he couldn't see anyone labouring in the pristine gardens, or sweeping the streets; no people, no bitek servitors, no mechanoids. The nearest anyone came to work was the café proprietors, and they seemed cheerful enough, chatting and laughing with their customers. All generals and no privates, he thought to himself. It isn't real.

He accessed the guidance block again. A green reference grid slipped up over his vision and he focused on a jetty at the far end of the town's clearing. The block calculated its exact coordinate and integrated it into the map.

When he checked his physiological status, the neural nanonics reported his haemoglobin reserve was down to half an hour. His metabolism wasn't producing it with anything like its normal efficiency. He ran through the guidance block's display one last time. Half an hour ought to be enough.

Chas started to crawl forwards again, easing himself down the muddy slope and into the water like an arthritic crocodile.

Twenty minutes later he judiciously parted a pair of snowlilies and let his rigid moulded face stick up out of the water. The guidance block had functioned flawlessly, delivering him right beside the jetty. A trim blue-painted rowing-boat was pulling gently against its mooring two metres away. There was nobody anywhere near. He reached up and cut the pannier with his fission blade, grabbing the end as it fell into the water.

The boat started to drift with the snowlilies. Chas dropped below the surface.

He waited as long as he dared. The neural nanonics' physiological monitor program was flashing dire warnings of oxygen starvation into his brain before he risked surfacing.

Wryde was out of sight round a curve, although the ordinary light which clung to its rolling parkland was spilling round the trees on the bank. When he looked at his prize it had changed from the well-crafted skiff he had stolen to a dilapidated punt that was little more than a raft. Tissue-thin gunwales, which had been added in what must have been a surreal afterthought, were crumbling like rotten cork before his eyes. They left a wake of dark mushy dust on the snowlilies.

Chas waited a minute to see if any other drastic changes were going to occur. He rapped experimentally on the wood which was left. It seemed to be solid enough. So with a great deal of effort, and coming dangerously near to capsizing, he managed to half-clamber, half-roll into the shallow bottom of the boat.

He lay there inertly for a long time, then ponderously raised himself onto his elbows. The boat was drifting slowly into the bank. Long slippery ribbons of foltwine were trailing from his splint. River beetles crawled over his thigh wound. Both the medical nanonic packages were approaching overload trying to screen the blood from the lower half of his leg.

"Apart from that, fine," he said. His grating voice provided a harsh discord to the persistent fruity rumble of thunder.

He crushed or swept away as many of the beetles and other insects as he could. Naturally there weren't any oars. He cut through the vines holding his splint together, and used one of the laths to scull away from the bank and back into the main current. It took a while, with the snowlilies resisting him, but when he was back in the middle of the river the boat began to move noticeably swifter. He made himself as comfortable as possible, and watched the tall trees go past with an increasing sense of eagerness. A keen amateur student of military history, Chas knew that back on old Earth they used to say all roads led to Rome. Here on Lalonde, all the rivers led to Durringham.

A bubble of bright white light squatted possessively over Aberdale. From the air it appeared as though the village was sheltering below a translucent pearl dome to ward off the perverse elements assailing the jungle. Octan circled it at a respectable distance, wings outstretched to their full metre and a half span, riding the thermals with fluid ease, contemptuous of gravity. The jungle underneath him was the same discoloured maroon as the sky. But away to the south a single narrow horizontal streak of bright green shone with compulsive intensity. Instinctively he wanted to soar towards it, to break out into the cleanliness of real light.

Tandem thoughts circulated through the bird's brain, his kindly master's wishes directing his flight away from the purity, and tilting his head so that he looked at the buildings in the middle of the illuminated clearing. Enhanced retinas zoomed in.

"It's virtually the same as Pamiers," Pat Halahan said. "They've got maybe fifty of those fancy houses put up. The ground is all lawns and gardens, right out to the jungle. No sign of any fields or groves." He leaned forwards blindly. Octan casually curved a sepia wing-tip, altering his course by a degree. "Now that is odd. Those trees along the riverbank look like terrestrial weeping willows. But they're big, twenty metres plus. Got to be thirty years old."

"Don't count on it," Kelly muttered in a surly undertone, covering subtler emotions. "In any case, this is the wrong climate."

"Yeah, right," Pat said. "Switching to infrared. Nope. Nothing. If there's any installation underground, Reza, then they're dug in way deep."

"OK," the team commander said reluctantly. "Have Octan scout further east."

"If you want. But it doesn't look like there are any more inhabited clearings in the jungle that way. He can see the light from Schuster quite plainly from his altitude. There's nothing like that eastwards."

"They aren't going to advertise with hundred-kilowatt holograms, Pat."

"Yes, sir. East it is."

A crucial urge to explore the as-yet-unseen land beyond the village flowed through Octan's synapses, and the big eagle wheeled abruptly, reducing landscape and injured sky to chaotic smears.

The mercenary team were also marching eastwards, but they were on the Quallheim's northern shore, keeping roughly parallel to the water, a kilometre inland. They had come ashore west of Schuster where deirar trees covered the ground as thoroughly as though they were a plantation.

Such regularity made the team's journey much easier than their first venture ashore when they had bypassed Pamiers.

The deirars' thick smooth boles rose straight up for twenty-five metres then opened into an umbrella of vegetation that formed a near-solid roof. Together they formed a sylvestral cathedral of enormous proportions. Everywhere the mercenaries looked they could see sturdy jet-black bark pillars supporting the dovetailing leaf domes. On this side of the river the usual deluge of vines and undergrowth was little more than a wispy clutter of straggly sun-starved weeds, long stemmed and pale, heavy with grey mould.

It was Reza who led the march, although he had sent Theo scampering across the treetop canopy on the lookout for hostiles. Few of them had escaped from Pamiers uninjured. He counted himself among the fortunate, with a burn on the rear of his skull that had scorched a couple of sensor warts down to the monobonded carbon reinforced bone; torso scores, and a spiral weal on his right leg. Of all of them, Kelly had borne the worst injury; but the medical packages had resuscitated her to mobile status. She walked with a small cylindrical shoulder-bag carrying her kit; her armour trousers protected her legs from thorns, and an olive-green T-shirt which the red light had turned a raw umber covered the bulge of medical packages on her side.

Pamiers had delivered a deft lesson, bruising their pride as well as their skin. But an important lesson, to Reza's mind. The team had learnt to give the sequestrated population a proper degree of respect. He wasn't going to risk probing a village again.

Fenton and Ryall padded tirelessly through the jungle on the southern bank, skirting Aberdale by a wide margin. Jungle sounds filled their ears in the short gaps between the red cloud's perpetual thunder peals. The organic perfume of a hundred different flowers and ripening vine fruits trickled through the muggy air, a vital living counterpoint to the stink of dead children.

Reza nudged the hounds further south, away from the

now-foreign village, from the smell of the small decaying bodies, its voodoo fence, away from the terrible price Lalonde's populace had paid under the invaders' regime. Narrow leaves, mottled with fungal furs, parted round the hounds' muzzles. Chilly distaste and shame—almost inevitably, shame—wormed its trenchant way into their minds along the affinity bond; they shared their master's susceptibilities, becoming as keen as he to leave the heartbreaker calamity behind.

New scents rode the air: sap dripping from snapped vine strands, crushed leaves, loam ruffled by footprints and wheel tracks. The hounds raced ahead, guided by primal senses. People had been this way recently. Some, but not many.

Reza saw a path through the jungle. An old animal track running north–south, enlarged some time ago—branches cut back by fission blades, bushes hacked away—only to fall into disuse again. Almost, but not quite. Somebody still used it. Someone had used it less than two hours ago.

Nerves and instinct fired now, Fenton and Ryall loped through the moist grass towards the south. After two kilometres they found a scent trail branching off into the jungle. One person, male. His clothes smearing the leaves with sweat and cotton.

"Pat, bring Octan back. I think we've got our man."

Reza kept the snatch mission simple. The team activated their hovercraft again when they were back on the Quallheim east of Aberdale and started searching for a tributary fork on the south bank. According to the map stored in his guidance block there was a modest river which ran south through the jungle, coming from the mountains on the far side of the savannah. It took them five minutes to find it, and the hovercraft nosed over the clot of snowlilies guarding its mouth. Plaited tree boughs formed an arched screen overhead.

"After the snatch we'll keep going up this river and out onto the savannah," Reza said when they had left the

Quallheim behind. "I want to get him and us out from under this bloody cloud as quickly as possible. We should be able to access the communication satellites as well once we're clear of it. That way if we can extract any useful information it can be delivered straight up to Terrance Smith."

If Smith is still up there, Kelly thought. She couldn't forget what the woman in Pamiers had said about the starships fighting. But Joshua had promised to stay and pick them up. She gave a cynical little sniff. Oh yes, the Confederation's Mr. Dependable himself.

"You all right?" Ariadne asked, raising her voice above the steady propeller whine and the rambling thunder booms.

"My analgesic blocks are holding," Kelly said. "It was just the size of the burn which shocked me." She resisted the urge to scratch the medical nanonic packages.

"Adds a bit of spice to the recording, a bit of drama," Ariadne said. "Speaking of which, you're not going to blow us out, are you? I mean, we are the good guys."

"Yeah. You're the good guys."

"Great, always wanted to be a sensevise star."

Kelly accessed her Lalonde sensevise report memory cell file and turned her head until Ariadne was in the centre of her vision field (wishing the combat-boosted could produce some halfway decent facial expressions). "What did you learn from the sample you took from the houses?"

"Nowt. It was dust, that's all. Literally, dry loam."

"So these ornamental buildings are just an illusion?"

"Half and half. It isn't a complete fiction; they've moulded the loam into the shape you see and cloaked it with an optical illusion. It's similar to our chameleon circuit, really."

"How do they do that?"

"No idea. The closest human technology can come is the molecular-binding generators starships use to strengthen their hulls. But they're expensive, and use up a lot of power. Be cheaper to build a house, or use programmed silicon like you suggested. Then again"—she tilted her head back to focus her sensors on the cloudband above the trees—"logic doesn't seem to be playing a large part in life on Lalonde right now."

The hovercraft eased in against the crumbling loam bank. Ryall was standing among the qualtook trees above the water, waiting for them. Reza jumped ashore and ruffled the big hound's head. It pressed against his side in complete devotion.

"Jalal and Ariadne, with me," Reza said. "The rest of you stay here and keep the hovercraft ready. Pat, monitor us through Octan. If we blow the snatch, I suggest you keep heading south. There's a Tyratca farming settlement on the other side of the savannah. It's as good a place as any to hide out. This snatch is our last stab at completing the mission. Don't waste yourselves trying to gather further Intelligence, and don't attempt a rescue. Got that?"

"Yes, sir," Pat said.

Jalal and Ariadne joined Reza on the top of the bank. The big combat-adept mercenary had plugged a gaussrifle into one elbow socket and a TIP rifle into the other; power cables and feed tubes looped round into his backpack.

"Kelly?" Reza asked ingenuously. "Not wanting to come with us this time?"

"It took eight generations of cousins marrying to produce you," she told him.

The three mercenaries on the bank activated their chameleon circuits. Laughter floated down to the hovercraft out of unbroken jungle.

Fenton watched the little clearing from under the sloping lower branches of an infant gigantea. The light here wasn't the pure solar white of the villages, but the universal redness had veered into a pale pink shade. A log cabin had been built in the centre, not the kind of frame and plank arrangement favoured by the colonists but a rugged affair that could have come straight from some Alpine meadow. A stone chimney-stack formed almost all of one side, smoke wound drowsily upwards. A lot of trouble had been taken to transform the clearing; undergrowth had been trimmed back, animal hides were stretched drying over frames, timber had been cut and stacked, a vegetable plot planted.

The man who had done it was a well-built thirty-five-year-old with inflamed ginger hair, wearing a thick red and blue check cotton shirt and mud-caked black denim jeans. He was working at a sturdy table outside his front door, sawing up wood with old-fashioned manual tools. A half-completed rocking chair stood on the ground behind him.

Fenton moved forwards surreptitiously out of the shaggy gigantea's shade, but keeping to the cover provided by bushes and smaller trees ringing the clearing. Between thunder broadsides he could hear the regular stifled ripping sound as the man planed a piece of wood on the table. Then the sound stopped and his shoulders stiffened.

Reza wouldn't have thought it possible. The man was a good fifty metres away, with his back to the hound, and the thunder was unrelenting. Even his enhanced senses would have difficulty picking out Fenton under such circumstances. He and the other two mercenaries were still four hundred metres away. Nothing else for it . . . Fenton cantered eagerly into the clearing.

The man looked round, bushy eyebrows rising. "What's this, then? My, you're a roguish looking brute." He clicked his fingers, and Fenton trotted up to him. "Ah, you'll not be on your own, then. That's a shame, a crying shame. For all of us. Your master won't be far behind, I'll warrant. Will you? Came down on the spaceplanes this morning no doubt, didn't you? That must have been a trip and a half. Aye, well, I'll not be finishing my chair this afternoon then." He sat down on a bench beside the table, and started to change, his shirt losing colour, hair fading, thinning, stature diminishing.

By the time Reza, Jalal, and Ariadne walked into the clearing he had become an undistinguished middle-aged man with brown skin and thin features, wearing an ageing LDC one-piece jump suit. Fenton was noisily lapping up

water out of a bowl at his feet, mind radiating contentment
with his new friend.

Reza walked over cautiously. His retinal implants
scanned the man from head to toe, and he datavised the
pixel sequence into his processor block for a search and
identify program. Although the earlier phantom lumber-
jack image had vanished, Reza saw the roots of the man's
black hair were a dark ginger. "Afternoon," he said, not
quite sure how to react to this display of passivity.

"Good afternoon to you. Not that I've seen anything like
you before, mind. Not outside a kinema, and perhaps not
even there."

"My name is Reza Malin. We're part of a team employed by the LDC to find out what's going on down
here."

"Then with every ounce of sincerity I own, I wish you
good luck, my boy. You're going to need it."

An ounce was an ancient unit of measure, Reza's neural
nanonics informed him (there was no reference to kinema
in any file). "Are you going to help me?"

"It doesn't look to me like I've got a lot of choice, now
does it? Not with your merry gang and their big, big
weapons."

"That's true. What's your name?"

"My name? Well, now, that'd be Shaun Wallace."

"Bad move. According to the LDC files you're Rai
Molvi, a colonist who settled Aberdale."

The man scratched his ear and gave Reza a bashful grin.
"Ah now, you've got me there, Mr. Malin. I must admit, I
was indeed old Molvi. Charmless soul he is, too."

"OK, smartarse, game over. Come on."

Reza led the way back to the hovercraft, with Jalal walking right behind their captive, gaussrifle trained on the
back of his skull. A couple of minutes after they left the
clearing the pink light began to dim back into the same lus-
treless burgundy of the surrounding jungle. As if immediately aware of the abandonment, playful vennals slithered
into the trees around the edge of the clearing. The more

venturesome among them dared to scamper over the grass to the cabin itself, searching for titbits. After quarter of an hour the cabin emitted a vociferous creak. The vennals fled *en masse* back into the trees.

It was another couple of minutes before anything else happened. Then, with the tardiness of a sinking moon, its surface texture leaked away to reveal a starkly primitive mud hut. Tiny arid flakes moulted from the roof, resembling a sleet of miniature autumn leaves as they scattered over the grass below; rivulets of dust trickled down the walls. Within twenty minutes the entire edifice had dissolved like a sugar cube in soft, warm rain.

Forget discovering Ione Saldana existed, forget discovering Laton was still alive, this was the ultimate interview. For *this* Collins would make her their premier anchorwoman for the rest of time. For this she would be respected and lionized across the Confederation. Kelly Tirrel was the first reporter in history to interview the dead.

And as the dead went, Shaun Wallace was agreeable enough. He sat on the rear bench of the lead hovercraft, facing Kelly, and stroking Fenton the whole while. Jalal kept a heavy-calibre gaussrifle levelled at him. On the front bench beside her, Reza was listening intently, making the occasional comment.

The trees were thinning out as they raced for the end of the jungle. She could see more of the red cloudband through the black filigree of leaves overhead. It too was becoming flimsier; there were definite fast-moving serpentine currents straining its uniformity. Strangely, for there was no wind at ground level.

Shaun Wallace claimed he had lived in Northern Ireland during the early twentieth century. "Terrible times," he said softly. "Especially for someone with my beliefs." But he had just shaken his head and smiled distantly when she asked what those beliefs were. "Nothing a lady like yourself would want to know." He died, he said, in the mid-1920s, another martyr to the cause, another victim of

English oppression. The reason the soldiers shot him was not volunteered. He claimed he hadn't died alone.

"And after?" Kelly said.

"Ah, now, Miss Kelly, afterwards is the work of the Devil."

"You went to hell?"

"Hell is a place, so the good priests taught me. This beyond was no place. It was dry and empty, and it was cruel beyond physical pain. It was where you can see the living wasting their lives, and where you drain the substance from each other."

"Each other? You weren't alone?"

"There was millions of us. Souls beyond the counting of a simple Ballymena lad like myself."

"You say you can see the living from the other side?"

"From the beyond, yes. 'Tis like through a foggy window. But you strive to make out what it is that's happening in the living world. All the time you strive. And you yearn for it, you yearn for it so hard, lass, that you feel your heart should be bursting apart. I saw wonders and I saw terrors, and I could touch neither."

"How did you come back?"

"The way was opened for us. Something came through from this side, right here on this sodden hot planet. I don't know what the creature was. Nothing Earthly, though. After that, there was no stopping us."

"This xenoc, the creature you say let you through; is it still here, still bringing souls back from the beyond?"

"No, it was only here for the first one. It vanished after that. But it was too late, the trickle was already becoming a flood. We bring ourselves back now."

"How?"

Shaun Wallace gave a reluctant sigh. He was quiet for so long Kelly thought he wasn't going to answer; he even stopped stroking Fenton.

"The way the devil-lovers of yesterday always tried to do it," he said heavily. "With their ceremonies and their pagan barbarism. And God preserve me for doing such things, I used to think what I did before was sinful. But there's no other way."

"What is the way?"

"We break the living. We make them want to be possessed. Possession is the end of torment, you see. Even with our power we can only open a small gateway to the beyond, enough to show the lost souls the way back. But there has to be somewhere waiting for them, some host. And the host has to be willing."

"You torture them into submission," Reza said bluntly.

"Aye, that we do. That we do, indeed. And, mark you, there's no pride in me for saying it."

"You mean, Rai Molvi is still there? Still alive inside you?"

"Yes. But I keep his soul locked away in a dark, safe place. I'm not sure you could call it living."

"And this power you mentioned." Kelly pressed the point. "What is your power?"

"I don't know for sure. Magic of a kind. Though not a witch's magic with its spells and potions. This is a darker magic, because it's there at a thought. So easy, it is. Nothing like that should be given easily to a man. The temptations are too strong."

"Is that where the white fire comes from?" Reza asked. "This power you have?"

"Aye, indeed it is."

"What's its range?"

"Ah now, Mr. Malin, that's difficult to say. The more of you that fling it, the further it will go. The more impassioned you are, the stronger it will be. For a cool one such as yourself, I doubt it would be far."

Reza grunted and shifted back on the bench.

"Could you demonstrate the power for me, please?" Kelly asked. "Something I can record and show people. Something that will make them believe what you say is true."

"I've never known a newspaper gal before. You did say you were from a newspaper, now didn't you?"

"What newspapers eventually became, yes." She ran a historical search request through her neural nanonics. "Something like the Movietone and Pathé reels at the cinema, only with colour and feeling. Now, that demonstration?"

"I normally prefer gals with longer hair, myself."

Kelly ran her hand self-consciously over her scalp. She had shaved her hair to a blueish stubble so she could wear the armour's shell-helmet. "I normally have longer hair," she said resentfully.

Shaun Wallace winked broadly, then leant over the gunwale and scooped up one of the long-legged insects scampering over the snowlilies. He held it up in the palm of his hand; a long spindly tube body, dun brown, with a round bulb of a head sprouting unpleasant pincer mandibles. It was quivering, but stayed where it was as though glued to his skin. He brought his other hand down flat on top of it, making a show of pressing them together, squashing the insect. Kelly's eyes never wavered.

When he parted his hands the prince of butterflies was revealed, wings almost the size of his palms, patterned in deep turquoise and topaz and silver, colours resistant to the red light of the cloud, shining in their own right. Its wings flexed twice, then it flew off, only to be kicked about in the air by the wash of the hovercraft's powerful slipstream.

"There, you see?" Shaun Wallace said. "We don't always destroy."

Kelly lost sight of the delightful apparition. "How long will it stay like that?"

"Mortality is not something you measure out like a pint of ale, Miss Kelly. It will live its life to the full, and that's all that can be said."

"He doesn't know," Reza muttered curtly.

Shaun Wallace practised a knowing, slightly condescending smile.

It was growing lighter around the hovercraft. Up ahead, Kelly could see the wonderfully welcome glare of pure sunlight striking emerald foliage. A colour that wasn't red!

She had begun to believe that red was all there ever was, all there ever had been.

The hovercraft skimmed out from under the chafed edge of the cloudband. All of the mercenaries broke into a spontaneous cheer.

"What is that thing?" Kelly shouted above the rebel whoops, pointing up at the cloud.

"A reflection of ourselves, our fear."

"What do you fear?"

"The emptiness of the night. It reminds us too much of the beyond. We hide from it."

"You mean you're making that?" she asked, scepticism warring with astonishment. "But it covers thousands of kilometres."

"Aye, that it does. 'Tis our will that creates it; we want shelter, so shelter we have. All of us, Miss Kelly, even me who shuns the rest of them, we all pray for sanctuary with every fibre of being. And it's growing, this will of ours, spreading out to conquer. One day soon it will cover all of this planet. But even that is only the first chapter of salvation."

"What's the second?"

"To leave. To escape the harsh gaze of this universe altogether. We'll withdraw to a place of our own making. A place where there is no emptiness hanging like a sword above the land, no death to claim us. A place where your butterfly will live for ever, Miss Kelly. Now tell me that isn't a worthy goal, tell me that isn't a dream worth having."

Reza watched the last of the jungle's trees go past as the hovercraft reached the savannah. The lush green grassland seemed to unroll on either side of the river as though it was only just coming into existence. He wasn't really paying much attention; the strange (supposed) Irishman was a captivating performer. "A closed universe," he said, and the earlier scorn was lacking.

Kelly gave him a surprised glance. "You mean it is possible?"

"It happens thousands of times a day. The blackhawks and voidhawks open interstices to travel through wormholes every time they fly between stars. Technically they're self-contained universes."

"Yes, but taking a planet—"

"There are twenty million of us," Shaun Wallace purred smoothly. "We can do it, together, we can pull open the portal that leads away from mortality."

Kelly's neural nanonics faithfully recorded the silver chill tickling her nerves at the naked conviction in his voice. "You're really planning to generate a wormhole large enough to enclose the whole of Lalonde? And keep it there?"

Shaun Wallace wagged his finger at her. "Ah, now there you go again, Miss Kelly, putting your fine, elegant words in my mouth. Plans, such a grand term. Generals and admirals and kings, now they have plans. But we don't, we have instinct. Hiding our new world from this universe God created, that comes as naturally as breathing." He chuckled. "It means we can go on breathing, too. I'm sure you wouldn't want to stop me from doing that, would you now? Not a sweet lass like yourself."

"No. But what about Rai Molvi? Tell me what happens to him afterwards?"

Shaun Wallace scratched his chin, looked round at the savannah, shifted the jump-suit fabric round his shoulders, pulled a sardonic face.

"He stays, doesn't he?" Kelly said stiffly. "You won't let him go."

"I need the body, miss. Real bad. Perhaps there'll be a priest amongst us I can visit for absolution."

"If what you're saying is true," Reza said charily, focusing an optical sensor on the cloudband behind, "then we really don't want to be staying here any longer than we have to. Wallace, when is this planetary vanishing act supposed to happen?"

"You have a few days' grace. But there are none of your starships left to sail away on. Sorry."

"Is that why you didn't resist, because we can't escape?"

"Oh, no, Mr. Malin, you've got me all wrong. You see, I don't want much to do with my fellows. That's why I live out in the woods, there. I prefer being on my own, I've had a bucketful of their company. Seven centuries of it, to be precise."

"So you'll help us?"

He gathered himself up and threw a glance over his shoulder at the second hovercraft. "I won't hinder you," he announced magnanimously.

"Thank you very much."

"Not that it will do you much good, mind."

"How's that?"

"There's not going to be many places you can run to, I'm afraid. Quite a few of us have sailed away already."

"Fucking hell," Kelly gasped.

Shaun Wallace frowned in disapproval. "To be sure, that's no word for a lady to be going and using."

Kelly made sure he was in perfect focus. "Are you telling me that what's happening on Lalonde is going to happen on other planets as well?"

"Indeed I am. There's a lot of very anguished souls back there in the beyond. They're all in dire need of a clean handsome body, every one of them. Something very much like the one you've got there."

"This is occupied, to the hilt."

His eyes flashed with black amusement. "So was this one, Miss Kelly."

"And all these worlds the possessed have gone to, are you going to try and imprison them in wormholes?"

"That's a funny old word you're using there: wormholes. Little muddy tunnels in the ground, with casts on top to show the fishermen where they are."

"It means chinks in space, gaps you can fall through."

"Does it now? Well, then, I suppose that's what I mean, yes. I like that, a gap in the air which leads you through to the other side of the rainbow."

Surreal. The word seemed to be caught on some repeater

program in Kelly's neural nanonics, flipping up in hologram violet over the image of a mad, dead Irishman sitting
in front of her, grinning in delight at her discomfort.
Worlds snatched out of their orbits by armies of the dead.
Surreal. Surreal. Surreal.

Fenton rose growling to his feet, fangs barred, hackles
sticking up like spikes. Shaun Wallace gave the hound an
alarmed look, and Kelly's retinas caught the minutest
white static flames twinkle over his fingertips. But Fenton
swung his head round to the prow and barked.

Jalal's gaussrifle was already coming round. He saw the
huge creature crouched down in the long grass at the side
of the water thirty-five metres ahead of the hovercraft. The
Lalonde generalist didactic memory called it a kroclion, a
plains-dwelling carnivore which even the sayce ran from.
He wasn't surprised, the beast must have been nearly four
metres long, weighing an easy half-tonne. Its hide was a
sandy yellow, well suited to the grass, making visual identification hard (infrared was, thankfully, a furnace flame).
The head—like a terrestrial shark—had been grafted on,
all teeth and tiny killer-bright eyes.

Blue target graphics locked on. He fired an EE round.

Everyone ducked, Kelly jamming her hands over her
ears. A dazzling explosion sent a pillar of purple plasma
and mashed soil spouting twenty metres into the air. Its
vertex flattened out, a ring of soot-choked orange flame
rolling across the river. The ululate crack was loud enough
to drown out the tattoo of thunder chasing them from the
red cloud.

Kelly lifted her head carefully.

"I think you got him," Theo said drily, as he steered the
hovercraft away from the quaking water sloshing round the
new crater. A semicircle of grass on the bank was burning.

"They're vicious bastards," Jalal protested.

"Not that one, not any more, as anyone within five kilometres will tell you," Ariadne said.

"And you could have dealt with it better?"

"Forget it," Reza said. "We've got more important things to worry about."

"You believe what this dickhead has been telling us?" Ariadne asked, jerking a thumb at Shaun Wallace.

"Some of it," Reza said noncommittally.

"Why thank you, Mr. Malin," Shaun Wallace said. He watched the burning crater closely as the hovercraft sped past. "Fine shooting there, Mr. Jalal. Those old kroclions, they put the wind up me and no mistake. Old Lucifer was on form the day he made them."

"Shut up," Reza said. The one optical sensor he had left focused on the edge of the red cloud showed him a lone tendril starting to swell out, extending along the line of the narrow river behind them. Too slow to catch them, he estimated, but it was a graphically disturbing demonstration that the cloud and the possessed inhabitants were aware of the team's presence.

He opened a channel to his communication block and datavised a sequence of orders in. It began scanning the sky for communication-satellite beacons. Two of the five satellites the blackhawks had delivered into geosynchronous orbit were above the horizon and still broadcasting. The block aimed a tight beam at one, requesting contact with any of Terrance Smith's fleet. No ship was left in the command net, the satellite's computer reported, but there was a message stored in its memory. Reza datavised his personal code.

"This is a restricted access message for Reza's team," Joshua Calvert's voice said from the communication block. "But I have to be sure it is you and only you receiving it. The satellite is programmed to transmit it on a secure directional beam. If there is any hostile within five hundred metres of you who can intercept then do not request access. In order to access the recording, enter the name of the person who came between me and Kelly last year."

The tip of the cloud tendril was a couple of kilometres

away. Reza turned to face Shaun Wallace. "Can any of your friends intercept a radio transmission?"

"Well, now, there's some of them living in one of the old savannah homesteads. But they're a few miles from here, yet. Is that more than five hundred metres?"

"Yes. Kelly, the name please."

She gave him a stonefaced smile. "Aren't you glad you didn't leave me behind at Pamiers?"

Jalal laughed. "She got you there, Reza."

"Yes," Reza said heavily. "I'm glad we didn't leave you behind. The name?"

Kelly opened a channel to his communication block and datavised: "Ione Saldana."

There was a moment's silence while the satellite's carrier wave emitted a few electronic bleeps.

"Well remembered, Kelly. OK, this is the bad news: the hijacked starships have started fighting us and the navy. There's a real vicious battle going on in orbit right now. *Lady Mac* got clear, but we've taken a bit of punishment in the process. Another story for you sometime. I'm about to jump us out to Murora. There's an Edenist station in orbit there, and we're hoping to dock with it to make our repairs. We estimate the damage can be patched up in a couple of days, after which we'll come back for you. Kelly, Reza, the rest of you; we're only going to make one fly-by. Hopefully you took my earlier advice and are now heading hell for leather away from that bloody cloud. Keep going, and leave your communication block scanning for my transmission. If you want to be picked up then you'll have to stay away from any hostiles. That's about it, we're battening down to jump now. Good luck, I'll see you in two, maybe three days."

Kelly rested her head in her hands. Just hearing his voice again was a fantastic tonic. And he was alive, smart enough to elude a battle. And he was going to come back for them. Joshua, you bloody splendid marvel. She wiped tears from her cheeks.

Shaun Wallace patted her shoulder tenderly. "Your young man, is it?"

"Yes. Sort of." She sniffed, and brushed away the last of the tears in a businesslike manner.

"He sounds like a fine boy to me."

"He is."

Reza datavised a summary of events to the second hovercraft. "I'm in complete agreement with Joshua about keeping clear of the cloud and the possessed. As of now our original mission is over. Our priority now is just to stay alive and make sure what information we have gets back to the Confederation authorities. We'll keep going up this river to the Tyrathca farmers and hope that we can hold out there until the *Lady Macbeth* comes back for us."

It was the rygar bush which had brought the Tyrathca farmers to Lalonde.

When they were searching for their initial backing, the LDC sent samples of Lalonde's aboriginal flora to both of the xenoc members of the Confederation; it was standard practice to try and attract as wide a spectrum of support as possible for such ventures. The Kiint, as always, declined to participate. But the Tyrathca considered the small berries of the rygar bush a superlative delicacy. Ripe berries could be ground up to produce a cold beverage, or mixed with sugar to form a sticky fudge; LDC negotiators claimed it was the Tyrathcan equivalent of chocolate. The normally cloistered xenocs were so enamoured at the prospect of wholesale rygar cultivation they agreed to a joint colony enterprise with their merchant organization taking a four per cent stake in the LDC. It was only the third time since joining the Confederation that they had ever participated in a colony, a fact which lent the hard-pressed LDC considerable badly needed respectability. Even better for the LDC board: to a human palate the rygar berries tasted like oily grapes, so there would never be any conflict of interest arising.

Five years after the dumpers had dropped out of the sky

to form the nucleus of Durringham the first batch of Tyrathcan breeder pairs arrived and settled in the foothills of the mountain range which made up the southern border of the Juliffe basin where the rygar bushes flourished. The LDC's long-range economic plans foresaw both the human and Tyrathcan settlements expanding from their respective centres until they met at the roots of the tributaries. By the time that happened both groups would have risen above their initial subsidence level and be prosperous enough to trade to their mutual enrichment. But that date was still many years in the future. The human villages furthest from Durringham were all as poor as Aberdale and Schuster, while the Tyrathcan plantations had barely cultivated enough rygar to fill the holds of the starships their merchants sent twice a year. Contact had so far been minimal.

It was late afternoon, and the savannah was already giving way to low humpbacked foothills when the mercenary team saw their first Tyrathcan house. There was no mistaking it, a dark cinnamon-coloured tower twenty-five metres high with slightly tapering walls, and circular windows sealed over with ebony blisters. The design had evolved on the abandoned Tyrathcan homeworld, Mastrit-PJ, over seventeen thousand years ago, and was employed on every planet their arkships had colonized right across the galaxy. They never used anything else.

This one stood like a border sentry castle overlooking the river. Octan glided round it a couple of times, seeing the vague outlines of fields and gardens reclaimed by grass and small scrub bushes. Moss and weeds were growing around the inside of the roof's turret wall where soil and dust had drifted.

"Nothing moving," Pat reported to Reza. "I'd say it was deserted three or four years ago."

They had gathered together on the riverbank just downstream from the tower house, hovercraft drawn up on the grass. The river was getting narrower, little more than a stream, down to about eight metres wide, and littered with boulders which made it virtually unnavigable. For the first time since they had landed that morning there were no snowlilies in sight, only the broken tips of their stems trailing limply.

"The Tyrathca do that," Sal Yong said. "A house is only ever used once. When the breeders die it's sealed up as their tomb."

Reza consulted his guidance block. "There's a plantation village called Coastuc-RT six kilometres south-east of here. The other side of that ridge," he pointed, datavising the map image to them. "Ariadne, can the hovercraft take it?"

She focused her optical sensors on the rolling land which skirted the mountains. "Shouldn't be a problem, the grass is a lot shorter here than the savannah and there isn't much stone about." When she looked west she could see another three of the dark towers sticking out of the bleak countryside. They were all in shadow; thick black rainclouds were surging towards them along the side of the mountains. The wind had freshened appreciably since they had left the jungle. Looking back to the north she could see the red cloud over the Quallheim forging the entire northern horizon; it was almost edge on, they had climbed steadily since leaving it behind. The sky above it was a perfect unblemished blue.

Kelly felt the first smattering of the drizzle on her bare arms as she clambered back into the hovercraft. She dug into her cylindrical kitbag for a cagoule, her burnt armoursuit jacket had been left behind in the jungle—in that state it wouldn't have been any use anyway. "I'm sorry," she told Shaun Wallace as he sat beside her. "I've only got the one, and the others don't need them."

"Ah now, don't you go worrying yourself over me, Miss Kelly," he said. The jump suit he wore turned a rich indigo, then the fabric became stiffer. He was wearing a cagoule which was identical to the one in her hands, right down to the unobtrusive Collins logo on the left shoulder. "There, see? Old Shaun can look after himself."

Kelly gave him a flustered nod (thankful her memory cell was still recording), and hurriedly struggled into her own cagoule as the warm drizzle thickened. "What about food?" she asked the Irishman as Theo goaded the hovercraft over the summit of the riverbank and started off towards the Tyrathca village.

"Don't mind if I do, thanks. Nothing too rich mind, not for me. I likes me pleasures simple."

She dug round in the bag and found a bar of tarrit-flavoured chocolate. None of the mercenaries had brought any food, with their metabolisms they could graze off the vegetation indefinitely, potent intestinal enzymes breaking up anything with proteins and hydrocarbons.

Shaun Wallace chewed in silence for a minute. "That's nice," he said, "reminds me a little of bilberries on a cold morning," and he grinned.

Kelly found she was smiling back at him.

The hovercraft moved a lot slower over the land than on water. Cairnlike clusters of weather-smoothed stone and sudden pinched gullies made the pilots' task a demanding one. The rain, which was now a solid downpour of heavy grey water, added to the difficulty.

Pat had sent Octan northward to avoid the worst of the deluge. Back out on the savannah it was still dry and sunny, a buffer zone between nature and supernature. Reza dispatched Fenton and Ryall to survey the ground ahead. Lightning began to spear down.

"I think I preferred the river," Jalal said glumly.

"Ah, Mr. Jalal, buck up now, this is nothing for Lalonde," Shaun Wallace said. "A little shower, that's all. It was much worse than this before we returned from beyond."

Jalal ignored the casual reference to the power of the possessed; Shaun Wallace, he thought, was playing a subtle war of nerves against them. Sowing the seeds of doubt and despondency.

"Hold it," Reza datavised to Theo, and Sal Yong, who was piloting the second hovercraft. "Deflate the skirts."

The hovercraft sank onto their hulls with flagging whines, crushing the sturdy grass tufts, settling at awkward angles. Rain had reduced visibility to less than twenty-five metres even with enhanced sight. Kelly could just make out Ryall up ahead. The hound was shifting about uneasily in front of a big sandy-brown boulder.

Reza took off his magazine belt, and left the TIP carbine he'd been carrying with it. He hopped over the gunwale and started to trudge towards the restive animal. Kelly had to wipe a slick film of water from her face. The rain was worming its way round her cagoule hood to run down her neck. She toyed with the idea of putting on her shell-helmet again—anything to stop this insidious clammy invasion.

Reza stopped five metres short of the brown lump, and slowly opened his arms, rain dripping from his grey-skinned fingers. He shouted something even Kelly's studio-grade audio-discrimination program couldn't catch above the wind and rain. She squinted, the rain suddenly chilling inside her T-shirt. The boulder rose up smoothly on four powerful legs. Kelly gasped. Her Confederation generalist didactic memory identified it immediately: a soldier-caste Tyrathca.

"Oh bugger," Jalal muttered. "They're clan creatures, it won't be alone." He started to scan around. It was hopeless in the rain, even infrared was washed out.

The soldier-caste Tyrathca was about as big as a horse, although the legs weren't as long. Its head, too, was faintly equine, tilted back at a shallow angle at the end of a thick muscular neck. There were no visible ears, or nostrils; the mouth had a complex double-lip arrangement resembling overlapping clam shells. The sienna hide, which Kelly had thought solid like an exoskeleton, was actually scaled, with a short-cropped chestnut-brown mane running along its entire spine. Two arms extended from behind the base of its neck, ending in nine-fingered circular hands. A pair of slender antennae also protruded from its shoulder joints, swept back along the length of its body.

Although it had a strong animal appearance, it was holding a large very modern-looking rifle. A broad harnesslike belt hung round its neck, with grenades and power magazines clipped on.

It held out a processor block, and a slim AV projection pillar telescoped out. "Turn your vehicles around," a synthetic voice clanged through the rain. "Humans are no longer permitted here."

"We need somewhere to shelter for the night," Reza replied. "We can't go back north; you must have seen the red cloud."

"No humans."

"Why not? We must have somewhere to stay. Tell me, why?"

"Humans have become—" The block gave a melodic cheep. "No direct translation available; similarity to: *elemental*. Coastuc-RT has suffered damage, merchant spaceplane has been stolen. Breeders and other castes have been killed by amok humans. You are not permitted entry."

"I know about the disturbances in the human villages. I have been sent by the Lalonde Development Corporation to try and restore order."

"Then do that. Go to your own race's villages and bring order."

"We have tried, but the situation was beyond our capability to resolve. There has been a major invasion of an unknown origin." He just couldn't bring himself to say possession. The processor block was quiet; he guessed he was talking to a breeder, the soldier caste were only marginally sentient—not that he'd like to go up against one. "I would like to discuss what can be done to protect you from further attack. My team are combat trained and well equipped, we should be able to augment whatever defences you have."

"Acceptable. You may enter Coastuc-RT by yourself to view the situation. If you believe you are able to increase our defences your team will be allowed to enter and stay."

"Reza," Kelly datavised. "Ask if I can come with you, please."

"I will need to bring two others to assess the area around Coastuc-RT with any degree of accuracy before nightfall," he said out loud, then datavised: "That makes us quits now."

"Absolutely," she replied.

"Two only," the synthetic voice agreed. "None may carry weapons. Our soldiers will provide protection."

"As you wish." He turned and walked back to the first hovercraft, feet sinking up to his ankles in slimy puddles. The processor block AV projection pillar began to emit the reverberative whistles and hoots which were the Tyrathcan speech. Answering calls shrilled through the rain, causing the mercenaries to up their sensor resolution to the maximum in a vain attempt to locate the other soldier castes.

"Ariadne, you come with me and Kelly," Reza said. "I'll need someone who can review the area properly. The rest of you wait here. We'll try and get back before dusk. I'll leave Fenton and Ryall on picket duty for you."

Two seemingly tireless soldiers ran alongside the hovercraft all the way to the village, antennae whipping back and forth (they were tail-analogues, helping with balance, according to Kelly's didactic memory). Kelly wasn't sure whom they were supposed to be protecting. The guns still appeared incongruous; for creatures that had evolved during the pre-technology tribal era to fight the Tyrathcan version of rough and tumble against enemy tribe soldiers bows and arrows would be more suited.

When she reviewed the entire didactic memory she found that the breeders (the only fully sentient Tyrathca) secreted what amounted to chemical control programs in specialist teats. A breeder would think out a sequence of orders—which plants were edible, how to operate a specific power tool—that would be edited into a chain of molecules by the teat gland. Once instructions were loaded in the brain of a vassal-caste species (there were six types) they could be activated by a simple verbal command whenever required. The chemicals were also used to educate young breeders, making the process a natural equivalent to Adamist didactic imprints and Edenist educational affinity lessons.

The rain was easing off when the hovercraft cleared the crest above Coastuc-RT. Kelly looked down on a broad, gentle valley with extensively cultivated terraces on both sides. An area of nearly twenty square kilometres had been cleared of scrub and grass, rebuilt into irrigated ledges, and planted with young rygar bushes. Coastuc-RT itself sat on the floor of the valley, several hundred indentical dark brown towers regimented in concentric rings around a central park space.

Reza steered the hovercraft onto a rough switchback track and set off down the slope. Numerous farmer-caste Tyrathca were out tending the emerald-green bushes—pruning, weeding, patching up the shallow drainage ditches. The farmers were slightly smaller than the soldiers but with thicker arms, endowed with the kind of plodding durability associated with oxen or shire-horses. They saw one or two hunter caste skulking among the bushes, about the same size as Reza's hounds, but with a streamlined fury that could probably give a kroclion a nasty fright. The escort soldiers whistled and hooted every time the hunters appeared, and they turned away obediently.

The first signs of damage were visible when the hovercraft reached the valley floor. Several towers in the village's outer ring were broken, five had been reduced to jagged stumps sticking up out of the rubble. Scorch marks formed barbarous black graffiti across the tower walls.

Fields on either side of the road had been churned up by fresh craters. EE explosives, Reza guessed, the village soldier caste had put up a good fight. The road itself had been repaired in several places. An earth rampart had been thrown up around the perimeter, a hundred metres from the outer turret houses. Farmers were still working around its base, using shovels which even Sewell would have been hard pressed to raise.

"Leave your vehicle now," the synthesized voice from the processor block told them when they were twenty metres away from the barricade of raw loam.

Reza cut the fans and codelocked the power cells. The soldiers waited until they had climbed out, then walked them into the village.

Up close the tower houses were utilitarian, each with four floors, their windows arranged at precise levels. They were made by the builder caste, the largest of all the vassals, who chewed soil and mixed it with an epoxy chemical extravasated in their mouth ducts, producing a strong cement. It gave the walls a smooth, extruded feel, as though the towers had come intact from some giant kiln. There were some modern amenities, bands of solar cell panels tipped most of the turret walls; metal water pipes lay bent and tangled among the rubble. The windows were all glazed.

Arable gardens encircled every tower, trellises and stakes supporting the grasping yellow confusion of native Tyrathcan vegetation. Fruit trees lined the paved roads, huge leaves providing ample shade.

Smaller rounded silos and workshops were spaced between the towers, each with a single semicircular door. Carts and even small power trucks were parked outside.

"I don't know who is jumpier, us or them," Kelly subvocalized into her neural nanonics memory cell. "The Tyrathcan soldiers are clearly immensely capable, to say nothing of the hunter caste. Yet the possessed have hurt them badly. The vassal-caste bodies you can see half buried in the rubble of the outer towers have been left untended in the haste to fortify Coastuc-RT. A large breach of the Tyrathcan internment ritual, they obviously consider the threat humans present to be of more pressing importance.

"But now we are inside the village I can see very little activity apart from those vassals working on the rampart. The roads are empty. No breeder has appeared. The soldiers seem certain of their destination, leading us deeper into the village. I can now hear a great many Tyrathca away towards the park at the centre of Coastuc-RT. Yes, listen, a whistle that rises and falls in a slow regular beat. There must be hundreds of them doing it in unison to achieve that effect."

The soldiers led them out onto one of the village's radial roads, cutting straight down past the tower houses into the central park. Right in the middle was a vast impossible dull-silver edifice. At first glimpse it looked like a hundred-metre-wide disc suspended fifty metres in the air by a central conical pillar whose tip only just touched the ground; another, identical, cone rose from the top of the disc. It was perfectly symmetrical, shining a lurid red-gold under the sinking sun. Six elaborate flying buttresses arched down from the rim of the disc, preventing the top-heavy structure from falling over.

The three humans stared in silence at the imposing artefact. Big builder-caste Tyrathca walked ponderously along the buttresses and over the surface of the disc. The pinnacle of the upper cone wasn't quite finished, showing a geodesic grid of timber struts which a rank of builder caste clung to as they slowly covered it with their organic cement. Another team were following them up, spraying the drying cement with a gelatin mucus that shimmered with oil-slick marquetry until it hardened into the distinctive silverish hue.

Kelly took the structure in with one swift professional sweep, then focused on the park. It had been reduced to a shallow clay quarry in the haste to extract soil for the disc and its buttresses. This was where the Tyrathca breeders had gathered; several thousand of them, circling round the outside of the disc. They sat on their hindquarters in the mud, short antennae standing proud, whistling in a long slow undulation. It sounded poignant, imploring even. Entities that had been needlessly hurt questioning the reason, the same the galaxy over.

Kelly's didactic memory didn't have any reference to a Tyrathcan religion. A more comprehensive search program running through her neural nanonics said the Tyrathca didn't have a religion, and there was no explanation for the disc, either.

"If I didn't know better, I'd say they were at prayer," Reza datavised.

"Could be the local version of the town meeting," Ariadne suggested. "Trying to decide what to do about us wild humans."

"They're not talking about anything," Kelly said. "It's more like a song."

"The Tyrathca don't sing," Reza replied.

"What's that disc for? There's no way in at the bottom of the cone pillar, not from this side, but it's definitely hollow. Nothing solid like that would be able to stand up, it's almost like a mock-up. I can't find any record of them ever building anything like it before. And why build it now for Christ's sake, when they need all the builder caste to construct defences? Something that size has taken a hell of a lot of effort to put up."

He put his hand on her shoulder. "Looks as if you'll be able to ask in a minute."

The soldiers halted when they came level with the innermost ring of house towers. All of the buildings had been sealed up, black lids capping the windows, cement slabs erected over the door arches. Colourful flowering plants swamped their gardens.

A lone breeder was walking towards them from the park. Male or female, Kelly couldn't tell, not even comparing it to the images stored in a memory cell—females were supposed to be slightly larger. It was bigger than the soldiers by about half a metre, the scale hide several shades lighter, dorsal mane neatly trimmed. Apart from its stumpy black antennae, the one physiological aspect which most distinguished it from the vassal castes was a row of small chemical program teats dangling flaccidly from its throat like empty leather pouches, although the long supple fingers intimated it was a sophisticated tool user.

She saw an almost subliminal hazy film twinkling

briefly on the road behind it. Superfine bronze powder, similar to the dusting on a terrestrial moth, was sprinkling down from its flanks.

The Tyrathca breeder stopped beside the soldier carrying the processor block. Its outer mouth hinged back, allowing it to whistle a long tune.

Flute music, Kelly thought.

"I am Waboto-YAU," the processor block voice translated. "I will mediate with you on behalf of Coastuc-RT."

"I'm Reza Malin, combat scout team leader, under contract to the LDC."

"Are you able to assist in our defence?"

"You'll have to tell me what happened, first, give us some idea of what we're up against."

"Starship *Santa Clara* arrived yesterday. Spaceplane landed, bringing new Tyrathca, new equipment. Much needed. Collect rygar crop. Amok *elemental* humans attacked; stole spaceplane. No provocation. No reason. Twenty-three breeder-caste killed. One hundred and ninety vassal castes killed. Extensive damage. You can see this."

Reza wondered how he would react if it was xenocs who had attacked a human village in a similar fashion. Allow a group of those same xenocs in afterwards to talk? Oh no, no way. The human response would be far more basic.

He felt mortally humbled as the breeder's glassy hazel eyes stared at him. "How many humans took part in this attack?" he asked.

"Numbers not known with accuracy."

"Roughly, how many?"

"No more than forty."

"Forty people did all this?" Ariadne muttered.

Reza waved her quiet. "Did they use a kind of white fire?"

"White fire. Yes. Not true fire. *Elemental* fire. Tyrathca have not been told of human *elemental* ability before. Many times witnessed delusion of form on attacking humans. *Elemental* changes of colour and shape confused soldier caste. Some amok humans stole Tyrathca hunter-caste form. Much damage before repelled."

"On behalf of the LDC I apologize profoundly."

"What use apology? Why not told of human *elemental* ability? Breeder ambassador family assigned to Confederation Assembly will be informed. Denouncement of humans in Assembly. Tyrathca would never have joined Confederation if had known."

"I'm sorry. But these humans have been taken over by an invading force. We don't normally possess this ability. It's as foreign to us as it is to you."

"Lalonde Development Company must remove all *elemental* humans from planet. Tyrathca will not inhabit same planet."

"We'd love to. But right now it's all we can do just to stay alive. These *elemental* humans now control the entire Juliffe basin. We need somewhere to stay until a starship can lift us off and we can inform the Confederation what is happening."

"Starships battle in orbit this day. Double sun in sky. No starships left."

"One is coming back for us."

"When?"

"In a few days."

"Does starship have the power to kill *elemental* cloud? Tyrathca scared of cloud over rivers. We cannot defeat it."

"No," Reza said forlornly. "The starship can't kill the cloud." Especially if Shaun Wallace is telling the truth. The thought was one he had been firmly suppressing. The implications were too frightening. Just how would we actually go about fighting them?

The Tyrathca let out a clamorous hoot, almost a wail. "Cloud will come here. Cloud will devour us; breeders, children, vassals. All."

"You could leave," Kelly said. "Keep ahead of the cloud."

"Nowhere is ahead of the cloud for long."

"What are you doing here?" she asked, raising her arm

to point at the park, the congregation of breeders. "What is that structure you have built?

"We are not strong. We have no *elemental*s among us. Only one can now save us from *elemental* humans. We call to our Sleeping God. We show our belief by our homage. We call and call, but the Sleeping God does not yet awake."

"I didn't know you had a God."

"The family of Sireth-AFL is a custodian of the memory from the days of voyage on flightship Tanjuntic-RI. He shared the memory with us all after attack by *elemental* humans. Now we are united in prayer. The Sleeping God is our hope for salvation from *elemental* humans. We build its idol to show our faith."

"This is it?" she asked. "This is what the Sleeping God looks like?"

"Yes. This is the memory of shape. This is our Sleeping God."

"You mean the Tyrathca on the Tanjuntic-RI actually saw a God?"

"No. Another flightship passed the Sleeping God. Not Tanjuntic-RI."

"The Sleeping God was in space, then?"

"Why you want to know?"

"I want to know if the Sleeping God can save us from the *elemental*s," she said smoothly. "Or will it only help Tyrathca?" Christ, this was beautiful, the story to end all stories; human dead and secrets the Tyrathca had kept since before Earth's ice age. How long had their arkships been in flight? Thousands of years at least.

"It will help us because we ask," Waboto-YAU said.

"Do your legends specifically say it will return to save you?"

"Not legend!" the breeder hooted angrily. "Truth. Humans have legends. Humans lie. Humans become *elemental*. The Sleeping God is stronger than your race. Stronger than all living things."

"Why do you call it " 'Sleeping'?"

"Tyrathca say what is. Humans lie."

"So it was Sleeping when your flightship found it?"

"Yes."

"Then how do you know it is strong enough to ward off the *elementals*?"

"Kelly!" Reza said with edgy vexation.

Waboto-YAU hooted again. The soldiers shifted restlessly in response, eyes boring into the obsessed reporter.

"Sleeping God strong. Humans will learn. Humans must not become *elemental*. Sleeping God will awaken. Sleeping God will avenge all Tyrathca suffering."

"Kelly, shut up, now. That's an order," Reza datavised when he saw her gathering herself for more questions. "Thank you for telling us of the Sleeping God," he said to Waboto-YAU.

Kelly fumed in moody silence.

"Sleeping God dreams of the universe," the breeder said. "All that happens is known to it. It will hear our call. It will answer. It will come."

"The human *elementals* may attack you again," Reza warned. "Before the Sleeping God arrives."

"We know. We pray hard." Waboto-YAU twittered mournfully, head swinging round to gaze at the disk. "Now you have heard the fate of Coastuc-RT. Are you able to assist soldier caste in defence?"

"No." Reza heard Kelly's hissed intake of breath. "Our weapons are not as powerful as those of your soldiers. We cannot assist in your defence."

"Then go."

Vast tracts of electric, electromagnetic, and magnetic energy seethed and sparked across a roughly circular section in the outermost band of Murora's rings, eight thousand kilometres in diameter. Dust, held so long in equilibrium, exploited its liberation to squall in microburst vortices around the solid imperturbable boulders and jagged icebergs which made up the bulk of the ring, their gyrations mirroring the rowdy cloudscape a hundred and seventy thousand kilometres below. The epicentre, where the *Lady Macbeth* had plunged into the drive-fomented particles, was still glowing a nervous blue as brumal waves of static washed through the thinning molecular zephyr of vaporized rock and ice.

The total energy input from the starship's fusion drives and the multiple combat-wasp explosions was taking a long time to disperse. Their full effect would take months if not years to sink back to normality. Thermally and electromagnetically, the rippling circle was the equivalent of an Arctic whiteout to any probing sensors.

It meant the *Maranta* and the *Gramine* knew little of what was going on below the surface. They kept station ten kilometres above the fuzzy boundary where boulders and ice gave way first to pebbles and then finally dust; all sensor clusters extended, focused on the disquieted strata of particles under their hulls. For the first couple of kilometres the image was sharp and reasonably clear, below that it slowly disintegrated until at seven kilometres there was nothing but a sheet of electronic slush.

The possessed who commanded the starships now had started their search right at the heart, the exact coordinate where *Lady Macbeth* had entered. Then *Maranta* had manoeuvred into an orbit five kilometres lower, while the *Gramine* had raised its altitude by a similar amount. They slowly drifted apart, *Maranta* edging ahead of the phosphorescent blue splash, *Gramine* falling behind.

There had been no sign of their prey. Nor any proof to confirm the *Lady Macbeth* had survived her impact with the rings. No wreckage had been detected. Although it was a slim chance any ever would. If she had detonated when she hit, the blowout of her drive tubes' escaping plasma would probably have vaporized most of her. And any fragments which did survive would have been flung over a huge area. The ring was eighty kilometres thick, enough volume to lose an entire squadron in.

They were further hindered by the way their energistically charged bodies interfered with on-board systems. Sensors already labouring at the limit of their resolution to try and unscramble the chaos suffered infuriating glitches and power surges, producing gaps in the overall coverage.

But the crews persevered. Debris was virtually impossible to locate, but an operating starship emitted heat, and electromagnetic impulses, and a strong magnetic flux. If she was there, they would find her eventually.

The soldier-caste vassals stayed with them until the hovercraft reached the top of the Coastuc-RT's valley. More tumid rain-clouds were approaching fast from the east, borne by the obdurate breeze. Reza judged they should just about reach the other hovercraft by the time they arrived. Both land and sky ahead were grey. Northwards, the red cloud cast a dispiriting corona, looking for all the world as though magma was floating, light as thistledown, through the air.

"But *why*?" Kelly demanded as soon as the soldiers were left behind. "You saw how well armed they were, we would have been safe there."

"Firstly, Coastuc-RT is too close to the Juliffe basin. As your friend Shaun Wallace said, the cloud is spreading. It would reach the valley long before Joshua gets back. Secondly, that valley is tactical suicide. Anyone who gets onto the high ground above the village can simply bombard it into submission, or more likely destruction. There aren't enough soldier and hunter vassals to keep the slopes clear. Right now Coastuc-RT is wide open to anything the possessed care to throw at it. And all the Tyrathca are doing to defend themselves is building giant effigies of spacegods and having a pray-in. We don't need that kind of shit. By ourselves we stand a much better chance; we're mobile and well armed. So tomorrow at first light we start doing exactly what Joshua said: we run for it, through the mountains."

Violent rain made a mockery of the hovercraft's blazing monochrome headlight beams, chopping them off after five or six metres. It obscured the moons, the red cloud, it damn near hid the drooping, defeated grass below the gunwale.

The pilots navigated by guidance blocks alone. It took them forty minutes to retrace their route back to the first tower house above the river.

Sewell plugged a half-metre fission blade into his left elbow socket and confronted the blocked-up doorway. Water steamed and crackled as the blade came on. He placed the tip delicately against the wind-fretted cement, and pushed. The blade sank in, sending out a thick runnel of ginger sand which the rain smeared into the reeds at his feet. Relieved at how easy it was to cut, he started to slice down.

Kelly was fourth in. She stood in musty darkness shaking her arms and easing her cagoule hood back. "God, there's as much water inside this cagoule as out. I've never known rain like this."

" 'Tis a bleak night, this one," Shaun Wallace said behind her.

Reza stepped through the oval Sewell had cut, carrying two bulky equipment packs, TIP carbines slung over his shoulder. "Pat, Sal, check this place out." Fenton and Ryall hurried in after their master, and immediately shook their coats, sending out a fountain of droplets.

"Great," Kelly muttered. The blocks clipped to her broad belt were slippery with water. She wiped them ineffectually on her T-shirt. "Can I come with you, please?"

"Sure," Pat said.

She turned the seal catch on her bag, and searched round until she found a light stick. Shadows fled away. Collins disapproved of infrared visuals unless absolutely unavoidable.

They were in a hall that ran the diameter of the tower. Archways led off into various rooms. A ramp at the far wall started to spiral upwards. Tyrathca didn't, or couldn't, use stairs, according to her didactic memory.

Pat and Sal Yong started down the hall, Kelly followed. She realized Shaun Wallace was a pace behind. He was back in his LDC jump suit. Completely dry, she noticed enviously. Her armour-suit trousers squelched as she walked.

"You don't mind if I tag along, do you, Miss Kelly? I've never seen one of these places before."

"No."

"That Mr. Malin there, he's a right one for doing things by the book. This place has been sealed up for years. What does he expect us to find?"

"We won't know till we look, will we?" she said coyly.

"Why, Miss Kelly, I do believe you're running me a ragged circle."

The house was intriguing: strange furniture, and startlingly human utensils. But there was little technology, the builders had obviously been given instructions on how to utilize wood. They were excellent carpenters.

Rain drummed on the walls, adding to the sense of isolation and displacement as they mounted the ramp. Vassal castes had their own rooms; Kelly wasn't sure if they could be called stables. Some rooms, for the soldiers, she guessed, had furniture. There was only a thin layer of dust. It was as though the tower had been set aside rather than abandoned. Given her current circumstances, it wasn't the most reassuring of thoughts. The neural nanonics drank it all in.

They found the first bodies on the second floor. Three housekeeper castes (the same size as a farmer), five hunters, and four soldiers. Desiccation had turned them into creased leather mummies. She wanted to touch one, but was afraid it would crumble to dust.

"They're just sitting there, look," Shaun Wallace said in a tamed voice. "There's no food anywhere near them. They must have been waiting to die."

"Without the breeders, they are nothing," Pat said.

"Even so, 'tis a terrible thing. Like those old Pharaohs who had all their servants in their tombs with them."

"Were there any Tyrathcan souls in the beyond?" Kelly asked.

Shaun Wallace paused at the bottom of the ramp to the

third floor, his brow crinkling. "Now there's a thing. I don't think there were. Or at least, I never came across one."

"Different afterworld, perhaps," Kelly said.

"If they have one. They seem heathen creatures to me. Perhaps the Good Lord didn't see fit to give them souls."

"But they have a god. Their own god."

"Do they now?"

"Well, they're hardly likely to have Jesus or Allah, are they? Not human messiahs."

"Ah, you're a smart one, Miss Kelly. I take my hat off to you. I'd never have thought of that in a million years."

"It's a question of environment and upbringing. I'm used to thinking in these terms. I'd be lost in your century."

"Oh, I can't see that. Not at all."

There were more vassal-caste bodies on the third floor. The two breeders were together on the fourth.

"Do they have love, these beasties?" Shaun Wallace asked, looking down at them. "They look like they do, to me. Dying together is romantic, I think. Like Romeo and Juliet."

Kelly ran her tongue round her cheeks. "You didn't strike me as the Shakespeare type."

"Now don't you go writing me off so quickly, you with your classy education. I'm a man of hidden depths, I am, Miss Kelly."

"Did you ever meet anyone famous in the beyond?" Pat asked.

"Meeting!" He wrung his hands together with fulsome drama. "You're talking about the beyond as if it's some kind of social gathering. Lords and ladies spending the evening together over fine wine and a game of bridge. It's not like that, Mr. Halahan, not at all."

"But did you?" the mercenary scout persisted. "You were there for centuries. There must have been someone important."

"Ah now, there was that, as I recall. A gentleman by the name of Custer."

Pat's neural nanonics ran a fast check. "An American army general? He lost a fight with the Sioux Indians in the nineteenth century."

"Aye, that's the one. Don't be telling me you've heard of him in this day and age?"

"He's in our history courses. How did he feel about it? Losing like that?"

Shaun Wallace's expression cooled. "He didn't feel anything about it, Mr. Halahan. He was like all of us, crying without tears to shed. You're equating death with sanity, Mr. Halahan. Which is a stupid thing to do, if you don't mind me saying. You've heard of Hitler now? Surely, if you've heard of poor damned George Armstrong Custer?"

"We remember Hitler. Though he was after your time, I think."

"Indeed he was. But do you think he changed after he died, Mr. Halahan? Do you think he lost his conviction, or his righteousness? Do you think death causes you to look back on life and makes you realize what an ass you've been? Oh no, not that, Mr. Halahan. You're too busy screaming, you're too busy cursing, you're too busy coveting your neighbour's memory for the bitter dregs of taste and colour it gives you. Death does not bestow wisdom, Mr. Halahan. It does not make you humble before the Lord. More's the pity."

"Hitler," Kelly said, entranced. "Stalin, Genghis Khan, Jack the Ripper, Helmen Nyke. The butchers and the warlords. Are they all there? Waiting in the beyond?"

Shaun Wallace gazed up at the domed ceiling partially lost amid a tapestry of shadows thrown by sparse alien architecture; for a moment his features portraying every year of his true age. "Aye, they're all there, Miss Kelly, every one of the monsters the good earth ever spawned. All of them aching to come back, waiting for their moment to be granted. Us possessed, we might be wanting to hide from the open sky, and death; but it's not paradise we're going to be making down here on this planet. It couldn't be, there'll be humans in it, you see."

It wasn't true daybreak, not yet. The sun was still half an hour from bringing any hint of grizzled light to the eastern horizon. But the rain-clouds had blown over, and night had sapped the wind's brawn. The northern sky glowed with a grievous fervour, blemishing the savannah grass a murky crimson.

Octan watched the dark speck moving along the side of the river, heading upstream towards the Tyrathcan tower house. Heavy moist air stroked the eagle's feathers as he dipped a wing, curving down in a giddy voluted dive. Pat Halahan gazed out at the lonely nocturnal wanderer through his affinity bonded friend's narrow peerless eyes.

Kelly came awake at the touch of a hand on her shoulder, and the sound of feet rapping on the hard dry floor of the second storey, where the team had rested up for the night. Neural nanonics accelerated her fatigue-soaked brain into full alertness.

The last of the combat-boosted mercenaries were disappearing down the ramp.

"Someone coming," Shaun Wallace said.

"Your people?"

"No. I'd know if it was. Not that Mr. Malin asked, mind you." He sounded cheerful.

"Good heavens, anyone would think he doesn't trust you." She shoved back the foil envelope she'd been sleeping in. Shaun Wallace offered his hand to help her to her feet. They made their way down the ramp to the ground-floor hall.

The seven mercenaries were clustered round the hole in the door, red light shining dully off their artificial skin. Fenton and Ryall were on their feet, growling softly as they were caught in the backwash of agitation coming from their master's mind.

Reza and Sewell slipped through the hole as Kelly reached them.

"What is it?" she asked.

"Horse coming," Pat told her. "Two riders."

Kelly peered round him just as Reza and Sewell activated their chameleon circuits and flicked into the landscape. For a few seconds she tracked them thanks to the circular medical nanonic package on the big combat-adept's leg, but even that was soon lost amongst the unsavoury coloured grass.

It was one of the plough horses favoured by the colonists. A young one, but clearly on its last legs; the neck was drooping as it plodded gamely along, mouth flecked with foam. Reza worked his way unobtrusively down the slope from the tower house towards the animal, leaving Sewell to cover him. His optical sensors showed him the two people on its back; both wore stained poncho capes cut from a canvas tarpaulin. The man was showing the first signs of age, stubble shading heavy jowls, temples touched with grey; and he'd recently lost a lot of weight by the look of him. But he had a vigour animating his frame which was visible even from Reza's position across the swaying grass. The young boy behind him had been crying at some time, he had also been soaked during the ride, and now he was shivering, clinging to the man in a wearied daze.

They didn't pose any threat, Reza decided. He waited until the horse was twenty metres away, then switched off his chameleon circuit. The horse took a few more paces before the man noticed him with a start. He reined in the lethargic animal and leaned over its neck to peer at Reza in bewilderment.

"What manner of . . . You're not a possessed, you don't have their emptiness." His fingers clicked. "Of course! Combat boosted, that's what you are. You came down from the starships yesterday." He smiled and whooped, then swung a leg over the horse and slithered to the ground. "Come on, Russ, down you come, boy. They're here, the navy marines are here. I said they'd come, didn't I? I told you, never give up faith." The boy virtually fell off the horse into his arms.

Reza went over to help. The man was none too steady on his feet, either, and one of his hands was heavily bandaged.

"Bless you, my son." Horst Elwes embraced the surprised mercenary with tears of gratitude and supreme relief shining in his eyes. "God bless you. These weeks have been the sorest trial my Lord has ever devised for this weak mortal servant. But now you are here after all this time spent alone in the Devil's own wilderness. Now we are saved."

11

Boston had fallen to the possessed, not that the rapidly disintegrating convocation of Norfolk's martial authorities would admit it.

Edmund Rigby looked out of the hotel window, across the provincial city's steep slate rooftops. Fires were still burning in the outlying districts where the militia troops had tried to force their way in. The Devonshire market square had been struck by a navy starship's maser last Duchess-night. Its granite cobbles had transmuted to a glowing lava pool in less than a second. Even now, with its surface congealing and dimming, the heat was enough to barbecue food. Nobody had been in the square at the time; it was intended as a demonstration only. A show of naval might: you there, ant folk crawling on the filthy ground far below, we angels above have the very power of life and death over all of you. As one, the possessed had laughed at the circling starships, rendered impotent by their lack of targets. Yes, they had the physical power to destroy, but the fingers on the trigger were snared in the perpetual dilemma of the great and the good. Hostages had always struck a paralysing blow into the heart of governments. The starships wanted to pour sterilizing fire down from the sky, the officers yearning to burn the loathsome low-life crop of anarchists and revolutionaries from the pastoral idyll planet, but the city hadn't been cleaned of decent people, the women and children and frail, kindly grandparents. As far as the planetary authorities and navy officers knew this was just an uprising, a political revolt, they believed the meek were still mingled with the wolves. The lofty orbiting angels had been castrated.

Even if they suspected, believed the rumours of atrocities and massacres flittering from mouth to mouth through the nearby countryside, they could do nothing. Boston was no longer alone in its dissent, it was simply the first. Edmund Rigby had planted the germs of insurgency in every city across the planet's islands, cabals of possessed who were already annexing the populace. A captain in the Australian Marines, he had died from a landmine explosion in Vietnam in 1971; but he had studied military tactics, had even been sent to the Royal Naval College in Dartmouth for officer training. And this vast space empire of Confederated planets, for all its awesome technology, was no different to the Earth upon which he had once walked. Vietcong insurgency tactics from the past were just as applicable now, and he knew them by heart. Securing the entire planet had been his principal objective since the vast merchant fleet had left Norfolk after midsummer.

Since he arrived he had been busy indeed. Toiling in the squalor and the horror and the blood which soiled the heart of every human soul. Those living, and those dead . . . and the ones trapped between.

He closed his eyes as if to shut out the memories of recent weeks and what he had become. But there was no respite. The hotel took on substance in his mind, walls and floors woven from shadows. People, us and them, glided through it, dopplered laughs and screams ricocheting through the grand corridors and sumptuous rooms. And, always, there, on the other side of the shadows, on the other side of everything: the beyond. Chittering souls clamouring for existence, silky insidious promises to be his lover, his slave, his acolyte. Anything, anything at all to be brought back.

Edmund Rigby shuddered in revulsion. Please, God, when we hide Norfolk from this universe let it also be hidden from the beyond. Let me have peace, and an end to all this.

Three of his lieutenants—selected from the more stable among the newly possessed—were dragging a captive along the corridor outside to his room. He stiffened his shoulders, letting the power swell within, giving his new body grandeur and poise, as well as a Napoleonic uniform, and turned to face the door.

They burst in, cheering and jeering, young turks from the worst of the backstreets, believing swagger and noise was an easy substitute for authority. But he grinned welcomingly at them anyway.

Grant Kavanagh was flung on the floor, bleeding from cuts on his face and hands, smeared in dirt, his fine militia uniform torn. Even so, he refused to be cowed. Edmund Rigby respected that, amongst the sadness. This one, with his conviction in God and self, would be hard to break. The thought pained him. Why oh why can't they just give in?

"Present for you, Edmund," Iqabl Geertz said. He had assumed his ghoul appearance, skin almost grey, cheeks sunken, eyeballs a uniform scarlet; thin frame dressed all in black. "One of the nobs. Got some fight in him. Thought he might be important."

Don Padwick, in his lion-man state, growled suggestively. Grant Kavanagh twitched as the big yellow beast dropped onto all fours and padded over to him, tail whisking about.

"We captured his troops," Chen Tambiah informed Edmund quietly. "They were about the last militia roaming free. Inflicted heavy casualties. Eight of us winged back to the beyond." The dapper oriental, in ancient black and orange silks, cocked his head grudgingly towards Grant Kavanagh. "He's a good leader."

"Is that so?" Edmund Rigby asked.

Iqabl Geertz licked his lips with a long yellowed tongue. "It doesn't make any difference in the end. He's ours now. To do with as we like. And we know what we like."

Grant Kavanagh looked up at him, one eye swollen shut. "When this is over, you mincing shit, and the rest of your friends have been shot, I will take a great deal of pleasure in ripping every one of your deviant chromosomes from your body with my own hands."

"Now there's a man's man if ever I saw one," Iqabl Geertz said, putting on an histrionically effeminate tone.

"Enough," Edmund Rigby said. "You put up a good fight," he told Grant, "now it's over."

"Like hell! If you think I'm going to let you Fascist scum take over the planet my ancestors sweated blood to build you don't know me."

"Nor shall we ever," Edmund Rigby said. "Not now."

"That's right, takes bloody four of you." Grant Kavanagh grunted in shock as Don Padwick put a paw on his ribs, talons extended.

Edmund Rigby rested his hand on Grant's head. There was so much resilience and anger in the man. It enervated him, sending the pretentious uniform shimmering back into his ordinary marine fatigues. The souls of the beyond were clamouring as he began to gather his power, flocking to the beacon of his strength.

"Don't fight me," he said, more in hope than in expectation.

Grant snarled. "Screw you!"

Edmund Rigby heard the vile rapturous imploring chorus of the souls beginning. Weariness engulfed him, there had been so much of this since he had returned. So much pain and torment, so wilfully inflicted. At first he had laughed, and enjoyed the fear. Now, he simply wished it over.

He hesitated, and the captive soul stirred in the prison he had forged for it within his own mind.

"There are ways," the other soul said, and showed, obedient as always to his captor. "Ways to make Grant Kavanagh submit quickly, ways no flesh can withstand for long."

And the desire was there, oozing up out of the prison, corrupt and nauseous.

"But it's a part of all of us," the other soul whispered quickly. "We all share the shame of having the serpent beast in our secret heart of hearts. How else could you have accomplished what you have the way you have if you did not let it free?"

Trembling, Edmund Rigby let the desire rise, let it supersede the loathing and revulsion that was his own. Then it was easy. Easy to make Grant hurt. Easy to commit the profanities which quietened his lieutenants. Easy to feed the desire. And go on feeding.

It was good, because it was freedom. Complete and utter freedom. Desire ruled as it should, unrestrained. It nurtured the psyche, these heinous abominations Grant Kavanagh was forced to endure. They were sublime.

Iqabl Geertz and Chen Tambiah were yelling at him to stop. But they were nothing, less than dirt.

The souls were in retreat, fearing what was leaking from him into the beyond.

"Weak, they are all weaker than us. Together we surpass them all."

Was that his own voice?

And still the savagery went on. It was impossible to stop. The other soul had gone too far, it had to be seen through now. To the terrible end.

Edmund Rigby rebelled in horror.

"But you did it yourself," said the captive soul.

"No. It was you."

"I only showed you how. You wanted it. The desire was yours, the yearning."

"Never! Not for this."

"Yes. You gave way to yourself for the first time. The serpent beast is in all of us. Embrace it and be at peace with yourself. Know yourself."

"I am not that. I am not!"

"But you are. Look. Look!"

"No." Edmund Rigby shrank from what he had done. Fleeing, hurtling, away, as though speed alone was proof of his innocence. Locking out the world and what he had been a party to, down in that empty vault waiting at the centre of his mind. Where it was quiet, and dark, and taste-less. Sanctuary without form. It hardened around him.

"And there you will stay; a part of me for ever."

Quinn Dexter opened his eyes. Before him the three pos-sessed, their exotic appearances bleached off to reveal young men with ashen faces, backed away in consterna-tion; their confidence in their supremacy jarringly frac-tured. Grant Kavanagh's decimated body quivered amid the blood and piss curdling on the carpet as the soul it now hosted tried valiantly to repair the colossal tissue damage. Deep inside himself he heard Edmund Rigby's soul whim-pering quietly.

Quinn smiled beatifically at his rapt audience. "I have returned," he said softly, and raised his hands in invoca-tion. "Out of the half-night; *strengthened* by the darkness as only a true believer could be. I saw the weakness in my possessor, his fright of his serpent beast. He is in me now, weeping and pleading as he denies form to his true nature. As it should be. God's Brother showed me the way, showed me the night holds no dread for those who love their real selves as He commands us to do. But so few obey. Do you obey?"

They tried then, Iqabl Geertz, Don Padwick, and Chen Tambiah, combining their energistic strength in a desper-ate attempt to blast the deranged usurper out of his body and into the beyond. Quinn laughed uproariously, steadfast at the calm centre of a fantastic lightning storm which filled the room. Dazzling whips of raw electricity slashed at the walls and floor and ceiling like the razor claws of a maddened gryphon. None of them could touch him, he was held inviolate in a cocoon of luminous violet silk mist.

The lightning stopped roaring, ebbing in spits and crack-les to disappear behind charred furniture and back into the bodies of the would-be thunder gods. Smoke hazed the blackened room, small flames licking greedily at the cush-ions and tattered curtains.

Quinn wished for justice.

Their bodies fell, cells performing the refined perversions he dreamed of, turning against themselves. He watched impassively as the terrorized, humiliated souls fled from the glistening deformities he had created, back to the beyond crying in dire warning. Then the second souls, the ones held captive, abandoned the macerated flesh.

Grant Kavanagh's body groaned at Quinn's feet, the possessing soul looking up at him in numb trepidation. The worst of the lacerations and fractures had healed, leaving a crisscross scar pattern of delicate pink skin.

"What is your name?" Quinn asked.

"Luca Comar."

"Did you see what I performed on them, Luca?"

"Yes. Oh God, yes." He bowed his head, bile rising in his throat.

"They were weak, you see. Unworthy fuck-ups. They had no real faith in themselves. Not like me." Quinn took a deep breath, calming his euphoric thoughts. His marine fatigues billowed out into a flowing priest's robe, fabric turning midnight black. "Do you have faith in yourself, Luca?"

"Yes. I do. I have faith. Really I do."

"Would you like me to tell you of the serpent beast? Would you like me to show you your own heart and set you free?"

"Yes. Please. Please show me."

"Good. I think that is my role now the portents walk abroad. Now the dead are risen to fight the last battle against the living and the time of the Light Bringer draws near. I have been blessed, Luca, truly blessed with His strength. My belief in Him brought me back, me alone out of all the millions who are possessed. I am the one God's Brother has chosen as His messiah."

When the tributary river finally spilled into the Juliffe it was a hundred and thirty metres wide. Villages had claimed both banks, buildings gleaming inside their safe enclave bubbles of white light. By now Chas Paske was used to the striking fantasy images of halcyon hamlets dozing their life away.

He had passed eight or nine of them during his slow progress down the river. All of them the same. All of them unreal.

Warned by the twin coronae ahead he had sculled his little boat back into the middle of the river, fighting the thick gunge of melding snowlilies every centimetre of the way. Now he was in a narrow channel of vermilion light which fell between the two pools of native radiance, crouched down as best he could manage.

His body was in a poor way. The nanonic medical packages had been exhausted by the demand of decontaminating his blood some time ago; now it was all they could do to stop the blood vessels they had knitted with from haemorrhaging again. His neural nanonics still maintained their analgesic blocks, delivering him from pain. But that didn't seem to be enough any more. A cold lethargy was creeping into him through his damaged leg, syphoning his remaining strength away. Any movement was a complicated business now, and muscles responded with geriatric infirmity. Several times in the last few hours he had been stricken by spasms which vibrated his arms and torso. His neural nanonics seemed incapable of preventing or halting them. So he lay on the bottom of the boat gazing up at the throbbing red cloud waiting for the ignominious spastic twitches to run their course.

At these times he thought he could see himself, a tiny shrivelled black figure, spreadeagled on the bottom of a rowing dinghy (like the one he thought he had been stealing), being borne along a sticky white river that stretched out to a terrible length. There was nothing around the river, no banks or trees, it just wound through a red sky all by itself, a silk ribbon waving in the breeze, while far, far ahead a speck of starlight twinkled with elusive, enticing coyness. Skittering voices on the brink of audibility circled round him. He was sure they talked about him even though he could never quite make out whole words. The tone was there all right, dismissive and scornful.

Not quite a dream.

He remembered, as he sailed on gently, his past missions, past colleagues, old battles, victories and routs. Half the time never knowing who he was really fighting for or what he was fighting against. For the right side or the wrong side? And how was he supposed to know which was which anyway? Him, a mercenary, a whore of violence and destruction and death. He fought for the ones with the most money, for companies and plutocrats, and sometimes maybe even governments. There was no right and wrong in his life. In that respect he had it easy, none of the big decisions.

So the river carried him on, that white band flowing through the red sky, ever onwards. The voyage was his life. He could see where he had come from, and he could see where he was going. Destination and departure were no different. And there was no way to get off. Except to jump, to drown in the vast guileful sky.

That will come anyway, he thought, no need to hurry.

The old resolve was still there, among the superficial self-pity and growing concern over his physical state, still holding together. He was glad of that. Right to the bitter end, that's where he was heading. The star glinted strongly, virtually a heliograph. It seemed nearer.

No, not quite a dream.

Chas jerked up with a start, rocking the boat hazardously. The twin villages guarding the tributary mouth were behind him now. He was out on the Juliffe itself. There was no sign of the Hultain Marsh which made up the northern side. The river could have been an ocean for all he could tell. An ocean paved with snowlilies as far as his enhanced eyes could see. This was their meridian, the end of their continental crusade. They were packed four or five deep, crumpled up against each other; decaying now, but wadded so tight they formed a serried quilt. It was a perfect reflector for the carmine light falling from the cloud, turning his world to a dimensionless red nebula.

The flimsy boat creaked and shivered as the current forced it deeper into the floating pulp. Chas gripped the gunwale in reflex. He had a nasty moment when something popped and splintered up at the prow, but the hull was so shallow it was squeezed up rather than in. He was sure it was riding on a patina of rotting leaves rather than actual water.

For all their stupendous mass, the snowlilies had no effect on the river's unflagging current. The boat began to pick up speed, moving further out from the southern bank with its near-continual chain of villages and towns.

Now he was sure he wasn't going to capsize, Chas relaxed his grip, and eased himself down again, breathing hard at the simple exertion of lifting himself. Up ahead the massive ceiling of red cloud became a bright tangerine cyclone with a concave heart, its apex hidden by distance. He could see the gravid billows of stratus being torn out of their constricted alignment, sucked over the lip to spiral upwards in a leisurely procession. It must have been twenty kilometres across at the base: an inverted whirlpool which drained away into the other side of the sky.

He realized its sharp living tangerine hue came from a fierce light shining down out of its secret pinnacle. Below it, the city of Durringham gleamed in empyrean glory.

Gaura floated through the floor hatch into the *Lady Macbeth*'s bridge. He took care not to move his neck suddenly, or his arms come to that; his whole body was one giant ache. He had been lucky not to break anything in that last agonizing burst of deceleration. Even watching the starships attacking the station he hadn't felt as utterly helpless as he had then, lying flat on the groaning decking of the lounge feeling his ribs bowing in, while blackness tightened its grip on his vision. Three times he had heard bone splintering, accompanied by a mental howl—it was impossible to make any sound. Together the Edenists had toughed it out, their minds embraced, sharing and mitigating the pain.

When it was over he hadn't been alone in wiping tears from his eyes. Aethra had followed their entire heart-stopping plummet into the ring, showing it to them. He had thought the end had surely come, for the second time in an hour. But the Adamist starship's exhaust had obliterated the ring particles as it crashed below the surface, eliminating any danger of collision; and the captain had matched velocities perfectly (for the second time in an hour), slotting them neatly into a circular orbit buried right in the middle of the ring. The swarm of pursuing combat wasps and their submunitions had impacted seconds behind them, kinetic explosions tossing out a ragged sheet of fire. None had penetrated more than a hundred metres below the surface.

It had been an astounding piece of flying. Gaura was very curious to meet the person who had such sublime control over a starship. It rivalled the union between a voidhawk and its captain.

There were three people standing on a stikpad around one of the consoles, two men and a woman, talking in low tones. It didn't help Gaura's composure to see that it was the youngest, a man with a flat-featured face, who had the captain's star on his ship-suit shoulder. He had been expecting someone . . . different.

Don't prejudge, Tiya admonished sternly. Most of the Edenists were using his senses to observe the scene. **Voidhawk captains are only eighteen when they start flying.**

I wasn't going to say a word, Gaura objected mildly. He swam past the ring of acceleration couches to touch his toes to a stikpad on the decking. "Captain Calvert?"

The young man shrugged. "It's Joshua, actually."

Gaura felt his bottled-up emotions come close to brimming over. "Thank you, Joshua. From all of us."

Joshua nodded shortly, the faintest blush colouring his cheeks. The woman beside him caught his discomfort and smiled secretively.

There, Tiya said in satisfaction. **A perfectly ordinary young man, if exceptionally talented. I like him.**

Joshua introduced Sarha and Dahybi then apologized for the acceleration. "But I had to stop us dead inside the ring," he said. "If we had gone through, south of the ecliptic, the other starships would have seen us, and come after us. Their drives could burn through the particles just as easily as *Lady Mac* did, then we would have been sitting ducks for their combat wasps."

"I wasn't complaining. In fact, we're really all rather surprised that we're still alive."

"How are your people holding out?"

"Liatri, our doctor, says none of us have acquired any fatal internal injuries. Melvyn Ducharme is helping her review my people in your surgery cabin. Metabolic scanning has revealed several broken bones and a lot of pulled muscles. She was most concerned about internal membrane damage, it could prove a problem unless treated swiftly. But Melvyn Ducharme is rigging up a processor block that can interface her with your medical nanonic packages."

Joshua blinked, nonplussed.

"Our own medical packages all use bitek processors," Gaura explained.

"Ah, right."

"Liatri says we'll pull through. Mind you, it's going to take a long fortnight for the bruising to fade."

"You're not the only one," Sarha grimaced. "And you should take a look at where my bruises are."

Joshua leered. "Promises, promises."

"That was an awesome piece of flying you pulled off back there, Joshua," Gaura said. "Eluding two starships . . ."

"It's in the blood," he said, not quite nonchalantly. "Glad to be of help, really. We certainly haven't been much use to anybody else since we arrived in this star system."

Go on, Tiya urged. **Ask.**

But suppose it's an illegal flight? He was carrying combat wasps, don't forget. We'd have to give evidence.

Then the law is an ass, and we'll all develop amnesia. Ask.

Gaura smiled awkwardly. "Joshua, exactly who are you? I mean, why come to Lalonde?"

"Er . . . Good question. Technically, *Lady Mac* is part of

the Lalonde government's starship fleet, helping to restore civil order. The Confederation Navy squadron has other ideas, and according to them we're under arrest."

"Navy squadron?"

Joshua sighed theatrically, and started to explain.

The Edenists crowding the cabin in life-support capsule D, which doubled as the surgery, listened with a mixture of gloomy dismay and confusion.

"This sequestration ability sounds appalling," Gaura said, summarizing the Edenists' unified feelings.

"You should see the red cloud," Joshua told him. "That really gives me the creeps. It's an instinct thing with me, I know it's *wrong*."

Gaura gestured to the console they had been consulting; its holoscreen was alive with blue and yellow data displays. "What is our current situation?"

"I'm playing a waiting game," Joshua said, and datavised an order into the console processor. The holoscreen switched to an image from an external sensor cluster, showing a very dark expanse of crinkled rock. Scale was impossible to gauge. "See that? That's the largest ring particle I could find at such short notice, near-solid stone about two hundred and fifty metres in diameter. It's twenty-five kilometres inward from the northern surface. We're keeping station directly underneath it, and I do mean directly; *Lady Mac*'s forward hull is about three metres away. Right now Warlow and Ashly are outside drilling load pins into the rock so we can tether *Lady Mac* in place with silicon fibre. That way I won't have to use the thrusters to hold our position. *Maranta* and *Gramine* would be able to spot any ion plumes easily when the rings calm down. Our on-board electronic systems are designed for minimal emission anyway, but with that rock as a shield we'll make absolutely sure we're undetectable to their sensors. It can also absorb our thermal output as well; I've deployed the thermo-dump panels so that they're radiating all our excess heat directly at the rock, it will take months to seep through. All the drive tubes and the five main fusion generators have been powered down, so our magnetic flux is negligible. We're operating on one auxiliary fusion generator which is well screened by the hull. All in all, it's a very reasonable position. As long as *Maranta* and *Gramine* stay north of the ring we'll be invisible to them."

"And if one of them moves to a southern inclination?"

"There is fifty-five kilometres' worth of particles between us and the southern surface. It's a risk I'm prepared to take, especially with the ring so electrically and thermally active right now."

"I see. How long do you think we'll be here?"

Joshua pulled a face. "Hard to say. Right now we're only a hundred and seventy thousand kilometres above Murora, *Lady Mac* needs to be at least two hundred thousand out before she can jump. So if we want to leave, we either wait until *Maranta* and *Gramine* decide to call it a day and quit, or hang on until their search pattern carries them far enough away to allow us to make a dash for a jump coordinate. Whichever one it is, I think we'll be here for some time. Weeks at least."

"I understand. Do you have enough fuel and supplies to last that long?"

"Yes, fuel's down to forty-seven per cent, those high-gee manoeuvres use up cryogenics at a hell of a rate, but what's left can supply our present consumption rate for years. So that's no problem. But we'll have to monitor our environmental systems closely given there's thirty-six of you. The limiting factor is going to be food; that'll have to be rationed pretty carefully. All of which means I really don't want you to take your children out of zero-tau just yet."

"Of course. They will be much better off in the pods anyway. But what about your mercenary scout team?"

Joshua exchanged a significant glance with Sarha. "Not a damn thing we can do about that. They're tough and they're mean. If anyone can survive down there, they can."

"I see. Well if the opportunity arises to go back, then please do not hesitate on our account."

"We'll see. It would be difficult jumping to Lalonde with *Maranta* and *Gramine* following us. Ideally I'd like to hang on until they leave Murora. Our major problem is going to be tracking them. When you came in we were discussing mounting a sensor cluster on the other side of the rock. Before we started hiding we caught a glimpse of their ion thrusters, so we know they're still out there. But we have the same problem as them, this ring is pure hell to see through. Without reliable data we're at a nasty disadvantage."

"Ah," Gaura smiled happily. "I think I may be able to help there." **Aethra? Can you see the two starships which attacked us?**

Yes, the habitat replied. **They are orbiting slightly above the ring's northern surface.**

An image formed in his mind, the dusky plain of the ring slicing across Murora, blanched of most colour. The habitat's external sensitive cells could just sense a broad zone agitated by heat and electricity. Two dull specks were poised slightly above it, ion thrusters firing intermittent tattoos to maintain their attitude.

Excellent. "Aethra can see them."

Joshua brightened. "Jesus, that's great news. They're both still here, then?"

"Yes."

"How is Aethra?" he asked belatedly.

"The shell was extensively damaged. However, there is no catastrophic internal injury, its main organs remain functional. It is going to require a considerable amount of repair work before it can resume its growth. My colleagues, the ones who were killed in the attack, their memories have been stored by the personality."

"That's something, then."

"Yes."

"Can Aethra work out the exact spacial locations of the other starships for me? If we can keep updated I'll know when we can risk breaking cover and flying for a jump co-ordinate."

"I can go one better than that." Gaura slipped a proces-sor block from his breast pocket. The slim palm-sized plas-tic rectangle had produced a spectacular gold and blue bruise on his pectoral muscle during the flight. "Aethra can communicate through the bitek processor, and if you can interface this with your flight computer you'll be able to receive the images directly. And the starships hunting us will never know, affinity is undetectable."

"Wonderful." Joshua accepted the block. It was slightly smaller than the Kulu Corporation model he used. "Sarha, get to work on an interface. I want Aethra tied in to our navigation processor array pronto."

"Consider it done." She plucked it from his fingers and datavised her systems memory core for appropriate elec-tronic module specifications and adaptor programs.

Joshua thought the Edenist station chief still looked wrecked. "You know, we come from Tranquillity," he said. "It's *Lady Mac*'s home port."

Gaura looked at him, a surprised light showing in his worn eyes. "Yes?"

"Yeah. I've lived there all my life, I was born there, so I know how beautiful habitats are, and I don't just mean their physical structure either. So I suppose I can em-pathize with what you're feeling more than most Adamists. Don't worry. We'll get out of this and bring help back for Aethra, and Lalonde too. All we need now is time, and we're home free. Fortunately time is one thing we have plenty of."

"So you're not Confederation Navy marines then?" Horst asked, trying to hide his disappointment.

"No, I'm sorry, Father," Reza said. "The LDC hired us to scout round the Quallheim Counties and find out what was going on down here. I believe you can say we've cer-tainly done that."

"I see." Horst looked round the simplicity of the Tyrathcan tower house's hall, its smooth curves illuminated by the light stick, solid shadows blending seamlessly with dark-grey arches. The red light outside was kept at bay, silhouetting the hole sliced into the doorway. In spite of the warmth he felt chilled.

"How did you know we were here?" Pat asked.

"I didn't, not that you were in this particular tower. We saw the starships arrive yesterday morning, of course. Then in the afternoon there was an explosion on the river."

"The kroclion," Ariadne said.

"Could be," Reza said. "Go on."

"Young Russ saw it," Horst said. "I thought it best that we keep a watch on the savannah; that morning was the first time the red cloud appeared, and with the starships as well—it seemed sensible. By the time I got my optical intensifier band on there was only the smoke left. But it didn't look like anything the possessed do, so I rode out to see. I thought—I prayed—that it might have been the marines. Then that bedamned kroclion was skulking about in the grass. I just kept going up the river to keep ahead of it. And here we are. Delivered up to you by God's hand." He lifted his lips in a tired victorious smile. "Mysterious ways His wonders to perform."

"Certainly does," Reza said. "That kroclion was probably the mate of the one we killed."

"Yes. But tell me of the starships. Can they take us off this terrible planet? We saw an almighty battle in orbit before the red cloud swelled over the sky."

"We don't know much about the events in orbit. But that was a fight between some of our starships and a Confederation Navy squadron."

"Your starships? Why did they fight the navy?"

"Some of them. The possessed got into orbit on the spaceplanes which brought us down, they hijacked the starships and took over the crew."

"Merciful Lord." Horst crossed himself. "Are there any starships left now?"

"No. Not in orbit."

Horst's shoulders sagged. He sipped listlessly at the carton of hot coffee they had given him. This was the cruellest blow of all, he thought wretchedly, to be shown salvation shining so close and then to have it snatched away as my fingers close around it. The children cannot be made to suffer any more, merciful Lord hear me this once, they cannot.

Russ was sitting in Kelly's lap. He seemed shy of the combat-boosted mercenaries, but was content to let her spray a salve on his saddle sores. She smoothed down the damp hair on his forehead, and grinned as she offered him one of her chocolate bars. "You must have been through a lot," she said to Horst.

"We have." He eyed Shaun Wallace, who had kept to the back of the hall since he had arrived. "The Devil has cursed this planet to its very core. I have seen such evil, foul, foul deeds. Such courage too. I'm humbled, the human spirit is capable of quite astonishing acts of munificence when confronted by fundamental tests of virtue. I have come to believe in people again."

"I'd like to hear about it some time," she said.

"Kell's a reporter," Sewell said mockingly. "Someone else who makes you sign contracts in blood."

She glared at the big mercenary. "Being a reporter isn't a crime. Unlike some people's occupation."

"I shall be happy to tell you," Horst said. "But later."

"Thank you."

"You'll be safe enough now you're hooked up with us, Father," Reza said. "We're planning to head south, away from the cloud. And the good news is that we're expecting a starship to come back for us in a couple of days. There's plenty of room for you and Russ on our hovercraft. Your ordeal's over."

Horst let out an incredulous snort, then put the coffee carton down ruing his slowness. "Oh, my Lord, I haven't told you yet, have I? I'm sorry, that ride must have addled my brain. And I've had so little sleep these last days."

"Told us what?" Reza asked edgily.

"I gathered what children I could after the possession

began. We are all living together in one of the savannah homesteads. They must be terrified. I never intended to be away all night."

There was complete silence for a second, even the red cloud's hollow thunder was hushed.

"How many children?" Reza asked.

"Counting young Russ here, twenty-nine."

"Fucking hell."

Horst frowned and glanced pointedly at Russ who was staring at the mercenary leader with apprehensive eyes over his half-eaten chocolate. Kelly held him a fraction tighter.

"Now what?" Sal Yong asked bluntly.

Horst looked at him in some puzzlement. "We must go back to them in your hovercraft," he said simply. "I fear my poor old horse can travel no further. Why? Have you some other mission?"

The combat-adept mercenary kept still. "No."

"Where exactly is this homestead?" Reza asked.

"Five or six kilometres south of the jungle," Horst replied. "And forty minutes' walk east from the river."

Reza datavised his guidance block for a map, and ran a search through LDC habitation records, trying to correlate. "In other words, under the red cloud."

"Yes, that abomination spread at a fearsome rate yesterday."

"Reza," Jalal said. "The hovercraft can't possibly carry that many people. Not if we're going to keep ahead of the cloud."

Horst looked at the hulking combat adept in growing amazement. "What is this you are saying? Can't? Can't? They are children! The eldest is eleven years old! She is alone under that Devil's spew in the sky. Alone and frightened, holding the others to her as the sky turns to brimstone and the howling demon horde closes in. Their parents have been raped by unclean spirits. They have nothing left but a single thread of hope." He stood abruptly, clamping down on a groan as his ride-stiffened muscles rebelled against the sharp movement, face reddening in fury. "And you, with your guns and your mechanoid strength, you sit here thinking only of saving your own skin. You should run to embrace the possessed, they would welcome you as their own. Come along, Russ, we're going home."

The boy started sobbing. He struggled in Kelly's grip.

She climbed to her feet, keeping her arms protectively around his thin frame. Quickly, before she lost all courage, she said: "Russ can have my place on the hovercraft. I'll come with you, Father." Retinas switched to high resolution, she looked at Reza. Recording.

"I knew you'd be trouble," he datavised.

"Tough," she said out loud.

"For a reporter you have very little understanding of people if you think I'd desert his children after all we've seen."

Kelly pouted her lips sourly and switched her visual focus to Jalal. That exchange would have to be edited out.

"Nobody is going to leave the children behind, Father," Reza said. "Believe me, we have seen what happens to children driven away by the possessed. But we are not going to help them by rushing in blindly." And he stood, rising a good thirty centimetres higher than the priest. "Understand me, Father?"

A muscle twitched on Horst's jaw. "Yes."

"Good. Now they obviously can't stay at the savannah homestead. We have to take them south with us. The question is how. Are there any more horses at the homestead?"

"No. We have a few cows, that's all."

"Pity. Ariadne, can the hovercraft carry fifteen children apiece?"

"Possibly, if we ran alongside. But it would put a hell of a strain on the skirt impellers. And it would definitely drain the electron matrices inside of six or seven hours."

"Running like that would drain us too," Pat said.

"I can't even recharge the matrices, not under this

cloud," Ariadne said. "The solar-cell panels don't receive anything like enough photonic input."

"We might be able to build some kind of cart," Theo suggested. "Hitch it up to the cows. It would be better than walking."

"It would take time," Sal Yong said. "And there's no guarantee it would work."

"Tow them," Sewell said. "Slap together a couple of rafts, and tow them back up the river. All you need is planks, we can get them from the homestead itself if need be."

Ariadne nodded her rounded head. "Might just work. The hovercraft could handle that. We could certainly get back here by the middle of the afternoon."

"Then what?" Jalal said. "Look, I'm not being a downer. But just getting them back here isn't the solution. We have to keep going. Wallace says the cloud is going to cover the whole planet, we have to find a way to outrun it, or this will all be for nothing."

Reza turned to look at the possessed man who had kept silent and unobtrusive up until now. "Mr Wallace, will your kind know if we return to the homestead?"

"Aye, Mr. Malin," he said sorrowfully. "That they will. The cloud and the land are becoming one with us. We can feel you moving inside us. When you pass back under the cloud the sensation will be like treading on a nail."

"How will they react?"

"They'll come after you, Mr. Malin. But then they'll do that anyway if you stay on this world."

"I think he's speaking the truth," Horst said. "One of them came to the homestead two days ago. She wanted me and the children. Our bodies, anyway."

"What happened?" Kelly asked.

Horst forced a vapid smile. "I exorcised her."

"What?" Kelly blurted in greedy delight. "Really?"

The priest held up his bandaged hand. The dark strips of cloth were stained with blood. "It wasn't easy."

"Shit Almighty. Shaun, can you be exorcised?"

Shaun Wallace had locked his gaze to that of the priest. "If it's all the same to you, Miss Kelly, I'd be obliged if you didn't try."

"He can," she subvocalized into her neural nanonics memory cell, "he really can! You can see it in his eyes. He fears the priest, this ageing worn-out man in shabby clothes. I can barely believe it. A ceremony left over from medieval times that can thwart these almost-invincible foes. Where all our fantastic technology and knowledge fails, a prayer, a simple anachronistic prayer could become our salvation. I must tell you of this, I must find a way to get a message out to the Confederation." Damn, that sounded too much like Graeme Nicholson's recording.

For a moment she wondered what had happened to the old hack.

"Interesting," Reza said. "But it doesn't help our present dilemma. We have to find a way of keeping ahead of the cloud until Joshua comes back for us."

"Christ, we don't even know when he's coming back," Sal Yong said. "And taking a bunch of children through these mountains isn't going to be easy, Reza, there are no roads, no detailed map image. We've got no camping equipment, no boots for them, no food supplies. It's going to be wet, slippery. I mean, God! I don't mind giving it a go if there's even a remote chance of pulling it off, but this . . ."

"Mr Wallace, would your kind consider letting the children go?" Reza asked.

"Some would, I would, but the rest . . . No, I don't think so. There are so few living human bodies left here, and so many souls trapped in the beyond. We hear them constantly, you know, they plead with us to bring them back. Giving in is so easy. I'm sorry."

"Shit." Reza flexed his fingers. "OK, we'll take it in stages. First we bring the children back here, get them and us out from under that bloody cloud today. That's what is important right now. Once we've done that we can start concentrating on how to get them through the mountains. Maybe the Tyrathca will help."

"No chance," Ariadne said flatly.

"Yeah. But all of you keep thinking. Mr. Wallace, can you tell me what sort of opposition we'll be facing? How many possessed?"

"Well now, there's a good hundred and fifty living in Aberdale. But if you race in on those fancy hover machines of yours you ought to be away again before they reach you."

"Great."

Shaun Wallace held up his hand. "But there's a family of ten living in one of the other homesteads not far from the children. They can certainly cause you problems."

"And you believe him?" Sewell asked Reza.

Shaun Wallace put on a mournfully injured expression. "Now then, Mr. Sewell, that's no way to be talking about someone who's only doing his best to help you. I didn't stick out my thumb and hitch here, you know."

"Actually, he's right about the homestead family," Horst said. "I saw them a couple of days ago."

"Thank you, Father. There now, you have the word of a man of the cloth. What more do you want?"

"Ten of them on open ground," Reza said. "That's nothing like as bad as Pamiers. I think we can take care of them. Are you going to add your fire-power to ours, Mr. Wallace?"

"Ah now, my fire-power is a poor weak thing compared to yours, Mr. Malin. But even if it were capable of shifting mountains, I would not help you in that way."

"That makes you a liability, Mr. Wallace."

"I don't think much of a man who asks another to kill his cousins in suffering, Mr. Malin. Not much at all."

Horst took a pace forwards. "Perhaps you could mediate for us, Mr. Wallace? Nobody wants to see any more death on this world, especially as those bodies still contain their rightful souls. Could you not explain to the homestead family that attacking the mercenaries would be foolhardy in the extreme?"

Shaun Wallace stroked his chin. "Aye, now, I could indeed do that, Father."

Horst glanced expectantly at Reza.

"Suits me," the mercenary leader said.

Shaun Wallace grinned his wide-boy grin. "The priests back in Ireland were all wily old souls. I see nothing's changed in that department."

Nobody had noticed the balmy smile growing on Kelly's face during the exchange. She let go of Russ, and slapped her hands together with surefire exultation. "Yes! I can get Joshua back here. I think. I'm sure I can."

They all looked at her.

"Maybe even by this afternoon. We won't have to worry about going through the mountains. All we'll have to do is get clear of the red cloud so that Ashly can land."

"Spare us how wonderful you are, Kelly," Reza said. "How?"

She dived into her bag and pulled out her communication block, brandishing it as though it were a silver trophy. "With this. The LDC's original geosynchronous communication platform had a deep-space antenna to keep in touch with the Edenist station orbiting Murora. If the platform didn't get hit in the orbital battle, we can just call him up. Send a repeating message telling him how badly we need him. Murora is about nine hundred million kilometres away, that's less than a light-hour. If he leaves as soon as he receives it, he could be here inside three or four hours. *Lady Mac* might not be able to jump outsystem, but if she can jump to Murora she can jump back again. At least we'd be safely off Lalonde."

"Can you get the platform computer to send a message?" Reza asked. "Terrance Smith never gave us any access codes for it."

"Listen, I'm a bloody reporter, there's nothing I don't know about violating communication systems. And this block has quite a few less than legal chips added."

She waited for an answer, her feet had developed a life of their own, wanting to dance.

"Well, get on with it then, Kelly," Reza said.

She ran for the hole in the door, startling Fenton and Ryall lying on the grass outside. The sky over the savannah was split into two uneven portions of redness as the cloud band clashed with the dawn sun. She datavised an instruction into the block and it started scanning across the dissonant shades above for the platform's beacon.

Joshua dozed fitfully in his cabin's sleep cocoon. The envelope was a baggy lightweight spongy fabric, big enough to hold him without being restrictive. Sarha had offered to sleep with him, but he'd tactfully declined. He was still feeling the effects of that eleven-gee thrust. Even his body hadn't been geneered with that much acceleration in mind. There were long bruise crinkles on his back where the creases on his ship-suit had pressed into his skin, and when he looked into the mirror his eyes were bloodshot. He and Sarha wouldn't have had sex anyway, he really was tired. Tired and stressed out.

Everyone had been so full of praise for the way he had flown *Lady Mac*. If only they knew the emotional cold turkey that hit him once the danger was over and he stopped operating on nerve energy and arrogance. The fear from realizing what one—just one—mistake would have spelt.

I should have listened to Ione. What I had before was enough.

He held her image in his mind as he fell asleep, she made it a lot easier to relax, floating away on the rhythm of night. When he woke, drowsy, warm, and randy, he accessed a memory of their time back in Tranquillity. Out in the parkland, lying on the thick grass beside a stream. The two of them clinging together after sex; Ione on top, sweaty and dreamily content, light glinting an opulent gold off her hair, skin warm and soft against him, kissing him oh so slowly, lips descending along his sternum. Neither spoke, the moment was too perfect for that.

Then her head lifted and it was Louise Kavanagh, all

trusting and adoring in that way only the very innocent can achieve. She smiled hesitantly as she rose up, then laughed in rapturous celebration as she was impaled once again, luscious dark hair tossed about as she rode him. Thanking him. Praising him. Promising herself for ever his.

And loving a girl hadn't been that sweet since he was her age.

Jesus! He cancelled the memory sequence. Even his neural nanonics were playing him dirty.

I *do not* need reminding. Not right now.

The flight computer datavised that Aethra was requesting a direct channel. Joshua acknowledged the distraction with guilty relief. Space warfare was easy.

Sarha had done a good job interfacing the bitek processor to *Lady Mac*'s electronics. He had talked to the habitat yesterday, which was engrossing; it came across as a mixture of child and all-knowing sage. But it had been very interested in hearing about Tranquillity. The images he received from its shell's sensitive cells were different to the *Lady Mac*'s sensor clusters. They seemed more real, somehow, bestowing a texture of depth and emptiness which space had always lacked before.

Joshua unsealed the side of the sleep cocoon and swung his legs out. He opened a locker for a fresh ship-suit. There were only three left. Sighing, he started to pull one on. "Hello, Aethra," he datavised.

"Good morning, Joshua. I hope you slept well."

"Yeah, I got a few hours."

"I am picking up a message for you."

He was instantly alert, without any stimulus from his neural nanonics. "Jesus. Where from?"

"It is a microwave transmission originating from the civil communication platform orbiting Lalonde."

He was shown the starfield outside. The sun was a white glare point, nine hundred and eighty-nine million kilometres distant; to one side Lalonde shone steadily, if weakly, a sixth-magnitude star. It had now become a binary, twinned with a violet glint.

"You can see microwaves?" he asked.

"I sense, eyes see. It is part of the energy spectrum which falls upon my shell."

"What is the message?"

"It is a voice-only transmission to you personally from a Kelly Tirrel."

"Jesus. Let me hear it."

" 'This is Kelly Tirrel calling Captain Joshua Calvert. Joshua, I hope you're receiving this OK; and if not, could someone at Aethra's supervisory station please relay this to him immediately. It's really important. Joshua, I'm not sure if the possessed can overhear this, so I won't say anything too exact, OK? We got your message about returning. And the time-scale you mentioned is no use to us. Joshua, virtually everyone down here has been possessed. It's like the worst of the Christian Bible gospels are coming true. Dead people are coming back and taking over the living. I know that sounds crazy to you; but believe me it isn't sequestration, and it isn't a xenoc invasion. I've talked to someone who was alive at the start of the twentieth century. He's real, Joshua. So is their electronic warfare ability, only it's more like magic. They can do terrible things, Joshua, to people and animals. Truly terrible. Shit, I don't suppose you believe any of this, do you? Just think of them as an enemy, Joshua. That'll help make them real for you. And you saw the red cloud-bands over the Juliffe basin, you know how powerful that enemy is.

" 'Well, the red cloud is swelling, Joshua, it's spreading over the planet. We were heading away from it. Just like you said we should, remember? But we've found someone who has been in hiding since the possession started, a priest. He's been looking after a bunch of young children. There's twenty-nine of them. And now they're trapped under that cloud. They're near the village that was our original target, so that gives you a rough idea where we are. We're going back for them, Joshua, we'll be on our way by the time this message reaches you. They're only children, for Christ's sake, we can't leave them. The trouble is that once we've got them we won't be able to run far, not with our transport. But we're pretty sure we can get the children out from under the cloud by this afternoon. Joshua . . . you have to pick us up. Today, Joshua. We won't be able to hold out for long after sunset. I know your lady friend wasn't feeling too well when you left, but bandage her up as best you can, as soon as you can. Please. We'll be waiting for you. Our prayers are with you. Thank you, Joshua."

"It is repeating," Aethra said.

"Oh, Jesus." Possession. The dead returned. Child refugees on the run. "Jesus fucking wept. She can't do this to me! She's mad. Possession? She's fucking flipped." He stared aghast at the ancient Apollo computer, arms half in his sleeves. "No chance." His arms were rammed into the ship-suit sleeves. Sealing up the front. "She needs locking up for her own good. Her neural nanonics are looped on a glitched stimulant program."

"You said you believed the red cloud effect was fundamentally wrong," Aethra said.

"I said it was a little odd."

"So is the notion of possession."

"When you're dead, you're dead."

"Twelve who died when the station was destroyed are stored within me. You make continual references to your deity, does this not imply a degree of belief in the nature of spirituality?"

"Je— Shit! Look, it's just a figure of speech."

"And yet humans have believed in gods and an afterlife since the day you gained sentience."

"Don't you fucking start! Your lot are supposed to be atheists, anyway."

"I apologize. I can sense you are upset. What are you going to do about rescuing the children?"

Joshua pressed his fingers to his temple in the vain hope it would halt the dizzy sensation. "Buggered if I know. How do we know there really are any children?"

"You mean it is just a bluff to trick you into returning to Lalonde?"

"Could be, yeah."

"That would imply that Kelly Tirrel has been possessed."

Very calmly, he datavised: "Sequestrated. It implies she has been sequestrated."

"Whatever has befallen her, you still have a decision to make."

"And don't I know it."

Melvyn was alone on the bridge when Joshua came gliding through the hatch from his cabin.

"I just heard the message," the fusion expert said. "She can't mean it."

"Maybe." Joshua touched his feet to a stikpad beside his acceleration couch. "Call the crew in, and Gaura as well. I suppose the Edenists are entitled. It's their arses on the line as well."

He tried to think in the short time it took for them to drift into the bridge, make some kind of sense out of Kelly's message. The trouble was she had sounded so convincing, she believed what she said. If it was her. Jesus. And it was a very strange sequestration. He couldn't forget the chaos in orbit.

He accessed the navigation display to see just how practical any sort of return flight was. It didn't look good. *Maranta* and *Gramine* had confined their search to the section of ring which was electrically charged, which meant one of them was always within three thousand kilometres of *Lady Mac*. The jump coordinate for Lalonde was a third of the way round the gas giant, over two hundred and seventy thousand kilometres from their present position. Out of the question. He started to hunt round for options.

"I think it's a load of balls," Warlow said when they were all assembled. "Possession! Kelly's cracked."

"You said it yourself," Ashly said. "It's a bad form of sequestration."

"Do you believe in the dead coming back?"

The pilot grinned at the huge ochre cosmonik clinging to a corner of an acceleration couch. "It would make life interesting. Admit it."

Warlow's diaphragm issued a sonic boom snort.

"It doesn't matter what name we choose to call the process," Dahybi said. "The sequestration ability exists. We know that. What we have to decide is whether or not Kelly has been taken over by it." He glanced at Joshua and offered a lame shrug.

"If she hasn't then we're all in a great deal of trouble," Sarha said.

"If she *hasn't*?" Melvyn asked.

"Yes. That will mean there are twenty-nine children we have to get off that planet by this afternoon."

"Oh, hell," he mumbled.

"And if she has been sequestrated then she knew we were coming back anyway. So why try and get us to come back earlier? And why include all that crap about possession, when all it would do was make us more cautious?"

"Double bluff?" Melvyn said.

"Come on!"

"Sarha's right," Ashly said. "We always planned to go back; as far as Kelly knew, in a couple of days. There's no logical reason to hurry us. And we know they try and hijack the spaceplanes which land. It's not as if we wouldn't have taken precautions. All this has done is make us even more cautious. My vote says she is in trouble, and they have found these stray children."

"And me," Dahybi said. "But it's not our decision. Captain?"

It was the kind of oblique compliment about his status Joshua could really have done without. "Kelly would never call unless she really was desperate," he said slowly. "If she has managed to avoid sequestration, or whatever, she would never have mentioned possession unless it was true. You all know what she's like: facts no matter what it costs. And if she had been possessed, she wouldn't tell us."

Oh, Jesus, be honest, I know she's in deep shit. "They need to be picked up. Like she said: today."

"Joshua, we can't," Melvyn said. He looked desperately torn. "I don't want to abandon a whole bunch of kids down there any more than you. Even if we don't know exactly what's going on below those bloody cloudbands, we've seen and heard enough to know it ain't good. But we're never going to get past the *Maranta* and the *Gramine*. And I'll give you good odds they've picked up Kelly's message as well. They'll be extra vigilant now. Face it, we've got to wait. They'll spot us the second we turn our drive on."

"Maybe," Joshua said. "Maybe not. But first things first. Sarha, can our environmental systems cope with thirty kids and the mercenaries as well as the Edenists?"

"I dunno how big the kids are," Sarha said, thinking out loud. "Kelly did say young. There's probably room for four more in the zero-tau pods if we really cram them in. We can billet some in the spaceplane and the MSV, use their atmospheric filters. Carbon dioxide build-up is our main problem, the filters could never scrub the amount seventy people produce. We'd have to vent it and replace it from the cryogenic oxygen reserve." Neural nanonics ran a best and worst case simulation. She didn't like the margins on the worst case, not one bit. "I'll give you a provisional yes. But thirty is the absolute limit, Joshua. If the mercenaries run into any other worthy cause refugees, they're just going to have to stay down there."

"OK. That leaves us with picking them up. Ashly?"

The pilot gave one of his engaging grins. "I told you, Joshua, I promised them I'd go down again."

"Fine. That just leaves you, Gaura. You've been very quiet."

"It's your ship, Captain."

"Yes, but your children are on board, and your friends and family. They'll be exposed to a considerable risk if *Lady Mac* attempts to go back to Lalonde. That entitles you to a say."

"Thank you, Joshua. We say this: if it was us stranded on

Lalonde right now, we would want you to come and pick us up."

"Very well. That's settled then. We'll try and rescue the mercenaries and the children."

"One small point, Joshua," Melvyn said loudly. "We're stuck in the rings, with one combat wasp left, forty thousand kilometres from the edge of Murora's gravity field. If we stick our heads up, they'll be shot to buggery."

"I was in a similar situation to this a year ago."

"Joshua!" Sarha chided.

He ignored her. "It was the Ruin Ring, when Neeves and Sipika were coming after me. Look at where the *Maranta* and the *Gramine* are right now."

They all accessed the navigational display, neon-sharp graphics unfurling in their minds. The two searching starships extruded curved yellow orbital trajectory plots paralleling the thick gauzy green slab of the ring which filled the bottom half of the projection. *Lady Macbeth* lurked below the ring surface like some outlandish slumbering marine creature.

"*Maranta* and *Gramine* are now six thousand kilometres apart," Joshua said. "They've got a reasonable idea of the general area where we have to be hidden, and they've changed altitude twice in the last fifteen hours to cover different sections of the ring. If they stick to that pattern they'll change again in another four hours." He ordered the display to extrapolate their positions. "*Gramine* will be about three hundred kilometres from us, she actually passes over us in another ninety minutes; and *Maranta* is going to be right out at the extreme, about seven and a half thousand kilometres away. After that they'll swap orbital tracks and begin a new sweep.

"So if we can break out when *Maranta* is seven and a half thousand klicks away, we'll be far enough ahead of it to escape."

"And *Gramine*?" Melvyn asked. He didn't like Joshua's quiet tone, as if the young captain was afraid of what he was going to say.

"We know where it's going to be, we can leave one of the megaton nukes from the combat wasp waiting for it. Mine the ring where it will pass overhead, attach the nuke to a large rock particle. Between them, the emp pulse, the plasma wave, and the rock fragments should disable it."

"How do we get it there?" Melvyn asked.

"You know bloody well how we get it there," Sarha said. "Someone's got to carry it using a manoeuvring pack, right Joshua? That's what you did in the Ruin Ring, isn't it?"

"Yeah. They can't detect one person fifteen kilometres deep in the ring, not using cold gas to manoeuvre."

"Wait a minute," Dahybi said. He had been running flight trajectory simulations in the navigation display. "Even if you did knock out the *Gramine*, and that's a bloody long shot, we're still no better off. *Maranta* will just launch her combat wasps straight at us. There's no way we can out-run them, they'll get us before we're halfway to the edge of Murora's gravity field, let alone Lalonde's jump coordinate."

"If we accelerate at eight gees, we'll have seven minutes fifteen seconds before the *Maranta*'s combat wasps will catch us," Joshua said. "Distance-wise that works out at about sixteen thousand kilometres."

"That still won't get us outside Murora's gravity field. We couldn't even jump blind."

"No, but there is one place we can jump from. It's only fifteen thousand kilometres away; we would have a twenty-second safety margin."

"Where?" Melvyn demanded.

Joshua datavised an instruction into the flight computer. The navigational display drew a violet trajectory line from the *Lady Mac* towards the edge of the ring, sliding round in a retrograde curve to end at one of the four tiny ring-shepherd moonlets.

"Murora VII," Joshua said.

A terrible realization came to Dahybi; his balls retracted as though he'd dived into an icy lake. "Oh, Christ, *no*, Joshua. You can't be serious, not at that velocity."

"So give me an alternative."

"An alternative to what?" Sarha asked petulantly.

Still looking at Joshua, Dahybi said: "The Lagrange point. Every two-body system has them. It's where the moonlet's gravity is balanced by Murora's, which means you can activate a starship's nodes inside it without worrying about gravitonic stress desynchronization. Technically, they're points, but in practice they work out as a relatively spherical zone. A *small* zone."

"For Murora VII, about two and a half kilometres in diameter," Joshua said. "Unfortunately, we'll be travelling at about twenty-seven kilometres per second when we reach it. That gives us a tenth of a second to trigger the nodes."

"Oh, shit," Ashly grunted.

"It won't be a problem for the flight computer," Joshua said blandly.

"But where will the jump take us?" Melvyn asked.

"I can give us a rough alignment on Achillea, the third gas giant. It's on the other side of the system now, about seven billion kilometres away. We'll jump a billion kilometres, align *Lady Mac* properly on one of its outer moons, then jump again. No way will *Maranta* be able to follow us through those kind of manoeuvres. When we get to Achillea we slingshot round the moon onto a Lalonde trajectory and jump in. Total elapsed time eighty minutes maximum."

"Oh, God . . . well, I suppose you know what you're talking about."

"Him?" Sarha exclaimed. "You must be joking."

"It has a certain degree of style," Dahybi said. He nodded approvingly. "OK, Joshua, I'll have the nodes primed. But you're going to have to be staggeringly accurate when we hit that Lagrange point."

"My middle name."

Sarha studied the bridge decking. "I know another one," she muttered under her breath.

"So who's the lucky one that gets to EVA in the rings and blow up the *Gramine*?" Melvyn asked.

"Volunteers can draw lots," Joshua said. "Put my name in."

"Don't be stupid," Sarha said. "We all know you're going to have to fly the *Lady Mac*, no one else could hit that moonlet, let alone its Lagrange point. And Ashly has to take the spaceplane down, I expect that flight's going to need a professional. So the rest of us will draw for it."

"Kindly include twenty of us," Gaura said. "We are all qualified in EVA work, and we have the added advantage of being able to communicate with Aethra in case the starship should alter course."

"Nobody is volunteering, nobody is drawing lots," Warlow said, using excessive volume to obliterate any dissent. "This is my job. It's what I'm designed for. And I'm the oldest here. So I qualify on all counts."

"Don't be so bloody morbid," Joshua said, annoyance covering his real concern. "You just plant the nuke on a rock particle and come straight back."

Warlow laughed, making them all wince. "Of course, so easy."

Now, finally, under the slowly spinning inferno and looking up into a glaring formless void. Journey's end. Chas Paske had to turn down his optical sensors' receptivity, the light was so bright. At first he had thought some kind of miniature sun lurked up there at the centre of the flaming vortex of cloud, but now the boat had carried him faithfully under the baleful cone he could see the apex had burst open like a malignant tumour. The rent was growing larger. The cyclone was growing larger, deeper and wider.

He knew its purpose at last, that knowledge was inescapable where he was, pressed down in the bottom of the flat boat under the sheer pressure of the light. It was a mouth, jaws opening wide. One day—soon—it would devour the whole world.

He gave a wild little giggle at the notion.

That heavy, heavy light was migrating from whatever (wherever?) lay on the other side. Weighty extrinsic photons sinking slowly downwards like snow to smother the land and river in their own special frost. Whatever they touched, gleamed, as though lit from within. Even his body, shoddy, worthless thing it was now, had acquired a dignified lustre.

Above the gashed cloud was a sheer plane of white light, a mathematical absolute. The ocean into which his white silk dream river emptied. A universal ocean into which Lalonde was destined to fall like a pearl droplet, and lose itself for evermore. He felt himself wanting to rise up towards it, to defy gravity and soar. Into the perpetual light and warmth which would cleanse him and banish sorrow. It would ripple once as he penetrated the meniscus, throwing out a polished wave crown, a single ephemeral spire rising at the centre. After that there would be no trace. To pass through was to transcend.

His remoulded face was incapable of smiling. So he lay there gladly on the boat, mind virtually divorced from his body, looking up at his future, awaiting his moment of ascension. His physical purpose long since abandoned.

Even though the red cloud's thunder had retreated to a muffled rumbling he never heard the starting gun being fired, so the first cannonball shattered his serenity with shocking abruptness.

They had known he was there, the possessed, they had been aware of him all along. From the moment he'd passed under the aegis of the red cloud he had registered in their consciousness, as an orbiting gnat might impinge upon a man's peripheral vision. His hapless journey down the river was of no consequence to them; in his miserable degenerative state he was simply not worth their attention nor a moment's effort. The river was bringing him surely to their bosom, they were content to let him come in his own time.

Now he was here, and they had assembled down by the docks to provide a maliciously frolicsome reception. It was a black-hearted jamboree suitable to celebrate the last possession before Lalonde escaped the universe for good.

The iron ball whistled low over Chas's boat with a back-lash crack that set the insecure craft rocking, then splattered into the snowlily mush thirty metres away. Purple smoke and ten-metre magnesium flames squirted joyously into the air like a jumbo Roman candle.

Chas shunted round on his elbows, looking in disbelief at the chromatic blaze. The snowlilies started to melt away around his boat, lowering it into sparkling clear blue water. Whoops and catcalls wafted over the river from the shore. He twisted round.

Durringham with all of its white towers and onion-dome spires and lofty castles and lush hanging gardens formed a magnificent backdrop to the armada racing to collect him. There were Polynesian war canoes with flower-garlanded warriors digging their paddles into the clear water; rowing eights with lean young men sweating under the cox's bellowed orders; triremes, their massed oars flashing in immaculate unison; Viking marauders sporting resplendent scarlet and gold sun-god sails; dhows whose lateens strained ahead of the fresh breeze; junks, sampans, ketches, sloops . . . and riding fast and proud out in front was a big three-masted buccaneer, its crew in striped shirts scrambling over the rigging. A quarter of the city's population crowded the circular harbours (now ancient solid stone) cheering on their chosen team in a boisterous rollicking carnival atmosphere.

Chas gagged at the sight of it all; the nightmare dormant in every human brain *the entire world is out to get me*. The whole city was chasing him, wanted him, hated him. He was their new toy, the day's amusement.

His body spasmed in massive quakes, implants faltering. Intolerable waves of pain from his leg crashed past the crumbling analgesic blocks. "Bastards!" he roared. "You shit-eating bastards. You don't play with me. I am your enemy. I am not a joke. Fear me. Fear me, God damn you!"

A dainty ring of smoke puffed out of the buccaneer's forward gun. Chas screamed, fury and terror in one incoherent blast of sound.

The cannon-ball hit the water ten metres away, sending up a sheet of steaming white water. Wavelets rushed out, slapping his boat.

"Bastards." It wasn't even a whisper. Adrenalin and nerves could do nothing more for him, he was devoid of strength. "I'll show you. Freaks. Zoo people. I am not a joke." Somewhere far away a soprano chorus was singing black canticles.

Chas datavised the activation code into the kiloton bomb strapped in its harness at his side. Good old faithful bomb. Stuck to him the whole time. That'll wipe the smile off their faces.

Nothing happened, his neural nanonics had shut down. Pain was burning through him, leaving only numbness in its wake. Fingers scrabbled feebly at the bomb's small manual control panel, prising open the cover. His head flopped to one side to follow the movement. He eventually managed to focus an optical sensor. The panel keyboard was dark, inert. It had failed. He had failed.

Almost forgotten natural tear glands squeezed out their very last drops as he slowly knocked a fist on the wooden planking in utter futility.

A couple of the triremes were gaining on the buccaneer. It was developing into a three-boat race, though one of the war canoes refused to give up, warriors pounding the water with their paddles, skin gleaming as though they were sweating oil. Back on the harbours the elated cheering mixed with songs and chants from across five millennia.

The buccaneer crew fired another cannon to terrorize their crushed victim.

"You won't have me!" Chas cried in defiance. He put a hand on each gunwale and started to rock the boat as the cannon-ball's wavelets broke against the hull. "Never. Never. I won't be a part of it, not of you."

Pain and numbness had gorged on his torso. His arms began to fail as the swaying reached a peak. Water slopped in over the narrow gunwale. The flimsy boat turned turtle, dumping him into the Juliffe. He saw bubbles churning past. The rumpled silver foil of the surface receded. Neural nanonics told him his lungs were filling with water. Pain diminished. His implants were working again. They couldn't reach him under water, he was beyond them here. He focused every sensor he had on the bomb whose weight was dragging him down.

On shore the audience had stopped cheering when their prey (so unsportingly) capsized himself. A groan went up. He'd pay for that.

Boat crews stopped rowing and slumped over their oars, exhausted and angry. The buccaneer's sails calmly rolled themselves up as the sailors hung like listless spiders in the rigging. They stared morosely at the tiny half-sunken boat bobbing about ahead of them.

Together Durringham's possessed exerted their power. The river around the hull of Chas Paske's boat began to ripple energetically.

"Hey look, it's Moses!" someone yelled from the harbour wall. A laugh ran along the spectators. They clapped their hands and stomped their feet, a stadium crowd demanding their sporting hero appear. "Moses! Moses! Moses!"

The waters of the Juliffe parted.

Chas felt it happening. His surroundings were getting lighter, pressure was reducing. Below his fingers the bomb's keyboard was a glowing ruby chessboard. He typed in the code, refusing to hurry, watching the numbered squares turn green. There was a loud gurgling sound building all around. Fast-conflicting currents sucked at him, twisting his lifeless legs about. Then the rucked surface came rushing down to seek him out. Too late.

The kiloton nuke detonated at the bottom of a twenty-metre crater in the river. Its initial blast pulse was punched straight up into the core of the transplanarity ferment raging above. A solar fireball arose from the water with splendid inevitability, and the entire river seemed to lift with it. Energy in every spectrum poured outwards, smashing solid matter apart. None of those lining the harbour wall really knew what was happening. Their stolen bodies disintegrated before the nerve impulses could reach the brain. Only after annihilation, when the possessing souls found themselves back in the bestial beyond, did the truth dawn.

Two seconds after the bomb exploded, a forty-metre wall of water moving at near-sonic speed slammed into Durringham. And the dead, ensconced in their beautiful new mansions and fanciful castles, died again in their tens of thousands beneath the usurping totem of the radiant mushroom cloud.

12

With his enhanced retinas switched to full sensitivity it appeared as though Warlow was flying through a dry iridescent mist. Ring particles still crawled with wayward spurts of energy; micrometre dust flowed in slow streams around the larger boulders and ice chunks. Despite the shimmering phosphorescence he was basically flying blind. Occasionally he could catch a glimpse of stars flickering past his feet, short-lived embers skipping from an invisible bonfire.

After leaving the *Lady Macbeth* he had moved twelve kilometres out from Murora, an orbit which saw him falling behind the sheltering starship. The big dark sphere, upper hull glinting in the livid red glow from its own thermo-dump panels, had been lost from sight in three minutes. Isolation had tightened its bewitching fingers almost immediately. Strangely enough, here, where he could barely see ten metres, a realization of the universe's vastness was all too strong.

The ten-megaton bomb was strapped to his chest, a fat ovoid seventy-five centimetres high. Weightless, yet weighing heavily in his heart—titanium and composite device though it was.

Sarha had given him one of the Edenist bitek processor blocks which she had modified with augmentation modules. The idea was to provide him with a link to Aethra in case the *Gramine* should unexpectedly alter track.

Makeshift, like this whole mission.

"Can I speak with you alone?" he datavised.

"Of course," the habitat answered. "I would be glad to keep you company. Yours is a fraught task."

"But it is mine alone."

"You are the best qualified."

"Thank you. I wanted to ask you a question on the nature of death."

"Yes?"

"It involves a small story."

"Go on. I am always interested to hear of human events. I understand very little of your species so far, even though I have inherited a wealth of data."

"Ten years ago I was a crew-member in the starship *Harper's Dragon*. It was a line cargo ship, nothing special, although the pay was comfortably regular. We had a new cadet lieutenant join us on Woolsey, called Felix Barton. He was only twenty, but he had assimilated his didactic courses well. I found him competent, and a reasonable messmate. He was no different to any other young man starting his career. Then he fell in love with an Edenist woman."

"Ah; this is, perhaps, a Shakespearian tragedy?"

Warlow saw thin ribbons of orange dust winding corkscrew fashion around an ice chunk straight ahead; a bird-kite's tail, he thought. They sparked pink on his carbotanium space armour as he splashed through. Then he was past them and curving round a mealy boulder, guidance and optical interpretation programs operating in tandem to steer him automatically around obstacles. "Not at all. It is a very straightforward story. He simply became besotted. I admit she was beautiful, but then every geneered human seems to be. *Harper's Dragon* had a regular contract to supply her habitat with specialist chemicals for one of their electronics manufacturing stations. After four trips, Felix declared he could not bear to be parted from her. And he was lucky, she felt the same way about him."

"How fortunate."

"Yes. Felix left *Harper's Dragon* and became an Edenist. He had neuron symbionts implanted to give him general affinity, and underwent specialist counselling to help him adapt. The last time *Harper's Dragon* visited, I spoke with him, and he was extremely happy. He said he had fitted in perfectly and that she was expecting their first child."

"That is nice. There are something like a million and a half Adamists who become Edenists every year."

"So many? I didn't know."

"Seventy per cent are love cases similar to your friend, the rest join because it attracts them intellectually or emotionally. Over half of the love cases are Adamists who form relationships with voidhawk crew-members, which is only to be expected given that they have the most contact with Adamists. It leads to many jokes about the voidhawk families having wild blood."

"So tell me, is the conversion absolute, do these new-found Edenists transfer their memories into the habitat when they die?"

"Of course."

His neural nanonics displayed a guidance plot, updating his position. Purple and yellow vectors slithered through his head, temporarily displacing his view of the irradiated dust. He was on course. His course. "Then my question is this. Is it possible to transfer a person's memories into a habitat if that person has neural nanonics rather than affinity?"

"I have no record of it ever having been done. Although I can see no reason why not; the process would take longer, however, datavising is not as efficient as affinity."

"I want to become an Edenist. I want you to accept my memories."

"Warlow, why?"

"I am eighty-six, and I am not geneered. My shipmates do not know, but all that is left of my real body is the brain and a few nerve cords. The rest of me perished long ago. I spent far too much time in free fall, you see."

"I'm sorry."

"Don't be. It has been a full life. But now my neurons are dying at a rate which is beyond even Confederation gene therapy's ability to replace. So, understandably, I have come to think a lot about death recently. I had even considered downloading my memories into a processor array, but that would simply be an echo of myself. You on the other hand are a living entity, within you I too could continue to live."

"I would be happy and honoured to accept your memories. But, Warlow, the transference must take place at death, only that way can continuity be achieved. Anything less would be that echo of self which you spoke of. Your personality would know it was not complete because its conclusion was missing."

He flew along a cliff of charcoal-textured rock. A virtual mountain of a particle, worn and abraded by aeons of murmuring dust, the lethal knife-blade spires unsheathed by its fractured formation now a moorland landscape of undulations, barrows of its youthful virility. "I know."

"Are you worried then that Captain Calvert will not be able to escape through the Lagrange point?"

"No. Joshua will be able to fly that manoeuvre with ease. My concern is that he is given the chance to fly it."

"You mean eliminating the *Gramine*?"

"I do. This mission to mine the rings is the weakest link in Joshua's plan to escape. It assumes the *Gramine* will not deviate its orbit by more than five hundred metres in the next two hours. It assumes too much. I propose to position the warhead accurately on *Gramine*'s orbital track, and detonate it while it passes. That way I can be sure."

"Warlow, neither *Gramine* nor *Maranta* have deviated their track by more than a hundred metres since the search began. I urge you to reconsider this action."

"Why? I have only a few years to live at best. Most of those would be spent with my memories and rationality slipping away. Our medical science has achieved too much in that direction. My synthetic body can keep pumping blood through my comatose brain for decades yet. Would you wish that on me when you know you yourself can provide me with a worthwhile continuance?"

"That is, I believe, a loaded question."

"Correct. My mind is made up. This way I have two chances of cheating death. There are few who can say that."

"Two? How so?"

"Possession implies an afterlife, somewhere a soul can return from."

"You believe that is the fate which has befallen Lalonde?"

"Do you know what a Catholic is?" A solid glacier wall of ice appeared out of the dust. The cold-gas nozzles of his manoeuvring pack fired heavily. For a moment he saw the splay of waxen vapour shiver as it was siphoned away into the blue and emerald phosphenes of dust.

"Catholicism is one of the root religions which made up the Unified Christian Church," Aethra said.

"Almost. Officially, by decree of the Pope, Catholicism was absorbed. But it was a strong faith. You cannot modify and dilute such an intense devotion simply by compromising prayers and services to achieve unity with other Christian denominations. My home asteroid was Forli, an ethnic-Italian settlement. It kept the faith, unofficially, unobtrusively. Try as I might, I cannot throw away the teachings of my childhood. Divine justice is something I think all living things will have to face."

"Even me?"

"Even you. And Lalonde looks to confirm my belief."

"You think Kelly Tirrel was telling the truth?"

Warlow's manoeuvring pack was nudging him gingerly round the rimed iceberg, loyally following the ins and outs of its gentle contours. Its surface was true crystal, but eventually it sank into total blackness, as though a wormhole interstice had frozen open at its core. When his armour-suit sensors scanned round they showed him the constellations returning to their full majesty through the attenuating dust. "I do. I am convinced of it."

"Why?"

"Because Joshua believes her."

"A strange rationale."

"Joshua is more than a superlative captain. In all my years I have never come across anyone quite like him. He behaves execrably with women and money, and even his friends on occasion. But, if you will excuse my clumsy poetry, he is in tune with the universe. He knows truth. I put my faith in Joshua, I have done so ever since I signed on with the *Lady Macbeth*, and I will continue to do so."

"Then there is an afterlife."

"If not, I will live on as part of your multiplicity. But Kelly Tirrel has been convinced that there is. She is a tough, cynical person, she would take a lot of convincing such a thing could be. And, as now appears likely, if there is an afterlife, I have an immortal soul and death is not to be feared."

"And do you fear death?"

He rose out of the iceberg's umbra cloak. It was similar to emerging from a dark layer of rain-cloud into clear evening sky, there was only a remote diaphanous shimmer of dust left above him. *Gramine* shone like a second-magnitude star, forty kilometres away and drifting towards him. "Very much."

The hovercraft slewed and bucked on the river, tossed about by white-water waves swelling over semi-submerged stones. Theo was concentrating hard on keeping them straight and level, but it was tough going. Kelly didn't remember yesterday's journey up this same river as being so difficult. She and Shaun Wallace were sitting on the rear bench, clinging on grimly as they were slung about. The propeller droned behind her.

"Already I feel wearied by the journey, daunted by what we are attempting. This is not even snatching victory from the jaws of defeat, although it might be termed a last vain attempt to salvage the team's dignity. We came to this planet with such confidence and high ideals; we were going to vanquish the evil invader and restore order and stability to twenty million people, give them their lives back. Now all we dare hope for is to escape with thirty children. And even that will tax us to the limit."

"Such a worrier, Miss Kelly." Shaun smiled congenially.

The hovercraft swerved, pushing her against him—for the briefest second the channel to her sensorium flek recorder block dropped out—and he smiled politely as they righted themselves. "You mean I shouldn't be worrying?"

"Now I never said that. But worry is the Devil's disciple, it rots the soul."

"Well, you'd certainly be the one to know all about souls."

Shaun chuckled softly.

Kelly glanced up at the red cloud. They had been under it for half an hour now. It was thicker than it had been yesterday, its constituent tresses twirling sluggishly. Somehow she was aware of its weight, a heaviness necessary to blot out not just the sight of space but the physical laws governing existence. A complex intertwining of associated emotions defeated her, as though she was sensevising some obscure xenoc ceremony. "That cloud means a lot to you, doesn't it?" she asked.

"Not the cloud itself, Miss Kelly, that's nothing, but what it represents, yes. That's like seeing your aspirations take form. To me, to all of us damned souls, it means freedom. A precious commodity when you've been denied it for seven hundred years."

Kelly switched her attention to the second hovercraft, with Horst Elwes and Russ sitting on the bench behind Ariadne, faces ploughed up against the biting slipstream wind. Cannonades of thunder thrashed overhead, as if the cloud was the taut skin of some gigantic drum. She saw Russ push himself closer against the priest. The simple act of trust was immensely poignant.

The privation dropped upon Shaun Wallace without the slightest warning. He experienced the dreadful exodus, the flight of souls expelled from the universe exerting a tidal force on his own precarious possession. Their lamentations and enmity spilled back from the beyond in that eerily pervasive chorus, and then came venomous anger of those who accompanied them on their expulsion, those they had possessed. All of them, preying on each other, hating each other. The conflict permeated his skull, wrenching at his thoughts. He gagged, eyes widening in shock. His face betrayed an emotion of uttermost despair, then he flung his head back and howled.

Reza never wanted to hear a cry like it again. The outpouring of anguish compressed into that one cataclysmic bawl spoke for an entire planet. Grief paralysed him, and loss, loss so profound he wanted the universe to end so he could be spared.

It finished as Shaun ran out of breath. Unsteadily, Reza twisted round on the front bench. Tears were streaming down the possessed man's cheeks. He drew breath and howled again.

Kelly's hands were clasped against her puckered lips. "What?" she wailed. "What is it?" Her eyes shut instinctively at the next outburst.

Reza tried to block it all out and project some comfort to Fenton and Ryall. "Pat?" he datavised. "Can Octan see anything happening?"

"Not a thing," the second-in-command answered from the other hovercraft. "What's going on? Wallace frightened the shit out of us."

"I've no idea."

Kelly shook Shaun's arm imploringly. "What's wrong? What is it? Speak to me!" Panic was giving her voice a shrill edge. "Shaun!"

Shaun gulped down a breath, his shoulders shivering. He lowered his head until he was staring at Reza. "You," he hissed. "You killed them."

Reza looked at him through a cross-grid of yellow target graphics, his forearm gaussrifle was aimed directly at the possessed man's temple. "Killed who?"

"The city, the whole city. I felt them go, thousands upon thousands blown back to the beyond like so much ash.

Your devil bomb, it went off. No, it was set off. What kind of creatures are you to slaughter so indiscriminately?"

Reza felt a grin reflex coming on, which his restructured face portrayed as a moderate widening of his mouth slit. "Someone got through, didn't they? Someone hit back."

Shaun's head sagged brokenly. "One man. That's all, one bloody man."

"So you're not so invincible, after all. I hope it pains you, Mr. Wallace, I hope it pains all your kind. That way you may begin to know something of the horror we felt when we found out what you did to this planet's children."

The flash of guilt on the man's face proved the barb had hit home.

"Oh, yes, Mr. Wallace, we know. Even if Kelly here is too tactful to mention it. We know the barbarism we are dealing with."

"What bomb?" Kelly asked. "What are you two talking about?"

"Ask him," Shaun said, and sneered at Reza. "Ask him how he was intending to help the poor people of this planet he was hired to save."

"Reza?"

The mercenary leader swayed as the hovercraft banked around a boulder. "Terrance Smith was concerned we might not get all the fire support we needed from the starships. He gave each team leader a nuke."

"Oh, Christ." Kelly looked from one man to the other. "Do you mean you've got one as well?"

"You should know, Kelly," Reza said. "You're sitting on it."

She tried to jump to her feet, only to have Shaun grab her arm and keep her sitting.

"Have you learned nothing of him yet, Miss Kelly? There's no human part left in that mockery of a body."

"Point to your body, Mr. Wallace, the one you were born with," Reza said. "After that I'll talk morality and ethics with you all day long."

They stared at each other.

Darkness began to fall. Kelly looked up to see the red light bleeding from the cloud, leaving behind a swollen slate-grey mantle massing sinisterly low overhead. A blade of purple-white lightning screwed down on the savannah to the east.

"What's happening?" Kelly shouted as thunder crashed over the hovercraft.

"You are happening, Miss Kelly. They sense you. They fear and hate you now your true nature and power has been exposed. This is the last mercenary team left, you see. None of the others survived."

"So what will they do?"

"Hunt you down, whatever the cost below the muzzles of your weapons."

Two hours after Warlow had left *Lady Mac* Joshua was accessing the flight computer's memory cores, looking for records of starships jumping from inside a Lagrange point. He and Dahybi had gone through the small amount of available data on Murora VII, using it to refine their computations of the Lagrange point's size and position, locking the figures into the trajectory plot. He could pilot *Lady Mac* right into its heart—no doubt about that: now he wanted to know what would happen when the energy patterning nodes were activated. There was a lot of theory in the physics files about how it should be possible, but no actual verified ZTT jump.

Who's going to be stupid enough to take part in an experiment like that? he asked himself. But he was lying on his acceleration couch, and Dahybi, Ashly, and Sarha were on the bridge with him, so he kept any qualms to himself. He was just wondering if there would be a reference in a history file, surely the ZTT pioneers would want to know the limits of their craft, when Aethra datavised him.

"Warlow wants to talk with you," the habitat said.

He cancelled the link to the memory cores. "Hello, Warlow. How's it going?"

"Superbly," Warlow said.

"Where are you?" The cosmonik ought to be back on board in another twenty minutes if everything was running on schedule. Joshua had helped draw up the flight vector through the ring.

"Twenty kilometres from *Gramine*."

"What?"

"I can see it."

"Jesus shit, Warlow. What the fuck are you playing at? The schedule doesn't have any margin for error."

"I know. That's why I'm here. I'm going to make certain that *Gramine* is destroyed by the blast. I shall detonate it when the ship is in an optimum position."

"Oh, Jesus, Warlow, get your iron arse back here now!"

"Sorry, Captain. *Maranta* will only be seven thousand three hundred kilometres away when *Gramine* is eliminated. But that will still give you an eighteen-second lead on the combat wasps. That's easily enough time."

"Warlow, stop this. We can wait until the end of the next sweep and position the bomb again. That's only another five hours. We'll still be at Lalonde before Amarisk's evening."

"Joshua, you have six minutes before I detonate. Make sure everyone is strapped down, please."

"Don't do it. Jesus, Warlow, I'm begging you."

"You know this has to be done properly. And I can ensure it is."

"Not like this. Please, come back."

"Don't worry about me, Joshua. I've thought it out, I will be quite all right."

"Warlow!" Joshua's face was crushed into a mask of anger and desperation. He jerked round to look at Ashly. The pilot was moving his lips silently, eyelashes sticky with tears. "Say something," Joshua commanded. "Get him back."

"Warlow, for Heaven's sake come back," Ashly datavised. "Just because you can't navigate properly there's no need for this. I'll do it next time, and do it right."

"I would like you to do me a favour, Ashly."

"What?"

"Next time you come out of zero-tau, in fifty years or so, I want you to come back here and visit me."

"Visit you?"

"Yes. I am transferring my memories to Aethra. I'm going to become one of the multiplicity. I won't die."

"You crazy old bastard."

"Gaura!" Joshua shouted. "Can he do that? He's not an Edenist."

"The datavise has already begun," Gaura replied. "He is doing it."

"Oh, Jesus wept."

"Is everyone in their acceleration couches?" Warlow asked. "I'm giving you the chance you really need to escape the rings. You're not going to waste that, are you, Joshua?"

"Shit." A hot steel band was constricting Joshua's chest, far worse than any gee force. "They're getting onto the couches, Warlow." He datavised the flight computer for an image from the cabin cameras, watching Edenists tighten the webbing around themselves. Melvyn was swimming about, checking they had done it properly.

"And what about the thermo-dump panels, have you retracted them? There's only five minutes left."

Joshua datavised the flight computer to retract the thermo-dump panels. Systems schematics appeared as he prepped the generators and drive tubes; mostly green, some amber. The old girl was in good shape. Sarha started to help him with the checklist.

"Please, Warlow?"

"Fly the bastards into the ground, Joshua. You can do it."

"Jesus, I don't know what to say."

"Promise me something."

"Yes."

"Gotcha. You should have asked me what it was first."

Joshua coughed. Laughed painfully. It made his vision all blurred for some unfathomable reason. "What is it?"

"Hard luck, you committed. I want you to be more considerate to your girls. You never see the effect you have on them. Some of them get hurt, Joshua."

"Jesus, cosmonik and social worker."

"Promise?"

"I promise."

"You were a good captain, Joshua. *Lady Macbeth* was a great way to finish. I wouldn't have had it any other way."

Sarha was sobbing on her acceleration couch. Ashly was clenching and unclenching his fists.

"I would," Joshua said silently.

Aethra showed them *Gramine*. The starship was traversing the ring surface with the suavity of a maglev train, straight and sure. Three thermo-dump panels were extended to the full, shining a dull vermilion. A long, narrow flame of blue ions flickered for an instant.

"Who'd have thought it," Warlow datavised. "Me, an Edenist."

Joshua had never felt so pathetically worthless as he did then. He's *my* crewman.

The bomb exploded. It sent a flat circle of sheer white light flaring out across the ring surface. *Gramine* was a tiny dark speck above its centre.

Joshua fired the restraint bolts. Taut silicon-fibre cables tethering the *Lady Macbeth* to its rock shield recoiled from the hull, writhing in serpentine coils. Lights inside the four life-support capsules dimmed and sputtered as the one active auxiliary generator powered up the four remaining primary generators. Ion thrusters fired, hosing the dark rock with unaccustomed turquoise luminosity.

A sphere of plasma inflated at the centre of the white shroud thrown across the ring, fast at first, then slowing when it was five kilometres across, diminishing slightly. Black phantoms migrated across its surface. *Gramine*'s lower hull shone brighter than a sun as it reflected the diabolical corona seething four kilometres below.

Thousands of fragmented rock splinters flew out of the heart of the fusion blast, overtaking the disbanding plasma

wave. They had the same riotous glow of doomed meteorites caught by an atmosphere. Unlike the plasma they
left behind, their velocity didn't fall off with distance.

"Generators on-line," Sarha called out. "Power output
stabilizing."

Joshua closed his eyes. Datavised displays filled his
head with technicolour dragonfly wings. *Lady Mac* cleared
the rock. Her radar started to fire hard microwave pulses at
the loose shoal of ring particles, evaporating snowflakes
and inflaming carbonaceous motes. Beams of blue-white
radiance shone out of the secondary reaction-drive nozzles, rigid as lasers.

They started to rise up through the ring. Dust currents
splashed over the monobonded-silicon hull, producing
short-lived surf-bloom patterns. Pebbles and larger stones
hit and bounced. Ice splattered and stuck, then slipped
downwards to fall away in the turbulent glare of the drive
exhaust.

A rock chunk crashed into the *Gramine*, shattering its
hull open and decimating the internal systems. Cryogenic
tanks ruptured, white gases scintillating from the dying fusion bomb's energy barrage. Four life-support capsules
raced out of the destruction, charred nultherm foam flaking
away, emergency beacons blaring.

Lady Mac cleared the ring surface. Fifty kilometres
above her a wave of scarlet meteors streaked across the
starfield.

"Stand by for high gees," Joshua said. The fusion drives
came on, tormenting the abused ring still further. *Lady
Mac* tilted round, and started chasing down the inside of
the tapering orange vector tube in Joshua's mind. He monitored the displays to ensure their course was aligned correctly as the gee forces built, then datavised an extra order
into the flight computer.

"Joshua, what—" Ashly's startled voice faded away as
the bridge trembled softly.

The last combat wasp left its launch-tube.

"Watch it coming, shitheads," Joshua purred. Jesus, but

it felt good to see the vector lines emerge as the submunitions separated. Purple threads linking *Lady Mac* with the tumbling wreckage.

It took eight seconds for the submunitions to reach the *Gramine*'s life-support capsules. A stipple of kinetic explosions boiled above the ring for a few scant seconds before the vacuum absorbed them as effortlessly as it did all human-born pollution.

The inside of the homestead cabin was even worse than Jay Hilton imagined hell must be like. She wouldn't let any of the other children go outside, so they had to use buckets in the small second bedroom when they wanted to go to the toilet. The smell was atrocious, and it got viler every time they opened the door. To add to their woes, the heat had reached a zenith which even Lalonde had never matched before. They had opened all the shutters as well as the door, but the air was solid, motionless. The cabin's timber creaked and popped as the frame expanded.

The physical ordeal was bad enough, but Jay felt so agonizingly lonely too. It was stupid, there were twenty-seven children crammed in around her so tight you couldn't move without nudging someone. But she didn't want other kids, she wanted Father Horst. He had never done this before, not leave them alone for a whole day, and certainly not at night. Jay suspected Father Horst was as scared by the night as she was.

All this wretchedness had started when the starships had appeared, and with them the red cloud. Yesterday, just yesterday. It should have been a wonderful time. Rescue was here, the navy marines would come and take them all away and make everything right again. The long dragging miserable days out here on the unchanging savannah were over.

The idea was a little bit scary, because there was always some comfort in routine, even one as difficult as the homestead. But that didn't matter, she was leaving Lalonde. And nobody was ever going to make her come back. Not even Mummy!

They had spent a happy morning outside, keeping watch over the savannah for the first sign of their rescuers. Though the growing red cloud had been a bit frightening.

Then Russ had seen what he claimed was an explosion, and Father Horst had ridden off to investigate.

"I'll be back in a couple of hours," were his last words to her as he'd left.

They had waited and waited. And the red cloud had slid over the sky above, bringing its horrible noise with it, as though it was hiding an avalanche of boulders.

She had done what she could, organizing meals and rotas. Things to do, things to keep them busy. And still he hadn't come back.

Her watch had told her when it was night. She would never have known otherwise. They had closed the shutters and the door, but red light from the cloud seemed to slide in through every crack and cranny. There was no escape. Sleep was difficult, the boomy thunder-noise kept going the whole time, mingling with the higher pitched sounds of crying.

Even now the youngest children remained tearful, the older ones subdued. Jay leant on the window-sill, gazing off in the direction Father Horst had gone. If he didn't come back very soon, she knew she wouldn't be able to hold her own tears back. Then everything would be lost.

I must try not to.

But she had been badly shaken by the way the red light had vanished ninety minutes ago. Now ghastly black clouds swept low and silent over the savannah, turning everything to funereal greys. At first she had tried to play the shapes game, to make them less sinister, but her mind's eye could only conjure up witches and monsters.

Jay turned round from the window, registering the frightened faces. "Danny, the fridge should have done some more ice by now. Make everyone some orange juice."

He nodded, happy to be given some task. Usually he was a real moaner. "Jay!" Eustice squealed. "Jay, there's something out there." She backed away from her window, hands pressed to her cheeks.

There was an outbreak of crying and wails behind Jay. Furniture was kicked and scraped as the children instinctively made for the rear wall.

"What was it?" Jay asked.

Eustice shook her head. "I don't know," she said wretchedly. "Something!"

Jay could hear the cows mooing plaintively, sometimes the bleating of a goat. It might just be a sayce, she thought. Several had gone by yesterday, driven from the jungle by the red cloud. She gave the open door a nervous glance, she'd have to shut it. With shivers in each limb she shuffled back to the window and peeked round the frame.

Lightning was playing along the horizon. The savannah's darkling grass was perfectly still, which made the movement easy to spot. Two ebony blobs jutting up above the blade tips. They were growing steadily larger. She heard a humming noise. Mechanical.

It had been so long since she'd heard any kind of motor that it took a moment to place the sound; and even longer for her to bring herself to believe. Nobody on this planet had ground transport.

"Father!" she shrieked. "He's back!" Then she was out of the open door and running towards the hovercraft, heedless of the stiff, dry grass slapping and scratching her bare legs.

Horst saw her coming and jumped off the hovercraft as Ariadne slowed to a halt fifteen metres from the homestead. He had told himself all through the trip that nothing had happened to them, that they would be all right. Praying and praying that it would be so. But actually seeing Jay alive and in one piece was too much, and the repressed guilt and instituted fear burst out, overwhelming him. He fell to his knees and opened his arms.

Jay hit him as if she was giving a rugby tackle. "I

thought you were dead," she blubbed. "I thought you'd left us."

"Oh, Jay, darling Jay. You know I never would." He cradled her head and rocked her gently. Then the other children came streaming down the homestead's ramshackle steps, squealing and shouting. He smiled at them all and held out his arms once more.

"We were scared," Eustice said.

"The sky's gone real funny."

"It's so hot."

"Nobody collected the eggs."

"Or milked the cows."

Bo narrowed her eyes as the mercenaries climbed out of the hovercraft. "Are these the marines you promised?" she asked sceptically.

"Not quite," Horst said. "But they're just as good."

Danny goggled up at Sewell. The big combat-adept had gaussrifles plugged into both elbow sockets. "What is he?" the boy asked.

Horst grinned. "He's a special sort of soldier. Very strong, very clever. Everything is going to be all right now. He'll look after you."

Kelly had kept her retinas on wide-field focus, scanning the whole reunion scene. There was a big dry lump forming in her throat.

"Holy Jesus, will you look at it all," Shaun Wallace said in a small demoralized voice. "What kind of a God could do this to us? Not the one I was taught about, that's for sure. Look at them all, little children. Crying their bloody damn eyes out. And all for what?"

Kelly turned round at the unaccustomed savagery and bitterness in his tone. But he was already striding towards Reza, who was watching Horst and the children impassively.

"Mr Malin?"

"Yes, Mr. Wallace?"

"You have to move these children away now."

"I intend to."

"No, I mean right now. My kind, they're over there in the edge of the jungle. There's a couple of hundred of them, if not more. They're meaning to get you, Mr. Malin, to end the threat once and for all."

Reza focused his sensors on the first rank of stunted, scrappy trees four or five kilometres away. The cloud over the jungle was still glowing a sombre red, giving the leaves a coral tinge. Heat shimmer and fluttering leaves defeated him, he couldn't tell. "Pat, what can Octan see?"

"Nothing much. But there's definitely a few people roving round in there, and . . . Oh my God."

The pages emerged first, young boys, ten or twelve years old, holding their heraldic banners high. Then the drums started up, and the pikemen marched out of the cover of trees. It was a long solid black line, almost as if the trees themselves were advancing. Following, and holding a tight formation at the centre, came the mounted knights. Silver armour shone by its own accord under the unbroken veil of leaden clouds.

The army assembled itself in front of the trees to the order of the drummer. Knight commanders rode up and down, organizing stragglers. Then when the ranks were neatly laid out, a single bugle note rang across the savannah. They started to tramp over the uneven grassland towards the homestead.

"OK," Reza said equably. "Time to go."

Along with all the other children Jay found herself being hurriedly lifted into one of the hovercraft by a mercenary and told to hang on. Boxes and equipment were being tossed out to accommodate them. Father Horst was in the other hovercraft; Jay wanted to be with him, but she didn't think the mercenaries would listen if she asked. Shona was plonked down beside her, and Jay smiled timidly, reaching for the disfigured girl's hand. Their fingers pressed together urgently.

There was a lot of shouting going on all around. Everyone was moving at such a rush. One of the big (really big) mercenaries dashed into the homestead and came out half a minute later carrying Freya.

"Put her in my hovercraft," Horst said. "I'll look after her." The limp girl was laid on the front bench, and he eased a bundle of cloth under her head.

Through all the confusion and bustle Jay saw one of the mercenaries strap a dark globe to the neck of a huge dog. A man (who she thought looked a bit like Rai Molvi) and a lady who had come with the mercenaries were arguing hotly in front of the cabin. It ended when she made a slashing motion with one arm and climbed into the pilot's seat of the second hovercraft. The other mercenaries were ransacking the ammunition boxes that lay on the ground, slotting magazines into their backpacks. Then the impellers on Jay's hovercraft began to spin and the decking wobbled as it rose up. She wondered where the mercenaries were going to fit, her hovercraft had seventeen children packed in between the pilot's seat and the fan at the rear. But when both vehicles swung round and began to pick up speed she realized they were jogging alongside.

"Where are we going?" Shona shouted above the teeth-grating buzz of the fans.

The small hairless pilot didn't seem to hear.

Aethra watched the *Lady Macbeth* streak across the ring. Triple fusion exhausts twining into a single braid of near-pure radiation that stretched for over two hundred kilometres behind the fleeing starship.

Murora VII was a thousand kilometres ahead of her. A battered sphere of grey-brown rock not quite a hundred and twenty kilometres in diameter. Along with the other three shepherd moonlets it brought a certain degree of order to the edge of the ring, creating a tidy boundary line. Dust, iceflakes, and pebbles extended out across the gas giant's ecliptic plane far past the immature habitat's orbit, although their density slowly dropped away until at a million kilometres it was no different to interplanetary space. But none of the larger particles, the flying mountains and icebergs, were to be found beyond the hundred and eighty thousand kilometre limit where the shepherds orbited.

Lady Macbeth's exhaust plume yawed a degree, then straightened out again, honing her trajectory. Three thousand kilometres behind her, five combat wasps, arranged in a precise diamond configuration, were accelerating at twenty gees. It had taken the *Maranta* a long time to respond to the break-out, its possessed crew wasting seven expensive seconds before launching the combat wasps—though they couldn't know that. Now the drones could never catch her.

Aethra had never known emotional tension before. Always, it had reflected the feelings of the supervisory station staff. Now though, as it watched the starship curving over the moonlet, it knew—understood—the meaning of trepidation. It *willed* the starship to succeed.

The station staff were lying on their acceleration couches, that wicked gee force squeezing them relentlessly. Aethra could see the ceiling of the cabin through a dozen sets of pained eyes, feeling the cushioning give below overstressed back muscles.

Three seconds away from the Lagrange point. *Lady Macbeth*'s fusion drives reduced to four gees as she skimmed eight kilometres above Murora VII, tracing a slight parabola around its minuscule gravity field. A couple of ion thrusters fired. The pursuing combat wasps cleared the edge of the ring.

Aethra prepared thirty-three storage areas in its neural strata. Ready to receive the memories of the Edenists on board. Although it would be so quick . . .

An event horizon eclipsed the *Lady Macbeth*.

Her fusion plume lingered briefly like a broken-hearted wraith before melting away. Then there was no physical evidence left of her ever having existed.

Five combat wasps converged on the Lagrange point. Their courses intersected, drive exhausts a dazzling asterisk, and they sped outwards on divergent vectors, electronic brains crashing in program overload confusion.

"I told you Joshua could fly that manoeuvre," Warlow said.

Aethra tasted smugness in the subsidiary mentality's thoughts. It wasn't used to that, but then the last twenty-four hours had contained a lot of unknowns. "Yes, you did."

"You should have more faith."

"And you're the one to teach me?"

"About faith? Yes, I could try. I think we both have the time now."

The hovercraft battered its way through the tall, heavy savannah grass. It had never been designed with this particular terrain in mind. The grass was too high, too resilient for the skirt to surmount; it all had to be ridden down. That took power, and they were overladen with the children as well.

Kelly datavised the vehicle's electron-matrix-management processor for a status review. Reserves were down to thirty-five per cent; not nearly enough to make it past the end of the cloud. Impeller monitor programs were flashing amber cautions into her brain as they struggled to maintain skirt inflation. Burnout wasn't imminent, though it was something she'd have to watch for.

A long mound arose out of nowhere, and she tilted the joystick exactly right to veer round its base. The piloting program Ariadne had datavised to her was operating in primary mode, enabling her to steer with the same consummate skill the mercenary had owned. Her weight—or rather lack of it—made her the ideal choice. Theo piloted the other hovercraft, and the priest was sitting behind her, but apart from them the team ran alongside. Even Shaun Wallace, though the few times she glimpsed him he was as red faced as a marathon runner on the home straight.

The mounted knights were pushing them hard, keeping a steady three kilometres behind, just enough to put them beyond the range of the gaussrifles. One or two would occasionally break rank for a charge. Then Sewell or Jalal would fire a few EE rounds to ward them off. Thankfully the sturdy pikemen were unable to match the boosted mercenaries' physical endurance (so how come Shaun could?); they had been left nearly seven kilometres behind. So far so good, but the situation couldn't hold stable for long.

Fenton was racing ahead of the hovercraft, scouting the land, his mass and brawn making easy work of the bristling grass blades. Reza looked through the hound's eyes, leaving a locomotion program to guide his own body down the trail left by the two hovercraft. He was developing a feel for the land beneath the rhythmic pounding of the hound's paws, anticipating the folds and abrupt rises which belied the savannah's facade of interminable mellow ground.

There was a small but certain change in the texture of the grass whipping against Fenton's blunt muzzle. The dead mat of decaying blades covering the flinty soil becoming thicker, springier. Water, and close by. Fenton slowed to smell the air.

"Kelly," Reza datavised. "There's a small stream two hundred metres ahead, steep gully sides. Head for it. Part of the bank has collapsed, you can take the hovercraft down."

A guidance plot filled her mind, all close-packed brown and blue contour lines, a computer image of how the earth would look stripped of vegetation. Neural nanonics integrated it with the piloting program, and she tweaked the joystick.

"Where does it lead?" she asked. So far all they had done was build distance between them and the homestead cabin, heading due south without any attempt to get back on the river which led to the mountains.

"Nowhere. It's cover for us, that's all. The knights are trying to wear us down; and the bastards are succeeding. We can't keep this pace going for ever, and the hovercraft electron matrices are being drained. Once we're immobile the pikemen will catch up, and it'll all be over. They know we can't fight off that many of them. We have to regain the initiative."

Kelly didn't like the implications leaping round inside

her skull at that statement. But she did her best to ignore them. Hunted beasts couldn't afford scruples, especially ones that knew exactly what lay in store if they were caught.

She datavised a query at her communication block. Since they left the homestead cabin it had been broadcasting a continuous signal up to the geosynchronous platform and the secure satellites Terrance Smith had brought with him. There was no need for secrecy now. But the darkened cloud was still blocking the directional beam very effectively.

Theo's hovercraft slowed as it neared the stream, then the nose fell and it went into a controlled slither down the scree of crumbling earth. The gully was three metres deep, with tall reed-grass growing along the top. Smooth grey stones filled the flat bottom, with a trickle of water running down the middle. A muddy pool had built up behind the scree.

Kelly followed the first hovercraft down, juggling the fan deflectors frantically to stop them from sliding into the opposite bank. She turned upstream keeping ten metres behind Theo. He reached the deepest part of the gully and killed the lift.

The mercenaries were jumping down from the top of the bank.

"Everybody out of the hovercraft," Reza said. "And sit with your backs to the gully here." He pointed.

Northern side, Kelly thought. She stood up—*don't think about it*—and helped to hand the children over the gunwale. They looked round in bewilderment, young faces lost and doleful. "It's all right," she kept saying. "Everything's all right." Don't think about it. She kept smiling too, so they wouldn't catch her anxiety.

Octan glided down into the gully, and perched himself on Pat Halahan's broad shoulder, wings folding tightly. Fenton was already nosing round Reza's legs.

Don't think about it. Kelly sat beside Jay. The little girl obviously knew something terrible was about to happen.

"It's all right," Kelly whispered. "Really." She winked, though it was more like a nervous tic. Flints in the gully wall were sharp on her back. Water gurgled round her boots.

"Joshua," Kelly datavised into her communication block. "Joshua, answer me, for Christ's sake. Joshua!" All she was given in reply was the oscillating ghost-wind of static.

There was a scuttling sound as the mercenaries sat down on the stones. Several children were sniffling.

"Shut your eyes, and keep them shut," Reza said loudly. "I shall smack anyone who I see with open eyes."

The children hurriedly did as they were told.

Kelly closed her eyes, took a breath, and slowly folded her shaking arms over her head.

As soon as the event horizon collapsed, Joshua accessed the image supplied by the short-range combat sensors. *Lady Mac* had emerged from her jump six thousand kilometres above Lalonde. There was nothing within two thousand kilometres. He datavised the full sensor-suite deployment, and triggered the fusion drives. They moved in at a cautious two gees, aiming for a thousand-kilometre orbit.

No starships were left in orbit, the sensors reported, even the inter-orbit craft from Kenyon had vanished. Victim of a combat wasp, Joshua assumed. There was a lot of metallic wreckage, most of it in highly eccentric elliptical orbits, and all of it radioactive.

"Melvyn, access the communication satellites, see if there's any data traffic for us. And Sarha, see if there are any low-orbit observation satellites left, their memories might hold something useful."

They both acknowledged their orders and datavised instructions to the flight computer. The starship's main dish found one of the secure communication satellites, and beams of microwave radiation sprang up to enmesh the planet in a loose web. *Lady Macbeth* started to receive data from the various observation systems left functional.

Everybody seemed to be working smoothly. Their flight to Achillea and the slingshot round its moon had passed off flawlessly. Jubilation at the successful jump from Murora had temporarily balanced out the loss of Warlow. Certainly Joshua experienced none of the sense of accomplishment which should have accompanied the Lagrange-point stunt. The most fantastic piece of flying in his life.

Gaura said he wasn't sure, but he thought the transference had worked, certainly a large quantity of the old cosmonik's memories had been datavised successfully into Aethra. The habitat had been integrating them when *Lady Mac* jumped.

The prospect of him living on as part of the multiplicity helped ease the grief—to a degree. Joshua felt a lot of regrets bubbling below his surface thoughts; things he'd said, things he should have said. Jesus, did Warlow have a family? I'll have to tell them.

"Nothing from the communication satellites, Joshua," Melvyn said heavily. "Thanks." The idea that Kelly and the mercenaries had been caught was unbearable. That would mean their own flight had been for nothing, and Warlow—"Stand by to broadcast a message from *Lady Mac*'s main dish, we'll see if we can break through the cloud with sheer power. Sarha, what have you got?"

"Not much. There are only seven low-orbit observation satellites left. They took a real pounding in the battle yesterday. But, Joshua, someone detonated a nuke down there earlier this morning."

"Jesus. Where?"

"I think it was at Durringham. The satellite only saw the blast as it fell below the horizon."

Joshua accessed the main sensor image. The red cloudbands over the tributaries had expanded dramatically. Individual strands had blended together producing a homogenized oval smear that covered the entire Juliffe basin. He realized the bright flame-glimmer Durringham had produced before was missing.

Then he noticed a large circular section of cloud in the

south-east had lost its red nimbus altogether, becoming a malaised grey. Interest stirred at the back of his mind; it almost looked as if the red cloud was being ruined by some cancerous growth. He datavised the flight computer for a guidance grid.

"It's south of the Quallheim villages," he said with a sense of growing confidence.

"That grey patch?" Sarha asked.

"Yeah. Exactly where Kelly said they were going."

"Could be," Dahybi said. "Maybe the mercenaries have found a way of damaging the cloud."

"Perhaps. Melvyn, focus our dish on it, and start transmitting. See if you can punch through and raise Kelly directly." Joshua centred an optical sensor on the area and upped the magnification. The hoary amorphous cloudscape rushed out to fill his mind. It wasn't giving any clues away, there were no breaks, no glimpses of the ground below. "Ashly, have you been following this?"

"Yes, Joshua," the pilot answered from the spaceplane cabin.

"We'll be in orbit in another three minutes. I want you to launch as soon as we finish decelerating. Loiter above those mountains in the south, and we'll see if the mercenary team can get out from under the cloud. Under no circumstances are you to go under it."

"No fear."

"Good." He datavised the flight computer to open the spaceplane hangar doors. "Anything from Kelly, yet?"

"Sorry, Joshua, only static."

"She said they wouldn't be out from under the cloud until the afternoon," Sarha pointed out. "It isn't quite noon there yet."

"I know. But that cloud is still growing, even the grey section. If it reaches the mountains they'll be in serious trouble. The hovercraft won't be able to handle that sort of country. They'll be trapped between the two."

"We can wait," Dahybi said. "For a week if we have to."

Joshua nodded vaguely, eyes tight shut as he flipped

through sensor inputs, desperate for any sort of hint. "Come on, Kelly," he murmured. "Show us you're there."

Ryall padded stealthily through the long grass. The scent of humans was strong in the air. Many had passed by very recently. But none were near him now.

After leaving his master he had run swiftly east, the big weight fastened round his neck jouncing about uncomfortably. After a couple of kilometres the masterlove thoughts in his brain had guided him to one side. He had traced a wide curve over the savannah, now he was heading back to his starting point.

When he reached a wide swath of grass, beaten down by many tramping feet, Ryall waited at the edge for a moment—listening, sniffing. Instinct told him he was alone. Satisfied, the masterlove thoughts urged him out. The swath led all the way back to the jungle, he turned the other way. Five hundred metres ahead of him, the homestead cabin jutted up out of the grassland. He hurried towards it, a hungering sensation racing through his blood.

The grass was beaten down all around the cabin. Fences had been broken. Cows wandered about, grazing placidly, paying no attention to him. Goats saw him coming and ran jerkily until they realized he wasn't chasing them. Chickens escaped from their smashed pen were scratching in the dirt; they scattered squawking when he trotted up to the cabin.

Height. The masterlove thoughts wanted him to have height. Ryall swung his big head from side to side, viewing the back wall of the cabin; then loped over to a pile of composite pods stacked at one corner. He jumped, bounding up the pods, then sprang for the eaves. Paws skated unsteadily on the solar-cell panels nailed to the roof, but he found his footing on the ginger qualtook-bark tiles and scampered his way up to the apex.

His master used his eyes to peer out across the savannah. The line of men carrying pikes were a kilometre away. And almost lost in the gloaming ahead of them the band of knights on horseback galloped after their prey.

Ryall felt a curious mix of excitement and sorrow. But the masterlove thoughts were full of gentle praise. He thumped his tail on the qualtook tiles in response.

Then the masterlove thoughts were guiding his left forepaw to the heavy weight hanging from his neck. He bent his head round and watched attentively as his extended nails caught the edge of a small hinged panel and eased it open. Glowing squares were revealed.

Masterlove adoration flowed through him. Very carefully his nail touched one of the squares. Once. Twice. Thrice—

The spaceplane stopped shaking as it dropped to subsonic velocity. It had been a fast, steep descent, Ashly had made the little craft stand almost on its tail to aerobrake. Now he levelled out and datavised the wings into their forward-sweep position. Nose-mounted sensors showed him the mountains rolling past below; the fringe of the cloud was fifty kilometres to the north. Short puffy fronds extended out from the main bulk, snaking through the air like blind searching insect antennae towards the foothills.

He datavised the flight computer for a channel up to *Lady Macbeth*. "Any word yet?"

"Nothing," Joshua replied. "Sarha says the observation satellites recorded that patch of cloud turning grey immediately after the Durringham nuke. We're not too sure what that means, but then I don't think normal logic applies here."

"Too right. I've got enough power in the electron matrices for a five-hour flight before I have to come back up and recharge. If you want that extending I could land on one of these peaks, they're fairly isolated."

"No. You keep airborne, Ashly. Frankly, if they're not out of there in five hours I don't think we'll see them again. And I've already lost one crewman today."

"You didn't lose him, Joshua. Silly old fart. Now I've

got to come back and wander through Aethra's parkland talking to the trees. Hell, he'll love that. Kill himself laughing I expect."

"Thanks, Ashly."

The pilot loaded a course into the computer, a patrol circuit along the length of the grey cloud section, staying at eight thousand metres. Thermals shooting up off the rocky slopes rocked the wings in agitated rhythms as the spaceplane flew overhead.

Jay thought it was a lightning bolt. Blackness suddenly and silently turned to bright scarlet. She sucked in a breath—it must have been frightfully close. But there was no thunderclap. Not at first.

The redness faded away. She risked opening her eyes. Everything seemed normal, except it was a lot lighter than it had been before. As if the sun was finally rising behind her back. Then the noise started, a dry roar which built and built. She heard some of the children start to whimper. The ground began to tremble, the gully wall vibrating her back. And the brightness behind her kept growing. A sheet of white light sprang across the top of the gully, throwing the floor into deep shadow. It began to tilt downwards, turning the opposite bank unbearably bright. Jay could just hear the lady beside her shouting what sounded like a prayer at the top of her voice. She closed her eyes again, little squeaks of fear escaping from her throat.

Lady Macbeth was passing over Amarisk's western coast, a hundred kilometres north of Durringham, when Reza detonated the nuke. The sensors caught its initial flash, a concussion of photons turning the grey clouds momentarily translucent.

"Jesus Christ," Joshua gasped. He datavised the flight computer for a secure communication channel to the spaceplane. "Ashly, did you see that?"

"I saw it, Joshua. The spaceplane sensors registered an emp pulse equivalent to about a kiloton blast."

"Are your electronics OK?"

"Yes. Couple of processor drop-outs, but the back-ups are on line."

"It's them. It has to be."

"Joshua!" Sarha called. "Look at the cloud."

He accessed the sensor image again. A four hundred metre circle of the cloud looked as if it was on fire below the surface. As he watched it rose up into a lofty ignescent fleuron. The tip burst open. A ragged beam of rose-gold light shone through.

Lady Mac's flight computer datavised a priority signal from one of the communication satellites direct into Joshua's neural nanonics.

"Joshua?" Kelly called. "This is Reza's team calling *Lady Mac*. Joshua, are you up there?"

Tactical graphics immediately overlaid the optical sensor image, pinpointing her communications block to within fifteen centimetres. Close to the blast point, very close. "I'm here, Kelly."

"Oh, Christ, Joshua! Help us. Now!"

"Spaceplane's on its way. What's your situation, have you got the children?"

"Yes, damn it. They're with us, all of them. But we're being chased to hell and back by the fucking Knights of the Round Table. You've got to get us out of here."

Vast strips of rank grey cloud were peeling back from the centre of the blast. Joshua could see down onto the savannah. It was a poor angle, but a vivid amber fireball was ascending from the centre of a calcinated wasteland.

"Go," Joshua datavised to Ashly. "Go go go."

Reza stood on top of the gully, bracing himself against the baked wind driving out from the blast. A mushroom cloud was roiling upwards from the cemetery of the homestead, alive with gruesome internal energy surges. It had gouged a wide crater, uneven curving sides spouting runnels of capricious magma.

He brought a series of filter programs on-line, and

scanned the savannah. A firestorm was raging for two kilometres around the crater. Pixels from the section of ground where the marching pikemen had been were amplified. He studied the resulting matrix of square lenses. There were no remnants, not even pyres; none of them had survived. He tracked back. Knights and horses had been hurled indiscriminately across the smouldering grass two and a half kilometres away. Encased in that metal armour human bodies should have first been triturated by the blast wave then fried by the infrared radiation.

He watched one silver figure struggle to its knees, then use a broadsword shoved into the ground to clamber to its feet.

Ye Gods, what will kill them?

A horse kicked its legs and rolled over, surging upwards. It trotted obediently over to its fallen rider. Slowly but surely the entire band was remounting.

Reza jumped back into the gully. Children were being packed back into the hovercraft.

"Joshua's here," Kelly yelled over the trumpeting wind. Her tear-stained face framed a radiant smile. "*Lady Mac*'s in orbit. The spaceplane's on its way. We're safe, we're out of here!"

"How long?"

"Ashly says about ten minutes."

Not enough, Reza thought. The knights will be here by then, they'll hit the spaceplane with their white fire, if they don't just switch off its circuitry with that black magic. "Kelly, you and Theo take off south. The rest of you, with me. We're going to arrange a small delay."

"No, Reza!" Kelly implored. "You can't, not now. It's over. Ashly will get here."

"That was an order, Kelly. We'll catch up with you when we've finished off these mounted pricks."

"Oh, Christ."

"Hey, Kell, stop fretting," Sewell said. "You've got the wrong attitude for this game. Win some or lose some, who cares, you've just gotta have fun playing." He laughed and vaulted up to the top of the gully.

Horst made the sign of the cross to Reza. "Bless you, my son. May the Lord watch over you."

"Get in the bloody hovercraft, Father, take the kids somewhere they can have a life. Theo, blast some grass, get them clear."

"Yes, boss." The jungle-rover mercenary fed power into the impellers even as Horst was scrambling on board. With the skirt bouncing against the gully wall the hovercraft turned in a tight curve and sped back up the scree.

Reza joined his team on the top of the bank. Out on the savannah the knights were mustering into a V-shaped battle phalanx.

"Move out," Reza said. There was a strange kind of glee running loose in his mind. *Now we'll show you babykillers what happens when you face a real enemy, one that can fight back. See how you like that.*

The six mercenaries started to march over the grass towards the waiting knights.

Sunlight and rain poured down on the hovercraft, surrounding them with a fantastic exhibition of rainbows. The clouds were breaking up, losing their supernatural cohesion. They were just ordinary rain-clouds again.

The rain sprayed against Kelly's face as she battled the hovercraft's inertia against the wind and damp cloying grass. Speed tossed them about like a dinghy on a storm-swollen sea.

"How big are the children?" Joshua asked.

"Small, they're mostly under ten."

"Ashly will probably have to make two trips. He can bring the children up first then come back for you and the mercenaries."

She tried to laugh, but all that emerged was a gullet-rasping cough. "No, Joshua, there's only going to be one flight. Reza's team won't be coming. Just the children, and me and the priest if the spaceplane can handle our mass."

"The way you diet to keep your image, you're into negative mass, Kelly. I'll tell Ashly."

She heard the first fusillade of EE projectiles exploding behind her.

Sewell and Jalal stood four metres apart, facing the apex of the charging knights. The reverberant thud of the horses galloping over the savannah rose above the hot squalls spinning off from the chthonic maelstrom of the blast's epicentre.

"I make that forty-nine," Jalal said.

"The lead is mine, you take the right flank."

"Sure thing."

The knights lowered their lances, spurring on their horses. Sewell waited until his rangefinder put the lead knight a hundred and twenty metres away, and fired both heavy-calibre gaussrifles plugged into his elbow sockets. Feed tubes from his backpack hummed efficiently. He laid down three fragmentation rounds over the knight's plumed helmet, and followed it up with twenty-five EE shells into the ground ahead of the left flank.

Jalal was laying down a similar fire pattern across the right flank, his two gaussrifles traversing the line, guided by a targeting program. Pamiers had shown that the possessed were capable of defending themselves against almost anything short of a direct hit by an EE round; he was going for the horses. Kill the mounts, chop the legs out from under them, slow them down. More fragmentation bursts saturated the air. The knights were veiled by smoke, fountains of soil, and riotous static webs.

Streaks of white fire ripped out of the carnage. Sewell and Jalal leaped aside. Four knights sped towards them out of the furore. Sewell spun round as he hit the ground, white fire was gnawing into his left leg. His targeting program locked on to the first knight; one of his gaussrifles was responding sluggishly, the other fired ten EE rounds. The knight and his horse vanished inside a tangled screen of rampaging electrons. Gore spat outwards.

Sewell's optical sensors were tracking more knights riding out from the first assault point. Several bodies were scattered on the crushed grass behind them. His neural nanonics automatically fired a salvo of fragmentation rounds at the renewed charge.

He tried to get up, but there was no response from his leg. One of the gaussrifles had packed up completely. Some of his sensor inputs were wavering. Horses were charging at him from three directions. His functional gaussrifle blasted at one. Another knight aimed a lance at his head, and fire squirted out of its tip.

Sewell rolled desperately. He flung a grenade as the fire caught him on the shoulder, punching him round. The grenade went off beneath the horse, lifting it clear of the ground. It crashed down, the knight tumbling through the air before landing with a bonebreaker smash.

The horse's outline imploded into an amalgam of purple flesh and pumping organs. Eight or nine sayce had been moulded together, like living dough, into a rough sculpture of the terrestrial animal. Heads stuck out of its sides and haunches, encased in thick vein-laced membranes, jaws working silently beneath the naked protoplasm.

Neither of Sewell's gaussrifles were working. He swivelled them down, and used them as crutches to lever himself upright. His medical program was flashing red caution warnings into his mind. He cancelled it completely, and drew a TIP carbine from its holster. The fallen knight was rising to his feet, crumpled armour straightening out. Sewell flicked the TIP carbine to continuous fire with his thumb, and pulled the trigger. It was like using a battering ram. The energy pulses kept smacking into the armour with jackhammer blows, knocking him down and kicking him across the ground. A violet corona seethed around the silver metal. Sewell pulled a grenade from his belt and lobbed it at the limp figure.

A lance caught him in the middle of his back, splitting his ribs apart then puncturing his lungs and an oxygenated-blood-reserve bladder before sliding out of his chest. The blow flung him three metres across the grass. He landed awkwardly, the lance jarring round violently and causing more internal damage.

The knight who had speared him reigned his horse round and dismounted. He drew his broadsword and walked towards the crippled mercenary.

Sewell managed to achieve a precarious balance on his knees. His right hand closed on the lance, boosted fingers exerting their full power, crushing the wood. It snapped off, leaving a splintered twenty-centimetre stump sticking out of his chest. A huge quantity of blood coursed down into the grass.

"Not good enough, my friend," the knight said. He ran his broadsword through Sewell's short neck.

Sewell reached out with his left arm and grabbed the knight's shoulder, pulling him even closer. There was a sharp grunt of surprise from the knight. Little crackles of energy skated over the surface of his armour. The broadsword penetrated up to the hilt, but Sewell opened his mouth slit wide.

The knight got out one frantic "No!" before Sewell's silicon carbide teeth clamped round his neck, slicing cleanly through the chain-mail.

The northern horizon was an uncompromising clash of turquoise and red, both colours textured as fine as silk, pressing smoothly against each other. Both unyielding. Beautiful, from a distance. Directly in front of the spaceplane, filth and fire was belching from a widening fissure in the rain-clouds.

Ashly altered the camber of the wings, and sent the spaceplane on a steep dive through the dank clouds. Water slicked the pearl-white fuselage, misting the optical sensor images. Then he was through, levelling out.

It was a small confined world of darkness and squalor into which he had come. At the centre, clouds reflected the diseased irradiation of the crater, tarnishing the land with the flickers of dying atoms. Wildfire scoured the malaised savannah around its base, eating its way outwards.

Twisters roamed the scorched earth, scattering soot and ash all around to form a greasy crust of embers over the flattened grass.

But further out the rain was falling, cleansing the land. Spears of sunlight wrested their way past the shredding clouds, returning cool natural colours to the fractal wilderness of greys.

Sensors locked on to Kelly's communication block. Ashly banked the spaceplane in a swift high-gee turn, riding the signal to its source. Ahead and below, two tiny hovercraft bounced and jerked their way across the uneven countryside.

Reza counted twenty-one knights escaping from the small holocaust Sewell and Jalal unleashed. That was good, he had expected it to be more. He and Pat Halahan were next. His sensors showed him the spaceplane sinking fast out of the sky a couple of kilometres behind him.

"Five minutes, that's all they need."

"They've got it," Pat said urbanely.

Reza fired his forearm gaussrifle. Targeting-program-controlled muscles shifted the barrel round as his sensors went into a track-while-scan mode. All his conscious thoughts had to do was designate.

He picked off three knights with EE rounds, and brought a further two horses down before the gaussrifle malfunctioned. Some of his processor blocks were glitched as well. Sensor resolution was falling off. He dumped the gaussrifle and switched to a ten-millimetre automatic pistol. Chemical bullets which produced a scythe of kinetic death, and nothing the possessed could do to stop it. Two more knights were down when he ran out of spare magazines. White fire hit his shoulder, blowing his left arm off. A two-metre jet of blood squirted out until his neural nanonics closed artery valves.

Pat was still sluicing bullets at a pair of knights off to Reza's left. Stimulant and suppressor programs were working hard to eliminate shock. Reza saw a mounted knight thundering towards him, whirling a mace around. A momentum prediction program went into primary mode. The horse was three metres away when Reza took one step back. His remaining hand came up inside the slashing arc of the mace. He grabbed, pulled, twisted. His carbon-fibre skeleton twanged at the severe loading as the inertia of the spiked iron club yanked him off his feet. Glossy armour shrieked a metallic protest as the knight was catapulted backwards out of the saddle, then clanged like a bell as he landed.

They climbed to their feet together. Reza raised the mace and started to walk forwards, a locomotion auto-balance program compensating for his lost arm.

The knight saw him coming and pointed his broadsword like a rifle. White flame raced down the blade.

"Cheat," Reza said. He detonated the fragmentation grenades clipped to his belt. Both of them vanished inside a dense swarm of furious black silicon micro-blades.

A hurricane squall of rain stung Kelly's face as the spaceplane swooped fifteen metres overhead. Its compressor nozzle efflux nearly overturned the hovercraft. She engaged the fan deflector and killed the impellers. They skidded to a rumbustious halt.

The spaceplane slipped round sideways in the air then landed hard, undercarriage struts pistoning upwards. Rain pattered loosely on its extended wings, dribbling off the flaps.

Kelly turned around in her seat. The children were huddled together on the hard silicon deck, clothes soaked, hair straggly. Terrified, crying, peeing in their shorts and pants. Wide eyes stared at her, brimming with incomprehension. There were no clever words left to accompany the scene for the recording. She simply wanted to put her arms round every one of them, pour out every scrap of comfort she owned. And that was far less than they deserved.

Three kilometres behind the hovercraft, EE explosions strobed chaotically, while antagonistic streamers of white fire curled and thrashed above the blood-soaked grass.

We did it, she thought, the knights can't reach us now. The children are going to live. Nothing else mattered, not the hardships, not the pain, not the sickening fear.

"Come on," she said to them, and the smile came so easily. "We're leaving now."

"Thank you, lady," Jay said.

Kelly glanced up as a figure hiked out of the rain. "I thought you'd left," she said.

Shaun Wallace grinned. His sodden LDC one-piece was shrunk round his body, mud and grass clung to his boots, but the humour in his eyes couldn't be vanquished. "Without saying goodbye? Ah now, Miss Kelly, I wouldn't be wanting you to think the worst of me. Not you." He lifted the first child, a seven-year-old girl, over the gunwale. "Come along then, you rabble. You're all going on a long, beautiful trip to a place far away."

The spaceplane's outer airlock hatch slid open, and the aluminium stairs telescoped out.

"Get a move on, Kelly, please," Ashly datavised.

She joined Shaun at the side of the hovercraft and began lifting the exhausted, bedraggled children out.

Horst stood at the bottom of the stairs, harrying his small charges along. A word here, a smile, pat on the head. They scooted up into the cabin where Ashly cursed under his breath as he tried to work out how on earth to fit them all in.

Kelly had the last boy in her arms, a four-year-old who was virtually asleep, when Theo started up his hovercraft. "Oh no, Theo," she datavised. "Not you as well."

"They need me," he replied. "I can't leave them. I'm a part of them."

Great bands of sunlight were raking the savannah. The fighting was over. Kelly could see three or four knights on horseback milling about. None of them showed any interest in the spaceplane now. "But they're dead, Theo."

"You don't know that, not for sure. In any case, haven't you heard, there's no such thing, not any more." He stuck his arm up and waved.

"Hell." She tipped her head back, letting the sweet rain wash her face.

"Come along now, Miss Kelly." Shaun leant over and gave her cheek a platonic kiss. "Time you was leaving."

"I don't suppose it would do any good asking you to come?"

"Would I ask you to stay?"

She put a foot on the bottom rung, the drowsy child heavy in her arms. "Goodbye, Shaun. I wish it could have been different."

"Aye, Miss Kelly. Me too."

Kelly sat in the cabin with one eight-year-old boy on her lap and her arms round a pair of girls. The children squirmed round, fidgeting, excited and nervous, asking her about the waiting starship. Lalonde was already half-forgotten, yesterday's nightmare.

If only, she wished.

The compressor whine permeated the overcrowded cabin as Ashly fed power into the fans. Then they were airborne, the deck tilting up, a press of acceleration. Kelly closed her eyes and accessed the spaceplane's sensor suite. A lone figure was trudging over the savannah, a well-built man with tousled ginger hair, wearing a thick red and blue check cotton shirt, collar up against the rain as he headed for home.

A minute later a stentorian sonic boom broke across the vast grass plain. Fenton raised his great head at the sound, but there was nothing in the sky apart from rain and clouds. He lowered his gaze again, and resumed his earthbound search for his lost masterlove.

TIMELINE

2020 . . . Cavius base established. Mining of Lunar sub-crustal resources starts.

2037 . . . Beginning of large-scale geneering on humans; improvement to immunology system, eradication of appendix, organ efficiency increased.

2041 . . . First deuterium-fuelled fusion stations built; inefficient and expensive.

2044 . . . Christian reunification.

2047 . . . First asteroid capture mission. Beginning of Earth's O'Neill Halo.

2049 . . . Quasi-sentient bitek animals employed as servitors.

2055 . . . Jupiter mission.

2055 . . . Lunar cities granted independence from founding companies.

2057 . . . Ceres asteroid settlement founded.

2058 . . . Affinity symbiont neurons developed by Wing-Tsit Chong, providing control over animals and bitek constructs.

2064 . . . Multinational industrial consortium (Jovian Sky Power Corporation) begins mining Jupiter's atmosphere for He_3 using aerostat factories.

2064 . . . Islamic secular unification.

2067 . . . Fusion stations begin to use He_3 as fuel.

2069 . . . Affinity bond gene spliced into human DNA.

2075 . . . JSKP germinates Eden, a bitek habitat in orbit around Jupiter, with UN Protectorate status.

2077 . . . New Kong asteroid begins FTL stardrive research project.

2085 . . . Eden opened for habitation.

2086 . . . Habitat Pallas germinated in Jupiter orbit.

2090 . . . Wing-Tsit Chong dies, and transfers memories to Eden's neural strata. Start of Edenist culture. Eden and Pallas declare independence from UN. Launch buyout of JSKP shares. Pope Eleanor excommunicates all Christians with affinity gene. Exodus of affinity capable humans to Eden. Effective end of bitek industry on Earth.

2091 . . . Lunar referendum to terraform Mars.

2094 . . . Edenists begin exowomb breeding programme coupled with extensive geneering improvement to embryos, tripling their population over a decade.

2103 . . . Earth's national governments consolidate into Govcentral.

2103 . . . Thoth base established on Mars.

2107 . . . Govcentral jurisdiction extended to cover O'Neill Halo.

2115 . . . First instantaneous translation by New Kong spaceship, Earth to Mars.

2118 . . . Mission to Proxima Centauri.

2123 . . . Terracompatible plant found at Ross 154.

2125 . . . Ross 154 planet named Felicity, first multiethnic colonists arrive.

2125–2130 . . . Four new terracompatible planets discovered. Multiethnic colonies founded.

2131 . . . Edenists germinate Perseus in orbit around Ross 154 gas giant, begin He_3 mining.

2131–2205 . . . One hundred and thirty terracompatible planets discovered. Massive starship building programme initiated in O'Neill Halo. Govcentral begins large-scale enforced outshipment of surplus population, rising to $2 million a week in 1160: Great Dispersal. Civil conflict on some early multiethnic colonies. Individual Govcentral states sponsor ethnic-streaming colonies. Edenists expand their He_3 mining enterprise to every inhabited star system with a gas giant.

2139 . . . Asteroid Braun impacts on Mars.

2180 . . . First orbital tower built on Earth.

2205 . . . Antimatter production station built in orbit around sun by Govcentral in an attempt to break the Edenist energy monopoly.

2208 . . . First antimatter-drive starships operational.

2210 . . . Richard Saldana transports all of New Kong's industrial facilities from the O'Neill Halo to an asteroid orbiting Kulu. He claims independence for the Kulu star system, founds Christian-only colony, and begins to mine He_3 from the system's gas giant.

2218 . . . First voidhawk gestated, a bitek starship designed by Edenists.

2225 . . . Establishment of a hundred voidhawk families. Habitats Romulus and Remus germinated in Saturn orbit to serve as voidhawk bases.

2232 . . . Conflict at Jupiter's trailing Trojan asteroid cluster between belt alliance ships and an O'Neill Halo company hydrocarbon refinery. Antimatter used as a weapon; twenty-seven thousand people killed.

2238 . . . Treaty of Deimos; outlaws production and use of antimatter in the Sol system; signed by Govcentral, Lunar nation, asteroid alliance, and Edenists. Antimatter stations abandoned and dismantled.

2240 . . . Coronation of Gerrald Saldana as King of Kulu. Foundation of Saldana dynasty.

2267–2270 . . . Eight separate skirmishes involving use of antimatter among colony worlds. Thirteen million killed.

2271 . . . Avon summit between all planetary leaders. Treaty of Avon, banning the manufacture and use of antimatter throughout inhabited space. Formation of Human Confederation to police agreement. Construction of Confederation Navy begins.

2300 . . . Confederation expanded to include Edenists.

2301 . . . First Contact. Jiciro race discovered, a pre-technology civilization. System quarantined by Confederation to avoid cultural contamination.

2310 . . . First ice asteroid impact on Mars.

2330 . . . First blackhawks gestated at Valisk, independent habitat.

2350 . . . War between Novska and Hilversum. Novska bombed with antimatter. Confederation Navy prevents retaliatory strike against Hilversum.

2356 . . . Kiint homeworld discovered.

2357 . . . Kiint join Confederation as "observers".

2360 . . . A voidhawk scout discovers Atlantis.

2371 . . . Edenists colonize Atlantis.

2395 . . . Tyrathca colony world discovered.

2402 . . . Tyrathca join Confederation.

2420 . . . Kulu scoutship discovers Ruin Ring.

2428 . . . Bitek habitat Tranquillity germinated by Crown Prince Michael Saldana, orbiting above Ruin Ring.

2432 . . . Prince Michael's son, Maurice, geneered with affinity. Kulu abdication crisis. Coronation of Lukas Saldana. Prince Michael exiled.

2550 . . . Mars declared habitable by Terraforming office.

2580 . . . Dorado asteroids discovered around Tunja, claimed by both Garissa and Omuta.

2581 . . . Omuta mercenary fleet drops twelve antimatter planet-busters on Garissa, planet rendered uninhabitable. Confederation imposes thirty-year sanction against Omuta, prohibiting any interstellar trade or transport. Blockade enforced by Confederation Navy.

2582 . . . Colony established on Lalonde.